The BRIDES of LONDON

The BRIDES of LONDON

VANESSA RILEY

Entangled Publishing, LLC
10940 S Parker Road
Suite 327
Parker, CO 80134
Visit our website at www.entangledpublishing.com.

Amara is an imprint of Entangled Publishing, LLC.

Edited by Erin Molta
Cover design by Bree Archer
Cover art by Tara Reed/The Reed Files,
Period Images, and Malkovstock/Gettyimages,
Interior design by Toni Kerr

Print ISBN 978-1-64937-029-7
ebook ISBN 978-1-64937-042-6

Manufactured in the United States of America

First Edition September 2021

AMARA

ALSO BY VANESSA RILEY

The BITTERSWEET BRIDE

Advertisements for Love Series

VANESSA RILEY

I dedicate this book to the memory of my beloved mother, Louise. Thank you for always believing in happy endings. I also dedicate this book to my loving hubby, Frank, and my daughter, Ellen. Their patience and support have meant the world to me.

I dedicate this book to my wonderful editor Erin, for believing in this story and pushing for it. I enjoyed developing Theodosia and Ewan with you.

I also dedicate this labor of love to my support team: Rhonda, Felicia, Erica, and Amy.

Love to my mentor, Laurie Alice, for answering all my endless questions.

And I am grateful for my team of encouragers: Sandra, Michela, Seressia, Piper, and Ms. Bev.

CHAPTER ONE

You Have Mail & Memories

Theodosia Cecil dipped her head, hoping her gray bonnet would hide her tall form amongst the crowd of Burlington Arcade shoppers. Her heart beat a rhythm of fear as her brow fevered with questions.

Could it be him?

Why was he haunting her now?

She spun, praying her wobbly legs would support her flight from the ghost. Spying a path between a chatty woman and her admirer, Theodosia claimed it and swayed toward the open door.

Safe in the shop, she put a hand to her thumping heart. Seeing the face of someone dead… It shook her, forced too many memories. The image of Ewan, her deceased first love, had to be a figment of Theodosia's conscience, nothing more. Why would this vision rear up now—questioning her resolve to be in town garnering letters offering matrimony from strangers?

Her hands trembled, puckering the stiff seams of her new kid gloves as she stuffed the sealed papers into her reticule. What if she'd dropped them in her mad dash? With all the people milling beneath the sparkling glass roof of the Arcade, the responses would've been lost, and with them, her dream of protecting her son. Hope in her plan slipped from her grasp, even with her onyx mitts. This time, there would be no kind Mathew Cecil to pick her up and wipe her clean.

She missed her late husband and his endless patience. He should be the only dead man in her head. Yet, there stood Ewan Fitzwilliam's ghost, vividly in her imagination. Perhaps it was her heart crying out at this unromantic way of finding a new husband.

"Ma'am, may I help you?"

Theodosia lifted her gaze from her gloves to a small cherry-red face.

"Our store has much to offer," the young girl said. "Did ye come for something special, Mrs. Cecil?"

Startling at the girl's use of her name, Theodosia raised her chin, then scanned from side to side at the pots. She took a breath and smelled sweet roses and lilacs. "What is this place? A perfumer?"

"Yes, Mrs. Cecil, and we use Cecil flowers to make the best fragrances."

The girl knew who she was, and the lilt in the young blonde's voice made Theodosia's lips lift. Respect always felt good.

A little less jittery, she nodded at the girl then turned to the walnut shelf and poked the lid of a greenish jar. The scent of lavender filled the air. Pride in her and her husband's accomplishment inflated her lungs. "Cecil flowers are the best."

The calm ushered in from the soft, sweet scents allowed her thoughts to right. Ghosts didn't exist. If they did, then it would be Mathew visiting her, guiding her, pushing her cold feet forward whenever she felt she couldn't do something, as he'd often done during their five short years of marriage. He had died almost a year ago.

The shop girl came beside her, dusting the shelves. "Would

you like some of the lavender, Mrs. Cecil?"

That beautiful name, the only last name she'd ever possessed—the repetition of it inspired questions. "You know me from the flower fields? Have we met?"

"Everyone knew Mr. Cecil. God rest his soul. And all the flower girls know you. If a Blackamoor... Sorry, if a shop girl could be more, then we all can."

Theodosia, dark skin and all, an inspiration to others? If those shop girls knew the whole of things, they would be scandalized. Horrified at the things she'd done, Theodosia became teary-eyed. She'd received unmerited favor catching Mathew Cecil's eye and his mercy.

"Sorry, I didn't mean nothing."

Theodosia nodded and tugged at her sleeve, hitting her reticule against her buttons, which clinked like serving bells. Her fine clothes hid the past, the fatigue and hunger of living on the streets. She forced a smile. "Becoming more is the beginning."

"Yes, ma'am. Quite a good 'ne."

From the outside, it must look like that, but some secrets were best kept in the grave. She turned from the almost-hero worship look in the shop girl's eyes and counted the brightly colored decanters in hues of salmon and cobalt blue lining a near table. "This is a lovely place. Have you done well since the shop's opening?"

"Some days. Some mornings, we're good and busy. Others, slow and easy. So much different than selling on the streets."

That worn-out heart of Theodosia's started moving within her chest. She caught the girl's shy gaze and said, "Slow days mean no money, but they can give ease to the back." With her palm, she cupped her mouth. "I meant selling flowers...long days." There were worse things for the back than an honest day's work selling flowers. Her mother's work at a brothel—that had been hard.

The younger woman nodded, but frowned as a shadow engulfed her.

A thick, portly fellow wearing a heavy burlap apron stepped from behind them. "Do ye belong here, m-m-miss?"

Theodosia blinked then stared at the man who stood with arms folded, disapproval flexing each meaty muscle. "Are you sure you're supposed to be here? Black servants don't come unattended. Blackamoor or whatever you are?"

"Sir, this is Mr. Cecil's widow," the shop girl said as her gaze dropped.

The man gawked as he glared at Theodosia. After an eternity of seconds, he said, "Oh...that Mrs. Cecil."

The pride she'd felt at hearing the Cecil name slipped away. It fell to the floor, ready to be trampled by her own short heels. With silk ribbons trailing her bonnet and an onyx walking dress stitched with heavy brass buttons, he still saw her as low. Was he thinking, as she often did: *mistress, half-breed, by-blow, whore*?

No matter what Theodosia felt about her past, she'd not let the sour shop clerk, or anyone else, stuff her into one of those names. She was a widow to a good man. "I'm not a servant, sir. In fact, you are one of the many vendors who use my family's wares for your livelihood." She took a step closer to the man. "I'm your business partner."

The man turned a lovely shade of purple, darker than fallen bee orchid buds. The veins on his neck pulsed.

As wonderful as it was to make him uncomfortable, it was never good to leave a bull enraged. Mathew had taught her that. She jangled her reticule, letting the *tink-tink* sound of clanging coins speak for her. "I'd like to be a patron."

The man harrumphed over his glasses. "We have many items." He pivoted to the shop girl. "Sally, go dust in the back. I'll take care of Mrs. Cecil."

The young woman nodded. "Good meeting you, ma'am." She offered another smile then pattered away.

Theodosia forced her shoulders to straighten and paced around the man. As a free woman and a proper widow with money, she could shop here. A glance to the left helped her settle on a practical item. "I'd like to purchase some soap."

The man nodded and pointed her to a table skirted in crimson silk. He dogged her footfalls, following close behind, as if she'd steal something.

She sighed. Hopefully, she wouldn't have to become used to this treatment again. The last year of grieving had protected her from outsiders, and the years of having her late Mathew's guidance had almost made her forget.

Almost.

She pressed her gloved fingertips against a jar colored lapis blue. "What type of soap is inside?"

The clerk pushed up his thick spectacles that had slid down his condescending nose. "A fine lavender. Very expensive, about four shillings a piece. Not so much for Cecil's widow."

Though she had the money to buy most things, years of thrift and haggling still pumped in her blood. She poked at the glass, tilting its heavy lid. The fragrance, honey-like, wafted from the pressed bars, stroking her nose. Surely, they had been made from Cecil spike lavandin—for nothing else could hold such strong perfume.

This had to be a sign from Mathew. He must approve of her actions to marry again in order to protect the son he'd so loved. She must buy the soap. She stroked the jar. "I'll take two pieces, and wrap it in paper. Make sure the scale is clear of fingers. I'd hate to pay more than what's necessary."

The man picked up the container. His head bobbed up and down as if it had taken this long to see past her face to her wealth. "I'll weigh this out...ma'am, without a finger on the scale."

Half watching the clerk, half watching the window glass, she decided the store front was more interesting than the man's balding head. She filled her vision with the sea of sleek top hats and crisp bonnets passing through the Arcade. None of them an apparition. She sighed again, the tight grip of apprehension further loosing from her spine. The vision had been her nerves.

Slowly, carefully, and in full view of the clerk, she dipped her fingers into her reticule pulling out the foolscap letters she'd retrieved from the stationer. She flipped to the first, a thin sheet of light gray paper, and mouthed the address. This was the second correspondence from a man with the rank of squire to her marriage advertisement. Though his crisp writing of her name, Mrs. Cecil, denoted elegance, their meeting last week had been far from elegant. It had been dull, lifeless, and made worse by his obvious discomfort in talking with her. He hadn't even had the courage to hold her gaze.

Surely, between the folds sat a polite *no*, and for that she'd be grateful. Theodosia was in want of a man's protection, but a new husband needed to be like Mathew, a Boaz protector. Yes, one of those gentlemanly fellows who cherished family above everything and who'd never be ashamed to be seen with her son.

What if it was a *yes*? She tapped the second letter to her bosom. If she had another offer she'd get her friend Ester to help pen a rejection to the squire. Ester's chaste brain had to be filled with clever ways of saying no.

Chuckling silently, she switched to the next response. This one addressed her advertisement number not her name. A first correspondence. New air filled her chest.

The primrose-colored paper felt thick beneath her fingers, and the thick glob of red wax sealing the note held an indentation of a crest. Could it be from a gentleman? Maybe someone titled? Maybe this could be the man who would stand up for her boy. The notion of such decency lifted her lips, even the bottom one she chewed when nervous or frightened.

"Mada...Mrs. Cecil." The shopkeeper's impatient voice sounded, cutting through her woolgathering. "I've more paper in the back. Another minute."

The heat from her kid glove made the wax melt a little. She should open it now and read the particulars, his age and situation, but having her dearest friends' dueling perspectives would help make sure she wasn't getting too excited. All the money in the world could not make a man want to father a sickly child and wouldn't help fight for the boy's interests.

Loud voices sounded from the backroom. The door opened and a shaking Sally came out. The blonde twisted her hands within her long apron. The stocky clerk passed in front of her and stood behind the counter. "That will be eight shillings."

Theodosia shoved her letters under the crook of her arm and fished out a half guinea.

The bright shine of the gold coin reflected in his widened eyes. They bulged like greedy hot air balloons. "Is there anything else you wish to buy?"

She shook her head and waited for two shillings and sixpence change. Everything her late husband had told her was true—money trumped questions. Pity all men weren't like her honest Mathew, or dreamers like her apparition. No, most were manipulative, lying as soon as they opened their mouths.

She picked up her package, shifting the treasure between her palms, and looked at the hurt painting the shop girl's face. She looked like Theodosia had used to look, contemplating the wrong choices. That couldn't happen. She flicked the edge of her parcel, making a hole. "Sir, might I have more paper? I don't want to lose these."

The man slapped the counter. "Aye. Picky. Seems money makes you the same as the rest."

Theodosia bit her tongue, then her lip, to keep a tart reply inside her mouth. She needed a moment alone with the girl.

As soon as the clerk headed into the back, Theodosia came alongside her. "Sally, was it? If you ever need an honest job, where you will be paid fairly for a good day's work, come visit Cecil Farms. Tell them Mrs. Cecil said to hire you. Whatever you decide, come to our Flora Festival in a few weeks." She dipped into her reticule and gave her three shillings to pay for transportation. The farm was a post ride out of London.

Amber eyes smiled at her. "Thank you, Mrs. Cecil."

The man returned, harrumphed, then settled the jar between

them on the shelf. "Here's your paper, ma'am."

Theodosia took the blue material and carefully wrapped her soaps. Feeling good at being able to help another, she turned to the door. "Thank you, sir." Keeping another woman from making mistakes would honor Mathew's memory. Even Ewan's ghost would smile, if the shop girl could find a way to dream.

As she stepped back into the crowded throughway, her letters slipped and landed near a man's boot. She bent to retrieve them, but the fellow grabbed them first and held them out to her.

"Thank you." The words crawled out slowly as her gaze traveled up his bottle-green waistcoat and broad chest, past his lean cravat and thick neck, to a familiar scar on his chin. She didn't need to see his thick, wavy, raven hair. She stopped at his eyes, the bluest eyes, bluer than the sky stirred clean by a thunderstorm.

"It *is* you, Theo," said the man.

Her heart ceased beating. Theodosia looked down to see if it had flopped outside of her stiff corset. Ewan Fitzwilliam stood in front of her. He wasn't dead. Didn't look the least bit distressed or deceased from the war. And he was no ghost, unless hell made apparitions look this good.

• • •

Six years had passed since Ewan Fitzwilliam had seen this beauty. The last time, the locks of her long, straight hair—a gift from her father, an Asian junk sailor, who'd been portside long enough to purchase companionship—had been free about her shoulders. Her deep bronzed skin, a blessing of the negress mother she'd barely known, had been exposed at her throat from a hastily put-on blouse. Her wide almond-shaped eyes, onyx pools of decadent wonder, had been afraid, like now. "Theo, the Flower Seller."

Chewing on her bottom lip, she nodded and blinked her lengthy, silky lashes, hiding the largest irises he'd ever seen. Before, those eyes had captivated him. He'd thought them passion-sated, but now, he knew them to be big with avarice, another of her deceptive guises. "It's been a long time, Theo."

She nodded and maybe took a breath, but still said nothing.

One look at her expensive frock, the tailored obsidian-colored walking dress that sculpted her hourglass form, and any doubt of her greed left his jaded heart. The sands of time had been good to her curvy form, and Theo had used her womanly wiles to attain wealth. Despite her humble background, she was no different than the ladies Ewan had met at the balls his mother forced him to attend. All were young women seeking advancement or larger purses, something a second son didn't possess. "Six years and you have nothing to say to me?"

"You died." Her alto voice dropped lower. "You are dead. An apparition."

"Very much alive. You look to be breathing, too. Barely."

She squinted and shifted the ribbons of her bonnet. "Whatever you are, can I have my letters? Then you may return to being dead."

Playfully, he waved the sealed papers fanning his chin. "Can you, or may you? A woman should know her capabilities. You know, like the ability to deceive."

He waited for her to respond. His Theo would offer a stinging retort, something with fire.

But this woman stood still, her fingers hovered inches from his as if she were afraid to take the letters. This wasn't his Theo.

Nonetheless, when she bit her lip again, he knew the folded notes held some importance for her. Out of habit, he swept them farther away, tucking them close to the revers of his tailcoat. Would this new Theo reach for something that was hers?

The woman glanced to the left and then to the right, but did not move. Part of him soured even more. Yes, she'd been shy when they'd first met, but never this cautious, not with him. This wasn't the girl he'd ruined himself over. Perhaps she had never existed, just a novel characterization his playwright mind had invented. "Are you sure these belong to you? Let me check for a name."

He read the markings on the folded papers and burned at the written name, Mrs. Cecil. "It doesn't say Theo the Flower Seller, but Mrs. Cecil. Is that you?"

She put a hand to her hip. "Yes. Give me those letters."

He waved at her again, fanning the pages near her cheek. "Then take them from your old friend. I don't bite. Well, not unless provoked or dared. Remember, Mrs. Cecil—my dearest Theo?"

She snatched the letters and stuffed them into her reticule. As she looked up at him again, her henna-colored cheeks darkened. "Too well, Mr. Fitzwilliam. How are you not dead? They said you died in Spain."

He extended his arm to her. "Perhaps we should get a bit of refreshment and have a long chat. You seem rather faint. Let's go to your shop. I recall you *scheming* to get a flower shop."

"I…I have no shop."

She did look faint and the part of his heart that should know better made him take the tissue-wrapped package from her lean fingers and support her palm atop his forearm. "There's a coffeehouse, Theo. Let me buy you a sweet. That will give you time to recover."

"No. No, I must go. I can't be seen with you."

She pulled away, leaving him holding her parcel. With elbows flying, reticule swinging, the daft woman dashed into the hustling crowd. He stood there watching until her form disappeared beneath the triple arch at the south entrance on Piccadilly Street.

She'd gone from the Burlington Arcade. Where? Where did she lay her head at night? And, whose pillow now possessed her?

He wanted answers. But chasing after Theo shouldn't be done. His pride wouldn't let him. However, he was holding the schemer's bag.

Like breathing, his fingers automatically sought to fist, but her bulky pack sat in his hands. A few nosy pokes released the strong bittersweet scent of lavender. The flower had meant something to him once, not a sop for the soul, but of being caught in a thunderstorm. The scent came to him in his dreams. Isolated in one of his father's carriage houses close to the Tradenwood flower fields, trapped with the business-minded flower seller who hadn't talked about bouquets when he'd finally taken her lips.

Who was this Cecil who had them?

Did he know lies lived within each kiss?

Or had Theo lied only to Ewan?

Craning his neck toward the skylights above, he warmed his chilled blood with the sunshine. Yet more questions filled his breast.

Why did Theo think him dead? Was it another of her false-hoods?

Slinging her package under his arm, he spun in the opposite direction she'd fled and marched out the north side of the Arcade onto Burlington Gardens. Seeing the past twice in one day would be too much.

With each step, Ewan stewed a little more. His gut ached. The words of his father's letter, recounting how Theo had run away with another man, mocking Ewan's choice for love, burned as badly now as it had when he'd first read them, laying near death in Spain. *And this Blackamoor harlot you wished to make a Fitzwilliam.*

Blood started to hiss and boil in his veins. He plodded down Bond Street, taking the long way back to where his brother's carriage awaited, all while repeating his father's slur.

Before a footman could jump down, Ewan gripped the pearl-black door and flung it open. Dragging himself into a seat, he prepared himself for questions and hoped his mind could swallow up the bitter dregs unearthed from seeing his past.

"Are you all right, Ewan?"

The concerned, low-pitch voice of his brother Jasper Fitzwilliam, the Viscount Hartwell, startled him.

Ewan gave himself a shake and dumped Theo's package onto the dark tufted seat. Theo. How could she still have a hold upon him? Hadn't he poured out all his anger at her lies into the lines of his latest play? He'd used his mad muse to re-create Theo as the perfect Circe, the goddess the playwright Homer had created to turn men into swine. Risking everything for Theo had made him low, like his father's hogs. No, he wasn't a fool in love anymore.

"Hello, in there." Jasper leaned over and thumped Ewan's skull. "Not creating your next masterpiece, are you? Have you tried selling the first?"

"Not my first, but by far my best. My first would have been exhibited at Covent Garden six years ago, if not for Father's influence on the manager. He made Thomas Harris renege on his commitment to buy my play."

His brother poked his lips into a full grimace, so different from the man who loved to laugh. "Please, not that again. There are more things afoot than six-year-old misunderstandings."

The way Jasper said *afoot,* made the writer in Ewan sit up straight. He leaned forward to give the man his full attention. "I'm listening."

"I asked you to help me with these newspaper responses, but there's more I need to involve you with. You've been in London these past three months and haven't come out to Grandbole, yet. Why haven't you seen him?"

The *him*, their father, the Earl of Crisdon, hadn't yet summoned Ewan, and he hadn't had the energy to volunteer for another dressing down. *A Fitzwilliam doesn't write plays. The theater isn't a profession for a Fitzwilliam.* "Jasper, please. It's difficult enough to visit with Mother and listen to her constant complaints of how I was cheated of Tradenwood. But I was not cheated. Only bad luck."

"Well, the report of your demise did make your uncle designate a new heir, who was not your mother. Their feud never ended."

Ewan stared up at the ceiling. Counted to ten. Yet, in his head, he heard his mother's soft-voiced lament of his uncle changing his will to leave Tradenwood and all its fields to a distant cousin—all because of the incorrect report from the battlefield. He shook his head, banishing the loss. "Another subject. Your mystery woman had already picked up her mail. Our clever note is on its way to the intended victim. And since you corresponded as one of Father's lesser titles, Lord Tristian for his barony, your identity is safe."

Jasper rolled his beaver dome between sweaty palms. "Who else should borrow but his heir? Being the eldest has its privileges."

"And its headaches." Ewan shook his chin, wanting nothing to do with his father's grooming or any of the ways the man sought to control Jasper. "But you seem to manage."

His brother nodded as his smile shrank. "It's my humor. It comforts me. So, no peek at what the grand woman looked like?"

Beautiful as ever, but Theo wasn't the lady his brother was asking about. "Pardon?"

"The newspaper advertisement owner. The woman who placed the matrimony request in the paper."

"The new shop clerk hadn't seen her. I waited past the usual time you said the widow checked for correspondences. Sorry, old boy, your stationer has things wrong. Don't let Father know a Fitzwilliam failed to obtain secret information. That would bring the earl such misery."

Jasper dropped his hat and folded his arms about his jacket, a hunting garment with oversized sleeves. It was hard to make someone so big look even bigger, but the man achieved the impossible with dozens of tiny diamond shapes running north and south upon his copperplate printed waistcoat. "That's what I get for sending a writer to do a spy's work. Should've sent Father."

The unflappable Jasper seemed nervous, a side of his half brother Ewan had never seen. With his brow rising, he felt his quill finger cramp as if preparing to write dialogue for a new play. "I am surprised the earl's encouraging you to find a bride like this. Maybe he *has* changed after all these years."

Jasper shrugged his shoulders. "He doesn't know that I am. I'm taking a turn at being the rebellious one and doing something Father wouldn't approve of."

"How is that working?" Ewan chuckled.

"A few disappointments. Mostly, I've exchanged letters with women of the wrong temperament or situation." His brother shuffled his boots. "You don't know how I've missed your assistance. You visit with your mother in Town, but what of us?"

The *us* was Grandbole and all that came with the grand house. Ewan did miss it. He missed the land and walking it to clear his head. He missed all the Fitzwilliams under one roof. "There are many things to remember, many things to forget."

"If I hadn't spied you at the countess's party, would you have let me know of your return?"

"I missed your wit whilst I soldiered in the Peninsula, even the jokes at my expense. But I didn't miss the arguments with the earl. It is he that gives me pause, not you."

Jasper looked down again, as if a humbled posture could wipe away the vitriol of their father's famed rants.

Ewan had given up on the earl. The pressure of never measuring up would build inside, until his lungs exploded. He was glad the scars on his chest bound him together, kept the rage from showing.

He took a small breath. The pressure released. He wasn't

that weak-minded person anymore. Hadn't the bad memories, the disappointments, become part of his sharpened sense of humor, the kindling wood for his farce comedies? Tweaking his cravat, Ewan sampled a little more air and sank into his beloved sarcasm. "Jasper, I would love to be the genesis of this rebellion, but take it from me, start small. Borrow the earl's hunting dogs without permission. Then work your way up to…oh, I don't know, petty larceny. Then you'll be ready to take a bride without his approval."

Jasper sat back and drummed the black leather seat beneath his thick fingers. "I haven't picked the lady yet, for it is so important to do this well. Once a gentleman proposes, there's no taking it back. What if she doesn't like children, as she says? What if this one is like the others, not as young as she stated in her advertisement?"

"If you are fretting, go about finding a bride the old way. Pick a chit during the Season and propose. Lady Crisdon will help."

His brother's face grew more serious with his jaw firming, his eyes drifting to the right. "I can't bear to hear how none of them are like Maria. I *know* that."

The man quieted. If his eyes moved more to the right they'd fling from his skull. It must be hard losing a good wife. From the letters the brothers had exchanged over the years, Jasper had cared for her himself until the stomach cancer had taken its toll.

"I'm sorry, Ewan. It will be a year next month." Jasper tugged at his sleeves, readjusting his cuffs over his thick wrists. "Have you asked for your mother's matchmaking assistance? That might get her to come back to Grandbole. We should be unified now."

Unity? At what cost? Ewan pushed at his temples with

fingers that now reeked of lavender, Theo's lavender. He put his palms onto the seat, gripping the edge, as if that would ground him from the memories of a fleeting romance with one of the Crisdon flower sellers. No luck. She'd be in his head tonight, tormenting him. "I've no time, or the finances, for a wife—not until one of my plays succeed."

Jasper rubbed at his chin. "What of that ginger-haired girl you danced with at your mother's dinner last week, the one with freckles? She didn't seem to mind the absence of a fortune."

That was unusual in London, to be sure. Mother must've whispered nonsense in the girl's ear. "She'll become enlightened by her own matchmaking mama. The second son from a second marriage can only do so much, particularly one recovering from banishment."

Jasper sat forward, folding his arms. "Father's irascible, but he only did what he thought was best. I will admit he is often misguided, but sometimes... Sometimes he's right."

Yes. The earl was right in the worst ways. He'd said Theo was after Crisdon money. He'd said she wouldn't remain faithful. Groaning, Ewan looked down again at his hands, his fisting hand. "The earl also does wrong. Lording his money over our heads, doling it out when we do as he wants. But then, he stops us from gaining the means to be independent. Not this time. My new play will succeed."

"How would Father put it?" Jasper held his nose up and made his voice strangled and low. "Fitzwilliams do military or religious service. We may go to the theater, but not perform in such. Ewan, use your writing talents for sermon making." He laughed and wriggled his nose. His voice returned to its normal energetic pitch. "That would've made Father very pleased."

Ewan's stomach churned, thinking of both the difficulty of doing as the old earl wanted and the image of himself being struck by lightning behind the pulpit. He spoke very slowly. "The black sheep can't wear white frocks, and I've already done my military service. Five and a half, almost six, years of service in Spain and the West Indies. My Fitzwilliam dance-card-with-bullets is jotted in full. I should be able to live as I want. I have stories to tell. They should be on the stage, no matter what the old man thinks."

Jasper dropped his hat as his shoulders slumped. "This new one is very good. It was a pleasure to read, but I hate being caught between you two. I'm not sure what has seeded the ill will, but this is a new day. We need family to pull together."

Not wanting to argue or mouth aloud Theo's name, Ewan sighed. "So, how do you intend to tell the old man of your plan for a new wife?"

"If advertisement number four lives up to the promise made in the newspaper, he won't mind adding another fortune to the family."

Ewan couldn't disagree with that logic, even if it felt wrong and unromantic. "Perhaps, but I still think you should give the traditional way a chance."

Jasper ran a hand through his curly, reddish-blond hair. His frowning lips turned up. "My rugged features do pale against yours, but I have three girls who will require dowries that my modest income will not profer. I don't want their fates to be under the earl's control. I need a young heiress who will be a good mother to my brood and add to my coffers. That can't be had at Almack's."

Maybe this finding-a-bride-by-newspaper-advertisement was a safe way for his brother to start living again. "A lovely brood, from what I can remember. Your wife gave you all she had. That is to be treasured."

Smoothing a wrinkle from his waistcoat, Jasper nodded. "I'm done with sentiment. You're only allowed one great love in a lifetime. The next will be a marriage of convenience."

That couldn't be true. His heart shuddered at the notion of only loving once. It would take a great deal of vanity for Ewan to convince himself that what he'd felt for Theo in those heady days before he'd left for war, was less than love. Oh, if only he were that vain.

What had started as an innocent, well, almost innocent, flirtation between the errand boy for the largest flower grower of greater London and a sassy street vendor had changed everything. Wanting Theo had cost Ewan dearly. He'd been disowned, dispatched from the family, and had almost died in the war. He grimaced, allowing his gut to knot and twist with the horrid truth. Seeing how things had turned out: she'd apparently married a wealthy man, he'd written a farce of Theo's love that would draw all of London. Perhaps she had been worth the sacrifice. Yes, his humor had matured.

"Pay attention over there." Jasper smiled. It was his infectious weapon. "Do you remember your nieces? You should see them. My eldest is now a petulant ten."

He stuck a hand in his pocket and shrugged. Staying away had cost more than time. Deep down in his heart, he missed his family, that sense of belonging. "Perhaps you can bring them to town. My flat is small but clean." *And not under the old man's control.*

Jasper raised his brow. "You should come see them today."

Ewan shook his head. "No."

"But I will need your plotting abilities. I could pay you to help write my correspondences to number four of the *Morning Post*. If this woman is indeed young, with a fortune, and not so bad on the eyes, there could be competition." He shuffled his boots. "And if you are not courting, who's the package for? Smells like lavender. What secrets are you keeping from your elder brother?"

"No. I bumped into a woman in Burlington Arcade. She left it. I'll toss them away."

"Pretty expensive wrapping. A pity to disregard. When did you have time to make a new acquaintance? Did you miss my mystery woman when you were flirting?"

"I'd hardly call a pleasant exchange flirting." But what would he call running into his past? Though Theo wore expensive garb, she could be like him, all outside trappings. These perfumed soaps shouldn't be abandoned. Perhaps he should return them to their owner and have that final chat. He whipped off his top hat. "Our mission is done today, Jasper. Drop me back to my residence."

"No, you must come with me for dinner with the girls...and Father."

Ewan slumped in his seat, wrinkling the vest he'd labored to pick out for an evening of cards at his mother's house in Town, not for seeing the earl. What type of mood would he be in after seeing Theo and his father in the same day? He shook his head. "I'm beginning to feel tired. Yes, very tired."

Jasper groaned, loud and long. "The chest wound?" His brother's voice raised an octave. "Does it still bother you?"

"Only on wet days...and during thunderstorms."

"Come to dinner, Ewan. So much has changed. The family needs to pull together. Don't be stubborn like Father."

Like the old man? His brother might as well have punched Ewan in the face to utter such horrid words. "I'm nothing like him. Stop the carriage. I'll walk."

Grabbing his arm like a madman, Jasper kept him from leaping out of the carriage. "I'm sorry, but it is true. I won't say it again. Have one meal. Get his complaints off my shoulders for a day. See my girls."

His brother had always tried to keep the old man at bay, even slipping Ewan a fiver upon occasion. "One quick meal, but as soon as he starts in, I'm gone. I'll steal a horse and return to London. In fact, give me money to stable a stallion now. For you know it won't take long for Father's harangues to start. It's about three jokes before he fumes."

"Fine, that will take care of one problem. For the second, you must also agree to help me with my potential newspaper bride, lady number four. I want to know more about her before I ask for a meeting. She'll respond to your quip. We'll need a clever note to follow. Help me write something to keep her attention. You're the clever one."

"You want to see her true character, then ask a question of substance. Let me think on it."

"Well, come up with something to match your riddle, Ewan. Maybe it will be so good you'll use it in your next play."

Avoiding the temptation to roll his eyes, Ewan nodded. "All right...I'll help."

"You think you'll find the owner of the package, or do you think my girls might like it? Is it too personal?"

Anything regarding Theo was too personal. Yet, returning

this package intrigued him. She had obviously purchased this in the Burlington Arcade. Perhaps, the perfumer knew where Mrs. Cecil resided. Ewan eased his head onto the seatback, preparing to sleep all the way to Grandbole Manor. Since she'd be in his brain, he piled up all the questions he wanted to know of Theo. Perhaps, he'd ask them the next time he saw the flower seller. "It should be returned to its rightful owner."

And there would be a next time. Fitzwilliams were good at finding things—weaknesses and secrets. Nothing else brought a smile to Ewan's jaded heart than the thought of improving his characterization of his play's villainess by visiting Theo, his personal Circe.

CHAPTER TWO

Family, Friends & Enemies

Theodosia's carriage rumbled forward. With each passing second, her lungs constricted a little less. Her driver and horse team didn't know she'd fled a ghost. Surely, they assumed she needed to hurry back for her dinner guests. She wouldn't correct them.

By the time she'd passed Tottenham Road, the jarring and swaying of her ivory seat had jostled every bone in her body. The ache, however, didn't compare to the pain of seeing Ewan again. All these years, and the man was alive. *How could he not be dead?*

Six years of mourning him, of feeling ashamed for living and finding some happiness with Mathew, all while thinking a bullet had felled her poor dreamer.

How many times had she looked in those fancy glass mirrors at Mathew's Tradenwood, the home they'd shared, and had seen a traitor to the future she'd envisioned with Ewan? The man with the crooked smile that had set her heart pounding. Today, that crooked smile had crushed the useless muscle in her chest to dust.

Wait.

If Ewan didn't die in the war, where has he been?

Why did he stay away when I needed him?

Her stomach soured, thinking and rethinking their foolish dreams. His plays would be performed on London's grandest stages, and her flower shop would provide roses, the best ones— without a single thorn—to his actresses. And Theodosia's Ewan wouldn't be tricked by those ladies' beauty. He'd said he only had eyes for *Theo, his Theo*.

Lies.

Dreams were lies.

Ewan had gone to war and hadn't come back to her. The life they had whispered in secret was nothing but deceit, lines from a play he hadn't yet written. Her heart burst all over again.

Had he laughed with his brother at getting her to love him? Did he smile to his circle of friends about taking her virtue? Had he said pretty words about loving her to lower her guard, making Theodosia forsake her vow not to be like her mother? Theodosia had given Ewan all of her, and then he'd left.

She'd become Theo the Harlot because of him.

Her pulse raced and whirled so loudly, her ears hurt. Almost panting, she forced air into her hurting chest and gripped her reticule to her bosom. Her eyes were already weak from sitting at her son's bedside till well past midnight. Crying now about lies would only make them sting. Ewan Fitzwilliam wasn't worth another droplet.

Her hand clenched. Her nails dug into the fringe of her reticule. That ache should have died six years ago. Ewan and his lies were no more. He couldn't affect her future or destroy the life she'd built for her son.

Another two hours of ridiculous fretting occurred before her carriage passed the Fitzwilliam flower farm. Squinting from her window, she could see their house, Grandbole Manor. The cold gray stone looked small at this distance, but it overshadowed the lilac-colored flowers in the orderly fields. Hard to believe it neighbored Mathew's warm Tradenwood, with its pinkish stacked stones. Tradenwood wasn't as grand, but she believed it held more peace and much more understanding. Things Ewan had always complained were missing at Grandbole.

She slumped onto the seat. Ewan couldn't be staying at his father's estate. She would've seen him at least once these six years if he'd resided there.

The urge to know why he'd played her false might cause her to be rash, to do something crazed. No, Theodosia Cecil didn't look for trouble anymore. She glanced at her rows of flowers. She thought of walking in those fields, of finding answers and strength there. She'd found Mathew there, or he'd found her. If she were to go out there now, she might find peace, the peace he had so often talked about growing, like buds in those fields.

Her carriage began to slow. Peeking out the window, she saw the grooms and proud horse teams of vehicles lining the drive of Tradenwood. Her dinner guests awaited her inside the parlor. They couldn't see her so broken. The ladies were there for an early meal to discuss the Flora Festival, the grand picnic Mathew had started as a reward for his workers, one that had evolved to also include every one of his vendors and their workers. She chuckled, wondering if the perfumer she'd met today would come. She prayed the girl Sally would, and she wondered if she would seek employment with Cecil's Farms.

The carriage stopped and one of her attendants came to free her from her stewing. Marching through the doors of Tradenwood, she slowed her steps and stopped at the console. Her butler stood near.

Pickens, with his starched livery of dark crimson and gold braid, held out his hands. "Welcome back, Mrs. Cecil. I'll take your bonnet and bag. Your guests are waiting for you in the parlor."

She unpinned her hat and gave it to him, but held on to her reticule. She wasn't prepared to relinquish her letters.

Pickens's brow raised, but he didn't try again for her bag. Six years had given them a routine and, hopefully, a measure of mutual respect. If memories hid in the wizened creases of his forehead, he knew Theodosia held on tight to things that were hers, only relenting when she was good and ready. "Thank you, Pickens."

He pulled a folded paper from behind his back. "This came for you while you were out. The footman said it was important. It's from the Fitzwilliams family. The earl himself."

Swallowing her newfound reservation upon hearing the name Fitzwilliam, she slid off her gloves, stashing them on the console, then clutched the thick parchment. "Thank you."

Emotionless, always about his duty, Pickens bowed his graying head and pivoted toward the long hall leading to the parlor. "And Mr. Lester is visiting. He's in the nursery with Master Philip."

Lester. The name sent shivers of fear and hate up her spine. Who knew Mathew's faithful steward would turn into a vengeful frog the moment he understood the powers Mathew's will had given him.

The tapping of the butler's footsteps moving toward her dinner guests sounded like a muffled drumbeat, but the decision to go to the birds in the parlor or to the vulture near her boy, wasn't a question.

In as dignified of a manner as she could muster, Theodosia's short heels clicked hard against the polished marble with its shiny cranberry veining. The moment her foot dropped upon the first mahogany tread, her false calm shredded. Visions of Lester taking her sweet boy and shaking him for a response froze the blood in her veins. She lunged up the steps and sailed on fretful wings to the door of the second-floor nursery.

She didn't see the leech in the hall. He had to be inside with little Philip. How long would it be before he discovered the boy's illness?

Theodosia couldn't blow into pieces like a dandelion in strong wind. She steadied herself, clasping the molding. The stupid parchment crunched against the raised wood before relenting and curling about it. With a strangled breath, she pushed open the door.

Scanning to the left and then to the right revealed nothing out of the ordinary. Polished pine planks on the floor and a thick jute rug of blue yarn warmed up the pale beige walls. A huge closet hid enough space to house a small family.

In the middle of the wide room, swimming in a pinafore of cream and blue threads, sat little Philip alone with his governess, Miss Thomas. No Lester.

Fanning the paper, hoping to chase away the fear fevering her brow, Theodosia took a few steps inside. A hungry panic of losing Philip was stirring, growing, pressing at her temples.

Lovely, honest Mathew had protected Theodosia and Philip, writing his will to withstand the challenges his young family would face in his absence. But a dead man could only do so much from the grave. Her own wit and a new, trustworthy husband, someone as honorable as Mathew —that would have to be enough to keep vultures like Lester away. Where was the pushy brute?

Coughing from the growing knot in her throat, she moved

closer to her son. She wanted to look in the closet or under the bed for Lester as she would hunt for a ghost. Lord knew she'd happened upon enough apparitions for one day.

Little Philip scooted forward, pressing his lean fingers against a carved block. His eyes were on the wooden toy, not looking at her.

That was good. He shouldn't see sadness on his mother's face.

She put a finger to her lips to keep the governess from announcing her. One heavy step after the other, clomping, stomping, she made her heels pound as loudly as she could as she approached his weak side.

The five-year-old didn't flinch. Never turned.

Her heart clenched.

The boy didn't hear her approach. The physicians, the old ones with gray on top, the young ones, trying to run experiments on the mulatto boy, even the ones who wouldn't see him until they heard his surname Cecil, all their words had been true. Philip was deaf on on his left side and losing his hearing on the right. This was the most painful consequence of her many sins.

Looking up to the ceiling, she counted her wrongs. Trusting Ewan—wrong. Holding on to pride too long—wrong. Not becoming a mistress to Mathew sooner, not trusting him sooner—wrong. Of keeping Ewan on a pedestal for so long, it had made it difficult for a good man to reach her heart—very wrong.

She lowered her gaze and looked at Philip. The boy jostled the toy between his small fingers. He still hadn't caught up to the size of other five year olds.

This punishment of barely hearing, of perhaps losing all of

it, tore her up inside. Would he forget the sound of words? Would he remember an impatient giggle? It was too much for an innocent boy. Living as she had, speaking lies, listening to her dreaming heart, were the reasons her child suffered. She cleared her throat. "How's my Philip?"

The governess tapped the little boy on the shoulder and pointed. "We had a good day today. No more fever from last night."

Philip spun toward Theodosia and showed a toothy grin. Her worn-out heart stirred. His bright blue eyes opened wider. He rushed to her, stepping onto her feet, embracing her legs. A smile she no longer thought she possessed lifted her lips. "Love you, son."

She scooped him up. His pinafore bunched in the crook of her arm as he wiggled his way to her cheek, placing his face there. His pulse pushed against hers. She wove her fingers into his dark, straight hair. She'd do anything for Philip, the only person in this world who was truly hers. For the first time today, she breathed easier. Maybe her withered heart had a little more living to do.

"*M-mmm-m*," he said, before giving her a big, wet kiss.

The boy offered another hug about her neck. Theodosia needed to keep him safe, to keep his world secure and beautiful, even if that meant selling herself in a new marriage.

Footfalls sounded behind her.

She spun with her precious cargo, tucking him deeper within her stiffening arms. Anger rose inside seeing Wilhelm Lester, her late husband's steward, smirking at the threshold.

"Well, isn't this lovely? Mother and son. The usurper and her spawn."

Theodosia leaned down and gave Philip back to his governess. "Come with me, Mr. Lester."

She squared her shoulders, tightened her grip about the paper, and waltzed past the scourge who had dared to be Mathew's confidant. She kept moving until she stood yards from the nursery.

The beast followed too closely. Was it onions and mutton on his breath?

"Theodosia, what was it? How did you bewitch old Cecil and convince him to make his mistress his wife? Usually only fools do that and Cecil was no fool."

"Maybe the same reason you've been asking to marry me? You didn't even wait for my dear Mathew to be cold in the grave."

The tall man laughed and flipped back a reddish-brown curl from his flat forehead. He would be handsome, if not for all the ugly evil spouting from his thin lips.

"No, can't be the same, my dear." His voice sounded like a fat cat's purr, one that had eaten its mouse. "You were penniless then. Now, you are a wealthy woman sharing the Cecil fortune. Yes, fifty-thousand pounds annually is more than enough reason to marry you, Theodosia."

"It's Mrs. Cecil to you. And I told you, you are not welcome in the nursery. Stay in the parlor."

"Can't. Your gaggle of hens is down there. Where did you find more educated dark ones?"

Ester and Frederica? Knowing her friends were near gave Theodosia more strength. "You heard what I said. Go downstairs."

"Then come with me." He held out his arm for her.

The thought of touching or being touched by Lester made

her skin itch. It'd be like fiery ants who had stung her hands in the fields when she hadn't been careful cutting flower stems. Around him, she needed to be extra careful. She scooted past him and started down the treads, but he fell in step with her.

"The boy? Is he breeched yet?"

"No, he's five."

"Well, Cecil wasn't that tall of a man, but this one seems a might scrawny. As his guardian, I will need to make sure you're not coddling him too much. He might need to be sent away, if you're not taking good care of him. That's a guardian's job to make sure his ward is well protected."

She lifted her chin as she cut her gaze to the fool. "Philip is fine. Growing well. Don't threaten me."

Lester grabbed her and yanked her close.

Her reticule swung around her elbow swatting him in his midnight blue waistcoat. "Let me go, you bounder."

His grip didn't slacken. He leaned near her ear. "Things would be better for the boy if we worked together. You're not so bad with that mouth of yours closed or given to a common purpose."

She shook free and stared into his beady blue-gray eyes. "Don't touch me. Some of the coloring of my hand may slap onto your sallow flesh. It will leave you black and blue. You wouldn't like that."

He clamped her shoulder, shaking her. "The hellcat protests too much. And I'm an improvement over an old man. It's been too long for you, hasn't it, dear? It's almost been a year since his death."

She made herself stone, forcing away the disgust threatening to spew vomit from her mouth. "How dare you? I'm not even out of my mourning for Cecil, the man you claimed to love. What would he say to you if he saw this?"

Lester's sneer shifted into a frown as if for a moment a bit of humanity filled him. Mathew's endless kindness had made him a weak spot for many. Theodosia had noted Lester's affection for Mathew during her husband's illness. At the man's first threat, she'd invoked Mathew's memory, Lester's Achilles heel, but how much longer would it work?

The blackguard lowered his hand and yanked the parchment away from her fingers. "This looks important." He ripped it open and held it to the light. "Another offer to buy our flower fields. You're not considering this?"

Theodosia put a hand to her hip. "All the fields are mine and Philip's. Cecil left you an income to be an advocate." She softened her tone to keep the man's fragile ego intact. "It's hard to consider something I haven't had a chance to read, but you know I will consult you."

He ripped up the offer into bits, balled them up, then stuffed the pieces into her palm. Lester stepped very close, his shadow falling upon her. "The Fitzwilliams ruined my father's business and took his lands. Land is everything. I won't let that happen here, and I've taken steps to ensure it." His brow rose. "The earl must think you stupid for such a low offer, though I think you know low."

He moved out of slapping range. "When you're done playing a lady and see that our interests align, mine for the Cecil business, yours for nurturing the heir, send for me. I'll come to you, Theodosia."

Lester grinned again, more evil than the first, and headed out to the hall. With a final smirk, he grabbed up his coat and cane. "See you soon, Mrs. Cecil, dearest woman. It will be good to see you out of your mourning garb. Maybe you and the lad shall come with me to Holland. Your head for numbers might come in handy."

No. Never would she go anywhere with him. Holding her breath, she made her response soft. "This is our first overture to those growers. You must go alone and represent us. I need you to do that."

"Yes, you are right. You do need me."

Even as he exited, his smirk stayed etched in her brainbox. Full of arrogance and condescension, it was a familiar response a Blackamoor woman faced in business. Exactly what she counted upon to be rid of him.

The footman closed the front door. The sound of the heavy thud made her hands tremble. If only Mathew had known Lester was vermin, worse than vine-rotting aphids. If he didn't go to the Dutch farms alone, her plan to outwit him would never work. How would she protect Philip then?

Pickens came near, squinting, creasing his brow even more. "Ma'am, do you need something?"

Yes, Mathew alive and here to keep me and Philip from harm. She shook her head and moved at the world's slowest pace down the treads. "How are my guests?"

"They are well. Enjoying your treats. I will go see if they are ready for more refreshments." The butler turned and left for the parlor.

Once she reached the console, Theodosia dumped the paper

pieces onto the mahogany surface. Her reticule slid from her elbow down the length of her forearm, but that didn't stop her from arranging the torn pieces. She swirled the paper with her pinkie and made out the sum, ten thousand pounds. The devil was right. The offer was far too low for anything she and Mathew had worked so hard to build. The earl, Ewan's father, must think her daft. She put the paper into her reticule. Later, she would toss it in the hearth and watch the bits burn.

She started to reach inside the satin and peek at her newspaper responses but decided against it. With a room of guests to attend, she needed to complete the planning for Mathew's Flora Festival down to the tolling of the small parish bells. He had so loved this event.

She folded her arms, her fingers clanging the brass buttons of her dark sleeves. These mourning shrouds had become her friend, a comforting hug, like now, when she was weak. It was a show of respect for a good husband gone too soon. Was marrying again the only answer? "Madam?" The butler stood beside her. Woolgathering, she'd missed his solemn footfalls.

"Your guests are waiting. Mrs. Cecil never keeps her guests waiting."

It wasn't censure in his voice, but something thick and noble, almost like understanding.

She nodded. "Cecils do what they must."

Pickens nodded. "Yes, even when things are difficult." He bowed, back as straight as a new fence post. "I'll go see if Cook's pastries have run out."

The loyal man proceeded down the hall. She watched his steady, easy gait until he disappeared around the corner.

Easy. Why did she think getting a husband by advertisement would be easy?

Go to the stationer's, pick up the latest response to her *Morning Post* advertisement, then return home safe and smiling with a suitable offer of marriage—all before dinner. Easy.

Easy, my eye. She took a breath, but it rattled within her chest until it found the right pipe to escape. She coughed, wiped her mouth, and tried to think of anything but fleeing. If Tradenwood wasn't safe, where would she and Philip find safety, find acceptance?

Still a little shaky, Theodosia commanded her wobbly legs to move toward the parlor. The meeting for the festival needed her attention. Tucking her reticule under her arms, she ordered her lips to form a smile. Once everyone left except Ester and Frederica—the Brain and the Flirt—she'd rely on her friends to keep her steady and follow through with their newspaper advertisement plan. Or... Theodosia would gather up all the coins she could muster and escape with Philip to the Continent.

. . .

Dining at Grandbole Manor after six long years wasn't as horrible as Ewan expected. His nieces grabbed ahold of him from the moment Jasper pushed him across the threshold.

Oh, how much time had slipped past? Three girls, three beautiful little girls. Only two had been here that last summer at Grandbole, before he'd joined his regiment. His heart burned, roasting with the memory of proud Jasper bundling two small girls in his arms as he escorted his pregnant wife to their carriage.

Maria hadn't wanted her laying-in here, but at her mother's home in Devonshire. Dutiful, appeasing Jasper had defied everyone, even shouting down the earl to please Maria.

Ewan had never been more proud or more jealous of his brother. He hadn't yet experienced the burden of that type of love. Ewan hadn't yet met Theo.

Anne, a ten-year-old with blonde-like-her-father locks, put a palm under her chin. She appeared to be the head inquisitor of the three girls and chose to ask questions rather than peruse the long cedar table that held more food than a regiment of a thousand men could devour. "Uncle, so what temperature is the West Indies?" she asked.

"Very hot, my dear."

Lydia, nine years old and very much math inspired, drummed the table with her little fingers. "Is it hotter than Grandbole on a summer's day or an autumn day?"

"Very, very hot—hotter than both."

The little one whose name also started with an L, Laura, no Lucy, cast a big frown. "That's not very descriptive, Uncle."

Ewan looked at the cute upturned nose and the strawberry-blonde hair and released a smile. "You are right. I can do better. The heat of the day starts warm and inviting. By noon, it's enough to positively boil the tea. There. Will that do?"

Lucy closed her eyes and nodded. Ewan smiled again. He'd discovered the dreamer in the mix.

Jasper chuckled and finished dumping a piece of bread into his mouth. "Girls, save your questions for later or Uncle Ewan won't come back. We mustn't frighten him away, and no tricks, not yet."

It wouldn't be the three angelic moppets who'd make Ewan flee. No, it would be a curmudgeon whose chair at the far end sat empty. With a sip from his glass of cool water, he couldn't exactly measure the disappointment roiling in his gut alongside the succulent duck they'd had for dinner. Scanning the dark polished floors, the high walls strewn with family portraits of Fitzwilliams through the ages, a dormant sense of pride wet his tongue. Though he'd never mention it aloud, Ewan had missed Grandbole and his family, even the earl.

A servant came and whispered in Jasper's ear.

His brother nodded. "Father's finishing up business. He wants to meet with you in the library."

Ewan chugged more water and wished the wetness possessed the tang of liquor. He'd been formally summoned. With a slow motion, he stood, bowed to each of his fine nieces, then turned to make the long walk through the quiet corridors. He filled his lungs, savoring the scent of polish, noting the absence of flowers. It seemed that the family livelihood stayed outside.

After several turns guided by the swords strewn across every inch of the dark paint, he made it to the library. He pushed on the heavy door, folded his arms behind his back, and marched inside, entering a room of fine emerald-colored silk walls.

He was alone. Again, a sense of disappointment stirred. Turning to the exit, he decided against retreat and sank upon the inflexible straight-backed sofa centered upon the wide gold rug.

The grand walnut bookcases still towered as they had six years ago. Both were filled with books, among them Aristotle, Bacon, and Descartes, titles meant to sculpt the Fitzwilliam men's minds. But did not the shelves also hold the gilded pages of playwrights Hensley and Broome? How was Ewan to know those ideas were out of bounds?

Not able to help himself, he popped up and moved to a perennial favorite, Shakespeare, and poked at the torn spine. One he'd probably injured. No smile pressed his lips. Memories of dressing-downs filled his head.

The door opened like a lid to an ancient coffin, slow and moaning. His brother entered and behind him, their father.

Archibald Fitzwilliam, the Earl of Crisdon, had aged. A thousand more white hairs rimmed the balding spot he'd long tried to cover with powders. Now, that battle had been lost. However, the sneer over his glasses, the condescension that only his narrow dark blue eyes could bring, none of that had changed.

"Good of you to come for dinner, Fitzwilliam, finally," his father said. His head dipped up and down as if scanning a rose for an aphid bug. "About time for you to slink back here. At least you've seen your mother in Town. Haven't totally abandoned family."

Ewan released a low, tight breath, then straightened to his full height. He refused to look at his brother who, obviously, still served as a trickster. "I was told you wanted to see me. Surely, I've been mistaken." He turned to the heavy door. "I'll see you in another six years, sir. You, too, Jasper. Oh, don't mind me taking your carriage back to town."

Before he could touch the knob, his Judas brother leaped in front of him with hands outstretched. "Father, you know you wanted Ewan here. And Brother, if you were truly against visiting you'd have jumped from my carriage earlier. You're both too stubborn. I tire at being caught between you."

Ewan had no desire to feel his peacemaking pain. In fact, he wanted to be numb. He wandered over to the sideboard, moved the false panel book that hid their father's prized brandy, and poured a glass of the amber liquid. Perhaps, if he drank enough, quickly enough, the anger trapped in his skin would evaporate. "I'm here. Tell me what you want me to know, Father."

The earl came up beside him and filled another glass. "Your service to the Fourth West Indian Regiment ended three months ago when it disbanded. Why didn't you return to Grandbole?"

"Did you pay for it to disband? Of course, you did. Something I was begrudgingly good at must have been horrid for you."

The tall man patted his thickening middle. "Son, you are being ridiculous."

Ewan took another slow swig, holding the honey on his tongue, missing the sweet rum of the Caribbean. "Well, you've done your best to stunt anything I've wanted to pursue."

"Your judgment has made me suspect."

Blinking, Ewan remembered how his actions had been judged in this room by the earl. *Your life will be a waste. She's a dalliance, nothing more.* With another slurp, his humor returned, for who couldn't laugh at the man being right? Theo's love hadn't lasted, but the memories of her, of shy, business-minded, insatiable Theo, had formed the play that would make Ewan a fortune, one independent of his father's. "You are right as usual, sir. I don't know why I came, either. That questionable logic thing is hard to outrun. The beefsteaks were good. Give my compliments to the cook."

Looking at the blank stare on his father's countenance re-minded Ewan that his father had a poor sense of humor, another thing they didn't have in common. "Time to leave. Father. Brother."

The earl coughed, then said, "Sorry."

Ewan froze for a moment. Then put a finger in his ear to unplug it. "Did you say something, sir? My eardrums could be lying."

His father gritted his teeth. He partially opened his mouth, exposing the canine fangs that had sunk into Ewan's hide and that of any man standing in the way of accomplishing something the earl wanted. "I said sorry. I shouldn't have demanded you to go to war to prove your merit."

The old man apologizing. Something wasn't right. The repeated word, "sorry." What did that mean? Shouldn't there be thunder crashing, maybe a flurry of villainous violin notes, as would happen in the theater? "What is this?"

"Your mother hasn't told you?"

Only a Fitzwilliam fool offered information freely, and Ewan was done being a fool. He didn't blink or move.

"Your mother blames me for you not inheriting Tradenwood."

Oh. The nonsense about inheriting his uncle's lands. "My uncle read the same letter you did about my demise. Pity he passed on before he learned the truth."

The earl frowned and stood uncharacteristically quiet. There must be something more.

But Ewan didn't want to submit to any of the man's games. "I am quite resolved, Father. For what would a soldier or a playwright do with all that land, anyway?"

Pushing at his forehead and the deeply etched frown lines, the earl gulped down his brandy and poured himself another. "Not the theater nonsense again."

Jasper jumped between them. "This is not a time for family to be fighting. We need to come together. Crisdon lands are under threat. The competition for flowers is more than ever. And Tradenwood is withholding water. They're building dams on the springs. If that continues, we'll lose it all."

"We?" Ewan folded his arms and kept his gaze level, resisting the call back to the sideboard. "You need to pay the new owner more money. Who is the lucky fool to have the land you wanted?"

The earl wrinkled his nose beneath his brass wire frames. "That blasted uncle of yours left everything to a distant cousin. The new owner passed away, leaving his widow with control of everything. If she doesn't take my latest offer I may have to..."

Ewan spread his feet apart, slightly enjoying the concern rattling the earl's grumbly voice. "You may have to what? Offer full value to my cousin-by-marriage, or is that once-removed?"

Jasper moved from blocking the doorway to perch on the large desk near the window. His face was strained, more serious than Ewan had ever seen.

"Father's done twice that on the last offer. I think she wants to ruin us. For a woman, she's a savvy one."

Back at the sideboard, the earl tapped the brandy stopper, but this time his hands shook. "Might have to resort to direct negotiations. It's been difficult, with her observing full and now half-mourning rituals."

There was something not being said by the old man. Something was in the air, heavier than the smell of dusty books or the warm cigar ash—the scents that stayed in his head embodying this library. "You've never had a problem being direct." Ewan lifted his gaze to the candles burning in the corner, counting flickers, counting direct slights.

No more playwriting nonsense. I didn't raise you to be a fool.

The regiment will make a man of you. Maybe even a good one.

If you serve with honor, then I'll turn my eye from your dalliances.

One dalliance was his first play. The second, Theo.

"Sir, I remember very well how you've made your opinion known. What's stopping you?"

His father nodded and downed his glass. "This situation is difficult, but Mrs. Cecil has a price. I have to figure out what it is."

Cecil? Ewan's pulse started to tick up.

His father stared at him as if hunting for something, but Ewan didn't know why, unless this Mrs. Cecil was the same Mrs. Cecil he'd met at the Burlington Arcade. Ewan's legs started him moving, even before he was ready to. He circled around the grand desk to the window. From the wide glass, in the tiptop corner, he could see the edge of Tradenwood. Could that be where Theo lay her head? Had Theo gotten herself a rich husband, a cousin to his mother? And now she owned Tradenwood?

Ewan pulled the curtain closed, keeping him from looking for her again. When he turned and saw the guilt painting the earl's face with those cocky brows flying high above his quizzing eyes, Ewan knew Mrs. Cecil was Theo. Making sure the shock paining his chest had drained away, he cleared his throat and forced his tone to be even and steady. "I'm sure that a fair offer will get the response you deserve."

With a tug to his waistcoat, the earl sank onto the stiff sofa.

"What do you intend to do now, Fitzwilliam?"

Was it too beneath the earl to ask his son to reason with an old lover? Perhaps. He scratched his nose and sniffed strong lavender. Theo's smelly paper package that he'd left in the carriage still stained his fingertips. Just like her to stay with him. "I...I'm working on a new play."

"Not much money in theater, Son."

Ewan jerked, tensing at the hint of a slight, then remembered his facade of not caring. "It's more than enough because it's earned by my hands, not yours. Except for the purchase of my commission, I haven't needed you—or your assistance."

Jasper chimed in. "This one is very good. He's created this villain. She's outrageous. London will adore this play."

"Ewan, you must stay at Grandbole and work on it. Become reacquainted with the land you once loved. The flower fields and its fragrances are in your blood, from your mother's family as well as my side. And you could be a help to Hartwell."

"My brother knows I welcome his help, but I can do more to manage Grandbole, if you let me, Father." His brother's voice sound unusually strained. "Your nieces would like to know more of Uncle Ewan, too. And they are getting started with their questions."

"Stay a while. Then, tell me of your desires. Maybe this time you can convince me of your passion for the theater."

Could the years have moved the earl from his harsh stance on the arts? Or maybe this war with Theo had changed him. Well, Theo had changed Ewan. "I turned down Mother's request to stay with her in London, I don't think—"

Jasper came alongside him and filled a glass with brandy. He drank one and then another in quick succession. "You're the perfect story crafter for the girls and for those whom *you* write."

Ewan sighed at the not-so-subtle hint at helping his brother with the newspaper bride stunt. With a shake of the head, he ignored the two faces waiting for his yes. It wasn't that easy. He set his glass down and again drew his hand along the bookshelf. These leathered spines written by playwrights had caught ahold of his imagination, never letting go, until he had spied a young woman gathering roses in the fields. Now, the thought of his Circe injuring his family wouldn't let go. Their common problem was less than a mile away. "I've missed a great deal. My nieces are fine girls. They make for a tempting offer."

Jasper clasped Ewan's elbow. "We need reinforcements. The girls outnumber us and with their pranks, we need you. Perhaps, we could have a chance at being a united family. Isn't that so, Father?"

The earl moved to the door. "Please stay, Son. You are welcome. Your room has been refreshed. Might even find a change of clothes to your liking."

He glanced at Ewan, dead in the eyes. It felt like an apology, but that was how it was between them, only going so far, never crossing the line. Respectable, distant, passionless. Yet, he'd never know if things could be different, if he turned away now. Ewan planted his boots apart and braced. "I'll stay for a few days. My flat and Mother's errands will keep."

The earl nodded. "Well, she's seen you enough these three months in London. If you stay, perhaps she will abandon her parties and return to Grandbole, too."

Being a pawn between his parents was an old game. One he'd

hoped they'd stopped playing when he'd gone to war. Ewan shoved his hands into his pockets and shrugged. He'd let the earl fight that battle. Ewan would focus on his Circe and the package of smelly lavender that needed to be delivered.

CHAPTER THREE

The Return of an Impassioned Ghost

Once Theodosia waved good-bye to her planning committee, she walked back to the parlor. Of all the rooms in Tradenwood, this one she liked the best. From the doorway, she scanned the gold-papered walls crowned with dented white trim. It felt regal and clean and held the largest fireplace she'd ever seen. Still better was the access to the private patio, a cobblestone wonder rimmed with flowerpots and overlooking a multitiered garden below. Majestic—it was the best place on earth. There, Mathew Cecil had made her an offer she couldn't refuse.

In this very room, he had offered her a name and his protection. The lowest moment of her life had become her best. Tonight, when everyone was in bed, she'd go out onto the cobblestones, smell the clematis they'd planted together, and listen to the night. Her lovely memories of a life with Mathew would stop her from fretting over her present troubles...and Ewan.

For a moment, she closed her eyes and clutched the heavy door. The bittersweet memories she'd tried to forget returned. Ewan's voice teasing her, as she had cried upon his shoulder after being cheated out of a guinea. How they'd snuck behind the coaching house and had danced in the rain. Even now she could the feel the strength of his arms as he'd twirled her till she'd lost her breath.

Theodosia tensed. She shook as if it were yesterday when she'd found out that the love of her young heart had died. The news had been tossed to her like trash. She'd fallen to her knees behind that coaching house sobbing until she'd become breathless, mourning his loss—Ewan had died in some foreign land. She never thought she'd see his face again, or bump into him at the Burlington Arcade.

His return could be a problem *Oh, who am I kidding?* His return *was* a problem. Could she pretend he was still dead and go through with her plans? She touched the letters in her reticule. There must be one decent offer from her newspaper advertisement, one that would keep her heart and Philip safe.

Pickens and a few grooms passed her as they returned the desk she used for business. In another moment, they exited the room with the excess chairs from her meeting. The butler bowed as she stepped into the parlor. He started closing the door then paused. "Will you need anything else for the evening, ma'am?"

"Nothing more tonight."

"Then good evening, Mrs. Cecil."

As if her surname was a magical elixir, a mixture of relief and wonder flooded her middle. Mathew would be proud of her planning. The meeting had gone well. The Flora Festival was one step closer to being perfect—with chimney sweeps and bell ringing, like when he'd lived. "Thank you, Pickens."

Once the door shut, she offered a smile, a small one for her two dearest friends. "So glad this dinner is over. Thank you for staying."

"Like w-we'd leave before hearing the news of your trip into town." Frederica Burghley popped another chocolatey bonbon in her mouth. It made her perfect pronunciation sound stuttered. "Did you get another answer to the advertisement?"

Theodosia patted her reticule, made her way across the room, and sank into an emerald chair by the fireplace. "Yes, but let me enjoy this moment. The last tradesman's wife has boarded her carriage." The faithful and the curious had had their fill of her hearty and expensive rabbit stew, a sixpence and a farthing a bowl. Then they'd eaten the best rainbow-colored jellies that could be had in all of England. "They had a good meal and surely enjoyed dessert. A shilling each."

With her short brown nose pressed in a book, Ester Croome put her feet up on the chaise. Her silky pale blue slippers peeked from beneath the creamy hem of her gown, like pollen stamens within a lily. The points of the Vandyke lace edging the pleats of her bodice matched the slim bonnet she used to cover her hair. Like a mobcap, she wore one all the time, each one more intricate and delicate than the next. "Theodosia, I see you counting with your fingers."

"You know I like knowing costs." Lord knows, life and death had taught her this. "But I think we did well. I saw many of the merchants' wives smiling with approval."

Ester, lovely, relaxed, always sketching—the brainiest of them all—turned another page in her book. "So how much did you spend on people hoping you'll fail?"

A little over one and sixpence a plate, but that wasn't her friend's true question. Theodosia sighed. "It's for Cecil's festival. I must honor him. His widow has to do this. I will not have anyone saying this wasn't done well or *she* didn't do it well."

Frederica wiped her mouth of crumbs, then smoothed her blush pink bodice. "Of course you must, but let's end the torture, Theodosia. Did my plan of a newspaper advertisement catch you a husband at the Burlington Arcade?"

Typical of her friend to get right to the point and take credit for things they'd all had a hand in, but Frederica meant no harm. Her heart was too big for that.

"I caught something." Theodosia unhooked her reticule from her wrist. The pouch sank to her lap. She didn't quite know how to explain about the ghost from her past. She couldn't even stop from chewing her bottom lip with all the uncertainty this day had brought. "The letters are in here, but I can't look. Not another surprise."

"Another? What is that supposed to mean?" Frederica sprang up from her chair. The blush-colored tail of her gown, layered with lace appliqués that looked like new growth leaves in spring, rustled as she paced back and forth in front of the oversized bookcase. "Did you get an offer or not, Theodosia?"

With a hand on her hip, Frederica stopped. Her perfectly coiffed sandy-brown curly hair bounced and fluttered as her large hazel eyes lifted. "It's not good for one woman to tease another. That's a man's job."

Despite everything—a ghost, a guttersnipe, a gaggle of guests—Theodosia laughed. "Frederica, the flirt. You're always good for a giggle. And I need humor today. We have letters, but the danger to Philip grows daily. I could lose my boy."

"No. We won't let that happen." Frederica crossed to her and held her palm out. "This plan will work, and end your suffering and ours, too. You look so drained. Let me read the letters."

Five years of friendship had surely taught Frederica to wait for Theodosia to bend. And she would for these women. No one knew her better, but none knew of Theo the Flower Seller, the waif who'd made horrible choices, doing things she'd sworn she'd never do, becoming what she'd sworn she'd never be. Only a ghost, whom she hoped to never see again, knew Theo. With his family up the hill, it would only be a matter of time before she saw Ewan again.

She pushed the letters into Frederica's hand. "Take them. If they are bad, burn them like weeds. My cup is full."

"Don't. Do nothing of the kind, Frederica," Ester piped up, though she hadn't put down her charcoal. "We are stronger than weeds or words on paper. We will give a proper response, fitting a respectable widow. Agreed, Mrs. Cecil?"

The magic of the name worked again, stirring up the dormant hope Mathew's kindness had planted and watered over the years. It couldn't be gone. The strength he'd given her had to live beyond the grave. Theodosia lifted her head. "Yes. A proper response."

Frederica nodded and waved the letters. She sorted them, flipping from one to the other. "Two responses. The squire sent one, and we have a new one. We'll start with the squire." She tore into the man's fancy gray paper, then mouthed a few words.

Seconds ticked by. The grandfather clock moaned from the corner. Anticipation built in Theodosia's chest, giving a little lift to her deflated lungs. With Lester's threats growing worse, the boring squire might be the answer, if he wanted to marry. Their meeting two weeks ago had not gone terribly. He'd sat very quietly through much of the coffeehouse visit and had not looked her in her eye. Had he been shy? Or had he been uncomfortable with her race?

"It's a yes. The squire wants to marry you." Frederica's voice didn't sound happy. In fact, it held shrill notes. "That's good, I suppose."

With wide eyes, Theodosia popped up and stared over Frederica's shoulder. "This is the answer. My boy can be protected by the squire. But you don't like him." She took a step back, lowering her desperate sounding voice. "What is it? What is wrong?"

Her friend started to pace again, this time with a hand to her hip. She frowned something awful and looked as if she'd toss the letter into the hearth. "He wants you to pay for the license. Does he have to be so cheap about it? This is not the man for you."

What else could a desperate Blackamoor expect? At least, he hadn't cursed at her or not sent a response after their meeting. Theodosia rubbed at her brow, but squared her shoulders. "I'm not perfect. None of these men are. Only my Mr. Cecil was. He was so generous. One of a kind."

Her flirty friend wrinkled her nose. "One of an old kind. Very old. Shouldn't a second marriage right that scale? Or are you afraid of young and virile?"

"Now you sound like that toad, Lester. He's almost forcing himself on me, even as he threatens to take my son."

"Well." Ester's voice rose, though, again, she didn't raise her pretty olive-colored face. Her gaze remained buried in her drawing. "Some men bluster because they fear rejection."

Theodosia moved to the patio door. She parted the curtains to allow the moonlight inside. She didn't need someone fearful. Her old love, Ewan, the one she thought had died, had feared his father more than he'd feared parting from her. No. No. She despised anyone who wasn't brave, even herself. "We've planned this Holland visit for Lester. It will give me enough time for banns to be read. Before he returns, I'll be a properly married woman with a husband who can advocate for Philip."

"So an old and cheap husband is fine for you?" Frederica's laugh grew louder. "Not for me."

Focusing on the patio, Theodosia let her eyes soak in the darkness dancing beneath the reflections of stars. Her arbor, holding the wonderfully growing clematis, let patches of moonlight onto the stone floor. This planting was Mathew's last great indulgence, so expensive to tend, yet so lovely. A cheap second husband couldn't be the answer. How would things fair when Philip's doctoring bills increased?

Despairing, she turned back to her friends. "If I had a choice, I'd choose another man, but only a man can fight for me at the Court of Chancery. A man will keep Lester from using his guardianship to take my son. Lester wants to control the Cecil money. By controlling me, he controls the fortune."

Frederica rubbed her palm along the back of the floral chaise, making the nap of the fabric darken. "It's such a lovely fortune." She chuckled again. "Very lovely."

Frederica was not shy about her want of riches. Though she'd been provided an extravagant allowance by her wealthy father, the Duke of Simone, the woman seemed to be on a quest to gain more. Her relationship with the duke was as well as one could expect between a father and his acknowledged bastard. Perhaps this need for coins was a way to attain her own security. Theodosia stepped close and put a hand on her shoulder. "I want honest and brave."

"Yes, but money is important. It gives us a say in this world, even if it's only a peep. You know it's a requirement for your next husband."

Theodosia picked up the poker and stabbed the logs in the snowy hearth, before leaning back against the heavy marble mantel and facing her friends. "I have enough. Cecil made sure of that."

With a clap of her hands, Ester lifted her face from her sketch. "This is so grand. We've been at this business for three months and we have our first offer."

She'd been selectively listening as usual, but she was right. At least Theodosia had an offer. "The squire is in his late forties and seemed honest. I need someone beyond reproach to protect my son. Philip Cecil had a good man who loved him. Is it too much to ask for another one?"

Nothing but silence and smiles of pity greeted her request. Maybe it was. Theodosia shook herself. Woolgathering was not to be had now, not with another letter to open. "Maybe the other letter will be better. There might be time for a new prospect, if we can get him up to scratch before the festival. The banns could be read, everything in place, before Lester figures out what I've done."

Frederica wiggled her small fingers under the wax seal of the second letter. When it broke open, she dipped her head and again her full lips moved. This time she put the letter on the table. "I don't know what to make of this."

Unprepared for another note filled with false praise, a request for funds, or addressing the wrong advertisement, Theodosia dropped onto the chaise and locked arms with Ester. "I need you to read it. I can't."

Ester put her feet on the floor. "What's going on Frederica? What is it?"

"It's a riddle of sorts from a man of good character, or so he states," said Frederica. "But he's a peer—a baron, I'd guess."

Ester slipped from Theodosia and pounced on the letter. Her brow creased more deeply. Surely, this was not a good match. Her friend waved the paper. "It's a riddle. This baron is either too clever or it's a test to figure out your character. We must be very careful in our response."

Stopping from biting her lip, Theodosia took the letter and became confused by what seemed like a poem. She laid it back down. "So we should take this seriously?"

Frederica shrugged her shoulders. "Why didn't he ask for a first meeting, Theodosia?" she asked. "I'm never afraid of first meetings."

Ester's forehead crinkled with more lines. With hands lifted, as if putting Frederica into her sights, she said, "I wouldn't be either, if my father was a peer, and my complexion was light like yours, Frederica."

Being caught between worlds was a sore spot for Frederica, not light enough for some, not dark enough for others. Lips in a full pout, the flirt sashayed over and scooped up the letter again. "Let me see if I can figure out what the brain cannot."

"Ladies, please. No fighting. I've had a horrid day."

Ester mumbled something that sounded like *Sorry, Frederica*. Her smirk-laced smile had turned to a frown. "What happened? You weren't at a safe store? The Burlington Arcade is very public."

The rise in Ester's voice would be followed by a scold of going without Phipps or another male servant. Theodosia didn't want to depend on someone else fighting for her. Like today, she'd been careful to pick shops that hated skin color less than they loved money. It was Ewan who had ruined things, but she couldn't say that. "No. Nothing untoward happened. I was able to shop, but I lost my expensive soap. It would have made for a nice bath, but nothing will wash this day away."

Frederica fanned herself with the stationery. "Oh, Theodosia. That's terrible. If you purchased them from the Burlington Arcade, I know it cost you."

Smile restored, Ester crossed her fingers. "Maybe we can discern what this new man is looking for in an answer. That is, if it's not a joke."

"A farce, like in the theater. That is what this sounds like." Frederica nodded then traced her pinky over the paper. "A baron? Could be a courtesy title. *Hmm.* That means he'll inherit something when his father dies. If he's looking for a wealthy bride, he could be either mouse poor or in a family given to scandal. That might not be good."

A title sounded nice, but how much worse could things get with family scandals? She'd had enough of those. Scandals caused families to split. The arguments she'd witnessed between Ewan and his father had been horrible—terrible like thunder. The day the earl had caught her and Ewan in the carriage loft, his anger had flashed. His words had killed her, and he'd made Ewan leave her. She blinked and closed off that stupid part of her heart, the part that remembered that fleeting summer love. "Is it worth the risk to think that this poet wants a marriage and not just games? I could spend my time getting used to the squire."

"I'm a hopeful cynic." Frederica waved her hand as if music

played. "A baron could be a more impressive advocate to the courts. With my shock of his approach gone, I think he is a poetic, romantic man. He put effort into this. Listen. 'Some say their love of children is unending, but how can that be proven to be permanent, unbending? What say you?' How very sweet."

Ester leaped up on her short legs, her gown swishing as she went to stand next to tall Frederica. "I get it now. He does not want to meet yet. He wants you to respond about children. Why is that important? Maybe your advertisement sounded too good to be true. What did we put again?"

Theodosia started to reply, but movement on the patio caught her gaze. Something sparkled in the evening light. A misplaced teaspoon or fork from her dinner guests?

It had been a long day of seeing undesirable things. She didn't need to look for more. She rubbed her eyes. "We said, 'Respectable young widow of means looking for honorable family man of good character for matrimony.'"

The grimace on Frederica's supple features was comical. Her nose wriggled as if she smelled dead fish. "Oh. I forgot we went the mind-numbing route. We should write back with more color. Something clever."

Trying not to turn back to the patio, Theodosia crossed her arms. "What should I have said? Blackamoor beauty with babe and loads of baubles, needs beau?"

Ester smiled wide, like Philip's governess did when he did something right during his lessons. Over the years, Ester's tutelage and Mathew's guidance had taken a barely literate street seller and taught her to sound as if she'd been brought up under the love and care of genteel parents, not a poor urchin with no last name. "Maybe this poet baron will have a wonderful last name. I hate giving up the surname Cecil. I've grown so accustomed to it. And maybe this flamboyant man won't mind the company I keep. The squire or baron must allow my friends to visit."

Now, Ester's face held a frown. She started twiddling her thumbs. "Well, if he allows you to continue to shop Croome's fabrics, I know my parents will be thrilled."

Frederica came over to Theodosia and Ester, linking hands—light, olive, bronze. "I remember the shy girls I met at a party thrown by my father. They held their heads high amongst all the whispers, like the day l went from obscurity to the acknowledged by-blow of one of the prince's favorite dukes. People will always talk or try to isolate us, but we are more than that. In fact, I now feed the gossips things to say, like what parties I will attend and which of the Croome's fabrics I will turn into the latest design."

"'Tis true." Ester's voice boomed with pride for her family's business. "We have the best silks of all the tradesmen. The best woolens in all of Cheapside. We probably supply some of the mantua makers in that fancy Burlington Arcade you went to today—but enough of this silliness. We have a proposal and a provocative response. I say we answer the new mystery man and delay the squire. Two offers definitely means more choices."

Considering all, Theodosia turned toward the doors that led to the patio. It made sense to have another option. One path was something to avoid. Again, she noticed movement outside. Something stirred in the dim light near her favorite rosebush. She was sure of it. *Could it be the wind?*

She rubbed her temples. "Anyone can write flowery words. Or lie with beautiful ones to your face. But you two think we should waste another week and delay a solid offer? Time is so short. Delay doesn't sound like a shrewd decision. It could be costly."

Frederica yawned as she rubbed her arms. "Business-minded as always. If the second letter is from a gentleman with a courtesy title, *he* can defeat Lester at the Chancery. The squire is riskier. And marriage, this second one, should be forever. You are young. Your math mind needs poetry. Listen to this line again. 'Love of children is unending, but how can that be proven to be permanent, unbending?' It's poetry. I know you are tired, but a couple weeks delay will harm nothing and could mean everything. You deserve a chance at someone who could love you and your son, forever."

Her dear friend possessed a generous heart, so Theodosia wouldn't correct her about love or marriage lasting forever. None of those sentimental things lasted. "Very well. I'll write something at my desk tonight. You'll be able to edit it in the morning before you head back to Town. Now go on to bed."

Ester wrapped an arm about her. The shorter girl reached up to Theodosia's shoulder, though her wisdom was taller than most. "You do deserve poetry and joy. Don't stay up too long. Get rest. The lines under your eyes are from staying up with little Philip. He'll not get better if you are not well."

Pulling away, Theodosia moved to the curtains and fingered the burnished gold cloth. As she was about to close them, she stopped. Someone hid by her rosebush. Dread mixed with anger in her stomach. She knew she wouldn't be able to rest tonight, not until she dealt with her ghost. "You ladies go on. I'll stay here and take care of business. I'll have the response ready for review in the morn."

Ester reached up and kissed her cheek. "Promise you will go to bed soon."

She nodded. "Go on."

Frederica dropped the baron's letter onto the chaise, picked up her goblet of madeira, along with a final bonbon, and headed for the door. "Do sleep, Theodosia. With the festival and your newspaper groom options, you need a clear head."

"Good night, dears," Theodosia said, hoping they'd hurry.

Frederica and Ester passed a shrug between them as they left. For this, Theodosia was grateful. She needed to face her latest problem alone. Once their footfalls disappeared, she locked the parlor door. She took a deep breath, and with a hand steadied on the brass knob of the patio door, she opened it. In a low voice, she said. "Come in, Ghost. Commence your haunting."

• • •

Ewan stepped from the shadows of the big rosebush. What had started as a simple quest to walk past, maybe drop her package off with a footman, had become an overwhelming desire to see the usurper in all her ill-gotten wealth. This was his uncle's house. Theo had married into his mother's family, *his* family. Outrageous.

His boot heels drummed on the cobblestones until he stood six inches from Theo—grabbing-her-and-shaking-her-for-answers or kissing distance. "I'm no ghost. I thought we established that earlier."

Her eyes widened. The dim light caused the pupils within to dilate even bigger. "Still a ghost to me. Nothing'll change that."

"I am quite alive, breathing the same fragrant air as you,

Theo the Flower Seller." He pushed past her and scooped up the note lying on the chaise. "So this is why you were at Burlington Arcade. Collecting your next swindle?"

Theo's henna cheeks darkened. He wondered if she'd fall over and faint, but as he moved closer to steady her, he didn't see weakness, but strength in her straightening posture, the leveling of her shoulders.

She reached for the paper and missed, almost slapping his chest in the process. "How dare you listen to a private conversation?"

"My apologies. But what makes the wealthy Widow Cecil seek a husband by newspaper?"

"It's none of your concern how I gain a husband. We both know that waiting for a man to profess his love for me but who then begs off of an elopement because of his father doesn't work. Does he know where you are? You should hurry back. Lord Crisdon might be snapping his fingers for you, or his dogs."

Now this was the woman he remembered—sharp-witted, expressing the precise sentiment to twist someone up. Shoving a balled fist behind his back, he shook his head. "That's not how it was. You know we had to wait until I served a year. That was all. But seems to me you don't know what it means to wait, Theo."

She bunched up her collar in the most prudish manner conceivable. "My friends call me Theodosia. Liars from the past, they call me Theo."

He gave her the letter, taking full advantage of clasping her hand, feeling her rising pulse. "Liar? I'm a liar because you thought me dead? I think you are mistaken. Perhaps liar doesn't mean what you think it does."

She slid her hand away from him, pulling back as if it hurt to touch him. "I've learned quite a few words since then. Like trespasser and bounder. Since you have no purpose here, other than to steal my peace, I suggest you leave."

"I have a purpose. Your soaps. Too feminine of a fragrance for me." He returned to the large rosebush where he'd dropped the parcel the minute he'd heard them read the lines he'd written for Jasper. Now, he saw his brother's brilliance in using the obscure courtesy title. Yet, the fool assignment of helping Jasper woo a newspaper bride had led to Theo. This was Ewan's luck, bad luck. "Here."

When she bit her lip, he knew the rawness of being face-to-face knifed her insides, too. A small part of him wanted her to suffer as he had, knowing she'd abandoned their promise. The other part of him was too busy concentrating on her delectable mouth.

"The soap was expensive, Ewan. But I can't risk you being here, can't be seen with you. Take it and leave."

"I told you. It's not my scent." He held the package close to her silky cheek that even now glowed in the soft light coming from the house. That creamy complexion had grown more beautiful. Kept women surely had an easier time of staying lovely. "It's yours, Theo. Or maybe I should say, Cousin Theo, since you've slept your way into my mother's family. Take it, Cousin."

Finally, her palm lifted. She touched his hand again before pulling the package to her bosom. "Please go."

She turned. The fine dark dress swathed her hips in a fashion that only Michelangelo could sculpt.

Ewan couldn't help but follow her inside.

Putting the package and the letter on a low table by the chaise, she faced him and winced. "Why are you still here?"

Her eyes were glossy and wet, not like before. *Is she crying?* Ewan wanted to kick himself for caring, kick himself for allowing her to still have a hold on him. "You don't think I'm owed an explanation? My father says you've been in mourning for Cecil for a long time. You're in gray—half mourning—that's months of paying respect for the dearly departed. You barely waited a few weeks to grieve little old me. And now you are hunting for a new husband. Why?"

"I owe you nothing, save a footman's coin for fetching my package. And is it so hard for you to think that maybe there is another man like Mathew Cecil who thinks I'm the marrying kind? Perhaps I'm longing for someone else who will treat me with respect."

His brow rose of its own volition. He leaned near her sweet ear. "Was respect required before or after you became a mistress?"

She stepped back, eyes widening, breath sputtering. "I've spent too much on you today. Leave."

Even as he said the slight, he knew it was wrong, but it turned her sullen eyes the color of flames, rich and dark, full of heat. Her fire was still there, merely trapped under neatly attired wrappings. And that heat made him press closer. "For six years, I wrote scene after scene in my head, why there was *us*. I didn't have money or titles or land. Was I practice? Was my teaching you to read enough to pretend to like me? Enough payment for an affair?"

"I was young and stupid, Ewan. So were you. Too much time has passed to do this now. They said you died. No one said you lived. Until today, you never came back."

"I was shot on the battlefield not even thirty days upon landing in Spain. It was bad. Names were mixed up and the regiment sent word I'd been killed. It took nine months before my full strength returned. Father wrote you'd run off with another man. I saw no need to return."

She blinked her long silky lashes. "I'm glad you're not dead. Maybe you can go live the life your father approves of and leave me be."

"Well, I am. You're in my latest play. I hope I've captured your appeal, your exotic heady beauty, your underhanded dealings—"

"Why must I be exotic? Because I'm not pale or white as a sheet? Mathew Cecil thought me pretty."

"Well, you do clean up nicely in such fashionable trimmings. But what rich man's fetish wouldn't? I suppose you saw an opportunity and seized it. Business-minded to a fault."

"Do you want to hear that I grieved you? I did. Your father said you were dead, before he ran me off. They... He said you were killed in honor, something a wench like me could never understand. But you are not dead. Probably not even a scratch and you are mad at me for continuing to live. You should be relieved that you didn't have to return to these fields to wed the ignorant flower seller. Can you imagine figuring out how to feed mouths while still waiting for your father's approval?"

He came alongside her, took her free palm, and flattened the fidgeting thing against his chest, sneaking it under his waistcoat to the smooth linen of his shirt, making sure her fingers covered the raised scars on his chest. "Do you feel those scratches? The physicians call them scars."

Her hand stilled a moment and a world of emotions twirled in her eyes, across her trembling countenance. She shrank backward. "I'm sorry, Ewan."

Her face became streaked in silent tears, and though Ewan wanted to provoke her, he didn't want her to cry. He coughed, clearing the knot of humanity that lodged in his throat. "I didn't come here for pity. I took a mortal wound but managed to live. Knowing you became a hot little piece for a rich man, that about killed me all over again. Didn't know you'd chosen my cousin."

She wiped at her face, then steadied her shoulders. "So after six years, you've come back to haunt me about things that can't be changed?"

He sat on the high part of the chaise's arm, still marveling at how much she had and had not changed. Still beautiful. Still determined, but with a new sense of calm or reservation that gave him pause. He smoothed his cravat back into place. "Father was right about so many things, including the military. I was good at it. I served in the West Indies until these past three months. I came back because I am a Fitzwilliam. Part of me missed family."

She folded her arms and turned toward the fireplace. "Family is important."

"And I was helping my brother, the viscount, with an errand at Burlington Arcade. I had no idea I would see you today."

She stormed to the patio door, opening it wide. "Well, now that you have, leave me alone. Go live your life, Ewan Fitzwilliam. Be that successful playwright you dreamed of becoming."

"I intend to, but not your way. Success won't be had by scheming, lying, or selling myself."

Theo stopped biting her lip and pointed outside with both

hands. "I may not be happy with my choices, but I own them. No one else. I did what I needed to do to survive. I have no luxury of a father to blame or surname to tarnish, for that matter. Now, leave. Don't sneak back here. And if you see me in passing while staying at Daddy's, call me Mrs. Cecil. That is my name. One I love."

He stood up and walked toward her. He wasn't in the habit of staying, if a lady requested him to leave, but Theo was no lady. She was a usurper intent to harm the Fitzwilliam family. "I will, if you stop threatening us."

She squinted at him as if he'd said lunacy. "What are you talking about?"

"I know you are threatening our farms by cutting off the water to our plantings. Relent and I'll do you a favor. I'll take your name out of my latest play."

"You've written a new play?" The hope in her voice suddenly dropped to nothing. "And you've put me in it?"

"Yes. This one centers on a woman who uses her womanly wiles to seduce and gain riches until all her schemes become announced to the world. Then, she's left with nothing."

Her frown deepened. She slunk backward until she clutched the doorknob, her beautiful tawny fingers pressing so hard against the brass, they almost blended. "And you've named this villain after me?"

"Yes, Theo the Flower Seller. I told you, I wrote you in every scene. How do you think you'll fare when that name is circulated?"

Her chest rose, up and down, as if she struggled to breathe. "Ewan." Her voice became airy and choppy. "My name, laughed at in London... You w-wouldn't be so cruel."

He rounded back, took her cold palm, and pressed his lips to them. "Ghosts are supposed to be cruel."

This time she did strike his face. It was a hard slap that jerked his head backward. His Circe wasn't a pushover. He'd always liked that about Theo.

"Go home to your daddy, Ewan. And never come back."

"Time is ticking away. The play is being circulated. Once it sells, it will be too late. Stop threatening the Fitzwilliam part of the family, Cousin."

He marched out of Tradenwood. With one foot over the low wall forming the edge of the patio, he took a last glance at her. Her back was to him, but her shoulders shook as she hugged herself. He'd surely left her crying.

If she were heartless and opportunistic, his threat should anger her, not make her hurt. It should be an opening for her bartering, something at which he remembered her excelling. Why did it still punch him in his gut, as it had so many years ago, when she cried?

He trudged back to Grandbole, reminding himself that this was the same woman who'd sullied herself with his distant cousin. She was a greedy woman who could only be made to heel with threats. This kind of female, as Lord Crisdon would say, only responded to money and power. Ewan lacked funds, but his pen was mighty, and he'd use it to protect his family.

The wind whipped a little, bringing the lavender smell imprinted upon his hands to his nostrils. It felt horrid to threaten someone he had once cared about. Lifting his gaze to the stars, they winked at him, reminding him of his humor. He remembered all the ways he'd coaxed a young flower seller into his arms. None of his teasing or affection had had anything to do with threats. He wasn't the earl and should only rely on such tactics as a last result.

Determined, Ewan walked a little faster. With a little poignant teasing, he could get Theo to relent about the water rights and not have to ruin her new name. She was family now, after all. He chuckled to himself, contemplating the joy of wearing her down. He'd need to do so quickly. His play could be bought in a fortnight.

CHAPTER FOUR

Love & Regrets

Theodosia sat in the parlor, pushing a translucent sliver of onion across her breakfast plate. The silver fork scraped and clanged, and she lifted her gaze to Ester's wide eyes.

"Dearest," her friend began, with a lilted voice dripping with the perfect blend of condescension and amusement. She lifted her pert nose from the parchment Theodosia had labored all night writing. "You get shifty and bothered when I review your correspondences, but there is no need to fret. I've corrected your letters these past four or five years. I know what to expect."

Theodosia nodded and began again her battle with the onion. This letter had to be worse than the others Ester had edited. Theodosia surely wrote nonsense after what Ewan had said. How could it be otherwise when he accused her of harming the Fitzwilliams, a family that had wanted her dead?

Why did he view her as a threat to his family? Hadn't the Fitzwilliams been the source of all her problems? They were a seed pod for stinky flowers, the perfume of her every regret. Regret. Such an awful R word. She caught herself stabbing the plate, the fork tines making an awful screech. "I tried very hard. I wanted it to sound personal."

"Everything should be personal, or at least sound as if it is." Frederica's voice held too much cheer, as if she hadn't a care in the world. Characteristically forty-five minutes late to breakfast, she sailed into the parlor with her eggshell-colored skirts floating about her thin ankles. The fabric moved about her as she danced to the window glass of the patio door. Her fingers tapped to an inaudible tune as she spread the curtains wide.

What would it be like to live in peace with violin music playing only for her? It must be great to awaken without anxiousness or doubts or that awful R word.

A noise from the patio, a branch twittering across the stones, startled Theodosia. Her gaze leapt to the spot where Ewan had stood. Then she remembered her hand pressed against the scars of his muscle-hardened chest. He had suffered. Maybe he had died. Maybe he *was* a ghost.

"Theodosia?" Frederica's tone sounded of concern, but one look at the minx's eyes foretold mischief. "Are you well? Did you get much sleep?"

"A little."

"Oh. That's good, very good." Again, the tone echoed like a purr. "I think you pattered on your patio too late." She popped a piece of toast, one she'd slathered in butter, into her mouth and grinned.

Her man grin. The one she wore when she received a note from an admirer.

Had she seen Ewan? So, he wasn't a ghost, only a former lover set on revenge. Was that better? She set down her fork. "What were you doing up so late? You couldn't sleep?"

Frederica cleared her throat and patted her lips with the starched linen napkin. "Too many bonbons. I regret that I had one too many."

Regret. If only Theodosia's were candies. She regretted loving Ewan. She regretted discounting Mathew's love, even as he'd held her hand during Philip's birth. She released a pained breath, one stinging from the jagged pieces of her broken heart. "Ester and I are working on a response to the riddle. I want the words to show *me*, what's true inside. This man needs to understand what I am, so he can either abandon these letters or move quicker to ask to meet."

"I knew it," Frederica said as she sweetened her tea. "You do need poetry, and this man will be better than the squire."

Ester's brow wrinkled as she dipped her quill into the ink. "You have hope in this suitor? Why? Is Fredericka-the-Flirt right about poetry, from a man?"

Something in the rhyme. Something in the inked signature. Something in Ewan's reappearance. It all reminded her of a soft spot hidden behind her lacy tucker, near her bosom where she stashed her hopes. Theodosia picked up her fork again and pricked a potato chunk until it smashed. "There's something in his words, in his way of asking the question. And a baron would have more influence than a squire. Silly thoughts?"

Frederica reached over and clasped Theodosia's hand midstab. "Put the fork down. What has that Wedgwood plate ever done to you?"

Releasing the silverware turned hapless weapon, Theodosia chewed her lip. "I'm not myself."

Flipping the page, Ester never looked up. Her matronly lace mobcap fluttered. The otherwise stylish girl kept reading.

Frederica sipped from her cup. "What—is his letter missing a comma? Is missing punctuation a poor indication of character. I think not."

Ester waved the baron's letter. "The gentleman has a rather

nice hand. Clever penmanship. He's educated. I'm glad you are answering him and not settling for the squire."

"I so agree. Options may be everywhere. Even next door." Frederica, picking through the platter of fruit for the ripest berries, stuffed a big one in her mouth. "Your landowning neighbor, the Earl of Crisdon. He has two sons?"

Theodosia's feet grew cold. The need to escape filled every inch of her lungs. She couldn't eat. If she picked up her fork again, she'd jam it through the table. "He has two. Lord Hartwell who is a viscount and a younger son, but they all hate me. They hate that I married Cecil, that I and Philip own Tradenwood. They mean to destroy me. The younger son, who happens to be Cecil's distant cousin, came here last night to tell me so."

Ester gasped.

Her smile gone, Frederica slammed her cup to the table. "No. I won't let that happen. I'll get my father—"

"To do what? To defend Cecil's mistress wife? The duke's a peer like the earl. He'll stay out of it, and I couldn't ask you to do anything that will put strain between you and your father."

Folding her arms about her, crushing the Mechlin lace of her bodice, Frederica shook her head. She picked up her fork and poked at another berry. "I would try for you or Ester. I could make the duke understand."

"No, sweetness. His world won't see I am an honorable man's widow. If I can't find a new husband to fight Lester for Philip's guardianship, I'm doomed." She lifted her dark palms, which still held stains from the past. "Why can't I take Philip and leave here? I could take care of us. Cecil left me money. I'm sure we could make a new start. I'd let you all know where we settled so you could visit. And you'd have to. You two complete my life."

Ester dropped her quill. Frederica her fork. "No," they both said.

Pushing back in her chair, Frederica stared ahead. "We have to give this plan a chance. You have one offer, a cheap one, but it is still a squire. Then there is the poetic baron. He might be the one."

"Mathew Cecil was the only man I could trust. They aren't him."

Blowing a curl from her eye, Frederica's light skin looked quite red. "Ohhh. You say this speech all the time. Might I remind you of all the hard work you and old man Cecil did to make these flower fields produce? Do you wish Philip to lose his inheritance? Cecil loved that boy. He'd want him to have everything."

This was true, and how could she deny what Mathew wanted, after all he'd done for them? "If Cecil knew how treacherous Lester was, he would have never left him as a guardian." That had been his flaw. He had trusted too deeply.

Frederica frowned. It looked so misplaced among her lean cheeks and a pert nose given to wiggles. But could she know that Theodosia feared ever finding someone who saw her as equal?

Ester put down her quill. "First pass, done. Dearest, it's not that bad. Quite improved. You impress me."

Impressions were momentary things, like a boy loving her... until his father changed his mind. And how would things fare when Ewan's play, the one he'd boasted of last night, played at the theater, offering lies and half-truths?

Even if, somehow, Ewan and Mathew shared blood, Ewan

was a Fitzwilliam and Fitzwilliams were nasty, evil people. How could she stop them?

Theodosia looked down and rubbed at her wrists. She'd gripped them too tightly with her full-on fretting. Resigned, she smoothed her thick cuffs and steeled her spirit with Mathew's words.

Theodosia, you are a light rising from obscurity. When you focus on helping others, the darkness you think you have will be like the noon sun.

"I need to get this letter sent as soon as possible, so I can focus on the festival. The workers and vendors will have a day like Mathew Cecil would give. I couldn't give them their due last year with Cecil so sick, then dying."

Frederica's brow lifted as she patted berry juice from her lips. "You both need to stop fretting. Ester, stop killing us with your slow edits."

Ester again waved her hand and frowned. "Final pass almost done. This can't be rushed, and Theodosia should know my opinion won't change because of a misplaced comma."

Starting to pace, Theodosia paused and decided to tell her truth. "Would your opinion change if it were made public that Mathew Cecil's widow had been an ignorant street beggar? That she made herself a harlot to survive and somehow managed to marry a wealthy man?"

The foul statement consumed all the air, burning up all the noise in the room like a greedy flame. Yet as she caught Frederica's gaze, her hazel eyes weren't filled with pity, but something akin to defiance. "Why stop at such a small insult? You and I are lucky by-blows and Ester's people would still be in Africa, if not for being such great sailors, coming before the slavers invaded." She stood up, marched to Theodosia, and gripped her shoulders. "We are misfits. And never good enough. With true friends, true lovers, none of this matters. You are decent, decent to us, to everyone. That's what matters."

As much as she wanted it to be true, it wasn't. The Court of Chancery would take her son from her and give control of his health to mean, horrible Lester. Unspent tears built in her throat, thickening it and drowning all hints of that R word. Sniffing, she nodded.

Ester's face lifted and a droplet rolled down her cheek. "Done. This letter is done. It's very good. We should still work on your spelling, but your teacher is proud of the formerly ignorant street girl, as you say. Frederica is right. You are a beloved friend. Theodosia Cecil is a kind soul, with a head for numbers, though not so much spelling and punctuation."

Holding her arms wide, Theodosia stood. "You're both such dears."

The chair screeched as Ester slid out, and she and Frederica rushed to Theodosia and embraced.

"I don't know how I'd do without you all," Theodosia said, still fighting a full-on cry.

Ester held her a little tighter. "You're too hard on yourself. If it were numbers, you'd best Frederica and me."

"You can't leave us," Frederica said, with a voice that didn't sound steady or cultured.

The love in their voices spoke to Theodosia more than words. She still had those who cared for her, and shoulders to cry upon when things became worse.

And they would worsen with the Fitzwilliams coming at her. She rubbed her jaw, smoothed the lace at her neckline, and decided to tell the newest threat. "The Fitzwilliams are threatening to scandalize my name if I don't agree to their terms, but I won't sell this place or the fields. You all are right about what my husband wanted. This is my son's home, his legacy. I'll do what I must to protect it, even marry a squire who can't hold my gaze."

Frederica moved and picked up the cut of foolscap that Ester had stewed upon. "You wrote this, Theodosia, because you know the squire is not for you. Your next husband could be swayed to sell the pieces of the business not entailed to your son. And what if evil Lester bribes him into siding against you? Philip's care could be in jeopardy. Don't accept the squire out of fear. Fear is the wrong motivation."

But the R word and humiliation were. Their power seemed greater than a vise, worse than horrible thunder coming for her. She mopped at her brow. "Let's get this draft ready, while I can still hope."

In silence, her friends nodded. They retook their seats and resumed their routines: berry selecting and reading.

Frederica leaned forward. "Well, maybe you'll attract someone at the theater next week. My father has agreed to let us use his box, if we promise to be discreet. And before you say no, Theodosia, you can go in gray or black. You should get used to being out again. Nothing's better at discretion than a dark theater."

Ester's nose wrinkled. "If it's dark, who will see us, or us them?"

Frederica twirled a strawberry on her plate. "We'll see them and enjoy the music, even if we must sit at the back of his box. It's not important to be seen, but to be there."

Theodosia nodded, but couldn't come up with a reason not to go. Outside of Tradenwood wasn't always welcoming. She'd have to find an excuse. The risk of leaving Philip alone at night was too great.

Her fingers tightened around the note to her fantasy suitor, coiling it within her palm. In her heart, she knew she'd met her new husband, the squire, for he'd already asked to marry her and she had a feeling he'd go through with it, unlike Ewan Fitzwilliam. She'd tell the squire after the festival, before Lester or the Fitzwilliams, especially her ghost, took her choices away.

• • •

Ewan pulled Jasper's gig close to the mews at the rear of the family's London townhouse. He stepped out and handed the reins of the fine beast to a groom.

The boy pulled the gelding into a stall and hitched him. The horse, pewter colored, with a high gait and a finely arched back, marched inside, as if this pen was something he owned.

Marvelous. Ewan almost envied the horse as it pawed at the earth, acting every inch the thoroughbred, not an animal with a layman's job. Maybe the horse knew something the *ton* couldn't conceive, that dignity and a profession weren't scandalous, but cleansing to a man's soul, even a jaded one. Not that he wished to be neutered. Ewan had big plans to be productive, with a wife and loving family—as he'd planned with Theo. Her handprint on his jaw, even the sting, had remained as he'd slipped into Grandbole. He could still move her. That would prove useful.

"Mighty nice horse, sir," the groom said as he brushed down the gelding. "Shall I wipe down the seat, give 'er a nice cleaning?"

"Yes." That would be a good thing to do for Jasper. Though Ewan had the money now to buy one of his own, the upkeep and stabling would consume his meager pension. A gig would be an indulgence he'd procure after his first author's benefit night. He'd be able to tell by the crowds if his play was a success.

Theo had taught him to be frugal. She had always calculated hidden costs, thinking about things others didn't notice. The way she reacted to his threat last night had the makings of a hidden cost. The sooner Ewan could figure out what that cost was, the sooner he could get her to relent.

He dug into his pocket for a coin and showed it to the groom. "There's an extra bit for a good job."

The boy smiled then went back to brushing the silvery coat.

No payment in advance of seeing the work—another Theo lesson. Ewan started down the alley toward the street. His nose wrinkled at the stench, the sourness in the air, the horse leavings. The city was nothing like the fields of Grandbole or those of Tradenwood. And every morning Theo awoke to the scent of fresh flowers.

He didn't have time to be jealous of her. No, he'd stewed most of the night on why? *Why hadn't mother told me?*

He waited for the butler to answer the door to the townhouse. The wind brought the smell with him, like it gave chase. Stewing, his gut knotted. What if Mother thought him incapable of handling another disappointment? Yes, he'd lost out on inheriting

Tradenwood because of an inaccurate field message of his death. He could live with that, but losing it to a cousin who had made Theo its owner—that was tough. His stomach turned again and not from the stench of the road behind him.

The door opened and an older man in shiny blue livery stood there. "Mr. Fitzwilliam."

"Yes, I am here to see the countess."

"She's taking breakfast in the salon." The man turned and pattered down the gilded hall, stopping at a heavily trimmed door. He ducked inside and then popped back out. "She'll see you now."

Ewan fumbled with his jacket button, one of the garments his father had stashed in the room he wanted Ewan to stay. It had stung, sliding it on after hearing Theo's accusation about him not being his own man, but he needed to hold his mother's full attention. Buttons and baubles easily distracted her and gave her the opportunity to meander away from facts. He needed truth. He needed it badly.

Entering the bright sunlit room, he stopped and saw a smiling cherub in a pale pink morning gown.

Mother touched at her lacy mobcap, then extended her hand. "Ewan? To what do I owe the pleasure?"

Stepping fully inside, he met her at the large breakfast table. "I came to see the best lady in the world."

Her dimples spread and made her lapis blue eyes sparkle. "Then I forgive you for missing my party last night. Sit down, sweet boy."

Ewan stumbled. *I am a man, one who fought death and won. How can I still be a boy to her—to Theo?* He sighed as he plopped in an open chair to her right.

"I wasn't too mad at you. Although Mrs. Whilton's niece was disappointed."

"I'm sure they both will live and find another impoverished playwright to pass the time with. Perhaps a better card player."

Her nose wrinkled. "So what has you out and up so early? Have you accepted my offer? Will you leave your horrid flat and come stay here with me?"

"No, Mother. That's not why I am here."

She put a flaky, pale biscuit that smelled of fine butter and orange bits on his plate. "I have plenty of room. I'm sure you could write dozens of things. It's so nice here, not so dreary."

Dreary? Was she comparing the small townhome to his flat or to Grandbole? He broke his biscuit up into bits. They would be easier to swallow once he steered the conservation to the street address he sought. "I'm content where I am."

Her chin lowered and she swirled her teacup. "I understand, but it's easier here."

Unease settled in his gut, mixing with the cinnamon of the biscuit. Her residence in Town sounded more permanent than staying for the Season. He caught and stilled her elegant hand. "I'm happy with my own flat, but you, you are the Countess of Crisdon. Even you must return from the ball at the stroke of midnight. Grandbole is at a loss without you."

"You look nice, dear."

"I take it you don't want to talk about Grandbole?"

She touched his coat, smoothing the lapel. "These full revers look best on you. I would love to send you to the tailor for more. I want to treat you."

The coddling he had enjoyed, as a protection against his

father's temper, had never stopped. It hadn't stopped after being breached at six, going to war at twenty, or returning now as a man. Probably would never stop, unless he did something. Patting her fingers away, he leaned close. "This is the earl's tailor. He's quite good. I borrowed it so I don't feel obligated or more leech-like."

"Your father's doing?" The small fine wrinkles that dared to touch her creamy countenance deepened as she seemed to stare through Ewan. "Well, you should've worn it last night. I had a very disappointed young lady here. It was awful moving things about to find her a new card partner. You hampered all my plans."

"Jasper changed my plans."

She set another biscuit in front of him, but he hadn't eaten much of the first.

Another distraction. He pushed the plate away. "Jasper took me to see—"

"You know, I introduced Jasper to his wife. God rest her soul. Maria was a dear. I only want you to be as happy."

"He was happy, but happiness is fleeting. It seems Grandbole is gloomy with her loss and now yours."

She picked up the pot of tea and poured him a cup. Mint floated to his nose, beckoning. Another distraction.

Mother set the silver service down. "Jasper won't let me introduce him to another lady, one with a bigger dowry than Maria's. I can do the same for you."

He shook his head. "I'm not hunting for a wife or a dowry. And you haven't asked how I know Grandbole is dull."

"Jasper told you. He doesn't lie. He's nothing like your father."

"I know. I saw them both last night."

Her lips thinned. Perhaps she was trying to think of another street to take him down, but he wouldn't be swayed. He needed to hear from her lips about Theo possessing Tradenwood and why his own mother thought him too weak to know. "Mother, why? Why didn't you tell me?"

"I thought you weren't going to see the earl until Yuletide. I have him considering wintering in Town."

"Jasper convinced me I needed to see Grandbole and Tradenwood."

She tossed her handkerchief onto the table. "Then I suppose you know."

"Mother, I've seen you once a week for the past three months. You lamented over your brother's passing, told me of Tradenwood going to a distant cousin because Uncle rewrote his will, thinking I'd died." He paused as his voice rose, almost shaking with the injustice rocking his windpipe, his soul. He'd lost everything—Theo, a fortune that would've funded his pursuit of plays—gone because of that false report from the battlefield. It had hit him hard, harder than he thought, seeing Tradenwood. Knowing another man had possessed Theo's curves, the henna-bronzed loveliness Ewan had thought only for him.

He took a breath and forced his tone to lower. "We've sat through dinners, or private moments like this, and no mention of my cousin's bride."

"It wasn't important. Tradenwood was lost to us. Nothing else mattered. Nothing could be done."

"The fact that I nearly eloped with this woman is not important?"

"No. No, it isn't. I don't mention her. The usurper who led you astray now has my Tradenwood." Her face twisted as tear-stained eyes drifted to the right. "I was raised in that home. I left for my come-out from those grand steps. Your father proposed on that patio. That she-devil and your cousin put up a trellis on my patio." Mother shivered, as if the covering were horse leavings. "Tradenwood should never have left the family."

"Technically, it's still in the family, in a distant cousin's hands. Well, now his widow's. How did that come about? Was she grieving me? Does grief make strange bedfellows?"

The crystals in Mother's eyes shattered, shaking in fury. "You can joke of this? That harlot made you wild, and you almost paid with your life."

Ewan chuckled to himself, for Mother didn't know wild. Wild was what he called his stint away. He'd been a dutiful soldier on the field, but he and his fellow officers had caroused, finding comfort in the towns and villages they'd encamped in Spain and the West Indies. Lots of willing arms had seemed to be enticed by his bright red regimental.

His mother's voice became more harpy-like. "The marriage should not have been allowed to happen. She's not worthy of Tradenwood."

"Their marriage was not legal?"

"That's not what I mean. Cecil's widow is a slut. A Blackamoor whore."

Ewan sat back and spun his teacup, covering the punch the slur made to his chest. "If she were a white harlot, that would be better?"

Mother leaped up with fists shaking. "That loose woman

should be cleaning the floors, or cargo on a slave ship, not making menus and being hostess in that great manor."

Anger makes people do or say things they shouldn't. Yes, that would be the excuse he'd make for his mother. He'd coddle her stupidity as she'd always coddled him. He caught her hand and tugged her back toward her chair. "It must've been hard grieving me, then Uncle, then the loss of your family home. I am sorry. Don't let grief push you into saying cruel things. I'm making peace with the past. You must, too."

Shaking and nodding, lace fluttering, she dropped to the seat. "It wasn't fair. My baby, my only baby was gone. You went to war because your father made you—because of her. He should've made her go. Then all would have been right. You'd own Tradenwood, not that harlot, Theodosia Cecil."

He lowered his voice to a whisper, but made his tone firm, resilient in Mother's tornado winds. "If I had stayed, her name would have been Theodosia Fitzwilliam. Would you have supported me or would you have called her names and torn down our love?"

"She wouldn't have loved you, never like you deserved. The creature is incapable of it. Hopping from bed to bed, gaining deeper pockets with each leap."

"Well, she didn't have a matchmaking mama to point her to the right pockets. But you are right. Mine are not as filled as Cousin Cecil's."

"You keep making jokes. You write funny plays, but it hides your pain. How can you stand to see her traipsing in your fields? Letting her heirs inherit it, not us."

It wasn't easy, but nothing changed the past. He closed his

eyes and drank the mint tea, hoping to get his gut to utopia so it would match the noise of forgiveness he was about to utter. "It doesn't matter. She's the new owner of Tradenwood. It's lawfully passed to her."

"It doesn't make you angered that it's not yours? I could help you make it great again, like when it was my home."

He didn't have the heart to tell her it was great and well-manicured. Theo had not, in any way that he could see, dishonored it. But nothing would console Mother from thinking she'd been cheated, just as when she realized most of his father's courtship of her had centered on her large dowry and the hope of getting closer to Tradenwood. Gut settling, he took a final sip of the cool mint. "You've always wanted that house. I'm sure it's a great loss. I suppose welcoming her to the family is out of the question. That would resolve the watering rights issue that has the earl all worked up."

"Your father has tried to buy it for me, but his offers are too cheap. Maybe you can work on him."

"Weren't you happy with my not seeing him?"

"I didn't want you distressed over being reminded of what going to war cost you. You'd have had Tradenwood. You'd never want for anything. You could write all the plays you wanted."

"Well, I will make my own way, by writing all the plays I want."

"I'm sure you shall, but head back to Grandbole. Convince Crisdon to get Tradenwood for me. Tell him I'll return, if he does."

"I'm not going to get in the middle of your spat."

She pouted and frowned.

Feeling guilty at causing her pain, he nodded. "But I'll mention it to him. If there is a price at which the Widow Cecil will sell, he'll find it."

"Tell Lord Crisdon I regret our argument. I realize that there is no sacrifice greater than Tradenwood."

Overly dramatic as always, Lady Crisdon wasn't going to be the route to find information about Theo and Cecil. No, he'd have to get that from the source, his new cousin, the widow Cecil. He rose and kissed Mother's hand, but she leaned up and clung to him, as if she was again sending him to war. Well, maybe she was. He marched from the drawing room to return to Grandbole, readying to battle his difficult father and an ornery widowed cousin-by-marriage.

CHAPTER FIVE

The Cost of Revenge

Theodosia waited for Frederica to climb into the carriage. Ester was already tucked inside, probably with her eyes stuck in a book she'd found in Mathew's collection.

Clutching her bonnet, Frederica popped inside then stuck her head out. "We meet two weeks from now at the theater. Don't make me come back here to retrieve you. Theodosia Cecil is good to her word."

"Yes." That was all Theodosia could muster. That and a wan smile.

Frederica nodded then took her seat.

The carriage started to move. The onyx vehicle with the Duke of Simone's golden crest jerked and jostled down the long drive. Two pairs of handsome horses headed them back to London and Theodosia's heart dropped. Saying good-bye to her friends felt so final this time. It shouldn't, but it did. Maybe that's why fleeing stayed on her mind.

She pushed at a curl falling from her mobcap and took a huge breath of air. The sweet aroma of roses overtook her, cheering her spirit. She hugged herself and that feeling of being unprotected and alone fled. Her friends said they would stand with her. She'd believe in them until she couldn't.

Like she had believed Ewan would marry her, until he didn't.

Clutching her elbows as if that would latch in her courage, she looked up into the darkening sky and saw a streak of light.

Then the sound that always brought dread pounded through her. Thunder. Fear filled her heart. It pimpled her skin all the way to her ankles. She couldn't have a panic in front of her pickers or tenants. The Court of Chancery would not look kindly on a mother so fearful of a storm. She would not be considered a good choice to raise a boy independent of his male guardian. No better than a harlot would.

As that feeling of again losing someone she loved swelled inside, the need to hold her son overcame her. She bolted for the portico.

Pickens held the door open for her, as if he'd been watching and had seen her panicked stride.

She ran on, lifting her heavy ash-colored skirts, and made it inside before the rain began to fall.

"Ma'am." The butler's voice made her stop and stand up tall.

"Yes, Pickens?"

He closed the door, shutting out the sound of the approaching storm. "Your letter has been sent to the Burlington Arcade."

Though he may not know what was on the inside of those sealed papers, he surely knew how important they were. She nodded to him. "Thank you."

In six years, Theodosia had learned the ways of Tradenwood, the roles and responsibilities. Yet, it always felt daunting. Thank goodness, Pickens was a stalwart butler who had served generations of Mathew's extended family. The staff Mathew had hired were all good people to her, ones who wouldn't cheat her and who knew how to help without making her feel ignorant. "I've lived here six years and I still feel lost sometimes."

"You do fine, ma'am. You are quite capable."

She didn't feel capable, especially when thunder boomed. It reminded her too much of growing up in the harshest parts of London, trying to see the beauty of roses from the papered-up windows of a brothel. Again, she wrapped her arms around her and went in search of her son, her happiness.

Philip always made her happy, like the fluttering big-winged butterflies in the fields. He must've seen the door open or heard her slippers with his good ear, for he turned to face her. He lifted his arms and came to her. She picked him up and swung him around until his little face exploded with giggles, silent ones at first, then full belly-jiggly ones.

And Theodosia lost her cares and laughed, too.

"Mrs. Cecil. It is time for Master Philip's lessons," said the governess. The spinster lady with dull red-and-white hair sticking from her cream-colored mobcap clapped her hands. "Master Philip?"

Theodosia pulled his little body close and completed three more turns. His little palms were about her neck, and she kissed "I love you" on his forehead. "Ready, Philip. School time."

Putting him down, she kept his hand within hers and walked to his governess. "Here's your student."

The woman smiled and pointed the boy to his shiny maple desk that she'd retrieved from a deep closet. "It is time to begin."

Philip pulled at his pinafore and made his way to his seat. He fingered the book laid upon his table. The governess went to him and kneeled close to his right ear, his good one, and read the page, sounding out each animal's name.

When Theodosia heard Philip's pitchy squeak reciting the word "chicken," a tear welled. She straightened her shoulders, approached, and kneeled to their left, like a pile of gray silk.

"H-o-g," said Philip, and her heart skipped a beat. Swine had never sounded so good.

The governess had been highly recommended to work with children with difficulties. She was worth the thirty-three pounds in wages, almost twice what she would pay a good housemaid. Philip needed someone to pack as many words into him before his right ear gave out, like the doctors said would happen.

"Is he doing better?" Theodosia asked when they finished the repetitions.

The governess looked over her glasses at Theodosia, as if she spoke in a foreign tongue.

Stopping the impulse to chew her lip, she tried again. "I mean, is he learning?"

Shoulders drooping, the woman's gaze lowered. If her head bent any further, it might fall off and roll around like a cabbage. "I don't want to get your hopes up. He's good at mimicking. I've gotten him to write his name, but it's hard. He's not like the other students I've worked with. He doesn't hear my questions sometimes. He can't—"

"Try using the mimicking more. If he follows what you do, that will be helpful. I know he's copied my figuring on paper, when I balance my ledger books."

The woman nodded and kneeled closer to Philip. She popped her chin atop the crown of his shiny black hair. "I'll try, Mrs. Cecil. That is all I can promise."

Theodora picked herself up, as if the governess had kicked her in the teeth. She backed up to the entry, waving and getting that last silent smile from Philip. Closing the door, she let her forehead bang upon it. Something had to help. Something had to get him to learn. He couldn't start in this world ignorant, as his mother had.

Her guilt shook her over the hurts she'd caused this sweet child by her choices.

A noise sounded from the hall. Her butler's voice alerted her of a guest arriving. It couldn't be her friends back this soon. She smoothed her hair, putting her lacy cap in her pocket and hoped her eyes weren't as red as the guilt rotting in her gut.

Then she saw him standing in her threshold in broad daylight. The ghost.

"Good afternoon, Cousin Cecil," Ewan said. His smirk was wide. He dipped his chin. "I'm sorry to appear without a note, but I am here to see about family."

As steadily as she could, she managed to come down the steps without falling. "Pickens. Can you show Mr. Fitzwilliam into the parlor?"

The butler's smile bloomed, a ready harvest of charm. "And bring a tea service?"

Ewan wasn't worth the shilling for the ounce of leaves. How could she politely ask to bring some that had been used two or three times? There wasn't a way, especially for someone announcing he was family. "Yes, Pickens."

She followed the men into the parlor, hoping this haunting would be brief and stay contained to the lower level. Philip's lesson did not need to be interrupted, especially from evil men or liars. Which category Ewan fell into, she wasn't sure.

• • •

After leaving London, Ewan purposed to come to Tradenwood, not slinking around in the dark, but as a man given to ending all the trouble Theo had caused.

"Why are you here?" she asked.

Not liking the wariness in her dark teak-colored eyes, he turned to the fireplace and poked the log. Orange and red embers danced along the wrought iron stick. He fanned the raindrops from his coat. The shower outside had slowed enough for him to leap under Tradenwood's portico. "I came for a number. You are very good at numbers, from what I remember. Good at a lot of things."

When she looked away with darkening cheeks, he knew she wasn't immune to his jokes or their good memories.

The door to the parlor opened and Pickens came in with a tea service. After the cup he'd drunk with his mother, Ewan had had his fill, but he'd partake with Theo. Keeping this meeting more social might move Theo more than bullying. He hoped.

"Thank you," she said to the old man, and with her graceful long fingers she pointed to the low table. "You brought biscuits, too? I don't think Mr. Fitzwilliam will be staying that long. He's no doubt needed up the hill at Grandbole."

"It's cousin now. Right, Pickens? And I'll take a cup filled to the brim. I intend to enjoy Madam's time."

The butler raised a furrowed brow. "Sir, do you still take only sugar?"

"Yes." Ewan couldn't help but smile. Pickens hadn't forgotten him. And maybe he hadn't forgotten that Tradenwood belonged more to the Fitzwilliam side of things than to the usurper flower seller. "It's good you remember."

Pickens moved close to the door, and he seemed to stare through Ewan. "Ma'am if you need anything, do not hesitate to pull the bell."

"Thank you. Thank you for everything." Theo smiled, maybe the first one he'd seen on her face since he'd returned. Deep brown skin, crinkling eyes, full kissable lips. She was a beauty when she wasn't fidgeting or sad. That charm had swayed his cousin and the butler, too. It had disarmed him once, but now he needed her to be relaxed, so he could act as if they weren't enemies.

Pickens left, closing the door with a thud. Ewan circled her as she sat calmly looking toward the patio doors and the falling rain. "I'm glad to find you about today. A woman with late night visitors might be inclined to lie around, becoming lazy."

Her gaze stayed fixed on the patio, not on him. "Why are you here? Skunks hunt at night. Pigs, too."

He stepped in front of the golden curtains, hoping to force her to look at him. "I need a number to take back to my father. What will it cost for you to sell Tradenwood?"

She laced her fingers together, creased gray cuffs enveloping her slender wrists. "Your play must not be any good."

"What?"

"You're already back here with a change of plans. A new scheme to coerce me, Ewan? It hasn't been a day and you're already altering plans. Oh wait. That is what you do."

Was that her game, to make everything that had happened his fault? Though he wanted her to own her unfaithfulness, to say it aloud, that would show his hand. He couldn't sweet talk a woman who was set against him. He moved close and sat directly opposite her chaise, in the chair by the fireplace. "There is nothing here that I want other than to restore peace to my family."

She didn't move or blink or breathe. "You mean the family who haven't been so supportive of you?" Her low tone magnified. "The one that keeps you around only when you are useful. That family?"

Maybe Pickens wasn't the only one with a good memory. Ewan had shared his Fitzwilliam frustrations more than once during their brief courtship. He ran a hand through his damp hair. "You can understand what it means to bring peace to all sides."

"So, for your peace, you offer to buy me off, to take the only home...to take *this* home from me."

"I can make sure my father pays you enough so that you can buy another. This was my mother's home. I remember spending yuletides in this parlor. Years and years of memories. You'll have what you wanted—money."

Thunder rumbled, deep and bone vibrating as the rain came down harder.

Theo looked frozen, almost doll-like. Moments passed but he dared not utter a sound.

He risked a slap, but he reached out and put his hand over hers. He sang, "Twinkle, twinkle little star. How I wonder what you are."

Those beautiful eyes of hers widened. Her shivers slowed. All these years and she was still afraid of thunder, and his ridiculous tunes again brought her from the darkness. If she were his, he'd hold her in his arms and sing to her again. But she wasn't his. Theo was his cousin's widow. "The storm will pass. You are safe."

She said nothing but picked at the plate of biscuits. Then Theo put one on a plate and handed it to him.

Surprised, he took it. He meant to set it down, but it had a deeply caramelized crust, probably the deepest brown of the pile. His mouth watered, and his heart softened further. She remembered those were his favorite. "Thank you, Theo."

He took a bite and the crunch melted on his tongue with that sweeter-than-honey taste. He wiped his face and hands on the napkin she stretched to him. "You were always so neat."

Another pound of thunder made her jitter on her seat, but she didn't turn from him. "And you, Ewan, were always a hearty eater in want of a handkerchief."

"I recall we were friends once. Can we be that again?"

"I don't know, Ewan. You did know how to make me feel safe." She gazed at him, her eyes soft, maybe longing for yesterday, too. "Never once did you belittle me for such a childish fear."

"Never, Theo. You were always brave. Do what is brave now. Sell this place so my mother can have her childhood home. Restore her good memories, and we can all live in peace. I know deep down peace is what you want. It's what you've always wanted."

She dipped her head and uttered no response. When the storm quieted, her voice returned. "I have memories, too. One of a man who pledged he would protect and honor me. Of reciting vows by that mantel. Of being welcomed into this house, which I shared with Mathew Cecil. My memories count."

If she had leaped up and slapped him as she had last night, that would have stung less. Hearing her talk of his cousin, of treasuring their love, pierced. It was easier thinking her money-hungry than loving another.

She moved to open the patio doors. A breeze swept inside and her cheeks flushed, turning a deeper shade of mahogany. "I want you out of here, Ewan. Run home to your parents and tell them no. I will not be run off. I have been civil to you. Something that your people have never been to me. Even when I begged."

"What are you talking about?"

"Ask Lord Crisdon how I was treated when you left."

Knowing how vicious his father could be, Ewan balled his fist. What had she endured when he wasn't around to make sure she wasn't harassed? He eased his palm against his knee. "Is that why you turned to my cousin? To get even with the earl?"

"You never understood me, did you, Ewan? Why else would you be here pretending to care, as you try to buy me off?"

"I knew you quite well, Theo."

He came close and took her hand away from clutching at her collar. Looping his finger with her fine ones he dipped his head close to hers. "Your mind is sharp. Your will is strong, but even you know that this feud with the Fitzwilliams is wrong. It won't end well."

Her eyes grew darker, the flecks of gold disappearing in the flames of her pupils. He could hear her heart beating. His heartrate picked up, too. "You don't want to be the center of this conflict. You and that next lucky fool who'll be your husband don't want that kind of constant tension. End this for me, for what we once had. I'll make sure they never bother you again."

A breath crossed her lips, then what started out sounding like a sob became a full-throated laugh. "You don't know me. Maybe you never did. If you had, you wouldn't come here and plea to me to think of your people, your senti...sensibilities. I will not sell. I need you gone."

He released her hand. Now she sounded like a Circe, one who would use her power to destroy the Fitzwilliams. The kindhearted woman whom he had cared for was gone. This was the earl's work. He'd known his father to be horrible to enemies. Yet Theo, strong Theo, had bested them all. She'd won. She had Tradenwood and control of the water rights.

He rubbed at his face. Her lavender scent sat on his fingertips. "We can't change the past, but we can set about a new future. Name the price to lease the waterway as before under your husband. The water is drying out."

"Water lease? Drying out? I'll check with Mr. Lester, Cecil's former steward."

Truth righted in his head, making his pulse race. "Perhaps, he is cutting off the water. Not you."

The sound of gentle taps of the rain on the stone floor of the patio was peaceful, serene, like the calm before a big storm. What was Theo readying to do? "It doesn't matter. If it was done in Cecil's name, it is my doing."

He came up behind her. He was close enough to hold her within his embrace, wrap his fingers in the curls in her chignon. "It wasn't you hurting my family. You haven't changed that much from the girl I once loved."

"I changed, Ewan. I had to."

"Theo, you can stop him. You can restore the peace."

"There will be no peace, not for free. You want a number. Ten times what Lord Crisdon paid Cecil. It will cost the Fitzwilliams something. I will be well compensated for their next revenge plot."

"Twenty thousand pounds is exorbitant. You don't need to be so vengeful. I won't let them hurt you."

She glared at him, with nostrils flaring. "I don't believe you. They'll be no different than the man who wrote a play to hurt me. You took your gift and made it a weapon."

He wanted to take her in his arms and shake her, but maybe he needed to shake himself. The play was his only leverage, since his charm seemed hopeless. Why wouldn't she think him trustworthy? "I wrote it thinking you long gone from here, not married to my cousin. I can easily take your name out to protect you, if you will only be reasonable. I remember when you were reasonable. When you were quite content to be reasonable with me."

Her lip trembled and her fists balled. "I remember believing that we would leave in the morn to marry. You changed your mind faster than I could pin up my hair. You say you'll stay, but you'll go away again. Then the war will begin anew. I'd rather stand my ground and collect the penalty money. When I tire of the war, when I say it is over, and go into exile, I'll take the bulk of the Fitzwilliam fortune with me. You'll never be able to hurt people again with your money. Do you know how many have starved because of the Fitzwilliams's need for revenge?"

Ewan could not answer, nor did he want to count. It hadn't mattered, for he'd wanted no part of the business. "I will be around this time. I'll show you. I'll haunt you to get you to be reasonable, to be better than my father."

She pointed to the doors. "Words. Words are the playwright's lies. Twenty thousand pounds. Take that to Daddy."

Thunder clapped and she shivered. Powerful and vulnerable and lovely, a Circe in the eye of his storm.

This wasn't how this moment should go, with her hating him, pointing out all the sins of his family. It was hopeless to make her see the difference now. He'd have to prove his resolve. "I'll be around, getting both sides to seek peace. You'll be sick of me, Theo. You may even grow to like your good old cousin again."

"I do know that I will never trust you. I see your flaws now. I wish that I'd known the truth while Cecil lived."

"Why?"

"I would've loved him more."

He watched her bosom heave. Waited for the knife to his gut to stop twisting. "Good day, Cousin."

That was all he could manage without arguing and showing how deeply her words had cut into his flesh. Ewan plodded down the hall and out to his gig, wondering why a woman he was done with still made him gnash his teeth.

When he climbed into the gig, the seat was wet, but maybe the soaking would quench his fire. Theo had loved Cecil. It wasn't his money that had drawn her. His family's treatment had pushed her to his cousin. How could he stop her from ruining his family when he truly couldn't blame her for hating everything Fitzwilliam? Knowing what they were capable of, he hated them, too. For believing they'd take care of her while he was gone, he hated himself.

But he was here now, and she'd see he wasn't going away. She'd see and even rue his attentiveness. He'd make her want peace just to be rid of him.

CHAPTER SIX

The Haunting Begins

Theodosia couldn't pace around the parlor to the nursery to her chambers and back again, and not upset her rattled household. Her prior thirty treks surely had worn a path through the rugs and dragged scratches across the polished floors. The doctor would arrive to Tradenwood in another three hours. One hundred and eighty long minutes to wait. Then she'd know if Philip's earache was a tooth thing or more progress in his hearing loss.

As she came from the narrow hall, Pickens stepped into her path. A grin that said *caught you* disappeared from his aged, battle-hardened cheeks. "Ma'am, Cook has been asking for your final approval. May I tell her you will see her after your next round of pacing?"

The festival... How could she concentrate on that after rocking Philip, hoping and praying that his tear-stained eyes would finally close in sleep? "Can... May it wait until tomorrow?"

The butler nodded. "No delay longer than tomorrow. She'll need to inform the butcher of cuts you'll need for the celebration at month's end."

Yes, festival preparation. Another thing to fret about. She wrung her hands then dropped them to her sides. "Thank you for keeping me on task. I'm not moving so fast today."

Pickens's brow rose. "You could outpace the fittest Olympian. You should take a drive. I've taken the liberty of having your gig pulled around. Visit the fields. You'll be refreshed by the time the doctor arrives."

"But Philip? He might need me."

"The boy is sleeping. The laudanum will keep him out of pain until the doctor is here." He picked up her gloves and hat, handing them to her as he shuttled her to the door. "Have a pleasant ride."

She started tugging on one glove then the other. They were close-fitting kid gloves, soft and thin. She'd be able to feel the power of her mount. Then she could pretend to be in control of something. "I'll hurry. I don't want to be late and miss being needed."

The butler handed her a knit shawl, acres of creamy stitches. "Master Cecil always said, it isn't about speed. It's about how you run the race."

Pickens was a dear and he must've studied Mathew, for he knew how to nudge her in the way she should go. His steady force, his apt words, had helped guide her these months without Mathew.

Waving off a groom, Pickens held the reins as she took her seat. "Go, Mrs. Cecil. Enjoy your ride. We'll see you in an hour or so."

She nodded. "Thank you. I'll stick to the paths so if I need to be... Thank you, Pickens. I will run this race the best I can."

He set the thick reins into her palm. "That's all anyone can ask, ma'am. It's all Mr. Cecil expected. Have a pleasant afternoon."

He turned and went back into Tradenwood.

Theodosia closed her eyes for a moment, then whipped the leathers, forcing the gig forward. The small buggy was her favorite. With one horse, her fastest one, she could fly through the fields.

Breathing the fresh air, free of ointments and laudanum

tonics, she let her heart smile. The doctor would fix Philip. He would be well. Theodosia had to hold on to that thought, as she did the reins.

Her horse, Willow, leaped over a gully, making the wheels bang hard, but Theodosia didn't care. This was as close to freedom as she could grasp and she relished it.

She'd have to do something nice for Pickens. He was such a dear. If a platonic marriage of convenience could be had with the butler, she was almost tempted to suggest it. Pity Pickens was as old as dirt and his position wouldn't have any sway with the Court of Chancery. Maybe she should get his opinion on the squire or the new suitor, the baron. Well, the baron hadn't replied yet, but he might. Finding someone as understanding as Mathew or Pickens—the hope of it was all she had.

Settling into her gig, she flew over the hill and through the fields. The glass greenhouses she'd had Mathew install glistened in the sun. No one could grow more exotic plantings than Cecil Farms. Zipping up the trail, she waved to a few of the tenants still out picking.

The morning was the best time to gather the flowers, unless you were slow or sickly. Theodosia used to be good at it, and she'd get on her small gig, the one financed by her mother, and make it to the Covent Garden area to sell flowers to the *ton* by ten. Those harried days had been so long ago.

A smile freed her lip from being chewed, and she slowed to enjoy the contours of the blooming fields. Rows of lavender waved, alongside sweet pink roses. The air felt crisp, tingling her cheeks. The day after a storm was the best. Everything felt cleansed.

Though yesterday's argument with Ewan had drained her, it had been good to admit to him that she'd loved Mathew and that Mathew had loved her. The poison Ewan's family had spewed about her had to have marred his thoughts of truth. It did make her chuckle, thinking of the old earl turning beat red over the outrageous sum of money she'd asked to be paid to continue the water rights on her land. He might've been more outraged at that than his son wanting to marry a Blackamoor.

Sighing, she let her *R*'s, her numerous regrets, be overtaken by a mix of lavender, roses, even manure. The blend of scents made a rich perfume. The Cecil fields would always possess abundance. Mathew would like that. Good. The first time today she thought of Mathew and not Ewan. She needed to be in the fields to cleanse her of thinking about Ewan and thunderstorms and his little nursery rhyme songs. Or even how much her son would enjoy them if he could hear the lyrics.

She wanted to strike at her chest and banish this foolishness. She should've given Mathew all the room in her heart, but she hadn't. Ewan was still in there.

Despairing, she pointed her gig to the tributaries that fed all the fields—Tradenwood's and Grandbole's. The main artery to the Fitzwilliam's flowers had been dammed with limestone bricks. Ewan hadn't lied and Lester was a bigger skunk than she'd realized.

Shutting off the water was wrong, no matter what they had done to her. Lester had no right to do this without her permission.

Driving one fist into her palm, she decided she must do something. But what?

Nothing. If she went against him, he'd take Philip. Lester

was his guardian. His word would overrule hers in the courtroom of men. She couldn't fix this until she and Philip were free.

The same sense of helplessness that made her check on her son every hour for fever invaded her soul. She bit her lip, to hold in the frustration she'd wanted to yell out last night, and stared ahead at the lonely limestone wall. It was as isolated as a widow, as a woman trying hard to hold on to everything.

"Coming to inspect your handiwork?"

She lifted her head and saw Ewan walking toward her. She hid her dismay behind a smile. "Morning. Needed to see this for myself. Fitzwilliams are proven liars, don't you know."

"That is ungenerous, Cousin."

"Good day, Ghost."

She turned her gig around and kept an even pace. Not slow enough to be caught but not fast enough to show fear. Ewan was a minor complication to her plans, a thorn in her floral arrangement. Lying must be contagious because now she was lying to her soul about Ewan being anything minor to her.

Willow neighed and clomped to the highest point, the place where Theodosia could see all the fields, hers and Philip's.

Her breath froze a little in her lungs as gratitude fell upon her. These fields had saved her life. She'd met Mathew here when she'd been broken and scared. He had protected her, fed her starving body.

To prove her love, she'd protect his fields as he had protected her and Philip. No ghost or Lester would wrest this place from her. Mathew had wanted it to be Philip's. Theodosia needed to make his last request come true, for he'd been the instrument to make her hopes true. "I'm sorry. Mathew, I—"

"Morning again, Mrs. Cecil." Ewan's sultry voice sounded again, heavy and soothing. "I hate to see a beautiful woman alone in such a picturesque place."

Her heart skipped a little. Then she remembered. They were at war. He swung a walking stick as if he were on a carefree stroll. But his top hat had been smashed onto his thick black hair. He'd run to catch up with her. She almost laughed, but she didn't know how she liked the thought of him pursuing her again.

"So what brings you here? Thinking of poisoning the Grandbole fields? Oh, I know. You are looking for that next husband. Am I interrupting a get-together?" He cupped his eyes and scanned. "Your new love is late? You must have quite a few advertisement responses to choose from not just... Who was it? Just a baron? My new wealthy cousin must have others writing to her. A duke in bad straights. Maybe a pauper prince in need of a healthy fortune?"

"Will you forget about my newspaper advertisement? It has nothing to do with you or us."

"It has everything to do with us. We are family now, Cousin Theo."

She bit her lip, hating that he knew of her gamble to find a husband. "Stay to the left, Ghost. You don't want to be on Cecil land. I'd hate to add fines to your fees."

"Grumpy? Only ghosts should be grumpy. Maybe you need a walk to refresh yourself. You have shadows under your eyes. That conscience you're suppressing is rattling you. Or is it my ghostly chains?" He held a hand to her as if to help her down. "You need to walk. I don't bite, much."

He *would* notice that she hadn't slept. How could she, with

Philip in pain? But to take Ewan's hand, and depend upon his humor or anything he offered, that couldn't be. "I'm safe—I'm fine here."

His brow rose a smidgen, followed by a broad smile that someone stupid would think charming. He pulled his arm back and wiped his fingers on his bulky black jacket, very different from his smart cut of yesterday. "Yes, you are, and scared of me, too."

"No, I am not, Ewan."

He stuck his palm out to her again. "Prove you're not afraid of ghosts."

It was dumb to accept his challenge and clasp his fingers. Dumber to let him lift her down to the ground. The dumbest thing was assuming he'd be a gentleman. He crowded her against her gig, with nowhere to run but deeper into his arms.

Brushing a fallen curl from her temple, he made his crooked grin bigger. "Cousin Cecil, have you thought of a more reasonable extortion? Maybe you do have some sense of charity."

She lifted her hands to push away from him but that would be touching him, something stronger than she. Instead she lowered her hands and braced for whatever he had in mind.

"So tense, Cousin." He gave her tired shoulders a little press. "Give me a reasonable offer so I can bring you relief. I could present it today and end this little family problem of the water. I'll assume selling Tradenwood is still off-limits."

"Yes, and why don't you rescind your blackmail? I might be more inclined to charity without your play nonsense."

He clasped her fingers. His other arm came up behind her, smoothing each bone in her wilting spine. "You need to relax, like you used to do." Changing the pressure of his fingertips, he spun her like a top as he used to do in the rain. "Has your dancing improved? I hear Cecil was rather old. He might not have had time for such trivial things."

"Let me go, Ewan. This is ridiculous with no music," she said, between twirls.

Her gripped her about the waist and waltzed her around her gig. "Always music in my head, when I'm with you."

Willow neighed and kicked her hooves, making a rhythm that Ewan seemed to adopt. For a moment, she let the memories, the ones locked away in her heart, leach out. Closing her eyes, they were young again, sneaking behind the coaching house. Ewan had purloined a bucket of oats for her old mare and had made her sit in the shade as he read her Shakespeare. It was her favorite remembrance next to hearing Ewan's heartbeat, his lips mouthing *I love you*.

"Your dancing has improved, Cousin," he said as he kissed her hand. "But it seems we are at an impasse. I call blackmail protecting my family from the woman bent on destroying it. You call it fines. What would the late Mathew Cecil think of you allowing the agreement between the two sides of the family to dissolve into bickering? I didn't believe you to be so petty. I remember you caring about people."

He dared to bring Mathew into this foolishness. She moved away, as if she'd done something naughty dancing with him, and scampered back atop her gig.

"Oh, Cousin, you don't have to run off. We were getting along."

Picking up the horse whip, she rolled it between her fingertips, then let the temptation to strike him and his teasing settle down. The old Theodosia didn't think, always forgot about consequences. She placed the snappy pole across her knees. "I think Daddy's been feeding you lies. Doesn't look like he's fed you much else. You look a little thin."

His lips pursed. Those blue eyes, big and full of stories and dreams tucked behind his long dark lashes, winked at her. "Ghosts need to be thin. That's how we slip about. But you've eaten well, if your rounded cheeks are any indication."

Ewan stood on tiptoes, and his hot gaze roamed over her. "And you still fit well in my arms. I suppose getting a rich *loving* husband was good for you."

He peered at her again and his gaze seemed to penetrate through her thick shawl. For once, she was grateful for the heaviness of her mourning robes. "You possess a very well-rounded figure. Yes, my cousin must have been very pleased with you, an apt mistress you made. I'm not ignorant to how this love began with Cecil."

The way he put it made her feel dirty. "Must you be crude? Or maybe that's what you bounders do. You convince a woman of your love, only to deflower her. How wrong I was to believe the words of a playwright. *I love you. We'll elope after the storm passes.*"

He looked down and kicked a rock with his boot. "I shouldn't make fun of such things. It is so hard to imagine you— vibrant-spirit-filled—with my cousin. They say he was very old. Very old."

Ewan took the reins of her gig from her. "The strap is not slack enough at the rein ring. You'll do too much work pulling.

The horse won't go any faster. I'll adjust it for you, like I used to do."

She watched his fingers work the straps, sliding fastenings, loosening sections, until it was at whatever tautness he felt was perfect for her, looking after her like he always had. Six years and Ewan still remembered. He had taken care of her, not with flashy things but in the smallest ways—a bucket of oats for her horse, adjusting her gig, a comforting rhyme.

He put the leather in her hands. "Was Cecil good to you?"

An odd question but he sounded sincere. How much did he still care?

A scream came from deep in her fields.

Ewan turned, cupping his hand to his eyes. "I think someone's fainted."

He started moving into her lavender fields.

Theodosia jumped down and followed. Which one of her workers could it be?

They pushed through stalks and fresh clippings and came upon an older woman. It was one of her tenants. Dropping to her knees, she fanned the woman's cheeks. "Mrs. Gutter, wake up."

Ewan bent and grabbed the picker's wrist. "She has a pulse. You know this person?"

Ignoring such a stupid question, Theodosia took off the picker's bonnet and waved it faster and faster over the stricken woman's countenance. "I know all my workers, and Mrs. Gutter's a stubborn one. She should have waited another week or two. She's been very sick these past few months. She should've started early morning when it's cooler."

Mrs. Gutter sat up and yawned, as if she'd taken a nap. Her

ruddy cheeks seemed even redder upon her ashy gray skin. "I thought I was fine, Mrs. Cecil, but I do have a thick head so I don't listen." She tried to sit, but fell back. "I'm so sorry, ma'am. Give me a minute. I don't mean to cause no problems."

Theodosia took off her gloves and stashed them in her pocket. "Silly, who means to faint? May I see if you have a fever? I'll have to touch your forehead."

The old woman nodded and allowed Theodosia's dark hand to brush her pale forehead.

Mrs. Gutter felt warm, warmer than merely picking under the bright sun. "You do have a fever. Come with me. Mr. Fitzwilliam, help me get this woman to my carriage."

"Nonsense," Mrs. Gutter said. "I just need to catch my breath."

Theodosia grabbed Ewan's hand and put it under Mrs. Gutter's shoulder. "We need to get her back to Tradenwood and get her something to drink. I need your help."

Ewan pumped Theo's fingers. "I will always be here to help you. My return is permanent. You can count on me." He held Theodosia's hand a moment longer then turned to Mrs. Gutter. "Ma'am, Theo—Mrs. Cecil is right. You need to go with her."

"Let me take you back to the main house." Hating the pleading tone in her voice, she shook free from Ewan. "The doctor is coming today, Mrs. Gutter. It would be no trouble for him to see you, too."

Ewan captured Theodosia's elbow and hovered over her as if to detect weakness. "Doctor? The shadows under your eyes. Are you well?"

She looked down to the rich soil, away from the bluer-than-blue eyes that had sent prickles up her skin when she'd first seen him, first spoken to him, in Grandbole's fields. Like they had this morning, dancing on the hill.

"Cousin Theo, you would tell me if you were not well?"

Must be the concern in his voice that sent a shiver now. "Fine. I'm fine. Mrs. Gutter is the one who is not. Help me get her to my gig."

Mrs. Gutter wheezed, but shook her head.

"No, my angel. I'm fine now. My son will be back any moment now with my cart." Mrs. Gutter gasped and sucked in a huge mouth of air. "He went to water the horse."

The lady was too big to pick up and carry to her gig. Theo needed to depend on the one man she couldn't. Swallowing doubts and bitter pride, she asked, "Please help me, Ewan? I need you."

Ewan didn't move, and his gaze upon her felt heavier than before. "You heard the lady, Mrs. Gutter. I'm not accustomed to denying one's request."

Did he see her as a lady now, not some lucky mistress, or was he talking about six years ago when she'd been stupid and had loved him more than herself. Theodosia put a hand to her bosom. Her cheeks felt heated like she'd leaned over flames. "Mrs. Gutter, I need you to allow Mr. Fitzwilliam to put you in my gig. Your son can meet you at Tradenwood."

"Fitzwilliam? Never. Leave me to dirt. I'm not disloyal to you, ma'am."

She couldn't stop the smile growing. Maybe Ewan would realize how awful his father would be to the tenants, if she sold to Lord Crisdon. She tucked the woman's hat under her arm.

"Mrs. Gutter, you couldn't be disloyal, ever."

Ewan's eyes told another story. They still seemed to be on Theodosia and they held fire. "Consider this an act of chivalry, not disloyalty. I'm sure Mrs. Cecil could tell you the difference." He lifted the woman in the air as if the portly picker weighed nothing, maybe a shilling's worth of foolscap.

Theodosia stopped gawking and, in her haste, her shawl dropped from her shoulders and tangled in the bushes. As she yanked it free, it wrapped around her feet.

His chortle from behind grated. "Do you need a little help, my dear cousin?"

She sped up, intending to get out of his reach, but the shawl dragged more and this time she stumbled.

Before she hit the ground, Ewan grabbed her arm, jerking her up. Then he seized her about her waist, pulling her into his chest, steadying her. His baggy jacket hid pure muscle underneath.

He didn't release her, forcing her to absorb his heat, his light scent of musk, the entire way back to her gig, all while supporting Mrs. Gutter in his other arm.

Back on the smooth dirt road, Ewan released Theodosia then swung Mrs. Gutter into the seat. Then he worked a strong hand about the middle of Theodosia's back. "Now it's your turn."

The ghost levitated her in the air. Hard, lean, chiseled hands hoisted her onto the platform to drive.

"Thank you." It was all she could muster. He was too close, too strong, and the heat of the day had surely made her weak. How could she keep contempt for Ewan in her head when his arms felt of safety, something she'd missed since Mathew's death?

All smiles, as if he knew he'd addled her brainbox, he leaned over the side. "Even a ghost can be helpful, but we return to haunting, if agreements aren't met."

If not for her pride or Mrs. Gutter's watchful eyes, she'd let him know that ghosts needed to die painful, horrible deaths. But that would be impossible to do to a true ghost or the wily Ewan Fitzwilliam. He had to be tough, if Napoleon hadn't done him in. "Nice to know you finally found your strength. Six years too late. Go home to Daddy. Tell him of your big adventure."

"No, I'll keep it a secret, but I will take the liberty of checking on Mrs. Gutter. I want to know this doctor's report, Cousin."

She gripped the reins tightly and rippled them, forcing Willow into a full run. The horse left him swallowing dust with each high kick.

"Dear, don't let a Fitzwilliam bother you. They think they own everything and they love to get into everyone's business. But you're Mrs. Cecil and everyone knows you to be fair and honest, just like the great man."

She nodded, but kept her eyes on the lane. Six years could change things. From a mistress to a wife. From a thief stealing flowers and food to one who owned the flowers and food. What had the six years changed in Ewan?

And would he change again if he knew the doctor's full report about Tradenwood's inhabitants? That must never, ever happen. Her son couldn't be caught in any more of these rows. "We'll be to the house soon."

Mrs. Gutter smiled and closed her eyes.

How was Theodosia to keep Ewan from popping up and finding out her greatest secret? As he had done in his play, he'd use it to destroy her.

. . .

Ewan rapped at Tradenwood's front door and waited for entry. The day had slipped away. Only a few hours of daylight remained, and from his frequent trips to the patio off Grandbole's library, he couldn't get a good view of the comings and goings down here, which meant he couldn't tell if a doctor had arrived or if one had left. All he knew was that the not-knowing had become maddening.

Before he knocked again, he stopped, lifted his top hat, and raked a hand through his hair. A piece of demolished porcelain Dresden fell to his boots, a parting gift from Jasper's girls for rushing off from Grandbole more quickly than they wanted.

His nieces, blessed demons, had started an endless series of pranks. The cuteness and questions offered with cherub smiles was an act. They were little masterminds, pranking anything that moved. Starting with swapping the sugar for salt, to more dangerous things like falling Dresden.

He touched his head again, searching for blood or scars. He had enough of both.

Satisfied that he had no new injury, he again knocked at Tradenwood's door.

Why was a doctor visiting? Six years could change a great deal. He now had a chest full of scars, aches that followed him into the cold winters. What could be wrong with Theo?

For a final time, he took up the brass loop on the door and knocked. No answer still. Should he look to get in by climbing a tree as Jasper and he had done when they were kids?

The door opened and Pickens came outside, pulling the massive frame shut, as if Ewan would sneak inside behind him. "Mr. Fitzwilliam, I need you to go away. The family is having no visitors today."

"I am family. I came to see my cousin, Widow Cecil."

"Is there something I can help you with, sir?" Pickens came down a step. His hushed tone continued. "She's not taking visitors, sir."

"Nonsense. She'll see me."

The butler's frown deepened as he shook his head. "No. No, she won't. She left specific instructions."

He felt like a caricature of his youngest niece parroting words. "Left?"

Gripping his lapel of his liveries, the powdered-haired man nodded. "No visitors."

Ewan turned and started down the steps, but he couldn't taste any satisfaction with these answers. Not a pinch. Something was wrong. He stopped and faced the butler. "Pickens. Did Mrs. Gutter need more help? Is that why Mrs. Cecil went?"

The older man stared at him, maybe even huffed. "Mrs. Gutter is well. A bit of punch and she was as good as new."

Something did not add up, and the way that Theo liked numbers, he knew things were amiss. Drawing up his coat as the wind shifted, Ewan's temper grew hotter. "I ask again to see Mrs. Cecil. Why are you pretending she is not here?"

"I'm hoping you'll tire and go back up the hill. The mistress is getting some much-needed sleep, but you'll wake up the late Master Cecil with your ruckus."

The butler was trying to get him to leave. Why? Much-needed sleep. It was obvious. She had shadows under her eyes. "Pickens, is she well?"

"You need to go home." The butler turned and marched back to the top of the steps.

Ewan had to stop him, had to know about Theo. "Pickens, you worked for my uncle and my mother's father. You remember who I am. I should know about this. This is family."

The man stopped but didn't turn. "Yes, I remember you, Ewan Fitzwilliam. You were your uncle's favorite. He grieved hard when he thought you'd died, but he was also quite fond of Mr. Cecil. Cecil knew what family meant."

"My concern for the widow is true. I am her family now, even if it is by marriage. I should know."

Pickens peered over his shoulder with a look of scorn. "Does a Fitzwilliam know the meaning of family, unless it's convenient?"

Ewan hadn't expected that moment of truth. There wasn't much to rebut in Pickens's words. He shifted his stance. "I see you've adopted Mrs. Cecil's quick tongue."

"Sir, I've worked at Tradenwood for many years. I've seen more than I'll ever admit to remembering. Your family was not kind to Mrs. Cecil. They did not even acknowledge the master's death."

The tension and the truth becoming utterly unbearable, Ewan put a hand to his neck. "They do hold grudges. I don't think they approved of her marriage."

"The new mistress of Tradenwood is worth the title, and she deserves her privacy. If you *remember* anything of the widow from six years ago, she does things when she is good and ready."

The way he said *remember* indicated Pickens knew more.

Did she tell that wizened-face butler that Ewan had ruined himself over Theo before she had attracted Cecil?

"The Mistress of Tradenwood is stubborn. I do remember that. It is still sort of galling to call her that, knowing how my mother, Lady Crisdon, wanted this estate."

"Your uncle chose not to leave it to her, but to Cecil. Now, Tradenwood is the widow Cecil's. Hers and her heir's."

Heirs? Could that be it? Was this sickness and doctors about Theo being with child? If so, she hadn't been devoted to Cecil any more than she had been to him. Had she hopped into bed with the next fool and was now with child? That had to be why she needed a new husband—to hide a pregnancy. "Her heirs?"

"Yes. Cecil didn't want the extended family to harass his wife."

The concern Ewan had started to feel for her was for naught. She hadn't changed her ways, despite the teasing fun of dancing with her or the warmth her claiming his hand in the fields had generated. His insides sickened, twisting with new frustration. "So much for hoping she'd changed. Good evening, Pickens."

That furrowed brow of the old man rose. "I hope she doesn't change. Never was a kinder or gentler soul. Good day, sir."

The door thudded closed.

Ewan walked away. Anger pressed on his lungs, making him pant as he paced. The lecture from the butler maligning his family was probably true. The fact that Tradenwood was Theo's, that was true. The jealousy and angst he felt over Theo, of not knowing of her health or if she carried another man's child, was true.

The reason for his current misery—unfinished feelings for Theo—that had to be a lie. If only he could convince himself that he was as over her as he had in writing his play. He took a few more steps and fought the urge to return, to find that tree, and see if it would hold his weight. He needed to stop lying to himself. He wasn't finished with Theo. That was his truth.

CHAPTER SEVEN

Pranks & Prose

Ewan stormed to his bedchamber door at Grandbole Manor, swiping at the cold liquid dripping from his face. He'd visited Tradenwood several more times in the past week only to be turned away by Pickens.

Theo didn't want to see him. He had no way of knowing if she were sick with an illness or suffering from the sickness that came from the changes pregnancy brought. He dabbed at his forehead, which felt sticky and ridiculous and blue.

He was wrong to expect the woman he had tried to buy off and scandalize in a play to tell him anything of a personal nature.

But that didn't stop him from wanting to know. It also didn't stop him from remembering the feel of her in his arms. Why did she still wind him up so tight? And who had Theo become these six years—the landlord whom all her tenants and servants loved? Was she the frugal business woman who knew all the figures? Was she an honorable widow?

The way she had forgotten herself when they'd danced—had she felt as he did, excited, wistful, or lonely? He swiped at his sticky fingers and tried to stop thinking about *her heirs*. Had that sense of isolation made her break her customary twelve months of mourning? Had it caused her to take a secret lover? She didn't look as if she was going to pop, so a new birth would be well beyond the time a child could be claimed as Cecil's.

Only a legitimate child could inherit. Lord knew, his mother and the earl would protest. Why would she be so reckless? He put a hand to his eye, his blue hand to his blue, now stinging, eye. He'd created a complete story for Theo without any shred of facts. His playwright mind needed to slow. And his face needed to stop stinging.

"Uncle?"

Blinking, Ewan turned toward the low, squeaky voice. "Yes, Lucy."

She fingered her snowy dress, which had indigo droplets on the hem and ribbon-trimmed bodice. "Are you much hurt?"

"No. You and your sisters didn't kill me this time."

She looked down and held her arms behind her back. "Does this mean you won't go away?"

There was a sad quality to the voice. Someone that small should be dancing to angel music. He stooped low to catch her gaze. "I have a place in the city. But you haven't frightened me so much that I will be gone forever."

A smile burst between two cherry cheeks. "I don't want you to go. No one visits anymore since Mama left and Lady Crisdon won't come back."

His playwright mind didn't need to write this story. It was obvious. The children were lonely and misbehaving for attention. In true Fitzwilliam style, their fits could be extremely pain-filled and somewhat lethal. "Come here, little one."

He offered a hug and she held tightly, even if he were squishy and blue. "Your uncle is pretty tough."

He released her and she now had indigo splotched all over. "But don't keep trying my patience. Let your sisters know."

The moppet nodded. "At least you are not frowning. Your

lips have been sad for a week."

He stood up straight. "Well, sometimes being an adult is sad."

"Then I want no part of it." She swung her head side to side, her blonde locks bouncing as she walked away.

Maybe Theo was as sad at this adult business as he. Maybe this love she claimed for Cecil was an act or a very good exaggeration. Would her pride let her admit it? Well, a baby for the widow would be a statement to the contrary. That made Ewan chuckle. Finding humor at her predicament was wrong, even if it proved Ewan right. No, he wasn't good at this adult thing.

What would it take for her to confess her regrets? Just one. And if she did, would that change the war between the families, or his feelings about her?

As surely as the muck drenching his collar, he couldn't take another day not knowing the truth. Maybe he should be more like a ghost and stop asking permission to haunt.

He grabbed the doorknob but stopped. The girls could've set another trap. He bucked up his spine, refusing to be terrorized by children, and females at that. He'd been to war, taken a bullet and metal shards to the chest. Yet, here he stood, as anxious as a rat in a field of wild cats. What if a pail of dye or dung awaited on the other side to drop upon him?

Shaking his head, he threw the door open, waited a minute, then barreled inside.

"Brother?"

Jasper's voice startled him and Ewan spun with fists raised to see the man sitting in his window with his feet up. "I needed to talk with you in private. Didn't mean to spook you."

"No, you have your daughters for that." Ewan moved to his

basin and dipped his hands in the water until they were clean. "So you are sitting in my room waiting. I mean, this room Lord Crisdon has let me use?"

Jasper rolled two pieces of sealed paper between his large fingers. "Yes. I hold a message from Mr. Brown. He's waiting to see your play today. He sent a rather impatient note. Is there a reason for your delay?"

The theater manager. Ewan had forgotten about that, so involved with Theo and the water wars. "I could see him today, but not blue. I'll need to change and borrow your gig again, if you don't mind."

"Of course not. If you are willing to return, you can borrow it as much as you like." The big man chortled with too much glee. "With your enhanced coloring, it's no wonder if my children's behavior doesn't push you out the door."

Ewan walked over to the chest of drawers looking at his choices in shirts, ones the earl had made for him. "Your girls are a handful. Aren't they supposed to be, as Southey said, made of sugar and spice, not antics?"

His brother chuckled as he picked up a glass that sat near his hip and took a sip. He waved the second letter as if his brow had fevered, then took another hungry gulp from his crystal goblet.

More liquor? And so early in the morning?

As if Jasper could read his thoughts, he put down his drink. "You mean Southey, the poet laureate. Ah, you and your love of poets. The girls are trying to get your attention. They will settle down once I've secured a stepmother for them."

Pulling off his ruined coat, Ewan shrugged, then untied his cravat. "Seems to me they need your attention or discipline more.

Have they had it?"

Jasper's gaze lowered. He seized his glass, sloshing it with a rapid swing of his arm, but he didn't guzzle. "What are you implying?"

"I've noticed..." Ewan wanted to say "drink," but couldn't, so he softened and started again. "You disappear a lot. Maybe they act out to get more of your time."

Putting down his brandy, Jasper harrumphed then slapped a hand on the sill, the movement causing the folded note to jostle. "You've deduced this after two weeks? Your attention to family care doesn't speak well. Not sure I should be taking advice from someone who's been away almost six years. You don't know them."

Ewan wanted to say something ungenerous, such as, his brother didn't seem to know them very well either, and he'd *been* here the past six years. Instead, he pulled his shirt over his head and said, "I'm merely wondering at their behavior. Their pranks could hurt someone."

His brother took another long drink. Then he slammed down the nearly empty glass. "Didn't you snicker when they swapped Father's sugar for salt? The man blanched over his ruined tea."

"Their antics were amusing, at first. Who doesn't love seeing the earl turn beet red? And it was a joy seeing you move at the speed of a fleet stallion to prevent another Fitzwilliam prized Wedgwood from falling to the ground." Ewan pivoted away from his brother whose lips formed a droopy frown.

Reaching into the closet, Ewan smoothed his fingers over the nap of a smartly cut jacket and matching waistcoat of dark blue.

"Lord Crisdon has fine taste. His bribes are the best."

"He wants you to be comfortable as you stay. He also wants to know if you've made any progress in your negotiations with Cecil's widow."

Ewan spun, his shirt barely clearing his head. "He knows I've been trying to see her. Has she sent any papers for the water lease?"

His brother's grin returned, making him the happy-go-lucky fellow everyone knew. "She hasn't sent anything. And Father hasn't said anything of a meeting. But your willingness to stay at Grandbole and the now-missing lavender package set my conspiratorial mind to work. A lucky inquiry to the merchants at the Burlington Arcade, the ones who sell that particular type of lavender soap, produced a familiar name, Cecil. I took a guess that you returned the parcel to Widow Cecil, our family's nemesis."

Jasper's eyes narrowed as if he were trying to see through him.

Then Ewan realized, with his shirt askew, the ten-inch nest of scars to his chest were visible. He started to yank the linen down as if covering nakedness, but he stilled his hand. He was half dressed, decent enough for a brother. "Yes, I returned the package. We spoke several times. Now she's refusing to see me. She's stubborn."

"Those look terrible."

The wounds from the field surgery were horrid, jagged, and bulbous. He'd grown used to them but not to how others reacted. Must be a shock for Jasper to see the aftermath of war. Probably more so for Theo. He'd pressed her finger to them, and she'd known his chest to be smooth.

It was days ago, but the anguish in her voice at his pain nested in his chest, alongside his wounds. She had truly thought him dead. But none of that sentiment would matter once a rich man caught her eye. They mattered even less with her new predicament, or she'd allow his visit.

"They are terrible, Jasper. All scars are."

His brother nodded and raised his glass in an invisible toast. The sun through the window cast amber diamonds onto the deep chestnut-stained floors, sad rainbows on the gray walls. "Sorry, Ewan."

Tying a new, starched cravat, Ewan stood straight. "Rather terrible than dead. Brother, why do so many pickers and tenants rave about Cousin Cecil? And his widow?"

Jasper set down the empty goblet, then shifted his feet along the floor. "Father is all about business. Cecil gave better terms to lease, and he also allowed women to pick his fields at advantageous terms. And those glass hothouses they've installed, well, they outdo us with exotic flowers available all year 'round. They've even grown pineapples in there."

Being better at business didn't answer all Ewan's questions. It certainly didn't explain all the love that seemed to shroud Theo now. Maybe being married to a demi-god had made her one, too? How would she fare with all her secrets exposed? "It seems to be more than that."

"Perhaps. But why don't you tell me how you know Mrs. Cecil other than a happenstance meeting at Burlington Arcade?"

Ewan put his back to his brother and finished dressing. "Why don't you tell me? You're the one with all the good guesses and conspiracies."

Something tugged at his collar, righting it. A scent of brandy took possession of the air. His brother now stood behind him fussing and pulling at Ewan's borrowed jacket. From the smell, Jasper had been drinking a lot, but he still seemed steady.

"So what is she to you, Ewan? An old acquaintance?"

"For a big man, you're light on your feet, even when sotted. I'll have to remember that."

Jasper settled a large palm onto Ewan's shoulder, but not a chuckle sounded. "I was away with Maria's laying-in for Lucy. They say you became involved with a low woman. Is Cecil's widow that Jezebel?"

Whatever Ewan thought of Theo, he didn't like Jasper calling her names. He gripped his brother's hand hard and flung it away. "She wasn't low when I knew her."

He turned and caught Jasper's brow cocked, one eye raised. "Ewan, she's a Blackamoor. From all accounts, illegitimate, with no money or connections at the time you were involved with her. What were you thinking?"

"I wasn't thinking. Not a thought about you, the heir in-waiting, or of anything Lord Crisdon held dear. I thought about me, about someone valuing me and what I wanted. And it didn't matter her origin or her connections. Only her love. Well, I thought it was love."

Jasper's lips parted then closed. He nodded and stepped backward. "I see. And she knew you were without fortune?"

"Yes. Not a dime to my name. Just a play to peddle. She didn't seem to care. We had a silly notion of building a life together, once I returned from war."

His brother went back to his perch in the window, picking up the folded letter by the edge, as if it were too delicate to sit upon, and leaned back. He eyed his empty glass as if it was the goblet's fault that it sat drained. "What happened?"

"Like everything else. The announcement a month after deploying that I had died set off the actions that changed everything—the loss of Tradenwood and her. She didn't mourn me and seems to have become Cecil's mistress before news of my living could spread. You'd think she'd have grieved a month or two, the way she appears to mourn Cecil."

Scooping up his ruined shirt and jacket, he sighed again. "I left her to go to the war. She didn't wait for me to return. This isn't a new story for a soldier, even if I am a Fitzwilliam."

"You must ask her why."

Dropping the clothes back onto the floor, Ewan locked his arms behind his back. "It doesn't matter her reasons. She found a rich man, my cousin, who made her wealthy."

He gazed at Jasper, hoping the man would stop. He could be as bad as their father when hunting for information. Ewan moved to the mirror at the edge of the canopy bed and whipped a hand through his hair to right his blue-tinged locks. "Hopefully, the theater will be dark tonight. I'd hate to lose this opportunity because of stained hair. But I've done my mother's bidding; I asked for a price to sell Tradenwood. Mrs. Cecil won't. I've also asked for a new lease. She's come back with 20,000 pounds per annum, a ridiculous amount. I suspect once my play is purchased, she'll see the light. She won't want her good name ruined."

Jasper slapped his knee and leaned on the window as he erupted in laughs. "She's in your play? You've written her in as one of the hilarious characters? Oh no. She's that Cleo, no Theo the Flower Seller. Oh, what a clever form of blackmail. Lord Crisdon will be proud. He'll pay for the theater, maybe even handbills, to watch her disgrace."

Ewan rubbed at a spot of paint on his knuckle, dabbing it with a handkerchief. "Don't say anything of her being in my play. Let him know I will get her consent. If she agrees to my terms, I want to live up to my end of the bargain. I am a man of my word. The earl would still want to ruin her name."

"True, but I'm surprised you care. You still do care, don't you?"

Not wanting to search too deeply into his scarred soul for the answers, he scooped up the letter. "I suppose you need my help with a new marital prospect from the newspaper. Your matrimonial chase continues. Another woman to court?"

"No, the same one. The one we sent our rhyme. Seems she's had time to respond."

Oh, no. Theo had responded, giving Jasper new hope. If his brother found out this advertisement was Theo's, his spirits would be crushed. Ewan should tell him straightaway, but the look in his eye—slightly desperate, slightly hoping—would become more troubled. That could not happen. He'd find a way to spare Jasper any more pain. "So what does the mystery woman say?"

"Go on, open it."

Ewan did. The letter wasn't a short few sentences. It was three paragraphs. "Well, it seems our advertisement bride has answered with a resounding yes. She loves children and details how they need good, moral examples." *That is rich coming from Theo.* "She sounds like she liked our little rhyme. I'll take credit for that. She admires that we would even take a child's needs into consideration."

Ewan stumbled at the third paragraph. It pierced his jaded heart.

Jasper rocked and coughed, as if to draw Ewan's attention. "What else does she say?"

"She talks of the sacrifices that one should make for a child, especially a sickly child." If Theodosia wasn't pregnant now, then those doctors were for her heir, a child who lived now, out of the womb. So maybe she wasn't scandalous but a blasted dutiful wife and mother? Had Theodosia borne Cecil a babe? And was that child sick?

He rubbed at his eyes and paced a moment, hoping to have read something wrong. He'd been in Tradenwood. She'd never introduced him to her child. But, why would she? He'd threatened her with scandal in his play. He'd accused her of trying to ruin his side of the family with the water leases. "She must have a child, one that's not well."

Jasper folded his arms, as if he was in deep thought. "That wasn't what I hoped for. Sometimes people don't get well."

A chill set in Ewan's skin. It wasn't what he hoped either. He'd rather Theo prove herself scandalous than with a suffering child, but a child to an old man could be sickly. She should've grieved a little longer and not taken up with old Cecil. Now she seemed like a good woman who'd fallen for his cousin and gave the man a child. No, that is not what he wanted at all.

He pounded his palms together as if that could warm him. "I still don't know why a woman of means would seek a marriage of convenience by newspaper?"

"Companionship. And as I need someone to mother my girls, she may need someone to father her child."

Still made no sense, nor warrant all the secrecy and doctor visits. Ewan closed his eyes and allowed memories of Theo to haunt him, unvarnished by his own disappointments and jealousy. She had been shy, except when selling flowers. It had taken time to make her comfortable, to see her laugh. They were supposed to elope and had gotten caught in the thunderstorm. She had been skittish and so unsure of herself. But she'd trusted him and had given into the love that bound them. Then his father had discovered them and their plans had changed.

Had Cecil seen her and pursued her, too? Had he been patient and found a way to make her love him? He'd never thought of that possibility. He'd believed Crisdon when he'd told him that she'd become a mistress and disappeared. Fitzwilliam half-truths had struck again. He moved to his desk and fingered the pile of papers, the play that branded her a harlot. Ewan felt shamed.

His brother interrupted his musings. "I hadn't thought of being a father to anyone else's children. Is that selfish?"

"Jasper, I'm no one to judge selfishness." He dragged his thumb over the edge of the pages.

Theo had to have truly cared for Cecil to give him a child. Maybe she'd loved Cecil as she claimed. That stung more than it should. Fuming on the inside, surely his guts turned black. Ewan read the third paragraph again, and again. "It definitely sounds as if she is a mother and to a sickly child. Do you want that? To father a child who is not well?"

Jasper took the letter back. "I've done sickbed duty before. It's not something I want, but I can't let this lady go. You must help me win her. I think she's the one. This is what I need for the girls. You've seen them. They need a caring mother. I'm failing them, Ewan. That's why they act out."

Ewan loved his brother, but he needed to give him a dose a truth. "The girls don't need a stepmother. They need more of you."

Looking to the ceiling, maybe counting the dark beams, Jasper was quiet, neither agreeing or disagreeing. Then he said, "You are always good at noticing things. You want to take care of things, but there is no more of me. Half of me is in the crypt with Maria. I'm doing what I can. Ewan, please stay at Grandbole. Come back here when your business in Town is done. Help me win advertisement number four. Ask her to meet. I am ready to paper this deal with solicitors."

A marriage contract? Ewan couldn't have that. As bad as it had been for Theo to marry his rich cousin and have a child with him, it was worse thinking of Theo with Jasper. Though her money might even make the earl welcome her with open arms, Jasper couldn't be what she needed. He still grieved Maria too much to be good to Theo. She needed more. But how much more?

One thing he did know, he had to make sure his brother never met this newspaper bride. "Jasper, you still don't know if you will like her. She could be playing on your sympathy. I'll pen a response and deliver it to her box today. You shouldn't meet with her until you are sure of her. The girls need you to be sure. If she writes back again, then you know she has passed all our tests. What she looks like won't matter so much, if her character is beyond reproach."

Vanity surely winning, Jasper nodded. "You are right. I still don't know what she looks like. She could be a rich hag. Or not so rich and more so hag. What will you ask her?"

"It will come to me, Brother."

Jasper moved to the door. "You are the best. And you will return here?"

"Yes, after delivering the note to Burlington Arcade, a dash to my own residence to gather my own clothes, and a meeting at the theater. Mr. Brown, the theater manager, needs to read through my play before making a decision. He said he'd know in a week. Once I've dropped it off, I will return here. Then we will wait for your widow's response together."

Smiling, Jasper handed him the letter. "I've missed you, Ewan. You've always had a way to make things not seem so bad, calming and reassuring, for a younger brother." The man stepped back, picked up his goblet, then wobbled out of the room.

Ewan's conscience roared, stabbing a bit at his gut. He'd do his best to make things good for Jasper, but his brother couldn't have Theo. Shaking his head, he looked at the foolscap again. This was her hand, steady with a curly E. Someone may have helped her. From what he remembered, she could read a little and write short notes, like, *I love you, Ewan. I'll meet you, Ewan. I'll wait for you, Ewan.*

But six years and means changed things. Why did she need a newspaper groom? She could still be all these things and pregnant.

He shook his head of foolhardy conspiracies and determined to draft something cute to appease his brother, but something that Theo would never answer.

It would have to be something difficult. Something transparent, something that singed her fingertips with its nakedness.

Then it came to him. He needed to hear of her regrets. Proud Theo wouldn't dare answer.

But what if she did?

Would she tell a stranger from a newspaper advertisement the answers to questions she'd never offer to him?

CHAPTER EIGHT

A Field of Truth

Theodosia bristled on her patio. Her weeklong list of busywork tasks had come to an end and with it the excuses to miss the night at the theater with her friends.

Her quick morning jaunt and several gold coins had secured the parish bells to ring for the festival. Hopefully, the wives of the merchants and pickers whom she'd hosted in her parlor would keep their word about inviting musicians and other cart vendors. Perhaps Mathew would hear the horns from heaven. How nice that would be.

With her shears, she trimmed the clematis and tucked each of the new runners about the trellis. The blooms were secure, the female and male plantings held hands as Mathew had ordained.

Maybe if she repotted her rosebush that would eat up more time. She could check on Philip. Then she'd check on him again. He was well, learning from his governess. No pain today for him, probably none tonight.

Not a single reason to delay this outing. Deep down she wanted one, something to stay close to Tradenwood. Even the faithful gray storm clouds appeared too small. The short rain storm hadn't lasted, leaving nothing but humidity. She took a breath of the heavy air. It wasn't enough to beg off, much too little to stop Frederica's pouts.

Theodosia wrenched at her neck, smoothing the lace of her high collar. She had a light gray gown of the nicest silk with starched Mechlin lace about its hem to wear tonight. It would be perfect with her onyx cape. She'd be demure, half mourning, maybe invisible in the dark of the theater.

With a sigh, she decided to focus on the good things in her life. A son who had no pain today. Plenty of food. Blooming clematis, purple and blush petals, vines holding hands, united in growth. She took another long breath, reveling in their fragrance.

She had been blessed. It had been a whole week since Philip's last earache. He'd been pleasant and without pain. Her heart had lifted when the doctor had said his hearing seemed to be at the same place it was when he'd last measured. Still not great, but no worse. The same pitiful hearing-from-only-one-side as before. She slumped against her patio knee wall. Nothing had yet been found to treat him or to keep these aches from returning. Nothing. Would he go fully deaf this year?

And a whole week without Ewan pestering her. What was he doing? Had he given up and gone back to town? Her stomach soured. It was a good thing for him to be gone, but that didn't stop that small part of her heart from beating fast when she thought him near, or the stupid part of her brain that leaped knowing he could visit any moment. She stomped her foot at her foolish, begrudgedly-missing-him heart.

A knock on the hall door made her pulse tick faster. Had she wished Ewan into visiting? Smoothing her skirts, she stepped back into the parlor. "Enter."

Pickens came into the parlor with a letter in his hands. "The footman retrieved this from Burlington Arcade. It looks important."

Her heart soared. The fancy paper with the bluish tinge. She opened her hands to receive it. A thrill coursed through her fingers as she saw the mark. The baron had replied. "Thank you, Pickens."

He dipped his chin but stared as if something made him cross. "The theater, ma'am. Might I suggest you start getting ready for the outing. It's a two-hour journey to Town."

She fingered the wax on the letter. What did the baron think of her answer? She flipped the paper over. "It's a long ride, too long of one."

His bushy brow rose. "You'll need to leave soon, so you'll not be late."

"I was thinking of not going. Philip might have another bad night. He'll need me."

"Master Philip has not had another upset. He will be well for this one evening." Pickens's face smoothed, showing the confidence that she'd come to depend upon. "I know how to contact the doctor. Your friends are counting on your presence."

She swiped at her brow. Fretting and humidity didn't blend. "It's not selfish to go? To leave Philip alone?"

"Ma'am, you've barely gone on your rounds. You can't stop living, waiting for the next upset."

It wasn't merely panic over Philip that made her hunker down in Tradenwood. Ewan had kept up his haunting. The man appeared everywhere, always wanting a moment of her time, but she couldn't give him any. He'd twist her like he'd done with Mrs. Gutter in the fields. She'd started thinking of him, missing his laugh. Why had she held his hand in the fields? That was how everything had begun, with him seeking her out. Would he stop by again tonight? No more being controlled by fear. She fanned the letter. "You are right. Miss Croome and Miss Burghley will be disappointed. I will go, but send for me if anything changes. If I am needed, I'll leave in the middle of the singing."

The butler chuckled, and then said, "Mr. Fitzwilliam stopped by again."

"What?" Her voice squeaked. "You know that I don't want him here."

Pickens's chest became big, as if he sucked in all the air of the room. "I know, ma'am, but this time he asked to meet your heir."

Theodosia blinked so hard it hurt. She must've seemed like a mad woman. Well, maybe she was, for everything felt as if the walls were closing in upon her. "What did you tell him?"

The butler took a cloth out and dusted the crystal knob. "I told him he was not welcome."

She coughed and let her heart start beating again. "Thank you, Pickens."

The butler's face became blank, and he took a few paces toward her. "I know you haven't asked my opinion, ma'am."

She startled and caught his gaze. "I haven't."

A part of Pickens's mouth lifted into a small momentary smile. "But I will offer it, this one time. The gentleman seems sincere. You may want to hear him out." The butler pivoted and walked back to the threshold. "Don't get so involved with your letter and forget the theater."

She waited for the door to close before pressing at the frustration that settled between her eyes. She didn't trust Ewan, and she could never ever trust him with Philip.

A noise sounded behind her. She swung, with arms raised, expecting to see her ghost lover, but saw nothing. The wind, not

Ewan, had knocked over her rosebush.

She put her letter down and bent over her toppled rosebush. With twitchy fingers, she scooped up the rich soil and filled the terra-cotta pot. The perfume of the dark, dark earth soothed her. It made her want to run out in the fields and find the spot where Mathew had claimed her. Mathew's ghost would push out memories of Ewan.

The man wasn't a caring cousin. He wanted to confuse her. He hadn't taken back his blackmail. He wanted her to sell Tradenwood, even as he'd danced with her in the fields.

She sat the pot up but couldn't take another second to enjoy it. New fear filled her. Ewan wanted to see Philip. That couldn't happen. She needed a husband now more than ever. Someone she could trust to keep all the people who could hurt her son far away. She picked up the baron's letter. With a prayer on her lips, she popped the seal. She scanned the lines. Her heart stopped, but not in a good way. She was mortified.

To love children is good, for a wondrous mother, the virtue understood.

It sounds as if you are a mother filled with love, but what lies lie in your heart? What falsehoods flow from your lips to aid your sleep? You don't have to answer this missive. You very well can be dismissive, but I'm seeking a life with a wife whose heart and actions are beyond reproach. Are you the woman I seek? If you are, tell me your greatest regret. Into your life, let me peek.

Another question? One sentence acknowledged her heart-felt response? How could he ask about personal regrets and not offer the same?

There was no way to unread what the letter said.

This would-be suitor, her newspaper groom, was all rhymes. How dare he want to know her deepest secrets, that hated R word?

The letter had to be a joke.

Someone found out about her trying to find a husband or maybe the baron liked games. Why hadn't she seen this before she struggled to pen three paragraphs to his last letter?

She started to pace, back and forth, patio tile, to parlor hardwoods, to cobblestones. A breeze swept over the fields, bringing inside a stronger scent of rain. The cooler wind stung her freshly chewed lip. She paced back into the parlor, picked up the letter, and crumpled the foolscap within her palm. This baron was playing games. Nothing was worse than a man who played games or who betrayed one's trust.

She should've stuck with the squire. His offer looked better and better. This fine-thinking rhymer offered nothing for her peace.

No. Not a thing. She lowered her head and waited for her pulse to slow, her thoughts to order. This mystery man did offer something. He'd give her a name that was as honorable as Mathew's and the hope that someone who asked such challenging questions would be a strong champion for Philip.

She wiped a horrible tear from her eye. Why was she crying? She didn't know this man, but she had foolishly put her hopes in him. She wanted someone stronger than Lester, than Ewan and all the Fitzwilliams. Then she wouldn't have to be strong all the time.

Theodosia had R's, big ones, ones that she lived with every day, ones she couldn't right. If she dared to pen one, would the baron use it to control her like Lester, like everyone else did?

Caged in her skin, she started to run. Anger at this new suitor boiled inside. She had labored long, writing and rewriting, surviving two Ester edits for the baron, being as transparent as she could about motherhood without saying the words—*my baby is almost deaf. And it's my fault.*

It hadn't been enough.

Her greatest regret was hurting Philip.

His deafness was her fault. All caused by her foolishness and pride. Theodosia's fingers shook. Her stomach churned as if she'd vomit. She needed peace. She needed to think. She needed to feel safe, like when Mathew had lived, or the night Ewan had sheltered her in the storm.

Not caring about her slippers or the hem of her dark mourning skirt, she trudged deeper into the field. The satin became damp in the fresh mud, but she didn't care. She stuck the paper against her heart and kept moving—all while the baron's reply repeated in her head.

Are you the woman I seek? If you are, tell me your greatest regret. Into your life, let me peek.

He toyed with her. Why? What was to gain from the baron laughing at her pain?

She stopped and looked up into the blue-gray sky. What if sharing the deepest part of her heart was the price to pay to gain a champion?

Was the cost too high or was her pride too much?

She was sweating, caught between crying and shouting.

Mathew had challenged her and so had Ewan, in different ways, but each had always made her think. Maybe this frustration was another way to challenge her. She swiped at her eyes, mopped at her temples. If the baron was moved at all by her letter, he would make a much better match than the dry squire.

Crumbling the paper, she stuffed it in her pocket. *A wife beyond reproach.* Could she ever be that woman, to any man? Mathew had understood her past, well, the parts she'd shared. Would he have counted her as beyond reproach?

Theodosia couldn't think anymore. She trudged deeper into the fields. Before she knew it, she was waist deep in lavender and couldn't move any further. Why was she tormenting herself? She should accept the squire. He had been the second response to her newspaper advertisement. All the lies, the regrets of the past would be put away if she married him. She rubbed at her arms, raised her face to the storm clouds. "I give up."

Horse's hooves pounded from behind.

She whirled to see who was coming toward her. With a blink, it was six years ago, and it was Mathew riding out to inspect his fields. He'd caught Theodosia picking flowers, stealing them, the week prior, but had then given his permission for her to take from his fields. He'd even had baskets waiting for her to carry away more than she could wrap in her skirt. It had been so welcome and unexpected. The Fitzwilliams had banned her from their land, but she'd had to earn some money to eat. And the low pain from the swell in her gut, the little one, had needed food, too.

She blinked again and was back in the present. She choked from the dust the rider kicked up as his mount almost trampled her.

The horse neighed like thunder. She was paralyzed in a cloud of horse sweat and dirt.

Laughing, the thick man jumped down and pulled tight on the reins, forcing the horse to obey. "You don't frighten easily, do you, Mrs. Cecil."

It wasn't Mathew's ghost but a very lively Lester hovering over her.

But she *was* scared. She shoved her shaking fingers into her pockets. All she could muster was, "Hello, Lester."

He leaned to the side and pushed his top hat back on his coal-black head. His narrow, pale eyes roamed as he gloated. "You do look a little scared."

Righting the hair starting to tumble down her back, she had to pretend to be strong. "You could've killed me. Was that your point?"

"Come on, boy." Lester tugged his silver horse. The horse neighed violently but submitted.

A moment of sympathy for the stallion swept over her. "I'm owed an apology and an explanation."

He tipped his brim. "I like to inspect what's mine, Mrs. Cecil. What are you doing so far from Tradenwood?"

She put a hand to her hip and lifted her chin. "Like you said. I am inspecting what is mine."

He chuckled in his typical menacing way, full throated and deep. "Well, our land. Yours, mine, and that mulatto of Cecil's—one big happy family."

Gall rising, she continued to glare at him. "Is there something you wanted?"

He grabbed her hand and clamped his hard palm about it. "There are many things I want from you, but for now I will settle for cooperation. Have the Fitzwilliams been bothering you?"

Lester had never showed concern for her before. And he couldn't know what Ewan planned with his play. Could he? She squinted at him. "Why do you ask?"

"They are a tricky lot, land grabbers. They may try to confuse you into signing things. When in truth, it's all to get their mitts on this place."

She wanted to say she read very well now, but it might be better to let Lester underestimate her abilities. "They haven't sent any new offers."

"Good. You'd show me, wouldn't you? I know I've been boorish to you, Theodosia, but viewing you now with the sun dancing upon you, I can see why Cecil took you as his mistress. You are built well. Your voice is pleasant. Yes. I see your appeal."

If this was a compliment, the squire had certainly run on with his praise, that is, with his mouth closed. "Thank you." That was all she could muster without laughing or spitting. It wasn't safe to engage the bull in a field alone. "I'm going back to the house. Continue riding like a mad person."

She turned away, but he seized both her hands. His rough gloves chaffed her palms, as he kissed each. After a nod, he jumped onto his horse. "Let me know what they are about, Mrs. Cecil. We keep this farm productive, we can own all the land. Land is what matters, and we should work together to win. Working together will be more pleasant. Don't make me an enemy. It won't do well for Philip, to see us at odds. Perhaps, the three of us should go away on my trip—the one that you set up but won't go on with me. He can help celebrate our wedding."

"I haven't agreed to marry you."

"Then perhaps I'll take the boy all by myself. It is my right to do so. In Holland, he will like looking at the bulbs, Of course, if he can keep up... Hate for him to fall, fall behind on my trip."

A tremor went up her spine, but she willed herself to stay put, not shaking. "Don't—Don't threaten him. Or me. Cecil wouldn't appreciate that."

"He's gone, Theodosia. Buried in the family crypt. I've been patient, but that all ends at the end of the month with your honorable time of mourning. Tell the boy I asked about him."

Would he take Philip to Holland without her? She hadn't planned on that. Dumbfounded, she watched Lester ride off. Her time of half mourning would be up in a few weeks—right after the festival. The fiend wouldn't be stopped by the mention of Mathew's name. Lester would be ruthless and abusive. She wouldn't have any recourse. She'd have to comply to keep Philip safe.

Breathing heavily, she headed to Tradenwood when another shadow fell upon her. It reached for her hand and steadied her, and this time she very much wanted to see this ghost.

Ewan was at her side. He held her hand gently as he had in the field with Mrs. Gutter. "What's wrong? Did that man hurt you?"

Everything was wrong. Every hope was being pulled from her, making her dizzy, and so unsure. She shook her head, but couldn't make words come out. Instead, she pressed their linked hands to her bosom.

With his grip tightening upon her fingers, he pulled her slowly and brought her close. "I'll kill him if he hurt you."

That didn't sound like Ewan. It was his voice for sure, but with a resolve she hadn't remembered him possessing.

He brushed her cheek. His thumb traced her neck before lowering his hand to her shoulder. "I mean it, Theo. I will."

Before she could stop herself, she fell into his arms. She needed something bigger than herself. Something to pin her hopes upon, even for a moment. And Ewan was here. His arms were tough, his chest solid, and his hold, everything she wanted when everything seemed wrong.

She stopped thinking. Didn't want to be challenged or scared anymore. She molded into her ghost and let her every fear absorb into him and disappear. Isn't that what ghosts did?

"I'm here, Theo. I saw him come at you. He meant to scare you." He kissed her temple. "I won't let him hurt you."

Her ear met the raised scars on his chest. They could be felt through his shirt and silky waistcoat. She looked up into those blue, bluer-than-the-sky eyes and saw an anchor. But anchors sunk to the bottom of things. Theodosia couldn't go lower. She couldn't have more regrets. "This isn't real. It's a daydream to replace my nightmares. Let me go."

His arms became heavy about her middle, his fingers kneading the stiffness of her back. "I'm here, truly here. I watched that big man coming at you. Who was he?"

Her ghost sounded as if he cared. Why? With the jitters caused by Lester draining away, she tried to step back, but his fingers met the nape of her neck and she became more breathless, more dependent upon him. "You've…"

She sounded strangled, but found some forgotten air in her weak body and pushed it out. "You've been watching me?"

A dimple popped on his lean cheek and the scent of him, sweet-like-cloves, haunted her nose.

"That's what ghosts do. And old habits in these fields are hard to break. And you've always been prettier than these flowers." His tone stiffened, hinting of possession. "The man who upset you? You haven't said who he was. Not a suitor gone wrong?"

She didn't owe Ewan an explanation. He was an enemy, right? With a determined shove, she broke free of his arms. Letting distance cool her racing pulse, she turned and started the slow walk back to the house.

"Who was he, Theo, I mean, Mrs. Cecil?"

At this she turned. She felt her face getting heavy in wetness, but didn't care. Who would Ewan tell that he found her crazed and weak in the fields? His father who hated her, the family who had pretended she didn't exist until they wanted to buy her land? "Mr. Lester is the man I am to marry, if my newspaper suitor doesn't come up to scratch. I will have to give up the only name I've ever had, one that is honorable and decent, beyond reproach."

He fished into his pocket and whipped out a handkerchief. "Here, Theo. I can help. Let me help."

"Don't make promises you can't keep." She mopped up more tears than she thought she had left. She felt him coming near, but held a hand up to stop him. "It isn't proper to be in your arms. You're not a beloved memory, only another man trying to convince me to do something." With a final swipe, she tossed the wet cloth at him. "Good day, sir."

He clasped her arm. "Sign Lord Crisdon's deal, Theo, and give us a reasonable lease. I'll protect you from everybody who is truly trying to hurt you. You know I don't want you hurt."

"I don't know anything about you, except that you are given to threats and careless dreams. And what do you know of me? I can tell you every memory of every dream you ever had, but what of mine? No, I was your secret little fancy. Good day, Mr. Fitzwilliam."

"Did Cecil trick you into becoming his mistress?"

She turned toward the house. "No more than you did."

He reached for her arm, and she shared his strong, alive pulse. "Theo, you loved Cecil? Did you love him more than me?"

She pulled free and then kept walking.

"Did he coerce you? Or compromise you? Did you go to him the moment I left or after you thought I died? I need to know why you didn't stay true to me, unless you never loved me at all."

Over her shoulder she saw him following, but she was done. No more explanations of her complicated world to a ghost or a baron. "If you knew me at all, you'd know the answer."

When she didn't hear steps trailing, her breathing returned to normal, in and out, in and out. That was good. If her ghost learned her truth, her deepest regret would make the hauntings worse, much worse.

• • •

Ewan watched Theo until she was safely on the patio at Tradenwood. He'd plodded through these fields every day, looking for an opportunity to catch her, to find a moment where she'd tell him what happened with Cecil, her child, or her health. It had become a sport, catching her here or there. Yet, each moment was a wonder. He'd seen the girl who'd been so shy caring for her tenants. He'd caught the number-wonder, bartering and calculating—she was as sharp in mathematics as ever.

Then she'd disappeared. She'd become the ghost, until today. That had saddened him more than it should. He swatted at his wilted cravat, crushed by the heat of her, and searched his mind for a memory, a word about her past. She'd mentioned her mother only once in passing. She'd then led Ewan by the nose into his favorite topic, himself. It had been far too easy to do for the attention-starved outcast. Pigheaded and selfish, that was what he was. He kicked a rock, wishing it was his head. He knew her, but not like he should've.

"Whoa there." Jasper had ridden up so close that Ewan's rock skipped right in front, almost hitting the pewter-colored horse. "Brother, you look like you lost your best friend. How could that be, since I am right here?"

"How did you sneak up on me?" He straightened his collar. "Where have you been? The coaching inn's tavern hasn't opened up yet."

"How droll." Jasper jumped down from his mount. "Been to Town meeting with glass makers. The hothouse ideas at Tradenwood. That's what we need here, but I must figure out how to convince Father, despite the expense. If only he'd let me run this place. I could do so much. *We* could be doing so much."

Ewan nodded, happy something captured Jasper's interest that wasn't brandy. "I'm sure you'll convince him. He might listen to your unpolluted opinions."

Jasper's face blanked, but he took some items out of his saddle. "Playwrights need to be direct or more generous in their statements."

It was unkind to drag his brother's nose in his liquor habits. But he couldn't think straight. Against his will, his mind locked on Theo and the boor who had nearly ran her down. Ewan looked down at his scuffed boots, the fresh mud from Tradenwood fields, the same darkness seemed thick on Jasper's boots. "You had a good ride? Tradenwood seems popular today."

"Yes, I examined one of our neighbor's hothouses. Funny thing. I caught a loving couple in the fields," Jasper said with a cocked brow and a smirk. "Interesting negotiation tactics. Do you intend upon seducing the enemy or was she leading you back into her web?"

"That's not what happened."

"You should be more discreet. You and the good widow or the good Jezebel, the one you wrote in your play. Is that how you intend to get her to sign the lease, beating her at her own game and bedding her? Maybe stash a bottle of ink by the pillow?"

Ewan felt his stomach fill with heat. His chest tightened, as did his fist. "Don't talk about her like that."

"Then tell me what you are doing. We were *close* once."

The way Jasper said "close" reminded Ewan of the other losses spurred on by his leaving for war. His brother was dear to him. They'd once been able to share everything. By accepting his father's ultimatum, Ewan had lost Theo, the fortune he would've inherited, and his brother's confidences. "I wasn't here to support you in the loss of Maria. I didn't come back. I stayed with my regiment. That's where I belonged."

"You belong with family, no matter what. And don't go seducing the widow and then blame us when things don't work."

Was that what Ewan was trying to do? Less comforting cousin, more carnal cretin? He shook his head. "'Twas no seduction. Mrs. Cecil has another enemy. That Lester character.

He threatened her. I couldn't leave her, not until I knew she was safe. She needed defending. What do you know of this man?"

"Yes, that embrace looked quite defensible. I don't think anything could get to her—beasts, air..." Jasper went around him and gave the reins to a groom. "Give my girl a good brushing."

The servant nodded and walked into the stable with Jasper's magnificent horseflesh.

When only the two siblings remained in the courtyard, his brother poked Ewan in the shoulder. "You be careful. You and Father are beginning to reconcile. You are back here at Grandbole. Don't destroy that for a fling."

Gritting his teeth to avoid snarling, Ewan thought of an apt way to phrase what should be obvious. "I was a gentleman. I have no designs upon her, and she has none for me. A gentleman has obligations to protect a lady. You're thick in size, not brains."

"But is she a lady? Father says she's a harlot who set her charms on the Fitzwilliams and then Cecil."

Unable to stop, Ewan reached out and jerked Jasper forward by the revers of his jacket. He shook the big man. "She was a girl, innocent and shy before I claimed her. If there is a harlot, it is me. Now this woman is a widow to my mother's cousin. She is family." He pushed him with all his might, forcing Jasper back two steps.

Ewan drew himself up, readying for another strike. "She's a lady, even if she's too dark for your tastes."

Jasper's smile faded but he didn't buck forward. Instead, he folded his arms. "I never said anything of tastes or hues. I don't know her, only the rumors, and after reading your play where you maligned everything about Theo the Flower Seller, I didn't think she still meant something to you. Thought you smartened up about her, her true character."

Ewan had been angry and hurt and had written his farce about Theo for all that loving her had cost. But every interaction he'd had since his return had proved her demure, very much the same woman who had drawn him years ago. Guilt ridden, he stuffed his hands into his coat. "I think I was wrong about her, about what happened."

His brother folded his arms and leaned in. "Isn't this the moment in your play where the hero realizes his undying love, then breaks out in song?"

"I don't write operas. All I know is Mrs. Cecil, my cousin's widow, is alone and unprotected."

"Father has called her every uncharitable name under the sun. She still threatens our water."

"She hates everything Fitzwilliam and I'm not sure I blame her. I hated everything Fitzwilliam for years, and I have the earl's blood. I can't quite imagine what it would be like... How he would treat someone he hated with different blood, with black blood."

Nodding, as if he could understand, Jasper pivoted toward Grandbole. "Father is ruthless to enemies, all races, all classes, even peers."

"Brother, if you could find happiness with someone different than what the earl or anyone else wanted, would you risk it?"

Shrugging, Jasper stomped his boots, one after the other, knocking off the mud. An odd dance, oddly in rhythm—for him, almost graceful. "I'm not you, Ewan. You've always bucked everyone and everything for what you wanted. But if I had the chance to be that happy again, I'd forget everything, take that woman in my arms, and promise her tomorrow." He stopped, smoothed his jacket, maybe a little surprised at the strength of his argument. "Don't you have an appointment in Town?"

Surprised at Jasper's stunning advice, all he could do was nod and hope to not let his jaw drop to the dirt. "Yes, I need to get cleaned up to see Brown again."

"And borrow my gig. This is your big day. You may sell that play in which you malign your cousin, the lady."

With a nod, Ewan sighed. "He wants to see me after the curtains open on his current play, Shakespeare's *Taming of the Shrew*."

Shoulders shaking with hollering laughter, his brother doubled over. "You're joking."

"I never joke about play openings." Ewan started up the stairs, but stopped. "When everyone thought me dead, did the earl take revenge on Theo? It was his bargain, for me to go away. I agreed to serve a year and prove I was a man. Then he'd allow us to marry with his blessings."

"Why did you need his blessings?" his brother asked. "It's not like you needed it any other time."

Ewan wasn't going to answer that. It didn't matter anymore. "Thank you for the use of the gig."

"Father's waiting for you on the patio off the library. Go see him. Give him a chance to tell you his side of things. Then make up your mind about who are your enemies."

"I think I know."

Jasper smoothed his sleeves as his frown deepened. "Father became unhinged when he thought you'd died. Your mother, too. It didn't get better when news came of you recovering but not wanting to return home."

"This isn't home for me. It hasn't been since I was given an ultimatum, one I was too weak to walk away from. That's your answer. I was a boy, too weak to say no to my father, the Earl of Crisdon. I accepted his offer and have lost everything since. But tonight, I win. I will sell my play."

"Your widow cousin is not going to appreciate that, but maybe your hold on her affections will allow her to forgive you."

Theo still had a hold on him. The frightened woman in his arms, the one who had drawn close to him, so much so he'd heard her fevered heart—that was the girl he remembered, the one he'd pledged to marry. Could he forgive her, if the truth was that she went to Cecil even before the false announcement of Ewan's death, that she wasn't faithful, not even a month? "I want to be done with her, Jasper, but I'm not."

"You're thinking of forgiving her? What about Father? He felt guilty for sending you to war. The loss of you ruined the sentiment that your mother had for him."

For a moment, maybe a half second, Ewan felt empathy for the earl, for his mother didn't seem to want to return to Grandbole. He rubbed at his face. "You've always seen a side of him I couldn't, but what if *he* drove off the woman I was engaged to toward Cecil? What if he made her life so horrible that she needed help? Whom would she seek? She has no family, not even a father's name. Would she have turned to a kind stranger? Could that be how Cousin Cecil caught her?"

Jamming his fists into his coat pocket, Jasper shrugged. "Sounds like something to find out, but you're a Fitzwilliam, Ewan, not just your mother's son. Find Father in the library. Ask him what he did to the woman who is now our enemy. Then forgive him."

Forgiveness? That wasn't a Fitzwilliam trait. Maybe if he had more of the stuff from his mother's side, that good spirit that everyone claimed Cecil had, then maybe it was possible. "I don't know about either. How does one forgive a hole bigger than his footfalls?"

His brother shrugged. "When you find the answer, let me know. Go clean up for your Town meeting, but see Father before you do."

Ewan walked slowly toward his room. Maybe his raging thoughts would catch him. He'd hear the earl out, maybe Theo, too, but in his heart, he knew neither would tell him anything he wanted to hear. That's why he liked writing plays. He could make his characters say the best things and know when they lied. An impossible task with either Lord Crisdon or Theo.

CHAPTER NINE

Trust & Thunder

Ewan shuffled with slow, small steps down the long hall, as if he'd been summoned by his commander. Being summoned by the earl was almost as bad.

A low grumble sounded. A storm brewed and filtered in through the window. It made the air feel moist. The wet heat of the air reminded him of sultry Jamaica. He'd recovered enough to keep his enlistment and journey to the other side of the world. He'd done well. The playwright soldier had turned into a useful man. Would the earl ever see him as such?

With a breath and a prayer for peace, Ewan popped his head in the library. Unfortunately, Lord Crisdon was there.

"Fitzwilliam," has father said and bounced up from his desk. With a wave of his knurled fingers, he ushered Ewan inside. "Been waiting for you...Son."

Though the voice sounded pleasant, Ewan knew better. He stood at attention and waited for review.

The man didn't move, and his lips went flat. Disapproval surely radiated. He moved to the patio. "Come, I have tea and biscuits waiting."

Hesitating for a moment, Ewan took another breath and pushed forward. "Thank you, but no. I'm journeying into Town shortly."

His father nodded and took a seat at the table.

A luncheon for two? "Sir, I see you are waiting for someone.

I'll leave you to your privacy."

"This is for you...Son."

Ewan's gut knotted three times over, a silent prayer to the Father, the Son, the Holy Spirit—anything to protect him from the fresh hell awaiting from the earl.

"Please sit."

Unable to think of a plausible excuse, such as Grandbole in flames, he puffed his scarred chest to the maximum. That way he'd still have something inside when his father's dressing down made it impossible to breathe. "I'll stand."

The earl stretched in his chair. His stylish coat and bottle-green waistcoat floated about his thin frame like kingly robes. With his nose lowered, he spoke over his glasses. "Have you solved our problem? Have you convinced the widow to lease the water rights?"

Ewan leaned against the balcony. "Nice day, Father. The weather seems to be turning. It may storm tonight."

"You have seen her?"

Deciding that looking down upon the man wasn't working, Ewan took a seat. "Yes, I've seen Mother."

"Not that her. The widow Cecil. Have you reasoned with her? Do we have a deal?"

Ewan chose a very brown and crispy biscuit from the platter and popped it onto his plate. "I did one better. I threatened her. I told her I'd ruin her if she didn't reconsider."

His father's eye grew large, the white part drowning out the beady blue dot one would call an iris. "Son, I didn't think you had that in you."

A smile crept over the man's typically annoyed features and

a part of Ewan hated to destroy it, since signs of approval were rare. "Don't get too pleased. That only gained a slap, and it may have pushed other things into being. Do you know a Mr. Lester?"

The earl didn't blink, but his biscuit crumbled in his fingers. "Yes. Cecil's aggressive steward. He's a conniving devil."

"Well, he intends to marry Mrs. Cecil."

His father turned all shades of a rainbow. "We can't let that happen. He'll ruin us for sure. Cecil and his mistress-wife have run things equitably until now. Lester must be influencing her. He must be the reason for the change. If he marries her, he'll control her. You must do something."

Chewing his treat that he'd amply spread with cream, he tried not to laugh at his father's belief that it was in Ewan's power to change Theo's mind. Until today, they hadn't been exactly civil. "What do you think I should do? How am I to stop her? She doesn't work for us. Maybe you've forgotten this."

The earl grabbed his hand. "You're clever. You can have anything you want. You have to put your mind to it."

"Like gaining your approval over my choice in professions. Yes, I seemed to have done well with that these past six years."

The man drew back and through gritted teeth, he said. "Ewan Fitzwilliam, you wanted her once. Go have her now. Take her and the land that would've been yours."

His father had told him what to do and where to go many times, most hadn't been pleasant, but never this. Ewan brushed a handkerchief to his mouth. "Not that I want or need to have your blessings to go seduce the widow, but I need clarity. You are giving me permission to court her, to bed, or even marry her? Am I correct?"

"You and the wench gave a good show six years ago about being in love. You've done your military service, my only requirement. Go take her, with my blessing."

Yes, Lord Crisdon had lost his mind. Fear over his money drying up with the water rights had pushed him to the edge of insanity. "You've been in the sun too long, old man. You should go inside and rest."

"You've done what I required, now pick up where you left off. And wear some of the fine jackets and dressings I bought. You'll have to beat Lester to catch her eye."

"I thank you, but I'll borrow a room for now. I have my own things." He wanted to shove the words, "I'm my own man" down his father's throat, but this might be his father's only way of showing kindness.

Ewan softened his tone. "You are giving me your blessings to attach to Cecil's widow. We must be in serious trouble."

"Lester will be the death of the Crisdon Farms. If sacrificing you to the Blackamoor is the answer, I'll pay that price."

Well, that wasn't a compliment, yet being reminded how expendable he was to his father's plans was normal. Ewan stood up and folded his hands behind his back. "Six years is a long time. I'm not sure what I…"

The blank look in his father's eyes, the thinning of his lips to a pale line, told Ewan that no logic would sway him. "I'll consider your thoughts, but tell me, does Mrs. Cecil have a right to hate us, you?"

His father looked out toward the fields as he jammed a biscuit into his mouth. "Yes" came out with crumbs.

"Why?"

"I was very cruel to her. I had no sympathy for her when I thought you dead. Her cart vanished, and I banished her from working our fields. I wanted her gone."

His father's tone held steady as he recited how he had given a flower seller a death sentence. Getting to town on foot was almost impossible and a guarantee to be robbed or assaulted. And what would you bring to Town? Twigs? She couldn't pick the fields. "So you made her life difficult."

"Yes. Your loss made things unbearable. Your mother blamed me, but your wench did us all one better. She went after Cecil and now she's taking her revenge."

Ewan worked the knots in the back of his neck, the new ones that the truth imparted. The villain of his life was not a Circe. Theo was a woman, grieving her lost fiancé and made destitute by his vengeful father. "She has every right to starve our fields as you did her."

His father grimaced and dipped his chin. "But I've made up for that in my offers, double market price."

"She wants twenty times."

Lord Crisdon snorted his tea. "No. That's outrageous. You must stop her. Go down to Tradenwood and convince her to relent."

"I know you prefer to snap your fingers and make problems and flower sellers disappear, but that's not going to happen. Do you think it easy to fix six-year-old damage? You ruined things."

The earl looked up with eyes that showed no remorse. "I know. Your mother will never forgive me. Even after learning you lived, she refused to come back to Grandbole. Her Tradenwood is lost to her. I've ruined this place for her."

"I'm sorry for you, Father. I saw Mother. She said to tell you she agrees with you."

Lord Crisdon's brows raised, but he said nothing.

Looking at his freshly polished slippers, Ewan stepped toward the railing. "Do what you can. Love is too much to let go of without a fight. Or so I am told."

Again, the man nodded in silence, as if he couldn't fathom what Ewan said or couldn't talk to him about things held close to his heart. Either scenario did nothing to fill the void in Ewan's chest. "I'm going to Town. I'm meeting with a theater owner. I'm hoping he'll want to produce my play.

"Sit, Son. Tell me about it… I want to hear about this passion that drives you. I'd like to help."

Like one of the characters in his play, Ewan began to recite generic lines about his play, the same ones he'd use to sway Mr. Brown the theater manager. His father nodded and smiled his crocodile smile. But in Ewan's core, he knew Lord Crisdon's actions were pretend. The earl needed his spare to win the rich widow. Money trumped race. Money made the man feign interest in his second son.

"Very good, Son. Your mother is proud of such creativity, too."

Ewan let his lips form an upside-down frown. He could pretend, too, and took his time relishing in the false praise, pretending each word, each labored syllable of his father's, carried enough heft to outweigh old disappointments.

Thunder crackled in the distance. He lifted his gaze to trace the lightning. He missed where it hit but became entranced by one of Tradenwood's chimneys, remembering Theo's passion.

His father moved from his chair and headed to the library doors. "Son, you seem lost in your words. Maybe you should rest and think about swaying Mrs. Cecil to our cause. Family is most important."

The man left and Ewan returned his gaze to Tradenwood's chimney. The sturdy dark brick offered puffs of white, seemed like it reached for something. Theo should reach for something. For a moment, Ewan wanted to be the person she reached for, even if it was merely for friendship. Maybe that would make up for his father's evil actions. Then they could see whether she'd be reasonable with the lease.

As a peace offering, he would change the name of his Circe without her signing anything. Flora sounded better, yes Flora the Flower Seller sounded much better. Would that be enough for her to trust him as she had years ago in a thunderstorm?

Lightning crackled above and he slapped the rail. *Reach for me, Theo.*

"Sir, the gig is pulled around and ready to go."

A groom had poked his head through the threshold. "Lord Hartwell wants you to leave early to beat the storm."

"Thank you." Donning his top hat and gloves, he climbed onto the driver's seat and took the reins—pondering if Theo would ever trust a ghost, a Fitzwilliam ghost, one who came to her, still doing his father's bidding.

• • •

Theodosia adjusted her gloves, creamy satin wonders with silver threads that shimmered in the dim light of her carriage. Sliding the cuff up and down, she tried to ignore each rumble of thunder. The rain had stopped before she could use it as an excuse to beg off. And the clouds had disappeared in the dusk. She shouldn't be nervous. This night would be over quickly, her friends would be happy, and Theodosia could return home to Philip.

The fear of Lester snatching up her boy tonight diminished. He wouldn't come harass her for a couple days, not after giving her a fright and a warning to think about. But he'd be unstoppable the minute he suspected her of plotting against him, and once he discovered that Philip was becoming deaf, he'd use his illness to make her do anything. She quivered. For a moment, she didn't want to be brave. She wanted to sink into the darkness of the carriage and hide. Against her will, her thoughts turned to Ewan. She'd heard the concern in his voice, felt the comfort of his arms, and had melted from the heat of his bluer-than-blue eyes.

He'd held her as if he cared. He'd pledged to protect her, as if she were special to him. That's how it had been so long ago, him seeming to care for her, and he had pushed her to new experiences, to depend upon him, to dream with him. She had wanted to elope and be his. Those eyes. It would be too easy to fall back into the caring, the holding, the needing of him.

Thunder clapped at the same time a tap pounded her door. Both made her sit up, shivering straight.

Her footman poked his head inside. "Mrs. Cecil, it will be only a few more moments. The entrance is being cleared."

She nodded. "Thank you."

When the man left, her knuckles balled, ready to rap the ceiling and signal to her driver to head back to Tradenwood and Philip. At least her boy wouldn't be upset by the noise. The flashes of light might even make him giggle, if he lay awake. Of course, he wouldn't be scared like her. You must hear thunder to be upset by it.

With Mathew gone, stormy nights sent her skittering. She'd scoot down the hall, scoop up her son, and tuck him into her big bed. It made the storm tolerable, knowing he lay safe beside her, and she by him. Snuggling in her arms, with his toothy giggles, Philip looked happy falling asleep, his bluer-than-sky-blue eyes slowly closing.

Goodness, she loved her boy, and she needed so desperately to be strong for him, but it was so hard with Lester counting the days to the end of her widowhood. And Ewan, pretending to care, only to get her to sign papers. Men. Maybe they could be bribed, given something to go away. Lester and bribery seemed a good mix. But what of Ewan?

She pressed at her temples, trying to push her fears to the back of her head, maybe into her tightly braided chignon. Lightning flashed in the distance. She gulped then counted the seconds before hearing the low moan. The storm could be right over her fields.

Hoping for rain, she opened the door a little and stuck a hand out. Nothing. Not even a tiny droplet, nothing to justify returning home, locking the doors, and sending the girls a note of apology.

The door swung and she froze until the face of a footman became clear. "Miss Burghley says to come, ma'am. Follow me. The crowds have moved inside. Your entrance is clear."

Girding up her strength, she banished her frets to the place she'd banished Lester and Ewan for the night. Fluffing the hood of her cape, almost hiding beneath gray fringe, she noticed the crowd had shrunk. Only a few stragglers stood at Theatre Royal, Covent Garden's main entrance on Bow Street.

The young man helped her down and guided Theodosia to the west side of the building. They would pass the king's entrance, and she prayed the Prince Regent wasn't there. She wanted to blend into the dark and not be seen by those looking for royal blood, not a mixed-up mongrel's.

Theodosia wanted to strike at her own temples. Such thoughts, such fears. That wasn't who she was, but insecurities always invaded during thunderstorms, when memories became inescapable. She picked up her skirts and paused at the door the man opened. "Are there people waiting inside this way?"

"A few, but this way is private. The duke makes sure of that."

Frederica's father was amiable. Theodosia had only met him once. He had looked at her strangely but was polite. Hopefully, the womanizing duke didn't see what she saw sometimes in the mirror. Bits of her mother. She dipped in her reticule and pulled out a coin. "This is yours if you lead me to the box."

The fellow dimpled as the shine of the bright pence often lent itself to creating love. "Yes. ma'am."

Doing this, going out in public without being on Mathew's arm, made her nerves tingle. It was harder than she thought. And tonight, after being in the fields with Ewan and Lester—it reminded her of how alone and unprotected she was.

The young man led her into the darkened stairwell. Thunder rumbled. It echoed along the walls that seemed to close in. *Just a passing storm.* She followed and tried to stop chewing her bottom lip, but that proved more difficult.

They climbed and climbed and climbed some more until they reached a landing that led into a nice-sized room.

The footman pointed and then continued inside. "Not much further. And you see, this lobby is empty. Always on dark money night."

She filled her lungs, in and out. Gladness from being out of the stairwell overcame her as much as finding this lobby empty, but she chose to ignore his phrasing of her outing. He wouldn't steal her peace. This is how things were in London and far better than what it could be, if you had no money.

Theodosia straightened her shoulders and strode across the carpet as the proud widow of a good man. Enough of ghosts, slurs, and Lester. She wouldn't let anyone stir up anymore uneasy inside.

Then a zigzag of light sailed at the window. The noise would come soon.

She froze, her feet unable to move. Not until she heard the sound.

"Ma'am." The footman tapped her elbow. "Your box is waiting."

It hit and she panted. She should turn from the window, the swords of light dancing and fighting. The next rumble shook the building and everything in her chest. It wasn't safe to move. No one said it was safe to move.

"Mrs. Cecil. All is well. Come with me, Mrs. Cecil."

That soft voice sounded like Frederica's. "Come along. The duke's box awaits."

Pearl-colored gloved hands claimed Theodosia's and unwound her fingers from the tight clasp she had about her arms.

Shaking, she stood next to Frederica.

"See, we only need to go a few more steps. Then we are in papa's box." Frederica, in lockstep with Theodosia, held on to her waist and marched her inside.

Before the black velvety curtain closed behind them, Theodosia stuck out her palm with the shiny copper penny. She gave it to the footman. "Thank you."

It wasn't his fault she let thunder scare her, but her word was good. Always good. Shamed, Theodosia drew deeper into her cape. "I'm sorry. I've made a spectacle of myself."

Frederica gave her another hug. "No one but a footman saw you. We are not in front of the theater, and in a few more minutes, Ester will be engrossed by her actor. The man took the stage, and she set down her book."

Ester offered a smile, then a giggle. "'Tis true. Mr. Bex has a lovely voice."

Still embraced by Frederica, she moved to the seats. Four chairs were pulled to the rear. Ester sat in the one closest to the corner with her crimson satin overdress swishing about pearl slippers and a pink skirt. She cupped her hand to her face and became engrossed by whatever happened below, the music and a baritone's direct address. No one would see them unless they made a scene. If the orchestra kept playing over the thunder, no one would know it was dark money night.

Sitting, she pulled off her cape and tucked her neat silver slippers beneath her. When Frederica nodded and smiled, she knew her gown, with dark silver cap sleeves and a misty gray bodice and skirt was a success. "I am so glad you came. You need something different from mourning."

"This gown is still half mourning. My Mathew is still honored."

As she took her seat, Frederica's face lost its natural glow, not upon her smooth skin but her eyes. They dulled in the dim light. "You can live and still honor him. That is what he would want for you and Philip."

Theodosia clutched the girl's gilded glove to her bosom. "I know he's honored by the friends I keep. I am honored to be here."

Frederica gave a nod and half a smile. She was a sensitive type of girl, but did she know how much of a struggle it was for Theodosia to be away from Tradenwood and Philip on such a horrible stormy night?

With no more cheer to offer, she closed her eyes and sighed inwardly, setting her hopes on hearing the dramatic lines and the swirl of the violins—all while wishing the storm would end and free her from fear.

• • •

Ewan stood in Mr. Brown's office at the Royal Theatre, Covent Garden. It was quiet now, most of the actors were on stage. The play had begun. He listened for Shakespeare's words to be recited in direct address. He closed his eyes. Oh, for that day when his play would entertain crowds.

How much would they love his current creation—Theo, as a saucy Circe? Or would they prefer the version bumbling about in his mind, the one about the woman whom he held in his arms, the one who needed him? Theo had changed. She'd never truly showed herself vulnerable, only scared of thunder.

Today, she had been different. And yes, his wary chest had

puffed up in pride when she'd turned to him. Yet, how long could a peace between them last? A day, a month, a year?

The roar of thunder blended with clapping. The first act must be over. The footfalls of the actors sounded, as did a violinist. The intermission between scenes—had Petruchio accepted his fortune by marrying Katherina? The farce made of Shakespeare's boastful idiot and his shrew bride was a sight to behold onstage or in Ewan's mirror. Yes, he was a boastful idiot to be thinking of Theo returning to his arms.

The storm boomed and rain pelted on the ceiling with a heavier rhythm. It was like a gong, echoing and cleansing him of wanting her. It helped him refocus on his purpose of being at the theater. He had come to sell his play without the earl's assistance or his blockage. Now, at least, his father wasn't using his influence to stop Ewan's plays. He hoped.

The door opened and Mr. Brown, a portly fellow with thick glasses and balding head, entered. "Sorry to keep you waiting."

"No problem at all."

The man flopped on a well-worn leather chair.

A hint of tobacco touched Ewan's nose. The man's delay, had it been a vice? There were flecks of rain on his coat. "You've come from outside?"

"We're making some dark money tonight and had a bit of trouble."

The term sounded odd. He felt his brow wrinkling. "What is that? Dark money?"

"The Duke of Simone pays me a little more to allow his by-blow and her Blackamoor friends to set up in his box from time to time. They usually sit quietly, not upsetting anything. Nothing harmed seating them in the highest box with the private staircase. If notable nobles sat in their boxes, they'd go unnoticed."

Ewan's gut twisted at the disdain coming from Brown's alliteration and his garish laugh.

At least when Jasper had asked of Theo, his voice sounded of curiosity or brotherly probing. This man's tone bristled with condescension, perhaps even masked hatred, like the earl's.

Ewan rolled his shoulder to allay some of the tension tightening his neck. "But tonight was different. What happened with the Blackamoors?"

The man scratched his chin hairs, then leaned back in his chair as if set to spin a long yarn. "Seems one of them, the one with slant eyes... She had a fit caused by a little thunder. The footman thought she was going to start screaming or crying." Mr. Brown rummaged through his desk, as if he hunted for something.

Ewan braced to keep his own composure. His pulse raced, then slowed, as he glued his low-cut boots to the ground. Could Theo be here?

Brown chuckled, then slapped his desk. "You should see them all gussied up like regular women."

"But they are women, sounds like women with means."

"I don't care what they are. If the duke is paying and none of my other patrons are aware, I keep the money, dark and lovely."

How money changes things. Theo, the rich widow, was now an acceptable choice of brides, to even the earl, but Theo the Flower Seller was not. One could be in the theater like *normal women*, if the price was right. Ewan soured immeasurably, wanted to walk away, but respectable theater was small. If he couldn't get his play here, there would be no chance at the Royal

Theatre, Drury Lane. "Well, hopefully, there will be no more complaints and your guests get to enjoy this play."

"I must say, the duke's by-blow could be mistaken for a lady if not for the thickness of her lips."

He obviously didn't know the joy of kissing such plump wonders. Ewan wondered if Theo's were still extraordinary.

The man stretched and laughed. "The one with the slant eyes, she could be a looker, too, if she wasn't so dark."

His pulse ticked up. "With straight onyx hair?"

Brown guffawed, then shot up. "Fitzwilliam, did you see her?"

"Yes." A thousand times in his dreams. There was only one Theo, with beautiful almond-shaped eyes, afraid of thunder. "She is some looker."

Brown shuffled more paper as Ewan leaned against the door. Theo was here, away from Tradenwood on a night like this. Why? She was so different, a ball of compelling opposites that drew his attention like no one else.

Thinking of her, feeling that old draw, made Ewan impatient. He twisted his hat within his palm. "So you've had a chance to review my play?"

Brown sat again. He searched his desk and finally settled on pages at the bottom of his pile. "I did. Outrageous. I think it will be the talk of London. Theo the Flower seller is outrageous."

"Well, I'm working on that character's name. I think Flora the Flower Seller."

"Don't change a thing. I like it."

"Well, I'll... keep that in mind, if you are going to buy the play, or Cleo the Flower Seller will bring in the allure of Egyptian culture."

"Perhaps. I do want to buy it. This will sell lots of tickets, but Fitzwilliam... How do I ask this without sounding condescending?"

With all the things he'd said about Theo and her friends, did it matter? Ewan stiffened his stance, all but locking his knees as he'd done in the regiment. "Say it. Shoot, then reload."

Brown started rocking in his chair. He tapped his fingertips together, as if he were praying, but this man didn't seem the type to have been to church in years. "I do a great deal for my wealthy patrons. I don't like getting crossed or my license to be threatened. Does Lord Crisdon approve of this? Your father can make everything difficult, difficult with tradesmen and creditors, if you cross him.

"I'm my own man. I can handle the earl. He'll be no trouble to you."

Standing, Brown stuck out his hand. "Then you have a deal. How soon can you get the final draft to me?"

Ewan shook the man's hand, pumping it with vigor and a sense of accomplishment. "A fortnight."

"Good. I can start planning. Work on getting the earl here for the opening?"

That would be a miracle. One with strings from the devil, no doubt. "I'll see what can be done, but this deal is based on the merits of the play. Nothing more."

Catching the man's sneer-like smile, Ewan donned his hat and pivoted to grip the door handle, but turned back for a moment. "A fortnight for the final play. Have the contracts ready."

"It's a good play. We stand to make a lot of money. And I still like that name, Theo, Theo the Flower Seller."

"It will be Cleo, Cleo the Flower Seller in the final draft."

Nodding, Ewan closed the door behind him. His moment of success felt a little slimy. He wiped his palms upon his jacket. This was the theater. Some wore masks and costumes. Others showed you who they were. Mr. Brown, as his father would put it, was a *necessary means* to accomplish Ewan's goals.

Thunder crackled loud and hard as Ewan exited the theater. The rain had slacked to a light pelting. The next hoarse rumble in the sky didn't make him dash to the mews for his brother's gig. No, Ewan turned the corner and sought out the lone stairs that led to the highest boxes. He trudged through puddles, sloshing cold water on his formerly buffed boots. It didn't matter. He needed to see if the story being written in his head was correct. That the heroine of his heart was misunderstood. The earl's wrath had made her vulnerable, easy pickings for Cecil. A grieving soul was easy to mislead by a rich predator or made a villain in a farce by a playwright who needed a villain for his own bad choices.

Six years ago, that strong, opinionated girl had become frightened by the storm. They couldn't elope, not in such a deluge. So, they had holed up together in the carriage house. It was the first time they'd ever been alone. Except for a holding of hands, a shared laugh in a thick grove nestled behind the carriage house, or a gleefully stolen kiss near Grandbole, he'd never fully given himself to her, never felt so much love in her dark eyes. Not until that moment.

Knowing how his father was, why had Ewan believed the lies and made Theo a gold-seeking mistress? Anger pained his breath as he pried the stairwell door open. He'd written the wrong fiend.

It wasn't a feeling of accomplishment for selling his play that drove him up those treads. It was that small lump in his scarred chest that tightened, thinking Theo was near and frightened— thinking of her clinging to him again like she had today made him take the stairs by two.

CHAPTER TEN

Night at the Theater

Theodosia shifted in her seat. The actor's voice couldn't drown out the thunder or the memories. She'd paid attention to the horrible story, wondering why Ewan could think this Shakespeare so fine. Fighting, complaining, tricks, and starvation—that felt a little too familiar, too Fitzwilliam.

A boom moaned above. The storm sounded as if it were gaining force, coming for her again. She shivered and pulled her wrap tighter about her arms.

The world around her rumbled. It sounded ghostly, as if it whispered her name. She pivoted in time with the next crash and caught the dark curtains swaying. The storm had to be atop her. Her gaze became glued to the velvet. It shrouded this box as it did the space she had hidden inside at the brothel. *Mama told her to be quiet, but how could she, trapped by the storm?*

A hand grabbed hers and she almost screamed, but she was too scared. And Mama would be angry.

"Theodosia, are you well?"

The voice wasn't Mama's, so Theodosia didn't move. She wasn't supposed to, not till she heard the signal. She hated the coal scuttle within the brothel wall and how it made every violent pound of thunder echo.

A gloved hand slipped onto hers, but she couldn't say anything; she hadn't heard Mama's knock. "Theodosia. You don't look well. Dear?"

The tones, the concern... It sounded like Ester, but why would she be here? Good girls like Ester wouldn't be in a brothel.

"Theodosia."

Something shook her by the shoulders, and she tensed. Blinking heavily made the world right. Frederica's arms were about her.

Disgusted by her fears, she shook free, not wanting to be touched, even by a friend. "I'm not feeling well. I need to go home."

Ester frowned deeply with her lips pressed tightly. "No. The new actor, the one who's all the rage. He hasn't come back out yet."

Frederica's fun face seemed blank, but she nodded. "This isn't any fun for you. I'll signal a groom, and we'll get you to your carriage."

She'd ruined her friend's evening out. Theodosia's insides hurt. "Stay. I've done enough to disrupt what should be a fun occasion. I'm ashamed...to do this to you two. I wish to make myself invisible."

Wrinkling her gown, Ester crouched down, pried off a glove, and applied the back of her hand to Theodosia's forehead. "You don't have a fever. Listen to me. There is nothing wrong with being frightened."

"Yes, nothing at all." The man's voice, the one that haunted her soul, introduced himself. "I'm Mrs. Cecil's cousin. I'll see her home."

A little damp, with a dark curl plastered to his forehead beneath his beaver-skinned hat, Ewan stepped fully inside. "I'm here for you Th— Mrs. Cecil. I'll get you safely to your carriage."

Why? Why was Ewan haunting her outside of Tradenwood and on a stormy night? Theodosia stood up and stared at him. "Not you."

Gripping her hand and not letting go, Frederica stepped toward Ewan. "This is a private box. You have no business here."

The grin on his face looked triumphant. Would he shame her in front of her friends by bringing up their tawdry past? Oh goodness, would he tell them of the loving, the leaving, and the lies? With lips pressed shut, he bowed. "Miss."

"Miss Burghley." Frederica kept her voice soft but her chin high.

Nothing intimidated her, but shy Ester had skittered to the side in the corner.

"Ladies, I'll make sure Mrs. Cecil gets home safely." He lowered his voice to a whisper. "From what I recall, she doesn't do well with storms."

Theodosia's cheeks heated. She'd fan her face but that would let Ewan know she was weak.

"No." Surely not understanding his reference, Frederica didn't move. She stood as an equal to the son of the earl. "I will send her to her carriage. You may leave."

But Ewan didn't move, and the heat of his steady gaze made Theodosia's pimpled arms feel warm, too. "My cousin can trust me."

With a brow raised, Ester came out of the shadows, looking back and forth between Ewan and Theo. "Frederica, why is your cousin here? Does he know the duke?"

"No, Ester, he means me. He was my Cecil's cousin. This is Mr. Fitzwilliam."

"Yes. We are cousins by marriage. My family is Mrs. Cecil's neighbor and sometimes business rival." He extended his hand again. "It is my pleasure to assist you."

Frederica smoothed her gloves. "Fitzwilliam," she said in a voice not as strong as before, "as in the flower rivals, as in up the hill from Tradenwood."

Theodosia forgot about the new rocking of thunder and focused on getting Ewan away from her friends. Signaling that she conceded, she nodded to her conquering ghost. "Yes, he is the second son of Lord Crisdon. He is my late husband's cousin."

"Guilty." Ewan's smile grew with bigger dimples, evil I-shall-now-embarrass-you-more dimples.

She braced for his worst and that made his grin worse.

He tapped the edge of her chair. "As her cousin by marriage, it's my duty and honor to be of service."

Frederica squinted at Ewan as if there was some sort of recognition firing in her brainbox. "The man from the patio. Seems you not only do night deliveries, but pickups, too." Frederica drew Theodosia's palm up to the small diamond necklace hanging about her neck and the creamy gold ruffles of her bodice. "If you wish to leave with your cousin you may. Ester and I will be fine. We'll have to do better with weather on our outings. The Cecil Festival must have perfect weather. I will put all my hopes on that and you."

The look in her friend's eye, the love and reassurance filled that spot in Theodosia where all had drained. With more confidence in herself, she determined it would be better to go with Ewan than to expose her friends to whatever tricks her ghost had planned. "It will be perfect, just as Cecil wanted. I'll accept your offer, Mr. Fitzwilliam."

Thunder crackled as she took his hand. The glint in his bluer-than-blue eyes surely meant she'd done what he wanted her to do. That was almost scarier than the noise.

The crowd below erupted.

Ester's mouth gaped, but then closed. She nodded and turned back to the stage. Maybe her dream actor had arrived.

Frederica bounced in front and drew the curtain open for them. "You make sure your cousin gets to Tradenwood safely, Mr. Fitzwilliam."

"Ladies, I'll see you Monday for the final preparations," she said, counting seconds after the latest streak of lightning.

"It will be my duty to see she's handled with care," Ewan said. "Evening, ladies."

Free of the box, Theodosia dropped his hand, adjusted her cape, and walked past him. "Good night, sir."

"Not so fast." Triumphant, smiling, and too handsome for words, Ewan clasped Theodosia's hand, pinning it to his arm, as if she'd escape. "Don't want you to fall. It's treacherous tonight. The stairs might be wet."

No, it was more dangerous to have her hand in his, to be nestled next to the scars upon his chest. Pulling away had to be done at the right moment to leave Ewan stewing. Patience, as Mathew would say, would win, or at least retain, her peace.

He laced his fingers with hers. "Not too much further."

They stood about halfway down, moving farther and farther from the lone window that let in light and stars, if there were any. She squinted and could see the exit, the door she'd entered. "Thank you for helping me out of here."

"My pleasure. Ghosts can be helpful, especially those bent on apologizing."

Without responding, she took another tread. Truthfully, she'd let horrible Napoleon help her out of here, if it meant getting her more quickly to Tradenwood.

"Theo, I remember how storms make you nervous. I'm remembering a great deal."

His voice purred against her ear, but she didn't have the luxury of swatting him in public. Who knew how much the slap would echo in the stairwell. "Ewan, no games. Please get me to my carriage like you said you would. Your word is good?"

"As good as yours, my grieving widowed cousin." He moved slower and held fast to her hand.

She tugged but he didn't budge. "Is something wrong?"

"I was wondering if you enjoyed the play? *The Taming of the Shrew*. Maybe the storm kept you from paying attention."

"I followed. A woman marries a beast who starves her. I didn't enjoy that."

He chuckled and hummed, but his hands tightened about hers, keeping her next to him all the way down to the last step. "Yes, Petruchio wasn't nice to Katherina. Perhaps he didn't understand how to get past her anger."

"I'm no shrew."

"I'm the shrew, Theo. I was so angry at you; I couldn't see past my anger. I forgive you."

A flash of light from the window above made the dark passage glow, framed his face with what looked like truth, but she didn't want that now. Too many things needed to happen to protect Philip without her growing weakness for Ewan putting things into jeopardy.

"I said I forgive you, Theo. Have you nothing to say to me."

"What do you want from me, other than a lease for your father?"

"I'm not sure, but I'm duty bound to find out."

Another bone-jarring thud of thunder groaned, and he slid her into his arms. Like in the fields, she hid against his chest. The world moaned outside, echoing in the darkened shaft, and she shook. When he pulled her closer, she didn't resist. She needed the storm to go away. She needed to believe that something sturdy could hold her up. Right now, Ewan served the part.

But wasn't he a part of her bondage? Initially, she'd kept her heart from Mathew by mourning Ewan. That time couldn't be returned. She'd wasted it on a love that hadn't been pure.

The thundering wouldn't quit and she drove her nails into Ewan's arm.

He didn't squeal; he merely flattened his palm atop her squirming digits. "I have you, Theo. Don't be afraid."

Nobody had her. "There is much to fear. It's called tomorrow. I can't face its revenge again, when minds are changed and promises are broken." She bucked up her spine and moved backward, away from him. She pushed open the door and went into the night.

She bristled beneath her cape and for an instant she wished she still stood sheltered.

"I don't disappear that easily, Cousin." Ewan came alongside her. "Now, where is your carriage?"

"I need no help."

"Of course you don't. This assistance is to keep me honest. I said I'd get you safely back to Tradenwood."

Rain drizzled overhead and began seeping into her hair. She chided herself for standing around like a nervous hen. She would ruin her expensive gown because of Ewan. He was too near, being too nice, talking of forgiveness, reminding her of the dreams of happy-ever-after that had led her astray.

He tugged her arm. "Your carriage is over here."

She chided herself but kept pace with his larger strides. The sooner he put her into her carriage, the sooner this haunting would end. Then, she'd be rid of her ghost and all the annoying butterflies twisting in her tummy.

"I should've asked you to stay in the stairwell until I retrieved your carriage. But then I wouldn't have you at my side."

Again, he tucked her close, as if he cared she felt fragile.

Any thought of protesting died, drowned with a flash of light and thunder crashing about them. The night smelled of rain. London smelled fresh like the fields of Tradenwood.

"Easy, Theo. Like I said, I remember."

She froze for a second, her mind swept back to six years ago, when a boy and a girl thought they'd found love. She'd held on to the sweetness too long before giving it up to find contentment with Mathew. She bit her lip, gnawing it raw. "When will this end?"

He raised his head and looked about. "This storm isn't done. Neither are we."

Her stomach dropped even lower.

Ewan leaned down, within nibbling distance of her ear. "Not much farther, Mrs. Cecil."

She looked out in the blackness. The link boys had settled down and huddled underneath overhangs. Cupping her hand to her face to focus, she finally spotted her footman at the front of the mews. "There it is. My driver must've known I might not stay. I debated upon turning around several times."

He steadied her as they traipsed to her carriage. He waved off her footman. "Easy now, Mrs. Cecil. We'll have you home in no time."

His expression hurt her heart, making her chest thump at the sparkle of determination visible in his eyes.

Now her feet felt cold and she fretted about how he'd found her at the theater. His play. Was his scandalous work about her going to be performed in Frederica's favorite theater?

She stiffened as his arms went about her, but she couldn't stop him from putting his hands on her hips and lifting her inside.

"Skittish? Six years too late, Theo?"

She sank back against the tufted squab of the seating. "Thank you, and good evening."

When she pulled at the door, he caught it. "Driver. To Tradenwood."

"Yes, sir."

She heard the words and almost released a sigh of joy, but then, Ewan barged inside. The door banged shut and he sat next to her. "I'm going to see you home, like a good cousin."

It was too dark to be alone with him. She bent and lit the carriage lamp on the floor. The light made things worse. It let her see how strong and virile he looked and how near he sat, with lips that were in want of a kiss.

She pushed at her temples hoping to free them of ridiculous ideas. "Get my driver to let you out then go away, cousin ghost. I'm in no mood for your haunting. The storm has upset me enough."

"I don't think you should be alone, and we are headed in the same direction. It's best to be at your side. Just a pleasant ride for Theo and her ghost."

The slow-moving cabin felt hot, and sitting so close to Ewan made her skin warm with anger. She dropped her hood to her shoulders, but it wasn't enough to cool down, not with molten temptation a hug away.

The last thing she needed was to become faint because of him staring at her. She drew her arms about her as if to add another layer of protection. "I didn't ask you to accompany me into my carriage, only to take me to it. You've completed this promise. Don't you have a flat in Town? Some other relative to bother?"

"It's less than two hours to Tradenwood which is practically next door to Grandbole. You can abide two hours, no? Much shorter than a month."

She stared at him and hoped her face didn't show how unfair that was, but it was better he thought her disloyal than know the truth. No, the truth remained hidden, buried with Mathew.

He took off his hat and sidled to the other side of the bench.

Thunder growled and he smiled a little. "Let me be helpful. This storm still has plenty of strength."

Trapped with him in a storm for two hours. Her fear would addle her. What if she accidentally admitted to things? The delicate balance she shared with her ghost would be eroded even more.

Her mind went to the embrace on the stairs and the one in the fields. Each felt more natural, reminding her of the stolen embraces of six years ago.

"So Theo, do we share? Or do we argue all the way to Tradenwood and share by default?"

Ewan, the Fitzwilliams—they were against her. She pushed at her brow. "Enemies don't share. You came into town some way. You can most certainly return to Grandbole the same way. I'm stopping this."

She reached up to tap the roof, but he caught her hand. He'd removed his gloves and pulled off one of hers. Bare hand to naked finger, he stroked her wrist, forced her to feel his lively pulse. It was too strong, too fast, like hers.

"You can't be here," she whispered.

He kept her hand and moved nearer. The dim light danced upon the angles and planes of his lean face. The set in his jaw tightened. Self-possessed. Strong. A determined Ewan was a dangerous thing. And unfortunately, it was catnip to Theodosia, making her voice purr his name. "Ew-wan, let go of me."

Why did she have to sound stupid—breathless and stupid? She pushed away.

That disarming smile that had made him so handsome six years ago grew. "Methinks, you are afraid of ghosts, too. Do you fear me or the truth, as much as you fear thunderstorms?"

Yes, to both. But the words never left her tongue.

He claimed her hand again and put his mouth to her wrist.

In a blink, he slid off her other glove, then kissed each naked fingertip. The motion soft, tender—bad, determined ghost. "I need to tell you something, Theo. My play will be produced."

His eyes radiated joy. Part of her was happy. He was living his dream. The other part, the sane side, boiled. She snatched her palm away from his coercion, his seduction. "Good for you.

Slander looks good on you."

He took her by the shoulders, forcing her reflection to swim in his eyes. "I'm taking your name out."

She'd been holding her breath when he touched her, and when his words started to make sense she gasped. "What?"

Nodding, he stroked her palm. "It wasn't right to threaten you like that."

The anxiety of what the play would mean to her reputation eased. Her chances at the Court of Chancery for Philip's guardianship improved. A sigh fled. But this was Ewan Fitzwilliam, and her heart tamped down to a near normal rhythm. "You're being kind to me? In exchange for what?"

The clap of thunder made her shiver, almost as much as when his finger slid under her cape to her shoulders. "I have you, Theo. I'm not ready to let go."

Trying to wriggle away made it worse. Her cape slipped, allowing his hands to be free. The heat of his palms wilted her cap sleeves. It was as if he stroked her skin.

"I still need my family protected, but that has to be done without hurting you. I don't want to be one of those people in your life who push you to do things. I'd rather be someone who you can turn to."

"And this is why you're in my carriage? With your hands on me?"

The pressure of his palms disappeared, but he never let go of her gaze. "Was your skin always so soft? I don't remember."

"Leave."

"When you turned to me earlier…it reminded me of something I'd missed. Our friendship. I sold my play, Theo, and there was no one to share it with, no one who truly understood the meaning. No one else has ever heard my dreams and encouraged me, and I have no one to take care of, no one to make sure she didn't work so hard that her ride and her burdens were easier."

Those big eyes of his, which looked even larger and more soul penetrating than ever, made her nod, made her remember, too. "I'm happy for you. You can stay until we reach the fields. Then out you go."

His arm moved to her back and slowly drew her closer, inches from his chest. "That's a poor congratulation. Can't think of a better way?"

"It's all I have for you or anyone."

His gaze lowered. "I know you are in trouble. I'm here now. I'm not going anywhere. I'll talk nonsense and make you laugh, like before."

He used to tell her nonsense about plays and Greek theater things. His face had been full of vigor…and love. Like now.

She gulped and looked away. The seam on her cape became safer and more fascinating.

Thunder shook. She shook. "We'll be getting to St. Martins Lane soon."

That arm of his tightened about her. As much as she didn't want to, she found herself pressed against his chest. The memories started. The laughs, the dancing, the joy of how special it felt to be near him returned. "We'll be getting to St. Martins Lane soon."

"You said already that, Theo."

Hating her weakness, she focused on the loud thud of his heart. His alive heart.

"Why do you hate thunderstorms?" He made his tone low and dipped his chin onto her forehead. "You know everything about me. But I know so little about you."

Fearing too much would be said, she tried to push on his chest to put distance between them, but her thumbs tangled in his cravat, skirting over his thin shirt, scraping his scars, deep and long scars. She froze, thinking of him suffering, almost dying, all while knowing her choice to keep living.

But no one would've suffered if he hadn't left her. Growing too warm, too hot with memories, and those *R* things, she moved his arm and sat back against the seat. "You know enough. Can't give you another thing to use to coerce me or blacken my name. That's the Fitzwilliam way. Is Fitzwilliam Greek, meaning to crush Theodosia?"

"Were you always this funny?" His lips pushed together for a moment. "Here's something that you won't hear a Fitzwilliam say and mean it. I'm sorry, Theo. I was so angry at you for not mourning, I wanted you to pay, but I was the shrew. I thought nothing but the worst of you. I raged and wrote. But I forgot how young we were and how easy it was to let fear affect us. You've been in my thoughts—some of them have been focused on revenge, some quiet like now, remembering what we had. I never once forgot you. Look at me. See the truth."

She didn't want to look up. It was too easy to become lost in those eyes. She shook her head. "I can't believe you."

"If I can admit regrets, can't you?"

No. She couldn't. To do that would steal Mathew's legacy, the man who had saved her, who had given her so much.

"I have regrets, Theo. Deep ones."

*R*s. He had them? Couldn't he see the turmoil churning in her stomach? Against her will, her face craned up to his. She put a shaky finger to his lips. "No. No more of this or you can leap out and find your own way to Grandbole."

His mouth opened. With his teeth, he raked her finger, shooting lightning down her skin. "I'll be brave and say it. I regret you thought me dead. I regret that my absence made you vulnerable and made you prey for others. I regret you weren't awaiting my return."

He leaned closer to her face. She could feel his breath, warm, sweet-smelling like sagebrush. The heat of it fell upon her cheekbone. "Don't you wish things had been different?"

That stupid part of her heart took over. She let her ghost, the man who symbolized the first kindness she had ever known, the first love of her heart, brush his lips against hers.

He took her face within his palms. "Well, I wish things were different, even if you can't admit it. I'll be transparent. I suppose that's what ghosts are good for. See through my misgivings. Know I've missed you, Theo."

His eyes had surely put her into a trance, for her palms were too weak to plant upon his chest to stop another advance. He angled her face then branded her mouth with his fire. He stole her peace, her sense, her air, as he took a second and then a third deep kiss.

Panicked and panting, she fell into his chest and let years of tears puddle in her eyes. She had loved Ewan, more than herself.

Ewan mopped her sobs with his thumbs. "Do you remember loving me? I remember."

He gave her no chance to respond to his whisper. His passion began again as his hands became more urgent.

She remembered his love and measuring everything against it. If she fell for Ewan again, there would be no Mathew to catch her. "No."

Her voice sounded small and weak and stupid. Why had she let Ewan into her carriage? Why had she given him room to tempt her?

His pinkie tugged a lock of her hair. "Is *no* what you want?"

Swatting at her stinging eyes, she sat up straight. "No. I—I can't do this. I'm a proper widow. I won't sit in the dark clinging to the past."

His head tilted toward her. The inches of separation she'd recovered disappeared. "Then cling to a future. I'm here, and I'm not scary." He took her mouth, tasting that raw lip that she'd nearly chewed off. "Trust me, Theo." The whisper was cool upon her jaw. Then nothing separated his kiss from hers.

With her resolve crumbling like a fallen flower vase, she bloomed, opening for him. She let him kiss her for yesterday, today, and tomorrow.

His hands went under her cloak tracing the lace of her tucker, sizing and squeezing, taking inventory of her shape, testing her lack of resistance.

He'd always been a good shut-up-I-can't-think kisser, but this was wrong and thoughtless. Anger at herself began to boil in her gut. Her desire waned. Reason, the better R word, came into her head, and she caught one of his hands.

That stopped one, but not the other. It took over, smoothing and tickling that patch behind her shoulders or that spot along a rib that made her sigh.

His fingers tugged at a ribbon holding her sleeves.

She broke from his kiss, shoved at his hands. "What do you think you are doing?"

"Exactly what you think. We are starting over, or where we left off. Father's not standing in the way this time. You only have to sign the leases to finish the peace."

He'd used her weakness to coerce her? "No, you bounder!" She drew up her cloak, hating how breathless and alive she sounded. "Seduction with Daddy's blessing? That's a new trick."

He undid his now-mangled cravat. "Theo, we've been apart six years, but I know you. I know you to be a headstrong beauty who'd rather chew nails than admit to faults or regrets. But I know desire even better. Etched in my brainbox is the way your eyes burn when you want more of me. You haven't changed. You need me. Does that scare you as much as thunder?"

"Yes."

Shrugging, he set his open palms on the seat. "Theo, I know my father did something that made you scared. You were left vulnerable, which went against everything he said he'd do while I served. I know you well enough to know that somehow Mathew Cecil came upon you in your time of need and took care of you, ingratiated himself upon you. If you weren't in trouble, my beautiful strong Theo would've never been snared by an old man."

"What? Who told you this? Your mother?"

His brow squinted then smoothed. "No one had to tell me. I figured it out. Tell me I'm wrong. Then tell me you don't desire me."

"This is what you figured out and now this story makes

everything that has happened matter less."

Ewan nodded, and her insides erupted in raw, hot venom.

She forced her voice to a purr. "You want to know desire, tell the driver to go to Beaufort Wharf."

His eyes widened and crinkled as a smile exploded onto his face. He knocked on the roof, stopping the carriage. He stepped out and then returned like a flash of lightning. Soon they were moving.

Ewan held her hand, drew her fully into his embrace. "We're both too stubborn, but I will say it again, I have missed you, Theo."

She didn't respond, and kept his hands locked upon hers where she could see them.

When she peeked out and saw the familiar buildings near the banks of the Thames, she climbed up onto the seat. Her knees sucked into the tufts of the squab and she tried to look happy and wild, while not losing her balance. "You are right. Why fight this feeling bubbling between us? Let me show you my desire."

She threw her arms about his neck and kissed him soundly, pretending that nothing mattered but emotions.

His fingers were in her hair, knocking pins, forcing her chignon down her back. "This hair. Silky and strong. The slight curl, not delicate. I still dream of it, of you and me."

Righting herself on the seat, she pulled up her cape, restoring her hood. "Let's continue inside. Help me down."

He jumped to wet ground, his low boots kicking up a splash. "Yes, I want to see you in the light, Theo, how time has sculpted you to perfection."

When he turned and reached for her hand, she held onto the

door. "Go inside to Adams Four, to room four."

He looked about. His face became more painted with questions. "A dark road? Dingy docks? Theo, not here. My flat is nicer. You and I—"

"Go in. Look for the crawlspace behind the curtains. It should still be there."

"Theo, I don't understand."

Scooping up his hat, she tossed it at him. "You wanted to know why I'm afraid of thunder. Because the sound is so much louder if you have to hide in a tight coal scuttle, as you wait for your mother, the harlot, to finish with the man who bought her for two bits."

He jammed on his hat, his face clouding in the shallow light of the moon. "I'm so sorry, Theo. I didn't know. We don't.... Let me get you home." He tried to climb back in, but she put up a hand in protest.

"Don't come back in here or come anywhere near me. You have your play. You're a handsome man. A Fitzwilliam. You shouldn't have any problems finding a bedmate."

"Theo. I shouldn't have—"

"Go on with your life, Ewan. That's what I've done."

"What if that life should have you in it?"

"No more lies or twisted truths. You made me a harlot once, by bedding me, then no next-day wedding. You changed our plans."

"But you agreed. You said it was the right course, given my father's offer."

"What choice did I have?" She wiped at her face, but held fast to her resolve. This mixed-up passion for a man who could never be all she needed, ended now. "Tonight, I changed your plans.

Pity your only consequence is finding a street hackney for a ride. And hear this from me. I chose Mathew Cecil. He didn't trick me. I decided to become his mistress. I came to him. I lay at his feet. And I offered him whatever he wanted."

Ewan's mouth dropped open. He wrenched at his neck as if that would make her statement of wantonness easier for his pride. "So you went after him?"

"Yes. I am everything that you wrote in your play."

"No. That's not true." He put his large hands on the door and pried it open. "Let me come back in. We can discuss this."

"Why? So, you can have another go at me? I don't want to be in your next play. My regret...is you. You said we were running away to marry, but the storm happened. And we had to wait it out in the carriage house. I was so in lo...dazzled by you. I believed you, I gave into feelings I didn't understand. Then your father caught us, and you told me to wait for you. Can't you hear your mother's laughter? You truly thought a harlot, the daughter of harlots, would wait for you? You are as big a fool as I am."

"Theo, that wasn't what it was. We weren't like that. Theo?"

She waved her hands wildly, pushed away his fingers, then slammed the door again.

He pried it open an inch, but she clung to the handle. "Please."

She wasn't letting him back inside. Angry tears flooded her throat, but she swallowed the itching fire. He needed to hear her, and she needed to be released from the second biggest regret of her life. "I'm no longer like my mother. I'm not going to be bedded like one 'cause of a storm and nice-sounding lies, you manipulative man. I'm an honorable woman because of Mathew

Cecil. He married his mistress and gave me a true name. Go on with your life, change all the names in your play back to Theo the Flower Seller, for that girl doesn't exist."

"You're hysterical." His voice fell softer. Maybe he could feel the anger she'd hidden in her bones for him not standing up for their love.

"I have regrets, too Theo. Even if you can't or won't admit to them, I will. Let's talk. Let..."

Regrets? Is that what he called leaving her unprotected to a family that would have her starve to make sure no black blood mixed in their bloodline? "No more *R* words about what we had, Ewan. That love vanished into thin air. It's a ghost to me." Theodosia tapped the roof and the carriage started moving. The door whipped shut, barely missing his fingers. He didn't hold on. Maybe her words made him not try.

She sank into her seat. Blanketing her cape tightly about her shoulders, she waited for her heart to stop pounding, for her lips to stop vibrating from Ewan.

Hopefully, he hated her enough now that he'd release her from his hauntings and his heart. For a determined ghost would destroy the only thing she valued: the honorable name of her son.

CHAPTER ELEVEN

The Depths of Hope

Ewan climbed down from his borrowed gig and stowed it in the carriage house at Grandbole. The morning sky had cleared, but the ground and air still smelled of yesterday's heavy rain. He stretched his stiff limbs, being dumped in the middle of the docks had left everything sore, including his heart.

With a shake of his head, he unhitched his horse and handed him over to the groom. The young boy looked as if he still had sleep in his eyes. "Thank you."

He headed to the door but stopped and examined the place, the heavy oak planks forming the walls. The old building might be the oldest on the family property. The loft was piled high with bundles and gear, but maybe there was still room up there for two.

He took another breath, gazing at the opening above and the hooks decorating the walls with harnesses, reins, and wheels, but he turned to the ladder leading to the loft, the quietest place to read and dream. Six years ago, he and Theo had waited out a storm up there. They had talked gibberish of what they would do when they married. Then they'd purposed to elope and they had decided, no, it was better to wait out the storm in the carriage house.

Touching the knurled ladder, he remembered the shy girl, the one so overcome by his telling her of his love, that she had allowed him every liberty. He hadn't coerced her. They'd been in love. Had Theo forgotten that?

Fisting his hands about the pole, he almost climbed the ladder but his legs weren't steady. Up all night, walking off a lifetime of anger, and even beating up a welcome footpad would make anyone unsteady.

His knuckles were raw, but he'd been thankful, ever so grateful, for something to thrash. Pounding his own skull wasn't the best option. No, Theo had done that enough.

One minute loving, alluring, responding to his touch. The next, tricking him out of her carriage. Accusing him of misleading her, of using her fear to take advantage of her.

She thought him a bounder.

But it was worse listening to her admit that she'd harlotted herself to Cecil. She hadn't grieved Ewan's alleged death not even a month before taking up with the rich man.

His father had been right. She'd become the Circe of his play, Theo the Harlot.

Yet. It still didn't feel quite right. How could the shy girl he'd once loved go on to another man so soon?

Jasper strolled through the door, his arms filled with cut flowers. "So this is where you spent the night. You look awful. Must not have gone well at the theater. Sorry, Ewan. I thought the play—"

"No. Mr. Brown wants to buy my play. I need to bring him the final copy. He's excited for it."

Nodding, a clear-eyed Jasper sniffed at the big bouquet in his arms. "Well, you look like you've had a rotten night."

The groom walked past them, yawning, and left. That left the brothers alone in the carriage house. This was bad, for Jasper had the questioning look upon his face with his happy, lopsided smile, his bright eyes searching for the right matches to set the Ewan tinderbox ablaze.

"Did you get caught in that wicked thunderstorm last night and take shelter here? Is it more comfortable here for successful playwrights? Not too drafty."

"No."

"Did the widow meet you here? I hear she came back late, very late. I was at the tavern this morning and heard some odd things."

"Tell your drunk friends she went to the theater, then returned."

"Seems one of her chatty footman talked of a lover's spat. Very unusual, since the woman has been cloistered in black and gray for months. She's been a monk, as far as they know." His brother's amused gaze disappeared. His pupils narrowed and fixed upon Ewan's hands. "You haven't been out carousing, as Father puts it. You've been in a fight, Brother. What happened last night? Did you have to defend the Blackamoor beauty from a bounder?

"No. Can we stop this conversation, Jasper?"

"Did you have to stop someone from attacking her, angry at her race? I'd assume with the Abolitionist movement starting, a buffoon might have the wrong idea. I hear they call slave mistresses fancies in the Americas."

Hot, blind rage crossed Ewan's eyes. Pulling his bruised hands to his back, Ewan spread his feet apart and prepared to strike his own brother. "Don't call her that around me. There's an unlucky footpad who stumbled upon me looking for money. He caught the bad end of my fists. I am unharmed."

Jasper's grin disappeared. "Sorry. You look mostly unruffled on the outside, but that's the outside."

Foolscap, on reams of paper, that was where Ewan wrote of his black insides. Not accustomed to talking things out with anyone anymore, he shrugged. "You look like you're getting ready to go court someone. Have you given up on your letter-writing widow? Going to try it the old-fashioned way? A matchmaking mama or my matchmaking mother taking the reins?"

"No. And no. I can wait to see what the widow answers. These blooms are for Father. He's going into Town to see your mother. He said it was your suggestion."

With a shake of his head, Ewan tried to dismiss an image of the old fool showing off his scowl to his poor mother, the gentle, sweet woman. Yet, Theo had lumped the lady into her list of complaints. Why? He rubbed his brow. "So the old earl is going to see her. Maybe there's hope of someone reconciling."

"Maybe he'll bring her back to help with the girls, but they've kind of scared her out of that grandmotherly role." Jasper moved from his post at the door, his head swiveling and studying, as if he'd never come to the carriage house before. "So this was where you secreted away, you and your flower seller before you were caught."

Ewan glanced at the loft and thoughts of Theo rushed his soul. He could still hear her laughter, her shattered breaths from his kisses.

So much like last night. He hadn't expected to rekindle things, but he hadn't expected to have her in his arms. Or that she'd dump him on the road, as if he were a blackguard. He swallowed the awful lump of gall filling his dry mouth. "Jasper, you have flowers to deliver. Don't let me keep you."

His brother came closer. Not a hint of brandy was in his breath. "We used to be able to talk. We used to see things the same."

Ewan touched the flowers, swirling the reds and pinks. "That was before you left for your grand tour, before you married, and before I took up with someone of another race. A Blackamoor. I loved her, Jasper. Maybe as much as you loved Maria."

The pronouncement startled him as much as Jasper, but it was true.

"Father said he caught you two here. He said he called her every evil name he could conjure up but you stood up to him, even more so than what you did with me. She had to be special."

"Aye. But then I did the unthinkable. I agreed to the earl's demands. He said he'd give his permission for us to wed if I served a year in the militia. I served, and I lost her. But the earl was right about her not being faithful. That she'd be ruinous to me. She admitted last night to seducing Cecil and becoming his mistress. I wasn't cold in the ground a month."

Jasper lips thinned. The big man swirled a long rose as if it was one of his swords. "Interesting. Why would Cecil marry his mistress? With a mistress, you get the benefits of the milk and cheese for which you've paid. One doesn't have to own the cow and put your name to it."

"The widow is not a cow."

"Ewan, I think there are answers you need to figure out."

"Why?" Ewan looked at the ladder, which led to loft. He climbed the first rung but stopped. She hated him, such awfulness had flowed from those wondrous lips. "What good would it be to hear the reasons? It wouldn't change a thing."

"Perhaps, perhaps not. But maybe she needs to hear why you agreed to the earl's demands. You loved her. You said she loved you. The two of you were set to elope, but then you agreed to the old man's demands. Why?"

The old reasons of wanting his father's approval had cost him. Ewan rubbed at his neck. "I wanted the old man to not hate me for loving her. I didn't want him savaging another play like he'd done with my first. But it doesn't matter anymore. I couldn't have made Theo happy. She once mentioned wanting to own a flower store. She has the money for several, but she's purchased none. Her dreams have changed. She's changed. It doesn't matter now."

His brother strode over to him and hefted the floral arrangement into his hands. "Maybe you can use these more than Father."

Ewan squinted at the big hulk of a man. "I don't understand."

"You've beat someone senseless over her. You've used your muse to write a play about her. Until last night, not a hint of scandal about Cecil's widow. I suggest you go to Tradenwood, apologize for everything, and tell her you want another chance."

Every bit of the frustration from last night still boiled his blood. It pumped and burned and stung every organ. Head down on the ladder, Ewan dropped the flowers, then jumped down upon them. "She called herself a harlot for loving me. She condemned herself and me for giving into passion."

He kicked the pile and sent more petals flying. "She is done with me. Maybe you should go to her. You both are widows. She seems to like neighbors."

Jasper bent and picked up a few of the undamaged buds.

"Maybe I should go court one of the young women your mother has foisted upon me at her parties. Seems newspaper advertisement number four hasn't written back."

"Good. You don't need anyone who can't admit regrets."

"But what of you, Ewan? You're besotted with Cecil's widow but won't go down to Tradenwood because you don't want to admit your own regrets."

"You mean go down there and say anything to have her sign away the rights to the waterway? Maybe you're more like the earl; her money now makes the neighbor acceptable."

Breaking stems in his hands, Jasper made a bigger scatter of red bits on the dirt floor. "I won't lie. I want our land protected, but I also want you happy. I know what love feels like. I know it. And I've watched it die. If I had a chance to regain that feeling I would, but you have to be brave to do that."

"I went to war. I am brave."

"On the outside, Ewan. Admit to her why you accepted Father's offer. You were set to elope, but then you changed your mind. Why?"

A sober Jasper meant all his acumen came full bore. His aim was deadly accurate. His brother shook his head. "Admit the regret, the one that made you turn from the woman you obviously loved."

"I didn't think I could support us against the earl's wrath. He'd threatened to make sure all my plays would never sell. How would I bring bread to the table? How would I be enough for her?"

Jasper lifted Ewan's hand and shook the scabbed thing. "With these. You've stood up to me with every slight I've thrown. You beat someone to a pulp last night, because of her. You should fight for her as you told Father to do for your mother."

Ewan blinked and he was on his sick bed reading the earl's gloating letter about Theo running off with another man. Dormant fury erupted. Knuckles stinging, he drew back his hand. "It doesn't matter now. That was a long time ago. She doesn't want me and I'm not so sure I want my cousin's mistress turned wife."

Jasper's face blanked. The man never showed any other emotion than humor, except when that long fuse tempering his anger was spent. He looked as if he'd explode, too. "It does matter. We all have pasts, but what about a future? What about being made new each day, because we are given a new day?"

"The elder brother holds the land not the role of a vicar. You're more loveable when you are less ministerial."

"I'm stating the obvious. Neither of you have resolved your feelings. You're both stuck in yesterday. I doubt if either of you know how to forgive."

"I forgave her when I thought she was a victim."

Jasper folded his arms, looking every inch the older, wiser brother. "Maybe it was easier to forgive your duplicity in deflowering her, thinking you died. The score sounds pretty even, in a tit-for-tat kind of way." His lips thinned to a line. "And if you don't get the widow's agreement before Father returns, he *will* coerce her. And you know how he is. It won't be pretty. Get the widow to see the light, before it is too late."

Hadn't the earl's dealings set Ewan and Theo onto this hopeless path? Ewan dropped his still fisted hands to his sides. "What did he threaten this time?"

With a shrug of his shoulders, Jasper turned. "Nothing specific, but I don't want to find out. Fix this, Ewan." Head hanging low, his brother walked out of the carriage house.

Alone again, Ewan felt a knot tighten in his gut. Theo was about to face the earl's vengeance a second time.

A sober Jasper, a fearless Jasper, not wanting to see the earl's schemes, meant the old man prepared for war.

How could Ewan get Theo to compromise when it seemed being compromised was the root of her anger at him? What Jasper had said, to tell Theo why he had changed their plans six years ago felt valid. Maybe things would be different if he'd told her then. Maybe things would be different now.

He bent and scooped up a single rosebud. Snipping off a bruised petal revealed a perfect flower. Maybe under their scars, the same could be said of the playwright and the widow.

Yes, there was a woman down the hill who needed to give him one last audience.

• • •

Theodosia stared out the balcony of her bedchamber at the sunny sky. The sun was high, casting short shadows over the rail. The morning had fled. It had to be past noon, maybe two or three o'clock, and she'd only written two words, *Dear Sir.*

She'd tried to prove Ewan wrong, that she could admit to the *R* words, but she'd failed. It was too hard to admit her greatest regrets.

A knock sounded on the door.

Theodosia pushed up from the writing chair, the one she'd taken from Mathew's adjoining room, and smoothed a drooping curl back behind her ear. "A moment."

Listless, she pulled back the flowing cream curtain around her bed. Her shawl lay there and she'd need its comfort. She was still drained from arguing in the rain with Ewan.

What if Pickens needed her to go to outside to the fields to check decorations for the festival? Her heart lunged forward then slapped back into her chest. Ewan would be there. She felt it. Pickens said he'd stopped by three times yesterday. *Oh, let this not require going outdoors.* She couldn't face him again. Not now, and never alone.

Another knock.

Resigned, she slogged forward, but before her fingers turned the doorknob, in popped Frederica. "Mrs. Cecil? Are you well? The butler said you haven't budged from this room except to check on Philip."

Pickens followed and his frown could've touched the floor. "I tried to stop her, ma'am, but I was busy dissuading Mr. Fitzwilliam."

Oh no. Ewan had come again. Why wouldn't he give up? "It's fine. Have Miss Burghley's room ready. She's here early."

Still frowning, Pickens left, closing the door with a gentle thud.

Frederica leaned against the threshold connecting the bedchambers. "What has occurred?"

Theodosia pulled at her shawl and shrugged. "I'm not in the best spirits, and you've arrived early. You were to come tomorrow morning. Is everything well with you?"

With her hazel eyes squinting, her friend slipped off her dark blue gloves. "I had a feeling you might need me." Frederica sashayed to the balcony and back. Her sleek indigo carriage gown looked like a uniform, with military fobbing and buttons about her sleeves. Was she coming to battle?

"Well, you are alone in here. There goes one of my ideas." A giggle fell from her lips, then her tone sobered. "So what happened with your *cousin*?"

Shaking her head, Theodosia backed up to the post of her canopy bed. "Nothing."

"The way the man stormed away from Tradenwood, something happened. Why is he desperate and why won't you see him?"

"How mad was Mr. Fitzwilliam?

"He looked like he'd breathe flames. Confess. What is going on with him, with you?"

Theodosia glanced down and folded her arms about her middle. She couldn't run from the truth. Now she didn't want to. "I deserved his wrath," she said. "I angered him."

"No one can be angered by you, dear Theodosia. You care too much for others."

"Oh yes, they can be. And Ewan Fitzwilliam has the right to be mad. I led him on, then dumped him without a care onto the side of the road. I knew it was wrong, but did it, anyway."

Frederica's mouth fell open and not in a snack-on-a-bonbon kind of way, but in a wide gape. "But you...you jest. I saw him at the door, here, applying to enter Tradenwood. Where did you leave him? At the gate? The edge of the fields perhaps?"

"I left him outside my mother's old brothel, the one I was born at near the docks. A most dangerous part of London."

Silence.

Frederica's eyes grew bigger.

Shame, almost as bad as the day she had been turned away

from Grandbole six years ago, rocked Theodosia. She had gone there to seek help and had been reminded that she was no better than her mother. The angry taunts rang in her head. She was filled with shame. Shame at her mother's profession. Shame at begging for a crust of bread to save her unborn child. "I wanted him to feel desperate and tawdry, like I had."

"Why would you?" Frederica's fair cheeks were ashen. "We never talk about the brothels...your mother's or mine. We don't."

For a moment, Theodosia closed her eyes, hoping to forget the hurt stirring in Frederica's irises. "This is why I hate talking of regrets. They are horrid and they remind people of their worst pain. I won't say it again."

"It's us. The lucky by-blows. The ones who escaped that life."

Theodosia rushed to her friend and lifted her chin. "I needed Ewan Fitzwilliam to see what happens to the unlucky ones. They have to go to brothels and sell their souls when men leave them unprotected."

With a nod, Frederica moved away, opened the balcony doors, and pulled back the gauzy curtains. "So you and this Fitzwilliam? He was a beau?"

"Yes. Then he went to war and died. I was left to figure out how to survive, me and my baby."

Frederica spun to her like a top. "Philip?"

"Only Mathew knew the secret, and he told me never to tell. My husband adored my son and loved him as if he was his own."

"I always thought Cecil was too old, but with Philip being so sickly—"

"Philip is sickly because I starved while I carried him—all because of the Fitzwilliams. They never approved of me and made things worse when they thought my beau, their son, had died in Spain."

Shock didn't look good on Frederica. Her features were made for lightness, nothing heavy or foreboding.

But Theodosia had to tell someone. As if to keep herself intact, she wrapped herself deeper in her shawl, the light cream wool bandaging over her gray widow's garb. "I regret believing my lover's lies, but not Philip."

Eyes growing larger, Frederica came near. "Fitzwilliam doesn't look dead now. He obviously still likes you. Maybe he could be the husband we need."

Turning her head like a mad woman, Theodosia said, "No. No. No. I can't trust him. He won't fight for Philip, not against his family."

"But you, and especially Philip, are his family, too. You should give him the opportunity to choose. The Peninsula War ended some time ago. He may have changed, and I saw how he looked at you when he assisted you from my father's box."

Refusing to agree, Theodosia shook her head faster. "That was lust. It will pass."

"But I saw your face and how you clung to his arm." Frederica paced from the bed to the desk and back, with her arms pinned behind her back, the picture of a barrister. She stopped at the desk and fingered the letter from the newspaper advertisement baron, then Theodosia's measly attempt at a reply. "Admit you still like Fitzwilliam. He's more interesting than the squire. Hopefully, he's as clever with words as this baron. Can't you see it in your heart to forgive your cousin?"

Theodosia took the notes from Frederica's fingers. "Forgive

and forget? I don't know anymore. I idolized him. I made our love seem so perfect and tragic. That was a farce, like that shrew play we watched. And poor Mathew. It took him too long to get through to my heart, because I kept comparing my dreamer to practical Mathew. I'm a fool. I had a perfect man who loved a child that wasn't his, while I wrongfully held on to lies."

"But Cecil won your heart. I saw you two. You loved him, and he knew it."

"Yes, but how many months, years, did I deprive him of my heart?"

Frederica wrapped her arms about Theodosia and held on tight. "You loved him, and he loved you. Don't you forget that. He chose you. He gave that boy a name, but Cecil wanted you happy."

"Mathew would want me to protect Philip. Maybe Philip and I need to leave here. I could take Philip and the means I could quickly garner and go. Do you think the waters of Bath will help him?"

Frederica tightened her embrace. "You can't leave. You haven't left because of Lester's threats, but this Fitzwilliam makes you so scared you want to flee? He can't hurt you. Philip was born during your marriage. He's Cecil's because he claimed him."

That was true but it didn't stop the fear of the Fitzwilliams figuring out ways to use the secret to hurt Philip or to steal him away as Lester had threatened. Biting her lip, she straightened and pried out of Frederica's hug. "I can't let them put out nasty rumors about my son. If I don't run, I must marry. The sooner I marry, the safer Philip will be."

She put her hands onto Frederica's shoulders, spun her

around, then steered her to the door. "You go settle into the guest room Pickens has for you. I promise to clean up and dine with you tonight. And we can talk about any nonsense you want, any *other* nonsense."

"Will there be bonbons?"

"Of course, so many we can forget what I've said."

Frederica stopped dragging her low-cut boots, but paused at the door. "Cecil had a look in his eyes that told me how much he loved you. His cousin has that look, too."

She opened the door and gave Frederica a light shove. "Bonbons. Now go on."

Her friend smiled and headed down the hall.

Closing the door, Theodosia took a long breath. Alone again, she felt lighter, maybe even motivated. She'd told her regrets and the world didn't crumble. She returned to her desk and picked up the cut of foolscap she'd started with *Dear Sir*. Her fingers tapped the smooth surface of the small pine desk. This was the ideal setting, tucked in the corner of her bedchamber, different from her business desk in the parlor. Through the billowy curtain covering the balcony, she could enjoy the sweet air rising from the fields, her fields.

Regrets didn't smell so fine. How did they look on paper?

Another knock sounded.

Frederica again? Did she think of another question to ask?

Two knocks sounded. The second echoed as it came from the lower part of the door.

Philip?

Pulse throbbing in terror, she rushed to the door and flung it open.

Her heart started to beat again as she saw her son standing in his blue pinafore next to Pickens. Then it stopped again. He was holding his ear. His pretty eyes were sad, filling with tears.

"Ma—ma."

Not caring about her dignity or station in front of her butler, she dropped to her knees and grabbed the boy. She massaged his head, the way that brought smiles once the pain went away. "It will be all right. I'll make it better, Son. How long has he been hurting?"

Pickens bent and picked up the boy and took her arm, helping her to stand. "Only a few minutes. The governess came to me."

The woman should've come to her directly. Philip's well-being was the most important thing. She scooped up her son and took him fully into her arms. "Can you have some hot tea sent? And send for the doctor."

The man's lips thinned. "Mrs. Cecil, the doctor will be here tomorrow at the festival. He won't do any better than what you do for Master Philip."

Why did Pickens have to be right? Why couldn't the answer be different for once? Couldn't any of the doctors do something to save her son? She spun from the butler, taking Philip with her, sailing almost half into the room before she faced the man again. "You say that as if there is no hope. Is that what you want to hear?"

Her butler stood in the threshold. His face was unreadable.

She clutched her son more tightly to her bosom hoping that the feel of her, the smell of her lavender would let him know that she was close, that she'd never stop hoping, never stop loving him.

Philip let go of his ear and hugged her neck. "Make—go away."

"Get the laudanum, Pickens. It will help him sleep until this passes. That's what all the doctors have done."

The butler nodded. "Master Cecil used to say hope was everlasting. That it lifted his head as he walked in the fields. He never feared, ma'am. Hope was on his side."

She looked down at the boy her husband had claimed for his legacy and snuggled her face against his shiny black mop. She'd never give up on trying to make her son whole.

As she rubbed his temples, she watched him breathe. He was small for his age and looked so delicate, but love overwhelmed her. He was the best part of her.

The need to gain the best advocate for Philip renewed. She'd wait for the medicine to take hold as he slept in her bed, then she'd return to her desk and answer the baron.

She wouldn't be afraid anymore. Her son needed her to be strong. She'd found a champion once, a kindly gentleman farmer, Mathew Cecil. Maybe she'd be that lucky again. Hope still existed for her and Philip. It had to.

CHAPTER TWELVE

The Flora Festival

The noise, *tap*, *tap* made Theodosia snuggle in her blanket. Frederica would have to wait for a decent hour to hear more gossip.

Tap.

It was too early for her chamber maid.

The rhythm continued. She sat up, pulling the bedclothes to her chin. Her eyes slowly opened to the ebony darkness. She struck a match and lit a candle. Gazing at Philip's sleeping form, her pulse slowed. He lay still beside her, hopefully enjoying pain-free dreams.

Before she could tuck the covering about his shoulder, the noise started again. This time she heard the *ting ting*. It was something hitting the balcony door glass panes. Something outside wanted in.

Blinking, Theodosia squinted at the curtains. Through the parting of the fabric, she spied an outline, a ghost, no a man. *Ewan?*

Like a cat, she sprung up, closing the sheers to her bed, hiding her sleeping son.

Fear pumped through her, her ghost...too near her boy.

Holding her breath, she pulled on her robe and cinched it tight. Starting to the doors on tiptoes she stopped. Philip wouldn't hear. Only if he were looking at you and concentrating could he make out noise with his good ear.

Sad and sighing, she stood at the glass doors, staring at the frowning man on the other side.

His hands were on his breeches. The man bent, half-hunched over, gasping air. "Theo. Open up."

"Go home." She hoped he'd heed and not wake the house, but the fire in his gaze said no. He wouldn't be moved. "Please."

"Not until we speak." He punched at the glass while still gulping like his lungs weren't working. "Not with this between us."

Unbelievable. Ewan rapped against the door, wheezing like an old fool. What did he expect climbing up here? And he could've fallen. Her chamber sat high on the second floor.

He banged this time, harder. "Let me in." His voice sounded louder this time.

Philip might not hear, but the rest of the house would. She couldn't have more whispers about her conduct, not after the footman had witnessed the argument outside the brothel. Resigned, she unlatched the door and pushed onto the balcony. "Be quick."

Ewan strutted forward, like a peacock, a panting peacock. "You don't look sick."

His shortness of breath filled her with unwanted concern. "You do. Are you very winded?"

"It will pass. It always does." He pressed at his chest in the spots where she'd felt his scars. "Overexerted myself climbing up here. Not quite the same as when Jasper and I did it as children."

"You shouldn't have done that, Ewan. It's too dark and dangerous to balance on my tree. Did you step on my clematis blooms to get here?"

Bright moonlight streamed about him, making his shoulders seem broader. He chuckled and leaned against the rail, dusting his hands. "Fretting over flowers? No regard for me falling?"

She folded her arms to keep from shoving him over the rail. "You chose to climb. No one made you. Why are you here? What if someone saw you sneaking in here?"

"From what I remember of our time together, you were consumed with lavender, not clematis."

"Good night, Ewan."

She reached for the doors, attempting to close them upon him, but this time he was faster and both his large hands covered hers.

Warm, rough, and alive. The heat of his skin seared her flesh, made her knees weak. "Leave me, Ewan. Please."

He opened the doors fully and sauntered inside. His brows popped up as his head dipped, then raised, as he circled her. "Creamy white silk is much better than dark, heavy mourning robes."

The glint in his eyes made her pulse race. His touch brought that dangerous, swirling, out-of-control feeling. It engulfed her, but she folded her arms about her middle like a shield. No matter how weak she was for him, he wasn't going to make her rash. "Say what you have to say then over the balcony and out of my life."

He leaned on the doorframe. "I have been trying to see you for days. I'm tired of waiting. You should understand that, Mrs. Cecil."

She refused to respond to his baiting and held all her retorts that it was *his* fault she'd needed Mathew. Ewan needed his say, if only to make it right that she'd dumped him at the docks.

Nodding, she said, "Continue, but be brief. I have a long day tomorrow. The festival begins."

"Yes, the Flora Festival. Pickens said you've exhausted yourself in the planning, but I've come with an ultimatum from the earl. He'll triple his offer. He will pay three times the previous amount for the water leases."

"Triple? And just for leases. Not to buy all my land." She tugged on her robe sash, almost turning toward her canopy bed but stopped. "Not my requested multiple of twenty?"

His eyes squinted. He pulled a folded paper out of his pocket and pushed it between her fingers. "This is reasonable. And take hold of it. Read it for yourself. I know my notions hold little weight, but this is a valid offer to continue the water use. This will bring peace between neighbors."

"But Lester won't let me agree. He wants..." She took the paper, and curled it within her fingers. "Even if what you say is true, I can't sign this yet. It will force my hand, literally." She moved to her desk and lit a candle. Using the light, she scanned the pages. It said what Ewan stated.

With heavy steps, he followed. She felt his breath on her neck before she turned.

"I can read it to you as in direct address. You used to like me reading to you, Theo. You used to like me."

She glared at him. "I don't want you haunting me anymore."

"Yes. You made that quite clear in your carriage. But I must resolve this before the earl does. I don't want him to hurt you."

The concern in his voice was palpable, heart stopping, and she had to remember that this was the same man who'd left her in fear of his father's wrath. "I'll manage."

His hand lifted, and she tensed, as if he were going to touch her.

Frowning, he grunted something then leaned past her and picked up her letter from the baron. "Oh, how droll, teasing you about regrets. I suppose you'll tell him how I misled you, poor innocent you."

He tossed the paper to the desk, then curled his palm under his chin. "Do be kind when you tell him how you never responded to my kisses, not even the ones in the carriage. No, that would be a lie, like saying, 'I'll wait for you to return from the Peninsula,' when you obviously didn't."

Breathing heavy in short bursts, as if he had touched his lips to hers, she slipped to the side of him. "I wish for you to take your mocking and seductions and go."

A smile lit his face and he moved to her again. "Seduction only works if the object is in the mood to be swayed. I'm no bounder. I've taken no liberties, nothing that wasn't freely offered."

"I never said you took anything."

"Theo, you made a great performance of it in your carriage. That kiss, the sizzling one that sent me flopping out the door like a happy puppy about to feast on the cook's soup bones—that was done well. You should manage theater. The production was quite fine."

"I was wrong to do that, but you used that storm to try to... confuse me. That was wrong, too."

He rubbed at his neck. "I didn't mean to take advantage. I remembered how you hated storms and meant to be of comfort. But I can't help my attraction to you. That doesn't make me nefarious; it makes me a man. I'm not seeking to ruin you, well, not like that. Admit that I'm no bounder. Six years ago, I was a man who was alone with the woman he loved."

Those pretty eyes of his held her captive, but it was easy to say this truth. "Yes Ewan, you are no bounder."

"Good. I like my sins known." His gaze raked over her.

She pulled at her lacy robe again, feeling exposed to his hungry, hypnotic gaze. "You chose your elegant words to make me believe a lie, that you would marry me, honor, and protect me. I forgave you when I thought you'd died. I only tried to remember the good, not that you'd abandoned me when I needed you. But now, I see the truth, how you will use your elegant words to ruin my reputation."

In slow motion, he put a palm to her elbow. "I took your name out. I will not put it back in because we are fighting."

"What of the carriage? Ewan, you're not in love with me, but you kissed me like you are."

He walked around her again, lowly humming to himself. "I'm still a man, Theo, and a little weight looks truly well on you."

"Haven't you ever seen a robe before? Or a mature woman?" She wanted to add that she'd had a baby, but she didn't, not with Philip sleeping a few feet away.

His grin returned. "Yes. But since I've returned, I've only seen you in dark billowy garbs. Sheer looks good upon you, and you're not pregnant."

What? Not ashamed of her curves, she lifted her chin. "Thank you, I think, but why would you..." She shook her head, knowing his new conspiracy would take today's peace. "Mathew Cecil thought me very pretty. You've delivered your message, but you being here is not proper. Someone could catch you. They'll think—"

A snore whistle sounded. Soft at first, then loud.

"We're not alone, Theo." Anger etched his jaw as it tightened. "Here I am trying to protect you." His voice deepened. "Thinking this Lester fellow is bad and he's trying to force his way into your bed, and he's already here. Let me congratulate him with my fists."

"No. Ewan stop."

Unable to grab him, he sprang over to her big bed and drew back the canopy curtain.

Theodosia came upon him and caught the shift in his face, the slacking of his jaw.

Ewan saw Philip.

But did her poor boy see Ewan?

Another sleepy snort whistled.

Philip didn't even awake with the commotion.

Relief sweating through her pores, Theodosia pulled Ewan's hands away and yanked the curtains closed. "Stop before you wake my son."

Ewan took another peek before turning to her. "I'm sorry, Theo. You make me cork-brained."

"I can't make you anything."

"Yes, you do. I've never been a jealous man. I'm a second son. I missed titles and wealth by the virtue of birth order." His palm curled about the knurled post of the footboard. "I lost this estate to Cecil by the premature reports of my death. None of this deeply cut, not until I found out he had you. And you have born him a son."

He looked as if he'd go back to Philip.

Against her resolve or even better judgment, she reached for Ewan and rubbed his forearm. "I'm sorry, but he's a good boy."

"Little comfort, Theo. I'm envious, stewing inside. Cousin Cecil married you. From all accounts, you two seemed happy and you have a boy. If I'd stayed, if you hadn't thought me dead, he could be my son."

Gulping in her guilt, she fought the urge to shout to him, *Yes, Philip is yours!* The truth dangled upon her tongue but so did the fear of what would happen next. More fussing, and Ewan would steal her boy's honorable name and not defend him to the world. His Fitzwilliam family would come first, not the flower seller's. She'd rather die than allow anyone to call Philip the names she bore, the names her dear Frederica had to endure. With a yank, she stole back her hand and clasped her elbow. "We can't look back."

"Well, now I know why Cecil married his mistress. He wanted his boy to have a name. Someone he could leave a legacy." He punched at his hand. "Blasted Cecil, you standup fellow."

She looked down at her robe and scooped up the sash. "This is for the best. You think your father would want a mulatto heir? I know he wouldn't. Your mother wouldn't want that, either."

Ewan ran his fingers through his hair. "My mother would love my son. She's nothing like Lord Crisdon. But it matters not what anyone thinks."

"It matters to you, Ewan. I remember how it tormented you not to have their blessing."

He frowned. "All I know is my cousin was the luckiest man." Ewan chuckled as if he'd gone mad. "I truly hate him."

She followed behind him out of the house and into the night, watching those broad shoulders sag. His emotions had to be as raw as hers. The man had seen his son. He said he was jealous of Mathew's claim to Philip. Even now, tears threatened at the costs Ewan bore. Once upon a time she was the one with whom he'd shared dreams. And she'd treasured those moments. Now, she was part of his nightmares. She put a hand to his shoulder. "I am so sorry. What's done is done."

He turned it and clutched her hand to his chest. "Is it? Or is it to be repeated. I can't deny my attraction to you is still alive."

"I'm a threat to your Fitzwilliam family, remember? You wrote me as a villain in your play. Go home. Maybe read some more of that foul Shakespeare you're so fond of."

"You remember?"

"Yes, Ewan. I remember. I remember everything. I did like you reading to me."

He didn't release her hand and swung her until the big bright moon seemed reachable. "Well, we are on a balcony. Come, gentle night; come, loving, black-browed night. Give me my Theo; and, when I shall die, take her and cut her out in little stars, that will make the face of heaven so fine. All the world will be in love with night."

It was hard to breathe. The cheek he touched burned as if branded. "You and your fancy words."

"They're foul Shakespeare's from his *Romeo and Juliet*, a forbidden love from opposing families."

"We're the same family now, sort-of-cousin."

Ewan lips brushed her forehead. "Let me make this plain. I still want you, Theo. And you should admit that part of your kisses were true. You still feel something for me."

Her heart stopped, and it would never beat right again if she started believing in him, if she again gave in to that desperate-for-her look in his eyes. She stepped backward. "You have your play. Once I'm married, I'll sign the papers you brought. Your father will be proud of you handling this."

"That solves his problems, Theo. Not mine."

With a slow step, he stood within inches of her, but kept his hands to his side, not wrapping her in those arms that would make her wilt against him like a lily lacking water. "Choose to kiss your cousin."

For a moment, she imagined pressing into his arms and waiting for him to take away her breath. In the carriage, Ewan had proved his kisses were the same as six years ago, dangerous and wild.

But she couldn't think of herself, only Philip. He needed a champion more than she needed to be held in arms that wanted her. Taking another step back, she shook her head. "Go home, Ewan."

"Theo. Everything has been frozen inside of me."

"You don't know me anymore. I still hate thunderstorms, but I'm different. I have a son who needs a mother he can respect. And I mourn a husband who made sure we were safe. He didn't care one whit about what others thought. He was our champion. I knew I was completely safe. His promises never changed."

"I was young. I had to be able to provide for us, and I didn't think we could survive with the earl against us. I should've believed more in us. He stopped my first play from being sold. That's the only reason I agreed. He never changed my mind about you. I left for war, thinking it would be a quick year and you and I would be free, with nothing to stop us."

She wanted to believe him, but too much was at stake. "We can't go backward. And it's not proper for you to be in my bedchamber or meeting me in the fields saying such things. Please, as your cousin's widow, if you care anything for me, go back to Grandbole as quietly as you came."

Standing erect, he reached for her hand and kissed it. "Then it's time to move forward." Gripping her palm high he spun her again, as he had at the beginning of his fine speech, as he had on the hill, as he had so many years ago. "I will court you again."

On the balcony, he twirled faster and faster until she clasped him tight to stop the world from spinning. He dipped his head atop hers and held her.

"I am Fitzwilliam. You know that makes me determined to win you. I will not be deterred. You need a husband and father for this boy or you wouldn't have placed an advertisement for one. Let it be me. Let me tend to you, Theo." He bent his head. His mouth neared hers. "Like it should've been before. Let me be the one. Turn to me."

His heart pounded in her ear and the scent of him—tangy sagebrush mixed with sweet oak from the tree he'd climbed—enveloped her. Right or wrong, she parted her lips, wanting to swirl away, lost in him.

"Open your eyes, Theo." Ewan pushed her shoulders and eased her rising tiptoe stance back down. "The right way this time. With a minister...and a bed, a wide bed. Let's elope now."

"Ewan, my husband's festival is tomorrow."

"Late husband, remember. You're querying for a newspaper

groom. Do I need to respond to your advertisement?"

It was good he didn't kiss her. One kiss might lead to another and tomorrow would disappear. She could feel herself falling for his teasing, but would he be there to catch her? "Ewan, we were young and not smart enough to keep our love. I must tell you. Something that I don't think you will forgive."

"It doesn't matter. It's the past, backward."

"But what I must say will ruin things. I must tell—"

He did kiss her this time, cutting off her words, her reservations, even the power to reason. His palms molded her against him and took possession of her breathing. He became air and she savored how he filled her chest with love. She levitated in his arms, so high, so fast that tomorrow didn't have to appear.

"No, sweet Theo. Not until the banns are read, then you'll be mine completely." He put her feet back onto the balcony and held her until his heart stopped racing. "Consider this a verbal application to your advertisement. I want equal, no, *all* of your consideration. We will elope after the festival. I'm not taking no and if I have to kiss you all the way to Scotland and back I will." With a safe kiss to her brow, he turned and threw a leg over the rail. "See you tomorrow, Theodosia Cecil, soon to be my bride."

He said her name, her whole one. "Fitzwilliams don't come to the Flora Festival."

"This one is. I'm coming to honor my cousin and his widow and formally meet his son. I am to be the boy's new stepfather tomorrow. He should meet me and get used to me. I will be around this time because we elope once the festival closes."

Her traitorous lips didn't say no. She watched Ewan lower himself into the tree and disappear into the night.

Going inside, she closed the door and leaned her head against the panes. The determination in his eyes was different than it had been six years ago. That scared her more than anything. How was she going to keep Philip safe, safe from angry in-laws, horrid business partners, and out-of-control passion?

She'd tell Ewan the whole truth tomorrow. Then he'd know why she couldn't marry him. Ewan would either despise her again or understand why she wouldn't expose Philip to Fitzwilliam hate.

If she couldn't marry Ewan, she still needed a husband. She dropped into her desk chair, pushed aside Ewan's lease paper, and began penning her greatest regret to the baron: she'd been so focused on the memory of a lost love, that she had fallen prey to hard times and almost starved to death, hurting her child. She'd send this note off tomorrow. If the baron dared to write back to newspaper advertisement number four, then he was the man who would stand by her and defend her to the Court of Chancery. If not, she'd marry the squire, anyone whose name wasn't Fitzwilliam.

A man who could be counted upon was who she needed, not a ghost who suddenly wanted to live again in her heart.

. . .

The musicians could be heard all the way up to Grandbole. Ewan had his youngest scamp niece dressed and ready to join the fun below, the Flora Festival. The air held the tart smell of fresh-cut hay.

They hopped all the way to the patio and spent countless minutes numbering the gathering crowds. The parish church bells rang and gonged in symphony with shepherds, who set and pitchforked hay bundles on the edges of Cecil property. It was medieval and wonderful.

Little Lucy tugged on his hand. "Anne and Lydia would like to come, Uncle."

"Well, they shouldn't have exchanged my ink for mud, dear."

"They didn't mean it."

The child's father came onto the patio, bent down, popped Lucy's drooping chin up with his finger. "No, they didn't mean to get caught." Chuckling, Jasper straightened, clear-eyed, energized. He reached out and thumbed Ewan in the chest right atop his deepest scar. "Literally, they've tried to scare him so much they'll give his weak heart pains."

"My heart's not that weak, just scared and cautious. Girls will do that, won't they, Hartwell?" Ewan swung his niece, her white dress floating about her short legs. Absolutely cute.

The wistful look in Jasper's light blue eyes concurred. "They've tormented your uncle Ewan enough. Missing the festival is fitting punishment. Besides, it'll take the two of us just to keep you from mischief."

Setting down the girl, Ewan looked down to Tradenwood. "Seems quite a show."

"One year, Cecil had chimney sweeps on his roof, dancing and singing with their brooms. They wore gilt paper and masks. It was a sight to see. Cecil had a fondness for extravagance and made his festival like a May Day celebration. It's crowded and noisy, perfect for an afternoon of ridiculousness."

Ewan scooped up Lucy and pointed to the fields. "Look at the milkmaids. I guess it's them with the wide skirts of red and gold."

"Uncle, they have huge pyramids on their heads." She put her hands above her head like she balanced something, too. "I want to do it. Mama used to make us paper hats, but with regular paper, not the gold stuff."

Jasper's countenance soured for a moment. "Maria did that? We never went. I didn't know she…" He took his dark top hat and popped it atop Lucy's bonnet. "You can use this."

The giggling girl put it on for a second then handed it back. "This is round."

Impatience winning over humor, Ewan started down the steps. "Let's go see the pyramids and all the gilt paper. You never went?"

"No, your mother hated it and pretty much convinced everyone it was low class and a travesty to Tradenwood. I'd never heard her scream before my oldest brought up going. But Maria liked fun and music. I should've known she would go."

Mother…screaming? Ewan shook his head, but realized Theo wasn't the only one mourning a legend, a mate who seemed more perfect than life. Was love possible again for one who had loved and lost so deeply? Ewan thought about his own heart and what he believed he had felt for Theo six years ago and now. There was a chance for them now. Right?

He had to get her to elope…in his brother's carriage. What type of man did that make Ewan? Shrugging inwardly, he picked up his pace. "I'll not tell Mother we are going. Can you keep that secret, Lucy?"

"Yes, Uncle. Now hurry. I hear a violin."

"I'll not tell Lady Crisdon." Jasper caught up and took his laughing girl from Ewan and put her onto his shoulder. "Perhaps,

I should blend in. Maybe borrow Father's other title again, Lord Tristian."

"No." Ewan lowered his tone and plastered on a smile. He didn't want to upset the letter-writing widow. She'd be humiliated and think he was up to tricks. She'd never trust Ewan, and her trust was important. He tugged his niece out of the way of a parade of toe-tapping musicians who rammed through the thick crowd, making their own path. "I think you should be your lovable viscount self. In fact, stay long enough to attest to our family only wanting the leases, nothing more. Not her land."

Jasper nodded. "Can you attest the same? Nothing else you seek?"

There was more, but Theodosia had to come away with him first. "Let's get to Tradenwood before all of London arrives."

Ewan let Jasper and Lucy lead the way as he followed behind. The rhythm of the musicians hit him first, the laughter, and buzz of the crowds. Then the heady smells of cooked pork called to his spirit and the breakfast he'd skipped. If it had the tart tamarind like the dishes of the West Indies, he'd dance himself dizzy. He'd missed that taste since his regiment disbanded.

His hungered spirit leapt when he saw Theo. Her hair was curled and pinned high, leaving her neck free for nuzzling. Yet, she stood on the portico wrapped in gray. Distant, lonely gray. She needed music and Shakespeare. She needed lightness.

With rainbow colors for paper patterns and bright pink table linens surrounding her festival, shouldn't she come alive with an emerald ribbon in her silky hair?

Staring at her like a schoolboy couldn't be done, so Ewan parted from his brother and niece as they became more interested in the hot air balloon hovering above the blooms. He headed to the food tables, slipping through the crowds separating him from Theo.

A wild cart owner pushed his wares too near his toes, so Ewan bounced out of harm's way and stood behind a man and older woman awaiting their turn at the carvers.

"Old Cecil would love this," one said.

The other sneered over her yellowing teeth. "The darkie got it right. The perfect amount of garish and finery."

"If you feel that way, Millie, why did you drag us here?"

"I wanted to see what she'd do and if she'd taken up with someone else. A rich widow is still rich, no matter how black."

"Stop it, Millie. She's a fairer vendor than Lord Crisdon, and you'd never see the likes of us invited to anything with their name on it."

"I hate the name of them."

Stepping away, a myriad of emotions swished into Ewan's throat like hot gall. It wasn't the insult on his family that burned, but the ones to Theo. These people ate her food, drank her wines, and did business with her, but still talked about her badly…

As he had in his play.

His gut twisted a little more. Theo wasn't stupid. She knew to the penny the cost of each morsel. She knew their sentiment. Yet she'd committed to this fair, all the trouble and expense. This Theodosia was indeed different from the girl he knew. He hungered to know her more.

He spun and glanced at Jasper running after Lucy who had Maypole ribbons. Lucy pattered up to a lady trimmed in a fine bisque bonnet and pale peach-colored gown.

Taking another look at her fair features, the indeterminate shade of brownish gold curls, she looked like one of Theo's friends from the theater. He cupped his hand to his eyes and looked again. Was that the Duke of Simone's daughter with Jasper and Lucy?

Mulatto or not, the woman and his niece had his poor brother twisted up in pink ribbons. Yet, Jasper was laughing, a full-bodied, belly-shaking laugh.

Jasper deserved to be happy. If only he could find a way to stay that way. Then he wouldn't be chasing after a bottle, a newspaper bride, or inadvertently, Theo.

Looking to the left and then to the right, Ewan saw revelers, and people pushing food carts, but where had Theo gone? Searching, his gaze fell upon Theo's son, a little boy with an ashy tan complexion. He played near the bottom of the steps of the portico. An older woman sat at his side. Maybe she was his governess.

The woman came closer to the boy right in front of his face. "I'm going to get us lemonade. Stay here," she said in a loud voice, before kissing his head and leaving him to play. The child was alone, a perfect time for an introduction.

Ewan's chest had no more room for what-ifs: what if he'd stayed, what if she'd waited for him, what if they'd married... instead he'd fill them with would-be's. She would accept him, he would be her lover, her husband, a stepfather to her child, and father to another babe. Well, he would enjoy trying for that one.

"Cousin?"

He turned at the sound of Theo's voice. Tipping his top hat to her, he bowed. "Is everything fine?"

She bit her lip for a moment then said, "I didn't think you'd really come. Fitzwilliams never attend."

Extending his arm to her, he waited for her to take it, but she didn't move. Disappointed at how wary she seemed again, he dropped his palm to his side. "I'm here and so is my brother, Lord Hartwell, and my niece. You should meet them, Cousin, as I am going to meet your son."

As he stepped toward the boy, she came close and took his arm. "He's playing, enjoying the fresh air. You can meet him later."

"Why? You're coddling him? The boy's still in a pinafore, even with his little knobby knees exposed."

Her fingers tightened about his elbow. "They're not so knobby, but he is little."

Ewan's gut was at odds. He liked her being so near, her holding on to him with the scent of lavender making him want to dip his head to her neck and inhale all of her. Yet, she was only touching him to keep him from her son. He pried at her thumb to be released and took two more steps to the boy. "Your son, he must be young or he'd be breached and in a full pair of pants."

A wince washed across her countenance. "He's not six, but I suppose your father tried to make you boys men as soon as possible. I want my son to enjoy every minute. I've no expectations of his growing other than health."

She had mistaken his fishing for an age as condemnation. He must have sounded judgmental, very much like the earl. He gazed at the boy again. He seemed frail as he rolled the hoop back and forth between his palms. Remembering Theo's first response to the newspaper advertisement he and Jasper had penned, about a sickly child, Ewan wanted to smack his stupid gut. The boy suffered and Ewan felt even more the blackguard.

"There's something I have to say." Tears were in her voice as she seemed to choke and sputter. "I need—to tell—"

"Let's go somewhere private." She couldn't accept his proposal between jugglers and musicians. No, it had to be in private, where he could kiss away any sadness. Her bold confession about wishing things were different, that she still felt love for him, that she wondered if they could start anew would be applause-worthy. Except, that would be the line he'd pen for one of his heroes.

Her other friend from the theater, the shorter girl with a pearl-laced bonnet, came to her side. "Mrs. Cecil. There's a young woman who says she must see you."

Theo raised her head. Her countenance cleared and his hope of her coming to her senses disappeared, too. "Take me to her, Miss Croome."

He clasped at Theo's hand but she slipped away. "But our talk?"

As soon as a dray cleared the path, the ladies started to move again, but Theo stopped. Over her shoulder she said, "We will, Cousin, after all is done."

He let her ominous tone sink in as he watched her walk away. Didn't sound like a confession of love was forthcoming. Was she going to reject him? No, he felt in his bones that this was right for them to wed. Something else was amiss.

Whatever it was, she would have to release it, forgive him, forgive herself, and then move forward. He'd tell her it was fine. No more guilt for what had happened. Things were finally on the right path. He was going to be a successful playwright, and this rivalry between the flower farms would be done as soon as Theo signed the papers. Everyone had a chance for peace, if they seized it with both hands and never let go.

Scanning, he found Theo again. Miss Croome had led her to the patio and up to the terraced gardens. The elegant negress with her creamy coffee complexion left Theo with a young blonde.

The girl's hand swung wildly.

His chest beat faster. He feared for Theo.

Something had to be amiss. Before he could stop himself, he started moving. He dashed to the side as a wobbly dray rumbled in front of him, nearly missing his leg.

Not waiting for an apology or acknowledgment, he moved closer to the gardens, navigating around a food cart. Everything was chaotic, like his beating heart. He raced up the terraces, past the laughing crowds, and stopped at the knee wall of the patio. He was within earshot of Theo.

"All can be made fine," Theo said. "You'll come work for me now."

"I'll take what you've given me and go to the country and have this babe. I have a cousin who'll help."

"If that's what you think is best. You have to keep this babe safe. You have to eat a lot, even if you don't want to." Theo's voice sounded weepy.

Ewan fought the urge to come out of the shadows. Something was dreadfully wrong.

"Mrs. Cecil, I should've listened to you when you came to Burlington Arcade. I shoulda listened. You said not to be his mistress."

Theo, giving mistress advice? Ewan rose from the wall and stared at them. He didn't care if he was discovered. He had to hear things correctly.

Theo had the girl in an embrace again.

The young woman snapped up, kissed Theo's hand, and fled down the terrace levels back to the revelers below.

Pivoting toward Ewan, Theo frowned deeply, her beautiful face marred with sadness. "You're supposed to only haunt me, not my guests."

He came closer and lowered his voice to a whisper. "Giving advice about not being a mistress? After we marry, I'm not sure I want women coming to you for the dos and don'ts of this business."

How was it possible for lips to disappear even more? She shook her head and dabbed at her eyes. The almond-shaped pearls quivered.

His gut froze with instant regret. Before he could take his boot from his mouth, she slipped past him. "Excuse me."

He should've reached for her hand, and apologized for the poor joke, but they both had pasts. He had forgiven her last night for not grieving him long enough, for letting her heart move on to his cousin. He had no choice. Unlike her, he hadn't forgotten her, hadn't stopped lov—

"She's too nice, you know."

Ewan lifted his head to see who watched him.

It was Theo's friend, the duke's daughter. She stood near, with her fan moving, frowning almost as much as Theo had. "I see how you are watching her. You care for her, more than a cousin should."

"Miss?"

"Miss Burghley." She crossed her arms. "If you don't intend to stick around, don't trouble her. Her heart's too big. It cares too much for others. It's too easy for her to be hurt."

"I'll keep that in mind."

"Miss Burghley." Her lips pouted, as if he should've repeated her name. "Why are you here now? Your cousin died almost a year ago."

"Seems your dear friend has been silent on things. Perhaps you should be asking her questions."

He turned to go back down to the party, when she swatted him with her fan. "She's silent on things and people who hurt her. Maybe that is why I hadn't heard of you until the theater."

Ewan hurting Theo? What, for a month? "I believe—

"Oh, no, that Mr. Lester fellow has her cornered. I don't know who I need to protect her from more."

As the musicians started again with a loud high-spirited tune, he turned to see where the blackguard had Theo, ready to pummel somebody like he had the night of the theater, but he spied something worse. "Move!"

Leaving the woman with her mouth open, Ewan shot down the terrace levels as if he'd become a bullet from a discharged flintlock, heading straight for a runaway cart. The big, barreling object made people jump out of its path and flee in all directions.

Everyone moved but one.

Theo's son.

"Move!" he yelled again. Ewan lengthened his stride, trying to become as fast as a racing horse. He huffed and puffed like a steaming tea kettle. The timing of Ewan snatching the boy had to be right or they'd both die, smashed by the cart. Mouthing a prayer, he leaped, clasped the child in his hands, and raised the boy high over his head—knowing the cart would hit him square in the chest.

Blam.

Something crunched inside as the cart exploded against him as the steel balls of war had done six years ago. The impact flung them like a rag doll. Sailing backward, he still clasped the boy about the ankle. He held on even as his own eyes began to dim, but he fought the pain.

Tucking the squirming boy into whatever remained of his chest, Ewan slammed into the grass, his head bobbing up and down. The boy wrestled free but stuck his face over Ewan's.

That's when he saw it.

Mother's irises, the same crystal blue, the same as his.

He tried to fight the darkness but lost the chance to see once more the light, the light in his son's eyes.

CHAPTER THIRTEEN

The Ghost House Guest

Theodosia paced outside of the bedchamber she'd had Pickens and Lord Hartwell put Ewan. Navigating the few chairs she had brought to sit on the deep burgundy carpet, she kept remembering the screaming, the impact of the cart, falling to her knees upon Philip's and Ewan's still bodies.

Everything inside her was torn up and grieving. She had almost lost her son today. Philip couldn't hear anyone's warning. And Ewan had risked everything to save Philip, and now he could die. He could be dead and not even know he'd saved his own son.

She stopped a few times and touched the door. It felt like six years ago as she'd waited for a shop owner to read the letter the earl had tossed in her face. The man had only gotten out the words "killed in battle" before the weight of losing Ewan had collapsed upon Theodosia. All her dreams had died, a day or two after she had discovered she carried his babe.

But now, Ewan wasn't far away.

Frederica came up the stairs. In her hand was a tea cup. She held it out. "Here, drink this and then go sit. You're pacing so much you'll wear your slippers clean through to the soles."

Pulling up her hem to make sure she hadn't already done so, Theodosia lowered her head. "I've been barefoot before. It doesn't matter. Why must women be stuck outside, waiting? Shouldn't I be with him? Or maybe I should go hug Philip again?"

Ester came from her son's bedchamber. When she closed his

door, the lights of the hall sconces danced. It was a hopeful sparkle, something Theodosia needed to keep her fears away. "Is my son awake? Does he need another hug?"

"Hugging Philip is always a good idea," Ester said, "but you've done that twice already. He's sleeping soundly. The jerking him out of the way and crashing to the ground, made him ache."

"But he didn't get an earache. And that jerking around had to be done. Mr. Fitzwilliam was the only one to risk his life for my son."

Dearest Ester came closer, stepping around Frederica. Her sprig muslin skirt held grass stains, as she had been the first to reach the accident. She took Theodosia's palms. "He's not some strange cousin, is he? I saw the look in your eyes when he came to the theater. It's worse now. How long has something been going on between you."

"Six years. I knew him six years ago."

Frederica put her palms over Ester's ears. "Does she need to know it was in a biblical sense?"

Ester swatted them away. "I heard, and I've read all the passages of Solomon and even romance novels. You don't have to—"

"Stop, you two." Theodosia wrapped her arms about herself, trying hard not to shake to bits beneath her shawl. "Yes. I knew him in every sense of the word. We were going to elope when his father convinced him to go to war. A report came back saying he'd died in the field."

A puzzled look crossed Ester's brows. "Six years ago. But you were Cecil's mistress then, right?"

Yes and no and yes. None of it mattered. She turned again

and touched the door. "It's too quiet. He can't be dying in there, not knowing."

Ester stepped to her. Candlelight shone in her eyes, as bright as her joy in finding solutions. "Not knowing what? That you're still in love with him?"

Bowing her forehead against the wall, Theo resigned herself. The truth burned in her throat. It needed to be freed. She'd said it to Frederica. She could to Ester, too. With a forced swallow, she nodded. "Something worse than that, but how do I tell him with the doctor, Lester, and Lord Hartwell, who is the heir Crisdon, keeping me away?"

Frederica came to her side. She clasped Theodosia's arm and forced her to turn the knob. "You go in and tell him. Make everyone leave, then tell him. You're not a waif or a servant but the owner of Tradenwood. Lift your head and say your truth. A man needs to know. He needs an opportunity to claim what is his, to take responsibility, even for a few seconds, of what is his."

Knowing Frederica's pain with her father, she knew her friend was right. Nodding, she opened the door. "Please don't leave, stay here to help me put the pieces back together."

Ester put her palms on Theodosia's shoulders. "Of course, we will. And Frederica is correct. You are Mrs. Theodosia Cecil, a free woman equal to any in your domain. This isn't the public or a private box where we must hide. Go see about your guest. You are strong enough not to crumble, and smart enough to fix things, if you break."

She gave Theodosia a push inside and closed the door.

The doctor, Pickens, and Ewan's brother looked up at her then returned to gazing toward the bed. Lester paced in the corner. He didn't glance her way at all.

The scent of sickness, tangy, and singeing mustard filled the room. The familiar perfume of laudanum hit next, as the doctor's fanning wafted it to her. She hated these smells—they always foretold pain and death.

Feet feeling like cold bricks, she forced them forward. "Gentleman, I must know how my cousin is doing. I owe him a great deal. He saved...my son."

The doctor harrumphed. "Couple of broken ribs. He's not breathing well. Can't tell if a lung is punctured. So much scar tissue."

She came closer and saw the valley and plains of the jagged lines upon Ewan's chest. They'd meshed about his heart and ran down half his stomach. Could they have been like iron to protect from the hit of the cart? Could they now keep him bound on this side, away from the hungry shadows of death?

She wanted her ghost to live. Ewan must. He had to recover. She stuffed her hands in her pockets to keep the trembling fear from showing. "Has he awakened at all?"

"He has, ma'am," Pickens said, as he shuffled to her side. The wrinkles of his face folded into deeper lines, thick like the night Mathew had died.

Pickens brushed her arm. "The doctor has given him a great deal of laudanum for pain. He'll have to be a guest for the next few days. Mr. Lester objects."

She felt her head nodding *yes* before any words could come out. "Of course, he will stay. Lord Hartwell and your daughter, too. You're welcome here."

Lester surged from the corner, almost running into Pickens.

"No. None of the Fitzwilliams can be here."

He whipped past Theodosia and stood, feet apart from Ewan's brother. "Take him up the hill."

The fool looked ready to fight. In her house? In front of Ewan and his brother. The viscount said nothing, only stared ahead.

Her butler straightened his silver-colored livery and moved to the doctor on the other side of the room. "Sir, he'll need to be a guest. He's very ill. Repeat your prognosis, sir. Mr. Lester may not have heard."

The doctor moaned again as he wrenched at his back. He sat back on the chair pulled close to the bed. "This man is not going anywhere, if you want him to live."

Visibly wincing, Lord Hartwell came from the footboard of the bed. His face seemed blank and he seemed a little lost. "My brother is horribly injured, Lester. Surely, even *you* can see that moving him would have dire results. Business is business. This is different."

Wanting to offer a hug to reassure Lord Hartwell, Theodosia raised her hand to him, but then lowered it as she approached. He was in a bad way and having her comfort, a Blackamoor's palm on a peer, couldn't be done, even if she offered humanity.

She looked down at her slippers, dusty cream kid leather with green stains, like the ones on her skirts from falling on her knees atop Ewan and Philip after the crash. Courage and fear, both demanded sacrifice. She chose courage and took a step toward him. "Mr. Lester has forgotten this is my house. My house. Mr. Fitzwilliam shall stay, if Lord Hartwell agrees."

Ewan's brother lifted his chin. His light blue eyes widened

as he ran a hand through his rumpled blond locks. "Thank you, ma'am."

"No," Lester said. "Mrs. Cecil is not thinking clearly." He approached and manhandled the bedpost in his sweaty palms. "Nearly seeing your son hurt has addled you. You're vulnerable. Philip doesn't need to see you like this, so out of control."

The only one who sounded hysterical was Lester, but there was no telling that man anything. And his voice. So harsh, it sent her brainbox spinning with fire, but she held her anger. She needed him to comply. "Lester, I appreciate the concern," she said, then swallowed gall. "You can stay, too. If you are so fretful."

"You know I leave for Holland tomorrow. I thought you and the boy would come with me. It would be good for Philip. Maybe he should come with me, since you will be busy with guests."

How dare he try to manipulate her when a man's life was at stake? She stopped twiddling her finger and made sure that her bottom lip was bite-free. "No. My son will stay. If not for Mr. Ewan Fitzwilliam, my Philip would have been killed. And you know what dear Cecil said about hospitality. *When I hungered, you fed me, when I thirsted, you gave me drink, and when I looked strange, you took me in.* There is no more need to discuss this. Fitzwilliam shall stay until he is able to leave on his own two feet."

She turned again to the silent viscount. "I have more than enough room. Your daughter is now in the nursery."

Lester spun her by the shoulder as if she would change her mind, but she wasn't a spinning top searching for direction. "They are our enemies, Theodosia. Lord Crisdon wouldn't do the same for you."

No, Lord Crisdon wouldn't. He'd shun her, like he had in the past, but she wasn't that evil man. "I have been blessed by unexpected favor. How could I ever be sucked into pettiness with my Philip still alive?" Knocking his hands away, she sidestepped out of Lester's reach. "Mr. Fitzwilliam is not the enemy, Lester. He's Cecil's cousin. Surely, my boy's guardian can see that? Today, we are indebted to the Fitzwilliams."

Lord Hartwell moved near, towering over Lester. "Bear this intrusion for now. We can go back to being enemies, fighting over water rights, after my brother recovers."

Lester's eyes grew big, and he looked like a cornered rat. With a shaky palm smoothing his wilting cravat, he swung his head toward the bed, then turned his glare her direction. "You have too many guests. I'll take Philip with me until this all settles down. He can go with me to Holland. Then you can join us."

"No." She stuck her hand against her bosom to keep her heart from bursting. "Don't take him. He was almost killed. I need him here."

Lord Hartwell put his hand on Theodosia's shoulder. The touch was light, comforting, everything she had wanted to do earlier but had been afraid of insulting him. "Leave the boy, Lester. My brother's been moaning for him. He'll need to see him safe and well when he awakens. I'm sure that viewing his little Cecil cousin will make him heal faster."

"This is none of your business, Lord Hartwell. You rule up the hill, not down here."

The large man started to laugh and slipped into the space between them, forcing her nemesis to move backward, one step closer to the door. "Lester, you don't look the wet-nurse type. The young boy should stay with his mother, if you want the

Fitzwilliams gone sooner. Unless you enjoy seeing Mrs. Cecil in distress."

Lester rubbed his chin, as if he hadn't thought any Fitzwilliams would come to her or Philip's defense. "Fine. I shall stay, too. I'll delay the trip."

"Stay tonight, if you must, Lester, but this trip has to go as planned. Holland is business. The first time I trust you to gain new advances for Cecil's fields, you disappoint me." She stared him dead in the eyes. "You know how much it cost to arrange: ten guineas for passage, eight pounds for a new suit for you to represent the business at your best, and now you will not go? I thought that you wanted the business to dominate. I thought I could trust you. You're costing me money."

His eyes darted as if she'd frightened him. "You are a mercenary when it comes to figures."

The man's greed and the need to one-up all the other growers was something Theodosia had counted on, plotted for. This trip would take exactly five weeks, long enough for banns to be read or an elopement to be done with a newspaper groom before his return. Well, that had been the plan, but now she just wanted him gone. She put a fist to her hip and glared at him like her knees weren't knocking. "You know I am right."

He nodded, but before she had a chance to enjoy the victory of him relenting, Lester tugged her hand, leading her to the door. His hot whispered breath scorched her ear. "Don't sign anything and don't forget where your loyalties lie, where Philip's loyalties lie."

She didn't push free, but she stood still and glared at him with every ounce of courage she possessed. He wasn't stealing her son today or hurting Ewan. "Go home, Lester. All is well here. Take care of *our* business."

With a little push, he released her fingers then nodded. "You win. I sail tomorrow for our business." The skunk stormed from the room.

The doctor closed up the sheer curtains. "Fitzwilliam needs to rest. All of you should leave this room until morning. I'll sit with him through the night."

"I will, too, once I check on my girl. Where is she, Mrs. Cecil?"

"The governess and my friends are keeping her entertained while my son sleeps."

"Take me to her. I'll tell her that her uncle is faring better."

Theodosia didn't want to leave the room, but she had to aid Lord Hartwell. With Ewan unconscious, it wasn't the time to have that private conversation about his son. She pulled the door closed once Lord Hartwell stepped through. "Funny."

The big man shortened his stride and walked in step with her. "What is funny, Mrs. Cecil?"

"Your daughter, she kept saying she didn't do it, like a small child could get that cart moving."

Hartwell stumbled, nearly bumping into Frederica. He recovered quickly and bowed. "Sorry. Of course, Lucy would not be responsible."

His brows and forehead squished together, as if he were doing math or numbering something, then he shook his head. "Again, excuse my clumsiness, Miss."

Frederica nodded then swept to the side. "We haven't been formally introduced, sir, but it is Burghley and you are excused. Your exit was nothing like Mr. Lester's exit. He almost ran into us like—that cart." Her face seemed half ready for a laugh, half remorseful. She covered her mouth for a moment.

So many formal rules. Theodosia couldn't think of them all at a time like now, but she needed to consider them, as Tradenwood would be crowded the next few hours, the next few days. "Lord Hartwell, this is Miss Burghley and Miss Croome."

Dipping a chin to each, he relaxed his shoulders. "It is a pleasure, but I wish the circumstances were different."

Different? So many things should be different. Theodosia rubbed her cold hands together. "We must manage as best we can, but time is no one's friend."

With wide eyes, Frederica grabbed her arm. "Is Mr. Fitzwilliam?"

Theodosia patted her fingers. "He's unconscious. The doctor and Pickens are still with him. It will be a long night. My lord, this way to the nursery."

"We'll show him, so you can go back to the less crowded room. Right, Miss Croome?"

Ester nodded and stuck her novel behind her back. "Yes."

"No, ladies," Theodosia said. "Go settle into one of my guest rooms. You all must be tired. You've already done so much to close the festival for me because I was with Philip and my cousin."

They smiled at her with waggling brows, probably hoping she'd spill what happened in the room and why Lester had bolted like a maniac. Not now, not with Lord Hartwell eyeing each of them like he compared them to invisible notes. Well, how many rumors had been started about them by Lord Crisdon or cruel people like him?

With a shake of her head, Theodosia started for the nursery. "This way."

When they entered, the governess was tucking a blanket around the little blonde girl on the chaise. "She just fell asleep," the woman said. "Philip is still sleeping soundly. I've checked on him every hour. No pain tonight. I will turn in myself. Good night, ma'am."

The woman swept past and closed the door behind them.

Lord Hartwell came closer to his daughter. He let his finger smooth the child's curls. "Is it not too much trouble? Having us here? I could take this bag of bones up the hill."

It was a sweet sight, this large, burly man being so delicate with the tiny girl. She turned to Philip's bed in the corner. "There has been enough trouble today, but you have to be here. Your brother may call for you."

"You are kindness, ma'am."

She'd like to think so, but fear gripped her windpipe and squeezed. Too afraid to touch Philip's face and find him a ghost, she stared at her son. A minute or two went by. She'd counted two hundred breaths, Philip's breaths, then heard his snore whistle. Nothing in the world was as sweet.

With her fingers, she swiped back perspiration that the laudanum sometimes brought, then put her pinky on Philip's cheek, his solid, warm cheek. He was a miracle, this time delivered by Ewan.

"Your son. He's not well?" Hartwell had moved near. He'd probably watched her show of weakness. "The governess talked of pain."

She bit her lip, but decided answering wouldn't harm

anything or put her more in jeopardy. "He suffers from severe ear pains, but the governess said he was good tonight."

He drew a handkerchief out of his pocket and handed it to her. If there were tears in her eyes, she hadn't noticed. She was too busy being thankful.

"May I ask why Mr. Lester would threaten to take a sick boy from his mother?"

"He's my son's guardian. His opinion apparently holds more weight than the boy's mother. He also thinks you are the enemy."

Ewan's brother scratched his chin. "My girls are my world. I couldn't be parted from them if they'd had such a harrowing experience. Your cousin, Ewan, didn't hesitate to help your son. He knows the difference between business and personal."

Theodosia did, too. It was the distance between safety and danger and what lengths she'd go to keep Philip well. After another swipe to her cheek, she bent and kissed her son's brow. "Lester's gone. And you, your daughter, and Mr. Fitzwilliam are staying. I can have tea and sweets brought up to the bedchamber."

Lord Hartwell smiled and turned back to his daughter. "Good. That will help the night pass."

Not feeling afraid to leave her miracle with Lord Hartwell, his uncle of sorts, Theodosia headed into the empty hall. 'Twas going to be a long night. Somewhere in the hours or days to come she must find a way to tell Ewan the truth.

What would he hate more, her becoming Mathew's mistress or not telling him Philip was his? She counted on her fingers, divided in the air but the sum came back the same. He'd hate her for everything.

· · ·

Light filtered into the room, sinking into the hairline cracks that were Ewan's eyelids. Everything hurt. It hurt to move, to breathe.

A look to the right, he saw a balcony and doors. Was it the one he'd climbed in his youth? He was at his uncle's Tradenwood.

He closed his eyes again, hoping that he'd dreamed everything, six years spent away from family, losing Theo, his rights to this house, had all been a nightmare. Perhaps he awakened with the world righted.

Yet, one push at his chest told the truth. Scars never lied. Nor did bandages and bruises.

A cough rattled in his lungs. The sputter made things feel like they worked.

Memories of Theo and the festival returned.

Then Philip.

The child, the one with crystal blues eyes—he'd saved him from the cart.

Could the boy be his? He wanted him to be his.

With nothing more than the raw desire to see those eyes again, those eyes like his mother's, like his own, Ewan pushed and tugged but the bedsheets held fast. With a mighty thrust he craned up, but the pain made him flop back upon the mattress. His fingertips brushed leathery ivy.

English ivy?

Had he died or gone insane?

He poked at a dark emerald leaf. The rubbery shape was true, but Ewan might still be crazed. He might have even imagined seeing the boy with his eyes.

"You're awake." Jasper's voice. Was he here in this dream, too?

Ewan turned his head to the left to see his brother, stretching then brushing sleep from his eyes. "Seems the same could be said of you."

Dropping a thick book upon the bed, Jasper shuffled his feet then rose from a chair that had been pulled close. "Resting comfortably?"

Ewan tugged at the strips of ointment-soaked cloth tied across his ribs. "As much as possible."

Jasper moved to the door. "I'll tell the doctor and Mrs. Cecil. They have been attending you without ceasing these past three days."

"Wait. Don't move. Three days?"

Releasing the doorknob, Jasper pivoted. As he came closer, the dim light revealed shadow on his jaw and rumpled clothes. Had he been sitting here, waiting all three days? Guilt and warmth danced inside. Ewan had not lost everything. He still had a brother's love.

"Why do you want me to wait? You are awake. Everyone's been anxious. I can get you back to Grandbole."

"No."

"What? Explain?"

He looked up at his brother and weighed the impact of what it would mean to say his hopes aloud. Another glance at Jasper and his withered cravat convinced Ewan. "My son may be here. I don't think I merely saved a distant cousin on my mother's side of the family, but her grandson. I think Cecil's boy is my son."

Frowning as if he'd eaten a tree of lemons, Jasper wrenched at his back, stretching again. "You definitely hit your head. You are seeing things that are not there."

"Go look at the boy and see his eyes. They're my mother's. I have them, too."

"Cecil is a cousin, Ewan. Surely those traits could be passed along."

Those eyes, could they have been imagined? New frustration stirred. He struggled to get up and fell to the mattress. "You think it is a coincidence?"

"I don't know what to think, but I do know her devotion to Cecil can't be questioned. And why does this matter now? The child is Cecil's by marriage. You claimed to be done with her."

"What if you were a woman—"

"I'm not."

"Jasper, please. You were a woman whose fiancé died in war and you find yourself heavy with his babe. What would you do?"

His brother's frown half disappeared. "I'd go to the country to family or turn to his. Or give up the moppet to Bethlehem Hospital."

"A mulatto baby might not be one of the lucky ones welcomed at that orphanage. If Theo did go to Lord Crisdon, what do you think he did?"

Picking up his book, Jasper plopped into his chair and stretched his stocking feet onto the bed. "You're a playwright. You are making up a story to suit what you want. I should not have read you Shakespeare these past three days. Maria, she liked a novel or a Psalm when she rested."

It was awful to put his brother back into the position of nursemaid. The man was still grieving, but no one had to lose anything if Theo confessed why she had not waited. Ewan swallowed and everything tasted of hope, bright and tart. "Only one person can confirm this. Only one knows the truth. If we stay, she might confide in me."

"She is very upset over your injuries."

"I have to know, Jasper. You have to help me."

"I don't know..."

"Her time of mourning is up soon and I asked her to marry me, but like you, she is corresponding to find a new husband. She hasn't fully accepted me. I think her hesitation is the boy. I need to show her I can be good to Philip."

"Well, almost dying for him is a good start."

"I've tried to let her go. I can't. I want her. I want the boy, even more so if he's my son. I need to know."

"Ewan? You're awake."

Theo had slipped into the room. She came closer. Her almond eyes were wide, maybe with joy. In her hands were a tray of tea and biscuits. "You've awakened."

Jasper said, "I am not sure what did it, ma'am. Between your ivy plants making him good air or this tome of Shakespeare's—all your suggestions have returned the man to us."

Her beautiful full lips seemed to tremble before she leveled her shoulders. "I'm so glad." She put the tray upon the bed table and came within an inch of brushing his brow. Instead, her fingers tucked the blanket. "You need to know how grateful I am to you. You saved Philip."

His gaze locked upon hers and he dared not blink. For a moment, he saw her eyes, dark mysterious pools opening for him, trusting him, believing in him again. If Ewan could grasp her hand, work his fingers between hers, he'd never let go. "I am glad to be of service."

When Jasper coughed, she blinked and backed away.

Their connection—it pounded in Ewan's chest—stronger than six years ago. He wished in his soul he could claim her hand right now.

"My brother wanted to know if Mathew Cecil looked more like his uncle or his own mother. I think, neither. Your son is too handsome to bear the stodgy bones."

Jasper's question couldn't have come at a worse time.

Biting her tender bottom lip, Theo moved away from the bed. "I'm not sure if they favor. I only met Lady Crisdon once. Is there anything that I can do for either of you while you stay?"

Ewan didn't quite know how to answer that. Everything ached, but a battle waged inside him. Was it wrong to want her, the boy, and to feel vindicated for believing everything he'd written in his play? But Theo, unlike others who'd confess or proclaim her innocence, had drawn deeper inside. He'd never win her if she shied away. "I thank you, Mrs. Cecil, for your hospitality. You remembered Shakespeare."

"It was Cecil's favorite. He liked the foul shrew, too."

Her smile, small and sweet—would it last for Ewan, if he pushed for the truth?

Beating her to the door, Jasper stood in her way. "Mrs. Cecil, when your son's lessons are finished, please bring him. My brother's been asking for him and, as we told Lester, it would benefit Fitzwilliam's health."

She seemed to wince, her shawl fluttering, as if Jasper's girls had performed a monstrous trick. "Later. Lord Hartwell, you have not slept in three days. Your room is ready. It's a few doors down the hall. I don't want another ill man in my house."

Almost in a full giggle, Jasper nodded. "I'll sit with the hero a little longer, but then I'll follow your orders. We are at Tradenwood."

She nodded and then slipped out the door.

Jasper put his ear to the wood panel. "Good, she's not an eavesdropper. And she seemed nervous when I asked about the boy. You may be right."

Ewan pushed at his brow. "I'm almost certain Philip Cecil is my son. She passed him off as Cecil's. She's wondering if she can trust me, but what about my trust in her?"

Jasper returned to his chair. "You must've hit your head harder than I thought."

Ewan glanced at his brother and found not a drop of humor in his stern face. "What are you talking about?"

"Mrs. Cecil nearly lost her son. That worm Lester threatened to take the boy if she didn't comply, but she stood up to him so you'd have the best care. I think you need to rest some more. Awaken and see the truth."

"What are you saying?

Jasper slumped more in his chair. "The widow isn't the enemy. I don't even think she's ever been one to our family. I think she is misunderstood."

"You defend her now?"

"You can't fake the fear of losing someone you love. I saw it in her, Ewan. Even when she knew her boy was safe, she still looked as if the world was about to end. It was the fear of losing you." He tapped his rumpled waistcoat, which showed three days of wrinkles. "It matched what happened in here."

Not knowing what to think or admit to his brother or even his own soul, he went with humor. "Didn't know you were so sentimental."

Jasper ran a hand through his unruly gold locks. "I watched the love of my life die. I remember the dread of missing that last moment, of failing Maria. I saw Mrs. Cecil pacing for you, while Lester threatened to take away her son."

"My son."

"That woman has been graceful and kind. You need to look at her through a lens that's not clouded by loss."

"What?"

Tugging at his neckcloth like it choked, Jasper gave up and stilled his hands. "You say you don't begrudge me for being the heir. Maybe that is true. But for Cecil to inherit what would have been yours, marrying the woman you wanted, and giving a name to the boy that might be yours, I'd say you have a right to be disgruntled. But it's not Cecil's fault he inherited Tradenwood or that a woman left unprotected found someone who was willing to marry her. If this boy you saved is yours, would you rather he be a by-blow bastard and not have a name?"

Ewan closed his eyes. The anger at being denied his son dissipated a little. Maybe Theo had done what she had to do. Ewan had not been here to protect her. "A name is important, but I'm here now. She should admit it. I've been here for weeks. Why withhold such a truth?"

"From the man who left her because he couldn't stand up to his father? From the man who wrote a whole play defaming her?"

Hating the list of his wrongs, Ewan wanted to strike out. Pain swelling, he tightened his fist on the blanket. "Well, I must have been unconscious for quite a while, if you are defending her. Last time I checked you held a very different position. Something about a lesser woman, one who'd been a mistress, of a lesser race, and illegitimate to boot."

"Yes. And I've been a fool before." Jasper swiped at his face before folding his arms. "I've spent three days at Tradenwood. Only leaving for a few hours to make sure that the girls haven't burnt down Grandbole before sending them to your mother. Mrs. Cecil and her friends have been generous and caring. Very good company. I've never been around women like them, educated and funny. And Mrs. Cecil has been kind."

"You take her side? Lord Crisdon would be pleased. You *are* looking to marry a rich widow with a love of children."

"You are looking for a villain. You created one in your play, but be mad at yourself or the folly of youth. One is not here."

The weight of truth in his brother's arguments was too great. Ewan dipped lower into the sheets, swatting the ivy as he did. "So what should I do? Walk away and not know if that boy is mine?"

Jasper picked up the book from the bed as he stood. "I think I'll finish this before I sleep; I want to read how things work out between Petruchio and Katherina. I can get the doctor to say you must stay for another couple of days. Make good use of them."

Book tucked under one arm, Jasper took a flask from his pocket and poured a bit in the tea Theo brought. "You're on the mend. The girls are with Lady Crisdon. I can relax a little."

"You didn't tell Mother or Crisdon I was hurt?"

Taking a sip, Jasper's face reddened. "I did, but when I told her we were here, she didn't want to know more. Get a bit more rest."

When the door closed, Ewan released a long breath, deflating what felt like shallow lungs. Would Theo trust him enough to tell him the truth? Was his soul ready to accept if the boy was Cecil's? In either case, could there be a future with Theo and the boy who should be his son?

CHAPTER FOURTEEN

The Lies We Love

Theodosia looked at her dressing closet, waiting for the sound of footsteps. Lord Hartwell's room was beyond her door—Mathew's old connecting chamber. With Ester and Frederica staying in the other wing of Tradenwood, she'd hear the man's boots, if she stayed quiet. Then she'd know Ewan was alone and could be told he'd saved his son's life.

Waiting, she fingered a pink gown folded in tissue on the shelf. It had stayed dormant in the closet. She'd purchased it years ago to wear for Mathew at his birthday dinner. He had liked the colors and the soft silk. But he wouldn't like Theodosia disclosing the secret he'd worked hard to bury.

Bam, *bam*, *swoosh*. Those sounds—they were a man's boots, followed by the sound of a closing door.

It was time. Shaking loose her doubts, she prepared to leave. One final glance to her mirror exposed shadows under her eyes. The angled corners were red. It had been hard to sleep, in the three days it had taken for Ewan to awaken.

She stepped out in the hall and spied Pickens coming up on the landing. He held a tray in his hand. The bowl on it steamed and smelled of broth. Bread was nicely buttered on a plate. "Evening, Mrs. Cecil."

"Who is that for? Lord Hartwell?"

"No ma'am. I gave Mr. Fitzwilliam the last of the laudanum. He mentioned wanting some nourishment."

The perfect excuse to be unaccompanied in his room had presented itself. She approached with hands wide. "I'll take it to him."

A brow rose on the butler's face. "Yes. And the footman retrieved this note."

Her breath caught until she saw the scrawl. The squire, not the baron. "Put it in my room."

He gave her the tray but took the letter away. "Shall I come for this later?"

"Yes. In an hour. I'll yell if I need you sooner."

"Good, but I was more worried about Fitzwilliam. You have left him on your doorstep so many days since his return to Grandbole."

Theodosia wanted to smile at the man's accurate memory, but she must focus on Ewan and saying the right words to him. "He'll manage."

Pickens held the door open for her. "Godspeed to both of you."

Chin up, she marched inside. The room was darker than before, no doubt from the sun finally setting. A sole candle flickered on the bed table. It cast a warm, healthy glow on Ewan. He didn't look so pale or as pained as he had before. That gave her energy. This wasn't a deathbed confession, though it would end the truce they'd formed. That saddened her to the core. She didn't want him to hate her again.

Leveling her shoulders, she strode all the way to the headboard. "Ewan," she said as she set down the tray on a bed table. "Are you awake?"

His eyes opened. Hypnotic, bluer-than-blue, his gaze grabbed onto her as it had before, when gratitude overwhelmed her soul.

"Theo, dear Theodosia, you don't look well. Is something wrong?"

"I...brought you some broth."

With a slow, jarring motion, he raised his hand from beneath the sheets and clasped hers.

The hold was light. She could break free if she wanted. "Ewan, I brought you some broth."

"You said that already."

"*Umm.* Would you like some?"

He nodded, shut his eyes, and released her.

Her freed fingers were like ice. She broke the bread, taking a small piece and soaking it in the savory brown liquid.

She looked at his strong jaw. The grown-up version of the button nose she saw every night. She stroked his cheek as she often did Philip. "Open."

He chuckled but complied. Two pieces down, he nipped her finger, suckling it before giving her palm a kiss.

Too surprised to move, she stood there, letting him have his way with her hand, nuzzling it against the light rasp of shadow on his jaw.

With a heart beating like crazy, she still didn't move her hand. It felt too nice. The joy she should've had when she'd seen him at Burlington Arcade, she let it free, one tear drop at a time down her nose, her cheek. Ewan, her first love, the father of her son, lived. And he'd almost died again saving Philip.

Grunting, he reached up and wiped a tear from her lips. "I don't want you crying for me. Have you come only to feed me? There are questions you have to answer, like will you marry me when I can stand?"

"I have to tell you about Philip. Your son, Philip."

There wasn't any shock in his expression. Instead, Ewan smiled wide.

"You know?"

"When I saw his eyes, my eyes, right before the cart hit me, I suspected. I've lain here torturing myself, wondering if you'd trust me enough to tell me. Wondering what it would be like to hear the truth from you. Now you have more reason to marry me. I want my son."

"I'm sorry, Ewan."

Hooking his palm behind her neck, he drew her closer.

She could feel his labored breath on her nose, but he went no further. "You thought me dead. You made your choices going to Cecil. He took a mistress who soon proved to be pregnant." Ewan tilted her and towed her into a deep embrace. "I understand."

She couldn't accept his truth, not when Ewan's forgiveness made Mathew weak. Stiffening, she eased his palm from her shoulders. "You think I fooled Mathew?"

"Did he know or did he feel guilty for impregnating a mistress when he was three or four times her age?"

The scorn in his voice sliced through her. It was fine for him to think her a jade, but to make Mathew's choices sound anything less than admirable was too much. She bolted up from the bed. "Don't you dare make this Mathew's fault."

"I know it's my fault. For dying, I mean, almost dying in the war."

"If there is a fault, it is mine. Mathew was good and decent."

"Theo, you don't have to protect him. You were confused,

alone, carrying my child. You wanted that babe to have a name. I understand. You have done nothing wrong. Once we marry, everything will be right."

She wrapped her arms about her waist to keep from slapping her hand across his face. "I told you about Philip because you needed to know, especially after saving his life, but I don't want this to be another thing between us to cause hurt. I don't want to always be reacting to you, to keep hurting you."

"It's fine to be reactive. It's called being alive. Not living so carefully. You used to like that."

"And what did I get for that? A ghost that hates me. A boy who can't hear."

"I don't hate you. But what about Philip? What's wrong with my son?"

She tugged on her shawl, pulling at the fringes, trying to hide, but she couldn't. The truth demanded that she face Ewan. Leveling her shoulders, she turned back to the bed. "When I discovered that I was with child, you were with your regiment. I didn't know how to write you. I thought maybe your father would send me to you. I went to him and he refused to see me. Then one day he saw me in Town and tossed a note at my head. I had a shop owner read me the most horrible news—that you'd died. I'd lost you and any hope of doing better than my mother."

"You weren't a prostitute."

"The streets don't make a distinction from a woman troubled by love or money. This baby wouldn't have a real name. Philip, the Flower Seller. How would that be? The one thing I promised myself—"

"Theodosia, if I'd known, I would've married you. I want

back every moment with you and Philip."

She held up her hand to block his words. "I trusted you with everything. Then you changed your mind and abandoned me with a promise of a year."

"I'm sorry. That was wrong."

She waved him silent. "I'm not done. You need to hear me. I must say this without thunder or fear twisting up my words. I thought I forgave you, when you died. I couldn't hold on to that bitterness, I had to survive. I tried to work to save money before Philip came but bad thing after bad thing happened. Your father banished me from picking his fields, and my cart was stolen. I couldn't get to Covent Gardens to sell in the mornings. I worked as a field hand but couldn't make enough money to eat and have a safe place to sleep. I began to starve."

The horror etched on his face made her heart hurt, but she had to tell him why Philip was deaf. He forced himself to sit. There was pain on his face, his breathing sounded rough. "No one would help. What about my mother?"

"One person helped." She returned to Ewan, picked up his bare feet, and swung them back in the bed. "Mathew Cecil caught me stealing from these fields. I thought he'd turn me in. They would have hanged me for stealing. That might have been a way out."

Ewan lay back but he kept his hand on hers, clutching it to his night shirt. "It was stupid to rise, but I didn't want you so far from me."

She freed her palm, but stayed at his side. "You will when I finish. Mathew had me come to his patio and he fed me sliced chicken and bread. The first full meal I'd had in months. We talked about flowers and how he wasn't watering his lavender right. He told me his favorite place in the summers was sitting on the patio. He smiled and let me ramble on with all my nervousness, wrong words. But he was a gentleman."

"So how did you become his mistress?"

"It was your mother's idea."

Ewan's lip twitched. He blinked liked he'd become crazed. "What?"

"She caught me leaving Tradenwood. She blamed me for you having gone to war. That you would be alive, if not for me. I told her I had your babe, I put her hand on my stomach, but she didn't believe me. She said harlots weren't faithful. She warned me to never mention your name again."

Her throat clogged, remembering her desperation. Swiping at her eye, she said, "I begged her to help. She said to starve or find a new mark. I went out into those fields and cried half the day. I wanted to die, but how could I let the only thing left of you go? I saw Mathew's carriage pass, and I thought about my mother and this babe in my body. So, I washed in the waters you and Lord Crisdon want. I snuck back to Tradenwood. Mathew was asleep on the patio. I lay at his feet."

"Voluptuous you, wet from the river, dropping at Cecil's feet. I already said I hate him, correct?"

"He woke up and I threw myself at him, tossed my arms about his neck, like I'd seen my mother do at the brothel, like I did to you in the carriage. But he didn't want me. He wondered why someone who knew how to grow lavender would do this. I sobbed as I told him about you, and you dying, and that I would do anything to have enough food to save this baby."

Remembering her desperation, she felt her eyes stinging, but she stood tall. She owned her mistakes. "He agreed. He said I would be his mistress. He moved me in to the room I sleep in now. He spent tuppence on vegetables, six pence on meats and cheese. I'd never eaten so well. Philip felt better inside. I had hope again."

"So then what happened?"

"He confirmed my story with your father and even your mother. And right before I was ready to pop, he came with a special license. He said family takes care of family and proposed to me."

"So he didn't coerce you."

"No. He was kind. So wonderful with Philip. Got him every doctor that could help. When he was born, he was perfect, but then the palsy set in. He has some hearing in his right ear. None in his left. When you were yelling for him to move, he couldn't hear you."

"Theodosia, I saw the child in trouble. That's all I thought of. I didn't want him hurt or for you to suffer. I didn't suspect until I'd saved him and saw his eyes. I'm his father."

"No. He is your flesh, but Mathew is his father."

"On paper, but that is only because I didn't know. I'm grateful Cecil aided you."

Shaking her head, she pulled his hands away. "I was grateful to him, but you were still locked in my heart. There wasn't room for Mathew. He wasn't you. He didn't like the gravel of his voice, so he hired tutors to read to me. He didn't do things like you, but when I saw how he took care of Philip, how he stood up for me, even listened to me to improve the Cecil lavender, installed my ideas about hothouses, I grew to love him. Yes, I loved him very much. I was safe, completely safe for the first time in my life."

Ewan dropped his chin, rubbed at his neck. "I didn't make you feel safe."

"No. Your mind was changed by your family. How could I ever be a safe again, when one word from your father could change your mind? Mathew didn't care what anyone thought. He gave me and Philip his name. I wasn't Theo the Flower Seller. I was Theodosia Cecil."

With his face blank, Ewan looked away. "You really did love him?"

He had to know it all, and Theodosia refused to hold in her feelings. She patted her broken heart. "I was a wife, in every sense of the word, to Mathew. He gave me honor. He loved my sickly child. He waited for me to love him. Yes, I loved him with all I had."

Ewan frowned and his eye held a light she'd never seen. "So what do we do now? I want to know my son. You haven't answered my proposal. I still want to marry you."

"You are Philip's cousin. You saved his life. You can always have an influence, but Lester is his guardian. He may not want you around. And once I marry again...things will be awkward."

"Marry me. I should never have left you."

"But you did. We are not the same people, those two stupid lovers caught in a thunderstorm. You don't know me now."

"I never thought I'd left you in such straits. You were so strong and determined. I didn't think you'd faced such things. My family should've sent you to me. I should've taken care of you."

"You didn't know what I needed, Ewan. And we should have thought of the dangers of what would happen when our love was illicit. I know you say differently, but I'll always wonder what test your family will have of me."

"Theo...Theodosia. I know my own strength now. I will fight for the dreams we share."

He tried to lay back but didn't seem to have the wherewithal.

"I don't dream anymore. I close my eyes and I see nothing. You should rest." She rose and tucked the blanket about him.

He grasped her hand. "I'm serious about marrying. We could find what we had. You loved me once."

Her heart remembered, and it beat as hard as it had in the carriage the night of the theater, or the balcony, but that would mean being vulnerable to him again. And his family. Though Lord Hartwell seemed nice, it wasn't worth the risk, even if the touch of him made her pulse soar. "Get some rest. I'll—"

The door to the chamber opened. Pickens stood there with Philip. Her boy cried hard and held his ear.

"Ma'am," Pickens said, "the pain just started up."

She held out her arms and gathered the boy up. "Philip, it's going to be better."

"What's going on, Theodosia?"

Ewan sounded angry but she couldn't help him. Philip needed her.

She bent and smoothed his thick black hair.

He held on to her leg. "Ma-Ma. It hurts. Hurt so bad."

"*Ssh*. It will be better. Pickens, the laudanum?" Her heart exploded. "We're out of laudanum."

"I sent a footman, but it will be hours. Perhaps there is some at Grandbole?"

"No. Nothing from there." She capped her mouth, then released it, and then scooped Philip up. She'd do anything for

Philip but beg at hateful Grandbole, but she couldn't leave her son in pain. "If I can't get him calm. We'll ask Lord Hartwell."

The mattress creaked from behind. Ewan had sat up again. "Get an onion. Warm it, cover it in cloth. Put it on his ear."

Her face surely showed every fret and concern her mind could conjure, but he slapped his palm on the bed. "Trust me. It's an old soldier's remedy."

Pickens came to her side. "Ma'am?"

Not knowing what to do, she decided to listen to the only person who sounded calm and reasonable. "Do what he said."

Pickens nodded and left the room.

Ewan heaved and waved. "Bring him to me. Bring my son here."

She stumbled a bit, bouncing Philip against her shoulder, but she brought the tear-stained boy to Ewan and laid him out on the bed. As usual, he cried in silence like the quiet world he was becoming a part of.

Her heart broke again.

Ewan ran a hand over the boy's chest, his little jaw and nose. He mumbled something, a prayer, a wish.

Theodosia clamped her palms onto the bedframe to keep them from trembling. She was afraid for her son, afraid of how content Ewan looked comforting Philip, afraid of the way her heart pounded at the sight of them together.

It was too much, and her fear too great. The letter from the squire might be the answer to keeping Philip and her heart safe forever.

• • •

Ewan passed another quiet week in Tradenwood. He spent the early mornings reading to Philip. The warm onion helped the first night and the two other times the boy had ear pain. It was hard seeing the little man suffer. And poor Theo, every time, she looked as if she'd fall over from fright.

Swinging his feet out of bed, he sent the English ivy jiggling. Whether it made good air or not, it showed Ewan that Theo cared. She never stopped his request to see the boy, but rarely did she stay. The woman was simply too stubborn or too afraid to admit the obvious, that he could be a good father to his son, and that they, all three of them, could be a family.

Why deny the attraction that was as sweet as the lavender in the hand lotion she used? Maybe she needed more convincing. He shrugged as he pushed aside the foul Shakespeare that he'd read to his son today. Philip was a lovey child, well-mannered but quiet, very unlike his nieces. Unfortunately, the few words the boy spoke had a heavy lisp.

To think, this boy might've been more perfect, hearing out of both ears, if he hadn't left for war or if his father had showed some compassion. And what of his mother? She had known Theo had his child and had turned her out to starve. He expected such cruelty from Lord Crisdon, but not Mother.

Tired of languishing even with Shakespeare, he rose and slid into his breeches. It took a great deal out of him to stand, but solitude was bringing him no closer to convincing Theo to trust him. And though he'd rewritten his play with the name Cleo and had made her Egyptian instead of a mulatto, it wasn't enough of a sacrifice for her. What would be?

He managed to head down the stairs, clinging tightly to the

banister with each step. The exercise felt good. His lungs didn't sting as badly as they had before. Maybe he'd have enough strength to kneel and propose.

At the bottom of the treads, he huffed and repacked his chest with the savory air of a roast of some sort. Music and laughter carried through the hall, and he turned his head to its source, the blue polished drawing room.

Peeking into the opening, he saw Jasper sitting close to the pianoforte. One of Theo's friends, the duke's daughter, played a jaunty tune vigorously on the grand instrument.

He heard clapping across the hall in the parlor. As stealthily as he could, he backed up and craned his head to spy inside. Theo's other friend read a book on the chaise. In chairs, holding glasses of wine were the doctor and a new older man, one with a receding gray hair line. A second glance didn't return the man's name to Ewan, but Jasper had so many physicians visit, it was hard to keep the names straight.

The last confirmed what Theo had said about Philip. He was going deaf. He didn't think it possible to be more angry at himself. If he'd stayed, all could've been different.

Leaning against the wall, he sighed and sucked air through his nostrils. Where was the lovely hostess?

She wasn't with the boy. She'd come for him and had put him to bed at his typical time of seven.

Then it hit him, the one place she would be. The place she seemed to love the most, the patio.

Not wanting to interrupt the music or get mired in small talk, he left the house and made his way around to the terraced gardens.

The wind stirred but he could still hear the lively tune of Miss Burghley's. In time with the beat, he cupped his hand to his face and craned his neck, scanning left and right.

There Theo stood, a beauty in a gray gown. Though he hated the mournful color, he loved how the bodice melted against her form, how the lacy cap sleeves showed forearms that held onto things with her strength and delicacy. Right now, he understood her.

She must've heard him and turned in his direction and started to descend, moonlight hitting her here and there, all the right places. A few steps away, her hands folded as if she wore a shawl, but no amount of wool could hide her loveliness. Her dark, shiny hair was coiffed in ringlets and sculpted her long neck. "Why are you out of bed?"

He took a step and came out of the shadows. "I needed to see a real flower. Mrs. Cecil the prettiest rose in Tradenwood or Grandbole."

She looked at her patio, hers and Cecil's place, as if she would flee, but didn't. "I thought you gave up haunting."

"How could I when it leads to a moment alone with you? Theodosia Cecil, may I have this dance?"

He held an arm to her. "It's not thundering. I'd like your hand given to me in trust. I won't let go."

A hundred seconds passed but she took his hand.

Slowly, he twirled her. She bit her lip then smiled.

He moved her farther from the steps. Nothing need interrupt them.

When the music slowed, she leaned her head upon his shoulder. "I always liked your height."

"I always liked you."

She reared back. "Don't talk like that. Be my good cousin."

He strengthened his hold, pushing her closer to the bruises on his chest. "Is that all you want, a good cousin? You had dreams. Remember owning your own flower shop? You were going to make blooms for my actresses."

Her face lifted and her eyes widened, beautiful pools of fine teak. "You remember?"

"I hope I wasn't always self-absorbed. Of course, I remember. What do you want now?"

"I want Philip whole, Ewan. I want him to have a full life."

"You and Cecil have done well. He's a great boy."

Her smile widened as he twirled her again. He kept at it, conserving his energy until she collapsed into him. Panting, she clung to him.

He ran a hand along her chin. "I dream, too, but mostly of a kiss. Just one. One without the fear of being tossed out at the docks again. One that you give because you trust me."

"Be serious, Ewan. What if we are caught?"

"I'll kiss you again in front of the voyeur. Indulge me, Theodosia. Your heart has moved away from me. And you have every right after how I left you, but I will praise you, for you are fearfully and wonderfully made. I marvel at how you've worked these fields, all the variety of flowers that you have bloomed. When I am with you, I know my soul is right."

She pushed at his hold, but he didn't have the strength to keep her, not if she wanted to go. "Please."

"I hid you. I made you keep our love a secret. That was the lowest, but I know that your pretty almond-shaped eyes saw my substance, how imperfect I was and you loved me still."

This time she pulled away and put her back to him. "Is that more Shakespeare?"

He approached and placed his palms on her exposed elbows, the beautiful skin freed of gloves. "No, a little King David, a great poet for only the best women. Lead me, Theo. Tell me what it takes to win your trust."

"I thought poets spoke of love."

"I know I have your heart, Theodosia. It's been in my breast pocket next to my scars. I know the truth about us. Trust, the lack of it, keeps us apart."

She looked down. "Your hands, they are light next to mine. You need sun, then maybe they wouldn't be so different."

"Theodosia. It's night. The moonlight doesn't show much difference. You married Cecil, a man whose age alone would make him paler than me. What is it?"

"Your father thinks we are too different. I won't put you in the position of having to choose. I remember how you needed your family's approval. Even now you've haunted me to get the water agreement."

Theo was sticking with all the old arguments. None of it mattered. She needed to be that daring girl, the girl he had once believed fearless. "Then kiss me good-bye. I will keep Philip's secret and be his good cousin. I want one kiss as payment. You know costs. You'll feel good paying. Then, we are done."

With a shake of her head, she turned to face him. "It's not right to kiss you tonight."

The music played but not louder than his heart. It thudded against his sore ribs, "My mind, my soul, neither has moved from that day you said you loved me. It's been that way since I saw you in the fields. Since you listened to my foolish dreams. If you are saying we are done, release me with one kiss."

She slipped her hands about the revers of his nightshirt. "One kiss good-bye?"

Maybe she was reaching up to kiss his cheek, but he intercepted the offering and tasted her lips. She was delicate and sweet like cloves. So vulnerable, in ways he'd never imagined. It made him want to bundle her up and hide her safely in his chest.

Pushing away, she took a half step but was still in the circle of his arms. "This must stop. You can't haunt me anymore. No more trying to get back to what could've been."

"I don't know how to rid myself of you. Teach me." He dipped his head to hers again and whispered good-bye across her mouth.

Like a wildflower, she bloomed. She stood up on tiptoes and kissed him. The passion was light, safe. If that was all she could give, he was prepared to accept, but then his Theo returned.

She grabbed hold of his collar and kissed him more deeply, demanding to cross the invisible line he'd allowed her to erect.

Her hands clasped about his neck. She held him tightly and searched him. She needed to find in him whatever she needed.

He clung to the curves that burned his soul.

Nothing tentative, nothing reserved in her response to him.

He cocked her head back and tasted her jaw, nibbling along her throat, the tender flesh exposed above her pearl necklace. "I love you, Theodosia."

He held his gaze upon irises so dark, so large and wonderful. "I have always loved you, always will."

She leaned up and took his kiss again.

Arms tightening, he lifted his chin above her head. He had

to get this right. "Marry me, Theodosia. Let's take Philip and go to Scotland tonight."

Stumbling backward, she tore away and began righting the pins in her bun. "That kiss was good-bye."

"No, it wasn't. Unless you are sending me to war again. That kiss said 'marry me and have at me'...in that order."

She dropped her head in her hands. "You make me out of control. I won't do the wrong thing for Philip."

"You know I'd never harm him. I would die before that happened."

She drew her arms about herself. "Mathew taught me to reason. There is nothing that tells me this time will be different. Your mother and father will never change. I accepted my squire's proposal tonight. We are engaged. Once the banns are read, we will marry. You and I will be formally done. Mathew would approve of him, and he has no family to please."

He saw it now as clear as the night sky. Theo was afraid and used the memory of her late husband as a shield. "Theodosia, there is still a ghost haunting you. Mathew Cecil. Do you think if you choose me, he'll disapprove from the grave? You're still in half-mourning garb, when your time has passed. He's not coming back. You can't earn his approval."

"He was a great man."

"He was much better than I. But he wouldn't want the woman he loved to live in fear."

Theo patted her lips, then smoothed her gloves. "You do. You want me to live in fear. How long before your father makes a new ultimatum, or how will you deal with a snub at one of your mother's parties, that is, if she even dared to invite me. I can't go back to that. I won't. Yes, let Mathew haunt me. I have to keep Philip as safe as he would want, and I hate to have to bear another name than Cecil to do it. Lester is Philip's guardian. Only a man, a new husband, will be someone the Court of Chancery will respect, and the Fitzwilliams won't be able to hurt us again."

It was suddenly very hard to breathe. Her truth had sapped his strength, made everything heavy.

"I can live without Lord Crisdon's blessings," he heaved. "But not your touch. I won't convince you. You have to see we've both changed, enough to make the love last this time."

He started back into the shadows, but turned and took a final look back.

She brushed at her face. Maybe she even cried a little for their loss. "Good evening, Cousin Ewan. I wish you happiness."

"If you truly did, you'd marry me."

He trudged back to the side door. He'd had that type of trepidation six years ago when his father had caught them in the carriage house. Being a soldier had given him the time to become brave, to learn how to live without Crisdon's blessing. But how could he live without Theo? Was there a way to change the family she feared? Well, he must work fast. Banns only took a few Sundays, then there would be no more time for Ewan and Theodosia.

CHAPTER FIFTEEN

Unveiling Truth

Ewan let Jasper help him down from their carriage as they arrived at Grandbole. Convincing his brother to leave Tradenwood seemed a more difficult task. Perhaps, he enjoyed the short holiday away from the girls, with them staying in Town with Mother.

Jasper held up his arm, though he didn't need it. Ewan was determined to leave the place as soon as possible. "You're very quiet. Not jealous of Mrs. Cecil's new company?"

"I am jealous. That is her fiancé."

His brother stopped halfway up the stairs. "Did you ask her to marry you?"

Ewan heaved heavily as he took another step. "Yes. I laid out my hopes and she trampled them like the runaway dray."

"No wonder you've been out of sorts since the good widow had that squire to dinner. You want to go back and put up a fight. I'll get my sword."

Even if he wanted to watch his brother change from his normal lumbering self to a fleet swordsman, how could Ewan spend another minute witnessing Theo accept another man, and a stiff colorless one, at that. One who probably did not see her beauty or humor. One who wouldn't appreciate her number calculations or her biting wit, though he would taste that tender lip she bit when nervous. "She doesn't trust that I will protect her or the boy's interests. She thinks they will become Fitzwilliam pawns. I haven't figured out how to convince her otherwise.

Would Father swearing an oath to her help?"

Jasper nodded. "Father swears a great deal sometimes, but I doubt Mrs. Cecil would want to hear that. Maria weathered everything with grace. I hadn't thought of how his attitude would make things difficult."

As the footman opened Grandbole's door, Hartwell walked in first, tossing his hat and coat on the side table. "I'm sorry. Truly sorry."

Ewan didn't even know what happened to his hat. Being laid up in Tradenwood, he hadn't even thought of it. Theo would think of the cost of it. "It's done for now."

"Done?" Lord Crisdon stood at the center of the hall. "What is done? Did you secure the lease or something more?"

Bracing his weight on the show table, Ewan shrugged. "Nothing was accomplished."

Jasper tugged off his gloves. "Well, Widow Cecil did assure me she will sign our lease. We won't run out of water."

His father harrumphed and strutted past a portmanteau. It sat alone near the end of the stairs. He must've returned from town. Yet with no sign of large ones or lots of maids, it meant his mother hadn't returned. Lord Crisdon had failed to convince her. "Mother's staying in Town?"

"She has other ideas and is trying to reform the grand-daughters."

His voice sounded sad, sadder than he'd ever noticed. Ewan had sympathy for him. Trying to convince a woman to trust you after disappointing her was a hard task. Theo would marry someone else while he stood by, alive, desperately in want of her.

"Why the delay in signing? You two have been down at Tradenwood for two weeks. Lying about?"

Ewan looked at Jasper, hoping his brother had something to say to stop the earl's accusations.

His brother only chuckled. Then with a fold of his hands, he launched into a Cheshire cat-sized grin. "Well, Widow Cecil is busy preparing for a wedding."

Lord Crisdon rubbed his chin as a smile of half-scrunched lips erupted on his face. "So you got the Blackamoor to agree. I suppose I'm happy. Not that my son will marry her, but that Tradenwood will be back in our control. Oh, the sacrifices."

Anger and humor bubbled up from Ewan's gut, threatening the air in his lungs. "I'm not the one she's marrying. She doesn't want the sacrifice of being a Fitzwilliam. We are beneath her."

His father blanched. All the color drained from his disapproving cheekbones. "You're not engaged to her?"

"No." Tiring, Ewan headed to escape up the stairs.

"Wait." Crisdon stormed ahead and planted a foot on the first step. "That goat Lester beat you to her bed this time?"

Gripping the banister, as if he could wring it like a neck, Ewan glared at the man. "No one's in her bed. She's an honorable woman who has accepted an honorable proposal."

"Son, you were under her roof and couldn't entice her. You did a better job six years ago with the harlot."

Not wanting to fight, Ewan swallowed the itch in his throat, the gall of the fool. "Pretty hard to be seductive while ill and fighting to breathe. I'm better. Thanks for asking."

The man paced back and forth. He seemed unhinged. "So

someone else will get her fortune. Why on earth did I put faith in you?"

That statement hit Ewan worse than the wagon, maybe even worse than receiving his father's letter so many years ago about Theo taking up with another man. "You brought me out here as bait. It wasn't about being a family. It was about a chance at reclaiming Cecil's land."

"If your uncle hadn't thought you dead, Tradenwood would've been yours. Your mother won't come back here until I get back what's ours."

"Ours? You mean yours. Everything is about you. If I had gone through with my original plans to elope, instead of taking up your bargain…maybe Tradenwood would be mine, but I'd have a wife and a son—"

"So now you'll let another man play father to the boy?"

He knew. The earl had known. Every last illusion in his head broke, ripped and tossed like edits to the page. Ewan grabbed the man by his coat. "You turned her away when she came for help. You could've saved my son such pain."

"Ewan," his brother said. "Let it go. It's done. Six years done."

Jasper's hands were on Ewan's trying to break his grip, but nothing could stop him from shaking the truth out of Lord Crisdon.

"I need you, Father, to say it. To be a man like you've called me to be. Say you tried to kill my flesh. That your hate made my boy go deaf."

Jasper let go and stepped down. "No. Father, tell him no."

Crisdon struggled but he couldn't break free. He caught Ewan's gaze. "Yes, I knew. Your mother told me. She wanted her run off, and I did what she wanted, everything she wanted."

Ewan tossed the man back. His hands shook with unspent anger.

A sneer started in Lord Crisdon's eyes and trembled down to his drawn mouth. "I didn't think you had it in you to finish me." He rubbed at his neck. "I don't target women, but your mother insisted on getting rid of her. I had to make it up to Lady Crisdon for sending you away. She virtually left me when the harlot got the benefit of her family's wealth. She won't come back until it's fixed."

"That's a lie, old man. Mother is not like you."

Lord Crisdon chuckled and righted his emerald-blue waistcoat, his freshly tailored coat. "We were united in getting it back at any cost, even sacrificing you for her Tradenwood."

Was Mother guilty, too? No, this had to be another convenient lie. He rubbed at the pain in his neck and moved to the door. "The bait failed. I'll tell Mother myself about failing tonight. Oh, and Mrs. Cecil wants twenty thousand pounds a year for the rights to water. Have fun paying that. I'm done with you."

Ewan couldn't tell if it was the absurdity of the number or the fact that he mentioned going to Mother's, which sobered the man, but Lord Crisdon ran to him, sputtering no.

Ewan turned his back on his father. "Jasper, I'm taking your carriage indefinitely. I'm going back to Town."

"No, Fitzwilliam," Crisdon said, "Stay. Your mother might come back to Grandbole, if you lived here."

He leaned upon the door and stuffed his shaky hands into his pockets. "Then you are both out of luck."

Lord Crisdon harrumphed and swung his hands desperately.

"Stay put or your play will never be performed. I was busy in Town, too. The manager at the Covent may buy it, but the committee won't approve it. No one will ever see it."

If he'd blinked, Ewan could've sworn it was six years ago. He'd just consummated his love with the woman who understood him better than any, but to curry his father's fleeting favor he had agreed to join the fight in Spain.

He turned back to Lord Crisdon and fluffed the cravat he'd mangled. "This is one offer I refuse. In fact, I will never darken this estate's threshold again, not until Jasper's made earl. And don't fret, old man, I need to confirm Mother's hand in this sorry affair, then she won't see me again, either. I did die six years ago. I'm a ghost to you."

Maybe the earl was shocked at Ewan's resolve, for his stone face broke a little with his lips poking out as if he'd swallowed pebbles. "An idle threat. You don't have it in you."

"I can be mercenary, too. There's some vengeful Fitzwilliam blood in here. Good day."

Crisdon shuffled about him. "Leave your mother alone. She's entertaining tonight. You can see her tomorrow."

Ewan kept moving. "She'll answer tonight."

His brother caught him by the shoulder. His big palms squeezed out Ewan's air, but he didn't know that only death would keep him from the truth. "You're both not rational. We should reason this out. Father say something. Don't let him leave like this."

Still ashen and pale, the earl groused and fisted his hands. "What are you soft, too, Hartwell? That's why you can't run this place without me."

Jasper turned from the earl and stared ahead. "Be the bigger man, Ewan. Don't separate from us again. The girls need their uncle. You can't be gone again."

"If you had to choose between Maria and this place, which would you choose?"

The shimmer in Jasper's clear eyes brightened; he pushed past Ewan and held the door open. "Take care of my horses. My gift. And get as far from here as you can."

"I'll borrow the horses tonight, but see me in Town, old boy, bring the girls, if they promise not to burn my flat to the ground."

With a final rap upon his brother's thick knuckles, Ewan strode out of Grandbole. The clean, free air hit him. If only he'd done this six years ago. *If only.*

Climbing into the carriage, he grunted, then motioned to the driver to head to Town. There was a countess he needed to see. His hope was that she was innocent or misunderstood, not duplicitous. He would not jump to conclusions or write the story in his head as he had with Theo.

With eyes shut tight, he lay back and took one long breath, then another. The memory of Theo's last kiss kept his mind right where he wanted it, centered on the rage building in his chest.

The two-hour ride to London seemed like minutes. Music could be heard outside Lady Crisdon's townhouse. Every window was bright with burning candles. He tugged his wrinkled coat, swiped at his missing hat. The musty smell of ointment and carriage leather would turn heads, but Ewan did not care. He hobbled up the steps and pushed inside.

At the top of the interior grand staircase, he saw three moppets. Dressed in fashionable ivory and pale salmon pink ribbons, they looked like Dresdens. His mother's work made them look perfect—perfectly trapped.

Lucy smiled at him. Then returned to her statue-like pose.

He nodded but he wasn't here for them. "Where is Lady Crisdon?" he asked Mother's butler.

The man dressed in a shiny satin blue coat pointed him to the big drawing room. "But I should announce you."

"No. I am her son. I'll do it."

Ewan didn't wait for a response and stepped inside. Tables were strewn about with the finest silverware and crystal. Even the gilded trim of the room sparkled. The fashionable ilk sat at the tables chatting over their dinner, something that smelled of fowl. They hardly noticed him.

When Mother lifted her head, her pretty blue eyes widened. "Ewan?"

"I came to see you after staying at Tradenwood."

She rose quickly and came to his side. "Dear boy, you didn't have to come tell me of your engagement. I have a party. We can discuss tomorrow."

"I need to know something now."

She took his arm and smiled as she giggled at each of her guests.

When they finally were alone in the hall, the joy faded. "Ewan, you could have waited, and you could have come more suitably attired. I keep different standards than what you may be used to."

"I have to ask you one question. You need to hear me."

She went to a console mirror and fluffed a curl, fingered the giant ruby necklace at her throat. "Yes, Ewan of course, but go refresh yourself, then join me—"

"Mother, did you go after Theodosia when I left to join my regiment? Did you turn her away when she asked for help?"

She lowered her gaze and picked at the folds of her fan. "Is that what she told you? They lie you know. I wasn't kind to her, but I suppose that is to be forgotten with you marrying her."

His mother played coy, and she could be as stealthy as the earl when it came to secrets. He straightened and offered her rope to hoist her canard. "So you will accept her and my son with the return of Tradenwood."

"Of course, dear." She put her satin hand to his cheek. "You've restored our loss, what was wrongly taken."

She didn't hesitate. She said everything in a calm tone, as if she were deciding menus.

He sighed, the sting to his gut worse than a mule's kick. "And you've broken my trust, Mother. You knew, too. You knew Theodosia carried my babe and yet you turned her away."

Her breath caught, and she started fretting with the lace on the handle of her fan. "I was grieving, and it was her fault you were sent away."

"No. It was *my* fault I went away." He folded his arms and sought the right words to make her feel his loss. "There is no wedding. You will never have Tradenwood. You don't deserve it. Probably why Uncle didn't leave it to you when he had the chance." He pivoted, leaving her with her mouth falling open.

"Ewan. Ewan?" Her voice was loud enough for guests to hear. "Wait."

"Mrs. Cecil wants nothing to do with us. I don't blame her at all."

He marched out the door and didn't stop. The family he wanted to belong to had ruined the family he could have had. How would he survive so many cuts? No play, no father, no mother, no Theo. He put a hand to his chest. His story wasn't going to end like this. He was a cousin to a little boy who liked Shakespeare. He'd not lose access to him, no matter what.

• • •

Theodosia gripped Philip's hand as she and Frederica ventured into the Burlington Arcade. Four weeks had passed since Ewan and his brother had left Tradenwood, and this was her last week as the widow Cecil. The final banns would be read Sunday. She and the squire could marry ahead of Lester's return. Her plan had worked. It had worked so well, she cried herself to sleep each night. When the picture book Ewan sent for Philip came in the morn, she cried all over again. She choked up when Pickens told her Ewan had left Grandbole, never to return. He'd broken with his family, something she hadn't wanted to happen. What pain this must be causing him?

Was it terrible to want her ghost to return and haunt her one more time?

Yes, it was. Engaged women couldn't have ghosts or regrets.

Frederica, dressed in a pale blue walking gown, strolled a few steps in front of them. Her head was high. Not a care in the world must be on her mind, but with all the colors and sights of the shops, who could blame her?

As if she knew Theodosia's thoughts were upon her, Frederica stopped and half-turned. "Why are we here again? Bonbons? You rarely come to Town unless on business. And I don't like the openness of this place, not without the duke."

Readjusting Philip's small hand within hers, Theodosia attempted a smile, but found her lips too heavy, or she'd moved to biting both the top and the bottom ones. "I needed to pick up a few things, maybe seek a designer for a wedding gown. Maybe check for a letter."

"You've accepted the squire, but you are rethinking the matter? Good. You shouldn't grasp at crumbs, when a bonbon might be on the next platter."

"Men and food? Well, one could never say your mind is fixed upon a single path. I want to see if the baron ever answered. With so much happening with the banns and my cousin, I forgot to have someone check. If the baron wrote, I need to tell him I'm no longer looking for a husband. I want to finish this advertisement business right. Correct. Rightly."

She shook her head. "That Fitzwilliam cousin of yours. He was scrumptious, a fine piece of bonbon. Now that he's returned to health, you haven't mentioned him."

"He's gone from the fields."

"Yes, you seem sad about that. Philip, too. During his convalescence, I awoke unfashionably early and found Mr. Fitzwilliam reading to his...your son. What exactly happened?" She pulled closer. "We've been friends a long time. It's fine to fancy him again."

Again? Have I ever stopped? "I don't know what to do. I marry the squire in a fortnight. Philip will be safe. The squire will represent me at the Court of Chancery."

Frederica's lips pulled into an uncharacteristic frown, all sour-lemon-puckered mouth. "You could go. You could do it. You're an honorable woman. You don't have to rely on a stiff bore. Stop selling yourself short. You know numbers. What value do you put on you? Pences or sweet pounds?"

The squire wasn't exciting. He seemed honorable and quiet, but hadn't Mathew taught her that quiet was better, better than uncontrollable fire. Irresponsible blazes burned and hurt too many. "I'm not a duke's daughter. The courts will look at me worse than how these shoppers eye Philip, trying to figure out which one of us is his mother."

Whipping her head from side to side, Frederica allowed her smile to return. "Or they are waiting to see if we have a pet monkey following our unusual entourage."

Theodosia cringed at the memories of selling flowers on the streets to ladies like Ewan's mother. They'd parade a Blackamoor page and exotic pets behind them on shopping days. "I want to scream at them to stop looking, but that would get us kicked out."

They passed the soap store and Theodosia peeked inside. Only the horrible manager was there, dusting his green glass vials. A smile rose inside. Sally was in the country, and Theodosia had given her enough money to feed herself and that baby to come. She bent to her own baby and straightened his coat. "I've saved one shop girl. Maybe I should be a reformer, too."

Philip cupped his hand to his ear as if he wanted to funnel in all the sounds. Theodosia wished she could put all the sounds in the world in a bottle for him.

"You rescued a desperate girl. You are bold in business

288 THE BITTERSWEET BRIDE

dealings. Why not be that in the rest of your life?"

Theodosia couldn't answer, not when a thunderstorm could reduce her to a quivering mess. Instead she leveled her shoulders and tightened her grip on Philip's small fingers. "Let's go see if there is a letter from the baron and then leave. This will be done. My newspaper search for a groom will be over."

As they rounded the corner, their path intersected with Lord Hartwell. "Mrs. Cecil. Miss Burghley, Master Cecil. How are you this fine afternoon?"

Her mood lightened as she saw the smiling man. Ewan's brother had been an amiable guest and so loyal at Ewan's side. He stuffed a paper into his jacket and came toward her. "Doing a little shopping?"

"Yes, picking up a few things. And Philip has never seen such architecture. He enjoys it as much as Miss Burghley."

Chuckling, he stared at her then turned to Frederica. "Yes, I can see her hazel eyes sparkling." His gaze lowered to Philip. "There is nothing quite like Burlington Arcade, is there, young man?"

Panicked that her son couldn't hear to answer Lord Hartwell, she stepped forward. "How is your brother faring? I haven't seen him in the fields." She bit her lip, realizing how stupid she sounded, admitting to looking for the man she'd rejected.

"I'll tell him you asked. I am dining with him tonight."

Frederica tugged at her gloves as if she'd suddenly become bored. "Where will you dine in Town? Maybe somewhere rife with intrigue."

Wanting to tap her friend and make her stop man-bubbling, Theodosia edged forward. "I suppose he is busy with his play."

"No, Mrs. Cecil. It's not going to be purchased. It seems the theater manager... His mind was changed."

"His play was rejected?" Her heart broke a little more. No. He was too good. Ewan must've said no. Could he have done that for her?

As if Frederica had read Theodosia's mind and read it wrong, she shook her head. "So sorry for Mr. Fitzwilliam. Was it not good enough?"

Lord Hartwell's brow rose. "It was quite excellent. The best I've read."

"It had to be excellent," Theodosia said. Her voice carried and more people turned and looked their way. Thinking of Ewan losing another play made her not care how loud she sounded. She stared straight into Lord Hartwell's eyes. "The theater owner couldn't see that?"

The man tapped his fingertips together. "Our father doesn't want a playwright in the family. And suddenly the offer for my brother's play disappeared."

Theodosia couldn't breathe. Somehow this had to be her fault. She swallowed and held onto Philip a little tighter. "He must be devastated."

"No, ma'am, something else had already bitterly disappointed him."

The look in his light blue eyes, wistful and sad, made her sadder. Ewan had surely told him of her rejection of his proposal, but it was for the best. "Your father has been known to have his way. Is there no way to appeal?"

"It would take hundreds of pounds and persuasion. That's a mighty sum while we are in the midst of this water war. Fitzwilliam says twenty thousand pounds is your sum."

She reached into her reticule and pulled out one of her cards with her mark. "I have given you my word on resolving the matter. There's a number that we can agree upon, I'm sure. After my wedding, I am sure there will be lot of things that can be agreed upon."

Lord Hartwell frowned. "All depends upon who you marry."

She'd said too much. Her hurt for Ewan clouded her judgment. She held out her palm and offered her card. "Take this and tell the theater person I will cover what is needed to get his play performed."

Frederica had that devilish grin on her as if she'd eyed the last bonbon. "I see you decided on pounds. Yes, Lord Hartwell, be her errand boy. That should be fun for you."

Something sparked in his eyes, and he turned from Frederica back toward Philip. "You are persuasive, Mrs. Cecil, but I don't make the best errand boy." He folded his arms. "You do know his play disparages a young woman, a flower seller who some might think is you."

She stuck her card in his face. "I know. But he deserves to have this play."

This time Lord Hartwell took it. His face reddened, and he coughed. "You have distinctive handwriting, Mrs. Cecil. Yes. I will take this to the manager and do my best to get the play purchased." He stuffed the card into his breast pocket. "Are you prepared for the excitement and gossip a play like this may bring?"

"Pounds worth. I'm not what people say I am. I am who *I* say I am. Your brother deserves to have his vision on stage. Please say you will take care of this. A Blackamoor woman may not be able to negotiate it, but I can definitely pay for it."

Jasper tipped his hat. "Character trumps a great deal of things, even rumors."

A crowd of ladies passed by, staring and giggling.

Frederica seemed above it all, as if they couldn't possibly be the object of their scorn.

But Theodosia knew. She felt it in her bones. "Not everyone can see that. And it doesn't matter how much strength one possesses. It's still in the same package. A woman needs a champion."

Frederica pulled closer, as if she tired of being ignored. "Yes, a champion to do her bidding, now go on, good little viscount."

Lord Hartwell's dimples popped as if he suppressed a laugh. "It's been a long time since someone's teased me or called me little, but I will handle this. I'll make sure Fitzwilliam gets what he deserves. Mrs. Cecil, Miss Burghley. Good day. The errand boy is leaving."

The grin on Frederica's face almost made Theodosia laugh. Her friend enjoyed tweaking everyone, but teasing a man. That was better than her beloved bonbons.

As they entered the stationers, the humor fled and Theodosia's fingers became ice-cold. She had to admit to herself, that she hoped for the baron to write. Truly, she didn't want to marry the dry squire. With Philip cupping his good ear as his head bobbed from side to side, they waited for the clerk.

Frederica played with the lace eyelets on her fan until the young man came forward. "Mrs. Cecil. There have been no new letters."

Even as the clerk moved and went to another customer,

Theodosia found herself stuck in place, hoping that a mistake had been made.

But she had no such luck. The baron had never sent a response to her reply. Her letter of regret didn't pass his muster or perhaps her sin was too great. It didn't matter. The imagined romance was done. "Let's go."

After winding back through the arcade, Theodosia heard humming. Not her classical pianofortes but something the fiddlers had played at the festival. Lively and in beat, as if she skipped around a Maypole, Theo sang, "So no baron, no playwright, but a squire, a boring squire. He will save the flower seller."

"You think this is funny?"

Frederica gripped her arm. "Your plan to get you a husband from the advertisement worked. But my plan to use it to get you to meet men and dream again didn't. You stopped dreaming when Cecil died."

No. Six years ago. But she'd had a waking vision of Ewan on her balcony, asking her to trust him again. "Frederica, I don't know what to do."

"You don't need a new husband. You need an errand boy and a good solicitor. Let's pay for a man to fight your cause."

"What?"

Frederica bent and scooped up Philip. "Yes. Let's find a man and pay for his services. We can even have a solicitor draft paperwork to buy off Lester. He has a price, too."

The girl had lost her mind, or maybe the lack of bonbons for the two-hour drive had reduced her to nonsense. She followed behind her flirty friend who spouted nonsense. "I accepted the squire. Why risk it all now?"

"Because you are worth the risk. If you could see the look on your face when the clerk said 'no new letters,' you'd know I speak the truth. You don't want the squire. You deserve the dream of what our riddle-writing baron offered. Let's go to my father. He can get you a solicitor. Then Ester and I will help you craft a rejection letter for the squire. This is one *no* I can't wait to write."

One of the most infuriating things about Frederica was her ability to transcend from silly to wise in mere moments, but she was right. She didn't want the squire. "Can this be done? Paying a man? What would that cost?"

"Less than what you paid for the play for your playwright cousin. You and I, we are daughters of women who were paid to entertain men. I think it quite fitting for you to buy one."

Frustrated, Theodosia picked up her pace to the carriage. Her thoughts whirled inside. A solicitor would still be representing a Blackamoor to the Court of Chancery. That hadn't changed, but buying off Lester was an idea. "How much would that cost again?"

"Less than selling all your hopes to the squire. You are strong, Theodosia. Mathew Cecil found you when you were in a bad way and needed protection, but you forgot about the girl who fought living on the streets. The girl who escaped brothel life without a duke's pity."

Theodosia spied herself in the shop glass. Older, cut in finer clothes, but where was that fighter? She'd made Mathew listen to her and now the Cecil farm grew the best lavender in the world. She'd made Ewan listen to her, and he had respected her decision and abandoned his haunting. Today, she had implored a viscount to do her bidding. If she could get three men to listen, was it so impossible to get another, like a magistrate, to side with her? She took a breath and counted her fingers, numbering every word of encouragement that Mathew and Ewan and her mother had ever poured into her, even the things her own mother had done to hide her from sin. "Yes. I will try. I will fight."

Frederica gripped Theodosia's cold fingers. "You will win, as easy as you do with math calculations and prices. Let's go buy a man."

After settling Philip in the carriage, she looked up at the blue sky and then down into his bluer-than-blue eyes. She could fight for Philip. She had to hope she was heard, not dismissed because of her race or her humble start at a brothel by the docks.

CHAPTER SIXTEEN

My Own Man

Ewan sent the toy horse across his desk one last time. The thing buzzed and rolled across the well-worn surface, almost loud enough to drown out the impatient knocking on the door of his leased rooms. He'd bought the toy the other day on one of his walks in Cheapside when, as now, he couldn't think of what to write. Where was the freedom words had always given him?

The knocks continued. It had to be Jasper. His brother had faithfully come each week to sup. It was something he treasured, but the man probably needed a respite from his daughters and Lord Crisdon.

Corking his bottle of ink, tweaking the position of the horse to his quill, Ewan sighed. "Coming."

Pulling at his rumpled waistcoat, he rose. His walk to the door held its own lethargy. When he unbolted the sliding lock, he was stricken by something worse than lightning—pure shock. "Mother?"

Lady Crisdon stood fidgeting, as if trying not to touch her white gloves to his threshold. "You haven't come to see me."

She had never left her salon all the time he'd been back. Now she stood at his entryway.

Mother sauntered inside, in her dark crimson carriage dress with gold fobbing, making him miss his uniform.

"Ewan. Your father says you won't return to Grandbole."

He shut the door and leaned against it. "Well, I suppose it's something we both share."

"That is different. I like being in Town for the Season, but you, you should be there, not here." Her pert nose lowered as she said, "On this side of Town."

"Why? Did you need me to make another go at widow bait?"

"You liked her once. Your father caught you bedding her. It didn't take too much of an imagination to think there could be hope—"

"Hope of what? Making my family whole or gaining Tradenwood?"

"Do you hate hearing the truth? If you hadn't been thought dead, Tradenwood would not have gone to the Cecils. It wouldn't be in the hands of that..."

"Woman. Is that the word you seek?"

She squinted and her face turned mean, diminishing her fair features. "Usurper. That is more fitting."

"But wasn't it you who told her to go to Mathew Cecil? It's rather cruel to castigate her for following your instructions." Going over to the door, he held it open. "Good day."

She didn't take the hint and moved to his desk. Picking up the carved toy, she traced the rounded lines of the horse's mane with delicate nails.

A new sense of anger hit his gut, swirling, tightening. How could she touch the toy he'd bought for his son?

She even spun the heavy wheels. "You don't care that this creature has what belongs to you?"

No charity remained in his soul, for it was clear Mother had never cared that Theodosia carried his child. He pried the toy away from his mother. Safely tucked in the crook of his arm, he released his breath. "She does have something that belongs to me, but because you didn't care six years ago, I'm rejected now."

She looked at him as she played with the fingers of her silky gloves. "I'll apologize to her, if that will make things right."

He smiled at her and leaned down. "Go whisper your apologies to the boy, Philip Cecil. Do it soon; he's going deaf. Seems starving makes for long-term problems, ones begrudged words can't make go away."

Her mouth opened, then closed, then opened again. "I'm a good person. There are charities that could've helped."

"Yes, I'm sure there are plenty waiting to help a Blackamoor carrying a mulatto baby." Fingers shaking with repressed fury, he put the toy down, whipping his hand to the door. "Good day, Mother."

"I'm sorry, Ewan."

Pointing again at the door, he watched her pout and sigh, reminding him of how she used to make him think Lord Crisdon had been cruel to her. "Go back to Father and make amends with him. You two are of the same mind. Use his money and buy the widow off. I want peace, and it can't be had caught in your struggles. Theodosia was right to not want to be a part of this family."

"Ewan." Her lips thinned and she poked at his sparse chair. "I wanted nothing of the usurper. But that was a long time ago."

"I love words; Shakespeare's the best. 'To thine own self be true, and it must follow, as the night the day, thou canst not then be false to any man.' To be true to me, is to know the truth of your cruelty. It cannot be forgotten. I wish I could choose to be a Cecil, not a Fitzwilliam."

"We are not all bad, Brother." Jasper strolled inside and headed straight for the toy. Moving it about as if he tried to avoid eye contact, he pushed the horse back and forth. "For Lucy? And am I interrupting?"

"No and no. Mother was leaving."

She wiped at her mouth and walked to the door, as if her short heels were mired in mud. "Lord Hartwell, you send the girls to me any chance you get."

"Will do, Lady Crisdon."

She grasped the revers of his brother's coat. "Convince him of what he owes to the family."

"Of course. Ewan, you must support...which side again? The Fitzwilliam side, the one that leads to bickering, or the other, like good old Cecil, who supported family. It's a tough choice."

Mother frowned and released him. "Remember who will help your horrible wee-ones get ready for their come-out."

"Good day, Mother. This is a threat-free dominion." Ewan took her palm and placed it on his heart. "Go in peace."

Head drooping, she traipsed away. She might be angry now, but Ewan didn't think it formed from the right things. That made him dour. He shut the door. "You are early to this side of Town. My neighbors must be curious to see such comings and goings."

"I had a busy day. Was a bit of an errand boy. How are you feeling?"

He leaned over his writing desk and again positioned the toy about a thumb's width from his papers. "Good."

Jasper tossed his hat on the chair and snaked off his gloves. "You don't look good, but I have some news that might uplift your spirits. I had a nice conversation at Burlington Arcade."

"Burlington Arcade?"

"Yes. I checked my box. It had a reply from my widow. You sure you are feeling well?"

Ewan spun around to see his brother hovering a bit close. "I said, yes."

"Good." Jasper reared his fist back and belted him in the mouth, knocking him flat. Ewan fell, barely missing the desk.

The man wiped his knuckles with a handkerchief from his pocket, then extended a hand, lifting Ewan from the floor. "You deserve that."

Rubbing his stinging jaw, Ewan nodded. "You still pack iron in your fists. Glad you went for the face, not the chest."

"Well, I do want you recovered."

"Sorry, Jasper, but I tried to keep you from the widow Cecil. It didn't seem right."

"You are not very Fitzwilliam. That's why you did it wrong. The conniving is supposed to advance things. Not waste my time or the good widow's. And we left the poor girl without a response for weeks."

He nodded, all while exercising his jaw, opening and closing his teeth. "So she sent a letter of regrets. Did she rail on about me seducing her, then leaving her in dire straits?"

Jasper's face lit up like bright candles in a chandelier. "No. That would have been more interesting. No, she said... Well, maybe you should read for yourself."

Ewan took the paper and scanned the lines. It said nothing of her complaints from the carriage. It read:

I have no clever rhyme, just truth. I grieved so long and hard over my first love, carrying him in my heart that I missed the joys in front of me. I live with the guilt of not being enough help for my child.

Something lodged in his throat. Remorse and a judgmental nature made for difficult mouthfuls.

I feel the weight of a sorrow-filled heart finding new love when I thought it closed. I feel so heavy.

"That's what she wrote."

His brother took the letter back and pointed at the last lonely sentence, a swirl of black ink on the very ivory paper. "The guilt of a surviving heart is mighty heavy." Jasper's eyes dulled. He pulled a flask from his pocket but then pushed it back inside. "She closed with: *If you can understand these regrets, I look forward to meeting with you and the mutual acceptance of our proposal.* That is bold; she's not even waiting for you to kneel."

"Not me. That's not my letter."

"You dolt. She is saying that she was in love with you. And she, like me, clung to sentiment too long. She has expressed her fears, yet she still reached for you, us."

Ewan couldn't give in to hope. She was engaged to another. He flipped his head side-to-side. "She has refused me to my face."

Jasper shook his head. "She refused the man who threatened her with a play and who originally left her in order to gain the old man's approval. She doesn't know the new Ewan, the one who's stood up to his father and, it appears, his mother, too."

Optimism started filling his heart but leached out. His lungs must still have holes. "Why can't she say these things to me? Not a letter."

"That is a minor concern, if you love her. You do love her, don't you?"

What did his feelings matter? He craved a dream so much he'd bought a toy for a boy he could never father. He shrugged. "She's made her choice. It wasn't me."

"Sad. That would make the errand I ran for her silly."

He stared at his brother, all while daring his own heart to slow its rush, a tiny bit of hope stirring it. "What did she have you do?"

"I've come from Covent Garden. She gave me her mark to pay any fees to sponsor your play. She charged me with spending up to a thousand pounds for a play that disparages her, for a love she can't forget."

"What? She can't fight my battles."

"Perhaps, but Brown is waiting to see you. The widow Cecil was right. He's open to bribes to withstand Father's threats. Go settle things with him and then go answer your newspaper bride."

"My play has to stand on its own. I couldn't let you bribe him. I can't let Theo—Mrs. Cecil pay my way, either."

Raising his arms to stretch as if he tired of being a busybody, Jasper yawned. "So are you going to go fight for the play? Our newspaper bride?"

If he could get this play sold, despite Lord Crisdon, and despite Theo's offer, that would be the way to prove his merit to himself. "Take me to Brown. I am selling a play today. Then you are buying me dinner."

"What of the widow? She isn't married yet."

"She has chosen her new husband. Perhaps, I should let her have her peace."

Jasper seemed downtrodden again, but he donned his hat and started to the door. "Perhaps, she'll get to that wedding day and change her mind."

Ewan spun the horse toy again before following his brother. If the good widow was ready to spend money on Ewan's dreams, maybe that was a signal that she was ready to trust him again. He'd haunted her to change her mind, but would she come to Ewan and bewitch him with her changed heart?

. . .

Holding his breath, Ewan stood at the side of the curtain. He mouthed the line in silence as the actress said Cleo's infamous line, "The price to my heart is a banknote you can't pen."

The actress did it, head held high, then strutted off the stage with her hips swaying. The audience erupted. The laughter and claps shook the place. This was the third week of the play, but the moment felt like the first time.

Brown came up to his shoulder and chuckled. "This play is a hit. I must admit, you coming to Covent demanding I buy this play for a measly fifty pounds was a gamble I was willing to take."

All smiles, Ewan tugged his coat. "I knew these words were gold. I knew how the audience would love them. Admit it, Brown, this was a great deal, only cost you a few more author's benefit nights."

"Yes. It took the fear out of me crossing Crisdon. He hasn't made a peep of problems. Yet, with this being the third night of your author's benefit to a packed crowd, minus my fees, you stand to clear a tidy sum. What are you going to do with this small fortune?"

He hadn't thought about it. *A bigger flat? A gig of my own, instead of borrowing Jasper's?* "I don't know, but I'll have to make it good."

"Well, maybe you should take some time and start thinking about your next play. I'll want it. You even got the old Duke of Simone to come, dark money and all."

Ewan's pulse raced, thinking of the last dark money night. That night when he'd first given in to his attraction, when he'd believed Theo would be his. So many things he hadn't known about her, hadn't thought to know about her.

She had trusted him in that moment and he'd taken the opportunity to seduce her again. What a foolhardy thing for a man in love to do. But if she were here seeing his play, the least he could do was thank her. If not for her trying to help him, he might not have pressed Brown. He wouldn't be living the dream of his heart, seeing his play performed. "I'm going to see if the duke has brought all his special guests."

Not waiting for the final act, he spun and was out of the theater, heading to the private stair before Brown's gobsmacked mouth closed, releasing cigar-tainted breath.

Conquering one tier of steps, then another, Ewan stood tall on the final landing.

What if she'd changed her mind, come to see his play, but the shy girl lost her nerve and couldn't tell him? That's how he wrote it in his head. His heart pounded as he made it into the lobby. A few people lingered, but most were in the packed boxes. He headed to the final one, Simone's box.

As he approached, Ewan heard laughter and hoped there was that one off-note in the tones, caused by someone biting her lip. Impatient, he pulled back the curtain. The duke's box was crowded, but to the back were two beauties, Theo's friends. Two, not three.

His heart dropped. He backed out, closing the dark curtains.

Disappointment wrapped about him like the shroud to this box. Of course, she wouldn't come. The stubborn woman was probably off with her squire on a wedding trip. She hadn't changed her mind.

Before he could turn and go back down, the curtains parted and Miss Ester Croome came out. She had a hand to her mouth as if she struggled to say something, but nothing came out.

"Yes, Miss Croome."

She took a breath. "Mr....Mr. Fitzwilliam, I thought that... you're well?"

He put his hands behind his back. "Yes, and you look well. How is Miss Burghley?"

"She's fine. She'd come say hello, if she wasn't afraid of disturbing her father. It's rare for him to come...with us."

Shifting his weight, feeling foolish, he nodded. "So I hear."

She waved her ice-blue fan that perfectly matched the lace on her long gown and crisp bonnet. "Your play is very good. Your Egyptian character Cleo. She's nothing like a certain friend of mine."

"I know. Your friend was never this character. Tell the new bride that, next time you see her."

Miss Croome's brows rose. "You don't know. She didn't marry the squire. She begged off. Miss Burghley and the duke, they helped her get a solicitor. They drafted things for Lester to sign, but he won't. Now she's fighting him at the Chancery to change the guardianship."

Ewan didn't know what to react to first, that Theodosia didn't marry or that she was fighting for Philip. His heart answered both. "She's still unmarried and she's in court. Did she get it done?"

The young woman looked to the floor. When she raised her head, he saw fear in her chestnut eyes. "She hasn't heard yet, but it doesn't look good."

Anger heated in his bones. He scrunched up his fists. "Can't they see Lester has no interest in the boy?"

Miss Croome yanked off her light gloves, exposing her smooth chestnut skin. "It's difficult for the courts to rule against a man for someone less-than. Lester has even used the accident at the festival against her. Mrs. Cecil is desperate. She's sending the boy abroad tonight, and she's selling Tradenwood to the Earl of Crisdon...your father, tomorrow. Then she is leaving for good."

He started backing up. "I don't think she's taken into consideration what her cousin thinks of this plan. Excuse me."

Ester rushed forward and hugged him. "Keep my friend and her son here."

"I'll try my best." He started down the stairs, only stopped at the office to collect his benefit even before the play was done. He had to hire his way to Tradenwood and haunt his cousin one more time. She needed to see he was his own man in need of the right woman. Surely, she'd let him prove he'd fight every hell to save their son.

CHAPTER SEVENTEEN

Getting Love Right

Theodosia tried to remain calm, but the maids couldn't pack fast enough. The Court of Chancery would rule any day now, but the solicitor she'd paid for, who had even hired a barrister—all said the same thing—no hope. Cecil's will was like iron, specifically naming Lester as Philip's guardian. A new husband might equal him, but now there was no time.

At this point, Lester would have to sign the solicitor's carefully drafted papers to give up his position. Why would he, when his goal was to control her *and* the Cecil fortune?

She went down the hall again, touching walls and trim. She hated leaving. Tradenwood was Philip's home. But at any moment Lester could come take the boy. He was so angry at her for refusing his proposal. If not for Pickens, he would have struck her when he learned she'd nearly married the squire.

All pretense of tolerating her was gone. He'd hurt her or Philip to have his way.

Wandering into the nursery, she saw Philip sitting in the middle of the blue rug.

"Ma—ma." He smiled then went back to flipping pages in the picture book Ewan had sent him.

The governess must've been careless, leaving things where he could pull them down. Yet, as she came closer, she noticed it wasn't that book, but foul Shakespeare. Philip must still remember Ewan reading it to him in those days he had recovered at Tradenwood.

"You miss him. You miss him, too."

Arguing, cursing sounded from below. Lester. He had barged into the house, again.

Scrambling, sliding in her slippers, she scooped up Philip and looked for a place to hide. Under the bed? A table? The closet? The dark closet.

Swallowing hard, she ripped open the door. "I'm so sorry, Philip. This has to be done." She put him up on a high shelf. "Stay quiet." Her voice sounded like her mother's and she didn't mind. "It's for the best."

He nodded as she moved a blanket to block the view of him. Watching the darkness cover her child—his blue eyes squinting as she closed the door—broke everything inside. It might as well have been a coal shuttle.

The footfalls on marble pounded like thunder. She froze for a moment then moved far from the closet and stood near the window.

The door to the nursery opened, slamming against the wall.

Lester stood at the threshold. "So, it is true. Portmanteaus everywhere. You are running. You actually thought you could take the boy without me knowing."

"Yes. I should've left yesterday." But she had wanted to see her friends one more time and hear how they had enjoyed Ewan's play. She shook her head and tried to push past him and lead him from the room. "My comings and goings are none of your concern."

"But the boy is."

She was still mistress of Tradenwood tonight, and she needed to bluff him out of the room. Chin high, she said, "You need to leave. You are not welcome."

"As his guardian, I should know his whereabouts, which means knowing your whereabouts."

She tried to pass him, but he blocked her. She huffed her frustration. "You were not invited in this house. You don't get a say."

"Yes I do. When will you learn to heel?"

"I'm no dog, Lester. Get out of my way."

He chuckled, hard and heavy, as he forced her back into the room. "So the dog is trying to run. You act so brave. I almost bought it. You're nothing but a lucky wh—"

"I am more than you will ever be. I have honor. Strength that you can't touch. Things vermin like you will never understand."

The sneer washed from his face. He gripped her hand and tugged her to him. "You've been nothing but trouble. And I'll inform the Chancery of your neglect. Shouldn't you be making me offers, not guff?"

Theodosia slipped from him, leaving her gray widow's shawl in his meaty palms.

She stood up tall. Didn't dare bite her telltale lip. "You and the Chancery are too late. He's gone. Your threatening ways are over."

Dumping the wool, he looked under the bed and the table. "You didn't have time to get rid of him."

She tapped her chin, playing the part of a conniving shrew. "How long ago did you last see Philip? When was that? Yes, before I tricked you into going to Holland—weeks ago?"

Fists balling, he charged toward her again and wrenched her arm. "Philip, come on out here before your mother is hurt. You hear me, boy? I'll break her arm."

He tugged on her elbow until she screamed, but Philip made no sound in response.

"Break it off, if you must, but my boy is safe from you. He's gone."

He tossed her to the ground and sputtered an obscenity. She landed hard on her backside, the floor stinging her hip. "Take my offer for money. You don't want me as a wife. You want money to buy your own lands. I'll give you ten thousand pounds."

"You think you can buy me off, you slut? Why settle for a slice? If I control you, I can control it all." He yanked her up from the floor. With a hand to her neck, he pushed her against the wall. "Where is the mulatto?"

She tried to buck free, then stilled, looking him dead in his eye. "Hit me if you must. But you'll never have my son. You'll never control me. I'm not afraid of you."

Lester cursed, spitting in her face. "You should be."

Theodosia closed her eyes to blunt the sting of his arm coming for her, but nothing came. When she opened her eyes, she saw a scuffle, flying fists. Ewan and Lester traded blows.

She blinked to make sure she wasn't dreaming, then ran to the door and screamed, "Help! Lester has lost his mind."

Evil Lester blunted Ewan in the back, smashing him against the closet door.

It shook, and her heart nearly stopped.

Nothing stirred or sounded. Philip had to be fine. He had to be.

The wind seemed gone from Ewan. He gasped and gasped, but he reared up. "That all you have?"

"No." Lester took a run and aimed his fists straight for

Ewan's chest.

Ewan groaned at the blow, then he turned his head her way, and laughed. "He has to do better. Ghosts are hard to get rid of."

Lester shook out his fingers. He moved again toward Ewan, but two grooms barged into the room.

"Get Lester," she said. Her shaky voice surely sounded pitiful.

The men grabbed him and kept him from moving.

Ewan came and took her palm. "Did he hurt you?"

Lester twisted and tugged but couldn't get free. "Theodosia, get them from me. I will make you pay. I'll get legal action on you for shipping off Philip."

Ewan's blue eyes clouded.

Would he judge her again and believe the worst?

He released her hand and her heart fell, crumbling past her stomach.

Wrenching his neck, he pivoted to Lester. "You are a pest to my cousin. What will it take to make you go away?"

"Why do you defend her? All the Fitzwilliams hate her."

"She's the only one of us beyond reproach. A caring mother and an honorable widow. If she sent him away, it was for his good." Ewan stalked over to Lester. "Mrs. Cecil, your grooms can let the man go. I think he is in control. Perhaps even reasonable."

In her head, not a doubt remained about Ewan keeping her from harm, but to let Lester go? A second glance at Ewan and his encouraging nod, she motioned to her footmen. "Let the fiend go."

Lester smoothed his dusty brown lapel with his red fingers, then he splayed them in the air. "What's in your coat, Fitzwilliam?"

"Scar tissue, my boy, can be quite hard. Or was it the blade in my pocket?" He whipped it out, a long knife with a pearl handle.

He made circles with it, before putting it away.

"The witch sent the boy away. I am his guardian. I have rights to know his well-being."

"Theodosia, is my little cousin well?"

"Yes."

"See, Lester. All you had to do was ask." Ewan started to laugh and winked at Theodosia. "There's a benefit to scars. They make you harder. More dependable. Perhaps they make one shrewd. Tell me what you need to go away."

"The Chancery will know that she denied me my rights. And running away won't do anything."

"The courts will be happy that Mrs. Cecil has packed her bags. She's eloping. Young Philip will have a new stepfather."

She wanted to object, but to do so would allow her enemy a foothold. So, she stayed quiet and nodded like a fool. Maybe she was one. She was depending solely on Ewan.

Lester's face broke. The shock made his chin drop to the floor. "What?"

Ewan came again to her side and lifted her hurting palm. "You were right, Lester. I have a tendre for my cousin. She has finally agreed to marry me. We are eloping." Ewan waved her letter to the baron in the air.

She felt her mouth pop wide, but she closed it and bit her lip. Something untoward had occurred, but the look in Ewan's eyes, one of *trust me*, made her nod again and say, "Yes. I did propose. You know the solicitor said the court will favor Philip having a father, more than a guardian. And Mr. Fitzwilliam doesn't have a conflict of interest. He's not trying to wrestle away Philip's fortune. Unlike you, he simply wants to love the boy. Who do you think the courts will side with, you or the son of a peer?"

Lester rubbed his hands together. He paced a bit. "Then I'm left with nothing."

Thinking about how Mathew would do things, she decided to allay the bull. "No, you are not. Sign the papers in the parlor, and I'll still give you ten thousand pounds. You can buy land. You take all the knowledge you've gleaned from me and Cecil and have your own. That's what you really want."

Lester paced some more. "I have to think about it. You wouldn't offer if you had no doubts of winning."

Ewan stepped in front of him. "The widow is trying to help you save face. She wants this over. For her peace, we'll offer a sum of twenty thousand but only if you agree now, and only now."

That was blackmail payment. Ewan had gone too far. She wanted to box his ears, spending so much. "That's too much. It's not—"

"To have him go away, so you can be free, the Fitzwilliam side of the family will repay this amount." He turned to Lester. "It's only a deal, if we do this now. Take your chances at the Chancery and get nothing. What say you?"

Lester's head swiveled from left to right. He flexed his fingers. "Yes." He sneered and pivoted to the hall.

"Follow him, Ewan. The papers are in my desk in the parlor. Then send him from my house."

"Theodosia, I will make sure he never harms you or Philip again. Where is my son?"

When her gaze went to the closet, Ewan shot there, too. He opened the door, sent a few blankets sailing, and brought out her sleeping boy. He kissed his forehead then handed the boy to her.

"Stay up here until this is over. I'll come back for you this time."

She waited until Ewan had left before letting her sobs free. As his footsteps faded, she hugged Philip tighter. "You were so good. I'm so sorry."

Tear after tear released, but she couldn't fully breathe until Ewan returned. Philip wasn't safe until those papers were signed.

"Don't cr-cry, Ma-Ma."

But she had to.

She'd hid her child from ugliness in a dark space, but he couldn't hear the ugliness. That was a blessing.

Something deep inside her opened, and she took a full portion of air. So many years ago, her mother had done the same thing, closeting away her babe in a coal scuttle. Today, she became her mother in a very good way, like she had six years ago, to protect her child.

The front door slammed, followed by more footsteps.

Ewan returned, he came inside the nursery and lifted her up. He put Philip on his shoulders and lifted her palm. "You are safe from him, Theodosia Cecil, but not from me."

She reached up and smoothed Philip's pinafore. "I'll take my chances with you."

His brow rose. "Why? Am I not so scary?"

She dried her face with her hands. "You should fear me. You overspent ten thousand pounds. You have some explaining to do."

As if she hadn't spoken, he spun and cooed at Philip. "I will buy you the best set of breeches. This year to come. You will be six then."

Waving at him to stop, she tried to step in front of him.

"Don't make promises. It is so hard to keep them."

He shrugged and spun faster. Philip tossed his head back and laughed. "Your mother is being stubborn." He moved closer to the boy's good ear. "I promise to fill you up every day with words. I'll make up for the years I've missed." He caught her gaze. "I can do the same for you, too, Theodosia."

She bit her lip, then followed him down the steps, giving chase all the way to the parlor.

Signed and blotted on the desk were the renouncement of Lester's right as a guardian and the contract giving him twenty thousand pounds. Her figure of ten had been crossed out. "Ewan, do you know how much one can buy with that amount?"

"I'm sure you do, Mrs. Cecil. The point is, he's gone. Lord Crisdon will pay."

She had planned on the earl paying Lester's portion tomorrow when she sold him Tradenwood, but that was tomorrow's trouble. Ewan had done it. He'd saved Philip. Smiling, she picked up the papers and held them to her bosom. "Thank you, Ewan."

The man wasn't listening. He was too busy taking Philip to the bookcase and having him put his fingers on the spines.

Pickens entered the room. "Ma'am, I made the arrangements for Philip's passage with the governess, but the footman said there had been some commotion while I was out."

A quick swipe to her eyes, and a check to her chignon, she turned to her butler. "It's over. Lester is gone."

A smile filled the old man's face. "May I start the unpacking?"

She shook her head. "No, Pickens. I'm still selling."

Ewan frowned as he lifted his lips to Philip's ear. "Maybe I can change her mind, or at least delay her, Pickens. Mrs. Cecil is eloping tomorrow. Make sure she is suitably packed, her and the boy. One bag each should do."

Her mouth dropped open again, wide enough to gulp all the air in the parlor. She recovered, tugging on her short gray cap sleeves. "Leave us. There is much to discuss."

Swiveling his head between them, Pickens backed to the door. "Will you require anything?"

Hugging Philip as if he were a delicate China doll, Ewan approached Pickens. "See that no one disturbs us. I want the widow to compromise me in privacy. But do bring some tea and biscuits."

Smothering a laugh, Pickens bowed and closed the door.

Setting Philip on the chaise, he motioned to her. "Your word is good, Mrs. Cecil. Is it not?"

She didn't move. "Yes."

He took a step to her direction. "You proposed to the baron?"

She squinted at him, but answered the truth. "Yes."

"Then you proposed to me. I answered your advertisement, initially giving my brother assistance. He's looking for a bride."

"So Lord Hartwell is a liar, too? Pity, he seemed nice."

He strode a little closer. "Lord Tristan is one of my father's lesser titles. He borrowed it. He is truly seeking a wife of convenience through newspaper advertisements. By happenstance, he stumbled upon yours. I do find it odd, that you'd attract another Fitzwilliam, but we are attracted to unforgettable women."

The things she wrote, thinking she'd found a kind stranger— it had been Ewan. She clasped her naked arms, hunting for her missing shawl, as if it would keep her from feeling so vulnerable. "Then it was him who I proposed to, not you. Did you like this joke? Did it give you both a good laugh?"

Ewan put his palms lightly to her elbows. "There's no laughing at you, but I did use the letters to test you. You passed. You astounded me. You exposed more and more of your heart in your responses. It frustrated me, tormented me, actually, that you couldn't be this free in my presence."

She dipped her head as her soul warred between disbelief and anger. "Those were private responses meant for someone else. Or at least the notion of someone else."

He closed the distance between them. "It made me jealous and crazy to know you couldn't say the same to me. I didn't understand before. I failed you in the worst way. Your letters gave me the chance to know you." He turned toward Philip. "Is it fine with you if I kiss your mother?"

The boy didn't lift his head. He picked up a book from the table and was turning pages.

"I'll take that as a yes."

She tried to move or duck but he engulfed her in his solid arms. He kissed her chin and worked his way to that spot on her throat that made her knees buckle. Weighing the cost of returning his passion or running, she clung to his lapels.

He stopped and held her. "My love will consume you, Theodosia. But I'll burn until you are sure. I want you only as my proper wife. Elope with me. I don't want to wait another moment to wed."

Breathing so hard from the air he'd stolen with his words, she shook her head. "This is reckless. We can't survive your family. Not six years ago, not now. You've freed me from Lester. That's all I want. Let me leave here with Philip."

"So you promised to marry me in a letter, will you compromise me in this closed room with a minor's supervision, and then leave?"

"You're twisting things, Ewan. I'm not a playwright so I won't try to best your words." She moved from him and headed to their son, but he clasped her shoulder, the one still smarting from Lester's cruelty. "Ouch."

He turned her, taking care to massage her arm. "I was fooled by or hadn't paid attention, to the fact that you act a great deal braver than you are. One of us must be brave enough to stay. Let me spend the rest of my life filling you with the words I should've six years ago. That you are loved. I believe in us, and I'll never leave your side."

He stroked her face. "You care so much for others. You're smart. No one can match you with numbers. You even let a fool save face."

"Mathew taught me to not let a bull run mad."

"I'm talking about me. You let me go to war, because you thought that's what I wanted. This fool didn't realize I should've put what you wanted first. I'll deal with my family, but my priorities are right here, you and Philip."

She grasped the revers of his deep chocolate coat. Too hesitant to draw near, too scared to turn away. "I can't put my hopes on something that will vanish. I won't have Philip caught in another war."

He patted her fingers and led her to the chaise. "Then trust me, a little more each day for the rest of my life. Don't let me haunt your memories. Let me be present every day with you and my son."

Whether she agreed or not, she was nodding yes between his kisses. His arms fit snug about her. Secure in his embrace, she didn't want to be released.

As his hands started to wander, he stopped himself and sat next to Philip. "Tomorrow won't be here fast enough. I'm going to sit here and read. This overnight stay should be enough to ruin my reputation. Then you'll have to make an honest man of me."

"But Lord Crisdon is coming then."

Ewan reached for her hand and eased her into a comfortable spot beside him, even propping a pillow behind her head. "We'll keep the meeting, then elope. If selling Tradenwood is what you wish, then do it. We need to be together in a place where I can write and get Philip the aid he needs. But I want you to keep Tradenwood. Cecil meant it for you and the boy, not the Fitzwilliams."

She closed her eyes. Maybe morning would never come. Philip was safe sitting between her and her dreamer. That memory she'd tuck into her heart. It surely made it hurt less than waking up tomorrow to lose Tradenwood and Ewan to the Earl of Crisdon.

• • •

Sunlight filtered into the room through the open patio doors. Morning had come. Ewan blinked and stretched. Philip slept in his lap. He fingered the boy's dark straight hair. Knowing that he helped keep him safe from Lester—that had to right some of the wrongs done to the boy.

He eased him onto the sofa and stood. Reaching up, he

relieved that tense knot in his back. Then it hit him. His fiancée had left without giving him a morning kiss. He searched the room but his chaise mate had abandoned him.

Scratching the light scruff to his chin, he wondered if she had taken to her bedchamber. Pride built in his chest. She trusted him with Philip. That made up for her less-than-wholehearted endorsement of eloping.

Theo wasn't one to be rushed. He wanted her to love him as deeply and as completely as he did her. Thinking of her, of what she liked, it came to him where she'd be. The patio.

She sat upon the knee wall. Wrapped again in her trademark shawl and yesterday's gray gown, Theodosia didn't quite look rested. Crinkles set under almond eyes. Her smooth bronze face held a frown. What a travesty for such a tasty mouth. "I know why you bite that lip. It's quite ripe."

She smiled for a second but stared at something.

He turned and saw the wonderful blooms of the clematis, sweet in purple and rose. "Why are you sad in such a place?"

"Mathew built this arbor. We planted the vines together. He was very happy here."

"We will keep it going, if you don't sell Tradenwood."

"Will we?" She shrugged. "Your mother hates it. Calls it weeds."

A few steps closer and he saw fear settling into the black pools of her eyes. "Go upstairs and dress. Get Philip dressed, too. Wear any color but gray or black."

She took his hand and held it to her heart. "I'll be ready before Lord Crisdon comes."

He almost wanted to check and make sure she didn't escape

out the front door. Theodosia wasn't convinced of his resolve but the walls, the curtain between them, had to fall.

He went to her desk, pulled out a quill, and began to pen corrections to the legal documents she had in a pile, including the bill of sale he'd found yesterday. Not deterred, he purposed to win. If they eloped today, and she made him a proper husband, he knew they would. She had to agree.

Within the hour, the sound of a carriage arriving rumbled through Tradenwood.

Pickens announced the Earl and Countess of Crisdon and led them to the parlor.

"Son?" Lord Crisdon asked, raising his head. "I didn't know you would be here. I no longer need your assistance. The widow is selling."

Mother rushed to him and wrapped her arms about him. "I've missed you so, Ewan. Your play is wonderful. I've seen it twice with all my friends. I told you, Crisdon, he would be great."

"Yes, you did, my dear. A Fitzwilliam, the talk of the town." Lord Crisdon folded his arms, wrinkling the sleeves of his pristine charcoal coat. "A Fitzwilliam in theater."

Lord Crisdon turned toward the hall. "There could be worse things."

Theodosia stood at the threshold of the room, holding Philip.

Ewan's breath caught, overpowering the anger boiling in his gut at his father's sneer. She'd changed into a fresh gown of blush. Bright and beautiful, with her silky hair way up in a shiny black chignon, she could be one of the pretty flowers on the trellis. And Philip, he wore a crisp white pinafore and sat safe and secure in his mother's arms.

"I see you are here, Lord Crisdon," she said, "I didn't think you'd come, too, Lady Crisdon."

His mother looked her way for a moment, then took a few steps Theodosia's way. Maybe she had to see the boy's crystal-blue eyes.

Lord Crisdon took papers from his pocket. "Here is the paperwork. I'll have my bank draft the amount."

Brow raised, Theodosia took the papers from him and handed them to Philip. Carrying the boy to the mantel, she pointed to the flames. "Philip, toss this rubbish into the flames. Lord Crisdon, we will use *my* paperwork, and you were to come with the banknote or there will be no deal."

"Crisdon," his mother said, in a voice that sounded weepy. "Don't cheapen out now. She's going to sell."

Ewan shook his head. "I have a better deal for you all to consider, and it will only cost twenty thousand pounds."

"Speak up, my boy." Lord Crisdon moved toward Ewan. "I am assuming, since you are here that you've already married her, and the land is ours."

"No. I am here to see about Mrs. Cecil and her son's best interest. I edited a few pages of the bill of sale to a lease, of sorts."

Theodosia bit her lip. She came to him and took the papers from him. "Ewan, this is not what I—"

"Trust me, Mrs. Cecil. Trust me now, or never."

With a nod, she handed the papers to Lord Crisdon.

His father took them and pressed his beady face close to the pages. He harrumphed. "Twenty thousand pounds to lease the water rights? How is this good? It doesn't give us Tradenwood."

Ewan took Theodosia's hand within his and she smiled, a big

true one. "The widow is eloping, but I will make sure her affairs are in order. Sign this, pay her, and make Jasper master over Grandbole. Then this lease is perpetual. You will never suffer from water rationing again; no further payment after this."

His father groused. "A lease that can be changed annually? Why would I ever do this?"

"You can simply pay a one-time fee and abide by the terms, or you pay annually. What was the amount each year you wanted, dearest?"

"It was twenty thousand pounds per annum," Theo said, turning Philip away from Lady Crisdon's slow advance.

Ewan took his son from Theodosia. He wanted Mother to see him, to feel the loss that he'd lived until yesterday. "Mrs. Cecil, if the Earl of Crisdon is late in his payments at 4 percent interest, what would that be?"

Theodosia didn't blink and said, "That would be another eight hundred pounds."

With Philip squirming, he leaned down and kissed her forehead. "She's a dream with numbers."

Lord Crisdon guffawed as he paced back and forth. "That's blackmail. Son, you are very sure of yourself."

"Never been more, my lord, never more."

The man smiled at him. "Didn't think you had it in you, my boy."

Catching Theodosia's gaze, he gave her hand a little squeeze. "I didn't either, not until I lost the one person who believed in me."

Mother sat on the chaise and pulled out her fan. "But what of Tradenwood? I thought she was going to sell it back to us?"

Lord Crisdon went to the desk and dipped the pen in the ink.

"No. Fitzwilliam has come up with a good plan."

Tears welled in his mother's eyes, and she fanned faster. "No. This was my home. I was born here. She doesn't—"

Philip fidgeted more, so Ewan set him down. The boy took the old book of Shakespeare from the table and climbed up onto the chaise, next to Mother.

Fanning harder, she looked straight ahead. "Do something, Crisdon."

"Mother, he *is* doing something by taking Mrs. Cecil's deal. If not, he knows Ewan Fitzwilliam-Cecil will personally ensure not a drop of water will flow to Grandbole."

Theodosia looked up. Her trademark lip bite had bloomed into a perfect smile. "Ewan, you would change your name, for me?"

"Yes. Cecil will be the name celebrated in Town, and it allows you to keep the only name you've ever known."

She gripped his arm tighter. "Thank you."

Something passed over his father's gaze. He pulled his note from his pocket and made the sum twenty thousand pounds, but he made it out to Ewan Fitzwilliam-Cecil. "You win. Lord Hartwell will now have full control of Grandbole, and I will join your mother in London. Come along, my dear."

Mother rose. "So you are marrying her? You will be master here?"

"It's none of your concern. I love you, Mother, but you are not welcome."

Her big blue eyes widened to a point of almost popping. "I'll say sorry. Have you no charity for your old mother?"

Ewan moved to the door and held it open. "My loyalties are to Theodosia and Philip. Maybe we'll visit you in Town at one of your fabulous parties, but not here."

Her jaw trembled. She clutched her husband's arm and left the room. Lord Crisdon paused for a moment and grasped Ewan's hand. "Hold on to what is yours. And congratulations. You bested me."

"Father, I made things right."

The man nodded and left the room.

Theodosia came to his side and put a palm on his arm. "I am so sorry, Ewan." She hugged him tight. "I never wanted you to choose."

Ewan scooped her up, pulling all her weight against him and spun her. "A man has to choose."

"I can't believe." She was winded, tearing up so much, but the last wall separating them had to be released. "Your mother looked so heartbroken."

For a moment, he cradled her against his silk waistcoat, against his scar-filled chest and restored heart. Setting her on top of the writing desk, he grabbed a handkerchief from his pocket and mopped up every droplet trailing her flared nose. "We have one thing to resolve. Now, that you've compromised me with this overnight stay, forced me to change my name, you must decide if we wed."

She hiccupped and furrowed her brow. "I thought you had decided."

"No. You need to ask me and mean it. Now, I am not opposed to you thoroughly ravishing me, if that will bring you assurance of my affections." He kissed her palm. "I need you to be very sure."

"I'm scared Ewan. What if we end up hurting each other again?"

Wiser than before, he shook his head. "That won't happen. My love for you is stronger than anything."

"But I'm not strong, not when it comes to you. Ewan, I'm weak. I'm fragile. I fear you walking out of my life, out of my son's life, and this time no miracle will bring you back."

"Love means being brave. There is no one braver than you, Theodosia." He put his hands to her waist, lifted her in the air, and twirled her until she clung to his neck. "My love means you can put your weight on me, all of your burdens. I love you, sweetheart." He set her back upon her slippers and took one step from her. "The strength of my feelings could overwhelm you. I could sweep you away in a wave of emotion so thick, that you'd float. I have enough love and patience to wait for you, until you are sure. You are worth everything to me, but I need to know if you want to be with me for the rest of your life?"

Swaying a little, she twisted her fingers. She stilled and put her hands to his face. "Ewan Fitzwilliam."

"Fitzwilliam-Cecil."

"Ewan Fitzwilliam-Cecil, will you marry me?"

He said nothing and stared at her.

Her forehead filled with lines, and she put a hand to her hip. "Well?"

"Was that it? What about the part about loving me forever? Your note said something about keeping me in your heart. I want to hear that aloud. A direct address is important. And do it loud, so Philip will hear."

Theodosia's lovely mouth opened but nothing came out. She shook as if she'd received a shock.

Maybe this was too hard for her. Maybe it was too much to

expect after all they'd been through. Loving her more than himself and his ego, he decided to make it easier for her to accept him. "I'm teasing—"

She put a finger to his lips. "*Shhh*. I need to say this. Be patient or I won't get the words out. You know I struggle with words. That day so long ago in the carriage house, I should've said the words, *don't leave me*, or *take me with you*. I should've begged you to not to part from me. I was so afraid of your father and so shamed for my own actions. I let fear steal my voice then; I can't let fear take it now."

He wanted to tell her he understood, but he knew her well enough to know she had to say her peace. "I'm listening."

Biting her lip, she stopped and grabbed ahold of his gaze. "Six years ago, an ignorant flower seller lost her heart to a dreamer, but what that wonderful man needed to know was that he was her best dream. Ewan, my heart crumbled when I thought you died. I wanted to die, too. Then I found I carried your babe. That part of you had to live. I had to keep alive any piece of you and the love that burned so brightly it scorched my soul. Know that even when you were dead, or far away, you were in my heart, haunting my memories with an everlasting love. When I couldn't grieve anymore, when I thought my soul was dry, you were there in my tears."

He took her hand and kissed it, then wove her palm against the scars on his chest. "I should have been here to dry those tears. I will never ever let you be far from me again. I'll never be parted from you, Theodosia. I love you more than anything."

Trembling, she fell into his embrace. "Mathew rescued me and Philip. I loved him for that, but I have always, always been in love with you. Not a day, not a moment passed without you being in my heart, and this time, I know you won't let me go. I can trust you with all of me, with the best of me, with our son."

He claimed her lips, whispering his love in each kiss, taking her mouth with a desire to assure her he felt the same, that she was a part of him, too—the only part that had worth.

She brushed at her eyes. "So, yes, Mr. Playwright. I love you. Marry me. Make me Mrs. Ewan Fitzwilliam-Cecil, a new name that I will love above all else."

"Yes," he said, hoping she heard the promise of forever in his tone. "We should be going. I want you to have our name as soon as possible."

Slipping from him, she went to her desk and rummaged inside until she pulled out her satin reticule. "That name, it's better than Flower Seller."

"You will be Theodosia Fitzwilliam-Cecil, the flower girl who made two men love her. For my vanity's sake, I'd like to think of the first husband as a placeholder, the one you needed until I grew up."

"Mathew wasn't—"

"I know." He brushed his lips against hers. "It's my goal, to make you secure in my love. I want to be your preferred husband. I hear it's difficult to beat a true ghost."

"You were my first love, Ewan, and now my last."

"Time for new memories." Grasping Philip in one arm, he clasped her hand and headed to his rented carriage. "It's time to go elope."

Pickens stood at the door, the one he'd stood guard on the many nights Theo had kept Ewan at bay. His smile was big. "Godspeed."

"Tell Lord Hartwell and my fiancée's dearest friends to have a wedding supper ready here when we return, in three days."

He settled his family inside the carriage and tapped the roof. As it started down the drive, Theodosia settled Philip onto his lap. "We could've taken one of my carriages. This is a long trip for a squirming child."

"No, I like it quiet and intimate here. Forces you to be near."

She frowned up and looked out the window. "I should go get medicine or an onion for Philip. He might have pain."

"I thought of it. It's in my stowed bag. I must be prepared to live life with you."

"That's a half a penny for the onion. At least ten shillings for the laudanum. That's a lot of money."

He reached for a bag on the floor and pulled out the little wooden horse and put it in Philip's small hands. "Well, this playwright will use his simple means to be of use."

"You are. You make me happy. We will be safe with you, Ewan. This time, I truly know it."

Blessed beyond measure, he waited for Theodosia to settle beside him. It was the place she belonged, next to his heart.

EPILOGUE

Theodosia yawned as the sounds from the first floor of Tradenwood, a pianoforte and laughter, finally started to quiet. Her open balcony door let the sweet smell of clematis inside her candlelit room. She sat at her vanity, staring at the gold band Ewan had purchased for her at Gretna Green. Simple, elegant, easily encompassing her finger. Her heart warmed at the sight of it. This meant security for her and Philip.

What a whirlwind the past three days had been. They'd journeyed to Scotland, only stopping for a meal or to water the horses. They'd arrived for a simple ceremony with a blacksmith whose coal-dusted hands had bested her own coloring. It all seemed too quick, and too short of a service to support the guinea Ewan had left the man.

Yet, maybe it was worth the stares they'd received. They did look different from other couples venturing to marry. Nonetheless, once Ewan had kissed her dizzy, she'd stopped paying attention to villagers and the footman. His love made the world disappear.

The door connecting their rooms opened, and Ewan came inside. The burgundy-colored robe draping his shoulders made his outline look royal, kingly, but the scars showed him as blessed.

Barefoot, he strode to her, took her hand, and spun her to Frederica's pianoforte tune.

"How is Mrs. Fitzwilliam-Cecil this evening?"

She looked in his eyes and didn't know quite what to say.

Happiness spilled from her heart, but so did nervousness. This was their first moment alone since the wedding.

He twirled her again. "Philip's tucked in bed. Your friends, Miss Burghley, Miss Croome, and Miss Thomas have assured me that they will take care of him, should he need assistance. And my dear brother is also in charge of making sure my theater friends don't stay too long."

Ewan stopped midstep. "I may have tasked the wrong man to chaperone. He's enjoys a good party."

"Lord Hartwell is quite capable. He chose my advertisement, after all. I feel quite confident in him."

"Yes, he does seem to have good taste, as does Miss Croome. She's beguiled by the actors. Maybe she has a future in the theater."

Theodosia muffled a giggle, thinking of her dear friend. "No, she's too shy, but she has a serious liking for Arthur Bex. She adores his voice."

Ewan tugged free the bow of Theodosia's nightgown. "He's a great actor, but she should take care. He's fighting something, not sure what, but something."

"Little Miss Croome is big with plans but too nervous to carry them out. You saw how she was mouse quiet through supper."

He spread the thin fabric of her robe and wove his hands underneath, cupping her shoulders. "Sheer does look good on you."

Her face heated and she took a half step backward. "I haven't changed too much. It's been six years since you saw—all of me."

"Shyness is one of your enduring qualities, too." Ewan scooped her up. His eyes, those bluer-than-blue wonders, glittered with candlelight. He carried her to her wide bed, separated the curtains, but allowed the gauzy fabric to sweep her face. "One of many and finally a bed, a wide one."

Soft and gentle, he laid her upon the mattress. He dipped out, blew out most of the candles, then entered from the other side of the canopy.

The music below faded. The beating of her heart overtook his. Six years since she'd been this close to him. Maybe she was dreaming, a wicked, delicious dream of the man who knew her soul, who was finally free to love her.

The sweetness of his gentle caresses almost distracted Theodosia from his fingers slipping off her robe, his thumbs flicking pins from her hair.

He splayed her locks between his palms. "You are the most beautiful woman. Six years have served you well."

She sat up with her hair dripping down her arms. She bit her lip and waited.

Smiling, he reached over, grabbed all the pillows, and turned back down.

"What? Ewan?"

He fluffed one and adjusted it underneath his neck. He worked a spot in the bedsheets smooth before stretching. "Good night, my love."

She hovered over him and shook him. "But technically this is our wedding night."

"I'm not rushing you, Theo. I made my father pay a large dowry for me, which cancels out the payment made to Lester."

"Yes, that was clever of you, but what does that have—"

He trailed his pinkie over her nose. "This being my first

marriage, shouldn't I be like the new bride awaiting discovery?" He leaned up and nipped the lobe of her ear, raking it with sensations. "You know what to do to help my motivation. I remember a vixen, a saucy Circe plying me with temptation in a carriage. Where is she?"

"Hiding. Wondering how things will be with us. Six years later."

He put her hand to his chest, forcing her to feel the wild thread of his heartbeat against the scars. "We will be better. We know better. We will love better."

The confidence in his voice reminded her how far they'd come. Finding joy in their strengths and vulnerabilities, she traced a circle, her unending love, for Ewan. "Perhaps, but I'll settle for love long-lasting. I just want us to be in love forever."

He eased his hand behind her neck, then traced her spine down to the small of her back. "Yes, but I will never settle, and I don't have to with you, not the way I love you." He tugged her to him. "This shyness is endearing, my sweet, but not exactly how the Circe of my play would go about enticing me. I'll have to give you plenty of direction, plenty of practice. Maybe a rehearsal every night."

She wanted to complain she wasn't anything like his Cleo character, but the playwright had abandoned words, sculpting Theodosia with his writing hands into a heroine besotted with love, one completely breathless beneath his weighty kiss.

ACKNOWLEDGMENTS

Dear Friend,

I enjoyed writing *The Bittersweet Bride*. It was a great deal of fun and a bit of a challenge to shape these meant-to-be-together characters separated by history and a lack of trust. I hope you enjoyed their journey to forgiveness and love.

My diverse stories showcase a world of intrigue and romance, and offer a setting hopefully everyone will find interesting, and a character to identify with, in the battle of love and life.

Stay in touch. Sign up at www.vanessariley.com for my newsletter. You'll be the first to know about upcoming releases, and maybe even win a sneak peek.

Thank so much for giving this book a read.

Vanessa Riley

AUTHOR'S NOTE

In 1819, Burlington Arcade was built by the Earl of Burlington. It is one of Britain's earliest shopping arcades. He designed it for "the sale of jewelry and fancy articles" and "for the gratification of the public." It is still in existence.

By Regency times, historians Kirstin Olsen and Gretchen Holbrook Gerzina estimate that Black London (the black neighborhood of London) had more than 10,000 residents. These were free, not enslaved, residents given to industry, mercantile, or in the service of estates around London. This population became absorbed into the culture by marriage.

During the 1800s, placing an advertisement in a newspaper like the Morning Post for a marriage of convenience was an acceptable way for single men and women to find a mate. For those new to the area or if the person had particular circumstances, like widowhood, small charges, etc., which could preclude a normal courtship, they turned to advertisements.

Editorial caricatures focused on the prevalent themes or societal worries of the times. A Woodward Devlin print from 1803, called "Advertisement for a Wife," shows a man surprised by the respondents to his marriage advertisement with one of the ladies being a Blackamoor. You can view the caricature and examples of advertisements at: http://vanessariley.com/NewspaperBride.html

The
BASHFUL
BRIDE

Advertisements for *L*ove Series

VANESSA
RILEY

Ellen, this is your fangirl book.

Hopefully, someday, you and John Oliver will meet, but don't marry him.

CHAPTER ONE

Ester Croome sank into the hammered copper tub and let the warm, sudsy water soak her skin, kissing her in her favorite lilac scent. A copy of the *Morning Post* sat on the floor of the bathing room with big, wet fingerprints atop her friend's advertisement for a marriage of convenience and a brutal review of her favorite actor, Arthur Bex.

"Miss Croome," Mrs. Fitterwall, the family's Irish housekeeper, said as she entered the bathing room with a silver pitcher high in her hands. "You must be part fish."

Bashful, even to another woman, Ester ducked into the suds until just her neck showed. "You should knock, Mrs. Fitterwall."

"I've been working here five years, and you're still a shy one, Miss Croome, but you can't lay about in the tub all morn. You've an appointment in town and then must come back and get ready for the party. No dawdling for a Croome."

The woman glanced at the walls. "Your mother has only a few more things to restore and then everything will be done at Nineteen Fournier."

Only an Olympian acanthus leaf indention in the molding needed fixing in the salmon-pink room. Her mother had three passions: Nineteen Fournier, newspapers, and knitting. Poor Mama. She needed something to be happy about.

"Come on, Miss Croome. I must rinse you off. Is that your

mother's *Morning Post*? She'll be looking for it."

Ester didn't reply as the woman carefully poured the pitcher over her. It wasn't time to wash her hair, and tender-headed Ester was grateful, but a splash too much of water would reduce her braided chignon to frizzy tangles. Wet Blackamoor hair could be unruly. At least Ester's curls were.

"Don't you fret. Not a drop of water will dampen your head. Your Mama's big party is tonight. Five years in this house. You must look your best." Mrs. Fitterwall gathered a robe and readied a fresh towel.

Ester unfolded her arms from about her bosom, a touch too large for her small height, stepped into the soft cotton, winding it tightly about her, then she dove into the robe the woman held out.

"The way you carry on, you'd think you hated baths." The woman chuckled, but Ester didn't think it funny. She was shy and small, but in her heart roared a lion. Someday she'd find the strength to show the world.

"I'll send the maid to your room to help you dress." She scooped up the paper and shook it as Ester rubbed lotion on to her hands. "And hurry. I think your father's discussing your birthday." The woman winked at her. "If you're quick, you might find out what big surprise he has for you."

But Ester was unmoved.

Papa always made a big to-do out of birthdays and holidays, but things hadn't been right between them for a while. With a sigh, she offered Mrs. Fitterwall a small smile, then dashed to her room to dress.

In her closet, she flipped past the bright hues to her silver-gray gown, perfect for the outside world still in mourning for the king.

Upon laying out the dress, she bathed once again in lotion, making sure to cover her elbows and knees. Mama said the ash on her skin could be so bad it would cut her stockings to ribbons.

She finished in time for the maid to come in and help. Once laced and properly corseted over her chemise, she slipped into her day dress then covered up in a dark spencer jacket and her favorite coral and pearl necklace. Pleased that she looked presentable, she fought the frilly lace covering her canopy bed to recover her sketchbook. Her friend, Frederica Burghley, would love this wedding gown. *Oh, please let the man she's corresponding with be the one.*

Bouncing down one set of stairs and then the last, she heard her father's deep voice. Remembering Mrs. Fitterwall's hint about a birthday surprise, Ester slowed her steps in the hall outside his study and listened.

"Ester will marry on her birthday."

The world stopped turning. Papa's voice. His awful deal-making voice.

Unless the great actor, Arthur Bex, sat inside Papa's study, Ester was doomed.

"My daughter will be so pleased—an April wedding. Your son is getting a diamond."

Papa's commanding tone stole her breath, made Ester crumple to the floor.

Almost sitting on her beloved sketches, she steadied herself against the creamy canary yellow walls.

This was a mistake.

That's what it had to be. No arranged marriage for her, but something of her own choosing.

As the Croome wealth had grown, she'd become used to more extravagant presents—silver slippers, her coral necklace with a pearl, but not a man. Craning her ear, she heard Papa confirm his foul agreement, "Ester will be a good match for him."

Who was the "him"?

Scooping up her sketchbook, she stood as Father's thunderous laugh bellowed down the hall. No names had been offered. No voices other than Papa's could she discern. To whom had he promised her?

Fear and curiosity twisted about her neck like the jewelry she wore. She looped the heavy cord of beads about her pinkie and waited. Truth, even a horrible one, always came out, like Papa's affair.

"Yes, getting married to a respectable young man is all she talks about," he said.

Her sketchbook dropped again, slipping from the crook of her arm to the floor with a splat. She froze. Papa's study was several feet away, opposite Mama's parlor. Either could hear her, demand her time, further ruining her already ruined day, but worse, make her miss her appointment and let Frederica down. Her friend counted on her. It would hurt her heart too much to disappoint her.

But how could she leave and not know more of Papa's deal-making?

So Ester waited, clutching the milk-white trim at her back, her nails sinking into the raised plaster fleur-de-lis rimming the hall of the family's Cheapside townhome. It wasn't Cheapside proper, but as close as Father could move them. Croome money wasn't enough to erase the limitations of Papa's dark hands.

"Yes. My son, Charles will be pleased, too." The second voice was masculine, but lighter, without an ounce of richness or gravitas, just pure smugness. "He'll ask her tonight."

Mama's party was tonight.

Mother's special celebration to honor Nineteen Fournier was turning into an engagement party. Ester scratched her brow, resettled her trim gray bonnet over her thick locks. There was only one of Papa's business partners with a son named Charles. Could it be Charles Jordan? She shuddered at the notion of marrying the known womanizer. No. This engagement couldn't happen, not at Mama's party. Not ever.

Heart pounding like it would break free of her ribs, she risked it flopping out from her stays and bent to pick up her treasured book. She tugged the worn spine to her bosom like it was a shield and covered her soul. She was one month from one and twenty and hadn't considered marrying. Not seriously. She'd been more involved in helping her friend Frederica craft a newspaper advertisement for a husband. That girl needed a good situation in the worst way and was to meet her first serious candidate today, with Ester as chaperone.

There was hope. One always had to have hope. The Croomes had been blessed by hope. How else could the family business grow without it? How else could they have come up from living above a warehouse to having a home? How else could they have taken this rundown place and made it bloom into a fashion plate?

Maybe Ester could hope to change his mind. Papa was reasonable, and until Christmas last year they'd had a perfect, doting relationship. Clenching her fingers in and out, she hesitated then tapped on Papa's door. Before her fourth knock, he answered.

Josiah Croome was a tall man with thick, jet-black hair, parted on top. He tugged on the lapel of his sleek lapis-blue tailcoat.

Endowed by God, he'd used his large dark hands and smart ebony eyes to build the family textile business from nothing. But Papa couldn't use those big palms to give her future away.

"Ester," he said with a toothy, winning smile. "Just the young woman I wanted to see."

He tried to claim her arm, but she stepped back. "Papa," she said in her honeyed tone. "Could you come out here for a moment?"

A frown appeared on his face, but he nodded. "Mr. Jordan, I'll be right back."

When he closed the door, Ester exhaled. "Father, no. I can't."

He folded his arms and stared way down at her short five-foot-four height. "You heard?"

"Yes, and I won't marry Charles Jordan, Papa. I can't."

"You met him once, Ester. You said the meeting was pleasant."

"I was being polite. He's horrible, and that evening cost me seeing Arthur Bex's last performance as Romeo."

With the wide span of his palm stretched over his face from ear to ear, he sighed. "Not the actor again. Ester, you talk about this Bex every day, as if he were truly your lover. Stop this. The man doesn't know you exist, and if he is as wonderful as you say, he isn't looking for a bride in the old Huguenot section of London."

Papa was being diplomatic, but it was his way of saying important men didn't go looking for Blackamoor brides.

A little unnerved by his use of the word "lover" and Bex in the same sentence, she clutched at the buttons of her short jacket. "You know how I love Bex's art. His theatrical performances are outstanding, and I missed one because of nasty Charles Jordan—a boy who never reads, knows nothing of Shakespeare, and needs a variety of women to stave off boredom. He cannot be a good husband to me."

"Ester, this is true life. You'll be one and twenty. I must make sure that you are well provided for, and Charles Jordan is a man you can build a life with."

"How can that be? Your choice is a womanizer. He's—" She bit her lip. Why would infidelity matter to Papa? The letters Ester had found last Christmas proved her father was an adulterer, too. She lowered her tone, looked to the polished floorboards. "He's not right for me."

Father claimed Ester's fingers, his big, meaty palms surrounding her thin ones. "You don't know what is right. You're young and sheltered. I've made mistakes, but this isn't one. The matter is settled, Ester. Tonight, at your mother's party, your engagement will be announced."

It sounded like a commandment from on high in Papa's deep, Moses voice, but he'd have to part the Red Sea or the Thames to make her believe that Charles was her fate.

"Come, Ester. Do your duty for the family. Be nice to Mr. Jordan. We are a respected family, too. We need to act like it."

Her pride kicked in, and she stood up straight. She'd act the part of a submissive daughter until she could plan a way to stop this, to become her own Moses and find a space, a promised land where she could choose her own husband. Someone who'd be truthful and not mock their vows of faithfulness.

Her father opened the door to his sand-colored study. The etchings of the old Huguenot fleur-de-lis were in here, too, making it feel stately—and the decisions made inside, so final.

"Ester, say hello to Mr. Jordan."

She fixed her frowning face, hid her sketchbook behind her

back, and followed her father in. "Hello to Mr. Jordan."

Papa stepped near his walnut desk, a reward for when the mantua-makers had started ordering his fabrics for the new Burlingame Arcade. "My daughter, Mr. Jordan, is a treasure with a good sense of humor. She'll make any man proud."

The man stared at her, reached for her, and Ester froze.

Bashfulness clamping her lips, she couldn't reply, not under Jordan's beady gaze. She lowered her gaze to Papa's orderly desk and spied the upside-down parchment that read Marriage Contract.

Now she truly couldn't breathe.

Mr. Jordan with his short height of five-foot-five, lowered his palm and tugged on his silken gray waistcoat. "My son, Charles, is made of quite good material, if I may say so to the fabric king." He bowed his balding head in Ester's direction, and she resisted the urge to look behind her for some other girl to be the recipient of this tragedy.

"Charles will be here tonight for your mother's party. He may have a question to ask you. Something that will change your life a month from now, on your birthday."

Gloating at her sentence of a horrid marriage was uncalled for. No matter how much she wished to believe this was a bad dream, that she still lay in her canopied bed, sketching dresses for Frederica, dreaming of reciting lines with Arthur Bex, Ester had to admit she was horribly awake and tonight she'd be horribly engaged to a womanizer.

"Ester, the Jordans are an honorable family. They've perfected gas-lighting as good as anywhere in London. My warehouses can run multiple shifts. More productivity, more jobs."

"And more money." Mr. Jordan winked and bared teeth in his

crooked smile.

Papa chuckled. "It's a perfect match."

For the Croome business, maybe, but not for the business of her heart. Ester refused to nod, didn't want to give any form of consent. She tugged her gray-colored gloves tighter. "Well…I… I'm meeting a friend in town. Mr. Jordan. Papa…pleasant meeting."

Her father picked up the spectacles he used for contract writing. "Ester, you should stay and become more acquainted with Mr. Jordan. There are ten-thousand reasons to be more acquainted."

Her dowry? The price on her head—and they said enslavement was finished in England. How could Papa expect her to want this? She wasn't like Mama. She wasn't like her sister Ruth, who had been happy with her arranged marriage in the country.

"Daughter, say something. I know you are terribly shy, but Mr. Jordan will be family."

Why did he expect a reply when he'd taken away her options? Ester had nothing for her father except a bucket of unshed tears. "Good day, gentlemen." She turned on wobbly legs and headed for the door. At least she stayed composed and held her voice even. Surely, she looked in order, not shredding apart like poorly tacked-on ribbons.

She put her back upon the door and ensured that it closed, that no one followed. The great actor Arthur Bex would be marginally proud of her performance. If only this were a play. Then that would've been the scene where the villains won, and her victory was bound for the last act.

If only.

"She'll come around, Jordan. Just like her mother, Ester is level-headed." The statement was harsh, vibrating the panel door as if her father knew she was still within hearing distance.

Like my mother?

The comment was a final slap, and it shook Ester more deeply than the idea of a bad arranged marriage. She wasn't like her mother, not in any way that mattered. It was an awful guilt-laden thought, but the sentiment was there, always there, more so since last Christmas.

Clancy, Papa's butler, slipped into the hall with a shiny silver tray of teacakes. "Miss Ester, you need to run on. You're going to be late. That Miss Burghley's going to start her trouble without you."

She half smiled at the man. He was tall and proud in his garnet livery. Papa had him powder his gray hair so he'd be as fine as the servants in Cheapside or even Mayfair. "Miss Ester, are you well?"

Ester wanted to say no, but that would make the man call a fancy physician and she'd not be able to go meet her friend. "I'm good. And you are right about Miss Burghley and trouble. I need to hurry. Can you see about the carriage, so I won't miss a moment? I'll take the tray in to Mama. I assume that's where these are heading. Father doesn't like the delicate treats. He says they are too small for his hands."

"You're not supposed to help me. Since you moved to this big house, you've been trying. It's not your place anymore. If I can't do it, there's an upstairs maid or Mrs. Fitterwall who can. I'll set these refreshments in the parlor for Mrs. Croome and Mrs. Jordan, then send the footman for your carriage."

She watched Clancy knock and then slip into the parlor. He worked too hard, but he seemed proud to be of service, proud that his employer, a man of color, could achieve so much. But how could Clancy ignore the unhappiness that seemed to suffocate this place?

Ester pulled her sketchbook to her stomach and moved to the front door. From the side glass, she looked at the calm street, the occasional carriage trotting by. If she were bold, she'd hitch herself to the back of one. *If I were bold.*

Clancy came out of Mama's parlor. "Mrs. Croome is asking for you. I'll go send the footman for the carriage. You won't miss that trouble. Go to your mother."

She nodded and went back into the small hall. She heard Papa and Mr. Jordan's laughter as she entered the adjacent parlor. The rich room of burgundy-papered wall was devoid of sound, so different from the room next door. Ester walked inside to the tapestry-covered couch where her mother sat.

Mama in her mobcap, which covered her straight dark hair, worked on her knitting. Mrs. Jordan, who couldn't be much older than Ester, was on the opposite end doing needlepoint. Not a word was exchanged. Were the ladies dutifully waiting on their husbands to tell them what to do, when to stand, what to think?

Of course they were. That's why Clancy's tray was untouched and the room had no conversation, no life. Ester couldn't turn into one of those women with no opinions about anything but colored yarn.

"Mama." Ester coughed to loosen her tongue then tried again. "Mama, I'm leaving for my appointment."

Her mother slowly turned her face to her. The woman's light skin had yellowed to a pale gold with age, and her eyes, forest green, looked small, as if she refused to see trouble. "You, should stay and visit with Mrs. Jordan."

Stay in the parlor? And make small talk about current and future cheating spouses? Not today, Satan. Ester tugged at her sleeve. "Mama, I am to meet Miss Burghley for tea. Remember?"

"You let her visit with Miss Burghley, the Duke of Simone's… daughter?" Mrs. Jordan sprang to life as her nose turned up in the air. "Mrs. Croome, is that wise?"

Ester held her breath and closed her eyes, hoping that her mother would say something to defend the prejudice that surrounded someone as dear as her friend. Frederica Burghley was Simone's illegitimate daughter, but that wasn't her fault any more than it was Mama's for Papa's failings—like what had been detailed in the horrible letters that Ester had found last Christmas. It had changed her father from a hero in her eyes to someone like the Jordans— known womanizers and opportunists.

When she heard the sound of tea pouring, drip-drip-splash, she blinked, then stared.

No words.

No defense of Frederica.

Nothing of what a good person Frederica was.

Nothing but brown liquid spitting from a fine silver pot into bone china cups.

"You should really stay, Ester," Mama said, "but I know you have an appointment. Be back as soon as you can. I'll need your help. My party starts at seven sharp."

As silent as a mouse, Ester turned. Out the door she started to run. She'd catch a hackney if Clancy hadn't ordered the carriage. Lucky for her, it sat at the steps. She climbed aboard the onyx berlin carriage. Its well-matched pair of ebony horses took off like their tails had been set on fire. One thing Ester knew right now. She couldn't be a couch woman waiting for a man to say when to jump, or move, or breathe.

• • •

It didn't take long to reach the White Horse Cellar, the coaching inn nearest the Burlingame Arcade. Ester sighed as she adjusted her bonnet again. She wanted to be supportive of Frederica's attempt at making a match by newspaper advertisement. It had been Ester's idea for her friends to solicit husbands through the *Morning Post*. She should've dictated one for herself, but that would be like cheating on her fantasy "lover," Arthur Bex, as Papa had put it. If only she'd spoken to Bex at Theodosia's party last year. Maybe he'd have noticed her, a girl from the wrong side of town.

Lifting her chin, Ester decided to do what she'd done at Christmas, to pretend to be happy. She'd be an actress and play the part of a dear friend, one with no troubles.

A groom helped her down. With her sketchbook in tow, she crossed the busy courtyard filled with travelers to the big gold and black carriage of the Duke of Simone. She tapped on the door.

Dark brown curls with sun streaks bounced as Frederica Burghley popped her head out. "I thought you'd abandoned me."

"Never." Ester meant that with every part of her heart.

Handed down by one of her trusted grooms, Frederica looked resplendent in a short indigo velvet pelisse over her gown, a fine ebony bonnet upon her head. "No, you'd never do that. You're loyal and predictable. Those are qualities I now treasure."

The two had grown closer since their friend Theodosia had married. And though Frederica tweaked Ester's nose about her caution, Ester knew the girl was right. Shyness and caution were weaknesses, ones her father had counted upon, so she'd comply with the sham marriage.

"You did remember to wear dark colors," Ester said.

"I miss color." Frederica sighed.

Ester did, too. They brought her sketches to life. "Mourning for the king is still occurring. Two women like us at a coaching inn are hard to ignore. Bright colors would be taken for an offense. We must be careful."

"I hear radicals meet in the cellar. If my newspaper prospect is dull, we could join a conspiracy." Frederica giggled, but the light tones fell flat. She tugged at the sleeve of her jacket with pleated butterfly embroidery at the waist. "Safety is an issue but so is security. This meeting has to work. With the duke thinking of marrying again, he's been looking into arrangements for me. Old men, friends of his, readying for a second or third wife, or *other*."

Frederica's voice could have been a bell, ringing of pain, foretelling every fear. The other…a fancy or mistress…as Frederica's mother had been to the duke—it was a fate worse than death for a girl who wanted honor and respect.

Ester gripped her friend's hand. "You will be all that you can be, and you will choose a great husband." She nudged Frederica toward the rugged door of the coaching inn. "I wish I were you."

Her friend stopped, planting her short boots in the dusty fairway. "Wait. You've never… All the years we've known each other, and you have never said that. What has happened?"

Jerking like she'd flubbed a line or been caught reading Mama's papers, Ester flinched. "It doesn't matter. Your newspaper groom is waiting inside."

With a hand on her hip, reticule swinging, Frederica shook her head. "No. Out with it."

People stared now, with scrunched-up faces and quizzing glasses, as if they wondered if Ester or Frederica had stolen some wealthy traveler's clothes. "I wish they wouldn't look at us."

"Who?" Frederica starting peering over Ester's head. "Who?"

"People," Ester said. "Maybe they think some imperial guests are about and we are their elaborate servants. That would be easier to accept than what we are."

"Lucky?" Frederica gripped her by the shoulders. "Don't curse our fates now by having secrets. I won't be able to concentrate."

Resigned, Ester lowered her head. "The Croome's money and the need to grow it have collided. My father has decided to sell me off in marriage to a bore because it will benefit his bank coffers."

Wide hazel eyes grew even bigger. "Wait. You. What? Who?"

"Jordan's son, Charles."

"The womanizer? He has mistresses. They say he's bedding a widowed countess whom he teaches fencing. That's the rumor." Frederica bit her lip. "It could be wrong. He might not be so bad."

Ester clutched Frederica's hand. "You're not going to tell me that the love of a good woman will change him. That he will behave once we wed." Tears clogged her throat. "I'm doomed. Accepting this fate is better than the hypocrisy of believing things can change. That Charles will change."

"You and Theodosia call me the dramatic one. There's always another way. Hope doesn't disappear because we are too frightened to look for it."

But Ester *was* frightened, terrified. Her sister's arranged marriage had made her live far away, never coming back to London, even for Yuletide. They'd been so close once, and happy when they'd lived above the warehouse. Moving up in the world had cost so much—was still costing. "I don't know what to do."

Frederica put her arms about Ester and drew her in tightly. "You could put an advertisement in the paper. We might be able to find someone for you, too, someone kind and faithful."

Ester shook her head. "Jordan's proposal will come tonight with a wedding in four weeks, on my birthday."

More travelers scooted by, fewer of them looking over at Ester and Frederica. Perhaps, for the moment, they blended into the deep brown of the coaching inn's facade. Ester wanted to disappear.

"You could say no, Ester. You could choose to say no."

The word *no* and Frederica seemed quite foreign to each other, and the concept was something Ester couldn't grasp, either. She whipped her head around. "I can't say no to my Papa any more than you can to yours." She exhaled, put on a brave smile, and began acting again. "Look at me getting us both flustered. This is your day. Everything will work out. I'm sure."

Frederica had that look of disappointment, a deep frown that made the luster in her hazel eyes dim to a sad sherry. "I pretend a great deal, too. In another few months, I won't have any hope, either."

Ester grabbed her and hugged her until a seam or two popped. "You listen well, Frederica Burghley. No one should count us out, not yet. We'll both be saved or go down in glorious flames. I may even enjoy knitting in silence."

"What?" A brow popped up on Frederica's fair countenance. "What does that mean?"

"Nothing, silly goose. So how do we meet this man?" Ester smoothed the rim of her bonnet in a slightly showy manner, something she'd seen Frederica do a hundred times. "Come on."

Ester led her friend into the crowded inn.

Crowds. Ester froze, her fake courage slipping to her boots.

People were packed in the lobby and at tables in the main area.

Frederica clasped her hand. "What's wrong, Ester?"

"So many travelers." A chill crept up her arm, but she accepted her friend's nudge forward through the dining room.

Too many strangers. She could feel her throat getting dry. "Frederica. How... How do we see your newspaper beau? It's easy for him, as we are the only ladies like ourselves here. The dishwasher or a maid doesn't count to most men seeking a wife of means."

Frederica pulled a sprig of lilac from her reticule and handed it to Ester. The bright purple of the tiny flowers looked like embroidery on the lapel of her jacket. "To gain more responses, I didn't exactly say I was Blackamoor."

What? Now Ester truly couldn't breathe.

"But the lilac will help us spot him. He will have a sprig, too. It will be all right, Ester."

Details like race were important. Ester shook her head as Frederica cupped the fragile flower in her palm.

"Ester, Theodosia Fitzwilliam-Cecil and her husband found each other again through the newspaper advertisement. Surely, I can be so lucky."

"Fitzwilliam?" A big man spun, and doing so, sent another fellow and his mug crashing into them. The foul beer stained Frederica's velvet pelisse.

Ester palmed the lilac to keep it dry, then she dug into her reticule and pulled out a handkerchief. "Dabbing at this won't help. We need to sponge it before sets in the nape. We need water."

Frederica's eyes became glassy with tears. "We can't ask, and my footman is outside. To go get him and then water, it will be too late for our meeting."

The tall man, whose face held a long frown, had joined them. "Perhaps you need an errand boy or errand man?"

Their friend's brother-in-law, Lord Hartwell, was the guilty man who'd started the commotion. He held out his hand, a trim leather glove, half covered in the billowing sleeve of his finely-woven greatcoat. "Come with me, Miss Burghley. I'll see that this stain is removed. It's my fault, but rarely do you hear the name Fitzwilliam in such lovely tones."

Her friend smiled up at him in the flirty way she did with nice looking men and took his arm.

Laughter cascaded to their left.

A round of shouts rolled over the top of everything, but a lone, muffled sound made it quiet.

Then she heard the word "Freedom" loud and clear.

Ester's skin tingled. That voice sounded familiar. She tapped her temple. Papa was right. She did carry Bex in her brainbox.

But the voice boomed out again, "Humanity and freedom for all."

The saving call became muffled like a door opening then closing upon a parish sermon. She whipped her head back and forth, searching, her heart beating hard. She looked but saw no one that could bear the weight of that voice, the voice she knew in her dreams.

A man stumbled out of what looked like a cellar door, and the masculine voice returned, the tones of a mythic god.

"There is one path. It is to the liberty of the soul."

That voice. It sounded like Arthur Bex.

Was he here? If the great Arthur Bex, the best actor in all of London, was in the coaching inn, then this horrible day would be better, much better.

When she saw Frederica smiling as a server mopped at her stain while Lord Hartwell observed and mentioned something about visiting his father in town—Ester knew her friend was in good hands. She'd look for Frederica's lilac-carrying suitor later, after she stole a moment to listen to Bex.

But she'd have to go down into the cellar for that.

It was dangerous to go alone, but if Arthur Bex was down there, it would be worth the risk. If troubles came, she'd hit them with her sketch pad and then run. Yes, that sounded like a plan. A fool's plan, but she'd be a fool for Bex.

She clutched the cellar door and started toward the voice. How Ester made it down without flying was beyond her, but she did it. Gripping the handrail, she searched. The room was lit with awful-smelling tallow candles. The stink of burning calf fat would stay in her spencer, but she didn't care. She saw Bex standing on a chair.

Bex, the love of her heart, was giving a speech.

Ester was in heaven.

Candlelight from the chandelier above made him appear to have a halo. Dark chestnut-brown hair graced his head. He possessed lightly sun-kissed skin and dreamy cobalt-blue eyes. The man was beautiful, even more so than that one time he had joined her at Theodosia's table. Ester hadn't been able to speak to him then. She had been too afraid of sounding weak and foolish, but now, being a few hours away from doom, she felt bold, almost brazen.

The man waved his arms, flexing the tan weave of his frockcoat, which hung upon a slightly askew cream cravat. The gold buttons on his chocolate waistcoat jangled as he stepped forward. "The human race is meant to be free, free to love," Bex said. "That freedom should not be denied by chains, by an origin of birth a continent away. The cry of freedom is in the hearts, the very marrow of every man. Who can shut up these bones?"

Not Ester.

She'd listen to his voice forever.

"Who among us can strangle the yearnings of any man? Race nor creed nor even allegiance to the king will not deny the desire to be free. If you believe as I do, join me at month's end to rally at the Serpentine. There, we will unite and be of one mind. Abolition should succeed and be the law in every colony."

Bex said the words in direct address, as if he were on stage. Ester sighed with bliss. She yearned to call out and encourage him to continue above the few boos and grunts of dissenters in the crowd.

Ester wasn't brave enough for that, but she'd applaud him. He had to know someone heard and was moved. She put her hands together and clapped loud.

A few men stopped their groaning and stared in her direction.

The danger meant nothing. Ester didn't care and clapped harder, cupping the stalk of lilac to not bruise it.

What harm could come from proclaiming her love of the great actor with applause? Her days of freedom would be over soon. The Jordans weren't theater-goers. This might be the last time she'd see Bex perform.

Ester had nothing left to lose, and clapped again and again, basking in Bex's voice.

CHAPTER TWO

A Rousing Response

Arthur Bex was used to tough crowds. He'd worked up from bit lines to the lead in farces and dramas over the course of three years. But those were other men's words he recited, not the ones he said today in the basement of White Horse Cellar. These were Arthur's, and they burned in his heart. It was time to show London that the time to fight for abolition was now.

A young negress stood on the steps, clapping. In that moment, he let the rhythm of her slapping palms command his full attention, away from the naysayers and those just looking for a reason for fisticuffs or, like Phineas, following him around to find a scandal. He nodded to her before stepping down.

The reporter with a hawkish nose, Hildebrand Phineas, who sat close, swilling beer, hissed at him. "Is that all you have, Gunpowder?"

Gunpowder burns up, consumed by its own power, and destroys everything it touches. That couldn't happen to Arthur. He had too much to do, too many wrongs to right. He glared at Phineas. "I've said my piece for now. Come to the rally at the month's end and hear more."

"He wants a Peterloo here in London," the reporter said as he sneered. "You want blood to run in our streets, Gunpowder."

"No massacre will happen in our fair city." Arthur made his voice louder than the Peterloo chants. Some did want blood in the streets, but not him. He'd seen enough death in his youth. He advocated for freedom. "We must stop the institutional massacre of our brothers by slavery."

Turning away from the annoying Phineas, he stared back to the rowdy crowd and the negress who still stood at the stairs. The young woman was too smartly dressed to be an errant server who had wandered down to an all men's meeting. No, she had to be there for a reason, for the lass wasn't disturbed at being the only female in the cellar, and the only Blackamoor at that. A bold woman.

Maybe she heard his call for abolition and believed his words.

Heartened, he rent his coat open and refused to stop pressing for the rally. "Abolition is the cause of the day, gentlemen and dear lady. If we do not hear the cry of the oppressed—our brothers in chains just beyond our shores—what good are we? I tell you, we must press Parliament, shake the seats of the House of Lords, do everything that is within our grasp to end the practice in our colonies that we have ended here in England. The barbarous slave trade needs to stop, with nary a slave ship in our docks, and none creeping into our ports. We must deprive our pockets to refill our conscience with goodness. How can we say we value freedom when coins take the freedom of others?"

Fists raised, almost daring someone to disagree, Arthur received nothing but applause. The young woman clapped again.

Blood pumping, he went back to his table and sampled the air, rank with swill and perspiration. He felt good. Someone was moved today from ambivalence to awareness of the plight of the enslaved. He sensed it. Maybe someone here would stand up for the fight.

Yet, no man in the cellar was called to fight abolition more than him. The passion had rooted in him early, for the sins of his bloodline must be righted.

One fellow got up and staggered first toward Arthur but then headed straight for the woman. The drunk grabbed her arm and dragged her close to the chair on which Arthur had just stood. "Get on up there, and we can practice selling her so Bex can save her."

"Let... Let me go." She struggled, but the drunk held fast to her wrist.

Arthur stood. "Let her be. Have you heard nothing?"

The fool blew him a kiss as he held her hand high. "So, this is what you fight for, Mr. Actor. A race scorched by the sun. A folk as dim as they are dark—"

Arthur had him by the throat before the drunk could say more hateful words and yanked him by the cravat away from the young woman. "Get some coffee and sober up. Miss, this is a men's meeting. It's not for females."

Her eyes were wide, like he'd said something profound.

"What gives, Bex?" The drunk broke free and snatched her elbow. "We have a prime example of womanhood here. Let's put her on the chair and sell the little thing for coming to the cellar. You said it yourself. This territory is for men alone."

"That hurts," she said. "Let me go you...you, Iago."

The drunk and Arthur stopped at the same time to stare at her, but Arthur was probably the only one to discern that she offered an insult—an Iago being the horrid villain from Shakespeare's *Othello*.

He almost smiled, but instead, he pushed the Iago drunk

away, flinging him into a chair. "Do you not hear her cry for freedom, Iago fiend?"

The girl, who'd now ducked behind Arthur, pressed her lean fingers into his side. That protective feeling that filled him when playing a hero on the stage welled in his chest. "Let's go, miss. I fear you'll need a personal escort before another Iago decides to test you. Yes, a personal escort, indeed."

Before they could take a step, the drunk careened into him. "No fun, Bex. Can't have the fancy all to yourself."

Temper rising, Arthur did a quick jab, coupled with a fast punch, which sent the man flat to the floor. "Good day, gentlemen. Come, miss."

She followed him up the stairs, even as others snickered as they passed.

"Miss, from the cut of your clothes, I can't imagine you need to be saved very often, but mind my friends. They can become very animated when disturbed. It was a men's only meeting."

"Maybe you need better friends." Her voice was low. Her olive cheeks deepened to henna when he turned his head and gazed upon her.

"You may be right."

"Arthur Bex thinks I'm right." She looked as if she was about to faint. When she stumbled on the last step, he took her hand, the one free of a notebook, into his. A stalk of lilac was crushed between their linked palms.

"Lilac is a wonderful flower," he said as he led her back to the main level of the coaching inn. His pulse raced. This was the woman he had exchanged letters with, his potential newspaper advertisement bride. "We have much to discuss."

She tried to leave him, but he steered her to his table. Her small frame was rather easy to navigate, putting a hand here and a nudge there.

Fanning her face, she looked very unsteady, so he took her book from her and guided her into a seat. Would she faint when he displayed his signal to meet, a matching stem of lilac from his pocket?

She looked caught. The sense of shyness about her made him smile inside. Even though he was applying through the papers for a marriage of convenience, his masculine pride demanded that it still feel as if he'd won someone's approval.

"I'm here with my friend. I should find her," she said. Her voice had a nice tone, clear and low.

"Of course, miss, but let us take a moment to get to know one another."

"You want to know me? Arthur Bex wants to know me." She put a hand to her bonnet and fanned. "I must be dreaming. This is nothing but a dream. The famous actor, Arthur Bex, is sitting with me, saving me from a drunk. And he wants to know me."

She pinched herself. "No. I still don't believe."

Phineas came up and tipped his hat. He looked ready to leave the coaching inn but then decided to take a table. It wasn't close enough to overhear, but it wasn't far enough for Arthur to let his guard down. Then he thought about the odds that a Blackamoor woman would answer his advertisement, a Blackamoor marrying an abolitionist. Anger swept through him. This might be a trap. He put his hand upon hers to keep her from squirming or leaving too quickly. "Who sent you?"

Over her creamy kid gloves, the exposed part of her wrist

pimpled. "I sent myself. This is obviously a mistake."

The blush, the fear induced bumps—that couldn't be an act, could it? He sighed. "Well, it is obvious that you know me, but I... Wait. I recognize you from the Fitzwilliam-Cecil wedding celebration. Your family's in textiles?"

Her eyes, glittering topaz jewels, grew wide as she pinched herself again. "You can remember that? You remember me?"

He caught her other hand. "You need to stop doing that."

She looked around, her cheeks darkening again, but deeper than before. "You have both my hands, Mr. Bex. As wonderful as this is, it's not right."

Self-conscious about their location and Phineas looking for scandal, he released her. "Sorry, Miss..."

"Miss Croome."

"Ester Croome, if I recall what Fitzwilliam-Cecil said."

She dug into her reticule and found a fan. "I barely said two words to you. I can't believe I am making complete sentences now. And you remembered my name."

"You have a very memorable face and figure, and now I hear a memorable voice to match."

Blinking ten times, like she'd just awakened, Miss Croome crossed her arms, then uncrossed her arms, then put her hands down. "Arthur Bex noticed me. I'm going to go back to mumbling and broken sentences."

She had wit, a sharpness of mind. Something he'd noticed at the wedding party when she'd spoken to others, but not him. He dipped his head closer. "I wish you would continue communicating, or how else am I to get to know you? How else will you determine to marry me? Well, you know of me. Have you made up your mind?"

"Marry you?" She dropped the fan to the table with a thud. "Arthur Bex, the greatest actor of the London stage, wants to marry me." She put a hand to her temple and rubbed like it held a smudge.

His latent sense of humor began to enjoy her shyness. He wondered what other ways he could tease her to embarrass her and how bright her cheeks would turn if she were thoroughly flattered by him. "What can I do to put you at ease? I'll look at your book. It's a sketchbook?"

"Please don't." She said as her dimpled cheeks, all her face, reddened.

"Now I have to look." He flipped it open and saw beautiful sketches of dresses and a page of signatures. Mrs. Bex, Mrs. Arthur Bex, Ester Bex. "You seem quite confident that we will agree to marry. You've practiced writing your marital name. You guessed I was the one."

"I'm embarrassed, and Arthur Bex is flirting with me. This has to be an illusion."

He put two fingers on each side of her squirming temples. "Is this an illusion? You act as if you have forgotten our exchanged letters." He dipped into his pocket and pulled out the fragrant lilac stem he'd purchased this morning from Covent Gardens after being given the part of Antony—his big next play.

The girl's face became crestfallen, her voluptuous lips sagged. "There's a mistake."

"Miss Croome," a woman said. "There you are, and you found...Arthur Bex?" She gasped, holding her mouth wide open for a few seconds. "Arthur Bex, the actor?"

"Guilty," he said. It was the other friend of Fitzwilliam-Cecil's bride. She was tall with a very light complexion, much lighter than Miss Croome's olive skin. In certain lighting, she wouldn't be taken as a Blackamoor woman at all.

Life might be easier for an interracial couple because of it, but the class differences, her being a duke's daughter, on such a higher rung than an actor, would be insurmountable.

He looked at Miss Croome again and was glad it was she writing him, someone in textiles, with humble beginnings like his own.

The standing woman squinted. "Arthur Bex. The man you… In the plays. The fellow—"

Miss Croome grabbed her hand. "Miss Burghley, this is the man who responded to the newspaper advertisement. He's the one with the lilac. The one you—"

"No, Miss Croome, he's the one you've been waiting for. Sir, don't keep my friend too long. I'll be in my carriage waiting for you, Miss Croome."

There had to be some confusion, something underfoot, for his table companion wouldn't release Miss Burghley's hand.

"But," Miss Croome said before being shushed by her friend.

"I know you're shy, but this is your one chance at marrying a man you admire. Mr. Bex, no one is a bigger student of your performances than my friend. I know you two have much in common."

Miss Croome didn't seem satisfied and still gripped Miss Burghley's glove in a seemingly desperate clutch. "Are you sure, Frederica? Your chance at happiness… Your father—"

Miss Burghley hugged her. "I still have time. And no friend could be happy at another's expense."

Now Arthur knew something was amiss. If these weren't Fitzwilliam-Cecil friends, he'd again think this was a plot by Phineas to trap him in a scandal. He swirled a thumb along a scratch in the table. "What does that mean, Miss Burghley? At another's expense? Everyone's happiness has some cost."

The woman's expression went from sober to impish in a blink. A wicked smile graced her light features. "It means I'll be very put-out if you don't declare to my friend all the reasons you wish to marry her. She's very busy. I wouldn't want her time wasted. She has other options."

Other options? Of course, other men would have answered her advertisement. Her race might put off some, but her family's money would make others forget the differences. As for Arthur, he didn't know. Would it be helpful to have a Blackamoor wife when he sought to be a leading voice in the abolition movement, or would the marriage be a distraction from the cause, another way for men to marginalize his voice? "Options are a good thing."

Miss Croome sat up. "This man has many options. He's Arthur Bex, the man whose performance as Romeo made the critics cry." She smiled at him. "Made me cry, too."

The woman, barely ten minutes into their discussion, had leaped to his defense. He had to get to know her better. He needed a wife who would attest to his character, who would believe in him above everything. Given his family's history, he wasn't sure a Blackamoor woman, even one that looked upon him with charity, would want to be his wife, but his goal was for that history to never be known. He craned his neck to find a waitress. "Let me get you all tea."

"None for me, Mr. Bex," Miss Burghley said, lightly tapping

the table with her finger. "What do you have to say to my friend? She's clever, a Shakespeare lover, and usually very articulate."

"Yes, when I'm not having palpitations in my chest." Miss Croome took her sketch pad and pushed air toward her face.

His seatmate possessed a sense of humor. That was something he treasured. Though she seemed shy now, it had been quite bold of her to come down to the cellar.

A woman like Miss Croome, who possessed a delicate nature, boldness, and humor, didn't come around every day, in any race. Arthur caught her gaze again and held on to it, as if reaching for polished gems. Delicate, shy, bold, pretty—though, she frowned as if she couldn't decide whether to stay, leave, or even be sick.

He hated to lose. It was the one unfortunate trait he shared with his uncle, the man who'd raised him. Losers straddled the fence. Winners decided. "I intend to declare myself to be of sound mind and body, and I want to marry this woman if she'll have me."

Miss Croome's cheeks were definitely darker now, and if she proved this easily delighted, the marriage might even be a happy one.

Whipping the lilac under her nose as if it were smelling salts, Miss Croome lowered her gaze. "I never dreamed to be sitting here with Arthur Bex. Are you sure, Miss Burghley, you don't want to change your mind and sit with us? Arthur Bex is a wonderful man. He'll make anyone a good husband."

"Not anyone, my dear Miss Croome. You. Upon seeing you look at him and how he's looking at you, I know this is right. When you are finished here, we'll head to the party where your other suitor will be." Miss Burghley offered a final pat to Miss

Croome's hand and left.

The meaning of the women's exchange was of no consequence. Arthur noted the important things. Miss Croome knew who he was, and unlike the last two women whose newspaper advertisements he'd responded to, she didn't seem to mind he was an actor...and she liked him. "I'll be honest, Miss Croome, when I thought of a marriage of convenience, I hadn't thought a Blackamoor or mulatto woman would respond."

"I hadn't thought of writing to a Blackamoor or mulatto woman, either, and my father wouldn't want me writing to an actor."

Her easy humor made the idea of them marrying more comfortable. "So, Miss Croome, my race does not matter to you or your father, but my profession and lack of fortune do?"

"The lack of a fortune, the profession, and your race will bother him, but my happiness seems...is no longer his concern."

"And those are not your concerns, Miss Croome?"

With wide, toasty, topaz eyes, she looked unafraid, even alluring. "No. Just my happiness."

Given to gambles, he'd test her, even though he had mostly made up his risk-taking mind. "In a jaded way, a well-spoken Blackamoor would cement my credentials for the cause that I fight for—abolition. Who could doubt my sincerity to end slavery if Miss Croome could attest to my heart? That's how the reporters will put our marriage."

"Or the fabric princess debases herself and her family with an actor—the gossips aren't kind on my part of town, either."

A sense of realism with her humor. That was something else he liked. Another good point in her favor. Arthur drummed the table again. "We should get to know each other over a pot of tea. How would you like that?"

"The same as you, with honey and a little lemon." Her voice was stronger now. She must be getting used to him. "And chamomile is my favorite, too, just like you."

"You know this?"

"I've studied everything about you, Mr. Bex, for a long time."

Three points in a row—she'd won the tally. Newspaper advertisement number eleven seemed more and more the one, despite the obstacles. He stretched and signaled to a barmaid.

Once the flabbergasted woman took his order, he returned his full attention to Miss Croome and her lovely eyes. "So why are you seeking a husband by newspaper? The fabric princess has other options, as your friend put it."

"I must be honest with you. Honesty and fidelity are the two things which are most important to me. You have been corresponding with Miss Burghley. I helped with the wording of her advertisement, but it was she who placed it, not me. But she, all my friends, know I am in awe of you. I have been for two years. She was the lucky one who you wrote to. I should just retrieve her or leave. Starting out under a falsehood is a bad omen."

He put his hand on hers. "You are the one who's here now. The one I wish to share tea with. Stay."

She nodded and slipped her palm to her lap.

Miss Croome with her button nose, and her noticeable figure hiding beneath the blousy spencer, blushed again, a deeper shade of henna, the color again commanding all of her face.

She smiled as she took her tea. Her long lashes fluttered as she gulped. "Done, Mr. Bex. Now you can send me home, back to reality."

She was definitely all woman, definitely attracted to him, and definitely a pleasing mixture of boldness and shyness. Unlike other theatergoers and sycophants who'd taken an interest in him because of his celebrity, this woman seemed cautious. Perhaps she needed convincing that a marriage of convenience could work. Point four, a challenge. A challenge was something Arthur appreciated, something inescapable in his foul blood.

He looked over at Phineas. The bloodhound nodded. He wouldn't stop chasing until he found Arthur's scandal. A respectable wife to recommend Arthur would deter questions, give the hounds a new story to chew. Miss Croome was the answer, but she needed to be swayed in this instance, or he'd lose her before they had a chance to begin.

CHAPTER THREE

A Surprising Proposal

Ester sipped the second cup of tea Arthur Bex had ordered for her. Arthur Bex. As hard as she tried not to rattle her cup, and to drink with an unaffected air as Mama had instructed her daughters, Ester failed miserably, clinking her cup, sloshing the sweet fragrance of chamomile.

But what could one expect? She was sitting with a demi-god, the man she had dreamed of almost every night, his voice luscious, thick, and sweet like honey. Arthur Bex sat beside her, discussing marriage.

"Miss Croome, while I do find the cups at the White Horse Cellar quite fascinating. I would appreciate it if you'd look up at me and tell me about yourself. It was Miss Burghley's advertisement that brought us here, but are you looking to be married?"

"Yes." Particularly since Papa's surprise this morning.

Bex was even taller and more handsome up close. Even sitting, he loomed above her, and she thought of how secure she'd feel snuggled in his well-built arms.

"Miss Croome, I met you at Fitzwilliam-Cecil's home. It seems to me that two consenting adults looking to be married could have spoken months ago."

"I'm painfully shy around strangers." She breathed deeply, looked up, and retook his gaze. There was kindness in his cobalt-blue eyes. It made it a little easier for her lungs to keep functioning.

"Words come easy for you, Mr. Bex. Your voice holds command even when ordering a pot of tea. I've a great imagination." She put down her spoon and tapped her bonnet. "But it never conceived of this."

"Then your imagination is limited, or perhaps trapped beneath that pretty bonnet."

He moved a little closer and fingered the ribbon beneath her chin. "You could take off your hat. If that will make you free."

"No, that will invite more stares. Curly thick locks compared to yours will get everyone talking. Can't you see how they are looking at us, wondering what Arthur Bex is doing taking tea with me?"

"Maybe they are pondering why Miss Croome is taking tea with an actor? My profession, as you've said, isn't quite what everyone wants for their daughter's husband."

"Not in this part of London, Mr. Bex. Closer to Cheapside in the old Huguenot areas, the Croome name is better known. Lord knows a few of my mother's friends would be running to tell her if they saw us."

"You mean the areas closer to the textile warehouses, or where the Blackamoor populations congregate?"

She looked at his sly, cutting smile, his dark chestnut-brown hair, and swarthy sun-kissed skin—not a trace of stupid. "You know what I mean, sir."

He nodded. His fingers brushed her hand again as he reached for a biscuit. "Yes, yes, I do. But I'm thinking that may not matter so much when it comes to compatibility."

He could've spoken French, though she was fluent, or Russian. It could be gibberish, and she'd still nod her head. His voice had wrapped around her and crushed her in warmth. There was no escaping her attraction to him, but she would for Frederica. "My friend Miss Burghley is very kind. Some consider her my prettiest friend. Her complexion is lighter, her connections are higher. She is looking for a lifelong companion. I've no problems going and retrieving her from her carriage. You both may have more in common."

He wiped crumbs from his mouth, and his deep smile captured her with a draw that couldn't be denied. "How would that sit with you, Miss Croome?" His voice became sultry as he leaned closer. "Would it do well with you if I whispered my intent in her ear, not yours?"

Her face felt hot. He was teasing her, and his confidence was alluring. She was her father's daughter, and she liked a confident man. "No. It would not. You're very sure of yourself."

"A good actor knows his audience. I can tell that you like me, Miss Croome. And I think I like you, too."

Her worst day had become her best, but now it was bad again for evening would come and this affair would be done. She'd be engaged to a troll, the son of a troll.

After another sip of his steaming tea, Bex said, "Fitzwilliam-Cecil, the playwright, says you can quote Shakespeare as well as he. What's not to like about that?"

He'd asked about her, then? Could one burst into flames from blushing? If he kept it up, they'd both find out.

"If you are done passing me to your friends, let's discuss your intentions. Are you wanting to be married, Miss Croome?"

How many times had she thought of Bex, heard his voice riveting her soul? But not once was he telling jokes. He wasn't being serious. Marriage was serious. If he wasn't focused on their union, distractions could come upon him. He'd stray like Papa. She sat up straight. "I'm not done with my questions. Just because I like you, that's not eeeeeenough. Have you ever been married?"

"No, Miss Croome. If we decide to pursue you liking me, you would be my first and only bride."

"Do you have a mistress?"

His face sobered. "Not now, not for a year."

Her brow raised on that answer. Bex was a handsome man, the rage of London. It was hard to believe he was alone. "So you'll take one after we wed? I hear that's what important men do. It makes them feel powerful."

He frowned for a moment. "I made jokes to put you at ease, but I'll be perfectly serious in answering you. I want your trust. I need a wife who will believe in me wholly, so I'll take no mistress. A man has no honor if he cannot stay true to his vows. The same for you. There should be no one other than me."

She swallowed, thinking of her father's failings. Anyone could fall, even with the best intentions. "You're not diseased or running from the law?"

He scratched his chin which held a little shadow. "Miss Croome, aren't you being a little dramatic?"

"Answer the question, if you can."

"Everyone knows Arthur Bex." He waved at a patron who seemed to be staring, then settled his hand back to the table, again next to hers. "I could hardly run from illegalities. Why don't you tell me your true objection? Am I not what you expected?"

"No. This is some cruel joke. I want to pinch myself again, but you stopped me from doing that."

"You could pinch me if that would help."

She rolled her eyes and peered around his broad shoulders at the other patrons of the inn. No one glared at her and Bex anymore. They'd faded into the noise. "This is the most I've ever said to you. Doesn't that concern you?"

"Not in the least. A shy woman will run from scandal. The widowed countess I last spent time with seeded the newspaper men with gossip about me. I want privacy for my home, my loved ones—if I had any."

His fingers lay so close to her hand. She could count the dimples in his knuckles or trace his off-kilter index finger, the one he'd injured last year when the skull of Yorick fell upon it during a rehearsal.

Yes. She knew too much of him and the Countess Devoors, the last woman the papers had linked him to. The countess seemed vivacious and was always in the gossip stories. Nothing like shy Ester. She gripped the gnarled table's edge. "I remember reading that your parents died at an early age."

He looked away, maybe for the first time. Had she offended him, or was the memory of such early loss painful?

"There is no one close to me, now. Just a would-be groom who runs errands for me."

His wondrous voice held notes of sadness. She couldn't let him stew in loss and pushed the saucer with the last biscuit his way. "You could have any woman, Mr. Bex. I've seen how they follow you. Even the barmaids here are ogling you. Why seek a bride by newspaper?"

"You've watched me?" He edged closer as he munched the last treat. His whisper fell across her brow. "You feel you know me?"

Skin heating from his biscuit-laced breath, she willed her chin to rise so she could bask fully in his close gaze. "Like you said. Everyone knows Arthur Bex, the great actor, but I wonder about the man answering advertisements for a wife."

"I'm a simple creature, Miss Croome. I love the theater, but I'm driven to right the wrongs of this day. I wasn't given my talents to squander them. I aim to make a difference, but it's time to have a wife. I wish for one that understands the demands upon me, one that's logical, and not compelled by the twists of a long courtship, one who is as resistant to scandal as I am."

"That is admirable and good. But a wife of another race could be problematic. I wouldn't want to cause harm to your reputation."

"There are worse things to harm a reputation than a different type of wife. You seem to keep saying why you're not the one for me. I say, why not you, Miss Croome? Fate, a friend, and a newspaper have brought us together. I say, why not us. What is your true hesitation?"

"My father has other ideas. He wants me to wed a business colleague's son."

He stopped toying with the shrinking distance of their fingers and took her hand, sending another spark up her arm. "Ah, the other option. I sense that the son is your father's choice and not yours? I still want to know why not you and me?"

She closed her gloved palm about his and dropped it to the bench. "We are not engaged yet. You can't be so familiar."

He chuckled, then swooped in. "I sense you are on the verge of deciding. I'll take an unfair advantage. Besides, I like the hint of henna that blooms on your face when I touch you."

She folded her arms about her as if that could keep her heart from racing. "Do you know what it's like to hear your deep baritone say those sweet words to me?"

"Then hear my soul speak, dear lady. The very instant I saw you, did my heart fly to your service."

He was quoting Shakespeare to her as he had quoted it on stage when he performed *The Tempest*, but those words of instant love couldn't be Bex's. They were Ester's. She closed her eyes, forgetting the noisy inn and even Bex's honey voice and said, "'The very instant that I saw you did my heart fly to your service, there it resides to make me a slave to it.'"

"No. No one is a slave, or they shouldn't be. No, you have choices. I want to be your choice, Miss Croome." His tone had hardened, then softened upon saying her name.

"I don't know what to think, Mr. Bex. I can't pretend not to be awed by you."

With a sigh, he sat back. "You are free to walk away from this moment, but I think we should try. Where else will I find a lover of Shakespeare's words? Yes, you are special. I think you should accept me. You, too, I assume, are not married, have no benefactor arrangements. I presume you are not sick or hiding from criminality. On your criteria alone, I think we are perfectly suited."

How many times had she thought of this man during theater season and hushed Frederica or their friend Theodosia, just to hear his voice, clear and true? How many times had she kicked herself for lacking the courage to say a few words to him at Theodosia's wedding celebration? Ester picked up her sketchbook and waved cool, sweet air to her face. "I don't have time to rationalize this, Mr. Bex, or think about it a hundred and five times. This is either madness or a dream come true."

"I hope for truth and righteousness. I feel that it is, but I won't rush you, Miss Croome. You can take—"

"No, I must rush you. If we are to do this, we must elope tonight."

"Tonight? There would be no time to get a license. The banns have not been read. We'd have to go to Scotland."

"Yes."

His brow wrinkled. "The blacksmith at Gretna Green who'll do the ceremony is at least four or five days away. It will be a ten-day trip in total to return to London. That is traveling day and night, unsupervised. It would be better if we waited for a proper license. We could get to know each other, without testing each other so soon."

"It must be tonight. A harrowing escape will bind us together. Doesn't adversity do that? It does for friends. Why not man and wife? But if you're not inclined, I won't push." She put her hand on the table to rise but his palm pressed atop hers.

"I'm inclined. And a woman who can make up her mind so quickly and in my favor is to be treasured. I was thinking of you. I don't want to run as if this were illicit, like we are wanted criminals."

His voice had changed. It seemed to hold the softness of a bad memory, one that he failed to repress.

Her weak-for-him heart softened more. He deserved to hear the whole truth. With a quick breath, she forced her tongue to admit it. "If we don't elope tonight, I'll be forced to marry my father's choice on my twenty-first birthday, a month from today. The man is a womanizing brute."

"Then you do need saving." He folded his arms. "If we make good time, we could return in time for the rehearsal of my next play. Yes, Miss Croome. Let me be the one. Let us elope, tonight."

"No one is safe from my father's wrath. Josiah Croome's temper is legendary. Once he figures it out, he will give chase. The more I think about it, the more I fail to believe we have a chance. Forget I said anything about eloping tonight. Thank you for the tea, Mr. Bex."

"I like challenges, particularly one with poor odds and dire consequences. Let's try, Miss Croome. Let's prove wrong the naysayers, even the ones beneath your pretty bonnet. I'll take a gamble on a fellow Shakespeare lover. Where do I meet you?"

"Come to Nineteen Fournier. At five minutes after midnight, I'll be at the far corner of the house, waiting in the parlor beside the wide window. I'll jump down from it, and we can ride off to Gretna Green."

Ester stood up, but he took her hand and pressed it to his lips. "I'll be there, five after midnight."

"I'll understand if you don't show, Mr. Bex."

"I'll be there to catch you, my future wife. And I'll knock on the door and come inside if you don't come down. Don't make me ascend a balcony for you. I will. You've seen me do it."

The smile he sent her made her knees knock, even more so than the eyes of everyone in the inn looking at Bex romance her. She shook her head and focused on him. "I remember your performance as Romeo in *Romeo and Juliet*. It was quite good. This isn't pretend."

"I'll be there, for we are now engaged, my sun."

This could be fun with endless references to theater plays. She smiled at her sweet prince. "Sorrowfully parting from you until tonight, Mr. Bex." She floated out of the inn, not looking back, not wanting this moment to be taken from her. Arthur Bex knew Ester's name and wanted to elope.

She leaned on Frederica's carriage door. Everything would change at the toll of midnight. This daydream of marrying Arthur Bex would surely go away. At five minutes after midnight, the truth would return and the arranged engagement set up by her father would begin. Josiah Croome believed he could run the world and that included his daughter's domestic happiness. The men who crossed him were doomed. One had even fled to the Americas. Would that be Bex's fate?

She hugged her sketchbook before taking the door handle. The naysayers in her bonnet, as Bex had put it, were robbing her of the joy she'd stumbled upon. Tonight, she'd be engaged, either to Arthur Bex, the man of her dreams, or the womanizer dreamed up by her father. Ester shook her head. The hours until five after midnight would be the longest ones in her life.

CHAPTER FOUR

Pacing and Partying

From the top of the stairs, Ester snuck unnoticed past the floor where the dining room was and on to the lower level. On the bottom tread, she took a breath and traced the glow of the tall beeswax candles in the Rococo chandelier in the main hall of Nineteen Fournier.

It had been old and dusty when Papa first took possession of the house, but Mama had cleaned it, found artisans amongst their old neighbors to make it shine, like she had done for the rest of the house.

Ester had been such a fool to think them happy. The grim look upon her mother's face when they'd first lit the chandelier should've been a warning. How could one be saddened by a fixture with gilded carved acanthus leaves made to suspend cut glass that looked like diamonds? With the long candles installed on the chandelier and even in the mirrored wall sconces, this party would go to three or four hours in the morning. Very good. She and Bex would have a head start—if he came—if she leaped to him.

Though indecision warred inside, she'd changed her dress to one she could manage without a maid and her undergarments to ones with a corset and ribbons in the front. Being on the run meant being quick, and she'd not be the reason they'd be caught. In her bag, she'd packed two easier buttoning dresses, a nightgown and robe, lilac soaps, a sack of charcoal, and her never-to-be-forgotten sketch pad. She was ready to elope. That seemed brave, but could she truly do it? Did that type of courage exist in her bones?

"Miss Croome, shouldn't you be upstairs readying for dinner?"

She nearly jumped out of her skin at Clancy's sudden appearance. "Yes." Her voice sounded like a croak.

"You have your traveling bag? You going to stay with your friend with the two names, now Cecil-Fitzwilliam Fitzwilliam-Cecil after the party?"

Ester never lied, but misdirection—that was something entirely different. "I'm planning to leave by the time the party ends or even before. You know how long these things go."

"Sounds like you're up to something."

Her eyes popped wide, but she relaxed at the wail of his laughter.

"I'm just jossin' with you. Here, I'll take that."

Ester's heart started to beat again. Time to act as if nothing was wrong. She handed the bag to him then adjusted her creamy silk gloves. They matched her robin's-egg blue gown with its high lace surrounding her neck. "You are a dear. Put it in the closet in the parlor."

"Yes, ma'am." He picked it up. "Your mother's upstairs in the dining room. I think she's looking for you."

"Thank you, Clancy. If I've ever failed to thank you for your service, for every kindness you do, let me tell you how much you mean to me, this family."

The old man dimpled and then headed to the parlor. He was a dear, and his humor would be needed to help soothe Mama and

Papa when they discovered Ester had eloped.

The upstairs grandfather clock's moans reached her ear.

Seven o'clock. Still trying to feign calm, she waited until she saw Clancy go inside and then come out of the parlor. Step one was accomplished. Her bag was in place. If Bex showed, she wouldn't have to think of anything or need any excuses.

Mrs. Fitterwall swished by, her strawberry-red hair matching her gingham skirts. "Good, you finally crawled out of your second bath. I swear you are going to be all wrinkled if you keep to that."

Ester put her arms about her shoulders and swayed to the music beginning to filter down the stairs. "Nothing helps to make sense of things like soaking in a lilac-scented bath."

The housekeeper stopped and pointed her finger at each sconce, then the chandelier. "The hired servants for the party lit that. One thing completed on your mother's list. She frets so much about her parties. I've known her since we first worked together as maids in Mayfair. She'd get like this about our employers' affairs, too."

Affairs? That was the last thing Ester wanted to think of. "What more is there to do? The dining room is set. The musicians have arrived. You hear them practicing."

Mrs. Fitterwall put a hand on her hip. "You know it's not done till Mrs. Croome says it is. Her celebrations have to be perfect. I think she gets her love of big to-dos from the sugar plantations where she's from." The woman clasped her hands together. "You know she'll make sure your upcoming wedding celebration is perfect. She truly wants to give one of her daughters a proper wedding breakfast."

Running away with Bex would deprive her mother of all the

things she seemed to enjoy. When Ruth's arranged marriage had happened so fast, Mama hadn't been able to plan a proper wedding. She'd been so sad about it. The family had lived at Fournier only two years then, after practically growing up in the two-room apartment above Papa's warehouse. Had those small quarters, with the peephole to spy on things below, been better days? Had it been the last time the Croomes were all truly happy?

Another fiddler's tune joined the first as more music filled the house. After dinner was done, they'd play full-on, and Nineteen Fournier would become a place for dancing. The perfect time to escape with Bex.

"Miss Ester," said Mrs. Fitterwall. "Don't doddle too long. Your mother needs you."

The housekeeper went back upstairs. She was a good addition to Nineteen Fournier, maybe the best, for she and Mama had a wonderful friendship beyond employer and employee. Sometimes, Ester wished she and her mother were as close.

With slow steps, Ester started for the stairs to the dining room, and Mama, but stopped and twirled under the candelabra. That first day Papa had shown them this house, before anything inside had been restored, she and her father had danced under it. With his big thick arms, he'd twirled her high as Mama and Ruth had looked on, laughing. He had been perfect then. She'd known of no wrongs, no transgressions. How long had they lived a lie?

"Ester."

She looked up and faced her father. "I see those dancing lessons I paid for have worked. You look like you could float."

Dressed in his onyx tailcoat and formal white silk waistcoat over dark pantaloons, Papa came down from her parent's second-floor bedchamber. His head swung from side to side, no doubt admiring the lighting, maybe remembering those easier times, too.

After tugging his white, white gloves over his big hands, he held out his palm. "May I twirl the loveliest daughter at the party?"

Ester stared at his pristine dancing gloves. This could be one of her last moments to spend with Papa before riding off with Bex. So, she'd pretend she was fifteen again and Papa was her hero. She took his hand, clutched it tight, and let him spin her until they both were laughing and breathless.

"Ester!" That was Mama's voice.

Papa put his big arms about her and gave her a large hug. "She probably needs you, but I'm happy, sweet girl."

"Happy about what?" Ester slipped away from him and smoothed the shimmering overdress that surrounded her robin's-egg blue gown. She fingered the matching thin bonnet to make sure the hat wasn't going to fall and unravel her thick braid. "Has something changed?"

Her father's smile diminished. "You've come around to the idea of an engagement."

"I am not happy about your arrangement. I won't marry him."

"Ester, this is best. You'll be happy."

"As happy as you and my mother?" Ester turned from Papa and the hurt in his dark eyes. She couldn't pretend anymore. She couldn't lie as well as Josiah Croome, either. "I need to go to Mama."

She left him standing under the chandelier. She wasn't fifteen anymore. Her new hero would come for her at five past midnight. But what if Bex's sweet talk was acting, and he proved to be no better than Papa?

The hairs on her neck rose. She felt dizzy and clutched the banister more tightly. Then she bucked up her spirit. Bex was better than her father's choice. At the second level, she moved toward the dining room and counted on her fingers the new servants she passed. Each wore crisp blue satin livery, no doubt some imported fabric that Papa had procured for this party. Four men, all tall, each with freshly-powdered locks. This party was even bigger than last Christmas Eve, when Papa had celebrated the new contract for the mantua-maker at Burlingame. Such a high moment for the Croomes. The next day, making room for Papa's new desk, Ester had found the love letters.

"Ester?" her mother said. "I need your help. You'll have your own home soon. You'll need to know these things."

"I'm not much for place settings. That was Ruth's job."

Mama looked off into the distance. Thirty seconds passed before she returned her gaze. "You will be under the scrutiny of the Jordans. I wouldn't want you saying something unwarranted."

Ester brow and her ire raised. "Unwarranted? Like what?"

"I don't know. Politics, or your theater nonsense."

"You mean everything that is worth anything?"

Mama stopped aligning the forks. "Mrs. Jordan thinks you are a tad bit spirited for her son. Charles Jordan is a handsome young man. How well his hands will look on yours as we give you the wedding I've dreamed of, one bigger, even, than what I wanted for your sister."

"Yes, Ruth had to go away with her husband. Did she try to rebel against the arrangement you and Papa made? It's so odd they haven't visited in two years."

Mama moved to an adjacent table and smoothed the white linens. "She's doing what's best for her family. You will, too. You're very level-headed."

She fluttered a napkin before folding a perfect square. "The gown I've planned for your wedding will make you look regal. The decorations for your wedding breakfast will be perfect. This will be the most celebrated wedding. You and Jordan will do well."

Burning inside, words and gall pitting in her throat, Ester threw up her hands. "We won't. He's not Arthur Bex."

"Not the actor again? I don't want that actor's or any actors' *hands* on you."

Something in the way she said "hands," made Ester angrier. "So, if Jordan were a mulatto like you or Miss Burghley, our hands wouldn't match well. Or if his skin were pale like your father's—"

The look her mother offered, blank eyes, mouth shrinking to a grim line, made Ester cringe. Her heart dove into her stomach. "I'm sorry, Mama. I've said too much. I didn't mean to bring up the memories."

Her mother lowered her head. She twisted one of her rings before latching on to a misaligned plate. "You have a mouth on you. But you know how we've fretted for Papa's business dealings—that he'd shake the wrong *hands* and never come home."

Ester knew. And could count on her fingers and toes, triple the times they'd feared that he'd disappear like some of their old neighbors, taught a lesson, a fatal lesson like Papa's brother. Yes. Ester knew, and her stomach knotted, and she swallowed bile. "Sorry, Mama."

Her mother pressed at her temples like she had a severe headache. "Tonight, we celebrate the anniversary of moving into this house. Perhaps, you and Charles can live here once you've married. It could help you settle into the marriage, knowing we are here to help. Mrs. Jordan thinks that will help her son settle in, too."

"You mean, stepson." Ester sank into one of the diner chairs and ruffled the tablecloth. The spotless silver service cast a sparkle on the pale blue walls. "The girl is barely older than me. And if that is true, that I'm so spirited, why do they want me to marry him? I can't do this. I won't twist up who I am."

"Who are you, Ester?" Mama stopped poking and sliding silverware and folded her arms in their elegant emerald silk sleeves. She glared, her forest green eyes narrowing. "Let me tell you who you are. You are the daughter of Josiah Croome, the granddaughter and niece of proud women who did what they had to, to survive. You've been brought up educated, and now have a taste for the finest things. You're a jewel. A man will strive to become what he sees blooming in your eyes. He'll want to be the source of your joy and pride. So, fix your face and lift your head. Do us honor tonight."

Ester drew back. That was the sternest thing Mama had ever said to her. "Yes, ma'am." She pushed a fork askew. "I can't set Charles Jordan's table or just be ready for his bed—that is, if he chooses to be there. I refuse to turn myself into nothing for some sort of status."

"You mean like me?" Mama pushed the fork back into position. "You were never really good at setting tables. That *was* Ruth's gift. Maybe she can be spared from the country and come back for a visit. Maybe as soon as your wedding. That would be an excuse for her to come." Mama twisted her rings, all gold, one with a jade stone. "You're young, Ester. You've been sheltered. You don't understand the cruelty of this world or its hard choices."

"I'm not naive. I see the world as it is."

There was pain in Mama's eyes. The little flecks of gold had disappeared in the glossy wetness. "No. If you truly saw the world, you'd know how hard it is to be a good wife, a good mother. You'd know the sacrifices I've made for the family. Then you'd respect my choices."

Mama turned and headed to the door, but paused in the threshold. "The Jordans are a decent, respectable family. For my party, give it a chance. Be kind tonight. I'll see what can be done, if you are truly against this."

Ester loved her mother, but she couldn't respect the choice of not even getting angry at Papa, of going through Christmas dinner with smiles as if nothing had happened. She had even chastised Ester for confronting her father over the affair.

Pushing a knife to align with the crystal goblet, Ester fought her own tears. She'd do anything for her mother—anything but marry a known philanderer.

Maybe things had changed between her parents. There were signs of true affection betwixt them, like the way he kissed Mama's cheek at breakfast. The way her eyes had lit up when he'd given her a pearl necklace for her birthday.

But Ester wasn't her mother.

Eloping tonight was the chance to ensure that she'd never become her. Bex played men of honor on stage, men so deeply rooted in love and principles that they would die rather than be untrue. With life, there were no guarantees. Yet, the way the papers hounded him, if he were a lout, something would've been printed about his wild life? The break with Countess Devoors was the worst gossip she'd seen, and that wasn't bad—just a woman throwing dishes because Bex didn't want to go to a party.

With a sigh, Ester moved into the drawing room, which had been opened for dancing.

A servant chalked the floor as they'd seen Papa's best client, a duchess, do. The woman had paid him well for importing special fabrics so she could be the fashion rage of the season, and the duchess had let Papa and Ester come by for a few moments before the rest of her guests had arrived. Papa had wanted to see her house. That was how he set his dreams, looking at what he wanted and pushing for it.

Walking fast, she almost leaped down the stairs. Back on the first level, she veered straight to Mama's parlor. Once inside, Ester closed the door then settled near the window. She peeked through the leaded glass. The waves in the pane made it look like it had rained. Fournier Street was lit up with link boys to guide the carriages to the house and the mews. The place would be filled with friends for Mama's party, but Ester wanted a light showing her the way to her dreams. What would be her path? Was it running away with Bex? What would she do if he didn't appear?

• • •

In the mews near the White Horse Cellar, Arthur stood at his phaeton and pulled his pocket watch from his waistcoat. It was four hours to midnight, four hours and five minutes before eloping with the future Mrs. Bex—

"There you are, Bex."

Arthur turned to the hoarse-sounding voice. Phineas, the dogged reporter, entered the mews. The man leaned against a wall with one of his trademark Hessian boots lifted onto the stall rail. "Are you sure you have to leave now? I could buy you a brandy, and we could chat."

Trying to ignore the hound, Arthur worked on his horse, checking the harness, tugging each ring and each strap. At his flat in Cheapside, Jonesy would do it, but away from there, he needed to be careful. Someone against his message of abolition might play tricks or create sabotage. He tightened the backhand and bellyband around his silver gelding. "I have an appointment, Phineas."

The man came to the other side of his gig. "A late-night rehearsal? Or a rendezvous? I hear it's not uncommon for men of the theater to keep numerous mistresses."

Phineas was an irritant, one who'd successfully become a burr in Arthur's saddle. The man wouldn't quit digging. "You should know. You follow me everywhere. Take a break from this chase and go interview the countess again. She's always ready for gossip."

The reporter started to laugh. "Oh, you saw my article in last week's paper. Mighty interesting, your being involved with a woman for two years and yet she knows nothing of your past."

Arthur hated that the woman had again tried to make a headline out of him, a year past their break. A woman who wouldn't seek scandal was what he needed. His quick gamble to marry the shy Miss Croome was looking better. "Phineas, why not report on matters like slavery in the colonies and help stop all the blasted slave ships that still roam the seas? That's a worthier fight to take on than the private life of an actor. Go fight wrongs. Do good."

The reporter chuckled. "Finding out the sins of famous men is what I do. You know those make the front page. That's what people want to read."

Tired of games, Arthur drew in a breath and readied his sore knuckles to come to blows. "If you have something to accuse me of, say it. The newspapers print sinful lies. They need to be sued."

Pushing away until he backed into the rails, Phineas frowned. "I have nothing yet. But there is a great deal of smoke about you, Gunpowder. No one had heard of you before your acting debut. You have no family or lifelong friends. No pretty little wife to talk of your good points. No children. You're in your late thirties, right?"

Barely thirty-four, but he'd not say that. Giving Phineas any detail could give the dog new life on his digging. Yet, what the man said was true. There was no one to attest to anything good or bad about him, except Jonesy, and most would discount the boy because of his disfigurement. Arthur had lost all connections when he had righted a horrible wrong, but no one fretted about those details when hunting juicy tidbits. "Over thirty. And I have not had the fortune to marry." *Yet.*

Phineas's lips drew to a circle. "Pretty peculiar to be at this point in your life with no one to attest to your goodness. You do like women, Bex."

"I do. I also prefer solitude. It helps to perfect my craft. Why are you pestering me? Is there a sister or niece you wish me to meet? I'm very picky but could keep them both entertained."

That got to Phineas because the man frowned, and his beak nose flared. "I have a gripe. Your debut, the starring role that made you—do you remember it?"

Arthur looked up at the sky, his heart pounding with the memory of taking the stage. The role of Hamlet wrapped about him. "Yes. It was a character meant for me."

"It was my brother's." Phineas pounded his fist into the post. "He's now reduced to bit parts."

Arthur rent his frockcoat open. "Then he shouldn't have been so drunk on opening night."

"So, yes. This reporting started as revenge, but my articles have added to my readership. Now, I'm more than curious. Give me your story, Bex. Be cooperative. I could make your interview in print be more forgiving. It's obvious you're hiding something. Confess to me. It'll make the medicine less painful."

"I am neither sick or stupid. I want to be left alone."

"A man in your position with no family or connections is rare. You should take care. Someone could make things up, and not a soul would be able to come to your defense."

Arthur fisted his hand. "Phineas, I'd be careful if I were you."

"Is that why your knuckles are red?"

The drunk from the cellar had come back at him after the young woman left, saying all types of crass things—slave-lover, fancy-thief, or the oddest one, accusing of him of wanting tar-water kisses. Arthur flexed his stinging fingers but reined himself in from slamming his fist into the reporter's face. "I don't take kindly to threats, or to people who threaten those under my protection."

"Who is under your protection? Was boxing in your past?"

Arthur stepped up upon his phaeton and bowed in dramatic fashion, as if he were leaving the stage. "This interview is over. Chase one of the folks in Parliament who are standing in the way of justice for a scandal. Write on freeing men in our colonies—then we'll have more to speak of."

"No, I'll stick with smoke, Gunpowder."

Gripping the reins, Arthur pushed his hat down. "Good evening, Phineas."

"When you're ready to confess, Bex, I'll be around."

Arthur's uncle would say something about ticks latching on to a dog's coat. Arthur didn't like ticks, Phineas, or memories of his uncle. "You'll be waiting a long time."

"Time is my friend. What is that actor's line about truth outing?"

Stewing, Arthur made his horse race forward, away from the determined reporter. He didn't want the man to follow him to the stables where Arthur would lease a second horse for the trip to Gretna. He couldn't afford the man asking questions that would lead to Miss Croome, especially when Arthur wasn't sure if she'd actually elope with him.

The girl was perfect—shy, articulate, well-curved. Someone who, in time, would attest to his good character.

If the truth "outed," she would need to say he wasn't a monster, that every speech he'd made was true, that he wasn't like his uncle, the man who'd raised him after the deaths of his parents.

Slowing his gig, Arthur dusted the seat beside him, slapping his glove against the worn leather. He had no one, not a soul from his past to attest to his mostly good upbringing. In his old shipping town of Liverpool, most only knew of the villain named Bexeley, the man who had been every inch a monster to everyone but his nephew, Arthur. If the truth ever came out, everyone would think Arthur a monster, too.

The question remained, was Ester Croome the woman who'd vouch for him? He'd know five minutes past midnight. If she appeared and escaped with him, that would prove she had mettle, truly tough insides to weather the scandal if his past came to light. Then he, the loner, had to figure out how to make her love him enough that she could say, without equivocation, that a man raised by a murderer wasn't one. That he was honorable and true.

He slumped in his seat as he navigated the streets by the glow of the gaslight. The role of a smitten husband wasn't going to be hard for an actor of his caliber to perform. And Miss Croome was not immune to his charm. He hadn't made a woman blush so much in quite a while. Could Miss Croome become a woman with complete faith in a husband with a shadowy past?

CHAPTER FIVE

Almost Midnight

After twenty minutes of pacing in Mama's parlor, peeking out of Nineteen Fournier windows and listening to Clancy announce each guest, Ester heard the names she had been waiting for.

"Mr. and Mrs. Fitzwilliam-Cecil." Clancy's voice carried above the lull of the music. Out of the parlor like a rabbit, Ester slowed her gait to a leisurely stroll until she grabbed Theodosia in a hug, crushing her fine indigo gown. "I've so missed you."

"Ester," she said, "I know I've been poorly of late, but I am feeling much better." She hugged Ester more tightly. "What is it? What is wrong?"

Her friend knew her well. "Come with me." She grabbed Theodosia's arm, almost dragging her into the parlor.

Her husband, Ewan Fitzwilliam-Cecil, followed. His gaze seemed locked on his wife, and he hadn't let go of her other hand.

Ester had grown more comfortable with him, and was even fond of him, but she needed to tell Theodosia alone. She released her friend and moved to the parlor door. "Mr. Fitzwilliam—I mean, Fitzwilliam-Cecil—I need to speak to your wife. Something for her ears only. It's a matter that cannot be delayed."

He puffed up his chest before kissing Theodosia's fingers. "Miss Croome, we are a well-matched pair tonight. You'll have to share this dark secret with both of us."

Theodosia smoothed his ivory cravat against his damask waistcoat. The man was handsome in black and white. "Ewan. I'm feeling much better. You don't have to hover."

Mr. Fitzwilliam-Cecil's countenance softened, filling with what Ester imagined any girl would want from a husband—a mix of concern and perhaps the desire that only the deepest love could bring. "I intend to crowd you, my dear," he said, "I haven't had my fill of you. Don't believe it possible."

Theodosia's pale cheeks darkened. Her coloring was off from her normally healthy bronze features. "There's no winning when he's like this, Ester. Not even Phillip's smiles can break his determination."

"Well, Phillip's good looks will break hearts. Just not his papa... stepfather's."

His smile dimmed at the truth of their son's parentage they'd been forced to hide, but a touch of Theodosia's hand to his cheek renewed the lift of his lips. The two were beaming, so entangled in each other's confidences that Ester wondered if they remembered she was still in the same room. She gave a cough. "Frederica's newspaper advertisement. Well, she gave the would-be-groom to me. I'm going to elope with him tonight."

"Elope tonight? Ester?" Theodosia's voice sounded low, almost cracking. "Why would she give him to you? A man isn't a handkerchief to be borrowed. And you. You haven't indicated that you were ready to marry, let alone elope. Is he here at your mother's party?"

"Not yet. The man, the handkerchief, is Arthur Bex."

"Wait. You ladies are still with this newspaper advertisement business?" Fitzwilliam-Cecil squinted. "Theodosia?"

She cast him a look, an arched brow above a sly, crescent-shaped eyelid. "Ewan, it worked out well for us."

Her husband paced with his hands behind his back, very much the picture of an elegant penguin. "And Bex is in this, too? I told you he's hiding something."

Something burned in Ester's chest at the insinuation. "What has he done? Name an instance of him being untrustworthy."

The playwright rubbed at his neck. "I know of nothing directly, but no one had heard of him prior to three years ago. Then he had a horrid break with a countess and it was in the papers."

"He's famous. I know it must be terrible having your every move scrutinized. I think that would make anyone seek privacy. But to accuse him of something nefarious without proof, that's wrong. You, of all people, should know to have proof."

Surely dwelling on his and Theodosia's bumpy journey back to love, he frowned. "I'm just concerned for you, as I am for all of my wife's friends. You ladies are special, and there are a lot more villains in this world than heroes."

Theodosia adjusted her deep blue gloves. "Ewan, Ester Croome's smart. You don't have to fret, but I must speak to her alone."

He nodded and went to the door. "Let me go find my brother and see if he's still looking in the newspaper for a bride, the next Lady Hartwell." The man stopped his grousing at the door, his countenance clearing of its frown. "Take care, Miss Croome. I know you're partial to Bex's voice, his stage presence. You deserve to be happy."

"Yes. I do. I think I can be happy with Bex, and he wants to marry me."

Theodosia walked her husband to the door. "Let me see what can be done. Pretend nothing is wrong. Is that something a successful playwright can do?"

"I won't betray confidences." He put a kiss to Theodosia's palm. "But convince Miss Croome to take care. There's something about Bex…his radical ties."

"Go out and save your brother Hartwell from receiving stares. He might not be as comfortable as you in these settings."

Ester knew what she meant. Theodosia's husband and her brother-in-law, the viscount, along with a banker and some representatives of Stephenson Clarke Shipping who'd enjoyed Papa's fabric trade from Jamaica, were the only pale faces in a sea of chestnut, olive, henna, and ebony. It could be uncomfortable for them. How would Bex fit into such a setting? Would he be beset with nervousness, like Ester? How would she do in his world full of strangers and other actors—all different from her?

Theodosia closed the door, came to Ester, and clasped her palms. "I know you have feelings for this actor. You've liked him since we saw him in that play, with Frederica, almost two and a half years ago."

"I'm in love with Arthur Bex, and now he wants to marry me." Her voice, to her own ears, sounded proud, and she was. How could she *not* be, with the man of her dreams coming for her tonight?

The sleek ebony hair of Theodosia's chignon bobbled as she shook her head, "Star-struck love…it's not the same as deep love. And it's not mutual. You must be logical. Think of what a wrong choice could cost. Your parents will disapprove of an actor."

The breath almost left Ester, and she wrapped her arms about her to keep her heart safe. "You are married to a playwright. How can you talk about an actor so poorly?"

Putting a palm on Ester's crossed arms, Theodosia said, "I have no parents to disapprove. You and Frederica are the only ones whose opinions mattered to me."

Ester pulled away. "Then you, of all people, should be supportive. Arthur Bex has dined at your table. He's been in one of your husband's productions. How can you stand here and talk about him as if he were nothing?"

Theodosia stopped reaching for her and lowered her arms against the shiny satin of her gown. Croome fabrics draped both of them, but they couldn't be more different.

"I respect Bex's profession, Ester, but I am not your parents. I know how important their approval is to you."

The approval of her parents had been everything until she'd discovered that they were living a lie. She shook her head. "This has nothing to do with them. It's about Bex. He wants to marry me. Maybe when he saw me, he loved me, too."

Theodosia nodded. "There is much to love about you. You're smart and thoughtful. Never rash. Why not wait a month, meet with him a few more times—"

"I don't have a month. Tonight, my father is to announce my engagement to a philanderer. Of course, he sees nothing wrong with that."

"Your father wouldn't do that. There must be some mistake. Mr. Croome adores you. He'd never do something that would make you so unhappy."

"I've seen the contract. He's told me so. The only mistake is mine, believing I had more time, or that my parents would afford me the opportunity to choose. I'm just a pawn in Papa's negotiations. Maybe now he'll make enough money to get that Cheapside home, perhaps even Mayfair, if they'll sell to Blackamoors."

"Ester. I know you are still smarting from the letters you found."

"Father's letters to his mistress. Those letters?" Ester moved to the window and wrapped the heavy purple tapestry curtain betwixt her palms, dragging the ribbon trimmings through her fingers. She had wanted her voice to sound calm, but the rage and disappointment of it all ripped through her again. She sat on the sill. "I thought things were so perfect. That my mother and father had found each other. I wanted a love like theirs."

"Ester, they love each other now. He's giving her this wonderful party."

"Perhaps, but I don't want his kind of love. Not any part of it. I'd rather listen to Bex say my name. I can live in his voice."

"What happens when the talking stops? It always does." Theodosia sat on Mama's couch, the side with no arm, and stretched out. "Whatever happened was a long time ago. You said yourself those letters were four or five years old."

Rubbing her temples, Ester exhaled. Too much tension had invaded her chest. Those were the ones she'd found. How many more existed? "We'd just moved into Nineteen Fournier. Mother was in the middle of restoring it to make it her dream home. Why would she leave him when he'd put a new roof over our heads? She never even became angry with him. Not an outspoken word."

"Nothing?" Theodosia cupped her elbows and rocked, as she did when she tried to figure things out. "Maybe you just didn't see it. Your mother is a very private woman. But what does this have to do with you? You're not marrying your father."

Ester peered out to the street again. More carriages lined it.

The link boys swung their torches like acrobats, big and bright and high. "Charles Jordan is just a younger, shorter version of Papa. Why are they forcing me to marry him?"

"Parents make choices for their children. They think they are doing the best." Theodosia's voice lowered, gaining a very solemn timbre. "Sometimes they make horrible choices, but that doesn't mean you should make a bad one. You'll know what it means someday, but don't do something now that could put you in a bad situation. You can't punish your father by doing something that could ruin you."

"Marrying Bex won't ruin me. It's a dream come true. You and Frederica both have tried to get husbands by newspaper advertisements. This is a man who we all know. I couldn't be any luckier than you finding Fitzwilliam again."

Brushing at her brow as if Ester's logic had given her a headache, Theodosia smiled. "We know of him, but nothing about what has made him the man he is. But I'll support you. My love for you is endless, Ester. I just want you to take care."

Coming close to the couch, she took Theodosia's hand. "Help me wait until Bex comes. He will be here five after midnight."

"The roads are so dangerous at night. When I sold flowers in town, I made sure to be off the streets by seven. I tried to be about my business during the daylight. Highwaymen are out there. Thieves and murderers prowl in the dark. You could be hurt."

"Theodosia, I know your stories, but rest assured, I'll not be alone. Bex will be with me. He'll take care of me. But, will you help?"

"Yes, of course. We'll even leave after you, so people think that you have left with us."

Unable to stand falsehoods, Ester shook her head. "I don't want you saying anything that is untrue. I can't have you lying for me."

"Ester, I won't lie, but I can't stop people from assuming you left with close friends." Theodosia smoothed her skirt over her stomach, fluffing the delicate pleats in her bodice. "Why five after midnight?"

"Because dreams and fairy tales last until then. If Bex arrives after midnight, then I know this is true. Our marriage is meant to be."

Theodosia rose slowly then linked arms with Ester. "Well, if the mysterious actor can keep this smile on your face, then he'll do right by you. I haven't seen you smiling so much since my wedding breakfast last year."

Ester put her hands to her cheeks. Yes, she was smiling, big and wide, thinking of Bex coming for her. She had doubts about many of the things Theodosia and Fitzwilliam-Cecil had said, but not about their care for her. If Bex appeared at five after midnight, she'd never doubt that they could be happy.

That was if Bex arrived and proved this wasn't a dream.

• • •

Arthur took a long breath as he leaned against the door of the stable, watching Jonesy prepare a second horse to harness to the phaeton he'd rented. The small carriage with four wheels and a roof should provide his bride the comfort they needed to make the long journey to Scotland, much better than his gig.

The mews was close to his Cheapside flat, so he was able to

pack a bag and his longhand pages for the script to *Antony and Cleopatra* for this unexpected trip.

Away from the noise of the cellar and the harangues of Phineas, he sifted through his decision to take a bride after one meeting. Though given to taking the riskier path, he typically wasn't a rash person. He prided himself on being methodical and thoughtful. The critics said it added depth to his portrayals, but it was also how Arthur lived. A snap decision to marry Miss Croome and elope tonight—it was uncharacteristic.

A loud whine and a slamming of a gate stirred Arthur from his doubts. He had to make it to Nineteen Fournier on time. He'd made a promise and wasn't one to go back on his word, even if it cost him everything. The promise to a dying mother that he'd always do what was right, and the same to a father, the vicar of their Liverpool parish, who had perished a month later, were always top of mind. Though their proper names hadn't left his tongue in years, these promises, like the ones he'd make to Miss Croome, were his bond.

"Not much longer, Mr. Bex," Jonesy said as he led a beautiful pewter horse from a pen and into place leading his team. Jonesy was a boy of thirteen or fourteen with deep red freckles and an easy manner. When Arthur had learned the young man had been abandoned and lived at the stables, he was determined to help him, tipping him well, seeing about him. No one should be on their own at such a young age, not like Arthur.

"Trying to hurry, Mr. Bex." The boy's scarlet hair fell forward, covering his eyes as he mumbled more words through the cleft in his lip. "In a hurry to leave at this time of night. Family problems?"

"No, Jonesy. I don't have a family, but I might soon."

The young fellow looked up. "You a good one, Mr. Bex. Jonesy will be happy you not alone no more."

Alone no more? The boy was concerned for Arthur. That's why he liked him, and that sentiment, alone no more…maybe that's why Arthur had agreed to elope. Unlike the countess, Miss Croome was shy. She wouldn't seek headlines or gossip. She seemed genuine in wanting to marry him. There was no talk of fortunes, or income, or invitations he should seek—none of that. He knew it wasn't because she wasn't aware of these things. From the cut of her stylish clothes, she was used to fine things. She simply didn't seem to care. That was refreshing.

And what a figure she cut in those clothes. Arthur strove to be an honorable man, but he was still a man. Miss Croome possessed a lovely bosom any husband would take pride in, a small waist worthy to take hold of, and a backside to admire and take a second or third look at. Her face was one of beauty—pretty eyes, generous lips. Her knowledge of Shakespeare rivaled his own—that was very intriguing to his soul. He'd never been drawn to someone outside of his race before, but he'd never met someone like Ester Croome.

"What is she like?"

"What, Jonesy?"

"Family begins with a woman. Jonesy knows that."

How should he describe her aloud? "She's pretty and has a sense of grace about her."

"That sounds nice. Almost done, Mr. Bex."

"Good." Arthur was excited to see her again. That had to be a good thing, to be in want of her presence so soon after their first meeting. If his past stayed buried, they could be happy. "Jonesy, you think two horses will take me to Scotland in good time?"

The boy stopped and looked up. "You asking me, Mr. Bex?"

"Yes. I want your opinion."

The biggest smile Jonesy could manage with his malformed mouth blossomed on his ruddy countenance. "No one wants Jonesy's opinion. Most look at me and think Jonesy's dumb." He stood up straight, maybe even puffing up his chest. "Yes, Mr. Bex. Jonesy put the strongest horses on this phaet...carriage. Much better than your gig. It's wheels and axles are reinforced. You'll make good time to a first stopping point near Stamford. But take care, it will still tip over if you drive bad."

It saddened Arthur that folks would discount a hardworking young man because of his looks. But that was the way the world worked. Anything different came under harsher scrutiny. "Stamford. Good, Jonesy. Well, my fiancée and I are off to Gretna Green. That is, if I make it to Nineteen Fournier on time, and if she hasn't changed her mind."

"Fournier. You'll make it to that part of town. It's not far." Jonesy went back to tugging and strapping the second horse in place.

"You know that part of town?"

"Yes."

"Then you have no opinions on my selection of bride? She's Blackamoor."

The boy was silent for a long time. Only hooves could be heard. Then he said, "You wantin' Jonesy's opinion again. Happiness is important. All folks but you look down on Jonesy. If you happy, that what matters."

It mattered a great deal to a lot of people. Arthur wasn't naive to that.

The boy brushed down the first horse with a stiff brown brush. "Jonesy would be happy being a footman with one of those shiny coats, but folks won't hire me 'cause Jonesy don't look right to them. That don't make my heart happy, Mr. Bex. Makes me sad."

The look in the boy's eyes—dull, covering pain—Arthur knew it. The ache haunted him, reminding him of everyone turning against him—the taunts, the fisticuffs, the busted lips—all for doing what was right. Yes, Arthur knew that look, and no matter how hard he tried, the pain always returned.

"Jonesy, you work hard. No one is more loyal than you. If I ever live in one of those fancy houses that need a footman or groom, I'll hire you. You do so well by me."

The boy handed him the reins. "Get Mrs. Bex's yes afore you go promisin'. She might not like Jonesy's looks."

"I have a feeling about her." He tossed the boy a good tip, several farthings. "I think she values honesty and loyalty more than looks." He hadn't known Miss Croome long, but there was something about her, the way she puzzled things out, that made him believe she was like him, knowing character outweighed all. Hopefully, that nature of hers wouldn't judge him too harshly if the truth came out. Perhaps, they could build enough of a life together that the past wouldn't haunt him so much anymore.

"You look like you still deciding, Mr. Bex...the route you want to go. Go the straightest route. That what Jonesy'd do. The Great Northern Route is best."

The straightest route would be to tell Miss Croome the truth about his past, but what if she became so upset that she told others? If the countess had known, she surely would have told reporters. Then everything he'd worked for would be taken away again. He'd kept the secret of his uncle for more than twenty years No. He couldn't risk it now. Arthur would take the secret to his grave. "The straightest route might not make the best path. Sometimes it is more trouble than it's worth, Jonesy."

Striking a match, the boy lit the lanterns on each the side of the phaeton, then handed Arthur the flint. "Use this to keep them lit as you travel through the night." He wiped perspiration from his brow. "Jonesy trust Mr. Bex to do what is right. You a good fellow."

Arthur wanted to believe he was good, but the whispers of the past made him believe he wasn't. He'd been careful at hiding and would let nothing take away the life he'd built. Arthur Bex had become a man people respected, and Arthur would use his talents to fight for abolition. That would forgive his family's sins.

He climbed on board his phaeton. "Thanks, Jonesy. I'll see you when I get back."

"Good luck, Mr. Bex."

He did need luck. Starting out with secrets wasn't the best. Yet, having just met Miss Croome, he could assume that she had secrets, too. Didn't most women have secrets? Yes, that was a good lie to tell himself.

Arthur waved to Jonesy as he turned the phaeton up Gracechurch Street. The crisp air cooled his brow. It was at least four days travel to get to Gretna Green. That time alone, just the two of them, would cement the foundation of their relationship. Then he'd know if he could go through with marriage, and if it was possible to trust Miss Croome with the darkest secrets of his past.

CHAPTER SIX

The Longest Five Minutes

At twenty to midnight, Ester stood against the wall in the drawing room. The musicians' tune sounded louder than the last. She tried smiling as Theodosia and Ewan twirled past, but the weight of what would happen and what might happen made Ester fret.

What if Bex was in an accident?

What if he was lost in this part of town?

What if he were set upon by footpads?

What if he changed his mind? That was her greatest fear—that somehow he had decided Ester wasn't worth the trouble of eloping after midnight. Had he decided that a full night of sleep was better than risking the mad dash to Gretna Green with a stranger?

Travel late at night could be dangerous, and they'd be on the run.

Ester looked down at her shiny satin gloves, spotless, without a wrinkle. They had been made for her. Was Bex made for her, too?

Frederica and Charles Jordan spun near. Her friend had rescued Ester from dancing with the rakish man again. Grabbing below Ester's waist and eyeing her décolletage had been two times too many.

Except for his manners and average height, she had to admit that Charles Jordan was nice to look at. A smooth complexion of warm bronze skin, with a muscular frame—probably from helping his father with gas lighting installations. But he had been too busy looking at every other girl at the party as he danced with Ester. He hadn't even pretended to be interested, not the way Bex had in their one meeting at the White Horse Cellar. No. Charles Jordan would never be for Ester.

Mr. Jordan, Charles's father, came to her side. "He looks so odd out there. Him and his brother." They were eye-to-eye, since he wasn't a tall man, but his gaze had narrowed. He looked distressed.

Ester fluttered her fan while glancing at the grandfather clock. "What is odd, sir? Is something wrong?"

"Seeing the famed playwright Fitzwilliam-Cecil and Lord Hartwell here. They are enjoying themselves too much, as if they owned the place."

Ester squinted and searched for the men. Nothing seemed odd. Just a man twirling his love in and out of the chalked lines, the other standing in the corner. "I see nothing amiss."

"Look closer, Miss Croome. You don't see how they size us up, looking at our women and our treasure for their taking?"

Cupping her hand to her eyes, Ester looked again and saw Theodosia's brother-in-law, the viscount, leaning against the wall with an expression that looked pained. He looked uncomfortable, only smiling when Clancy brought the punch tray around. She saw nothing of what Mr. Jordan saw. Maybe a man no taller than Napoleon saw conspiracies everywhere.

She lowered her arm. "Mr. Jordan, I am confused. I see none of the aggressions you see."

"Maybe with gaslights in here you would." He chuckled, a sneering laugh. "You are young, girl."

So, age made one see things that weren't there? "Fitzwilliam-Cecil is a very pleasant man, and Lord Hartwell—" Ester became distracted at Frederica's turn with Charles Jordan. She was pulling at her sleeve as if it had been manhandled. Ester's gut twisted with guilt. "My friend, Miss Burghley, has missed a few steps in this set. I wish this dance was over so she could refresh herself."

"Good, I see you looking at Charles. He's a good dancer. You'll have him to yourself soon enough."

She wanted to say aloud she didn't want him, and to point out how rude and awful he was being to Frederica, but Ester wouldn't make a scene. That would embarrass her Mama. Protective hackles raised, Ester moved to save her friend. She'd take the abuse and even a lecher's harassment to save someone she cared for.

"What is Lord Hartwell doing?" Mr. Jordan's gruff tone deepened. "He's cutting in on Charles."

The viscount had moved from his spot and was taking Frederica's hand from Jordan. Her friend's lovely face looked bright, like a pixie, when she and Lord Hartwell twirled by.

Ester sighed in relief and Charles moved on to another girl, maybe one with virtue to match his appetite. "Don't be concerned, sir. Your son has found a new place to warm his hands."

Mr. Jordan frowned, his upper lip covering the lower one for a moment. "If you can't see the problem, Miss Croome, then you are naive. Don't worry. My Charles will protect you when you are wed."

From what could a future adulterer protect Ester? Not from couch-sitting and wondering if and when he'd be home, or worse, like Papa, the pretense of happiness, only to discover later the lies in old love letters. Stomach turning, she nodded. "Yes, I saw how he protected Miss Burghley from a chill with his wandering hands. And she heated them by hitting them with her fan. Lucky for her, Lord Hartwell's not cold like your son. Her shawl will stay unwrinkled."

The man's eyes went wide, shocked at the directness of her words, and Ester was surprised she'd said them.

The dance came to an end. Frederica gave her new partner a bow before heading to Ester. "Charles Jordan is a monster," she said behind her fan. "How can he be so aggressive in front of you on the night of your engagement?"

"I'm not marrying him, Frederica."

"So, you're standing up to your father? Or are you talking about eloping with Bex?"

"I tried to tell Papa, but he's still set on this match. Once I elope with Bex, well, he'll come around. He'll have no choice."

Ester fluffed up the languets, the oval silk butterfly-like wings that she had designed for Frederica's silver dress, but her friend pursed her lips. "Your mother will be so hurt."

"At first, but she's forgiven Papa for worse without even raising her voice." Ester flicked another languet in place over the sheer lace that formed the overlay of Frederica's gown. "I'm sorry you were manhandled by Jordan."

"It's what men like him expect they can do to someone like me, one borne of an illicit nature." Frederica covered up with her long creamy shawl of fine silk, as if her gown were indecent.

"You are lovely, Frederica. Don't let anyone make you feel less."

Her friend's countenance cleared. "You believe Bex will show? And after talking with him for an hour, you are ready to elope? Are you sure?"

"Yes, I am, Frederica. We leave five minutes after midnight."

Ester's tone must not have convinced her, for the girl took a punch glass from a servant and sipped like she'd thirsted for days. "That's ten minutes from now." She took Ester by the shoulders into the hall. "How can you be so calm?"

"You just danced with Charles Jordan. Do you see him as anyone who could be a faithful husband? I'm calm and reasoned about Bex because I let him know how important honesty and fidelity is. It seemed just as important to him."

Frederica squeezed her hard. "I want the best for you. If you are determined to elope, tell me how to help."

"Yes," Theodosia said. She waved her husband off, who left, shaking his head.

Fitzwilliam-Cecil surely knew the three friends needed to plot.

Theodosia embraced Frederica. "I'll never ever say you are stingy."

Ester leaned in and joined the tangle of arms. "Never, ever from my lips again. She gave me Bex."

"Men aren't bonbons." Frederica laughed. "Of course, I'd share. Well, maybe not the bonbons... You two know what I mean."

They all did. They were more like sisters, each looking out for the other. This love had helped Ester when she missed Ruth. Maybe she and Bex could go visit her in the country if they could manage around his plays. "This must be meant to happen."

Theodosia waved her lacy fan. "Last chance to count the costs, Ester? You could remain up here or hide on the third level in your bedchamber. We could get word to Bex."

Her friend didn't understand; maybe no one would. Sighing, Ester looked at the floor, at how each of their hems floated about their pretty slippers. The delicate lace, the tiny stitches, all gliding above the polished floors. The Vandyke points of Theodosia's gown almost touched her shoes but remained inches away. Not wanting to be inches from a dream, Ester raised her head. "I'll take my chances with Bex."

Theodosia reached into her reticule and pulled out gold coins. "Take these with you. It's enough to catch a stage if things don't go well. I want you safe. If, for any reason, you change your mind, you will not be at his mercy."

"I can't take your money."

She put the money in Ester's hand and closed up her palm. "Consider it a wedding gift."

Even in a happy marriage, Theodosia still carried money with her, still planned out everything in great detail, as if she were alone.

The way Bex had protected Ester from the drunk, she felt safe with him. "I can't go into this looking for an out."

"This isn't about quitting," Theodosia said, "It's about safety. When you leave your father's home and are away from your friends, you become a girl who some will see as foreign, a thief who has stolen a gentlewoman's clothes, a servant to mistreat, or worse, a runaway slave."

Ester's eyes popped wider. "Slavery is illegal in London."

Frederica shook her head. "Tell that to slave owners who still have men enslaved in vessels offshore. Some of my father's friends joke about it, when they think I'm not listening."

"That's what Bex was fighting for in the basement."

Theodosia voiced real concerns, ones Ester had no way to argue. Both of them were privileged and faced fewer of the evils that many who looked like them did. Ester put the coins in her reticule. "I'll be safe, but I'll come to you if something goes wrong. I'll be like one of those shop girls you rescue. I'm too old to be one of Frederica's urchins she sends to the charities."

Theodosia hugged Ester and held on tightly. The air seeped out of Ester's lungs when Frederica wove her arms around them again.

Frederica gave Ester an extra embrace. "I hope this is the love you've waited for, the love you deserve."

The clock moaned. It was midnight. Each friend released their holds and dried their eyes. Five minutes to Ester's appointment.

Slowly, Ester, followed by her two friends, dipped down the stairs and slipped into Mama's first-floor parlor.

Frederica went to the window and pulled back the curtain. "The glow of the link torches is bright enough to see Bex arrive. Not the gas lighting we have about Mayfair."

"Don't mention gas lighting." Ester took her bag from the closet. "That's the Jordans' livelihood."

"I don't see anyone," Frederica said. "Just carriages, with more of your parents' guests."

All Ester's big talk, her fight for a dream, crushed in upon her. She sat on the back of the couch to keep her balance. "He has a few minutes."

Frederica wore a wide frown. She turned back to the window. "There's still time."

A knock on the door echoed in the silent room. "Come in," Ester said. Her voice warbled.

A servant entered. "Miss Croome, your father wants you in the main drawing room. They're about to cut Mrs. Croome's cake."

She nodded. "Thank you. Tell him to do so without me. I'm out of sorts."

"I'll let him know." The man left, closing the door behind him.

"I'm leaving here, with or without Bex. I won't be given away to this marriage, not for a business deal, never to Jordan's son."

"Well, I think you will be leaving with Bex." Frederica's voice had recaptured its normal lilt. "A fellow in a gig—no, a phaeton—has arrived. A surprisingly tall man just parked across the street."

Ester's heart pounded as she flew to the window. Even in the moonlight, she knew Arthur Bex's athletic six-foot form. "Seems I am off to get married." She scooped up her bag, moved to the window, tossed open the sash, and climbed onto the sill. "Help with a delay?"

"Of course. Yes." Her friends' voices blended.

"Miss Croome?" Bex's rich baritone floated inside. "I'll catch you."

She let her bag go, and he seized it in his big hands. From the shine of the candlelight in the near sconce, Ester saw his kind eyes and the smile that made her heart flip-flop. She was ready to jump, ready to leap into a future with Bex. She put her feet out first.

The breeze whipped about her, lifting the light netting of her gown. "Not the ideal dress to elope in."

"Nonsense," Theodosia said. "You'll make the prettiest bride in robin's-egg blue. Take care."

Frederica gave Ester the shawl from about her shoulders. "Make haste. One of my friends... She was caught by her guardian halfway. There was no marriage, and she lives with endless shame."

"I'm here, Miss Croome. Jump."

Taking a quick breath, Ester pushed from the sill. The air squeezed out of her lungs as Bex caught her. She now balanced in his strong arms.

She opened her eyes and saw Bex's smile. He scooped her bag up in one hand while he carried her in the other. "Glad you could drop in. My small chariot awaits."

In the dark, they slipped across the street to his phaeton. He put her feet on the platform. "I'm not a wealthy man, but this carriage should take us to Gretna Green and back."

Ester stared at Nineteen Fournier. The window had closed. The sconce had gone out. This elopement was starting.

Bex climbed next to her, crowding her on the seat. And she liked that.

Could picture a lifetime of that.

She trembled, half wanting to snuggle closer. "When my father figures out what has occurred, he will give chase."

"Then let's hope he doesn't figure out things for a good while. Our destination and marriage are days away. This phaeton will only go so fast, but we'll make it. We will."

   She closed her eyes and hoped he'd speak a little more. His voice outweighed the growing fear of her father's wrath. One thing was worse than not eloping, that was being caught in the middle, with no marriage and no hope of stopping one's name from being forever linked to scandal.

CHAPTER SEVEN

Regrets and Chances

The phaeton moved steadily along White Chapel Road heading to Gracechurch Street, the easiest route of escape from Nineteen Fournier, but close enough to turn back around. His bride-to-be looked like she was ready to leap off or grow sick. He reached a hand out to her, and she startled. "Are you all right, Miss Croome?"

"Yes. I just don't believe...I did it."

He took his eyes from the road for a moment to look at her again. Fashionable bonnet, expensive gown, revealing a figure that was pleasing...*very* pleasing.

Pity she was hiding under a billowing shawl.

More of a pity was the sad expression gracing her face. Her gaze was that of a lost rabbit, and he felt unsure of his plans again. "I can turn the phaeton around, Miss Croome. I don't want you doing something you're not ready for."

She fiddled with her gloves. "Of course, I'm ready. Would I have leaped into your arms if I wasn't?"

"Maybe. I don't know you well, Miss Croome, but I want to know you better. I'd love to know you better."

By the time they hit Gracechurch Street, street lighting had become more prevalent. The scattering of lamps brightened the farther they went from her neighborhood, probably highlighting the transition from coal-fired posts to gas. Yet, nothing matched the glow of the torches the link boys had lit around Nineteen Fournier. It could have easily rivaled what they had outside

Covent Garden or The Theatre Royal the night of a play.

The Croome townhouse had seemed quite large, larger than he'd expected. The house could've easily been located in Mayfair, like the ball he'd accompanied the countess to after his first run as Romeo in *Romeo and Juliet.*

He hadn't expected that the Croomes were that well-off. "You said you were the fabric princess. My lifestyle will seem very meager compared to your family's, Miss Croome."

"Is your life happy, Bex? That's what I want."

Another point for Miss Croome, but did she truly understand the differences in their stations? Unease rolled again in his gut. He pulled on the reins, slowing the horses. "Do your parents give parties often?"

"Yes, every few months. This is the second since the king's passing. It was so strange to see the dark armbands, and so many dark colored and gray gowns at the first one. It was good to see people in a little more color again."

She liked parties? Half a point deduction. Absent everything else, he'd just run off with a rich girl, one who might hate his little life. His stomach soured at the thought of her reacting like the countess, sneering at the gifts he bought, belittling his offerings— the pearls not big enough, perfume not fine enough, clothes not created by the right mantua-maker. Hard-earned money wasted had proven difficult for a frugal man.

He adjusted his hold on the reins, again slowing the horses. "Many think the life of an actor is wild, with extravagance every night. I don't live like that."

She didn't look up at him. Maybe her glove was more interesting.

"Mama likes her parties." Miss Croome's voice, low-toned and sweet, rose. "Papa likes to be showy. He even hired more servants, just to make the evening seem bigger. I don't think it necessary, but it makes them happy."

He needed to make things clear before they left London so his fiancée wouldn't react like the countess. "Miss Croome, I have no servants. My household is just me."

"Not one?"

Full point deduction. His gut soured more. "Not even a man-of-all-work."

"Oh."

She might not mind his profession, but maybe she did not understand his lack of a fortune. His reservations slammed his middle like opening night, except with sledgehammers in place of butterflies. He swiped at his chin. "Miss Croome, we don't have to do this. I could return you to the party that you left. You could walk back in through the front door. It's only been about thirty minutes of travel."

Fumbling with her folded hands, she shifted her gloved fingers in her lap. "No. That wouldn't do. Mama might not have cut into her cake. I won't have eyes on me, ruining her moment."

"It's a poor beginning if you can't look at me when I'm telling you I understand my situation might be a little less than you bargained."

She wrapped her arms about her, further obscuring the outline he'd admired. "Bex, I'm a shy person. And I've never done anything like this. And the shame I'll cause my family, if… I've never, ever done something like this."

Shame was a terrible thing, a stain that wouldn't go away,

like Shakespeare's Lady Macbeth's stained hands. He needed to make Miss Croome laugh. He needed to laugh to not think about shame. "Well, this would be my first elopement, too, Miss Croome."

"I've never, ever gone against what my parents wanted. Never, Bex. I suppose it is different for men."

He tightened his hands on the reins. "My parents died when I was very young. But I had to go against my guardian once. It wasn't easy."

From the corner of his eye, he saw Miss Croome's face fully. Half hidden by long lashes, shadowed topaz eyes reflected the sparkle of the gaslights. She liked him, but what would it cost for her to trust him? And what price was he comfortable paying?

She spun in her seat as they approached a few of the warehouses lining Lower Thames Street. "Bex, this is Papa's warehouse. Can you slop for a moment?"

"We are supposed to be fleeing, Miss Croome. Are you changing your mind?"

"This is it. The home I grew up in. I haven't been back in years." She leaned over, her hand atop his and tugged on the leather strap. "Please stop the carriage."

Curiosity outweighing caution, he stopped the phaeton in front of a large stone building with boarded-up windows. "Is it abandoned?"

"No. Papa doesn't like people looking in. I was born in the small rooms at the top. I lived here until age fifteen."

The way she said it, "until age fifteen" sounded wistful, but how could that be in this section of town? Wealthy folks didn't stay here. Maybe she wasn't a spoiled little rich girl. It felt wrong to be proceeding without knowing more. He leaped out, came to her side, and held a hand up to her. "Come down, Miss Croome."

"I just wanted to see it. We can keep going."

"You wanted to see this place until I came for you. Do I make you nervous, or are you having doubts? Maybe I'm having doubts too."

"What?" She took his hand and came down. The lady was small in height, coming up to the middle of his chest. "Bex, I don't understand."

"I'm not a wealthy man, Miss Croome. I have rooms in Cheapside."

"You are allowed to lease in Cheapside? Papa couldn't."

He knew what she meant. Her father's means didn't open all doors. His race surely kept many closed.

Arthur fisted his hand. The injustice whipped through him. He knew a portion of what that felt like when his name, the one given to him at birth, made doors slam, made grown men curse that he'd been born. He forced his fingers to unclench and rubbed at his neck. "I live by actor benefit nights based on the success of my plays. I am a saver, very frugal, but even all my savings cannot compare to the home I took you from. Now you say you lived here above a warehouse. Are you ready to live this simply again, with no servants?"

"Bex, you don't misunderstand. I love the house at Nineteen Fournier. I'm fond of Mrs. Fitterwall and Clancy, the best housekeeper and butler I've ever known. I love my frilly room with the softest linens, and the chance to have a warm bath with lilac soap anytime I want." She pointed to the roof of the warehouse. "But I also loved living here. Life was simpler. It was honest. It was true."

She clasped his hand and took him to the door. "Papa has an office on the main level, but we lived in two rooms upstairs."

Compelled to look at her beginnings, he pried at the door, but it was locked. "There's no entering here." He slipped betwixt her and the doorway. "You liked living here."

"My parents worked hard and built a business. They fiercely loved and protected our family. My sister Ruth and I laughed so hard in our small room, peeking through the floorboards at the workers below. I miss those times, but I'm not afraid of building a new life with you, Bex."

Concerns starting to subside, he took her hand in his. Her shimmering cream gloves in his worn, tanned-leather ones looked different, but no different than if he'd taken the countess's palm. "It's good not to be afraid."

On the vacant street, he twirled her to the long horn sound of a barge sailing up the Thames. The air had that sour smell of waste, nothing like the freshness of the sea in Liverpool, yet the sounds of the boats—that was the noise he missed most—the noise he couldn't quite forget. "I don't want you to be afraid of me, Miss Croome. I want your trust."

He stopped when they walked under a streetlamp. "Did I mention how lovely you are, and how inappropriately dressed for travel?"

"Thank you. I think."

She held his gaze as he unwrapped her shawl and saw the glitter of the silver, like angel wings, swirling above her light blue dress. "Very inappropriate. Very beautiful. I'm glad to dance with you under this streetlight."

She looked back toward the warehouse, then at him. "Life was simpler here. My family was whole. Yes, I'd love to live like that again in a house filled with honesty. We are both coming to this marriage with nothing to hide. That is what I am most thankful for."

At that moment, there was nothing he'd rather give, but he was hiding something so awful, it would ruin this marriage as much as it had ruined his life. "That's an awfully big promise. I don't know—"

"*Shhh*." She giggled. "I've been in love with your voice so long, but I need you to be quiet and listen. The Croomes didn't always have money. I remember being hungry, but I also remember being happy. The fact you care enough to consider my feelings, speaks volumes about your character. I want to get to know you, Bex, and I want nothing more than to be a good wife to you. Have no doubts about that."

The shy girl had a palm upon his lapel, and it blew away his internal scoring. The street lighting on her face revealed a hint of snow-white teeth between plump lips that had become a great deal more fascinating. "Now, let's continue, Mr. Bex. Help me back in the carriage."

He wanted to stay in that moment, examining her mouth a little longer, but that wasn't wise. "We are supposed to be eloping. I guess we should continue." He put his hands around her waist and lifted her back to the platform.

Again, he noticed she was firm in all the right places that his hands could attest to and not cross a boundary. "Yes, ma'am," was all he could muster. His thoughts were divergent, dashing between failing her trust and what would it take to win her love,

love beyond theater infatuation. "Let's keep going."

Pushing his top hat down, he climbed aboard and sat beside her. His conscience wouldn't let him make the horses go. He couldn't be completely honest, so he put the reins down. "I think I should turn the phaeton around. You could tell your parents that we just took a drive by the river. They will be angered that we did so without a chaperone. Then perhaps they'll allow me to court you the right way. We could take more time to get to know each other."

She took up the reins, put them in his hands, and kept her fingers on his, trying to force him to flick his wrist and make the phaeton move. "I can't go back. People will see me returning with you. Unchaperoned. I'll be shamed. My mama won't be able to lift her head. No there's no sneaking back into Nineteen Fournier. Let's go, Bex. I'm ready for our new life."

Nothing would make his horses move without a firm hand. "Miss Croome, I'm not sure that you and I are ready. We haven't been alone that long. We could—"

"Then why did you come to Nineteen Fournier, Bex? If you've changed your mind, you didn't have to arrive and raise my hopes. I didn't have to risk my reputation for you to quit now."

"I came because I said I would. I am a man of my word."

She gripped his lapel and leaned up. "That is what I want. Not the money or the servants, but a man of his word. I want someone who I can count upon to be honest and faithful. So unless you have decided you can't be that type of man for me, I suggest we head to Gretna, because I know I can be that type of woman for you."

"I like a brave woman, Miss Croome. I'm a little older, maybe a little wiser. We've reached the point of no turning back. There could be things that we learn of each other that will make you unhappy. I don't want you ever to be unhappy about choosing me."

"Bex, you have changed your mind." She released him and covered herself in her shawl. "You're the famous Arthur Bex. You've decided you are not interested in marrying me, a Blackamoor bride. I'm not a desperate woman. There are easier marriages. One of the same race as you would be easier for you."

That was what she thought the hesitation was. Yes, he was white, and she wasn't, but she was also pure and devoid of scandal. He wasn't. His uncle had done so many atrocities to people who looked like her, but he couldn't risk saying it aloud.

He bent and lit the small lantern and held it up to his face. "Ester Croome, I want to marry you, but I can tell you are the type of woman who is used to more and deserves more. I want you to be happy with your choice—that is all. He put the lamp on the seat and slipped a glove off, then put his bare hand upon her face. The glow of the light exposed tears which he flicked away. "There's nothing about you that is deterring me, only my wish to be assured that this is the best path for you."

"You are the best, Bex. I know that more than ever because you are so caring about me—a stranger." She put her moist lips together and blew out the lantern. "Now drive us. Let's get as far from the past as possible. I want our future."

Being away from the past was what he'd become good at. Maybe his secrets would stay buried, and he could live his life with a woman who seemed to believe only the good about him. With a nod, he pulled on the reins and started the horses moving.

"The rest was good for the horse team. I think I can get them to a greater speed. I want to be far from the past, too. You can be brave when you want to be, Miss Croome. I see that."

"When I have to, Bex, when I have to."

He could feel her smiling at him, but he couldn't turn and confirm. He couldn't risk Miss Croome guessing he wasn't being fully honest. Marrying her would finally be a way to close off his past, to have a new family. They just had to make it to Gretna without being caught.

• • •

When she felt the phaeton move at a faster speed, Ester took an easier breath. If Bex had sought to measure her resolve, he must have found it sufficient. It was good to know that he felt strongly enough about her welfare that he refused to leave without assurances.

Having no servants did frighten her a little, more than she'd let on. Her hair could be very temperamental to style, easy to tangle, because it wasn't straight like her mother's locks. Yet, Mama had made due for years without Clancy and Mrs. Fitterwall. Surely Ester could.

And she was scared of being caught and being shamed as a woman of loose morals. Frederica was flighty but respectable, and folks still always talked about her.

No. No getting caught. No shame. Just a marriage to the man of her dreams.

Ester looked at Bex, so big and tall in his seat. His shadowed profile seemed so filled with fortitude. Maybe someday, he'd be as sure about Ester as she was about him.

Yes, she had no doubts. He had come for her on time and had caught her in his big strong arms, the same strong arms that seemed as if they wanted to embrace her for a kiss under the streetlamp. Did Bex want to kiss her? What would that be like?

In an hour or two they made it beyond the city. The clear night sky showing above the trees showcased stars that twinkled like seed pearls in a fancy veil, like the one she'd drawn for Frederica. She patted her bag that sat near her feet, feeling the heavy board cover of her sketchbook. In the daylight, maybe she could work on a new dress, something special for her bonbon friend.

"When do you think your parents will notice your absence, Miss Croome."

"It must be at least two in the morning. The party at my parents may have just ended. Papa will think I was pouting when I did not appear to stand by my mother to cut her cake. Seeing me absent probably made Papa furious. Good."

"*Hmm*. You want him to be more furious?"

She didn't want to tell Bex all the sordid details, but she had to say something. "He disappointed me most cruelly with his deceit and then arranged a marriage without my consent."

"So, I'll be your first act of revenge? I don't like the sound of that."

"Is it so wrong to expect your father to be honest and true?"

Bex cleared his throat as he turned onto a darker path. "No, that is reasonable. I didn't have to worry too much about that. My father was a vicar, and I think honesty was a requirement of the position."

"My butler, Clancy, might have assumed from my packed bag that I left with my friend, Mrs. Fitzwilliam-Cecil. Maybe you and I will be wed before my parents discover I've run away."

Bex yawned, fully and loud. It was the third one he'd released, but this one he did not fight to hide. "We'll stop soon to change horses. I hadn't planned on eloping today. My schedule was a busy one. Perhaps, we can spend the night at a coaching inn. Then start again at first light."

Her heart thumped at the thought of staying alone with him unmarried. Being on the road, they had a mission to keep them focused. What would happen between them if they stopped? What if one of Papa's business associates saw? What if they were caught? Ester would be shamed. "Can't we go farther?"

This time he stretched an arm. "I'll try, but we are going to have to stop at some point."

"Bex, are you prepared for the difficulties we'll face at coaching inns outside of London? Faces like mine are less seen. It could be more difficult to secure *two* rooms." She emphasized the need for two rooms because they weren't married yet, and he may not be fully aware of the issues presented with traveling together.

"You don't have to be alarmed. I intend to take *two* rooms until we are married."

She wanted to smile at him, but he stared ahead.

"Miss Croome, there is a flint in my pocket. Can you get it and light the lantern? It's going to get darker before we get to a coaching inn."

She did as he said but couldn't find it.

"My coat pocket, Miss Croome. I've no pockets at my thigh."

She lifted her hands as if they'd caught fire, and he laughed so hard the phaeton swerved.

"You are a treasure, Miss Croome. Will you always be this nervous about me?" He reached into his jacket pocket and grabbed matchsticks and flint. "Here."

"Probably."

Taking them from his palm, she lifted the lantern from the floor and lit it.

The light showed that Bex chuckled even as he yawned.

"Is there anything I can do to help you stay awake. Can we recite lines?"

Bex stuck his hand out to her. "That will only tire my voice. Would you mind pulling off this glove? My knuckles are starting to sting."

With great care, she slid the worn leather off his fingers. His hand seemed swollen; one knuckle looked cut. "What happened, Bex?"

"Nothing really."

"Bex. Have you been in a fight?"

"A small one."

Without a thought, she tucked his hurt hand against her chest, cradling it as if it were a babe. "Who did this? Are you much hurt?"

He tugged at his hand but then stopped. He must have become resigned to let her keep it. "Well, your drunk came back to say a few more words to me after you left."

"He said something dreadful, and you decided to do more fisticuffs."

He leaned closer. "Miss Croome, you might want to be

careful where you hold my hand. Your party gown has a thin lace up top, not enough to keep my fingers from wandering. You truly should have changed into something sturdier, particularly when you are concerned about *two* rooms."

Flinching from her thoughtlessness, she released him. "I brought a carriage dress, but that doesn't answer my question."

His dark rich laughter surrounded her, and it took at least another minute before his hand moved. "It was a small fight. A few punches."

"You could have been hurt. Bex, those kinds of men don't play fair."

"What do you mean, those kinds of people?"

He didn't know what he'd face with her as his wife. She folded her arms. "The loud ones, the ones who think it is their right to say whatever mean thing they think. Don't they know we just want to be let alone?"

Bex put a hand upon hers. "I won't allow him to disrespect you, Miss Croome. And I'm not one to walk away from injustice. I'm big enough now... If I turn my eyes away, who will help? Who will make things right?"

Could she admire the man more? What a pleasure it was to know that he wasn't just handsome with a voice as sweet as honey, but he was kind and forthright—everything she ever wanted. "Making things right—is that why you are so passionate about abolition?"

As if he was startled, his palm flew away, back to the reins. "Yes... Yes. If no one says anything, the practice will continue."

"Your voice, Bex, as lovely as it is—you think your lone arguments will be enough?"

"It was enough for you, a prim and proper miss, to accompany a stranger at night on a long and dark road."

She wanted to roll her eyes, but it was probably too dark for him to see her displeasure. "It's not as though I took off with a highwayman. Just London's most famous actor."

"Well, some say the price of admission to the Covent Theatre is highway robbery."

"Bex, don't even joke about that. Mrs. Fitzwilliam-Cecil, she says it's not safe on the road at night. She says highwaymen or thieves could lurk in the shadows."

"Things can be dangerous, but that is why I'm careful. I'm careful in London, too."

"You're not being serious, Bex. I know of families whose loved ones never came home because they upset the wrong person. My uncle never came home, just his battered coat. He upset the wrong man. Abolition upsets a great number of people. Bex, why does it have to be you leading the fight?"

"Because." His voice lowered as he sat up straight, as if a hot poker had touched him. "It just is. We'll keep going as long as we can, but why don't you settle in. We'll be at a coaching inn before you know it. I'll get us two rooms. We aren't married *yet*."

She'd upset him. When they'd stopped at the warehouse, it felt as if she'd passed some sort of test, but now she'd failed one. She didn't care. His safety was important to her. She folded her arms about her. "Arthur Bex shouldn't be engaging in common street fights, no matter what someone says about me. You'll have to learn that. It's what we all learn, even my father. It's the price of the freedoms we do get to enjoy."

"It's not right, Miss Croome, and I won't allow anyone to

disrespect my wife."

It was an admirable thought, but that was the difference between them. "You were born with no boundaries, and you have the right to question the world, even pound through doors. I don't have that right. No one that looks like me does. And if we have children, the brown ones won't be able to, either."

"It's still wrong, but I do like that you're thinking of our children." His humor had returned, and his voice held a sultry tone, one that made the hair on her neck curl with anticipation.

Adjusting her skirt about her slippers, she refused to be distracted by his charm. This was for his safety. "You know I speak the truth, Bex. Even Fitzwilliam-Cecil has to be more careful, and he's the son of a peer."

"I know, Miss Croome, but I must do something to change the world. I owe it to you and those future children you don't want to talk about."

He was teasing her, and she wanted to box his ears. Yet, she couldn't help but admire his conviction. Nonetheless, words meant nothing in the face of brutes or bullets. Ester was better at holding her peace in public than in private. Bex probably never had to live so carefully. What if this was too much for him, having to learn to act not only on the stage, but in public with his Blackamoor wife?

CHAPTER EIGHT

On the Road Again

Arthur stormed out of the Bear Claw Inn. His hands shook but there was no one to punch. The innkeeper actually offered him some choice advice about bringing his fancy to his inn.

A fancy.

Referring to Miss Croome by the crude American term for an enslaved mistress. Miss Croome was no loose woman. She was enslaved by no one.

He trudged to the stables where she waited on his phaeton as the horses were changed. Had he known about the prejudice of the innkeeper, he would've tried to make it farther and dusted the dirt of this place from his boots. How would he tell her?

From the threshold of the stable, he saw her clutching her bag in her lap as if she feared it would be taken. He wiped his face with a handkerchief from his pocket. Injustice, complications, sharing bad news—all had a way of making him perspire.

He walked to the phaeton. The glow of the stable lamp showed on her face. Her lips were pinched, her grip on the bag, deathlike. The girl sat in fear. He didn't need to wipe his brow anymore. That sense of injustice had turned to sadness. Time to act, acting for her benefit, so she'd know the world he was drawing her into would be safe. He'd make it that way for her. "Miss Croome. Sorry for keeping you waiting."

Her eyes went wide as she looked up. "You look happy. Does that mean you rented two rooms without any problems? You were right. I'm fretful. I have to learn to trust more."

Wrenching at his neck, he took the reins from the groom and tossed him a coin, then climbed aboard.

"What? We're not staying?"

A quick tug and a click of his tongue made the phaeton start to move. "No. We're not. The place is subpar, and I began to think we've not made enough progress."

"But you were tired? You said we'd get a few hours of sleep then start fresh in the morning." She tugged on his sleeve. "Bex?"

Looking for an excuse other than the obvious, he scanned the sky. The scant bit of clouds seemed far, far away. "Red sky at night, a sailor's delight."

"What Bex? What did you say?"

"Nothing, just an old poem came into my head." He wanted to punch at his skull for letting a kind thought about the man who had raised him after his parents died enter his head. His uncle had been a monster even if he had been nice to Arthur.

He glanced at Miss Croome, prim and proper with her blue dress with its sheer netting. She was fancy, not *a fancy*, and not chattel, as his uncle and his ilk would claim.

"Bex, I can tell you are trying to protect me, but if you can't be honest with me about the inn, what type of marriage can we have?"

She was right. Not just about the inn, but about his past. But how could he tell her now, miles from her home? What a lout he'd appear to be. So far from London, Miss Croome wouldn't be able to be affronted, slap him silly, and leave him like the countess had done when she was mad. "I'd like more miles between us and Nineteen Fournier. Then you could catch a coach back to London if you feel we can't make a good marriage."

Her lips became an O-shape. "I'm not changing my mind about us. I'm a little nervous. Since we stopped, I have the odd feeling we are being watched. Doesn't make sense, does it?"

He pushed the brim of his hat back a little. It felt weighty on his tired neck. "You must not be used to long travel."

"The Fitzwilliam-Cecils live outside of town. That is about as far as I typically go. And this trip will take us about two or more days? I've never been this far, not without Papa."

Her hand shook as she wrapped her arms around her bag, and she squeezed it tight like a found lost puppy.

His gut twisted up. Didn't she know he'd protect her with his life? No. Maybe she didn't. "Miss Croome." He made his voice deeper. "You have nothing to fear. You're with me, my wife-to-be. No harm will find you."

Her grip didn't loosen so she must not be convinced.

"How long before we stop again?"

He counted the hours on his fingers. "With fresh horses, we can go another four hours. It will be morning before we stop again."

"Morning? Did you want to make more progress because you think we are in danger of being caught or because the last coaching inn wouldn't rent you rooms?"

He nodded, not that she could see in the low light. "Yes, Miss Croome. I had trouble at the last inn. The keeper and I exchanged some choice words, but no rooms for us."

She didn't respond.

He heard nothing but the knocking of hooves.

"You mean for me, Bex. No room for me."

Now it was Bex's turn for silence, for what could he say to make it better? He'd been denied services, even humanity, because of his testimony against his uncle. Things hadn't gotten better until he'd left Liverpool and changed his name. By wedding Arthur, Miss Croome's name would change, but not her lovely face.

"Travel outside of London is different." Her voice was low and steady. "Very different, Bex."

"Nothing ever goes smoothly. I think you've led a bit of a sheltered life."

"You make that sound bad, Bex. It just means someone thought enough of me to protect me."

Their acquaintance, talking and sharing, was less than a day, but he already knew he wanted to banish her fears. He took her hand in his, felt the strong coursing of her blood within her pulse. "Well, now you have me to protect you. I'll get you safely to Scotland."

"It's possible we could be caught. Papa has a barouche with two teams. They are fast."

"Two pairs, aye. Miss Croome, not staying at a coaching inn is actually helping us. We'll make it."

With her free hand, she drummed her nails on the seat, then offered a laugh. "They'll be slowed checking every inn. They won't know we were denied. Won't catch us sleeping…in a bed? Maybe we won't be caught. Maybe?"

Her voice diminished, and it brought new humor to his tired lungs. "For a woman set on eloping at five past midnight, you seem very unsure of the success of our plans." He yawned. "Would it be so wrong to be found in bed, our separate beds, sleeping?"

"Yes. We are alone, unchaperoned. It will be hard for anyone to believe that an actor was respectful, or a prodigal daughter wasn't promiscuous. Oh, maybe we should practice what we say when we are caught. We'll have to convince them to not shoot you and to let us still marry."

"Shoot? What?"

"Yes, Bex, we'll need to have a convincing speech."

She avoided his question, but since there were many questions he wouldn't talk about—such as his horrid connections— he didn't press, but he wondered if she could withstand the scrutiny of their marriage by reporters like Phineas?

Miss Croome sighed. "Papa has a temper. What if he shoots you, whether you're sleeping in a bed or not? No speech will fix that."

"Being shot is sort of hard to fix." Arthur didn't like the fear he heard in her voice. His inability to convince the innkeeper of her humanity had shaken her faith. He slowed the horses, looking for a safe place to pull over. "We can't go on like this."

"What are you doing, Bex? We have to keep going."

"No, we don't. I can't have a wife who is nervous of her shadow, one who's not sure that I can protect her. Today, we had problems because of an ignorant innkeeper; tomorrow a milliner might abstain from making your prim bonnets. If you really think your father will shoot me because I won't be able to convince him otherwise, then I won't think any less of you if you decide we should turn back. It will be full daylight when I drop you at Nineteen Fournier."

She folded her arms. The drumming of her slipper grew louder. "I wouldn't have you drop me there and shame my Mama, but at the Fitzwilliam-Cecil's. That's cowardly, but it would spare Mama some humiliation. She's delicate, and my father would force my marriage to someone probably even worse than the Jordans. Bex, I don't want to quit. We can't stop now."

"We didn't even try to get your parents' approval, Miss

Croome. I'd hate to be missing sleep right now when your parents could have been reasoned with."

"Papa wouldn't accept you unless you had ships or something to add to his wealth.

"Ships?" It was good that it was still dark. Maybe in the low lantern light, she'd miss Arthur choking on her words. He tugged off his remaining glove and swiped at his neck. "I don't have ships."

"And Mama wouldn't accept you at all because—"

"Because what? Because I'm an actor?"

Her voice lowered. "Because you're not Blackamoor."

His race was a concern? Stunned, he almost dropped the reins. His profession and class, maybe, but never had he thought *his* skin would be an objection. Finding a safe spot on the side of the road, he stopped his phaeton. "So, an actor, who's not one of you, has stolen the fabric princess. That is how you put it over tea. I've accomplished more than I thought."

"Don't be so smug. You're not what my parents would expect, any more than I was what you expected when you saw the lilac in my palm—my olive palm. I know Miss Burghley's advertisement did not mention race."

"You had on gloves, Miss Croome."

"You know what I mean, Bex."

"I was stunned at the reply being from a Blackamoor. My first thought was that you were part of an elaborate ploy, a Blackamoor and abolitionist. Very rich. When I discovered you were serious, I noted how charming you were, compared to the other advertisements I'd answered. Then I noted that glorious figure you keep trying to cover up. I am very attracted to you, despite our differences."

"You're attracted to me?" She stopped fidgeting with her shawl and sat up straight. "You haven't said that before."

She couldn't tell that he was soundly entranced by her, and that made him like her more. "A modest, beautiful woman is a blessing as a wife. Let's take a walk."

"But you said we need more distance."

He jumped down and came around to her side. "You need to stretch, too." His outstretched hand remained lonely, so he shoved it to his side. "We should clear the air. Get a few things settled."

"Like what?"

"I can't do this with you still up there." He put his hands around her waist and lifted her up from the bench.

Her arms scrambled about his neck as if she feared falling, but Arthur never let anything that he thought was his go away. The way she'd felt in his arms as she jumped to him from that window, and now with his palms encircling her waist, hers snug about his neck, he could easily think of Ester Croome as his. "I have you. You don't have to be uneasy."

He lowered her to the ground but didn't move his hands. She didn't seem to mind, either, for she didn't swat at his fingers as she had over tea at the White Horse Cellar Inn. "See. Much better. No stiff limbs."

"You are wonderfully tall." She released him and stood directly under the lantern attached to his phaeton. The light shone in her toasty, topaz eyes.

His hand was bare, and he placed it on her cheek. "Such supple skin."

"Lotion." Her voice sounded breathless. "Plenty of it. Always after a bath."

"I take it you enjoy a good soaking."

Her cheek burned beneath his fingers. Surely, if it were daylight, he'd catch her blushing again. "I like your confidence and your vulnerability, Miss Croome."

"Then why do you keep wanting me to give up?"

"I won't lie to you, Miss Croome. I had no expectations outside of a woman of grace with kind eyes and humor in need of a husband. The fact that you are a Blackamoor and I'm not doesn't seem to matter to either of us anymore."

"It doesn't, does it? I've been infatuated with you since the first time I saw you on stage, but I like the man in front of me now. I like you, Bex."

He lifted her chin, bringing her lips closer. "Miss Croome, my attraction to you doesn't care about our differences other than the important one."

"What's that?"

"I'm a man with eyes, and you're a woman. I delight in your delectable curves, which are noticeable even as you try to hide beneath layers of fabric."

With his other hand, he tugged at her shawl, freeing one shoulder. "I'm growing more curious about other secrets you have."

Pushing at his hand, she turned away. "You like making me blush."

"I like a lot of things." He circled her until he captured her eyes and put his arms about her, pulling her to him. "You're not afraid of being alone with a man by the side of the road at maybe four or five in the morn? Nothing fearful about being in my embrace?"

Her fingers went to his mangled cravat. "Not with Arthur Bex."

"What if I weren't Arthur Bex? Would you still feel secure?"

She puffed the loops of the tie, but only starch and an iron could save it. "Would you have the same melodious voice?" Hers was a purr.

"Yes. I suppose. You wouldn't have accepted anyone else's advertisement to escape your father's suitor, just mine?"

Her slim index finger stilled, very close to the vein on his neck. His pulse ticked up. "Just you, Bex. If you must leap into a fire, why choose a match light over a hearth flame? Both will burn you, just one more so."

"Am I the match or the hearth, Miss Croome?"

"Time will tell. You should give my name a practice. Ester Croome Bex. Ester Bex. Ester."

Did she know how alluring she was? Or how well her curves fit against him? "You must truly like me, Ester Croome."

"Yes. But say my name once more, with feeling, as if you were on stage."

Arthur moved one hand from the glorious perch at her waist to stroke her neck. Round the curve and along a ribbon, he traced the lace at her throat that led to an ample bosom. "Is there a reward for saying your name in direct address, Miss Croome?"

Concentrating on her plump lower lip, he dipped his head closer. "A reward should be in order—"

Harsh galloping sounded from behind. A large carriage sprinted past them on the road where they were pulled over to the side.

Miss Croome ducked her face, hiding against his abdomen. She shivered against him. The lass truly feared being caught, and it reminded him how vulnerable they were.

"Bex, we should get back on the road. I don't want to be found here in the middle of nowhere with no chaperone."

"You're eloping, Ester Croome. No chaperone required."

She held on to him tighter; her words came out half muffled by his waistcoat. "If we fail and my father doesn't kill or maim you, you will still be Arthur Bex. I'll be a fallen woman. The limited choices and freedoms I have now as Josiah Croome's daughter will be no more. No coaching inn will ever allow me to rent, not the infamous Ester. Not to mention that no respectable family will want anything to do with me. That shame will hurt Mama. She'll forgive me, but the shame will cut her deep. We have to marry, being out here—all alone with you."

"Then we can't fail at making you my bride."

"We can't, and I know you can and will protect me. I don't want us to fail."

Her words were sweet, sweeter than the kiss he'd wanted to take. "We won't." He put his hands around her waist again and carried her back to the phaeton. He hoisted her up onto the platform. "We won't fail, future Mrs. Bex."

When he climbed in on the other side, she had the reins in her hand. "Bex, I've driven my friend's gig. It's small, with only two wheels, but I could drive this, and you could sleep. We could get more distance."

He hadn't thought of her being useful like this. Taking his gloves from the seat, he offered them to her. "These are a little worn, but they will protect your hands. He tugged off one of her gloves, taking a moment to clasp her fingers—long, piano-playing-digits. "Let's not ruin these silky things."

"That is satin with Mechlin lace." She took off the other and stuffed them both into her bag before pulling on his gloves. "Do I keep to this road?"

"Yes. Stay the course unless you are ready to quit. I hope you're not ready for that." He sank back into the seat.

"Bex, I'm staying the course."

When she safely made the horse take to the road, he relaxed a little more.

Chin held high, arms taut, blasted shawl again wrapped about her, she had the phaeton moving smoothly, the horses' gait steady and straight.

Surprised at her skill, he sank a little more into the seat. "Your friend taught you well."

"Mrs. Fitzwilliam-Cecil believes horse skills are essential for women."

"But not your parents?"

"Rest, Bex. I'll keep us on the path."

She hadn't answered his question, but his eyelids refused to let him seek further counsel. He'd have to find out more about her parents later, and perhaps figure out a way to smooth things over. Miss Croome wasn't like him. She needed her family. Since the age of twelve, after his uncle's trial, he'd been forced to live by his own means. If Arthur could spare her the pain of giving up her relations, he would.

The world became quieter as his lids drooped. A little sleep would help, but if Ester was right, how would things work if they were caught here, days away from Scotland?

CHAPTER NINE

Women Drivers

As they drove farther north, the wind started to pick up, blowing chilly air at Ester. While Frederica's shawl offered some protection, Ester's wildly inappropriate travel gown didn't. She shivered on the seat, partly from the cold, partly from the occasional touch of her napping companion. She should've changed before she leaped from the window, but Bex hadn't seen her in her pretty blue gown with the netting.

Though Ester designed dresses for Frederica and Theodosia, the gown she wore had been her mother's choice. Mama had beautiful, elegant taste, and the gowns Ester usually sketched were for taller, bolder women.

Mama must have thought Ester was being disrespectful for missing her cake cutting, and Ester remembered how she, Ruth, and Papa had always stood near Mama when she'd cut the cakes at her parties. How hurt had she been when she'd discovered Ester had actually run away?

Bex's hand touched hers again, and at the same time, a memory of Mama crying shot through her. The words "his hands" repeated in her skull. For that's what Mama kept saying on the stairwell leading to their rooms above the warehouse.

Ester remembered, for she and her sister Ruth had been naughty, staring at the hardworking men below through a knot in the floor. Ester had heard the noise, strained her eyes, and had caught Mama sobbing.

Odd, Ester hadn't thought of this memory before. Odd, she'd never asked what "his hands" meant or why those words had made Mama cry?

Another breeze felt like ice water on Ester's legs. She should've changed from this dress to the frumpy burgundy one when they had stopped at the coaching inn, but she'd had that feeling of being watched. No show would be given to a voyeur or a thief.

Snort. Whistle. "Leave 'em alone." Bex shot up straight from his sleep. His eyes were wide, almost crazed in the lantern light.

"Bex, are you all right?"

He took a handkerchief from his pocket and swiped at his mouth. For a moment, he stared at her as if he didn't know her, as if he didn't know himself.

"Bex, it's me. Ester Croome. We are heading to Scotland."

Sinking back on the seat, he covered his face with his hat. "I must confess, Miss Croome, I've been told that I snore a little and talk in my sleep."

"Would it be lines of Shakespeare?"

"Clever, Miss Croome. And I remembered you and this venture to Scotland."

"I hadn't doubted that, but who said you snored? You're an only child."

"I'd rather not say."

"Perhaps the Countess Devoors?"

He pushed his hat away and sat up again. "You read the newspaper too much."

"Blame my mother. She collects all the papers. Every scandal caricature, she saves them. There was a funny one of you and the countess throwing a set of Wedgewood platters when you broke off your...arrangement."

"The papers get things wrong all the time. It was one bowl, maybe a vase. No heirlooms were destroyed in our parting."

"Why didn't you marry her? You courted for a while. Definitely more than a day."

He coughed, then said, "The widow wasn't the marrying kind."

"Then why were you with her?"

The seat lantern exposed a look on his face, brow rising over his eye, suggesting she'd asked one question too many. Ester turned back to the road, studying the couple of feet in front of them illuminated by the phaeton's side lanterns. "Well, I don't mind you snoring."

"That is good. I don't intend to sleep in separate chambers."

She couldn't look at him now, not when her questions could lead to such dangerous territory. "I don't mind so much. My father snores. When we lived above the old warehouse, that hard noise meant Papa had made it home safely, that nothing had happened to him in his business dealings. Those long nights with the moon high over the Thames, I'd wait on my mat for the door to open, to hear the mumbles of my parents, then that harsh sound of his sleeping. That was safety."

"You'll be plenty safe with me." He yawned big, surely pushing out all the air in his big chest. "Your father lives with danger?"

"Some don't take kindly to the Croome's advancing wealth. Mama, all of us, were gleeful when Papa hired solicitors to do his negotiations. And someone must not have liked my uncle's advancing. Nothing save a bloody coat came home."

"Miss Croome. I can imagine...the pain—"

"Say no more of it." She remembered her uncle's quick laugh—his never-to-be-heard-again-on-this-side-of-glory laugh. Her fears for Papa returned. Ester almost wished she could walk past her parent's bedchamber and hear Papa's snores. "Look at the bruises on your hands, Bex. We live in dangerous times."

"We do. I remember the first rally I attended. I don't know what I feared more at St. Peter's Field, being shot or trampled."

"Last year. You were at the St. Peterloo Massacre." Her heart thumped hard, remembering the horrible reports of those killed. She jerked to stare at him and rocked the cart. "Fifteen people were killed, hundreds injured. How many bloodied coats were sent home? Bex, you can't be so reckless."

"The road, madam." He grabbed her hand and steadied the reins. "What you call reckless, I call finding my purpose. I saw Henry Hunt speak. The great orator of the people used his voice to try to create change. I can't live just to be in a costume on the stage. I can't be quiet to appease my wife's fears."

"Hunt was arrested. They say he may serve time in prison. Maybe he should've listened to his wife."

Dousing the seat lantern again, he leaned back and put his head near her side of the phaeton. "You won't come visit me in Newgate?"

She dared herself not to look at him and risk her heart melting at moonbeams dancing on his grin. "I won't be a couch woman, Bex. I won't sit around and not have my opinion heard."

"Not sure what a *couch woman* is, but I hear you just fine." His voice was a yawn again. Soon his nostril made another heavy noise, a sawing sound like workers raising a new section of the warehouse. His sleep-warm face pressed into her shoulder. His lips moved again against the skin exposed by her cap sleeves.

A breath caught in her throat when he moved away. Why was her skin so aware of him? Why did she feel foolish and scared for Bex? How would she protect him from the dangers she knew to be real?

Bex's hand joined hers, tugging to the right. "You're drifting, Miss Croome. Are you tiring?"

"No, getting tangled in my thoughts."

"Regrets? So soon? If I were arrested, you wouldn't have to come to Newgate every day."

She cast him a frowning look, but it was probably too dark for him to see. "My hope is that you never put yourself at such risk. Is that why you broke from your countess—your rallying?"

He sat up and steadied the reins, his naked hand atop her wrist. "She's not my countess. It was an affair many months ago. Your mother's papers should have made you aware of that."

"My mother's not aware of everything. She didn't discover my father's affair until last Yuletide."

Bex straightened. "You could tell me about it. I'm up now."

Opening up to Bex or keeping quiet warred in her head until she felt the warmth of Bex's hand. This man was to be her husband. She needed to be open to him. "I love the Yuletide. The smell of cinnamon, ribbons on wreaths. My father still gave us presents to make up for when we were poor. He'd always hide the tiny parcels. I thought I was so clever finding one in his study. It didn't have a tag, but I thought I could guess if it was for me."

"So, you opened it?"

"Yes."

"And could you tell, Ester?"

"Yes. They weren't for my or Mama's consumption. They were letters to my father's mistress."

"Oh."

Was that all Bex could say? She could still see the brokenness in her mother's face, still feel the twist in her gut when Mama took the box of letters Ester showed her. "That was the worst holiday ever. No morning songs, no lighting of candles—just pain. And no explanation, if there could be a reason to be an adulterer."

"Did your mother forgive the transgression? She must have. She hosted a party with him last night? Right?"

She jarred the horses, making them run faster. "There was a party for the New Year, just six days after the discovery of the letters. Fake smiles and a strand of watercolor pearls seemed to be the price of making it all better."

"I'm sorry, Ester." He clasped his hand about hers and the reins for a moment before refolding his arms and getting comfortable again. "Maybe he repented, and your mother found a way to forgive him."

"I'm not my mother, Bex. I'm not an easy spirit who will do or think as you want me to. I am no couch woman."

"You said as much when we discussed my going to prison. Ester, I haven't said I want a couch woman. And what I've come to know about you, I highly doubt your mother to be that easy with a betrayal."

Bex didn't know her mother to be weak and so concerned about public opinion. "We are nothing alike, mother and I."

"If you say so. Thou doest protest too much, Ester."

"You would use Shakespeare against me? Though, with your voice, I'll forgive you."

He chuckled, something wicked and knowing. "What else can my voice do?"

Skin to skin, his fingers had slipped beneath her shawl and wound about her arm, sending a deep shiver through her. "What things do you want, other than for me to give up my principles and my rally-making."

Biting her lip, she warred against the butterflies doubling inside. "I said it before. Your honesty and fidelity are the most important things."

"What if an omission was for your protection?"

"No, that won't do for me, Bex. I need to be able to trust you."

"Miss Croome, no riddles. I'm not sure my brainbox is fully awake. You seem to be a smart lass, so this definitely isn't fair, but since you are speaking of what you want, I need to know what type of marriage I should expect?"

Foot jittering, she righted the carriage's rumble off the road. "What type of marriage is it you seek?"

He settled beside her, a little closer than before. From the heat of his breath on her cheek, he'd nestled near her ear. "I believe one with you, my dear."

Ester wasn't a little girl, so she couldn't act like one. She'd leaped as she had through the window with everything at risk. "You're wondering if I want a marriage purely of convenience or one of occasional affection?"

"Never occasional, my dear. I'm inclined to passionate relationships. Surely, you read that in the papers. That part was no lie."

Cheeks fevering, she focused on the closest horse. "You are trying to set my face on fire, aren't you?"

"Perhaps, but I need to know if Ester Croome is inclined to a passionate relationship. You could let a fellow down easy if you aren't interested."

There was no way she'd change her mind, but what did he mean? "You wouldn't marry me, if I weren't inclined?"

He tapped the soft, ticklish spot along her ribs. "It would make things more challenging, and of course, I would take great pleasure in changing your mind. There's an attraction between us which cannot be denied."

His chuckle was arrogant, and melodious, and deadly accurate. How could she not be attracted to someone she'd loved from a distance for two years?

"What? Miss Croome? No response?'

There were plenty of responses—her stomach was tense, her head was light. She'd jump out of her skin if his elbow tapped her again. "I'm not a couch woman, one of those wives waiting for a carousing husband to find his way home, hoping for a gift to make his lies better. Not me, not that type of relationship."

A long sigh came from Bex. "Well, it seems a mistress or extramarital affairs have been ruled out. That would make our marriage very limiting, very dull, for a man of passion. What do *you* want, Ester Croome?"

"Boring isn't what I want, either."

His hand clasped hers. "Good answer. No one should want boring."

"Mr. Bex, you know I'm infatuated with your stage presence. I've watched you in so many plays—the ones my friends and I could attend."

"That is a profession. That's not me."

She nodded, not that he could see. "I know. I want to know you. The true you."

"I could make a joke about biblically knowing, but I won't. Your tone sounds too serious. My hope is that the true me is someone you like."

"I pretend a great deal, particularly when I'm frightened. I hope you get to know me, Bex."

"I like you, Ester Croome, but the question becomes: the more that you learn of the man as opposed to the actor, will you like what you see?"

"It's dark, Bex, but I can still see your character. I like you, Arthur Bex, well enough now."

"Well enough to allow a kiss the next time there is an opportunity?"

So, she was right. He had wanted to kiss her before the racing carriage had reminded them how vulnerable they were on the side of the road.

Her head screamed yes, but until today Ester had never been so bold. "I suppose you'll have to wait and see."

"If we keep to this path, it should be interesting."

His tone was a mix of arrogance and promise. He surely knew she was vulnerable to his charms. That unsettled her. The gulf between their feelings seemed wide. Would he use it to his advantage?

His hand slacked its hold. The abrasion on his knuckle scraped against her elbow. She should've changed her outfits, to be less sensitive to his touches. Ordering her thoughts to the mission of getting to Gretna without being caught, she focused on the road, which seemed to be narrowing. "I still can't believe you chose to fight within hours of our elopement."

"Sometimes, the fight picks you. You don't always have the luxury of choosing."

"I suppose."

"Miss Croome, I learned to box at an early age. It comes in handy—with drunks, theater critics, reporters." He wriggled his head, his forehead finding that space between her ear and collarbone to perch. "It will come in handy for those who are rude to Mrs. Bex."

It warmed her heart that he was already protective her, but how would she fit into his world? "Bex," she said in a voice she hoped was low and easy, "How will your friends take that you are married."

"Just fine. If I had any. Well, Jonesy did wish us well."

"Jonesy? Another actor?"

"A stable boy."

No friends? "Bex, you are so wonderful on stage, larger than life. How can you not have friends? No one from childhood? No one from before you made a splash in London?"

He bristled and turned further away. "It can happen. I like to be alone."

"With a preference for being alone—how exactly will that work for our marriage?"

His restless turning made the seat squeal. "Another thing we'll have to wait and see."

More distance separated them, and she instantly missed the heat of him and the smell of his soap. Maybe a spice?

Up a hill and down the other side, she kept the phaeton moving. Taking a glance at him nodding off, Ester didn't like the imbalance between them—she infatuated, him not so much. "Why were you answering newspaper advertisements for a wife?"

Sigh. *Snort-half whistle.*

"Thanks, Bex."

"Just." His voice sounded weary, half audible. "Just felt...I just felt it was time."

It was a small, unsatisfying confession. Stewing, she concentrated on the horses, but couldn't help looking over at him for better answers. He should use his melodious voice to set her at ease, to say that he saw something special in her other than desperation.

Yet, each casual peek made the phaeton veer. She couldn't resist.

He stretched. "Miss Croome, you're not driving smoothly. Pull over and let me take control."

Him taking control wasn't what she wanted. "I haven't driven that long. You need to rest. Won't we be near a coaching inn soon?"

His hand tightened on the leather strap. "In another hour. But I'd like to make it there unharmed. You're swaying. Pull over to the side. I'll drive."

"My friend, Mrs. Fitzwilliam-Cecil, she says it's not safe to stop on the road. Highwaymen or thieves could lurk in the shadows."

"Your friend is right, but her warning might be making you unduly nervous. Rest assured, you are safe with me. I'm a boxer, remember."

One glance and Ester knew she wasn't safe. Not from his humor, his condescension, or the lightness his presence caused her stomach. "The loner boxer who now wants to be a husband. Should I be nervous or cautious?"

"I don't know. You're the one driving backroads with a stranger. Again, I think you protest too much. It's fine to be nervous. It's lovely on a woman."

She should focus on the *lovely* part, but the condescending tone—that could have come from her father. "Fine. I'm stopping. I'm cold and I need to change." Ester pulled to the side of the road. When the horses stopped, she flung the reins at Bex then jumped down.

He lit and held up the lantern. "Miss Croome, where are you going?"

She scooped up her bag and yanked out her carriage dress. "I'm going to put on this more sensible gown. It's warmer, and I need a moment alone. You should understand that."

"Oh... Well, don't take too long or wander too far. Dawn is breaking, and your friend's highwaymen could be about. We could be their last run before going to bed."

Without a look back, Ester moved forward. She knew she was being ridiculous. She knew it, but the feeling that she could be marrying a man as patronizing as her father didn't sit well.

In fact, it burned her inners. She went into the edge of the brush guided by the hints of orange from the rising sun. Mama would be arising soon, inspecting Nineteen Fournier for damage from her guests—a scuffed floor, a broken glass, a missing daughter.

Mama would be so hurt. Would this elopement cut her as badly as Papa's love letters? When those notes had fallen from her mother's fingers, there had been so much pain on her face.

The poor woman had expected a present, only to be gifted

with the truth of her husband's failures. If Ester had known what the letters said, she'd never have given them to Mama, never hurt her so bad.

But hadn't Ester hurt her mother by eloping?

Ester stumbled over a root, her breath sputtering as she lunged against a trunk. Her irritation at Bex had been replaced with guilt about her own treachery.

She'd deprived Mama of a chance to fix things and the opportunity to throw a big wedding breakfast.

And she'd find out at full light with the scuffed floor, the broken glass, the horribly ungrateful missing daughter.

Ester was guilty.

She folded her arms to keep her heart inside. She loved Mama but couldn't trust that she'd fix things. And if Papa hadn't forced Ester's hand with this betrothal to Jordan, she wouldn't have had to elope. She and Bex could've courted normally.

But the elopement was Ester's doing, not her parents. She'd chosen this path. She chose Bex. Whatever happened—getting caught, disgraced, or worse, a poor marriage betwixt strangers— the fault would be on her shoulders, hers alone.

Things would work out. Maybe Mama could offer a celebration once things calmed. More hopeful, Ester stretched then wiggled one button at her neck open, then a second, and a third of the lace caressing her neck. Satisfied, she slid off her shawl and laid it on a branch, then she began her dance again, wriggling to loosen the outer gown's lacings. The pretty overgown fell but caught on a bush with thorns, a plant with spiky leathered leaves, emerald green like a hawthorn shrub, but taller. Ignoring the noises behind her, she picked her netting free, only being poked once. The bush found out she'd fight for what was hers.

Bex wasn't hers but there was an attraction between them. At this point, the actor was all she had. And he was her choice, not Josiah Croome's.

Scanning the trees behind her, she saw nothing and continued undressing. One shimmy and two shakes helped Ester climb out of the rest of her party gown. She was careful to save the brass pins that made the fit perfect. The pretty thing might make an excellent wedding gown, though she wondered how she'd ever get the pins in again without assistance. Bex wouldn't help her into the gown but more so out of it, if she took his suggestive words seriously.

Standing in her chemise and corset in the middle of the lush woods, with the sunlight starting to spread, she felt naked. She wasn't, but the richness of her garbs was armor, built by being Josiah Croome's daughter. Would being Mrs. Bex offer the same protection?

Sighing, not crying, she slipped the carriage dress onto her shoulders, tugging until it fit properly at her bosom, covering it more discreetly than the sheer lace of the party gown.

Done. Warm, covered, and matronly in one of her old gowns from their life above the warehouse, when they'd had no servant to help dress. Collecting her things, she started to walk back to the phaeton, but stopped and covered her mouth to hide a scream.

Bex wasn't alone. A man dressed in ebony held a gun to his head.

CHAPTER TEN

Highway Robbery

Arthur stared at the end of the gun. It wasn't the first time his nose had been so close to the smell of gunpowder, the feel of the cold iron, but this wasn't merely his safety at risk. Now he had Miss Croome to keep from danger. "I've no more gold," he said to the fiend. "I've given you all my guineas."

The bandit laughed. "There's always more. Been trailing you since you stopped at the coaching inn. Your pace is too leisurely a speed for a poor man and the only man not in a hurry is a rich one."

Miss Croome hadn't come from the bushes. Surely, she saw the robbery and would stay in hiding. Perhaps the shyness he'd seen in her would surface and keep her from jeopardy.

Yet, something in his gut said that wouldn't happen. He needed the fiend to flee before she took notice. "Look, you've taken what I had in my pockets. Be on your way. Surely, you've some other fool to rob."

"Where's the woman?"

The man had a handkerchief to his face, but it didn't block the gravel in his voice. With Arthur's lantern still aglow, he could identify him. This time, being a witness against evil might again cost the life he'd built. "She isn't here. Go on."

"I decide when it's time to leave." The thief hoisted his gun and rummaged in the gig, but he'd find nothing of value—just Arthur's clothes and the script he needed to memorize. "I saw a woman, and I smell lilac. You didn't leave her at the inn. Where is she? She looked well-to-do. Scarves or lace can fetch a penny or more."

Arthur balled his fist behind his back, calculating when to strike to subdue the fool before Ester returned. "You need to leave my wife out of this. Go on—"

Ester stood at the edge of the brush.

He wanted to yell for her to leave, but that would alert the fiend, giving him more leverage. "Look, you have everything. Go on your way."

"Come out, little woman. I've your husband." The bandit dumped Arthur's bag on the ground. "So where is the little woman?" He cocked the hammer again and put it against Arthur's temple. "She has to have a ring or a little jewelry. Here, little sweetheart. Come nigh and save your husband."

"Don't hurt him, sir." Ester's voice sounded full of tears.

The fiend slugged Arthur with the gun and knocked him to the ground. His vision was blurred, but he saw Miss Croome waving her arms like she was distraught. "Stay back. Let this man be on his way before you come close."

The rising sun shined upon her. She looked frail, helpless, and Arthur's gut twisted. "Run, Ester."

The bandit kicked at him before turning to her. "A maid? No, a prostitute. There's no wife. Oh, no wonder your driving was crazed. You've ditched the wife for a hot little piece. I hear her kind gets hot and bothered quite easily."

"You have all that was in my pockets." He tried to rise, but the man's boot pinned his leg. "Go now. We won't follow."

"Of course, you wouldn't. Your hands are far too full." The

bellicose laughter grew worse. "Come on over, little woman, and let me take a look at you."

She threw her head back, and in a voice that sounded calm said, "I'll come if you lower that gun. Don't hurt him."

"I don't take orders, especially from the likes of you. Now come over here before I blow his face off."

The barrel was again at Arthur's head. The smell of the gunpowder, the heft of the muzzle setting creases above his eye, reminded him of long ago, walking his uncle's ship with the sailors who didn't want the kid too near the cargo hold. "Don't touch her. Leave her be."

"Mr. Bandit, sir, why don't you come here?" Her voice sounded husky, not proper and prim or scared, as before. "I'd like a look at you."

That tone made both the bandit and Arthur stare in her direction.

Her hands fluttered about her hair. Then her braid came down. She looked wild, almost savage with her chignon waving down her back as she swiveled her hips to music that only she heard.

"Oh, I see why you took off with her, mate." He pointed his gun at the phaeton. "Why don't you go on and leave me and the maid to play hide-and-go-seek in the woods."

Arthur leaped to his feet and started for the man, but he again cocked his gun and pointed at him. "Go with your life. I'll only tell you this once."

The bandit started for her. "I'm stealing your plaything. Come on, lil' Wowski, or shall I say, Rapunzel. Let me play. If your kind is good enough for Prince William to bed, then you'll do fine for me."

"Go, on love," she said with a giggle, a nervous one. Your wife's waiting around the bend. Let her know her maid won't make it in today." She fumbled with the top button of her dress. "Go on, lover boy."

That's when he knew it was an act to distract the bandit. "Fine, I was tired of you anyway. The likes of you cost me four guineas."

He got into the phaeton and pushed it up the road a few paces and into the thicker grove around the bend, just far enough to pretend to leave. Arthur jumped to the ground, took a knife and rope from his seat storage and went back to save his brave bride-to-be.

Huffing, he charged through the brush. When he saw his brave Ester, she'd slipped deeper into the woods, but the bandit was now halfway to her.

"What game is this, lass? I've come this far, now you come out to me."

Hips swiveling, Ester continued her dance, edging more into the woods. "You know my kind will say anything. And I'd say anything to keep you from my man."

The sunlight wasn't Arthur's friend, but it slipped behind a cloud, giving him a little time to get closer to the woman who was risking her neck for him.

The highwayman cussed, as if that kind of talk would convince a peach like Ester to come closer. "I'm done with the games, Wowski. I don't pull guns out on women, but there is a first for everything." He lifted his gun and took aim at her. "Come now and dance for me, close and easy."

No more space to go—Ester was against a tree. "Put down

your gun and come get me." She fingered the top button of her dress, popping it and one more. "'Less you're scared of little old me?

The air sucked out of Arthur. She was brazen and wild, but smart as a fox.

"Sure, love. A little busty thing like you is no threat. We'll play it your way, for now." The fiend set his gun down but pulled a knife from his boot. He took the final steps and dangled it in front of her wide eyes. "You like to tease." He drew the knife point down her bosom. "But I think you won't disappoint."

Dropping the rope, barely in control of the rage pumping through his veins, Arthur balled his knuckles and pounced. He leaped and knocked the knife, sending it far away. Then he punched the man, three blows for every one the highwayman could muster. He wasn't going to let the thief have any part of her. "She hasn't disappointed me ever."

One deep blow after the other, Arthur sent the bandit careening backward.

"I'll kill ye both."

But Arthur wasn't done. He was back on *Zhonda*, his uncle's ship, but he was finally big enough to pummel the first mate, the one leading the charge to toss the cargo overboard.

Hands went up about Arthur's neck, but he broke the choking hold. He beat the man below him until blood splatted his hands. All was silent below him, but Arthur fought against the sailors who kept him from reasoning with his uncle. If he didn't stop the crew, the killings would continue. The cargo below wouldn't be saved, all tossed into the ocean to drown.

Arthur took his knife and put it to the first mates throat. "It's over. No more will die."

The cock of the gun sounded, and again he smelled gunpowder. "Bex?"

A soft palm touched his cheek. "He's done-in, Bex. You don't have to kill him. Look, you saved me."

Blinking, he came back to himself, stashed his knife in his pocket, then stood.

She handed him the gun. His hand shook while he fisted his fingers about the barrel.

"Bex?"

He yanked off the highwayman's scarf and wiped his hands clean, but couldn't say anything to her. His mind hadn't settled. It was still in the past, still haunted.

With a better grip to the gun's stock, he fought the temptation to blast holes in the highwayman, but that wouldn't cleanse Arthur's memories.

"We are all right, Bex."

Lowering the gun, Arthur turned and snatched her about her waist and held her until his heart slowed. "You're crazed. What if I were a lesser man?"

"You're not. You're Arthur Bex, and I'm safe. We are safe. I never lost faith in you." She reached up as he bent his head, and she kissed his cheek. The softest lips planted on his jaw as the words she'd said blessed his lonely soul.

She hugged his neck again before pulling him toward the phaeton. "Now, let's get out of here. Someone will think it's my fault."

"I'm going to tie the highwayman up first. Get the rope from the bushes over there."

Her lips had pressed to a thin line, but she nodded and ran like a rabbit then bounced back with the jute in hand.

Arthur practiced breathing as he did for a direct address, focused and in control, even as he pointed the flintlock pistol at the bandit's head.

Not trusting himself and his fight with the past, he handed the gun to her. "Hold this, Ester, while I bind up your highwayman." Taking the rope, he twisted it about the bandit's hands and feet, then dragged him to a tree.

Ester stared as if she'd seen a ghost when he'd finished. All the bravery she'd had seemed to disappear. "The coils about his wrists, his ankles. You've hung him up like an enslaved man."

"What?"

"Something my father once described." She touched at her bosom. "You don't know how frightening a thing is, not until you see it."

Arthur looked back at the highwayman. The man's blonde hair caught the morning sun as he lay with his hands and feet bound like shackles to a boat hull. Sweat beaded and rolled down Arthur's face as he struggled to contain the venom in his heart for his memories, for his uncle. "I...I don't want the highwayman to escape before a constable can find him."

"Bex, let's go." Her hand shook as she picked up her bag. "I knew you'd come back to save me."

Her gloves were off and she put her free palm against his brown jacket sleeve. In the early light, he and this lovely woman were barely distinguishable, like they were one. They had to be one, for no one had seen him so weak—not in a long time. He forced a deep breath. "That was dangerous, Ester. He could've hurt you, or worse."

"He was going to hurt you." She moved from him too soon, but before he could object, she went to the bandit and pulled Arthur's guineas from the man's jacket. "These are your coins, not his."

"You're not mine officially yet, either, Ester. Let's get back on the road to make it true, you as my wife."

A shaky curl lifted her lips. "He can't die out here tied to a tree. That shouldn't happen."

"Compassion on a man who just called you low names, who threatened to assault you, maybe kill you when he was done?"

"I'm safe. We are both safe. I can't focus on the bad. Frankly, there is just too much."

After putting the gun in his waistband, he took her bag and led her through the woods to his phaeton. "I'm sorry, Ester. I was careless. I forced you to act...that was an act, right?"

Her smile hadn't quite returned. For the first time, he couldn't read her emotions. "No greater love hath a man than to lay down his life for another, for his friend." Her voice was low. "I think of you highly. I hope you know me as a friend, too."

He put her bag into the carriage and then spun to crowd her against the wheel. Tapping the two brass buttons she'd opened to entice the bandit, he drank in her beauty. "May I."

"Yes. I mean, what?"

Her eyes went wide as he buttoned the first one, then the second. "No one sees you but me, Ester. I'm claiming this figure that has me intrigued beyond a mere distraction. Don't risk yourself, this loveliness. I'm not worth that sacrifice."

"Maybe you are to me."

"Because you're in love with an actor on the stage?"

"Maybe. But the man, the one who promised he'd come at five minutes after twelve, the one who I knew wouldn't truly leave me with a highwayman, has me in a serious state of bliss. I'm in serious like for Arthur Bex."

At this moment, he wished he were Arthur Bex, the one she saw with her topaz eyes. His throat tightened a little. "There is a coaching inn another hour or two ahead. We'll send word of the highwayman's capture. No doubt, he's taken advantage of others. He has to be a wanted criminal."

"Good, and you'll tell them. You'll be a hero. And no one will think it's my fault."

He dove his fingers into her loosened hair. Her tresses were silky with heavy curls. It was something to clasp, perhaps strong enough to keep them bound together. "You think they will blame you because you're Blackamoor?"

She backed away, moving from his hands that wanted more of her.

Fingers working fast, smoothing her locks behind an ear, she nodded. "Yes, and I'm also a woman. The rules are always different for us."

"They shouldn't be." He took her back into his arms and held her for a moment, then lifted her to the padded seat. He climbed up next to her. Before he could stop her, she reached for the reins.

"I could drive for a little longer, Bex."

"Oh, no. I'm wide awake now." He'd lowered his tone, but it was too late.

She drew back from him.

"Sorry, Miss Croome, but I'll drive." He forced the horses

forward. "My emotions are a bit scattered. I need the hum of the road to collect myself."

"Your voice, Bex. You sound quite angry."

"I'm angry at myself. I put you at risk. I made you feel as if you had to coerce this man to spare me. I'm not worth your safety."

As the phaeton moved from grass to the gravel path, Ester looked small again, deflated. It was a long time before she took pins from her pocket and finished righting her hair.

Prim and proper again, and he felt more the heel. He was a good actor; he had to be able to make her smile again. He smoothed the edges of his temper. "Ester."

"Yes, Bex."

"Have you done any theater? That little performance was quite good. Makes me wonder of an encore."

"You were in danger, and I went with the myth about Blackamoors and mulattoes being loose and wild. The horrible man fell for it. I only wanted you out of harm. I knew you could figure something out if a gun wasn't being waved in your face."

"Well, save the theater for me. I'm the actor in the family. But thank you for caring so much, so soon about me, Arthur Bex, the man."

It took about a mile before she offered a hint of a smile.

He put his eyes back on the road, not this mysterious girl who'd just risked everything for him. The countess would never have risked herself like this. That one *surprise* dinner with Phineas in tow, the woman had detailed their every argument and had even seemed to side with the reporter, asking questions about Arthur's past. She had even cast doubts on his sincerity about his push for abolition.

But the countess hadn't known the truth. He had certainly not shared the haunting memories that never went away.

A glance at Ester, fidgeting with all her buttons done, made his chest swell. She was with him even to her detriment. Her loyalty couldn't be questioned. If he opened more of his life to her, would her sympathies remain?

Part of him wanted to confess to her now. Yet, his healthy skepticism screamed, *don't do it, remember how you were shunned*. The stakes had risen. He wouldn't merely be losing someone he found attractive, but perhaps the only person who found him worthy enough that she'd risked her life to save him. That kind of person was too rare. No, he'd not gamble and lose her over things long buried in the sea and in Liverpool's prisoner's field. Arthur didn't think she'd smile at him, not even a hint of one, if the horrid deeds of his uncle became known.

• • •

Ester sat back against the seat, waiting for Bex to come from the main building of the Travelers Coaching Inn. The noon sun burned outside the limestone walls of the stables, highlighting the pink and gray blocks. She was grateful for the shade and the quiet of the stable hands. No questions about who they were or why, only silence and hard work scrubbing lathered horses, strapping in fresh ones.

The hearty scent of fresh hay overcame that of stale horses and muck. She felt comfortable enough to close her eyes, but she couldn't. She had to wait for Bex to come back with two rented rooms.

"What city are we near?" she asked one of the grooms who stared at her.

The young man swiped at his light brown hair. "Close to Sheffield."

It was a place she hadn't heard of, but it didn't sound like any city near London. Maybe they were making progress, getting closer to Gretna. Too afraid to ask how far Scotland was from Sheffield and give away their plans, she dipped her head.

Ester inhaled long and deep. Creating a distraction for Bex to subdue the highwayman was the craziest thing she'd ever done, save eloping. What else could she have done, seeing that gun pressed to Bex's temple?

Never could she sit by and hope things would get better. She had to act, even if it meant pretending to have more courage than she really did. Her hands shook as she clasped her elbows, remembering the fear that had wrapped around her as she'd chosen to dance for the gunman. If Bex had been anyone other than an honorable man, Ester would be dead, or worse than dead.

"All finished up," the groom said as he clunked his brush in his pail and moved on to another carriage.

She watched the metal bucket slosh soapy water as he carried it away. Could she be envious of a brush because it soaked in water that she imagined was warm and soothing? If Ester were home, she'd be in her room atop her big canopied bed, waiting for her turn in the copper bath. She'd be the second to use it, after Mama, as was her rank in the household of Nineteen Fournier. The sides of the copper tub would still be warm, and Mrs. Fitterwall always brought Ester fresh water.

Curling deeper into the seat and the silky shawl, she closed her eyes. The care of everything drifted away except her hope that Bex would hurry to get them rooms.

The carriage rocked, and when she opened her sleepy eyes, the Travelers Inn was disappearing in the distance. It took at least another minute for her weary soul to realize that there would be no bed, not now.

She forced her eyes to open and focus on Bex.

His hat had been tossed to the floorboards, and his handsome face seemed blank.

Her heart beat hard, and she bolted up. "Did you get in trouble over the highwayman? Are we on the run?"

"No, for his capture, I was thanked."

That feeling that he was leaving something out pressed at her middle, grounding the butterflies inside that had taken flight upon seeing Bex.

"I can't stand it." Bex said, "You're a wonderful woman, Ester Croome. You risked your life for me, but no single room for you. It's not fair."

"So, you think I'm wonderful."

He turned to her with a forehead riddled with lines. "Is that the only thing you heard?"

"It's the only thing that matters. Sleeping inside a horrible small inn does not mean as much as hearing you say I'm wonderful, Bex."

With a shake of his head, he turned back to the road. "Women."

Almost grinning, she settled back down on the bench but found his arm scooting her closer. "It's only fair. Put your head on my shoulder if you can reach it. I used you for a pillow yesterday before our highwayman. I still think you shouldn't have put yourself at risk. Now have at me."

She trembled at the teasing command, worse than any shiver she'd tried to suppress. "Once we are married, things will be better. We'll get to know each other without all the differences of our worlds coming between us."

"Ester, is this what it's like for you and your friends outside of London? Denial of your humanity? Being treated worse than a criminal?"

"Sometimes. Sometimes it's that way in London. We mostly try to stick to our own. We don't venture too far from London, not without setting up the trip far in advance. Some will refuse, but others won't care because our money is gold. That's the only color that matters."

She could hear the fury growling in his chest, and in his eyes she saw the want of something, or perhaps the haunting of being powerless. Then she remembered waiting for Papa to come home, waiting to hear his snores. She hated that feeling, but it was too common, too ingrained in her soul.

Ester sighed. "Bex, this is how it is. I'm grateful for what I have, for you. You look at me and your mind doesn't see foreign or exotic, or loose morals. Hopefully, all you see is a girl going with a boy to Gretna Green to marry and live happily ever after."

"I see that, but I also see the injustice, and it burns. Prince William, the new king's own brother, is rumored to have kept his enslaved lover offshore because she'd be free if she stood on our soil. Things must change." He swiped at his neck as if it was bathed in heat. "Perhaps when abolition is law in every part of this world, then this attitude held by the innkeepers will change, too."

"It's so difficult to change the world, difficult and dangerous.

Bex, I just want to know you'll return to me safely."

His fingers massaged the tired muscles of her shoulder. He made the horses move so smoothly it lulled her. Her eyelids grew heavier.

"I'll take better care, Ester. Definitely take better care of you. But I won't stop speaking out against enslavement, not until it is done."

"With your dreamy voice, and some well-placed providence, all things are possible." Another yawn pushed out. "Will you promise to think about your safety?"

"Let's talk on this later. Sleep, my sweet fiancée. I'll wake you at the next coaching inn. Maybe we'll have better luck then."

Bex's idealism was heartwarming, but Ester saw the world as it was, not as she wanted it to be. And people like Bex, they got hurt with their do-gooding. She didn't want him hurt, and she didn't know how many times she could see him get knocked down, put in his place.

"Sleep, Ester. Know that you are safe with me. We're halfway to Scotland."

Blinking, she snuggled against his thick arm. His voice sounded so comforting, like it always had on stage, but this was only a moment in time, a respite between storms. Halfway was a point of reflection. There was time to change minds, to come to new understandings.

Ester wanted to marry Bex, but if he persisted in putting himself at risk, how could she stand it? Marrying her might not be best for him, his career, or even his safety. And she cared about him enough to protect him, even use the money Theodosia gave her and take a coach back to London. That would save Bex, but what about Ester?

How could she live with the shame of almost eloping, of being that brazen girl who ran off with an actor? Frederica struggled with the stigma of being a loose woman because of her courtesan mother, but nothing would save Ester from the cuts-direct, the awful whispers, the hurt of seeing Mama's proud, crestfallen face.

There was no escape, not now. Ester would be branded low, as if Bex had taken a heated iron and smote the words on her forehead. She'd enslaved herself to this path by eloping,

"Ester, you don't look like you're sleeping. You look pensive." Bex's voice was soothing, like hot tea, warm crusty bread, or a dip in a steaming bath. "Do I want to know your thoughts?"

"No." He didn't need to hear of her want of a bath or of the need to convince him to take a quieter path and merely focus on his acting so she wouldn't fret about receiving his bloodied frockcoat and have no hope of him coming home. "The world is dangerous, Bex. Things happened to Papa's brother, and a few family friends. Their murders never made it into Mama's papers."

Bex put his arm about her. "We'll just have to take more care but keep moving in the right direction."

She shivered again, and his hold tightened.

Would he ever understand the danger? Would he promise to be sensible? Ester needed to convince him before they took their vows. She wasn't going to sit on the couch hoping to never hold his battered frockcoat.

No, that wouldn't do for Ester at all.

CHAPTER ELEVEN

Rocky Roads

Arthur drank the hot coffee he'd procured at the last inn. It wasn't good to drink too much of it, but he had to. They'd gone another full day and night with only stops to change horses and to get something to eat. The strain of it all wearied his soul, but he'd not give up going north, not until they made it to Gretna.

His seatmate nibbled on an apple. Ester's appetite seemed small, and that smile she'd had at first had waned. Eloping without a plan for how to travel had been foolish. He had never thought it would be so difficult, so draining, but now this was a battle he must win. "Eat some of the mutton stew, Ester. It's quite good."

"The apple is filling, Bex. It's hard to swallow watching you suffer." She put down her charcoal from the new sketch she was drawing.

"Done with your art?"

"Bex, could I have another go at driving?"

The poor girl asked every time they stopped, and now every twenty minutes or so. "You've done enough with the highwayman. That can't be the highlight of this trip. And I'll not ruin your buttery soft hands on these straps. Ester, enjoy the scenery. Smell the cooler air."

"How do you know my hands are so soft? I've barely been without gloves."

"I've touched a little; the rest is imagination."

Her face frowned up, her lovely lips puckering. "Tell me more of your upbringing, Bex."

Maybe the lack of sleep made him giddy, but she had said something that didn't involve stopping or letting her drive. "My father was a vicar. I heard he had a voice on him."

"Well, like father, like son. Who raised you when your parents died?"

There was always a choice in what he confessed to another soul and how bad things would become if his words ended up in the papers. The reporters who had covered his uncle's trial had made caricatures of Arthur's testimony—one showing him on the stand, half devil, half human. That image lingered. Though he felt close to Ester, how could he risk her seeing him as such? "I was passed to an uncle who died a few years later. I raised myself. I had to. I don't want to say more."

"Is it that painful?" Her frown became a line of sadness and sympathy.

Arthur hated pity.

"So you've learned to be independent and alone."

The statement was small, but like a pinprick, it stung, echoing the truths he'd rather deny and avoid. "Smell the air. It's different from London."

Her eyes never shifted, but the slight nod of her chin indicated a willingness to let him be on this matter. "I smell rotten egg. Is that sulfur from the coal? There is ash in the sky above the trees. I like London. The stench is familiar. In a way, it is comforting because I know it. I don't know what it's like to be alone, but I've chosen a path that may separate me from my family."

"You're not much of an optimist are you, Ester? They'll come around. Let's be hopeful."

The furrows on her brow deepened, and she took another small bite. "I'm more a realist. I think it is easier."

"How very dull and unromantic. Do you dream? Surely you do. You liked me well enough all from the majesty of the stage. That's a dream."

Her eyes drifted to the left, and he hoped she remembered the things that had drawn her to him, that they would sweep away the doubts which he knew had grown.

"I do dream. Right now, I'm dreaming of a hot bath. The water's the perfect temperature, almost steaming, maybe a hint of rosewater or lilac fills the room. Yes, I dream, Bex, but maybe my dreams are too simple."

She grabbed at the reins. "Bex! You're looking at me and drifting. It's not safe to go on when you're so tired. You're weaving more than I did."

He was tired, bone aching tired, but she had done too much for him. As a man, he needed to show her he could protect her... that she could depend upon him, no matter what they faced as a husband and wife—even the loss of her family. "I suppose I should stop glancing at you. Staring at the road is a safer bet than thinking of you in a bath."

Her olive cheeks darkened, and it delighted him as much as her hand, tiny and strong, winding about his.

"Bex, you are struggling. Let me help."

"A little suffering is good for the soul. ''Tis nobler in the mind to suffer the slings and arrows of outrageous fortune than to take arms against a sea of troubles.'"

Her topaz eyes brightened. "Your Hamlet was very good, but our sea of troubles is the lack of sleep. Maybe we could pull over for a few moments. You could nap in the sulfurous air."

"The last time we did so, your highwayman found us and you danced for him. Though I am not opposed to seeing those hips of yours in a fit of fancy, I won't put you at risk again."

He'd done it again. Her whole face fevered. A stranger might not've been able to tell, but he could. It meant he'd come to know a little more of this woman who was so concerned about his welfare. "I am finding you a good sport and a pleasure to tease, but you can help me."

"Oh yes, Bex. Let me help."

"Dig into my bag by your feet and pull out the long pages."

Her expression changed. The edges of her plump lips lifted as she dove into his things and retrieved the script. Lean fingers flipped through the pages. "*Antony and Cleopatra*." She drew the papers to her bosom, and he envied the parchment. "Is this your new play?"

Loving the light sound of her voice, he smiled. Good, the distraction of Shakespeare. "Yes. I'll be General Antony. As long as we are back on time for rehearsals, I'll get to keep the leading role in one of the greatest love stories."

Ester's pert flared nose wrinkled. "If you say so, Bex. You'll be wonderful in anything."

He scratched at his chin but returned his eyes to the road. "I sense you are not impressed. Have you read the play?"

More pages rustled. "Yes, I've read it. Shakespeare's plays were some of the first books Papa bought for his study. I saw this one performed a couple of years ago. It wasn't that fine."

His curiosity was piqued. He thought a Shakespeare lover would enjoy all his works. "You don't find the story of a great warrior totally enraptured by the queen of the largest African country to your liking?"

She shook her head and pulled the pages to her bosom. "No, Bex. I do not."

The woman was quite adorable holding his script with such a serious pout. Was she again fretting? He needed to become better at engaging her, even as his own attention drifted from the road. "I am at a loss, Ester. I thought we were of like minds, yet how could you not find the story of a Roman soldier and an African queen not similar to, say, us? Albeit, I'm from Liverpool, very close to where the Normans, the Roman's descendants, came through."

His jest didn't seem to amuse her, not if her spreading grimace was an indication. "It's not like us, Bex. It should never be anything like us."

Glancing at her and her rising tone, he saw her fingers tightening about his papers. "But their love was so powerful. Aren't you looking for a love like that?"

"No, Bex. I'm not. Their love was deceitful. Antony was married when he took up with Cleopatra. He was with the queen when his first wife died. How disloyal can a fellow be? Maybe Antony thought he'd get his wife pearls upon his return to gain forgiveness. Pity the wife never collected."

Arthur fanned his hat. "Uh, yes, Antony was a bit of a scoundrel at first, but you must concede he was devoted to Cleopatra."

Ester made a horrible laugh before shoving his papers back

into his bag. "How devoted could he be? And to whom—the second woman he married, or the queen he returns to and with whom he continues an adulterous affair? I think Antony is horrid."

"Maybe you are missing the point. It's a classic love story. His marriages were political."

"Bex, don't tell me they were marriages of convenience. That still wouldn't make me have sympathy for Antony or his portrayers."

Arthur hadn't thought about the play like that, and with Ester still smarting over her father's infidelity, he heard the pain she hadn't forgiven. He rubbed at his neck. "I can see your point. It was wrong to engage in the illicit affair, but that is how Shakespeare sculpts the web of their relationship."

Ester tossed her head back onto the seat. "Webs are sticky. You do things for one reason, but you become entangled in another until you can't break free. A neglected spouse, working all the time, too much to do to come straight home. Webs are ruinous."

Yes, they were. This wasn't going well, but at least she wasn't fretting at his driving. Might as well push farther down this hole. "Do you think the queen was at fault?"

Cutting her eyes at him, Ester said, "Antony is responsible for his choices, but I wonder why he chose her, other than for her beauty. Every time Antony needed her help, Cleopatra was untrustworthy. She left her great love in need, and his ships were defeated. How can there be love, even a little love, if there is no trust? I hope we are never like them."

One forbidden glimpse at Ester revealed tears in her eyes—wet, topaz eyes. His chest ached as he turned back to the rocky road. "It's just a play, dearest, not our story. I'm not Antony. You're not Cleopatra. What's the matter?"

She fished in her bag for a handkerchief. "I don't know why it matters to me. I mean it happened years ago. Mama has forgiven my father. Why can't I? Why am I holding on to the grief?"

They were getting to the steeper parts of the terrain. It was either pull to the side now or have to wait hours. One look at Ester and there was no choice. He slowed the carriage to a crawl then edged over to the side of the road and parked. Slipping his hand about her, he tugged Ester, small delicate Ester, into his chest. His lips found her brow, and he kissed away the creases. The sweet scent of lilac from the soap she used to wash her face was still there. The sweetness so fragrant, so enticing. "Don't cry, Ester. Your father's a flawed man. Most men are."

Fisting her hands, she beat upon his chest, but he did not let go. "You can't be like that. You can't lie to my face and say we are everything and then risk it all for a Cleopatra. Papa was perfect. Tall and strong. You can't be like him."

Arthur rubbed her back, settling Ester more firmly against him. "Your father, Antony…neither thought of the risks. If your father had properly weighed them, I am sure he'd have chosen the right course. But that is your parent's marriage. Their lack of happiness or discord will be nothing to us. We won't be foolish, Ester. We won't squander what we have."

"What do we have, Bex? A response to a newspaper advertisement that wasn't even mine? You don't know anything about me. You just mentioned you were from Liverpool, but what else do I know? You raised yourself, nothing of your connections. Nothing but what has been in the newspapers, the caricatures of the scandals. Will you leave me when things get tough? Things always get tough."

Lifting her chin, he spoke of what he did know. "Ester, I've known you for two days. It's not a lifetime, but I've never felt more like sharing a life with someone than I do with you. I'm not promising a grand passion, or that we'll never argue. We've already done that."

"Yes." She sniffled. "You can be condescending."

He tapped her nose, tracing the slight arch until he met her cheek. "And you, my dear, will not think of your own safety, in spite of my wishes."

"'Tis true, Bex. I can be stubborn like my father. That has to be bad."

"Ester Croome, I know I can depend upon you. That's important to me. You're right. I have to learn how to not be a loner, but you are the one I want to learn that with."

Any doubts about them not being of one mind had diminished to almost nonexistence. Ester was a quiet person, but not passive, and if she truly loved him, Arthur knew she'd fight for him. Wasn't that what he wanted in a wife above all else—someone to believe in him and recommend him?

Forgetting his past, stuffing it away to the rear of his brain, he gripped her delicate palm, her graceful fingers, so warm and full of life. "I promise you fidelity, Ester Croome. I promise to tell you the truth to anything you ask. I'll cherish what we build. I won't take it for granted."

She pushed away to the edge of the gig as if she'd jump.

"Please don't make promises, Bex. I know things change. One minute everyone is happy. The next, not so much. I've admired you for two years. Maybe that has blinded me to our incompatibility. Maybe this crazy trip and lack of sleep has blinded you, too."

"Ester, I'd rather you not see my flaws. They're daunting."

"What if I'm your Cleopatra and every time you need me to defend you, I shrink away? I'm a private person. You'll push for abolition and you'll keep fighting, but it is so dangerous. What if you need me to support you, and I can't because I'm afraid of you getting hurt?"

He swallowed hard as his gut tightened. That couldn't be. He knew that she was the one. Scooting over to her, he put an arm on her shoulder. "So tense, Ester. You think that I have doubts about a woman that danced in the bushes, placing herself in danger for me? You knew I would come back for you. Ester, what's between us is new but it feels right."

Turning to him, she looked up, and he captured her gaze.

He wasn't ready to call what he felt love, but it was more than passion and thankfulness. "We have a beginning, Ester Croome. Something thick and rich to build upon. Yes, I am an actor playing parts in the theater, but my trust in you is no act. I hope to keep earning yours."

"Maybe, but I'm sure my parents must suspect something is wrong. Hopefully, my absence has ruined my chances of marrying Jordan. You've done enough, Bex. Send me home by coach at the next inn."

"Ester, your reputation. No one will think—"

"I know, Bex. I know. I hope this won't end up in Mama's scandal papers, but I need to protect you. Without me you can take a room and rest. You'll get a great deal of sleep and make it back to London for rehearsals.

No.

He couldn't lose her over sleep. She cared about him, perhaps more than she did herself. No one had done that in a while. The last woman he'd cared for, the Countess Devoors, had liked his fame and the attention his name brought, but she would have sold his hide for her name to be put in the papers. That's why bashful, brave, beautiful Ester was perfect.

"Put me on a stagecoach, Bex. Then go on being London's best actor."

"No. I will not send you away unless you have decided against me as a husband. Do you not care for me?"

"You know I do, but this is not right."

It hit him like a dropped line, a bad review. Somehow, she'd taken up the notion that this was too hard for him. She surely thought he couldn't do well in a mixed-race marriage. He slipped a frizzy curl behind her ear. "You're wrong to give up on me, Ester. In four hours or less, I'll have you in Scotland. We'll marry as planned. I'll not send you back to face the scorn of the world. I care too deeply for you."

He framed her face within his palms, claimed her wide-eyed gaze, and came within a whisper of her mouth. "You still wish to marry me, Ester Croome, don't you?"

"I...maybe...yes, yes, Bex."

The garbled words scented in apple were like a sultry kiss, exactly what he wanted. He started the horses. "Good, I want to be married to you, too."

But Bex knew the matter wasn't settled. As the horses

regained speed, he looked over at her fanning herself with a sketchbook, perhaps a little breathless, like he was.

He wanted Ester, the right way, to be given to him in marriage. His past, like the miles ahead, was just an obstacle to overcome. He had to prove himself to her today, to wed her today, or lose her forever.

CHAPTER TWELVE

Almost There

Ester sat in the phaeton as Bex paid for the horses to be changed. She saw a couple traveling with a girl maybe a few years younger than she. The mother figure hugged the young woman, combing through the girl's ash-blonde hair, as they climbed into their carriage.

She wanted to turn back to her sketch, but Ester couldn't and watched them sitting behind the window of their carriage, laughing, enjoying each other's time. The picture sank her heart as she remembered Mama's soft laugh, her knitting on the couch. When had their laughter stopped? When was the last time Mama had done her hair?

Unable to help herself, Ester eased her charcoal from the dress she'd started, to glance at the back of the ebony barouche pulling away from the coaching inn's courtyard. A sob collected in her throat. Ester wanted her mother. She couldn't wait for this elopement to be done to see Mama again.

Bex climbed back onboard, and she caught his half-closed eyes. "Not much farther, my future wife."

The yawn in his voice could not be denied.

Her heart sank, hitting the bottom of her soul. She grasped his hand. "Bex, you are putting yourself at risk. An hour will change nothing. It'll barely get us to the blacksmith at Gretna or back to London any sooner. Let's stay at Carlisle, pull into a grove, and you can sleep for an hour. We'll still have plenty of light left to make Scotland."

He shook his shoulders as he took up the reins. "Carlisle is ten miles from Gretna Green. Ten miles. We are thirty minutes away. I'll sleep well in a room with my wife. Not in a stable or by the side of the road, but a proper room with my proper wife."

There was no reasoning with him. Though his determination to marry her touched the deepest parts of her, his bloodshot cobalt eyes ruined her peace, made her pulse race with fear. How could she stop someone so set on killing himself?

If she didn't voice her objections, did that make her a couch wife—or perhaps a phaeton wife, but without the knitting needles?

"I'm fine, Ester. Put away that frown. We're so close. We're pushing through. Now don't wear yourself to ribbons fretting. Why not finish the sketch you've been working upon. What is it, a dress?"

He swayed and peered over her. "My, with a trimmed low-cut bodice. What color should it be? Scarlet? I think you'll look so pretty in it."

Her pulse raced a little more as she absorbed his smile. Yes, she was a phaeton woman with charcoal instead of yarn. Resigned, she picked up her charcoal and positioned it within her fingers. The ride jarred too much for her to work on the delicate lace of the dress, but the contours of the hem could be refined. "I couldn't wear something like this, not without adding lace up to the neck and maybe some sleeves—and in pink, not red. It would look too revealing on someone...of my height."

"It will show off that beautiful neck of yours and the delightful figure you try to hide. Maybe you should wear it for me, and me alone."

Was he trying to make her spark like a flame with such notions? "Please keep your eyes on the road, Bex, but thank you. This dress is for my friend Frederica Burghley. I make designs for her and Mrs. Fitzwilliam-Cecil."

"Pity. That scooped neckline would be quite fetching."

"No...I'm a bit..." She found her hands floating closer to her bosom before she forced them down.

Passing a yawn, he waggled a brow. "Buxom? Beautifully buxom."

She swallowed, but the unease lodged in her throat. "Yes."

"Ester. You seem embarrassed, but you're beautiful."

Cheeks burning, she covered up with her shawl, rolling the silk tight about her neck. "I have a pretty face, but I think I'm..."

"Well-endowed? A woman of substance? Possessing a round figure? You don't need to be embarrassed. I think the cut of the gown would accent your curves."

"You noticed."

"Oh, I noticed. I'm sleepy, not blind."

If I hit him with the sketch pad, will he wreck the phaeton?

"A man in the company of a woman sees many things—her modesty, her manners, her loveliness. I'll be very proud to have you on my arm and in them."

His voice sounded so strong and overpowering, but Bex's fine posture had become slumped, curving into a C-shape. More than once, before they'd stopped, she'd seen him blinking his eyes and shaking like he'd been caught napping.

If only they'd pull over again. He could nap, she'd draw and not have to fret about him. "I won't think less of you if we stopped for a rest."

Bex yawned loud and long. "Don't ask. I'm fine. Just a little tired, but we are almost there. So close."

His hand jerked as the ride became uneven. The high slope of this section of the path seemed hard for the horses and for stubborn Bex.

She tugged on his coat sleeve. "I think you should stop on the side of the road. You're very unsteady and the horses, they don't look so good, either."

"We're not at our best. Don't fret, my dearest Ester. I'll rest soon, with my wife at my side."

The phaeton swayed again as Bex looked over at her. He latched a finger on to hers. "We've a few more miles of travel. Once we are married, I'll sleep for days before we head back to London. I'll make it up to you. Will you trust me to make amends later?"

"Bex, you give good speeches about freedom, but I'm not free if you won't listen. My voice and concerns should matter to you."

Maybe it was her bluntness, but he swerved a little and the horses left the road. Their hooves kicked up choking dust.

"Sorry." He blinked a little then straightened his posture. "How do you and your friends make do? Every time I see Mrs. Fitzwilliam-Cecil, she is smiling."

"She's in love with her husband. They don't always agree, but they listen to each other."

"I mean, how do they make do? How do they navigate society?"

"My friend is very smart. She knows the best days to shop, when merchants will be more amenable to us. She makes arrangements or utilizes her footman or butler to accomplish tasks. We all make do."

"It's not right. Should never have to be this way. Men are equal. We bleed and die the same." His voice rose, roaring like thunder. "We both drown if we're bound in chains." His palm flew to his face like it perspired.

"Bex, what is wrong? Are you feeling more ill?"

"Do you think of marrying me as a loss?" He sounded more in control, his tone had lowered. "Are you losing things by being with me? Tell me, Ester."

The way his lips moved as he said her name felt like a kiss. As sweet as a marriage to Bex would be, Ester would lose some of her freedoms. She couldn't say that and bruise his ego, but she'd never lie, so she nodded. "A woman exchanges her father's house for her husband's. Seems, at best, a draw, unless she marries poorly. With my parents surely fuming, no dowry will be paid. Yes, marriage is a loss."

"I never thought of it like that. The female perspective seems depressing. Ester, you keep telling me to slow down, to wait. It seems that the closer we get to Gretna, the more out of favor the idea of us marrying is to you." He scooped up her palm and held on to it and the reins. "Do you still want to wed?"

"Bex, I'm scared. This feels wrong. I left my parents to fret because I was angry. I disappeared without a word. It must be awful for them. They don't know if I am alive. I've caused my mother so much pain by running away. Then I look at you, and I feel the pressure of your hand on mine, and everything is good again. I think there's a chance we could be happy. Maybe all these mixed-up feelings happen when you elope."

His lips became pensive, thinning to a line. "Ester, what if something was in my past. Something that could prevent us having a future, or a good future. Would you want to know?"

"What are you saying, Bex? "

His lips pressed to a line, and then he opened his mouth. "Ester—"

The phaeton veered sharply to the left.

Knock, bump.

Everything was out of control. Ester held to the seat, which jerked and threw her as if it would vault her into a tree.

"The horse. It looks lame. Hold on." Bex reached forward and started undoing some of the harness strapping.

The screech of branches hitting the sides smothered the noise of the hooves.

Pine and oak limbs swatted at them, and she ducked. The scent of kicked-up mud and fresh-cut pine branches filled the air.

Bex tugged on the reins, but the world kept moving. The gig hit a bump, and soon everything went high into the air.

"Got it. Go horses."

With one hand, Bex pushed at her back. "Jump, Ester."

The horses released but the gig kept going. The bumps rattled everything. Her sketchbook flew up and went over the side.

"Please, Ester, jump."

She looked at his face, heard the pleading in his voice, and did what he said. She leaped away from the phaeton. Rolling in dirt, kicking up moss, she finally stopped spinning.

But Bex.

His carriage flipped up in the air then flopped over. It rolled and rolled then righted itself with its roof smashed in.

"Bex!" She ran to wreckage. "Please be well. Please be well."

She climbed up next to him, pushed leaves and branches

from his still form. He was wedged into the floor beside the seating. His body wasn't crushed like the phaeton's roof, but he wasn't moving. Waving a finger under his nose, she felt a breath, a slow, hot one. He was unconscious, but alive.

There was a lump and bruising on his forehead, but she saw no bleeding, no open wounds. He needed a physician.

Blood pumping, ringing in her ears, Ester smoothed his dark brown hair. "I had doubts, but I'm sure you holding my hand will give me the courage to say those vows. You hear me. You have to live. You have to be all right."

The road was a good forty paces away. The lame horse was kneeling. She couldn't do anything with that one, but the other was munching grass. It could still pull, if she could hitch it to the phaeton. "You can depend on me, Bex. I'm depending on you to recover and make me an honest woman."

She kissed his forehead then climbed down.

Her sketchbook lay halfway between the gig and the horse. She scooped it up, thankful that Bex had made her jump. If she hadn't, she might be too injured to help. He saved her, and now she'd do the same for him.

Shaking, she approached the standing horse.

It neighed at her and stretched its mouth wide. Ester hoped that the noise and the teeth were its way to show consent.

"Horse, if you're spooked, then we have that in common." She grabbed the rein ring. "Come on boy...or girl...or horse." Trembling, she brushed at its gray mane. "We have to get Bex to safety. It's just you and me. We have to do it."

Leading the horse back to the cart, she felt better that it followed, but her heart ached, and her head, too. A hundred questions invaded at once. Could a single horse pull the smashed phaeton back up the hill? If they made it to the road, would they find help at the coaching inn?

Only one way to find out. Ester had to get Bex to the inn and then beg.

One sniffled breath filled her lungs with the sweaty-lather scent of horse. Gagging, she tossed her sketchbook onto the seat and she tugged the beast in place and threaded the rein hooks as best as she recalled, from observing Theodosia with her gig.

Ester should've paid better attention. So much she'd taken for granted.

With a prayer in her heart, she yanked on the horse's bridle.

The animal neighed.

She looked at the damaged phaeton. Bex still hadn't shifted or turned.

"Please, horse. He needs us."

Her eyes began to water, but the building tears turned to hope when the horse took a step. With a little more coaxing, the horse took another one, then trailed behind her.

Relief swept through her, but there was still much to do. The gig had to be freed from the bushes. "Come on, horse. Bex's counting on us."

The wheels screeched, and the noise clawed through her, but the carriage moved.

Forty agonizing steps with the horse neighing every inch of the way rattled a shaken Ester, but the phaeton finally pulled onto the road. A big sigh left her lips, her heart skipping a beat or two. "Bex, we made it this far. You're going to be saved. Please know I'm here. I haven't left you."

He still hadn't moved or said anything. She missed the sound of his voice, even if it was teasing her. "Bex, you said it was only a mile or two to the last inn before Scotland. I'll get you help there."

The wind picked up, and it cooled her brow. Stumbling over a rock, she kept her balance. Her slippers would be so worn, but maybe that would be a good thing. Not looking like Ester Croome, a runaway bride from a wealthy family, but a poor Blackamoor servant would get them more help. That was the role she'd play next.

She took her shawl from her shoulders and wrapped it like a turban about her head. "Ester Croome, the exotic servant to the great actor." The innkeeper would like this role. It was far more plausible than a bashful Blackamoor bride to the great actor Arthur Bex.

"Horse, when we get to the inn, I don't like falsehoods, but I'll have to play the part of Mr. Bex's maid. Then they'll help him." She looked back at her fiancé. Her throat clogged. He still hadn't moved.

"Bex, know you are worth this price. Don't be mad at my choices when you awaken."

After walking for an eternity, her tired bones rattled into life when she saw a big limestone building with a few carriages outside. It might not be the inn he talked of, but it would definitely be the place she'd go to ask for assistance.

Ester stiffened her spine and drew back her shoulders. She would suffer whatever indignities necessary to save Bex. He was worthy. He had to live long enough to know it.

CHAPTER THIRTEEN

An Inn and a Miss

Arthur opened one eye, then the other. Whitewashed walls greeted him, not endless stretches of dirt and gravel roads like the strange dream that repeated in his ringing skull. The haunting notion of losing something, something special and beautiful, churned inside.

The world seemed fuzzy, and he was lost. He fought to put an arm under his head, but it was wrapped in place. Was he chained, like the shadows that lurked in his head, the memories he'd never forget?

Pained from flexing his arm, he found it bandaged, not shackled in irons. Perspiration crossed his brow, but the screams of the lost—those stayed in his soul. Fighting to be free, he sat up with a grunt.

"Sir. You're awake." A boy of six or seven, the same age as Arthur when he had first boarded his uncle's ship, the *Zhonda*, sat at the end of the bed.

The little fellow jumped, causing his rumpled blond locks to flutter. "Let me go tell."

Tell? Arthur's pulse raced. "Who are you? And tell who?"

"I'm Timothy," the lad said. "My papa, the innkeeper, and my grandpapa Smythe. He doctored you. Your maid told me to tell her when you awaken, too. She promised me a farthing to let her know."

Maid?

That's when Bex knew he was still dreaming. His cut of the benefit nights at the theater were huge financial boons sometimes, but he was too frugal to hire a servant. He closed his eyes again. "Yes, tell the world, Bexeley is dreaming."

The boy came near and waved his tiny fingers over Arthur's face. "You seem to be awake to me, sir. Maybe you have the 'nesia. The maid said Bex, Arthur Bex."

Arthur touched the bump on his head. It was inflamed and tender at his crown. "'Nesia, you say? Amnesia?"

"Yes. The 'Nesia," the boy said. The little fellow's leaping up and down was too loud for a dream. "Think on it, sir. Who are ya?"

Arthur swiped at his mouth. "This is no dream."

"No, it isn't, sir."

But he wished it was a dream, for Arthur had said aloud his birth name. Oliver Arthur Bexeley was the name given to him by loving parents who had died of consumption when he was six. He smoothed his hand over his bandaged arm. "It's coming back to me now, lad. Yes. That name I said, that was a role I'd performed years ago when I was about your age. My name is Bex, Arthur Bex."

The boy grinned up big. "Good, sir. The girl said you were a famous actor. Don't want you sick no more, or with the 'Nesia. My mama read a novel where the hero had that. She says he shoulda went to Bedlam."

"No, I don't want to go there, right, Es—"

Ester? Was she well? Did she get hurt in the crash? He thrashed until he sat up. "Where is she? Did she get injured?"

The boy waved his hands. "Sir, calm down. You're going to

hurt yourself or get more of that 'nesia."

How could he? Ester could be hurt because he had pushed too hard. With his good hand, he grabbed the boy's shirt collar. "Tell me if Miss Croome is well? Where is she?" Head pounding, he settled back down and released the boy. "She can't be hurt because of me."

"Sir, calm down. Your maid is in the servant's quarters. She didn't seem no hurt."

It took a moment to understand what the boy said, for the blood rushed hard in Arthur's ears. He fell back, pained in his chest. Ester was not hurt, but they thought Ester, his Ester, was a servant. "See if she'll come to me. I must see her now."

"Papa has her doing duties. He says she's not very good at much, but she tries hard. I'm sure when she's done, she can come, but I'll tell her, her and Papa. Want that farthing."

The boy walked to the door and stopped. "She was nice to me. Read me some more of Mama's novel. She's not stupid like what Mama says about them. She's not dark as pitch, either." With a shrug, the forthright scamp was out the door.

Arthur should feel better that one young mind had started to be changed about the races, one who had a lifetime to influence others. But Ester was no maid. She didn't need to pretend to be one.

Oh, woman. She had donned another role, just to save Arthur's sorry hide. She should've let him rot before debasing herself. Arthur had to right this now. He sat up all the way this time, but the throbbing to his head made him sink back upon the mattress. Nausea swept over him, and he hoped whatever was in his gut remained there.

The door opened, and an old man entered the room, but behind his hunched shoulder was Ester.

Arthur's pulsed raced at the sight of her. She was not injured, no bandages or slings on her person, but she'd made a turban out of her shawl to cover her head. Did it hide a bandage or some other injury? Maybe she knew it would kill him to know he'd caused her to be hurt.

"Mr. Bex." Her eyes looked glossy and bright as he sought her gaze.

The tap of the old man's cane became louder as he crossed the floor. "Young fellow, my son who runs this place is busy. My grandboy, Timothy, said ye were awake."

"I am, but is Miss Croome well?"

"Fine, Mr. Bex," she said, "Brought you tea."

"That was quite an accident, young fella. Took the men in the stables quite a while to fix, a day and a half."

Arthur swallowed hard, but he couldn't take his eyes off of Ester as she made a slight turn to the window.

"It will be dark in a few hours, sir."

His stomach sickened. "We've been here a day and a half?"

"Yes, sir. Almost two days you've—ye been unconscious." She said. "I paid the grooms with your purse. Been managing your expenses as usual, sir. Mr. Smythe here has been helpful finding me things to do."

"Yes, your maid has been doing good, not lying about," the old man said.

Ester smiled. "To serve, that's me purpose."

The accent she'd tried to master was off, but perhaps passible for the untrained thespian. His heart sank. She felt she had to do this for him.

Feather turbans of silk were fashionable headdresses. He'd seen more than a few at the countess's parties, but none were like Ester's shawl surrounding her face, as if it were a sin to see her thick locks free or swirled in a braided chignon. To complete her guise, she wore a voluminous cotton apron that swallowed whole her delectable form. Maybe that part was best. With one arm not working right, he wasn't in the best position to defend her.

He glanced at her, straight posture illuminating the outline of a worthy bosom, the flare of hips that could not be denied. Yet, if anyone touched her, he'd die for her.

Ester came near the bed and set the tray in her hands down on the table. "Hot tea with lemon is what he likes. Very particular, very eccentric about his requests."

This time the masking of her smooth tones sounded better, a cockney variant. The lass wasn't a bad actress, but she shouldn't have to do this. "I'm glad, Miss Croome, that you were not injured. I should've slowed as you requested. I am very, very sorry."

Ester poured a cup of the steaming liquid. "They had no honey. I know that is how you like it, Mr. Bex."

The old man clicked his teeth. "You shoulda listened to this one. Her people know about slow." The man cackled as if he'd said a joke but there was nothing funny about his prejudice.

Smythe pushed on Arthur's bad arm by his shoulder. "Just making fun. The maid told us she weren't a slave, or nothing but in your employ. That you're one of those abolitionists."

Everything hurt when the man stretched Arthur's wrapped arm. "Ouch." He tried to hold in the grunt, but the pain was too great.

The old man tapped his shoulder again, sending a shock down to the bone. "Shouldn't be in such a rush. Life doesn't need this jumpin' about from here and there." He pattered back to the foot of the bed. "This time it's a dislocated shoulder and bang to the skull. The next time it could be worse. And I heard how dangerous those rallies for abolition or the right to vote can be."

"It's not that dangerous." Arthur cleared his throat. "Not that dangerous at all."

"Remember Peterloo last year. Lots of good people died. You need to be very careful, young man."

Ester's eye grew wide. "Yes, rallies are dangerous, aren't they?"

He had only known Ester for a few days, but that creased brow, the softening of her voice, that was fret and fear, two things he didn't want her to feel. Rubbing at the scruff of his chin, he tried to capture her gaze. "I wasn't thinking. I won't do anything so rash again. We were in a hurry and that exceeded my caution."

"Where are you heading?" The old man looked at him then toward her and back. "Your maid wouldn't say."

"Yes, sir. I said you were debating where to go next."

Arthur had a feeling she wasn't acting anymore. Her doubts about going to Gretna had probably tripled with his recklessness, but he wouldn't expose her to these strangers. She needed to know he supported her as much as he wanted her to support him. He raised his wrapped arm, and it hurt a little less. "I'm having problems recalling. The boy said it might be the 'nesia. The ports of Liverpool are not out of reach."

The old man eyed him very curiously. "We're from Liverpool. A little out of your way from here. You could've chosen a more direct route than crossing the River Sark." He grunted and tapped his chin. "You from those parts? You do look a little familiar now."

Arthur's heart started to pound. He forgot how well known his uncle had been in Liverpool, and how many people used to say Arthur was the very image of his uncle.

Scratching his bald head and wiggling his thin glasses, Smyth asked, "So, you going to visit relatives back there?"

The man surely wanted answers, perhaps a name or connection he'd know, but Arthur wasn't giving away anything. He only wanted to be alone with Ester and exchange their thoughts in privacy. "May I have some tea? My throat is dry."

Smiling with her perfect pouty lips, surely masking her concern, Ester lifted the cup to his mouth. The sweet smell of the calming chamomile tea, the soft lilac smell of her skin, tickled his nose. He could drink them both up.

After a good gulp, he lay back. "Two days will cost me. The delay will hurt my return to London or Liverpool. Miss Croome, could you take dictation in your book?"

The old man clicked his tongue again. "In a hurry again? Perhaps your maid can convince you to stay at least another night resting. You might be able to get some sense in him. That shoulder's not broken, but it was a bad hit to the head."

"Yes, sir. I'll try." She took her sketchbook from the tray. "That correspondence, Mr. Bex. I should write as you dictate."

"She writes, too? Well, you said Mr. Bex was eccentric in his choices of help. London actors." The man shook his head as he went to the door. "I'll leave you two to write. I'll tell my son that you're now awake. Maybe send for the boy when your maid is done. We should watch you and make sure that 'nesia doesn't get worse."

After a few more taps of his cane, the door shut. Arthur let out a sigh of relief.

Ester clapped her hands before folding her arms about her sketchbook. "Is this what it feels like to take on a role at the theater?"

"You've done quite well with acting since we've begun this trip. The temptress in the woods and now a nursemaid." He sat up with a grunt and took the sketch pad with his good hand and set it down, clearing the one physical block to holding her. "You could've just said the truth. You are the one who advocates truth and fidelity."

Her pacing began again. "Between us, between husband and wife. Acting is merely acting, becoming a persona on the stage. My stage just happens to be small, and it opens when I'm panicked." She put a hand to her hip. "What sounds more plausible, Bex? A famous actor is eloping with a Blackamoor bride, a famous actor was attacked by a treacherous Blackamoor, or a famous eccentric actor is traveling the countryside with his exotic maid?"

"None of them sound ordinary. You're not ordinary. Far from it, Ester."

She sat on the edge of the mattress then sprang back up. "You've been unconscious for almost two days because of this accident. I was so scared. I couldn't take the chance that they wouldn't help you because you chose to consort with me, and I'm not going to rot in some jail because you weren't able to defend me. I chose the easy path, and I acted a part I know others would accept. We are so far from London, I didn't trust that things would be different. I wasn't taking a chance—with your life or my own."

He reached for her, but she was six or more inches beyond his fingertips. "I'm sorry. I know you're trying to help, but this is wrong. You're a lovely young woman who saved her fiancé's life—again."

Sweeping to the window, she batted the muslin curtains between her palms. She started to weep. "Bex, I was lucky that the phaeton had landed back on its wheels. I was able to get the one good horse to pull it and lead you up to this inn. I would have said anything to make sure you got well."

When she came near, he grabbed her arm. Sitting further up, he gritted through the pain and drew her near. "I put you through something awful." He pulled her against his nightshirt, held her sobbing form against him. "You are resourceful, but I never should've caused so much distress. Now, help me get dressed. We need to get out of here and go get married. Two days is enough time to be caught."

"Maybe we should be caught. Maybe we should end this. I was scared out of my wits. I almost lost you, Bex—all because I had to elope right away. We didn't plan this. We didn't think through each step. This is my fault."

"No, woman. The fault is mine alone. I wanted to prove myself to you, and instead, I caused you more grief."

She pushed to be released, but he wouldn't let her go, not yet.

"I must be bad luck, Bex. Since we've met you've been in a fight, a robbery, and now, an accident. What is next? Attacked at a rally? Will I have to stand by and see you wounded at another Peterloo?"

"*Shhh.* Don't speak of such." He cradled her until she stilled.

Her face found that spot between his shoulder and neck. Her heavy breaths sent tingles into his skin. "This is just a rough start, Ester. It can only get better, and maybe we'll be able to change minds. Then folks like these people will know it is more plausible for you to be my love than my servant. I won't push tonight, but in the morning, we'll walk to Gretna Green. We'll take our vows before the blacksmith."

"You still want to marry me? You are crazy, Bex."

Maybe he was. He lifted her chin and captured her beautiful topaz eyes. "Hopefully, you are, too, and you will agree. Ester Croome, let's marry, if you'll still have me."

Her fingers rose to his cheek, and she stroked the scruff that had to be three days of growth. "I'll ask the boy to come help you shave. Must be clean shaven when we leave here tomorrow."

"Yes, for our wedding, Ester?"

She stood, but words of agreement did not leave her mouth, though she did use those lips to kiss his forehead. "I'll send the boy."

"Ester."

She picked up her sketchbook. "Hearing you say my name too many times might make me rash."

"Ester, you are too levelheaded to be rash. Ester, dearest Ester."

She waggled a finger at him as she moved to the door. "If we leave here tomorrow, Mr. Bex, you can still make it to your play on time."

He'd forgotten about that. Yes, there was still time, if they rushed, but that was the last thing he wanted. "I'm not rushing anywhere with you. The play will wait. If I lose this role another will come. Why don't you come back and sit next to me?"

"No. If I stay too long, they'll think I am a different type of servant."

He tried again to get up, for he knew in his gut she'd decided against him. "Ester, where are you off to?"

She put her hand to her stomach as she looked at him. "The servant's quarters. It's clean there. I can sketch and nap in a bedroll, and it has to be my turn in the bathtub. I want a bath so badly."

"Don't stay away too long. Come back so we can walk to the Gretna's blacksmith tonight."

Those eyes of hers went big again. "Oh, your coat and shirt are on the chair. I washed them clean of stains, No blood this time. This time."

Before he could reply, she had ducked through the door.

The girl was scared, perhaps too doubtful of him to marry. Ester was wonderful, supportive, resilient—exactly the kind of woman he wanted. How could he convince her to go through with the marriage?

Knowing his past, knowing he'd still have to take risks to fight for abolition, maybe she was right to be skeptical.

He lay back down and covered his eyes. She'd lost faith in him. After all this trouble, he'd allow her to beg off. That was the sensible thing to do.

But Arthur had not been sensible since he'd agreed to elope with Miss Ester Croome at the White Horse Cellar Inn. Nothing he felt right now was sensible.

Everything inside said to fight for their union, but he'd do what was best for her. The notion of putting her on a coach back to London ripped his heart in two.

· · ·

Ester waited for the footman to give her the fresh water for the kitchen. She took an easier breath now that she was out of Bex's room. Joy had filled her soul that he'd awakened and was in his right mind and didn't have the amnesia the boy said.

But danger was still awaiting them. Her father could catch them now, five days gone, if he hadn't given up looking. And if she and Bex wed, a Peterloo attack spurred by his rallies was a true and present danger. Eloping was the stupidest thing she'd ever done. This harrowing trip had been foolhardy. Tears threatened as the servant gave her the bucket. Ester didn't know whether to curtsy or run. She offered a mumbled, "Thank you," and took the water.

She shook herself as she headed for the stairs. No more fretting, no more pacing between chores, no more wondering how she'd care for an ailing Bex. He was awake, and she was about to have a bath.

The water steamed. The heavy bucket sloshed each step, so she slowed and took it tread by tread. None of the precious water for her bath could spill; she'd not get more, and this was the first moment the innkeeper had allowed her access to the bathing chamber.

Finally, at the door to the room housing the copper tub she set her bucket down and wiped her eyes. Her hands were rough on her face. Bex had clasped her palm. Could he not tell her fingers were raw? Of course he couldn't. He hadn't seen the list of tasks the innkeeper had given her, the awful things she'd scrubbed, just to stay in a horrid cold room on the floor.

No dawdling, Ester. She chided herself. She needed to bathe before someone of perceived higher rank arrived and took her turn.

A warm bath, soaking in heavenly water with the lilac soap in her pocket would make the world good again. Then she'd remember the greatest actor in London was alive and still wanted to marry her.

She popped open the door with her elbow and powered inside. Ester set the bucket down and locked the door behind her. Then she tore off her apron and started to undo the front of her gown in anticipation.

Then she turned, intending to stare at the copper tub as if it were an old lost friend.

But it wasn't.

It was strange and awful, and it felt like a horse had kicked her in her middle.

Strands of red hair curled over the hammered wall of the tub.

She grasped her stomach. *That could be wiped away.*

Of course, the tub wasn't ready for her as Mrs. Fitterwall would have had it at Nineteen Fournier. She came closer, ready to use her apron to give the tub a cleaning, and stopped.

Scum floated at the surface.

Heavy stains ringed the walls.

And more strands of other colored hair bobbed in the murky water.

Nausea flooded her throat as Ester's heart crumbled, shattering to bits.

The tears started.

From her eyes, past her nose—plop, plop into the tub.

Every salty drop she'd hidden in her bosom was wrung out of her soul. How could she dip in the dirt of every person who'd bathed today, every person of higher class than a Blackamoor maid?

She couldn't.

The hot water she'd lugged from downstairs would have to be used to clean the tub, not for a bath.

Ester sobbed harder.

She cried for Bex and the injuries this elopement had caused him.

She cried for Mama and Papa, who must think her dead or debased, five days gone.

She cried for herself, her stinging pink fingers, and for not valuing what she had. Why was it so easy to discount her family's love, their care, as pride?

At Nineteen Fournier she was second. The tub and room had always been pristine when she stepped inside, and she could always ask Mrs. Fitterwall for fresh hot water.

And the housekeeper never seemed to mind, for at Nineteen Fournier, Ester was worthy.

Ester was worthy, a daughter sheltered by love.

She'd forgotten how special her life had been and how valuable the freedom she'd possessed truly was. Could her parents ever forgive her?

She needed to be back home, not here. The prodigal daughter needed to beg for entry at Nineteen Fournier. If only they would take her in, shamed and all.

And if Mama could forgive her, forgive every traitorous

thought Ester had ever held inside, then maybe Ester could forgive herself.

A knock on the door made her startle. "Yes."

"Papa said there's a guest who needs to use the tub. He says it needs to be cleaned."

Done with everything—the pretenses, her own stubbornness— Ester dried her eyes and stood up. She was Josiah Croome's daughter. She had been birthed from a line of strong women, as her mother had claimed.

And it was time to go home.

She took her shawl down, exposed her curls, pinned up her dress, then opened the door.

Timothy was there with his ruddy eager face.

"Young man." She reached in the pocket of her gown. "Here is a farthing to clean the tub. Then tell your papa Bex's maid has quit and is going home."

The boy's gaze rose to hers then lowered to her shiny coin. "Yes, Bex's maid. No problem."

"Thank you." She moved to the door. "When you are done, have your father rent me a coach back to London. I have enough money to be its only passenger."

"Yes, ma'am." The boy jumped inside, picked up a rag, and started cleaning the swill.

As fast as she could, Ester ran to the attic room and collected her bag. She didn't speak to the other women up there. She couldn't. They didn't have parents to run home to and be saved from this life. Knowing this was right, she yanked out her carriage dress, the one she'd cleaned and pressed after taking care of Bex's coat. This dress would suit travel better than the thin one she'd worn to be a maid. That one, and all these memories, would need to be burned.

Once changed, she pushed her sketchbook and her simple gown into her bag and clasped the handle. Lifting her chin, she left the servant quarters and headed to Bex. She'd release him from their engagement and say her goodbyes. It was only right.

Her steps slowed, and Ester let her mind dream once more of loving Bex and him loving her. Then she let that notion drown in that tub of murky water. Heart aching, she kept her slippers moving all the way to his door. She cared for Bex the man deeply, but this life of being last wasn't for her. She knew that now. She deserved more, and she wanted more.

Before her strength abandoned her, she knocked on his door. Another quick pound led to a husky, "Enter."

Bex sat on the edge of the bed. He'd exchanged his night shirt for breeches and his shirt with a collar. The one bad arm was tucked inside, but not in the sleeve. The bulk of the bandage could be seen through the white material. "Ester, I am glad you have come back. I was coming to look for you."

She put down her bag, but picked it back up, holding it like a shield against her heart. "I have something to say to you." Her words were rushed, but she had to tell him this elopement was over before his voice or the way he smiled at her made her go silent.

"Me, too," he said, "but you first."

She thought about sitting across from him in the chair the boy had used to keep watch over him as they directed her away, but that would only remind her of the fear she had of Bex dying, of how much him living meant to her. Sucking in a breath, concentrating her strength, she put the bag down again. "I'm taking the next coach back to London. I'll tell my parents that I started to elope and changed my mind."

"I see."

Folding her arms across her bosom, she felt her pulse beat faster as his frown ripped into her chest. "I think our worlds are too far apart, Bex. You don't want me to pretend I'm a servant to be accepted where we go. And I can't have you pushing yourself to exhaustion to prove a point. This won't work."

He crossed the room and stood near her. The mustard ointment on his forehead around the big purple bruise in his chestnut hair overpowered the laundered smell of his shirt, the shirt she'd washed with her two hands. "You are worth the extra mile, Ester. But it's not just you rethinking this. There are things about my past, about being a loner, that disqualify me from being a good husband to you."

Taking her hand in his, he held it against his chest. "My haste has left you unprotected. That's wrong, Ester. For all you've done for me, I have to be a person you can count upon to do the right thing. Letting you go is the right thing."

He spewed nonsense, probably just words to make her feel better. That was sweet, for he had to know this hurt, cut like glass, slicing up her silly dream of a happily-ever-after with him.

"Arthur Bex is a famous actor, probably the best in the theater. I spent what feels like a lifetime loving your stage presence. With this trip, as harrowing as it has been, I've come to know you. This feels like another lifetime. You are a wonderful man, but we aren't good together. I guess we are saying the same thing." She reached up, tugged his collar forward to kiss his cheek. "It was a fun adventure, Bex. I'll remember it always."

"Are you going back to the arranged marriage, the one set up by your parents? Is there more safety in marrying a philanderer of your own race than in marrying me?"

She didn't want Jordan. Hopefully, he didn't want *her* now. She looked to the floorboards, to his onyx boots flecked with sandy white dust. "That's not a fair question."

"Life isn't fair, Ester. It's hard, filled with difficult choices." He pulled her close. "Why does it feel as if we are stepping away from something that could be wonderful if both of us weren't so stubborn?"

"Because we are, but it is for the best." She loved the strength of his hold on her waist even with only one arm.

"Goodbye, Bex." A final stretch to kiss his jaw led to him leaning down. He intercepted her and took her mouth.

The kiss was slow and patient, lingering, teaching.

When she thought it done, his embrace tightened. His one arm sculpted her to his chest, angling her until it felt natural to cling to him.

Her toes tingled in her worn slippers as the kiss deepened, and it felt like one of his speeches, wrapping her heart in warmth like she'd never known, not even in a steaming bath in a sparkling clean copper tub.

Her hands collapsed about his neck as he backed her to the wall. "Yes, Ester," he said between breaths, before tasting and taking her lips again and again. "This will never work."

His hand ripped away the heavy scarf that separated them. His fingertips traced the scallop lace of her collar. He spun the big pearl of her necklace and dragged a thumb along her throat, tweaking the ticklish parts, racing her pulse faster than his speeding phaeton.

"Two handed you'd be mighty dangerous, Bex."

"*Shh*. I'm trying to remember why we won't work. Maybe another kiss will tell me."

With his one hand, he sandwiched her between the wall and his solid chest, tasting her lips, as if they were covered in honey. "How do we let this go? I think we reconsider. We must, Ester."

Her name sounded like a prayer.

But there was no folding of her hands, no room between them to allow it. And she was too busy holding on to a dream, kissing him with eyes shut tight to savor the last, luscious moment.

"Tell, me Ester, darling Ester, that you'll reconsider."

He didn't let her respond. His mouth was upon hers, speaking of things she didn't understand, things that tasted like sugar, and chamomile, and heaven.

She was crazed against the wall, feeling each deep breath he took with the rising of his chest. Her fingers danced in his dark brown hair, trying to cling to a dream that was bigger than her, bigger than everything but her fears.

"Oh, Ester. I can be everything that you want."

And Bex could be. He could be Romeo, Antony, a hundred others if she said yes.

"How can we both think to end this elopement with passion such as this? Ester, we can be so good together. Marry me."

Did she love him enough to fight for this union? She didn't know, not anymore. But no kiss, nothing but a full-throated direct address saying he loved her would salve her raw fingers.

But none would come. He didn't love her. And she'd finally

remembered she was worth everything her parents had sacrificed for.

"No. No, Bex."

He stopped, stared, then stilled his wandering fingers.

Reason and a slowing pulse had to prevail. "Bex, passion passes the time until the next problem. It doesn't fix anything. I have to say goodbye. That's the reasonable thing to do."

He nodded and eased her to the ground. "I don't want to be reasonable. Nothing about us is reasonable. I suppose I'll tell Jonesy that I lost my greatest role, the husband of a remarkable woman."

"Careful who you tell, Bex. I don't want to be in the gossip section of *The Morning Post*, Bex's Blackamoor Lover."

He took her hand. "I hate the papers. I'll never let them hurt you." He put his jacket half on, draping his injured shoulder. "Let me escort you downstairs and make sure you get on a coach back to London. Maybe in a week or two, we could start again. This time with your parents' approval."

She couldn't agree, only stare down at the weathered threshold. It hurt too much now, walking away from him. Seeing him again, even on stage, would keep this ache always in her heart.

Picking up her bag, Bex opened the door but then marched backward. A gun barrel was in his face, and an angry Josiah Croome, her father, held the trigger.

CHAPTER FOURTEEN

Vows of Duress

Staring at the gun barrel and the shaking onyx hand pointing it to his chest, Arthur stepped backward into his room and drew Ester behind him. "I think you have the wrong room. Don't hurt her."

The large, angry man pushed deeper into the room, kicking the door closed. "You stole my daughter, and you're worried about *me* hurting her? Do you know what side of the gun you're on and where my sight is pointed?"

"Papa, please. Put the gun away."

"Mr. Croome?" Arthur had dealt with a few jealous husbands of women who'd claimed to have fallen in love with his stage performance, but never did he think the men's anger would lead to his death, not until now. "Your daughter is unharmed."

The man put the gun barrel atop Arthur's nose. "Take your filthy hands from my Ester."

He dropped her bag but stayed in front of her. "Mr. Croome, your daughter is safe. Please lower your weapon."

"Safe! You take my daughter to a remote coaching inn, share a room with her. Defile her. How is that safe?"

Ester came from behind, leaning against Arthur's hurt arm. "I stayed in the servants' quarters. Bex has done nothing to me."

"What? My daughter was good enough to steal from her home but not good enough to stay in a room?" Mr. Croome cocked the pistol.

"Papa, you're not listening. The servants' quarters were my idea. Bex didn't want me there, either."

Croome's jaw trembled, as did his finger on the trigger.

Arthur swallowed hard. "You're not helping, Ester. The man just needs to know you have not been injured or taken advantage of."

Mr. Croome gritted his teeth. "Don't tell my daughter what to do. I'll do that. You defiled my girl, took her without permission from my house. A man would have had enough respect to come and *ask* to marry her."

Ester left Arthur and grabbed hold of her father's muscled arm. The bulging strength of it was barely hidden beneath the gray-weave greatcoat. She forced him to lower his hand. "Papa, I left on my own. I chose to jump out that window."

"A window? Not even dignified enough to leave through the front door." He raised the gun again. "You stole her from my house and defiled her."

"Sir, nothing has happened. I've not dishonored your daughter."

"Bex, I can speak for myself." She tugged on her father's coat again. "Papa, nothing has happened. Put down your weapon."

"Bex?" The man's hand dropped to his side. "The actor? Arthur Bex, the actor you always talk about? You were serious about being in love with him?"

Ester had tears in her eyes. "Yes, I talked foolishness, Papa, about Arthur Bex, but nothing happened. Bex has been a gentleman to me."

"Nothing?" Croome shook his head. "Ester Croome, you disappear from my house during your mother's party. You have me thinking you've been kidnapped or lost to the violence of the streets. There's a brothel with Blackamoor women that caters to the lords. I don't want that for you."

Knowing the things that they'd faced on their travels, he couldn't fault the man's fears. Arthur tried to make his bad arm work a little to pull his coat back on, but it was bound too tightly. "Your daughter's safe. I'd let nothing happen to her. I was escorting her to make arrangements to send her home on a coach. No one will know that this elopement occurred or that it never came off. You have my word."

Ester came back to Arthur and swiped up his good hand in hers. "He's telling the truth. I wanted to elope, and we are only a few miles from Gretna Green, but we've called it off.

Croome's finger eased, but he could easily still lift and fire. "I don't know whose word to believe—you, who ran away, or your Bex, who changes his mind after all the trouble of escaping with you from my house. What happened, Bex? Did you come to your senses and realize she wasn't wife material for the likes of you?"

Oh, Ester was wife material, more than he'd hoped for. "*She* changed her mind, Croome. She decided to end things, perhaps with the hope of starting a new courtship—with your consent."

The man frowned and put his gun into his coat, but Arthur dared not move. He might change his mind again.

"Ester, why would you do this to me and your mother? Why did you believe this actor's words and risk all to leave with him?"

"Papa, the elopement was my idea. I chose to come with Bex. I wanted to elope because I wanted to choose my husband. I chose Arthur Bex, and you and Mama didn't."

Croome patted at his pocket—his gun pocket. "Bex, you let a slip of a girl drive you to this? How long has this romance been going on?"

Arthur had a feeling that Mr. Croome didn't know about the advertisement in the paper. He'd at least protect her from that. "Long enough for me to ask her to marry me."

"That's not an answer, Bex. Ester, how long? Tell me how long you've been running around behind my back."

Ester slipped in front of Bex and now was a wedge between them. "I've been infatuated with Bex for at least two years. You know how I've talked about him. So longer than a day, but less than the timing of your indiscretion."

Croome swiped at his brow then clasped a big hand about Ester's arm. "We'll discuss this later. Forget about her, Bex, about all of this. Girl, you'll be lucky if Jordan takes you at all. We've already started installing gaslights in the warehouse. Our businesses are already in bed together. Maybe his son will still want you, and you will be back with your own."

Shaking her head, Ester pulled free and stepped next to Arthur. "I'm not getting in bed with anyone but him."

Arthur waved his arm in protest. "Figure of speech, sir. Nothing happened. Don't shoot."

"Papa, you don't need me to do deals with Jordan. You have already done them." Ester looked up at Arthur, and she had that look in her eye, the one where she made up parts to play. She slammed into him and tossed her arms about him. "If I marry, it will be to Arthur Bex. The man I've loved for more than two years. Every one of his performances, whether at the Theatre Royal or Covent Gardens, they've been coded messages to me. Every word he's said on stage, it was for me. Like Antony for Cleopatra, he's made war for me. I have his heart, for he has mine." She planted a kiss on Arthur's lips.

Her words—he didn't have time to examine them for truth. Arthur knew he was a goner now, so he embraced her boldly, a daughter in front of a father with a gun. But if he was to die, why not let it be in the arms of this African queen? He didn't hold back on this performance. He kissed Ester with everything in him. It was the perfect way to die, with Arthur as Antony in his Cleopatra's embrace.

• • •

Her father groaned. She smelled the scent of black powder but didn't care. Papa would never take the shot with her arms wrapped about Bex. And this kiss was different. It didn't feel like goodbye, but something amorous and thrilling. It had to be the threat of the gunpowder.

"Stop it, Ester. Unhand him. You've made your point."

Clinging to his neck, she held Bex more tightly, and he wound his good arm about her. "Only if you promise not to kill him. As you see, I'm a very willing participant."

Bex's heart raced against her cheek.

He lifted his head. "Sir, nothing happened between us, but I can't deny the attraction. I want no harm to come to her. I'll do what you think is right."

If her father was still determined to give her away, then it would be to Bex and only Bex.

"No, Bex. Don't step aside." She took Arthur's hand in hers as she claimed his gaze. "I'm not ready to marry yet, but if I were, it would only be to you, Arthur Bex. That is my vow to you."

Bex's gaze softened. His hand tightened about hers.

The door swung opened and then slammed shut.

She turned, expecting her father to have left, but a new pair of eyes stared at her.

Her mother's.

The stoic woman stood just inside with her back to the door. A scarlet cape shrouded her, and a thick, dark ebony bonnet covered her straight black locks. "Get your hands off of her. You can't know her love. It's not possible for the likes of you."

Mama had an off look about her. Her fury seemed deeper than Ester had ever seen, as if she were unbalanced. "His hand. Get his hands off her." She came over and beat on Bex, punching his hurt arm with her reticule. "Get 'em off her."

Papa came to her side and pulled her back. "Horatio. Stop it. They say nothing happened."

"He can't touch her. Can't put his hands on her. He can't hurt her."

Papa tightened his hold, almost yanking Mama off her feet. "Don't go off, woman. This is Ester and that actor, Arthur Bex. Nothing from Jamaica, girl. No slave master going after his enslaved woman."

But Mama wouldn't stop. She kept swinging at the air. "Don't touch her. You've no right. It's started again. He's got no right."

Her father put both arms about her mother, lifting her in the air. "Horatio, come back. This isn't the past. This man Bex ain't from where you're from. Ester says she loves this man and won't marry Jordan. That's why she ran away. Come back to yourself. Reason with her and him to keep this quiet, and for her to do her duty."

Blinking, Mama's stricken face cleared. "No, Josiah. Charles Jordan won't have her now. He'll be mean to her once he learns of the scandal. No, this one, the man from London, is the one she wants. This is the one she'll have."

Ester focused upon her mother's blank face. If one could age a hundred years in a day, her beautiful mother looked as if she had. Her cheeks had sunken in, probably from grief and that heart of hers that Ester had broken again.

Longing to make things good with her mother swelled inside. "Mama? I'm so sorry." She released Bex like he was fire. "I have given you such concerns." She tried to smooth her wrinkled dress. "But nothing has happened."

"Horatio," Papa said, "Bex said he didn't defile her. They both say nothing has happened. We can still go on with our plans. We can buy his silence."

With her hand to her hip, Mama stared at each of them, her head snapping back and forth between them like the clicking minute hand of a grandfather clock. Her forest-green eyes were black ice. "Silence, Josiah. You threatened the duke's daughter to learn of Ester's plans. You think one of the duke's maids didn't hear? You don't think Clancy won't accidentally say the wrong thing? What about one of those fancy servants who saw your angry tirade when we discovered Ester missing? No, this story will be out, and she'll be ruined like Ruth, but at least she won't be pregnant and deserted like her sister."

If eyes could explode—splat on the wall from shock—Ester's might. Hers stretched so wide they hurt. "No one ever said Ruth eloped and that it didn't work. She has an arranged marriage, doesn't she?"

Papa lifted his gun again and aimed toward Bex. "I don't want my daughter to marry an actor. Actors are the lowest class."

Seeing Bex endangered again, Ester linked arms with him,

and he whimpered for she'd chosen his injured one. "Sorry," she said to him before turning back to her father. "He's not any actor. He's the best. Mama knows. She's read about him in her papers."

Mama clasped her father's arm and made him lower the gun. "The scandal papers." She shook her head. "She's chosen him, Josiah."

Papa stomped his feet. His big arms looked as if they'd break through his great coat. "I'll not—"

"Yes, you will Josiah. You owe me. I told you that you'd honor one request from me if I forgave you for your sins. This is my one request. Let them elope. Let us take them to Gretna Green and see that it is done. She won't be jilted and used up like Ruth."

"Mama, tell me about Ruth."

Her mother's hand waved, the jeweled rings flashing as if she'd thrown fire. "Silence, Ester. You have brought shame to the family. I don't want to hear anything from you."

"We've too many secrets, Mama. Just tell me."

Her mother looked up at her father. When he nodded, Mama said, "Your sister Ruth had no wedding. The blackguard bedded her and tossed her aside. Your father made up the story of a strict husband that forces her to live in the country to explain her baby."

"That is why she's banished, because she's disgraced?"

"Yes. Because she didn't value what we have, what your father and I have worked for, just like you."

Ester turned to Bex. "They said my sister eloped. They lied again."

Bex wiped at his mouth. "They had their reasons." Even his voice had lost its confident swagger. Papa's happy trigger finger would do that.

Pounding her skull, Ester couldn't take it. "Is anything true?"

"Your sister eloped, too, but the man used her, then dumped her like trash. Papa had to rescue Ruth from a brothel, where her beau had left her. Your sister didn't trust that we knew best. Ruth learned the hard way that she did not know best, either."

Ester reeled. Another lie had been spun about the Croomes, and Ester had been shielded from the truth. "Why didn't you tell—"

"Hush, daughter. I'm waiting for your father to answer. Josiah, this is my request. You promised me."

Papa raked a hand through his thick jet-black hair. "Can't I just kill him?"

Bex retook Ester's hand. His palm felt warm against her freezing fingers. Shock must do that, too. "I'd rather you not shoot. I want to marry your daughter if you will allow me. If Ester—Miss Croome will have me."

"Josiah, if you hurt that actor, the magistrate you think you're cozy with will string you up faster than you can blink. Then those same sympathetic people you do business with will try to use the courts to take away your legacy. Or worse, they'll come for me. A widow with half your money is still a prize."

"You win," he said under his breath and put his gun in Mother's hands. "You always had a way with reasoning."

"No one could ever call you stupid, Josiah. Go down to the carriage and wait while I speak with the lovebirds."

Papa looked cornered, with his neck swiveling between Mama and Bex. He didn't look at Ester.

"Don't take too long, Horatio." With his head lowered, Papa thumped from the room.

Ester moved to her and put her arms about her mother's stiff form. "Mama, I've never seen you stand up to him."

"You've never had to. Your father and I know our responsibilities. Your father's not perfect, but he is a good man."

"No, he isn't. Those letters of his affair."

Her mother frowned and stared in Bex's direction.

His blank expression gave nothing away, but he was part of this now. He didn't need to leave.

Stepping away from Ester, Mama pulled off her reddish-brown gloves and stuffed them into her satin reticule. "That is my business, Ester. Mine. Not yours. We worked through that long ago. I don't know why he kept the letters."

"You knew? But you looked so hurt when you read the letters."

"Your papa told me when he ended the affair. He told me and promised me to never let anything break us again. Those letters brought back that hurt, but that debt had been forgiven."

"I don't ever remember you even getting mad at him. You knew of his failings. Why didn't you stand up for yourself?"

Mama grabbed Ester's hands and led her to the mirror. "I had you and Ruth and an evil family on a sugar plantation an ocean or two away. Could I leave to go back to Jamaica—with two girls—so your cousins or uncles or even your grandfather could have at you as an enslaved mistress? 'Cause I was born enslaved. Those that look like Mr. Bex in Jamaica can claim you as their property and use you up for nothing but evil. That's why this very actor fights for abolition. You remember the articles on Mr. Bex's cause in the papers."

Ester knew Bex's stories, but her mother had never said much about her upbringing in Jamaica. When Ester had asked, it had made Mama's face fill with pain. "Mama...I..."

Her mother picked up Ester's bag and set it on the bed. "I forgave a man who was repentant, and we rebuilt the trust we had when we married. Yes, I was mad, but your father is a good man. He's a big man, with beautiful black hands, and we've created two beautiful, ungrateful girls."

Bex went to the door. "I could step outside."

"You leave this room, Mr. Bex, and Josiah may find his other gun from the carriage and shoot you. There are a lot of woods outside this inn, the kind you could be shot in and buried with no questions. That happens to our people all the time, so it's best you stay here, where I can see you. That is, if you want to live."

Ester winced and reached for Bex before she lowered her hands. "Stay, Bex. Mama's right about my father's temper." She turned back to her mother. "Why didn't you say something about this, or even about Ruth? I am old enough to understand."

Mama gripped her shoulders and shook her. "Because it was my business, Ester. Mine. It was private until you got a hold of those old letters. And Ruth didn't want anyone to know about her failings. Her little baby has no name, just a fake one. It is hard enough to be Blackamoor, but illegitimate, too? It's too much."

Wanting the world to stop moving, Ester stepped into Bex's shadow. If only she could fall into his arms and have him hold her to stop the shaking. "You could've explained instead of offering lies. I would've listened, Mama."

"You don't listen, Ester. You're like your father in that way. You judged me weak. You don't know what type of strength it takes to hold a marriage together, to be the bigger person and forgive. The way you two are starting off, learning to forgive will be a necessity." Mama rifled through Ester's bag until she whipped out the party gown. "Put this on. It's the one you will marry him in. Mr. Bex. What is your full name?"

"Bex…Arthur Bex," he said, "But your daughter has changed her mind. I was getting ready to put her on a coach to send her home."

Mama came near and swatted her on the bottom. "You haven't come this far to change your mind. If you or Ester have cold feet, stick them in the fireplace. This wedding is happening. I made your father agree. There's no going back on this. Now put this on."

Ester looked at Bex, and he caught and held her gaze. "Yes, Mrs. Croome. if your daughter will still have me."

"I already told you she accepted. Now turn around so she can put this dress on."

Bex nodded and turned to the door. "I could step outside."

Whipping through the buttons on Ester's carriage dress, Mama shook her head. "Step outside, Mr. Bex, and you could get shot. Just face the wall."

Ester clasped her hands. "Mama, he's…"

"You ran away with this man. In a few more minutes, he'll be legally able to see everything, if he hasn't already. Don't be modest now. You're a runaway bride. I'm getting a wedding out of one of you girls. I won't have you looking like an urchin."

Beet red across her bosom, face fevered, Ester stood in her chemise and corset as Mama dragged her carriage gown to her hips.

"These shoes are horrid, Ester. They'll show under your ball gown. But that can't be helped."

Bex had his good hand to his face as if to shield his eyes, but the shadows of the ribbon loops of her chemise were obvious on the wall.

She couldn't think about what was to come, marrying Bex, not with her dress at her knees. "Hurry. I can't stand here like this."

"Don't be shy now, Ester. You've been five days with this man." Mama pulled the party dress up the rest of the way, then slipped on the shimmering overdress, tightening the laces, fluffing the netting. "Your chignon is horrible."

She took Ester's locks and smoothed them with her palm. "There is no time to redo this. It will have to do."

Ester grabbed at her hand. "Please, Mama. Fix it."

She nodded and undid the chignon, then made a quick new braid and pinned it up again. "A little better, but not what I wanted. This isn't what I wanted for you at all."

Sighing as if she could barely contain her emotions, Mama placed the wrinkled shawl on Ester's arm. "It's not the beautiful beaded silk gown I had planned for you, but it will do. Now you are ready to wed. Come along, Mr. Bex. My husband and I will take you both to Gretna Green."

He scooped up Ester's hand. "Right behind you, ma'am."

She couldn't tell what he was thinking, but it was hard to have a cohesive thought with her mother now forcing her to marry Bex. "We don't have to do this, Mama. If you want me to say I made a mistake, I will."

"You'll not shame the family any more, Ester. I'm going to watch you marry the man you chose above the Croomes."

Ester had always wanted to see her mother get angry, but to be furious at Papa, not her. The determination she heard in the woman's voice was resolute, chilling.

"Run off now, Ester, if you can." Bex said in a whisper. "Your father won't shoot you, and your mother doesn't have a gun to your head."

But she did. The weight of ruining the Croome name was as good as a flintlock, and the look of disappointment on her mother's face was enough to break any resistance in Ester's spirit.

"Stop buzzing, you two." Mama held her head high as she pushed them out the door. "Remember, this is what you wanted."

They walked past Mr. Smythe and the grandson—both staring with mouths open. Mama tossed a guinea to them but never stopped.

"Mr. Bex, Miss Croome, you'll have time to say everything after we see the blacksmith at Gretna Green."

This marriage was about to happen. It wasn't going to be stopped. Not by Papa, not by Bex, or by Ester's doubts. Little Mama was the power. She drove things now, and Ester could only nod and agree.

They climbed into the carriage, the three of them joining her brooding father. The silence in the cabin made her pulse loud within her ears.

What a curious group they made. Ester beside her stoic mother, Bex with a coat half draping his bandaged arm, sitting next to her sulking father. Five miles of no talking, the rumbling of the big carriage's wheels, the pounding hooves of the two pairs of horses sounded loud, definite. The trip was five miles too short.

The carriage stopped. Bex didn't wait for the footman and jumped out. He stuck his hand back inside and helped Ester down. "So, we are going to do this." His tone teased her ear, but he moved her forward, not waiting for a reply.

Then she realized it wasn't a question. He was committed.

An older fellow stood at the anvil. "I assume..." He stared, and Ester wondered if he'd ever seen so many dark faces together in his establishment. "I assume ye want to be married. It's late. Come back tomorrow. I have a suite of rooms next door for the ceremonies—"

"It must be tonight," Mama said and put coins into his hand. "They must wed tonight."

"Very well. I'm Mr. Elliot, the blacksmith and the anvil priest who will marry the *happy couple*. I need the parties' names and places of abode."

"I am Arthur Bex. I stay in London."

"I am Ester Croome, I stay near Cheapside."

"Are you both single persons?"

"Yes," Ester said.

"Yes. I'm single." Bex took her hand in his and gave it a little squeeze.

"Did you come here, Miss Croome of your own free will?"

Sort of yes, and sort of no, but the anvil priest didn't need the particulars. "Yes."

The man leaned forward and stared in Bex's direction. "Did you come here, Mr. Bex, of your own free will?"

"Yes. I'm pleased to marry Miss Croome."

Mr. Elliot turned and started jotting in a book. "How do you spell Bex?"

"B-E-X". Her fiancé said it loud and bold, a perfect direct address, the climax of the tragedy in this play, only this was true. It was Ester's life.

"There that is done." The blacksmith said as he turned

around. "Do you, Arthur Bex, take this woman to be your lawful wedded wife, forsaking all others, kept to her as long as you both shall live?"

"I will."

"Do you, Ester Croome, take this man to be your lawful wedded husband, forsaking all others, kept to him as long as you both shall live?

She looked up at Bex, caught the sparkle in his cobalt eyes. "Yes."

"A ring, Miss Croome."

Bex swung a hand to his forehead "Can I buy one for her?"

Mama pulled off one of hers, the one with the jade stone, her favorite. "Use this, Ester."

Willing away tears, she handed it to the priest and just breathed in and out, the ash and sulfur of the hearth and the melting tools.

"Now give it to Mr. Bex." Mr. Elliot put the ring back into Ester's palm.

She did, her fingers vibrating every moment of the exchange.

"Now give me the ring." The blacksmith tugged his hands upon his stained apron and stretched for it.

Nodding, Bex gave it to him. The anvil priest held it up in the light of his hearth. The band reflected the fire. He pushed it to Bex. "Now put this on the fourth finger of her left hand and say these words: with this ring I thee wed, with my body I thee worship, with all my worldly goods I thee endow in the name of the Father, Son, and Holy Ghost, Amen."

Bex cleared his throat. He turned to look at Ester. "I..." He cleared his throat and took sole possession of her gaze. "I thee wed, with my body I thee worship, with all my worldly goods, I thee endow, in the name of the Father, Son, and Holy Ghost, Amen."

The blacksmith took her hand and put it on his bandaged shoulder. "You're supposed to link right hands but that seems impossible. Hope you put up a good fight before landing in the parson's trap, Mr. Bex." He winked and chortled.

Papa groaned.

Then Mr. Elliot turned to Ester. "Repeat after me, Miss Croome: what God joins together let no man put asunder."

These were the last lines. If she would rebel, this was the time. But with Papa looking as if he'd be sick, and Mama wiping her eyes, there was nothing else to do but play the part she'd begun. Pulse raging, she said, "What God joins together let no man put asunder."

"Good," the priest said. "Forasmuch as this man and this woman have consented to go together by the giving and receiving a ring, I, therefore, declare them to be man and wife before God and these witnesses in the name of the Father, Son, and Holy Ghost, Amen. Go in peace."

Ester's mother kissed her on the cheek. Her father just shook his head and left the shop.

She wanted to go after him, but she'd let her mother soften him. She now understood the woman's power. "Perhaps, Mama, we can come to dinner in a week or two. Then you can get to know Bex."

Her mother kissed her again on the forehead. "No, Ester. You chose to leave us for him. I've given you your wish. But you are cut off this day from the Croomes."

Ester's heart stopped at least thirty seconds before it started again with a jolt. "But you forgave father for worse. I want to come home."

"Your father is my business, as much as this man you chose is yours. You wanted his hands on you. Go to him like you left us, with the clothes you smuggled out. No dowry. You will live as he lives. You're not a Croome anymore, Mrs. Bex."

"Mama?"

The woman pushed away, head up, but she stopped at the blacksmith's door. "If you think this is your father's doing, then you don't know me. You punished him enough for his flaws, broke his heart every time you washed his nose in it. Now, you've done it again, and ripped up mine, too. Take care of her, Mr. Bex."

"I will, Mrs. Croome. I don't want a dowry. Don't let money come between you. She's your daughter."

"No. She's your wife. You're all she's ever talked about. Now she has you. Be good to her." The voice sounded strong but also winded, like it held back a forthcoming sob. The hurt in her mother's face was worse than the day Ester had found those letters. She reached for her hand.

But it was too late.

Mama had turned her back on her and left.

Ester wanted to run after her, but what could she say? All this time she'd thought Mama weak, and the woman had been the strongest Croome.

Bex gathered up the document from the priest and they had a low conversation, something about names, but all she could hear was the sound of the great carriage going away. Her parents had left. She was cut off from them.

With a wistful look in his cobalt blue eyes, her new husband took her hand. "We have a five mile walk back to the inn. The evening air will do us good. Come along, Mrs. Bex."

She walked beside him. Without the energy to act happy, she couldn't put a smile to her lips. All she wanted to do was cry.

CHAPTER FIFTEEN

The Long Walk Back

Keeping his stride small so his little wife could keep up, Arthur held her hand and walked away from the blacksmith at Gretna Green—a married man.

He'd wanted to marry Ester, wanted to stay with their original plans to elope, but had decided to let her go. He'd failed her with his reckless driving, his lack of planning, but now they had a new start. He'd make the disappointment cresting upon her lips go away.

He gave her hand a little squeeze. "Ester, Ester Bex, a farthing for your thoughts?"

She didn't look up but gazed down like she hunted for her slippers in the evening light. "That sum of money doesn't seem like enough." She folded her arms about her. "I don't think it wise for you to know. It may doom our path more than we already have."

Her gentle spirit was breaking, and that hit him squarely in the gut. He had to make it better for her and bring her back to that hopeful moment when she'd first leaped into his arms. He stopped, tugged her hand from the voluminous scarf that she tried to hide behind, and spun her. "You made a pretty bride, Mrs. Bex. This is the dress in which you floated down to me, a sun come to earth. Good to see it in the evening light."

Pushing away until he dropped her arm, she brought her hands to her face. "I gained you." Her voice was low and full of pain. "I'm happy of that, Bex. There's no one I'd rather marry. But I lost my parents today. I've learned more secrets and lies about the past than I ever wanted to know. I'm robbed of joy. I'm so sick over this."

A lump formed in his own throat. He had secrets, too, and telling her now would ruin her. He yanked at his drooping tailcoat. "Maybe it was best that you didn't know all the bad. Maybe they thought not knowing was a way to protect you."

She glanced at him with glassy, wet eyes. "They didn't think me strong enough, so they sheltered me with lies. The way I hurt my mother, maybe they were right. I'm horrible."

"You're not anything but courageous. We'll find a way to reconcile with your parents. I don't think it's a permanent break. Look, Ester." He pointed to her father's onyx carriage. It's evenly matched team sat out front of the coaching inn. "They waited for you. Perhaps they have already had a change of heart."

Her head rose, but then her pretty face became sadder with a bigger frown, then unreadable. "No, they just wanted to see if we made it this far. They're leaving."

He turned in time to watch the big carriage drive off. It was cruel to see them abandon her again. Thinking how to make this better for her, he came up with nothing. He swiped at his dry mouth and tried to sound the role of an encourager. "They surely waited to see if we made back to the inn safely, but they are still angered. It will pass. They still care, Ester. You can see that?"

"I see them leaving like I left them, but not through a window. They left in a comfortable fashion, hours before midnight."

He took her hand, the one with the shiny gold band, and kissed her fingers. "I was there to catch you, Ester. I'm here now."

She drew back and put her arms about her. "With a bad arm? I'll take my chances walking."

Arthur saw her swimming in regret. The concerns that made her decide to end the engagement were still there, unresolved. "Ester, you chose me. I'm not ignorant to think it was my charm alone. You agreed to spite your father."

She put a finger to her full lips as they entered the inn. "*Shhh*. Not now."

Old man Smythe, who'd doctored his shoulder, looked over his glasses and pushed a pile of coins at him. "Your *father-in-law* paid for your room and the keep of your horse, even the repairs. Interesting he'd do that for you. I never forget a face or the likeness of a captain. A Liverpool captain."

The man knew or suspected. Well, his uncle's trial had been big news for areas close to here. Picking up the money, Arthur braced and puffed out his chest. "I think it was a gift for his daughter."

The old man shook his head. "I think you should be inclined to leave tomorrow. We don't want no trouble."

Slinging his coat back over his hurt shoulder, Arthur nodded and absorbed the warning. "We need to head back to London as soon as possible."

He put Ester's arm on his and led her to his room.

He closed the door and leaned against it. "Well, it's done, Mrs. Bex."

"Yes." She stood with her back to him, inches from the bed. She sank onto it softly then sprang up as if it were hot coals. Pushing at her shawl, not catching his gaze, she looked miserable with a frown almost as wide as her thin face. "It is done."

She looked miserable. Time to make it better.

"*Tsk. Tsk.* I always thought the future Mrs. Bex would seem happy about our nuptials. That she'd be waiting for me with open arms, not a refuse bucket ready to vomit."

Ester looked at him then crumpled onto the bed, crying.

His attempt at humor had the opposite effect of what he wanted. A rose only needed so much water to bloom. Flinging his coat to the chair, he sat beside her. With his good hand, he stroked her back. "Time will make things right with your parents."

"Bex, how do you know this? Have you ever had to reconcile with your parents?"

"No, but then, I was orphaned at six."

Chin lifting, she curled toward him. "Then you don't know."

Her pretty eyes, large topaz-brown pools with flecks of henna and gold, had said so much on their journey, but now they read of pity and disbelief. He didn't want that from her. She, of all people, had to believe in him, in their union.

"Ester, I do know that sometimes there is no reconciliation. Sometimes the crimes are so great you have to part ways."

"Crimes? Bex, now you are being dramatic. We've done nothing heinous by marrying. And I suppose they've done nothing heinous by cutting me off."

This wasn't how he wanted to broach this subject of his past. She deserved to know, and there was no one he felt like telling, ever, except Ester. "They're very upset, but you and I, we are family now. It's us against the world."

"Us Bex? Us against the world?" She wiped at the tears staining her face. "Some wedding day."

Ester was miserable. He'd signed the marriage certificate

with the name he'd chosen and had made famous, not his birth name. If he couldn't make her happy, he'd tell her so she could annul the marriage for fraud. It was her only way out of this situation. But Arthur felt he could make her happy. He'd captivated her on stage, and he could captivate her now. "Today was not all bad. I met your parents. They allowed us to marry. Then there was that moment when you kissed me."

She tugged at her shawl, her fingers tensing on the folds. "I think it was you who kissed me."

"What? My bashful bride... You seem to not have a long memory. That might be good for us."

"Maybe that means you will never be bored with me."

He looped his fingers with hers, stilling her fidgeting. "Not likely. You're an enigma, changing from shy to bold, from scared to brave. Enigmas are hard to take hold of."

Her face had dried, and she looked as if her mood had lifted a little. "What do we do now?"

There were plenty things that came to his head, with Ester the incredible kisser sitting so near him on the very comfortable mattress. "Ester, I told you that I wanted a full marriage."

She wiped at her eyes. "Yes." Her voice sounded strained as she smoothed the hem of her skirt. "I suppose it is too late to get to know one another better."

"Bashful again." He kissed her fingers. "That skirt has been beaten of wrinkles. Don't be frightened around me. I can be a patient man."

"Bex. I... You said if I asked you anything, you wouldn't lie."

With a brow raised, he sobered his expression and nodded.

"Why did you marry me? Do you love me?"

He didn't know how to describe what he felt—part gratitude, part hope, part glad to be chosen—that she cared so much for him. He stood up, pulling her to her feet. "I care for you more than myself. Perhaps that is love. I know what it cost for you to go through with this wedding and to even jump through that window. Your reasons for saying yes matter less to me, only that you did say it."

She hooked her hand about his neck and draped her head against his bum shoulder. "What does matter to you, Bex?"

"You. You do, Ester."

She peered up with her mouth slightly open, maybe in want of him.

He put his hand in her hair and flung off the bonnet that covered her tight curls. Grabbing hold of a loose tendril, he drew her face to his. "Say yes again, Mrs. Bex."

"What are you asking, Bex?"

Part of him wanted everything, but she was far too wary. Like an audience on opening night, she needed to be cultivated, made aware of his presence, enraptured by his words until she asked for more. "Tonight, it is yes to a kiss. Let's congratulate ourselves on the opening act of this marriage."

Her eyes were wide and glossy with tears, but then she closed them and leaned in. "Yes."

Smiling inside, he dipped his head and removed the space between them. He had intended for the kiss to be small, chaste, but Ester was too delicious. Her curves against him felt so fine. She molded to him in all the right places. He loosed the shawl from her shoulders and exposed smooth, creamy skin that his fingers would explore if not for the high lace at her throat. That wouldn't do. "Let me undo the laces of your dress, so you can change for bed. We leave here early in the morn."

He spun her and loosed the bow her mother had tied.

She bounced away. "I can handle the rest. Remember, I changed in the woods."

"Yes, with that lovely dance."

She pulled a dressing gown from her bag then stared at him. "Are you going to step out?"

"No, but I'll turn." He faced the door as he had before. "Ester, I have a two-room flat, probably as small a space as the warehouse you once lived. I'm frugal with my money, so you'll have to become used to me. You need to become used to me."

He heard her rustling and watched her engaging shadow on the wall.

"I'm done, Bex."

He turned to find her in another high-necked gown of cream. Graceful and demure, and his pulse raced at the site of her.

Holding her party gown, she began to fold it. "This is so delicate. I shouldn't have worn it. I washed, but I haven't had a bath."

"You were lovely in it, and your lilac soap is quite distinctive on your skin. I could inquire with the innkeeper about a bath in the morning."

She shook her head and sat on the side of the bed. "No, Bex. Don't. I'll be the last to use it. The negress wife of an actor ranks the lowest. The tub will be horrible and dirty before it's my turn." She offered a nervous giggle. "I'll stick to my bucket and pretty soap.

His heart broke for her. The life he had to offer her was so different from the life to which she'd grown accustomed. "That's why you originally changed your mind? The changes you'll have to go through to be with me?"

She shrugged. "Yes, and the changes you will have to endure for marrying me. I'm not sure either of us is ready."

He crossed to her side and saw her clutching the blanket. It wasn't in anticipation. Fear was not a good lover. "Do me a favor, Ester? I need you to free me of this shirt and the bandage. I have to get my arm moving."

Ester was tentative in touching him, but she lifted his shirt with great care. Still looking like a scared rabbit, she undid the knot on his bandage.

"I'm free. Thank you, Ester." He leaned in and kissed her cheek.

Her eyes were wide as she stared.

Flexing his arm, he leant over and blew out the candle. "You go on to sleep. I'm going to practice my lines. By the time we are back to London, I'll have missed most of the rehearsals."

She inhaled deeply as he moved to the small desk. "You're Arthur Bex. You will be wonderful."

If she believed that about him completely, she wouldn't be digging her fingernails into the blanket. "Get some sleep."

She lay back and maybe released a yawn from her lungs as she hit the mattress. "Good night, Bex."

"Good night, my dearest Ester. You can call me, Arthur. It's allowed to be more familiar with your husband."

He sat at the desk and drew the script from his bag to study his lines.

"You don't have to be quiet, Bex. I love your voice. It will help me sleep."

He pushed his arm out of the bandaged sling she'd loosened and stretched it. He needed it strong and flexible, to do everything to woo his wife and make Ester love *him* as she loved his characters on the stage. Yes, he was ready to take on his greatest role. For Ester was his, and she needed to want him whether his name was Arthur Bex or Oliver Arthur Bexeley. Once he was sure of her love, he could tell her the truth and not fear losing her.

Losing a woman who'd just given up everything for him should never happen.

. . .

With wide-awake eyes, Ester watched Bex and listened to his dreamy voice recite Shakespeare. His tones were clear, and her heart pounded when he said words of love. Like in the theater, she imagined that it was her name he said, not Cleopatra's.

She wanted Bex to love her. Then she wouldn't feel so fretful, so vulnerable. Then she wouldn't be concerned about him straying like Papa, or worse, abandoning her like Ruth's beau had done.

Everything still ached from the lies and revelations. She smiled at her husband pacing and saying lines. He was the only one who hadn't lied.

Her breath caught when Bex stretched and yanked off the remaining bandages. Bare from the waist up, he groaned as he flexed his shoulder. Another small moan ushered from him as he rotated his hurt arm. "Don't fret, Ester. It's better, just a little stiff."

Having been caught gazing, she closed her eyes but

remembered how she and Ruth had peeked at Papa's workers through a knot in the floorboards at the warehouse—sweaty bulky arms in all shades, from beige to deep ebony, lifting crates and drying wool near the big furnaces.

Through her lashes, she glanced at Bex again. He was a sight to behold, tall with a lean stomach and solid muscles in his arms and chest. The bulky costumes of the stage hid much of his masculine beauty.

Bex moved to the fireplace. With his hurt hand, he clasped the onyx poker and stoked the flames. The odds his shoulder would be permanently lame had diminished. With no lasting damage from this escapade, Bex, a thing of beauty, would remain whole.

Ester tried to roll over, but she couldn't help herself, watching him stir the fire and recite his lines. This was her husband. She had chosen him, and he'd chosen her. Could their attraction grow into something more? Could they both be faithful to their marital promises, even if they had been made under duress?

Bex came over to the bed. "Have you fallen asleep?"

"No." Her pulse ticked up.

"Good. I won't feel bad when I force you to scoot over."

He sat on the side as she shuttled to the other edge.

The mattress wasn't so big, so he'd be touchable. "You're going to sleep in this bed?"

He slid on his nightshirt, grunting as he lifted his hurt arm. "That is where one sleeps."

"But."

He lay back and took the pillow from her. "And I hear that married couples do that all the time. It is a rumor. I haven't confirmed it." He touched her cheek. "Your skin does flame when you blush."

When he moved back to his side, she missed his gaze upon her.

"Good night, Ester," he said.

It took a moment to become used to the way the bed swayed when he moved, for he shifted the bedsheets and then ended up very near her side.

"Bex, you will do well as Antony. You have nothing to fear."

His hand found hers, and he tugged her so that she shared the pillow. "There is always something to fear. Sometimes fear is good. It tells you what to value. Makes you hold on tight to the good in your life."

"Well, Arthur Bex will be brilliant. On the nights I can go, I'll be cheering for you. I'll talk to my friend Frederica Burleigh. Her father, the Duke of Simone, lets us use his box."

"Nights you can go? By us, you mean your friends Mrs. Fitzwilliam-Cecil and Miss Burleigh? You'll have seats opening night, or maybe you can sit off stage."

"No. No. I'll be too nervous for you. I'd rather watch you like I always have, at a distance. You'll be so great."

He sat up, hovering over her, and was so close she could trace the curl of dark hair over the night shirt. If she sketched Greek statues, Bex could be an excellent one, and she was within touching distance, her to him, him to her.

"Ester?"

"Yes." She blinked away her distraction by the muscular lines of his form. "Yes. Bex."

"You want the truth, Ester, but I expect the same about

anything I ask."

She pulled at the blanket as if he could see through her robe. "Yes."

"It's not that you would be nervous for me. It's that you don't think you belong, and you are trying to protect me again, this time from the reaction of others."

Ester closed her eyes for a moment. "This marriage cost me my family. I don't want it to cost you your profession or your reputation. If Arthur Bex is destroyed because of his wife—I'd never forgive myself."

"You're a queen, Ester, but not an untrustworthy Cleopatra, not the way you keep trying to shelter me."

Still hovering above, he touched her cheek again. "Warm again. A blushing bride. Well, I believe someone thinks I should be well rested before we start back to London. I'm surprised you hadn't already insisted."

"It's good to see that you learn quickly."

Chuckling, he punched the pillow then reclined, reciting lines the whole way down. Then his voice grew louder. "Let Rome in Tiber melt, and the wide arch of the ranged empire fall: here is my space...next to you."

The resonance in his voice, the clarion call of Bex claiming his spot, the space next to her, made her toes wriggle. "You sleep, Ester. We've a long way to go."

He started practicing Shakespeare again.

Ester loved it. It was a performance just for her. Right now, Bex was just hers, not shared with the world on stage.

When his voice grew lower and slowed, she couldn't help herself, moving a little closer to hear each word.

His fingers clasped hers. "Ester, if reciting Shakespeare is what it takes for you to be at ease, I'll willingly become hoarse."

"Then I'll make you more chamomile. Good thing you're not that manipulative, Bex."

"Good thing your toes are warm. They are touching my shin."

"Oh, I …"

"Don't move a muscle. That's your place now, at my side. I'll have to get you to say Arthur and learn how to make you love saying it."

That sounded like a challenge, and that should bring her some concern, but she was too comfortable sharing Bex's pillow to look for trouble. It would find her soon enough. It always did.

CHAPTER SIXTEEN

A Simple Life

The final leg of the trip to London was slower than Ester wanted, for the familiar buildings of the city made her anxious. When the scent of the Thames, the tart fog with the hint of horses' leavings greeted her, she relaxed on the seat. The city was safer for Blackamoors, so it had to be better for her and Bex.

Yet, her husband didn't look relieved. He seemed cross, with a deep frown on his face.

She put her sketch pad onto her knee, her charcoal into her bag, then linked her arm about his. "Bex, we are back in London. Is it much farther to your home?"

"Not much farther." He patted her hand but pulled out his pocket watch. This was the second time.

"Well, I've missed rehearsal again. That four-hour wait to change horses at the last coaching inn has done me in." His smile was thin but there for her. "I hate missing appointments. I gave them my word. I sent a messenger from our stay in Newcastle, saying I'd return today. I don't break promises easily."

Their marriage had already started to cost him. She fretted for him but tried to encourage him with another squeeze to his forearm. "They'll understand. You've just come back from a wedding trip. Funny, I always pictured sailing away on a boat."

"No. No boat for you...or me."

His tone had sharpened, but he kissed her hand before she could pull away. "I don't like missing appointments. My word is

550 THE BASHFUL BRIDE

all that I have. I committed to being there."

"They'll understand. It's not as though they'll give your role away to someone else."

He tugged on the reins, and the lead horse pranced a little faster, but there was no room to move with the other carriages. "You don't know how fast someone can turn on you." He rubbed his neck and glanced again toward the road. "There is always a new bright light, some new actor waiting for a chance."

"No one can replace you."

"Let's hope that's always your take on things. I seem to be replacing your pillow at night. Maybe I could compete with a blanket to keep you warm. London nights can be cold ones."

Heat flushed her cheeks.

The need to box his ears didn't leave her when he chuckled, but it was good to know that he desired her as his wife.

"I do wonder how much I can make you blush, my bashful bride. I'd like to try."

Heat spread now, racing the length of her, down to her toes. "I wonder if you will still speak to me with such enthusiasm once our marriage progresses."

"Only one way to find out, my dear. And with no rehearsal, it seems we have a whole evening to determine...progress."

She tried to combat his wit, but how could she with his lips puckered into a knowing smile.

"I'll talk to you the whole time, Ester."

His whisper dripped like honey or thick coconut oil along her neck and stirred her pulse to thrash within her veins.

"Ester. Dearest, Ester. We'll just hold hands or find something else to do. If you trust me."

His tone was light, but there was no jest, not anymore.

And her heart couldn't pretend anymore that she wasn't as affected by Bex the husband as she was Bex the actor, not after sleeping at his side each night for the last three. She'd even become used to his snores. She loved his snores. "Tell me about your flat."

The simmering expression in his eyes did not diminish. "It's two small rooms, each in need of a woman's touch."

"Your countess friend never touched it."

"No. No one comes to visit."

Ester felt as if she had touched upon something, something raw. Perhaps the man who liked to tease couldn't take teasing. She drummed her fingers upon her lap. "Two rooms? A bathing room and bedchamber?"

"No. A sitting area and a bedchamber. There is a room in the building with a copper tub, but it is shared by the residents."

Shared? Her heart sunk. "That means it will have a rank for its use." In her reticule were the two guineas Theodosia had given her. "I have a little money. Perhaps I could order one. It wouldn't be a frivolous purchase. I can also wash my dresses in it. I only have one simple gown and this carriage dress. The party dress, my wedding dress, is too delicate for everyday wear."

"Perhaps, we should consider purchasing new garbs for you. You've come to me with little. Then on my next benefit night, if we haven't made arrangements, I'll buy you a big copper tub with my money."

"But I have clothes. Lots of clothes. We only need to stop at Nineteen Fournier."

His smoldering smile turned into a solid frown. "No. Ester, we cannot. Not without a proper invitation."

He was being silly. Those were *her* things in her room in her closet.

When the gig turned onto Lower Thames Street, getting close to Papa's warehouse, she tugged Bex's arm. "Let's stop. Papa may be inside. We can ask him about my clothes."

He picked up the reins and moved the gig faster. "No, Ester. You're going to your new home, my flat. It's too soon to press your parents for anything."

"I want to try to make amends, Bex."

He shook his head. "It's only been a few days. Their anger hasn't cooled. We haven't proven that we are right in this marriage."

"But I want to try."

"I know Ester, and we will, but you made a choice by eloping out of that window. Now you are dead to them. Not much will fix that."

His words stung like a kick to the gut, but she couldn't accept it. "No, Bex. You know not what I feel."

"Yes, I do, Ester. I, too, made a choice once that made everyone disown me."

His posture seemed tense. There was still so little she knew of him. What past hurts did he hold inside? He had to be a loner for a reason, and that made her sad for him. "Your parents didn't disown you. They died and died young. Is that how you feel about their passing?"

His jaw tightened, then he eased his grimace back to a simple frown. "No."

"Then what are you talking about? Bex, tell me. I think I should know."

"My guardian disowned me. My uncle believed I had turned against him, but I was only doing what I knew to be right. I know how it cuts, Ester. I know the pain of separation."

"Was that what happened when you chose to be an actor? I know some look down on it, but not me."

He wiped at his face. "One of many decisions he found difficult. The point is, Ester, he felt my choice was a betrayal, but I could never do what he wanted. Never."

Bex's hands shook on the reins. His pain seemed raw, right under his gloves.

"But you reconciled? There's a happy ending to your story?"

He shook his head. "No happy ending. He hated me until the day he died. I don't blame him for that. Betrayal looks different, even to the guilty."

A gasp left her lips before she could stop it.

"Ester, there is a very real possibility that we may never reconcile with the Croomes. I haven't demonstrated I'm a good choice. I'm some actor that stole the fabric princess. We've just come back to London. We haven't lived as man and wife yet. There's much to prove."

"You're not *some* actor, but the best, and we've been married for three days. We've been amiable."

Swiping at his brow, as if her logic had overwhelmed him, he shook his head. "And we've slept as friends. Not as husband and wife. There's still much to prove."

Maybe that's what men did—wrap everything in a moment of passion. What of tenderness and care and concern and fidelity? "Who better to be friends than husband and wife?"

"I suppose that is true, friend." He pushed his hat down and slowed the phaeton, turning onto Gracechurch Street. "My flat's not far. If you want me to keep going to Fournier, I will. I'll be by your side, even if the front door is slammed in your face."

Would her mother cut her again? And would showing up be an admission that Ester had been wrong to elope and her parents right in telling her lies? Anger swam in her stomach, engulfing the ache of missing Mama and Papa. "They lied, allegedly to protect me. Would you do that, Bex?"

He leaned forward as if he needed to inspect the horses. "Ester, I won't lie to you. I promise to be faithful, but there may be things I won't tell you."

"What?"

"If a colleague makes cruel remarks about our marriage, I won't tell you. If I'm disparaged for marrying you, I'll seal my lips. If I have to have fisticuffs because someone makes a statement that's offensive, I'll not say a word. I'd rather keep things that would pain you to myself than put you in a position which compels you to dance with highwaymen or play a maid. Your acting days are done."

"Lying is to be preferred?"

"No, but omitting something painful is. I care enough about you to keep you sheltered from the bad. I care a great deal for you, Ester."

She should be outraged that he wouldn't tell her things, as if she couldn't handle the truth, but the second thing he said, about caring for her—well, that outweighed everything. "You should be glad I have selective hearing. For I care a great deal about you, too. Let's head to your flat."

Bex's laughter was low, and she laughed, too.

Minutes later, he turned onto another street, something called Fenchurch Street, and the neighborhood looked foreign. No hint of the Thames. No warehouses. No Huguenot homes. Nothing but lines of neat looking town homes. Her foot began to tap in anticipation.

"It's best that I miss rehearsal tonight, Mrs. Bex. Means I can focus on getting you settled. Not much farther. We'll be turning into the mews in a few minutes. Then I'll take you to our flat and properly welcome my wife home."

It wouldn't be the home she knew, in a neighborhood where she didn't know if she belonged. She tried to slow her pulse, but too many knots built inside at the thought of living with Bex as man and wife.

• • •

The wind whipped a little as Arthur headed down the final street before his flat. Ester sat on her hands, her cute chin turning this way and that way.

She was a beautiful woman, delicate, sophisticated, but right now she seemed fragile, more fragile than at any point in their short acquaintance.

But he was too anxious and unbalanced. He should've told her. The opportunity had been there in her questions. How could he say aloud that he'd witnessed atrocities, and that his testimony about such had led to his uncle's hanging? The truth had cost Arthur what was left of his family and his good name. Now the truth would take his Ester away before they had a chance to discover what their marriage could be.

"Bex? Are you all right?" Ester's voice was low. "Bex?"

"I forgot how hard it was those months after my parents died. I was isolated from everyone." Then he had endured it again with his uncle's imprisonment. "But, unlike me, Ester, you're not alone."

Her lips lifted from their sad pout. "I know, Bex. And you've been very sweet. I like you sheltering me."

She put her hand on his again, this time smearing a little dark charcoal on his glove from her sketching. She wet her thumb on her tongue and swiped the smudge away.

His chest felt lighter as he marveled at how comfortable she'd become with him. Barely a week had passed since they'd met over the newspaper advertisement, and she'd become more at ease with him, even reaching for him as she slept. He'd taken his time driving back to London, taken his time letting her become accustomed to his weight shifting beside her and his arm draping her, holding her about the delightful bosom she was so shy about sharing.

He grasped her hand as he made the final turn into the mews behind his flat. "We're here. Your new home."

Her shy smile had returned, with those ever so soft lips opening. If not for seeing Jonesy approach, he'd take the invitation. "Wait for me, Ester, to help you down."

He jumped down and handed the reins and a coin to his red-haired young friend.

The boy fingered a scratch on the side. "You had a bit of an accident?"

"A small one." He could feel Ester rolling her eyes, but he kept his focus on the young man. "There's an extra farthing if you can buff it out."

"Yes, sir."

The boy started unhitching the horses but stopped when Arthur handed Ester down."

"A new maid, sir. Miss, let me tell you. Mr. Bex like his things clean, cleaner than new."

"Jonesy, this—"

"Come along, Mr. Bex. Let me see this new place I have charge of." Her fake cockney accent came out again, and he shook his head and extended his arm. This time he wouldn't allow her to pretend. With an arm draped about her waist, he turned her to Jonesy. "Young man, this is my wife. She's a bit of an actress. If ever she needs anything, you see to it. There will be more than a farthing in it for you."

"You married...her?" The boy looked down then up. "More than a farthing. Sure thing, Mr. Bex. Pleased to meet you, Mrs. Bex. Mr. Bex is a good tipper."

Ester stared in Jonesy's direction a few seconds longer, and Arthur hoped she wouldn't ask about his cleft lip. The sheltered girl probably hadn't seen anything like it.

Arthur held out his arm again to Ester. "Shall we?" He put her hand in the crook of his arm. "We can't usher in change if we hide. Now let's go. Jonesy, when you are done, bring my bag."

The boy had one horse unhitched. "Sure thing, Mr. Bex. More than a farthing?"

"Yes. Jonesy."

Ester tried to retake her bag from him. "I don't want you hurting that arm."

He could only shake his head and admire how she wanted to

protect him. It was a nice feeling. "Come along."

They walked out onto the street, and Ester stopped, her mouth gaping.

Arthur looked around but saw nothing amiss on the street, only storefronts and pedestrians. "Ester, what is it?"

"I'll be living in Cheapside. Papa will be impressed."

"Well, there is nothing as grand as Nineteen Fournier around here. You'd have to travel to Mayfair to see the likes."

"The groom Jonesy, was he hurt in an accident?"

"No, he was born with a defective lip." Hoping she wasn't being missish, he stopped and looked at her. "Oh, please don't think less of him. He's been abandoned and on his own since he was twelve. He is such a good worker."

"Abandoned like you? He must be so hurt."

Arthur had accepted being alone, he just hadn't focused on the hurt part of that kinship with Jonesy. "Perhaps, but he dreams of being a groom at a fancy house like your parents', but no one will hire him because of his looks."

"Bex, why don't you advocate for him and people like him? That is something you are much more connected to than abolition. It might be safer."

He grasped her hand and walked her to his building. "Abolition is the cause of my heart. Not abandonment. And can you question it, Ester, after hearing your mother? You and your sister would be enslaved back in Jamaica. Slavery must end."

Her gaze never strayed. Her topaz eyes cut through him as if he'd said something stupid. "I know of its importance. My whole family knows. My mother is a quiet person, but she shared some of the horrors of growing up on a plantation in Jamaica. Her father treated his enslaved people as if they weren't human. The slave ships from your Liverpool stole her mother and her brothers, her whole family from Africa and brought them to Jamaica. It's a death sentence for those that work the sugar cane fields. And a different kind of death to be kept in the master's clutches. Yes, Bex, I know."

"Slave ships from Liverpool?" The blood froze in his veins. "I'm sorry. I didn't think. I'm sorry."

She brushed at a braid that had escaped her bonnet. "I've heard how vicious my flesh-and-blood grandfather was to the people he owned, who looked like me or with darker skin. So vicious. My grandfather would have you killed for your push for abolition. He'd do it. Others here might, too. I don't want to live in fear, waiting for you to come home." She fingered the lapel of his coat. "Or open your door and this coat comes to me, battered or bullet ridden."

He pulled her into him, and he just held on to her until her trembles stopped. There wasn't much to say. She spoke the truth. These were dangerous times. "Ester, I know the risks, but I will be careful, and I've a wife to come home to. Don't fret, Mrs. Bex."

"But I will, Bex. I always will."

A feeling close to love filled his head as he led her to the third floor. He dropped her bag in front of his door. "Well, I've quite recovered from the accident, and I'm well-rested, and I'm welcoming my wife home." He slipped his hands about her waist and lifted her in the air. "I'll carry you across the threshold."

She sniffled and giggled like he'd done a great feat.

"You are easy on my ego, Ester."

Her lips parted as if she was going to respond, but instead

she ducked her face behind him as if to hide. "We aren't alone."

Clapping sounded from behind. He eased Ester to the floor and spun to see Phineas.

"So Bex, the saint does have a morsel on the side, a chocolate bonbon. I guess the great actor isn't a saint. Man cannot live by pages alone, aye, Bex?"

Arthur's fist balled. "Phineas, please do not disrespect my wife. No matter what you think of me, she is good."

The man's busy brows raised. "My apologies, ma'am. So how long have you been married? Wait—the girl from White Horse Cellar?"

Ester stayed behind Arthur, her nails had clawed into his coat.

Arthur clasped her fingers and pried them to the front, weaving his with hers. "We just married."

Phineas tapped his chin. "A quick courtship?"

Remembering how Ester had portrayed their relationship to her father, he decided to say the same. "Some could say that this has been in the works for two years, right, my dear?"

Ester said nothing but drew deeper into his back. Though he didn't mind her breath heating that center spot on his back, he'd hoped for a more spirited defense.

He gave her hand a little squeeze. "Go on, tell him like you told your father."

Again, she said nothing, only planting her face deeper in his back.

"Seems you have a shy one, Bex."

"Why are you here, Phineas?"

"Your big rally tonight. You're the star of it. I wanted to get a statement, beforehand since you never like to talk afterward."

"Phineas, that's not until the end of the month, days away. Could you please—"

"The thing became organized after your big speech. I believe you were there, Mrs. Bex, to catch the end. No wonder you felt so at ease coming down to the cellar where the radicals gather. Your beau was on stage."

"Radicals? That means danger?" Ester's voice was low as she peeked around Arthur's arm.

Phineas grinned. "Very, very dangerous, but tonight's rally could be deadly. A blowhard could get shot if he isn't careful."

Pulse raising, anger boiling over, Arthur pointed to the stairs. "Unless you've become my personal secretary, Phineas, you need to be on your way."

"Well, I tried to find you at the theater, but when you didn't show, I assumed you were working on a big speech, something to make the crowds go wild. There will be terror in the streets incited by the man who loves the limelight."

"I've returned from getting married. And please, my wife doesn't understand that you're exaggerating the danger."

"Just come back? *Hmmm*. Well, the rally starts at seven, but you'll miss it getting the wife settled. All talk, Bex, or has the abolition cause been something you've used to woo a negress woman? A fancy one at that."

Arthur raised his arm to punch the reporter senseless, but Ester clutched it, as if she didn't want to see him violent. "Leave my wife out of your columns and out of your mouth."

The reporter sobered. "It'll be hard to do, but perhaps an interview given by you, Bex, could sway me. Your story has just become even richer with this shy wife. If she's what you've been hiding, you should've said so."

"I've nothing to say to a nosy reporter, but 'leave.'"

"You're hiding a secret, and I'm close to exposing the truth."

Fury ripping through him, Arthur took a step toward Phineas, but Ester held on to his tailcoat.

"Please, Bex. Don't." Her whisper was soft, smothering the fire in him, at least the one to pummel Phineas. "He's not worth it."

The reporter clapped his hands. "When you change your mind about an exclusive story, Bex, send for me. Same for you, Mrs. Bex. I love informants equally. See you tonight, if you can bear to get away. *Bang. Bang.* Gunpowder."

Phineas marched away, all while almost singing, "Exclusive: Arthur Bex is married to a bashful Blackamoor bride. Will the sham last beyond the rallies? The ones he feels are worthy of his presence."

Arthur's anger raged again. "He better not put you in the papers."

"Bex, you said it yourself. We can't hide if we are to create change. I suppose that also includes from the reporters who want to do you harm."

With a sigh, he turned to unlock the door but caught her big, wide eyes. The pique Arthur had felt over her not defending him subsided. She was fearful...for him. Again, that protective nature of hers had come out and made a play for his heart. "Phineas is a nuisance, but harmless."

"He's not harmless. He's out to hurt you. He's baiting you to go to that rally where you could be hurt."

There were no words to comfort her. He had to go to the rally. He'd promised to be there, had encouraged others to go. Slipping his other hand in his pocket, he dug for his key. "I still think you are much bolder when you think our lives are at imminent risk."

"I don't want to be at risk. I want to be happy. I want you safe. Don't go to the rally."

No pleading or soft lilting voice would deter him, not from his calling. He jiggled the fob, metal clicked against metal, and the door opened. "Welcome."

With her chin high, his bride entered. Her head turned from side to side as she took a lap about the freshly papered pale-yellow walls that he'd helped the widowed boardinghouse owner finish a few weeks ago. "Very clean for a bachelor."

The scent of pine soap wafted as he lugged her bag inside and closed the door. "The landlady must've come through this morning. But you are right, I like a clean house." He took off his tall-crowned felt hat and set it on his desk. "Saturday morning chores to swab my decks are not out of the question."

"You sound like a sailor." She took a full circle about the sitting room. "Papa likes a clean warehouse, but some of his workers don't seem to know what clean is. This is very nice," she said in a tone that reeked of *is-this-it?* before she sat on his sofa.

"I'm a simple man. I live within my means."

Ester stood and came toward him. "This isn't my father's house. I didn't marry him or the rich man he hand-picked." She put a hand to Arthur's cheek. "I could learn to be happy here. I like clean and honest, too. I like safe more."

"Safe is fine. But risk made you jump out a window and into my arms. Taking a risk made me come to Nineteen Fournier to catch you. Taking a risk can be worthy."

Her bright topaz eyes were light and filled with hope among the ribbon flecks of gold. "You are worthy."

If he could dip into those molten pools and come out dripping of virtue, he would, for he wanted to be what she saw. He kissed her palm. "You believe I can make you happy?"

"You already do."

She tugged him to a chair and stood upon it. They were now eye to eye. "I'm happy, Bex." With arms about his neck, she kissed his jaw. "Bex, I know you want to go to the rally tonight, but we just made it here. I want you home and safe. Is that too much to ask on our first night in Cheapside?"

Her lips went to his, and she kissed him. Soft, tentative, encouraging. "Choose me, Bex. Let's begin our life tonight."

Arthur slipped off her shawl and stepped closer to the little woman, fingering the lace and buttons that separated them. He wanted his wife. He wanted to love and care for her. With his blood pumping faster, swooshing in his ears, he needed to draw near the woman who had risked everything for him.

But the rally needed him, too.

He broke from her kiss and sat his chin on her head. "Ester, this rally is of my making. I have to go."

"You've birthed it, Bex, but it can happen without you."

It could. The rally might have other foot soldiers that could lead the movement forward.

"But what if it fails, Ester? How do I look at myself in the mirror, knowing I could have helped but didn't?"

"Don't go, Bex."

His neck bathed in sweat, he took a step away from the chair.

"Ester, my mind won't be with you tonight. It'll be out on that field. I'll be thinking of the words that need to be said to make those in power understand. To sway the ambivalent to action"

"Why does it have to be you? Why you, Bex?"

He should just tell her. Maybe if she knew of how his testimony had made a difference and had given justice to those who'd died, she'd understand. Maybe she'd understand the guilt he bore at being on his uncle's ship for six years and not wanting to recognize that his cargo wasn't crates, but men. "Ester—"

"You could be hurt. Bex, I need you."

He needed her, too. But if he told her the truth, she'd think him a liar, like her father. He'd rather be a risk-taker than a deceitful lout who should've told her something so vital before they wed.

She tugged on his shoulders and pulled him closer, again eye-to-eye. "I want you to choose me. I chose you over my parents, Bex. I need you to choose me over these dangerous rallies. I must have you here, snoring in my arms."

Big topaz irises sated with passions enchanted Arthur, for Ester wasn't talking about merely sleeping. He knew it, and his mouth salivated. His fingers tingled at the thought of tucking his arms about her and finally claiming every bit of her, every inch of olive skin. She'd be all his, once and for all.

Ester was that one person to recommend and love him. Wasn't that what Arthur always wanted? If he stayed, wouldn't he have that?

"Please, Bex. Don't go."

If he kissed her now, he'd not make it to the rally. She'd be in his arms. He'd be unwrapping her from the carriage dress and tasting her goodness—all night, until dawn broke through yonder glass. Ester was his sun, his bright moon, the love he'd always wanted.

The woman he loved.

Perhaps her love would smother the screams that met him in the night, the unquenchable memories that tormented him—all the wrongs he hadn't been able to right.

"Bex." Ester clutched his lapels, wove her hands about his neck. She wasn't shy anymore. With this kiss, bold, encompassing, heated—her intentions to keep him were explicit.

"I need you to you stay, Bex."

But the voiceless needed him, too. He'd promised to be at the rally. He'd given his word.

"Bex?"

"A man is no better than his word. I want you to be happy. I'm committed to that." He played with the cravat that choked his hot skin, then scooped her up and set her feet on the ground. "There's a small closet and a chest of drawers in the bedroom. Go settle in, and I'll retrieve something to eat."

Before her sweet lips opened, he fled the room.

• • •

Ester paced in Bex's flat. Unpacking had not taken long. Two dresses, a nightgown, and a robe made little work. Placing her bonnet and gloves upon his small chest of drawers also took no time.

The small clock on his mantle read four minutes after six. He couldn't have gone to the rally this soon, could he? Well, he hadn't promised that he wouldn't. "Bex said he'd be back. He's a man of his word."

Saying her thoughts aloud didn't diminish her fears of him being killed at the rally.

After she'd taken three more turns about his sofa, the door opened.

The boy Bex had called Jonesy lugged in two big buckets of steaming water. Bex was behind him with something that smelled like beefsteaks. He put the basket on the table and handed Jonesy a key. "Go clean that other thing for me."

"Yes, Mr. Bex." The boy took one of the buckets, turned, and ran out of the room.

Bex was up to something, but since he hadn't gone to the rally, she didn't care. His causes were important, but now she knew she was important to him, too. She walked over to him, reached up, and tossed her arms around him. "You didn't go."

Before she could stop herself, she stretched and claimed his mouth. She kissed him with all the love she had for him—not the worship she had for the actor on the stage, but true feeling for a man who stayed true.

His hands were in her hair and had unpinned the braid of her chignon. Wild spirals probably bloomed like flower petals raining down on her shoulders. She wanted to stop and pin up her tresses, but this was truly her, and he needed to see it.

Still kissing her, he picked her up in his arms and started toward the bedchamber.

It was time to be his wife wholly. Her hands clawed into his cravat. She wanted to be close to him like they were at night.

But he stopped moving and set her slippers on the ground.

"Ester." His voice was husky. He pulled both her hands to his chest. "Ester," he said again, panting. "I've a surprise for you." He laced his fingers with hers.

She didn't want a surprise. She wanted Bex, but how could she say such a thing?

Cheeks on fire, she let him lead her.

When he reached the flat's door, she panicked. "My hair's not up. I'm not fit to be in public."

He kissed her ear. "Listen to me. You're beautiful, every inch of you, from the soles of your feet to the crown of your head. I ache to behold all of you, but not until everything is perfect."

"It is now. You stayed."

"Come with me." His arm was about her waist, her feet barely touched the ground—partly from the strength of his arms, partly from floating on love. "Bex?"

"*Shhh.*" He blew the sound over her lips and brought her to a door at the end of the hall.

Jonesy came out even before he knocked. "All clean, Mr. Bex."

"Good, go get the other bucket, Jonesy."

As the boy left, her husband opened the door. The white room was small but in the center was a glistening metal tub. A pile of snow white towels sat close by and a fresh bar of lilac soap. The scent of it was sweet. "Bex, you did this—"

Jonesy came back with the bucket sloshing and dumped the hot water into the tub. "Anything else, Mr. Bex, Mrs. Bex?"

"No," Bex said and pulled a coin from his pocket.

"You're a good tipper, Mr. Bex." The lad seemed to skip from the room.

Her husband pushed the door closed and clicked the lock. Before she could thank him, he had her in his arms, kissing her, unbuttoning her buttons, whispering her name against the pulsing vein along her neck.

When her carriage dress hit the ground, she couldn't breathe. She was alone in a chemise and corset with the man she loved.

His hand wandered the length of her, and she stood up tall. She trusted him. This was the beginning of a communion between them, of how things should be, the mystery of a husband and wife.

Loosening the lacings of her corset, his fingers smoothed her skin. He stood back and gazed at her, but Ester wasn't afraid anymore, for she was his and he was hers. "You're beautiful."

He took a step back and folded his hands behind his back. "I need to remember how hopeful you look." A loud sigh fled his nostrils. "You're first in this clean tub, Ester. First. You deserve to always be first. He scooped up her dress. Take a long soaking bath. I know how you love them. Get good and wrinkly and enjoy the water and know how I wish to kiss you everywhere."

She breathed hard, but he had the fortitude to part from her now, and that built the anticipation of what was to come.

At the door, he turned. "When you are done, knock three times. When you hear the same repeated, know that it's me, and I've come to take you to our wedding bed. Not as friends or roommates, but as man and wife. A man very infatuated with his beautiful wife. Soak a long time and think of me."

He stepped outside. "Lock the door, Ester, and enjoy."

Her pulse raced as she turned the lock.

"Take your time. You're worth the wait." His steps disappeared, and she stayed by the door a few moments until all was silent in the hall.

Turning to the metal tub, she looked at the hot water condensing moisture on the sides. She moved to it, and her eyes felt moist. Stirring the clean, hot water, she fought the tears wetting her cheeks. Bex did this. He must love her. *Lordy, how did I get so lucky, so blessed?*

She brushed at her face and inhaled the lilac soap. Bex knew what a hot bath meant to her, what this night would mean to them. Giddy, she took off her chemise and corset and climbed into the warm water.

The bath was hot, permeating her tired muscles. She let the water, the clean water, baptize her arms and legs. The dirt and sweat of their travels melted away in the suds.

She lay against the side of the tub. The copper had taken on some of the heat of the water and it felt so good against her back. Her husband had done this for her.

Ester was so in love with Bex that she was frightened. Did he love her like this—so much so that the strength of it shook him to the core of his soul?

He hadn't said the words, but the bath and prioritizing her over a rally that could get him injured or killed—was that the deepest love?

Maybe she should find out.

But what if she wasn't perfect like he said? What if he looked at her, short and busty and brown, and wasn't pleased?

With her palm, she cupped water and drizzled it down her neck. It felt so good, heating her spine with courage. Bex said that he wanted her as his wife. He'd never lied to her or made her feel as if his word couldn't be trusted. She needed to stop being afraid.

Though he wanted her to take a long bath, she couldn't. She was ready to be loved. She was ready to commit everything to him, and that meant now, not an hour from now.

Leaping out of the tub, she toweled off. Arms and head through the chemise, she tugged on the muslin. She scooped up her corset but didn't put it on. The boned linen garment was just another thing separating her from the man she loved.

She giggled. She loved Bex, the man, her husband, and he'd have all of her to cherish, the short height, all brown and busty, everything.

Against the door she laid her head, barely able to catch her breath. She loved him.

Forming a fist, she knocked on the door three times like he'd asked.

One-two-three, the reply sounded, and her heart echoed with the same force.

The door opened, and she scrambled behind a big towel.

It wasn't Bex, but Jonesy, grinning as he stood there. "Mr. Bex said to make sure you made it back to his rooms.

Raking a hand through her hair, she followed. Maybe he had expected her to dwell longer. The way she went on about the importance of a bath, he surely thought he had time to review his lines.

Jonesy opened the door.

"Bex. Bex," she said as she ducked inside, through the empty sitting room and into the empty bedchamber. Her carriage dress was folded on a chair. It had been put there with care and forethought. Hope still lived. She pulled on her robe. "Jonesy, did Mr. Bex go run an errand?"

"No, ma'am. He went to the rally." He put his hands to his mouth. "Don't tell him I told. Not supposed to tell."

The rally.

The dangerous rally.

She couldn't breathe. He'd be killed, without knowing of her love. And she'd be alone with no Bex and no parents.

"Mrs. Bex? You look faint. You sick?"

Ester put a hand to her head and sank onto the sofa. "Jonesy, I won't tell." Her voice sounded reasonable and calm, though she seethed inside. But maybe she could save Bex. "Can you get me a jarvey? I'll be ready in less than a minute."

Jonesy scurried out the door, and Ester started to braid and pin her hair. It was all she could do to keep from exploding. She wasn't a couch woman, or a sofa girl. She wasn't ready to play the part of an unconcerned wife, a woman tricked by a deceitful man.

CHAPTER SEVENTEEN

Rally to Danger

The jarvey let Ester out at the Duke of Simone's residence in Mayfair. With her prim bonnet and smooth gloves, she hoped she looked calm and elegant, but how could she? Her heavy silk carriage dress was wrinkled, her hair was only partially tamed.

Oh, and her heart was breaking.

Bex had deceived her. He had used a bath, her special treasure, to trick her. She swiped at her brow, rubbing away the perspiration of fury. He had put himself at risk. She didn't even know where to go to protect him. The man could die of violence from the rally. How could he do this to her?

When the butler asked who called upon Frederica Burghley, she offered the name, Ester Croome. The man should recognize her as much as she visited, but the butler was stodgy, conforming to rules. Those unwritten rules, such as: do not fool your wife, don't hurt your mama.

"Wait here. I'll go see if Miss Burghley is taking visitors.

If Frederica were home, she'd help. Ester fidgeted, but her bold friend would know what to do.

The man came back down the long hall of polished mahogany floors and detailed, gilded trimmings. His shiny, powder-blue livery held nothing to Clancy's uniform. "Follow me, Miss Croome."

Musical scales filtered to her, happy loving tunes, but Ester grieved too much to be moved. She focused on her slippers, which now appeared worn and old. Nothing like a fairy princess, as they had looked a week ago.

The butler escorted her inside to the music room, where Frederica practiced her pianoforte. The man held open the door, and Ester went inside.

Frederica lifted her spry head. The music stopped. She stood up from the polished chestnut instrument and floated to Ester in an emerald silk gown with epaulette braiding about the sleeves, a dress Ester had designed.

"If you are going out, Miss Burghley...I'll..."

Her friend was at her side, holding her up as the tears fell. "Templeton," she said, "bring some tea and a hair brush."

The man looked at her as if she'd lost her mind.

Ester surely had.

The grandfather clock moaned thirty after seven, and she trembled. Bex could be dying from an angry mob, and she didn't know where or how to save him.

Helping Ester to the sofa, Frederica sat beside her. She gathered her in her arms and just rocked her. "When you're ready, tell me what happened. And who I have to bribe to go beat the tar out of Bex. Lousy actor. I should've told him so. How dare an actor answer my advertisement."

Shaking her head, Ester wiped her eyes. "He's a great actor, but I don't know where he is."

Frederica smoothed her hands on the velvety nape of the indigo sofa. "Tell me what has happened. Did you marry? Did your parents stop you? Are you sure I don't need to have someone beat the tar out of him?"

Though, she didn't know about the last one; maybe a good

shaking was all that he needed, Ester waved her hand. "Slow down. I'll tell you everything. Yes, Bex and I married. Yes, my parents caught us. They are the ones who insisted we go through with it, then they disowned me."

Her brow crinkling with questions, Frederica popped up. "You're married, so you successfully eloped. Your parents were there? I don't see the problem. Was Bex mean to you? Was he violent? Do I need to tell my father?"

"Frederica, you're not listening. Oh, why doesn't Theodosia live in town, not hours away. She's easier to talk to about these things."

Frederica's lips turned down like she'd bitten beetroot or a turnip. "Our friend doesn't need to be upset right now."

"Why?"

She waved her hand across her mouth as if she'd given away a secret. "I'll tell you later, but first tell me very clearly and precisely what has happened."

"Bex and I married. He's kind and funny and never laid a hand on me except to kiss me. He's dreamy at it. The best kisser, all I could want, but he doesn't understand the danger he faces. There's a reporter who wants to destroy him, and tonight he's attending a rally."

Folding her lean fingers together, Frederica said nothing for at least a minute. "You came here looking like a drowned rat not because he left you, or was mean to you, but because he went to a rally. *Hmmm*. A man given to speeches went to a rally. Shocking."

"You don't understand. He can be hurt tonight, and no will be there to help him. I'm not there to protect him."

Frederica went back to her pianoforte. She flexed her fingers and plunked at the keys, doing her scales higher and higher. "Perhaps you should go there."

Ester put her hands on her head, squashing her bonnet and making more of her shaggy chignon sputter out. She didn't care. Concern for Bex's safety had her near tears. "I don't know where *there* is. I came here because I didn't know what else to do. I thought you could help me reason. Maybe I should've stayed in Cheapside."

"You live in Cheapside now?" Frederica made a harsh bang at the keyboard. "I don't know if that is an elevation. Nineteen Fournier is a palace in comparison. Ester, you came here because you want action. You want Bex. Let's go to the rally and find him. It's at the Serpentine at Hyde Park."

Shocked, Ester raised her head to the coffered ceiling. "How do you know this?"

"An old friend of my father's. He's an earl. I met with him today because the duke asked me to. The rally was all he could talk about." Frowning deeply, she shook her head. "I think he thought that attending the abolition rally would impress me, since I am mulatto with a Blackamoor mother." She plunked another horrid note that haunted and rang with finality. "Abolition is a worthy cause, but why not talk to me about poetry and dancing, something light and fun, like I'm a potential match or a friend. The earl won't do. I'll have to place another advertisement. I'm trying not to fret, but I'm running out of time to find a husband."

Walking to the piano, Ester smiled at Frederica. She put a palm to her shoulder. "You will find the perfect respondent to your advertisement. It will happen. You're meant to be happy."

Her friend started playing again. This time it was a bittersweet melody. "Father is dining with Miss Stevens again. An engagement will come any day."

"Has he said so?"

"No, but this woman is different. She's biding her time so carefully, being nice to him and me while she measures the curtains. She's my age, but I know she will be the mistress of this house. There will be no place for me. I won't be happy losing my father."

Ester sat by her side. "What if Miss Stevens makes him happy, too? What if being with her makes him feel young and alive?"

"He's not. He's my father. The duke should be at home drinking hot milk for his gout."

"Frederica, that's not fair. The heart wants what the heart wants."

Her friend played a few more chords, her long, elegant fingers traipsing the ivory keys. "Of course, it does. So why don't you go after what your heart wants. Bex is at the Serpentine. I could take you."

Ester bounced up, pacing in her worn slippers across the expensive gray silk tapestry running the floor. "He should not have gone. Why can't he be home and let me listen to him snore?"

Frederica hit an off note. "What?"

Stopping mid-step, Ester folded her arms about her. "It's silly, but that's how I knew my father had made it home safe when we lived above the warehouse. His snores vibrating the walls let me know he'd come home. We were still a family. I don't even know why I'm here. I should be at Nineteen Fournier begging to be forgiven. I should admit my parents were right to shelter me and right to choose someone for me. I've made horrid choices."

"If Bex isn't at your side, you at least know he's fighting for an important cause, not out carousing. We are lucky to be born in London, Ester. Your mother's people are enslaved in Jamaica. I often wonder how she's here and free."

Those wonders should've been Ester's, but she'd taken for granted so many things about her Mama and never broached the subject, too often thinking the woman delicate. Her mother was a lioness. Would she ever forgive Ester? "Mama was born in Jamaica, but her mother was kidnapped from Africa and transported on a slave ship. I think an earlier run of that horrible ship the *Zhonda*. She may have even had relatives that died on that ship's last run."

Her friend folded her arms but barely covered her trembling. "The *Zhonda* killed so many. That trial, I believe my father followed it so carefully, he kept the clippings. I found some documents while rifling through his papers, trying to find birthday presents."

"Neither of us is allowed to rummage through our father's things ever. Too many horrible secrets."

"Yes. I don't know if it does anything to know how big of a hypocrite the duke could be. He was an investor in the insurance company the captain of the *Zhonda* tried to defraud by killing his enslaved cargo. What if my mother could be related to one of the enslaved men who died? But I couldn't ask him, Ester. Just realize how lucky we are and how hopeless life is for those that look like us but are not born in England."

"We are lucky, Frederica. I didn't value what we have. I admire the fight in Bex, but I want him safe, too. I don't want the fight for abolition to cost his life. What if he's killed and nothing changes? Then what?"

Frederica lifted from the pianoforte and wrapped her in a big embrace. "It's the fight that he wants, but he also wants you. You love him, right?"

Ester did—more than she thought possible. That was why she was so furious he would risk his life, their happiness, *and* leave without telling her.

A sharp knock announced Templeton's return to the room. He entered bearing a large tray. In the middle was a setting of tea and a silver hairbrush. He set it down on the low table in front of the sofa. "Your items, Miss Burghley."

Frederica came to him, the short emerald train of her gown swishing at her low heels. She picked up the hairbrush and waved it like a wand. "Templeton, draw the carriage around. We have an emergency."

The man looked at them beneath his spectacles. "It's late, ma'am. Are you sure?"

"Yes, Templeton, I am. Please hurry."

He made a stiff bow, maybe an inch with his chin, and then he backed from the room.

"The man isn't happy. He's no Clancy. Frederica, are you sure you want to be mistress here?"

Her friend picked up the brush and started undoing and unpinning Ester's poor braid. "Templeton will do what I ask. That is why the duke pays him so well. He's a gruff servant, but this is my home. This is all I know." She sighed. The notes weren't light. They were dull, and hollow, and Ester's heart broke for her, but she was in no position to prove that happy endings were possible, not with Bex in danger.

With another few twists, Frederica had Ester's hair in order. She wouldn't look disgraceful chasing after her husband.

"Ester, we'll be on our way so you can claim your husband and take him home."

"If he'll come home. But how will he make amends? He distracted me so he could go do this. It was deceitful. I can't stand lies."

"Did he tell you he was not going, but went anyway?"

"No, Bex didn't say he wasn't going. He just made me believe he would stay with me." He gave her the treasure of a hot bath, with clean water and fresh soap. The perfect gift—an illusion like her dream of a wonderful marriage. "I don't know if I can forgive him."

"Ester, if that were true, you'd have gone home to the Croomes. You're in love with a man, one who knows his own mind. You can't control that, any more than I can control my father. If Bex wants you, he'll come home, but let's show him the way."

Wanting to nod, Ester looked out the window and waited for the sound of the carriage. They had to get to Bex before he was hurt. And before she'd fully committed to this marriage, he'd have to promise to take none of these risks again.

Ester dropped her face into her palms. She didn't have much hope. Her heart was his, and he'd already risked breaking it.

• • •

The crowds at the Serpentine grew thick, gathering around the sand and the partially dried lake bed. Arthur had butterflies in his stomach. It would be his turn to speak soon, and he hadn't written or practiced anything. How was he to speak his mind, when it was focused on Ester?

Ester.

Delicious kisses.

Welcoming arms.

All ruined by his deception.

Arthur had tricked her. He hadn't lied but he'd made her a bath, made her comfortable, then left her alone. He shook his head. It was well past eight. She wasn't still soaking in the tub. She had to know he'd left. A groan left his lips. The woman deserved to be the center of his world, and he'd deceived her. How would she ever trust him?

He was horrible. How would she ever be the woman to defend and believe in him, if she never trusted him? Tonight, he'd tell her everything and beg for one more chance.

No secrets would be between them, but she would have to understand his fight. Was that too much to hope for, to have understanding, trust and support?

The noise of the crowds whipped up again.

Arthur looked up and saw the rail-thin Wilberforce take to the bench that the organizers had made into an impromptu stage. With hands to his dark coat, he lifted his head, staring toward the growing crowd, the fire torches of the organizers. "Gentlemen, this stain on our hands, enslavement, it does not go away because it is an ocean away. This blot must be removed. The road to change is fraught, but let us not despair. Abolition is a blessed cause, and success will crown our exertions."

A rumble swept the crowd as a fight broke out. A few men who looked thick, like Bow Street Runners, pulled the trouble-makers apart.

Wilberforce raised his arms, capturing the onlookers, directing them to listen. "We have gained one victory; we have obtained, for these poor creatures, the enslaved, the recognition of their human nature, which we have shamefully denied. This is the first fruits of our efforts; let us persevere. Our triumph will be complete."

The crowd howled as he stepped down. His footing looked less sure than it had in past years. The black armband engulfing his arm made him seem fragile, but how could a powerhouse for change be anything but strong? The man came over to Arthur and shook his hand. "The fight needs more young voices."

He clung to the grip for a moment, as if it were a baton from an Olympian run. "Even an actor, sir?"

Wilberforce put a palm to Arthur's shoulder. "Only a loud voice is heard over the noise. Don't stop until this stain is no more. You know, Parliament can use loud voices, too."

Arthur nodded. Parliament wasn't for him. Too much scrutiny. He barely stayed above the likes of Phineas now.

Speaking of the reporter, the pest was off to the side. He fanned himself in the still air with the flyer created by the artist Wedgwood. The medallion printed on it was the dark outline of an enslaved man encircled with the words, AM I NOT A MAN AND A BROTHER. It pricked Arthur's conscience. The plight shouldn't be reduced to a throwaway.

Am I not a man and a brother? If only Arthur's uncle had

realized that. He'd never have murdered fifty men. He wouldn't have been hanged for it, and he could've remained Arthur's doting uncle, someone to admire.

A man shoved Phineas and the flyer fell from his hands.

Arthur bent down and scooped it up like it was a script. The paper, the image of the man, stirred words in his chest. Arthur leaped onto the bench.

"Brothers..."

"Yes, let's listen to the actor," Phineas said. "He married today. Bex, is the little wife about?"

"Brothers..." Arthur paused as he witnessed Ester and her friend coming toward the crowd on the same side as the reporter. They were easy to pick out, the only faces of color, the only women in the mix.

Ester's arms were folded across her chest.

Arthur could tell she was fuming by her stiff stance. He didn't know how to fix that or what to say to inspire the men of the rally.

"Choke." Phineas roused a few to start the chant.

"Choke. Choke. Choke."

Their incantation worked. Arthur's throat closed up. The muscles tightening, until everything became locked inside.

"These men came to hear a message, but the actor can't deliver. Tell them about the wife, Bex. That'll calm things down."

The taunts, the threats to Ester worked. Arthur pivoted to step down, but he saw Ester with her hand to her mouth. A few paces behind Phineas, she looked so nervous, so scared for him.

Arthur had put her in this position. He should have known she'd be rash and her fear for him would lead her here. The cause, his fight, had put her at risk. But still she was here, pulling for him.

He couldn't let her down. He must speak to this angry crowd about what was right.

"Gentlemen." He coughed and filled his lungs. "Gentlemen, I'll tell you about a relationship of black and white, about love and hate. They're the most important relationships. Right and wrong have a marriage. They need each other. They aren't the same without the other, for how can we judge what is true without knowing the consequence of falsehoods? Neither partner is the same. Neither can replace the other. They both have a place."

He took the flyer and waved. "If this was your brother, your father, your uncle, would you stand for the injustice? Are you not your brother's keeper because you don't see him in chains in London? Do you love your brother any less because you are here, and he's in Jamaica or South Africa?"

Pointing at the flyer, he let his voice boom. "This man on the flyer asks a simple question. One that is as clear as black and white. Is he a man? Yes."

Arthur's voice grew in power, and he glanced at Ester as if she were the only one in the audience at Covent Garden. "Yes, he is a man. For he loves like you and me, he'll bleed for what he believes in, like you and me. This man will lay down his life for the lover of his soul—just like you or me. I'll lay down my life for what is true, for the lover of my soul."

Ester began to clap but her friend grabbed her hands.

His wife heard him. Maybe she understood.

Arthur shook the poster again. "He's your brother. Enslavement is our problem, even if we don't own slaves. It's the scandal of our lifetime, the stain on our humanity. You must press. You must push. You must do what you can to right the wrongs. For at the end of your life, you will give an account. Let abolition or indifference not be your haunting shame."

He felt the hiss of the bullet even before it struck the paper. Where it came from he didn't know but he knew the crowd would descend into chaos. He leaped down as another shot was fired.

He lunged past Phineas to Ester and her friend and surrounded them in his arms. He pushed them back until they were behind a tree.

Out the corner of his eye he saw a gun leveled in their direction. The bullet would hit Phineas. He stood to warn him, but Ester held his coat.

"No, Bex."

"Not when I can help."

Arthur started running. The hate he had for Phineas fled to the back of his mind. He was a brother to be saved. In a running leap, he jumped as the gun fired, and knocked Phineas to the ground. The bullet whizzed past.

The crowd swarmed the fellow shooting. Chaos engulfed the Serpentine.

Phineas jumped up and offered a hand to Arthur. "Bex. You saved my life."

Breathing hard, Arthur stood on his own, brushing sand from his coat. Then he headed back to Ester.

Phineas caught his arm, the one that still smarted. "Bex, I said thank you."

"I heard. Use your power for good, Phineas. That's how you can thank me." He trudged away toward the women.

He lifted them from huddling behind the tree. "Miss

Burghley, where's your carriage? I am going to make sure you are safely on your way before I take my wife home.

Miss Burghley nodded. "This way." Her eyes were big as saucers, bigger than Ester's.

He put his wife's palm on his arm, but she pulled away. "No. I'll go with Miss Burghley."

This was the first time she'd ever done that. Her jaw was tight, her posture stiff. She was furious. "You're safe. That's all I wanted, Bex."

"No, Ester, you're coming with me. There is much to say."

He kept both women close until they found Miss Burghley's carriage. Helping her inside, he sent her away.

Now just his wife remained. He wasn't letting her go, not until they talked.

When they walked to his phaeton, he set her atop and climbed beside her. "I know you are angry. Let me explain."

"No, Take me home, Bex."

"I am, Ester. At Cheapside we'll discuss everything, even things I've never said."

"No, Bex. Take me to Nineteen Fournier. It's time to end the charade. We've failed." She folded her arms. "No, *you* failed because you couldn't trust me enough to tell the truth of where you went tonight."

Her words kicked him in the stomach, but he wouldn't argue with her until they left Hyde Park and were as far from the Serpentine as possible.

Yet, he could not lose hope. Ester had started to clap for him. Surely, she felt the importance of his message, and if he told her why it was his fight, everything of his uncle's scandal, maybe he could win another chance.

Yet, the sadness in her eyes, the line stealing her soft lips, foretold that her love for him was lost. No. That couldn't be. He'd fight for her love. He'd make her understand.

CHAPTER EIGHTEEN

The Fiery Inferno

A weave of ebony and smoky purple seemed to blot out the stars the farther they drove from Hyde Park. Ester was furious, her arms folded, and she wished Bex would take the streets faster. The sooner she was at the door to Nineteen Fournier and begging for forgiveness, the sooner her heart would be safe.

Being with Bex wasn't safe, not at all.

He sat next to her with his tan frock coat stained with dust, and he smelled of gunpowder. Yet, he had the audacity to look sad, his mouth drawn in a line as if *he'd* been hurt or deceived.

"Do you know how scared and how angry I am, Bex?"

"I have some idea, Ester."

Turning away, she clasped her elbows.

"But I'd like to tell you everything. I don't want to lose you, Ester."

His voice, deep, maybe steeped with regret, vibrated through her. The ache in her chest became greater with images of that bullet whipping by him. It repeated in her head. "I can't live like this, not knowing when you'll lie to me just to put yourself in harm's way.

Bex slowed the carriage when they came close to the Thames and more stars disappeared, making the brightness of the gaslights more prominent. Something would guide her home, for love wasn't enough.

"I was wrong to deceive you. I should've just told where I was going, but I didn't want to disappoint you when I said I had to go to the rally. I had to, Ester. Forgive me."

"No. Take me to Nineteen Fournier. You left me before. I'm leaving you now."

"There's nothing I can say that would make a difference? How much I care, how I wish to make amends. You don't want to hear that?"

She stared at him and his fists clenched about the reins. How could he be angry when he was at fault? "I commend your ruthlessness, Bex, but how long did you think I was going to bathe? It's well past ten. I think I'd be a prune waiting for you. Do you know what it felt like to go from feeling loved to being tricked? Why did you trick me?"

"I know. I know. I thought I was giving you a perfect moment, a bath fit for a queen. My queen. I know you, Ester. I know how baths make you happy."

She wanted to cry and throw things at him. "That's why it hurt so much. You used something I treasure as a ploy, just so you could sneak away."

"Yes. It was wrong. So wrong. If it hadn't been for the rally, the rally that I called for the day I met you, I would have stayed with you. And we would have consummated this marriage. For what it's worth, I approve of the lengths that you will go to keep me home."

Her breath went away. His jest ripped right through her. "How can you joke about this? Before you surprised me with the bath, just seeing you come back through the door had taken away all my doubts. I wanted to be everything for you, Bex. I thought you had chosen me above your rally. I wanted you so much in that moment."

He rubbed at his face. "Don't you know how I burn for you? It killed me to leave, but I had to do what was right. They needed my voice at the rally."

"I needed you." She dropped her face into her palm. "But you want me pacing, wondering if you'll come home. I've done that for years, waiting to see if Papa would come home. Now you want to sentence me to the same purgatory, hoping some fool never shoots you at a rally. You, Bex, want me pleading on my knees, praying you aren't trampled by a mob."

"Ester, I need you, but the cause needs me, too."

She wanted to stand up and leap off the gig to be away from his voice of lies. "You didn't have to go. Mr. Wilberforce was there. He could've led the rally. You're good, but he's the man who championed the law banning slavery in England."

Bex reached for her. "I know you are angry, but I have to be a part of this fight for abolition. The cause, this righteous cause, needs new soldiers. We can't depend upon others. We have to fight."

"It wasn't *we*. It was you."

He took off his felt hat and fanned his face, which had reddened. "It had to be me, alone. You shouldn't have been there. You and Miss Burleigh were the only women to attend. It was a men's rally. You could've been shot, or targeted, or worse. That shooter doesn't want change. He'll take his anger out on you, because of your sex or because you are Blackamoor."

"Then maybe you'd feel a tenth of what I did, my heart ripping in my chest at seeing the bullet fly through your paper. A few more inches and you'd be gone. What would I do then?"

"Go home to your parents, like you are doing now. Nineteen

Fournier is where you want to live, instead of staying with me."
He lowered his tone. "I know there's danger. I've seen it. But I
know what happens if you say nothing. If I don't try to stop evil."

"Bex, what are you talking about?"

He tossed his hat to the bottom of the gig and raised his eyes
to the sky. "I've been afraid to lose you if you knew the horrible
truth. But you must know. I can't keep this from you, not anymore."

Was the actor being overly dramatic? Or was there a dark
secret that kept her love from reaching him? "Tell me."

His neck craned upward. He picked up the reins and started
the phaeton. "No. God. No."

What? She turned to see what had captured his attention.

Her heart stopped.

A plume of smoke billowed from the top of the building.
Papa's warehouse.

The place the Croomes owned, used to live above, was in
flames.

Bex stopped the phaeton in front and jumped from the
phaeton. "There are people inside. I hear their screams."

She heard it, too, and they'd parked behind Papa's big
carriage.

Before she could say anything, Bex had run straight for the
warehouse door. He aided other men trying to get it open.

"Bex!" Ester went as close to her husband as she could. "My
father's in there."

Bex turned to her. His face was grim, nothing lit his eyes, just
the reflection of the fire. "It's jammed. A beam may have fallen.
Stand back."

As if he had superhuman strength, he started to ram the door. With the same shoulder he'd hurt on their trip, he hit the doorframe until it began to creak. Others joined in.

The door began to yield.

"Stand back, Ester. I'll get him."

Paralyzed in fear, she couldn't move away. Her father was in there. His workers were in there. Her childhood home was consumed in flames.

Bex and the men finally broke through. A cloud of black smoke poured out, and the heat, the heat, singed the air about her.

Powerful arms wrapped around her and carried her to the phaeton. "Stay this time, Ester."

Before she could cry, plead, or mumble, Bex ran inside as men, coughing, fighting for air, staggered out.

Neighbors started coming with buckets of water. Everyone seemed to want to help, but she just sat there, hoping Papa and Bex would be well.

Minutes passed.

Nothing. Hungry scarlet flames danced on the roof. She jumped down again and went halfway. The opening billowed. Nothing could be seen in the black smoke.

Then Bex came out.

His face and coat were covered in ash, but he dragged Papa with him.

Her father's grooms, the men he paid, reached them at the same time she did.

Bex laid Papa on the ground. She hugged her father's neck, but part of his face had been burned. Red scars covered his jet countenance.

Papa said nothing, but he gripped Bex's hand.

"Sir, I'm going back for that last man."

"No," Papa said, struggling to breathe. "He dead...already."

Bex turned and went back to the opening. "Got to save 'em. Won't let them kill him."

"Bex, wait!" she called to him. "It's too dangerous."

His face was blank, ghostly. "Not another man can be lost. No more being tossed overboard."

He charged back in.

She rose to go after him, but her father grabbed her arm. He coughed and coughed but still had a bear's strength in his palm. "Too dangerous, girl."

A doctor-looking man had started poking at Papa when Phineas the reporter showed up. "Where's Bex?"

"Don't be useless. The man who saved your life tonight keeps going back into the burning building."

Phineas jumped down from his horse and tossed the reins through the phaeton's big wheel. "He saved me. I'll save him."

The man charged into the structure that was spewing ebony smoke. A window exploded, showering glass like snow.

The flames belched with a new explosion on the roof. The rooms upstairs collapsed, taking her old home. Now the fire would take her husband.

Why hadn't she told Bex she loved him?

Why was the man so determined to get himself killed? She looked at Papa, the doctor ripping away his fine coat to get to the burns on his arms and chest.

Bex had saved Phineas and Papa, two men who hated him. Two men Bex felt were his brothers.

The scent of ash closed in upon her. Nausea burned her throat. She'd lost Bex, for how would he be lucky enough to make it out a second time?

• • •

Arthur yanked his cravat off and covered his nose. The thick, heavy smoke made it difficult to breathe. He heard someone calling him his nickname. Telling him to get out of the hull. He couldn't heed. No one could be lost. Not one.

"Bex, get out of here! Anybody left in here is dead."

The voice wasn't Uncle Bexeley. It had to be one of his murderous crew members. "There are men to save. Men are not cargo or ballast. Men! Tell Bexeley he's wrong. Tell my uncle, he's wrong."

"Bexeley? Who is that, Bex?"

Arthur moved from the ghost voice and fought deeper into the flames. He saw a figure on the floor. "See, there's one you haven't tossed away. I'll save him."

Dropping to his knees, Arthur crawled to where a beam had fallen and pinned the man. Arthur pushed, his fingers circling the crumbling girth of the wood. The sky moaned above, dropping wood around him.

"Bex, you're going to take the rest of this roof off if you move that beam." The ghost touched the imprisoned man's neck. "He's dead, Bex. It's too late."

Choking on the air, Arthur couldn't quit. "Get up, man. I won't let them toss you away. Get up."

The ghost clawed at the man's sleeve until his dark wrist

showed. "See, Bex. There's no pulse."

"I just have to get this beam from him. Can't you see it's chaining him in place?" Arthur lifted with all his might, but he couldn't get the beam free.

Someone caught him by the coat. "Bex, the place is about to fall in. That man is already lost."

They'd killed another one.

Another man had died, and Arthur couldn't stop it. He couldn't breathe. He coughed on foul air and drowned in the sense of loss.

Phineas shook Bex hard. He was the ghost following him. "Come out of it, man. You're in shock."

"Not on the *Zhonda*."

He shook Arthur again. "You're playing a role, or you've hit your head. You're not on a boat. You're at the warehouse on the Lower Thames."

Angered, he punched at Phineas. "It's a trick. You'll say anything. But I saw the cargo hull. I saw the men chained in there. I won't let you kill any more."

Arthur turned back to the fallen man pinned by debris. He clawed at the beam. Char broke free and flaked in his hands.

"Bex, you have to go." This new voice sounded loud and strong behind him. Not a ghost. A woman's cry. It wound its way to his heart and made it beat faster. "But the men?"

"Bex. I love you. I'll die with you, then. If I can't convince you to come out, then I won't go, either. It's Ester, Bex. Whatever dark place you are, come back to me. You never wanted me hurt. Save me, save you."

Arthur came to himself. His wife was in danger. "Save you,

Ester?" He scooped her up in his arms.

Phineas yanked on his sleeve. "This way, Bex. The whole place is going to fall any minute."

It was the reporter, the one who'd been a pest, the one whose life he'd saved at the park. He wanted to turn back, but there was nothing but flames, the stench of choking death coming to take Ester. Arthur had to trust his enemy to get his wife to safety. He trudged forward.

Ester's coughing became worse, but she clung to his neck.

The heat. The smell of sulfur and burning flesh almost over-took him before seeing the light. They made it to the doorway.

He set Ester's feet down but turned back to the flames.

She put her hands about his waist and held him. "I can't lose you, Arthur Bex. I can't lose you. You want to save others. Sometimes, you have to save yourself. Papa won't let his grooms leave, not until he knows you've come out."

Bex looked at the man stretched out on the sidewalk and Phineas waving him forward.

Coughing, he took a step over the threshold and then another.

"Come on, Bex."

Heart beating fast. The smoke swirling about his eyes. His fingers slacked away from hers.

The warehouse collapsed, sending fumes to suffocate him. He dropped to his knees looking for the sky. Air couldn't get to him and smoke filled his lungs.

Arthur fell flat on the sidewalk.

CHAPTER NINETEEN

Saving All My Love

Ester soaked in the deep copper tub. She was home in Nineteen Fournier, at her parent's house, in the bathing chamber upstairs. The acanthus carving in the upper molding had been finished, as if to say, *Welcome home, conquering hero.*

But Ester was no hero.

She was a lucky fool who'd almost lost the two most important men in her life, two men she'd held in bondage, not forgiving them for things that didn't matter.

She pushed at the water; the lilac soap wafted about her, relaxing her taut muscles, but her fears wouldn't quit. Papa grew worse, his speech had become more difficult by the time they'd put him in his carriage, and her husband hadn't yet awakened.

They'd cut away Bex's shirt, cleaned a wound to his shoulder, and he'd just lain there, motionless.

She had sat with him as long as she could in the guest bedchamber before Mama and the doctor kicked her out, fearing she'd faint from fretting. Bex wasn't a pale man. His skin was swarthy and tanned from the sun, but now he was so gray. He must've breathed in so much smoke, too much smoke.

Ester lay her head back and let the warmth of the metal work on the knots in her shoulders. Mrs. Fitterwall had made the water extra hot. That was good. The steam could hide the path of her tears.

The door to the room opened. Ester ducked for a moment before remembering she was home at Nineteen Fournier, not in some shared public place.

Mama came inside. Her perfect mobcap topped her perfect curls and a sweeping pale pink robe. But Mama's lips held an imperfect half smile, and her eyes were red like rubies.

The muscles in Ester's stomach tightened. "Is Papa better?"

Mama shook her head. "The doctors are still with him. Seems your husband lifted a beam off him before carrying your father to safety. The beam did damage to Josiah's hip." Mama's voice sounded wet with tears. "He may never walk again."

Ester dropped her gaze to the sudsy water, for if she kept glancing at her mother she'd cry. Holding her knees, she tried to breathe evenly. "Thank you for letting me and Bex stay the night. I couldn't handle things alone at his flat in Cheapside. I wouldn't know what to do."

"My, my, Cheapside." Mama sat near and began unpinning Ester's hair. "There's soot in your hair. I'm sure you could handle anything. You're strong."

"No, I'm not. I'm a horrible failure. My marriage is a horrible failure."

Stoic Mama snapped a tendril, and it hurt. "What? That man, Bex, may have saved your father and some of his workers, but if he's been mean to you, I'll fix him good while he sleeps. I'll show you—"

"No, Bex is very sweet to me, but he takes unnecessary risks, and he refuses to tell me things he knows will upset me."

Mama unwound the chignon but left the braid intact. "You married a man, Ester. Not a little boy to shape his mind, or a puppy to tell him what to do. That willingness to take risks saved your father."

Ester knew that, but it still didn't make the knots in her stomach go away. She hit at the water. Suds, sweet lilac smelling suds, landed on her nose. "Yes. For that I am grateful, but he could've died there or at the abolition rally."

"It's been in the papers for two years, the great actor's fight for abolition. How did you miss it? Your father says you two have been sneaking about for two years. You should've known." Mama put fluffy white towels from a shelf closer to the tub. "Surely, you talked of it. Or did you do other things to pass the time."

There was tension in her mother's voice that sounded of hurt. Ester and her mother had problems, but she needed to know the truth. Truth was everything. "Mama, the two years I told Papa was an exaggeration, to make him feel cheated as I had felt when I found those letters."

Mama took a whole breath, maybe her first deep one since entering the room. She lifted the edge of the towel and wiped Ester's nose. "The sneaking was a lie to punish your father more. We've been through this. That's my business."

"I know, Mama. I know that now. I've been watching Bex on stage for two years and loved him from afar. We didn't meet until Theodosia's wedding, but I was too shy to say anything to him then. We met again the day of your party. The elopement was planned then."

Mrs. Fitterwall sailed into the room. She brought a comb and the jar of coconut oil. "Your chignon is horrid, Mrs. Bex. That won't do. Mrs. Croome, I burned that burgundy carriage dress of hers like you asked. It was threadbare and smelled of burned tar."

Covering up, Ester ducked further into the tub. She was tender-headed, and she dreaded the heavy-handed woman combing through her knotted tresses. Though, that would be a fitting punishment.

"I'll do my daughter's hair, Mrs. Fitterwall."

Ester's eyes went wide. She blew air out her mouth and re-laxed again. Though her hair was thicker and curlier than Mama's straight locks, Mama knew how to handle it without whipping through it as if it were a horse's mane. "Mrs. Fitterwall, has Mr. Bex awakened? I left him with Clancy when the physicians came."

"That's a brave one, there. But no, no change. Just snoring away, even as we scrubbed the soot from him. That made the snores worse." The woman offered a smile, maybe of sympathy, but those happy noises were the only reason Ester had left his side. It meant he was safe, and alive, and she could still get to him.

Mrs. Fitterwall went to the door. "The doctors gave Mr. Croome more laudanum. He's resting more comfortably."

Mama nodded as the housekeeper left them alone. She started undoing the braid Frederica had whipped together. "You met and convinced him to run off. Did you throw him hopes of a dowry? He's an actor. I doubt he has much."

"He lives comfortably, but he was in want of a wife. I came up with an idea from your papers, reading advertisements for husbands. I thought that might be a way to help my friends. They were both in need of marriages of convenience."

"Advertisements in the paper?" Mama sighed heavily. "What of their connections, their families, their races? Was none of that a consideration? Anyone who can read could respond? And if someone figured out that Blackamoor women of means were using the papers, they could be nasty. It could be very unsafe. For one talking about avoiding risks, you certainly have allowed your friends to take them.

Ester hadn't thought about that.

She was lucky that Bex hadn't been vicious. He was far from it. "Frederica Burghley had been corresponding with him. They were to meet for the first time the day of your party, the day Papa announced he'd arranged for me to marry Jordan. When Frederica saw it was Bex she had been corresponding with, she gave him to me. Bex and I, more so I, cooked up the elopement." She grabbed her Mama's hand. "It was never meant to hurt you."

"Meaning and doing are two different things." Mama pushed Ester's hand back into the water and kept working through her hair, holding the tendrils at the root to keep from tugging too hard. Mama knew how to get things done without hurting.

Ester realized that now. Her heart sank to the bottom of the wide tub, soaking up more sorrow like a sponge. "Mama, I'm so sorry."

"I know. I am sorry, too. I should've let you see that I'd take care of you." Mama continued brushing, then massaged her tresses in the soap until the scent of ash had gone away. "Let me go get some water to rinse you, then I'll oil down to the root."

Her mother's footsteps faded, and Ester was alone again, with all her doubts and fears. Yes, Bex had lived through tonight's misadventures, but could she live with him always taking such chances with his life?

Tears fell, plopping from her chin to drop into the water, and Ester wanted to blame the soap dripping from her hair, but this sob was all the thoughts in her head of how he could be hurt. Her tears kept falling, more than could be counted.

Her mother returned, carrying a yellow bundle of satin and another bottle in her hands. Mrs. Fitterwall bounced behind her with a shiny pitcher.

The housekeeper dumped the picture of warm water over Ester as Mama worked it through the curls.

"There you go, squeaky clean. Let's get you out," Mrs. Fitterwall said.

"Not so fast," Mama said. "I have to oil her scalp. Ester will dry out faster than anything."

Mrs. Fitterwall nodded and yawned. "If you don't need anything further, ma'am, I am going to turn in."

"I can handle Ester. You rest well. Tomorrow will be another hard day. Mr. Croome's recovery will be long."

The red-headed sprite yawned again. "God bless him. He's a good employer. He'll be a good father-in-law, so don't be breaking his heart again."

"That's enough, Mrs. Fitterwall. Rest well."

The housekeeper nodded and left the room.

"Mama, Mrs. Fitterwall is right. I hurt Papa, and I hurt you, too."

Her mother said nothing and opened a jar of the coconut oil, a rich cream she'd made from mashing up the insides of the big nut. She rubbed it into the parted locks, baptizing her scalp in the sweet scent, then towel-dried the hair. "There, let's get you out of this tub."

Ester rose and stepped from the tub into the soft white towel, but more so into Mama's arms. She clung to her, hoping the unsaid words in her soul touched her mother's.

"Here, Ester, put lotion on your knees and ankles. You

always forget."

"Mama, will you ever forgive me for eloping? For not respecting you?"

The woman walked to the small table she'd set her bundle upon. With golden rings glistening, she undid it. "It's amazing that you want forgiveness just for asking, yet you punished me for forgiving your father. He asked to be forgiven, his sorrow was true, and I forgave him. I believe he knew what it meant to hurt me. Funny, your Bex saved your father and his workers. Not once did he ask your father for Josiah's sorrow in threatening to shoot a hole through him. You might learn something from Bex."

"Mama, I—"

"Put more lotion on those ankles. Otherwise, you'll ruin this." Her mother held up the softest yellow nightgown. She walked back to her and helped Ester into it. Then she tied a bow under her bosom with the sash of the matching robe.

"This is beautiful. Mama, is this one of yours? Did the seamstress make it too short for you?"

"No dear. I had it made for you when we returned."

That was after her parents had disowned her. "I don't deserve this."

Mama kissed her brow. "I was angry at you. But nonetheless, Ester Bex, never ever forget that you will always be Ester Croome, one of the daughters I love."

She touched Ester's elbow that showed beneath the puffed sleeve of the fairy-like nightgown. "You always miss your elbows—dry and ashy."

Water streamed down Ester's face, harder than before. The deep, ugly cry only stopped when she was in her mother's embrace again. "You don't mind that Bex is my choice?"

Mama's light gold fingers gripped Ester's olive ones. "If his hands are the one you want on you, and if those hands treat you well, then he's my choice, too. Your husband has awakened. He asked for you. If you go to him tonight, tell him he is welcome in this home."

Her mother went to the door and grasped the knob. "Your husband's waking up in a strange place. The doctor said he'd uttered some strange things, but will be fine, and we'll pray that your father will be fine, too. Good night, Ester."

Mama left the chamber, and the soft close of the door took all of Ester's strength. She sobbed anew. Her stomach ached at how deeply she'd wounded the woman and how great was her forgiveness. It wasn't weakness to forgive. Maybe someday she'd be as strong as Mama. Maybe she could start now, by forgiving Bex.

She slipped into the hall. The house was quiet. A sconce flickered, but nothing else moved. The grandfather clock began to chime, bellowing up to her on the third floor. It had to be midnight.

For a second, Ester thought about going to her room—her canopied bed with the perfect pillows and satin ribbon trim—but she couldn't hide from Bex. That's what scared little girls did.

The clock tolled. It was after midnight. Fairy tales ended at midnight. She needed to see Bex and discover if the love she felt— that feeling that maybe he loved her, too—was still there.

• • •

A door shut. Arthur rolled over, smelling coconut. He just had to accept that he'd lost his mind for good this time.

"Bex?"

A match struck, chasing the sweetness away with rotten-egg sulfur.

Then the glow of a candle made his eyes blink, but he promptly sealed them. "Doctor, I'm no longer beside myself. There's no need to be concerned."

Soft footsteps continued, then stopped a few feet away. "Let your wife be the judge of that."

Eyes opening fully, he sat up. "I thought that Clancy had returned to scrub on me some more, or the doctor, to see if I had my wits." He smiled at this angel in yellow leaning against the bedpost. Her locks were free, moist, taking the shine of the candles—something to be touched. "Ester, it's late. You should rest after the night I've put you through."

"It's after midnight, Bex. The best things happen then."

"At least five after. I remember." With his thoughts running wild, he coughed and lay back down, turning his head into the pillow. "How's your father?"

"He's in pain. Mama says the doctor has him on laudanum."

"I'm sorry, Ester. Mr. Croome is a strong man. I'm sure he'll recover."

She came closer and put her hand to his cheek. "Will we recover?"

He wove his fingers between hers. "I'd like to think so. You look wonderful, like an angel."

Her laugh was easy, unhurried, and it lingered in his ear. "Well, I had another hot bath."

"I'm so sorry that I took something that makes you so happy and used it to deceive you."

"I know, Bex."

"Baths make you happy and forgiving. I'll buy you one for your own use. I'll even fetch the bath water."

"Will that put Jonesy out of a job, Mr. Bex?"

Now was Arthur's turn to laugh, but the rumble hurt his chest. "No. Someone that loyal will always be with me."

His eyes were heavy, and it still hurt to breathe. He lifted a hand to scratch his chin and slapped himself with the bandage on his palm. Peeking at her, he saw her face blank, lines growing on her creamy forehead. "It's not as bad as it seems. Barely hurts."

Ester picked up his palm and cradled it to her bosom, his finger tangled in her flowing robe. Soft and smooth, the material swirled about her, like a river around her mountains of curves.

"If you're going to tell me not to fret, that won't work. I'm beyond fretting, Bex. I'm frightened. You could've been killed twice tonight."

"I have but one life to give."

"No lines. No Shakespeare."

"That's Nathan Hale, Ester."

"You know what I mean, Bex."

"No, Ester. No, I don't know what you mean. I want you to call me Arthur to reflect a newfound closeness in our relationship. You still say Bex."

"It's the name I've loved since I first saw you on stage." Sinking onto the bed, she sat beside him. "It's just so natural to say."

"I'm not that man. That's an actor, Ester."

"One who likes a clean room, one that's stubborn and too clever for his own good."

"Maybe you prefer the actor. His lines are scripted. He'll always do and say what's written on the pages."

She put her soft lips on his knuckles before returning his hand. "I don't want paper. I want my husband who is kind. So kind to Jonesy, to even my father, and to me."

"It's easy to be nice to you. You're easy on me, Ester."

"When you first woke up, you said some strange things. The doctor had to convince you that you weren't on a boat. Was it a role? For when were you ever on a boat?"

She had to know. It was time. He closed his eyes again. "A long time ago. I was on a boat. My uncle's boat."

She kissed his cheek.

He wanted to pull away, but it was her mouth, soft and plump like a juicy pear pressing against him. It had a hold on him. He needed to tell her why he had to fight for abolition and why he almost died trying to save a dead man. "I can take critics and sneaky reporters thinking ill of me, but not you. Not now or ever." He pulled her closer. "Ester, you're not twenty-one."

"That'll be in three weeks."

"Your parents could withdraw their consent, and we could annul this marriage."

Her face became blank as she stepped backward. "Lie to the world? Never. My parents were there, Bex. They are the reason we married. You don't want to be married anymore?"

"I want you, Ester." He gazed at her, focusing on the lips he needed to claim and the waist meant for his hands to cling to. "In every sense of the word, I want you, but I'm not the man you want me to be. I cannot give up fighting for causes to secure your love. To do so makes me a bigger fraud than I already am."

"I am in love with you, Arthur Bex. That's no lie."

He reached up to smooth the lines on her forehead, but she was out of reach. "Those marks will become permanent if you continue to fret. That's a crime for someone so young, so beautiful."

With a shake of her head, she turned to the window. She opened the curtains, letting the moonlight inside. It shadowed her, her curves, her fine neck, and rich skin. "A rose by any name is still a rose. Bex or Arthur, it is all you. I'll practice saying Arthur. Arthur. Arthur. I know you were confused by the fire, but don't be confused in what I am saying. I'm in love with you."

If her logic were true, then he'd be free to love her, but it wasn't. His past would always be looming, waiting to destroy all they built. He sighed, inhaling her lilac that remained on his fingertips. The hunger inside to be loved like she claimed overpowered all but his reason. It was good that she stood inches away, far out of his reach. He stroked his nose. "I'll make you miserable. You'll always be concerned that I'll become injured or killed."

"Maybe you are right." She offered a yawn and started for the door.

His gut twisted, wringing with a sense of loss. He'd pushed her away. That made his insides cave in.

Then she turned at the bedpost.

She took off her robe, exposing more of herself, more of her waist, the full bosom, her thicker hips. She hung the satin on the footboard. Whipping back the heavy blanket and sheet, she climbed in the bed and laid her head beside him, against his shoulder.

Her locks smelled of coconut. Her skin was perfumed with lilac. "What are you doing?" His voice sounded hoarse, almost a toad's croak. "In a place this big, don't you have your own room?"

"I do, on the third floor, with a beautiful view of Fournier Street. But my place is here with my husband. I've one roommate, and he's here. We've slept in the same bed since we wed. Will you deprive me of enjoying the heat of you? I need to hear your snores. Don't deny me the shiver when my palm feels the rhythm of your heart."

His shy Ester put her hand to the nightshirt he wore. The fine silk was probably one of her father's.

"Bex, I need to hold you. I need to remind myself that you're here and alive."

With her pinkie, she circled his heart.

The thing beat for her like it had for no one else.

A sharp release of air left his lungs when she moved away.

With those soft lips puckered, she blew out the candle she'd lit. Then she settled onto her side of the mattress, inches away.

Coconut and lilac, her heady scent had control of him. He reached for her, and she fell in his arms.

"Move from me, Bex, if you don't love me. I know you, Arthur Bex. With every inch of my heart, I love you, and I know you love me, too. If I'm wrong, you have permission to move."

"I need permission to sleep in this bed? I was here first."

She lifted her face from his chest and stroked each nostril with her thumb. "I know you, Arthur Bex, better than I know myself, but sometimes the talking has to stop."

That's all he ever wanted, for someone to believe in him. "But Ester. I have to tell you—"

"*Shhh*." She put a finger upon his mouth. "I know, and I love you, too."

Ester was right. He loved her, more than he thought possible. He reached for her and took her lips.

It wasn't a slow kiss.

Not one for good night.

It was one of forever, with her trembling in his arms, her wantonly stealing his breath, with her taking everything he had to offer and more.

Nightshirt gone.

Nightgown floated away.

Nothing mattered. He'd be Arthur Bex for her forever. For that man was loved beyond belief and had a temptress, a warrior, a caregiver, and a lover melting in his embrace.

CHAPTER TWENTY

Get Your Newspaper

The sound of rain splashing the windowsill made Ester awaken. Her eyes were tired from too much watching Bex, too much not sleeping. She stretched and found the bed empty. That saddened her. She wanted to see him smiling at her again. Maybe he'd say aloud the whispers that nipped her ear. Snuggling his pillow, she pressed it against her bosom with her heart racing at the memory of him, the thought of his touches. The scent of ash and pine soap were faint, but the memories of his arms holding her, of him breathing life into her—those were vivid and warm.

The door opened, and she shrank into the bedsheets to cover her bare shoulders.

"Mrs. Bex, I thought you up," Mrs. Fitterwall said as she walked in with a green silk gown in one hand and a poppy-colored one in the other. "I am here to draw you a bath. Mr. Bex said that a warm tub was your favorite, as if I didn't know that."

Ester sighed with relief that it wasn't her mother coming to wake her. Though she was married, she'd die of embarrassment if Mama had barged in upon her. Fishing for her robe with her toe, she seized it and pulled it on. "Is it drawn already?"

"No, Mr. Clancy will bring the copper tub here. I'm going to fetch the hot water. You just need to relax and decide which dress you wish to wear." The woman laid the beautiful morning gowns on the bed then dashed out the door.

Ester scrambled to her feet and wrapped her sash about her

tightly. She formed a bun of her hair. The locks that Bex didn't seem to tire of sinking his fingers into were wild and frizzy. A stiff brushing was in order.

A knock on the door made her dizzy. Was it Bex come to kiss her good morning? "You may enter." She said, hoping her voice sounded dignified, not lost in love.

Clancy came into the room with another servant hoisting the metal tub. They set it down by the fireplace.

The housekeeper waited on the threshold until the men were done, then she brought in a bucket of hot water.

Clancy came back in with another bucket. The cheery smile she was used to seeing on him was missing. In fact, his long face had a frown. "Clancy what is wrong? Is Papa worse?"

He looked at Ester then toward the housekeeper. "An actor up in these parts. He should go back to his own."

Mrs. Fitterwall gave him a frown, her lips looking as if she'd pressed them flat between book pages. "I suppose that you don't want me here."

"No, you're different. You're one of us. You know the struggle. What does London's most famous actor know?"

It was good Clancy stepped away, for if he was closer, both Ester and Mrs. Fitterwall would have hit him.

"Mrs. Bex," the housekeeper said as she moved to the door. "Your father is still in a great deal of pain. There's no improvement."

Ester clutched the post. How could she be so happy with her father doing poorly? "Perhaps Mr. Bex and I should stay while he recovers."

"I'll be back in an hour to help you dress. Enjoy your bath." Mrs. Fitterwall handed Ester her soap and fresh towel, then swept from the room.

Ester grew happy inside as she looked at the heat rising from the water. She was back home with her family, like nothing had happened, except Bex was here, too. Would he want to stay? Would his man's mind want to be on his own, back in Cheapside?

Part of her wanted to dress and find him, but maybe he'd see that she—that *they*—needed to be here. She kneeled beside the tub and dipped her finger inside, making rings and hearts, soaking her whole hand in the warmth. Surely, Bex had to love her to be so thoughtful. Why else would he draw a bath for her?

Unless it was to distract her.

Had he gone again, or was he like Ruth's beaux, bedding her just to leave her?

All the happy feelings inside her began to disappear.

No. She shook her head. She'd trust him. They'd found each other last night. Nothing would change that. They'd started their marriage again holding on to each other in arms of love. She wasn't going to stop trusting her husband after she'd given herself totally to him.

Ester would enjoy her bath, then take her time to dress and keep hoping that Bex was worthy of her trust. She stroked the hot water and made suds with her soap. She sighed, hoping the hot water and lilac scent would wash away the fear drowning her heart.

• • •

Arthur stood outside the door to the bedroom chamber. He'd walked Nineteen Fournier up and down, feeling every inch the heel. He'd given in to love, the desire to have Ester, but he'd done so without giving her the one thing she'd ever wanted. Truth.

But that ended now.

He opened the door, and as he'd hoped, Ester was in the tub. Her beautiful neck craned against the side. Beads of moisture dripped from her chin. Suds obscured the best view a man with hands could ever want. "Ester?"

She opened her topaz eyes and smiled. "You're here and safe."

"Of course. I'm done going into burning buildings for now."

"And how about rallies?"

"Ester, I won't lie or trick you. Not after today. I have to tell you what I started to say last night."

She turned away and looked toward the fireplace. "You don't, Bex. Not if it's going to steal us. We're happy right now. Maybe I don't need to know, ever."

Arthur went in front of her and sat so they were almost eye-to-eye, he at the hearth, she pulling as many suds over her décolletage as possible. "Ester, I'm not Arthur Bex."

Her fingers gripped the sides of the tub. Her beautiful face looked so pained. "Then who did I marry? Who did I consummate a marriage to? A stranger?"

"My name is Oliver Arthur Bexeley."

"You changed it for the stage. That's common." She sighed and smiled. "That's nothing."

"I changed it because of my uncle. Oliver Bexeley. The captain of the *Zhonda*."

Her eyes grew large. It looked like she wasn't breathing. "Not the monster, the ship captain who threw twenty-five enslaved men overboard to collect insurance money?"

"Yes, but it was closer to fifty men."

"Fifty." She fell back in the tub. Water splashed out wetting the rug. "Fifty men."

"Yes. Fifty enslaved men."

"Do you know what the *Zhonda* means to my family, to my mother? It carried her family from Africa to be enslaved in Jamaica. Someone that shares my blood, her blood, could have been one of those fifty men."

He cupped his brow, the weight of his guilt, the weight of the sadness in her eyes smashing against him. "I was on the *Zhonda* since I was six, as Uncle's cabin boy. I knew something wasn't right with the cargo. Not the way his crew joked about. Not the way Uncle Bexeley made sure I didn't watch the loading. I know I was young, but if I had bothered to look, or hadn't loved the bliss of ignorance, I could've said something that could've stopped him."

"But you were six."

"Twelve is the age of reason, Ester. I was twelve on the Zhonda's last trip. I finally saw the cargo, all those poor bound men. I tried to stop them, but nothing would stop my uncle and the crew from tossing the cargo. I saw men, not cargo, screaming as they sank."

"Mama." She put her hand to her mouth and covered a scream. "How could I have brought a killer's nephew into this house? I married a slaver's nephew."

He hung his head. "Yes, Ester, that is true."

"You lied to me, Bex. When Mama discovers this, she'll toss you out. Don't give her the trouble. You leave now."

He stood up, his limbs still shaky. "I didn't tell you. I'm sorry for that. I left my past behind. I put it away and became Arthur Bex. Now that you know, the past has nothing more to do with us."

She shook her head. "The past is the best indication of the future."

"I am not a slaver, Ester."

"No, but that's why you fight for abolition. Do you think your sacrifice makes up for all that was lost? Is that why you chose to marry a Blackamoor? Doesn't it burnish your credentials? Wait until the world learns of your little wife. 'Good for you, Bex,' they'll say, and won't think another moment of those that were lost by the *Zhonda*—all the pain, all the loss it caused."

"It wasn't like that. I wanted a wife who would believe in me, who could love me despite my past."

She wiped at her face as sloppy tears fell, ones he couldn't wipe away. He couldn't touch her. Not now. She hated him...like he hated himself.

"Did it bring you some type of joy lying to the world about who you are? Did it make you feel special to trick me into marrying you, the daughter of an enslaved woman to the nephew of a slave-killer?"

"No. Ester, inside, I'm the same man you said you loved. The same man who cradled you in his arms last night. Does a name change that?"

"Lies do. Do you think I would've married you if I had known? I'm not a trophy to assuage your family's guilt. I wouldn't hurt my mother like this."

He stood, turning away to the roaring fire. "Ester, I'm in love with you—funny, headstrong you. The fact that you are

Blackamoor and I'm not did not matter to me. *You* matter. The hope of having someone to believe in me, to build a family with to replace the one I lost. That's what I see when I look at you."

But her gaze held loathing and contempt. "Bex, Bexeley. I'm a Blackamoor woman. A proud one. One who will not sweep a lie under the rug. One untruth begets another. I won't live like that. I won't be a bathtub woman who looks the other way. I need you to leave here."

Her breath was ragged. She was as affected by him, by the love between them that couldn't be denied, as he. "If you had known, you wouldn't have married me, and I'd never have known true happiness. For that, I'll never be sorry."

"You didn't give me the chance, Bex-Bexeley. I know the difference between an actor and a slaver. The man who deserves my love should've trusted me enough to tell me the truth."

"I lost everything once because of the truth. Ester, I wasn't prepared to lose you."

"You have. If you'd told me, I could've chosen. We could've reasoned through this, but you took that from me. We married under false pretenses."

"You don't mean that."

"The name on the certificate. Is it Bex or Bexeley?"

"It's Bex. That is the name I have chosen, the name I am known by."

"That is fraud, Oliver Arthur Bexeley."

He turned and walked to the door. "Then you do have a choice. You can have this marriage dissolved, just as I suggested before we consummated it last night. You remember, Ester, being with me, loving me fully and completely. That's what you said.

Was that a lie?"

She sank into the tub, splashing water his way. "Go."

"I'll agree to whatever you want. I thought we were good together. I still believe that." He put his hand on the doorframe and turned to look upon her one more time—wet glistening skin, tears flowing. "Ester, I can't change the past, but I won't let you enslave me to it. I've done that enough to myself. I should've told you, but this mistake doesn't change a moment we spent together, or how I feel about you. Know that no man will ever treasure how your lips part when you smile, the crinkles in your forehead when you fret, or the low moan in your voice when you're kissed well— not like me."

"But who are you? What's tomorrow's lie?"

"The one I sign to annul this marriage and accept your wishes." Gut shredding, Arthur left the room and plodded down the stairs.

Clancy stood at the entry. He picked up Arthur's hat and held it out. "There's a reporter here for you, a Mr. Phineas. He wants to talk about the fire, but I wouldn't let him in."

Arthur took the tall-crowned felt hat and slapped it on his head. "Tell Mrs. Croome and Mrs. Bex I'll do my best to keep things out of the papers."

The butler shook his head. "Actor people. You know she's too good for the likes of you."

"It doesn't make me love her any less." Arthur took a deep breath and marched outside.

Phineas was sitting on the steps. "The butler wasn't letting me in to get a statement about the warehouse fire. I thought maybe you'd give me one."

The last thing the Croomes needed was to be dragged into the papers. "Phineas, I have a better story for you. One that should've been told by now. But for the exclusive, you have to leave the Croomes out of the paper."

"I have to investigate the fire, but I'll protect them as much as I can. You have my word on this. But what is your story? And why do you look like your best friend died? Is Mr. Croome—"

"If you want the scandal of the season, follow me to my flat. I'll tell you everything."

Arthur walked down Fournier Street to the mews. It was time to stop living a lie, and if he could tell his scandal without hurting the Croomes, he would. The pain of his past, of hiding, was nothing to the gut punch of losing Ester, the woman he loved.

CHAPTER TWENTY-ONE

What Light Breaks a Heart?

A knock woke Ester from her light sleep. Her bedchamber at Nineteen Fournier was dark, only lit by the moonlight. She punched her pillow. It was hard to get comfortable without Bex's shoulder to lie upon or the rumble of his snores teasing her ear.

And she still fretted that he would put himself in harm's way.

Was he well?

Was he out risking his life at more abolition rallies, or running into burning buildings?

Was he sleeping?

Or had the newspaper men robbed him of that?

In the week since she'd asked him to leave, his horrid connection to the *Zhonda* had been printed in every paper. Headlines like WAREHOUSE FIRE CLAIMS LIVES AND UNMASKS HERO were everywhere. The vile Countess Devoors had suggested he, too, was a murderer. Poor Bex.

Ester rolled over but couldn't find comfort. Papa was no better, and Mama had gone silent again, only rousing from her blank-faced knitting to check on Papa or to go with Ester and Mrs. Fitterwall to bring food to the women widowed by the fire.

Heartbroken, unable to sketch anything, she turned over again and put her face in the pillow.

Another tap made the window creak. It sounded as if it would break.

Ester sat up. Her pulse raced. At her window stood a man.

A few blinks revealed a tall, muscular outline, and she struggled to breathe.

Bex. He was outside her third-floor window.

"No." She leaned over and lit a candle then pulled the curtains back fully.

The crazed man was on the ledge. She stared, transfixed, at his lips. He mouthed her name, and she felt his voice rip through her heart, even before she heard it.

He wasn't moving away, and Ester feared he'd fall, so she opened the window.

One of his big legs plowed in first. Then the rest of him in a costume—tights, a pointed hat, and a leather mantle that looked like what he'd worn as Romeo in Shakespeare's play. Had he just left the stage to come to her? "I thought you were to be Antony of *Antony and Cleopatra*?"

He smoothed his rumpled shirt sleeves. "I've a bit part right now. I lost the general's role. It seems the theater owner didn't want a slaver's son in the part.

"You're not that, Bex."

He stepped an inch or two nearer. The heat and hurt in his eyes pained her soul, made her almost pant. "Details don't matter when a scandal is available. This room is very pink. Pink suits you. Yellow does, too. Pity you've taken off your wedding ring." He leaned and spun the gold and emerald band on the coral necklace she wore. "Forget me so soon?"

Like that was possible. She tugged at her salmon-colored nightgown, covering her throat and her vulnerable heart. She wished she had on a robe to hide from his gaze.

But her own expressions probably gave her away, for he was

gorgeous and tall and here. She pinched at her cheeks. "Why have you come?"

"I have returned many times, Ester, but Clancy won't let me past the door. You haven't returned a single note."

"Notes?" She shook her head. "I haven't received any."

"I sent Jonesy. I know he wouldn't deceive me."

His voice sounded accusatory, as if she had, but only one person hadn't been truthful. "Clancy must be trying to protect me, sort of like you, omitting everything to protect me."

"It's not the same. He doesn't love you like I do, and he's never lost everything. At least, I hope that's not his plight. I did want to protect you, and I still am. I've let the dogs have at me, to keep the Croome name out of the papers. There've been only a few lines about the warehouse fire. Nothing at all about our marriage."

"Bex, I look every day for a cartoon or interview about you. I've seen the horrible articles."

He put his arms on her shoulders. "I've sacrificed my privacy for you and the Croomes. It was the least I could do. I want no more harm to touch you. Just me."

His fingers sent a jolt through her limbs. His palms were warm, and she wanted so badly to go back to the night they'd loved each other.

But there was no going back, not for her. She couldn't trust her heart. "Why are you here, Bex?"

"It's after midnight. Our marriage still exists. No legal papers have come, Ester." He brushed a curl of her unbraided hair about his thumb. "I hoped that was a small sign you'd reconsidered. Perhaps you could love me again."

His eyes, hungry and hurt, stole what air she could breathe. He was too close, towering over her.

"Ester, I know we didn't start this marriage right. I should've told you everything. But do you know what it has been like to live in fear that I will say the wrong thing to the wrong person and then be judged to be just like my uncle. I'm still paying for his crimes."

"You know how I live, Bex. I know the fear of saying the wrong thing, but I know more the fear of hoping my loved one comes home. I want to be safe. I want you safe. We can't work."

"But we've found each other, Ester. Can you deny the love that is between us?" He took her palm and placed it against his chest, smoothing it against his leather vest. "I can't sleep without reaching for you. I don't want us to end."

He took the candle from her icy fingers and put it on the sill. "I love you, Ester. Love should conquer all. You're my heart's dearest love."

Oh, no he didn't... Coming here, looking dreamy, twisting up lines of Shakespeare to confuse her—she could do that, too. "Bex-Bexeley? This love is too rash, too unadvised, too sudden. It had no choice to be like lightning, to be a flash then cease to be."

His brow popped above a dark, cobalt-blue gaze. "Why do you want to leave me so unsatisfied?"

She wasn't about to ask, as Juliet would, what satisfaction he wanted, not with him standing so near, so touchable, so desiring of another chance. Ester inhaled deeply, enjoying the scent of sandalwood and ivy vines on his person. "Will you give up rallies and danger? And be a man that I can depend upon? That's the price for my love."

"That's a fine price." He hoisted her high in his arms and kissed her, gently at first, then with an almost ruthless passion that made her cling to him. He was dangerous with two hands, so dangerous.

Clutching at his neck as if nothing in her world was solid or true, she couldn't help but return his kiss. Maybe she wouldn't fret this one night, not like she had without him. "I love you, too."

He scooped her up and made her float in the air. His mouth, so sweet, so set on teasing her lips, never relented. Not a complaint could be uttered, not with his ardor sweeping her away.

With a kiss to her jaw, he settled her on the mattress, his finger dipping into her tresses. "You are beautiful. I've missed you. I love my wife."

Her eyes were wide, anticipating and waiting. "Then commit to me, Bex, and let's live without danger. No more rallies or burning buildings. Then I'm yours. London knows your secret. We don't have to hide. We can build again."

"Is it that easy? I say no rallies, no more fights, and I'll have a wife who loves me?"

"Yes, Bex. Yes." She reached up and took his mouth, wrapped her hands about his neck, intending to never let go.

His kiss was deep, soul stirring, tying tighter the bonds between them, but he stopped and stepped away from her embrace, her bed. "No."

"Bex?"

"It's Arthur." Heaving as much as she from their denied passion, he moved to the window. One leg was out the opening before she could sit up.

"Bex, wait."

"I can't, Ester. I'm not a couch husband, as you defined it, passive, waiting to be told what to do with my passions."

She ran to the window. "But you said you loved me. If that was true—"

"I do, but it's not enough. I'm a man who needs you, who wants to love tenderly and completely, but I have to be a man who can still look in the mirror and respect what he sees. I can't do that by giving up my calling or living half a life because of your fears. You have no faith, Ester. I believe in us, but you don't."

"I have faith, Bex—"

"No, you don't, not in us or me. My bounty is as boundless as the sea, my love for you is deep. I give it to thee and only thee. But it's not enough to pay your price. Good evening, Ester."

"Bex, wait."

He pulled his other leg through and started down the vines. "If you change your mind, come to me in Cheapside. We can begin again. We'll find a way together to make our love last."

Head against the window frame, she watched him and waited until she knew he'd climbed down without falling. Cheated and alone, she bristled and slammed the window shut.

But he was right.

She feared for his safety, like she feared for Papa's. The trip to Gretna Green had shown her how fragile the life she lived truly was and how easily everything could be taken away. If Papa didn't get better, things would change again. Ester had never felt more vulnerable in her life.

She had no faith.

No faith that she could take care of her mother. None that Bex would shy away from danger. None that he'd be happy with just Ester's love. He was a man given to fight, to save someone.

It was wrong to ask him to give up everything, but that was what she needed to feel secure. How else would she?

Somehow, Bex still believed in her, their marriage, or he wouldn't have climbed three stories or denied a passion that she'd regret in the morning.

With a sad sigh, she looked once more to see Bex, but the dark street had swallowed him whole. A glance at the night sky revealed a netting of stars, so many, like when she had eloped. Stars knew how to fly and keep soaring. They had faith.

And Ester was jealous of them for being so easy and light and secure where they lived.

She touched her lips and sank to the floor. Bex's kiss, his respect of her person, had poisoned Ester.

It had.

She was Juliet to him, dying inside, without the hope of holding on to his love, and almost too weak to survive without it. But Ester was her father's daughter, stubborn. She was also her mother's child, so survival was in her blood. She'd find in herself an antidote for wanting Bex. She would, for there had to be a cure.

. . .

Arthur heard the knocking on the door of his flat. In his heart, he hoped it was Ester, that she'd come to forgive him, but two days had passed since he'd climbed in her window. She wasn't coming. His notes weren't being delivered to her. Another desperate visit would come to nothing but frustration.

The knocking persisted.

He leaped up from his desk and opened the door.

Phineas was there, top hat in hand, rolling it between his meaty palms. "Bex."

"Yes, Phineas, was there more you needed? My guts have been spilled all over your parchment."

"I researched what you said to me about the *Zhonda*. Are you sure you want the whole story out?"

Shrugging, Arthur let the man inside. "It's the story you wanted, and it keeps my end of our bargain to keep the Croomes out of the paper."

"I know, Bex, but I owe you my life. I don't want to make things worse."

"Some already call me the son of a slaver. How much worse can things get? I suppose it's better than 'Gunpowder'."

"The story of your testimony at your uncle's trial could change things or make things worse. I don't know how this will play out in London—brave hero or traitor to his flesh and blood."

Arthur folded his arms and leaned against the wall. "I've lost everything, Phineas. But you've held up your promise. I suppose I'm grateful."

"The talk will die down if nothing more is published. Bex, you could take your wife and travel the continent until things are better. How did you meet her, anyway?"

"An advertisement in your paper. Funny. The papers which are ruining me brought us together."

"I wish it could do more to fix things. I saw how she went into that fire after you. She wanted to die with you that night if you wouldn't leave. She truly loves you."

Ester only had strength when she thought him in danger.

Fear was no way to live. "She still reads the paper every day. Maybe I'll place a new advertisement. Perhaps she'll see it and forgive me." He chuckled to keep from grousing on how hopeless everything was.

"If I found a love willing to die for me, I'd do anything to keep her." Phineas went to the door. "This new story will publish in a couple of days. And I'm still looking into the fire. Warehouses don't go up in flames like that. Arson or gross negligence will do it."

Arthur, put a hand on the door. "Just spare the Croomes any more pain."

"I'll do what I can, but the cause has to be known. Bex, you are the one who called on me to do things that actually help."

The man started to turn but stopped. "I went after you because of a perceived injury, but for what it's worth, you were a hero at the warehouse and long ago on a boat and in the courtroom. At twelve, I can't imagine the courage to stand up for what was right."

"I still wonder, if I'd been a more courageous child at eight or ten and discovered that the *Zhonda*'s cargo was men, could I have persuaded my uncle to take a different course."

"Bex, you put too much on yourself, even over thirty."

Staring at Ester's sketchbook on his desk, Arthur shrugged. "We live in the real world, Phineas. I'm gunpowder, and I've burned up everything I've ever cared for. Travel may return perspective or humor."

"But the fight, Bex?"

There wasn't much left in Arthur. Heartbreak and leaving Ester that last time had extinguished much of his flame. "The cause won't have me anymore, nor will any theater. Time and distance is a cure-all. Good evening, Mr. Phineas."

Arthur closed the door. Soon London would see the whole story. Everyone would read it. Everyone including Ester, for she still loved newspapers. Maybe seeing the whole truth would move her.

He pried open his door and chased after Phineas. He did have one more advertisement to place. Maybe a woman as stubborn as himself would read it and regain faith in their future.

CHAPTER TWENTY-TWO

No Happy Birthday

Ester descended the grand stairs. Servants scurried about, readying for the party, but thoughts of her birthday made her head hurt. What type of celebration would it be with her heart in shreds?

Her birthday was two days away, but Mrs. Fitterwall had everything glistening, as if the party was starting within minutes. Remembering how Mama would cut a slice of her cake with Papa at her side made Ester miserable. If Bex-Bexeley hadn't lied, he'd be there, holding her hand, maybe even making some sort of speech, so Papa could rest. He still couldn't walk but a few feet before tiring.

A knock at the entry door brought Clancy from whatever hallway he'd been polishing to open it. "Mrs. Fitzwilliam-Cecil and Miss Burghley."

What a joy it was to see Theodosia and Frederica. Ester needed them to rally her spirits. She almost jumped the final steps and met them in the hall. "Let's go into Mama's parlor."

Trimmed in fine blue, Theodosia entered. Her steps were slow, and her bronze skin had a tinge of green. Odd.

Frederica, in a wonderful chocolate-brown cape, swept off the thing like it was a bad dance partner. Underneath, she wore a pretty peach-colored gown with large pearl buttons lining the front. A shawl like the one she'd given Ester would set her outfit off, but that one was at Bex's residence, with her sketchbook and her heart.

She sighed, depriving her lonely chest of air. "Clancy, can you bring tea and biscuits?"

Theodosia patted her mouth. "Dry toast, if you don't mind."

Her friend looked very green, and not the envious kind. The women wandered into Mama's parlor.

Frederica took a seat on the couch and dove into Mama's pile of newspapers. The headlines—ARTHUR BEX IN HIDING. BEX REPLACED AS THE LEAD IN *ANTONY AND CLEOPATRA*—were in full display. "Your mother loves her papers." She frowned, "I'm very sorry my newspaper advertisement has cost you so much."

To agree was to admit that all her time with Bex was horrid. Far from it. Things had been almost perfect when he was here. One night of not fretting. He'd been safe in her arms. She'd been loved in his. Maybe when he'd returned through yonder window, she should have forgiven him. "It wasn't all bad."

"Have you spoken with Bex?" Theodosia asked as she fanned herself with a foul paper.

"Yes. A week ago." Ester closed her eyes and she remembered the look on his face, leaving through her window. "I...We...We couldn't reconcile."

Clancy came into the parlor with one of his fancy silver trays. Three cups, three saucers, three silver spoons—all for serving Ester and the best friends in the world.

"Mrs. Fitzwilliam-Cecil, there's no dry toast, but Mrs. Fitterwall says crackers are best to calm the baby woes. Shall I bring some?"

Theodosia nodded. "Yes. Please bring me some. I'll try anything."

Clancy made a quick turn and left the parlor.

"Baby?" Ester covered her mouth. Her voice sounded weak and simple. A baby is what happened when a couple was in love.

"Yes. I might be older than you two, but apparently not too old."

Frederica giggled and waggled her thin brows. "Nope, not too old."

Ester froze in her chair. It had been only one night between her and Bex—that couldn't be—no, Theodosia and Ewan had been married at least seven or eight months. Yet, the thought of holding a baby with Bex's eyes wasn't bad. But what would it be like to rock that child, fretting about his father not coming home? She wrapped her hands about her stomach. A baby was a reason to reunite, a sad one if neither could compromise. But would Ester be like her sister, Ruth, having to go to the country to raise a child by herself?

Theodosia put down the paper, flipping it over to page two. "So how long are you going to wait before you respond to Bex's new advertisement?"

What? He hadn't even waited for their marriage to be annulled before he was looking for a new woman? She ripped the pages from Theodosia's fingers and scoured the print. With her finger, she jumped from one advertisement to another until she spied it.

"Humbled man of modest means looking for woman of esteem who must be a Shakespeare lover, lilac wearer, and sketch artist with initials ECB. Inquire in Cheapside." Ester swallowed hard. "The only thing he left out was 'must love baths.' How long has this has been in the papers?"

VANESSA RILEY					633

"A few days," Frederica said. "He still loves you. Don't you love him?"

Clancy returned with a plate of crackers then disappeared again, but not before Theodosia had stuffed two crispy bits into her mouth. "Who needs bonbons when dry, non-nauseating crackers abound?"

"Bonbons are everything." Frederica giggled. "So how long are you going to punish Bex? He made a mistake. He's clearly sorry."

"Why can't he just come, apologize, and say he'll avoid danger?" Ester tossed the paper back to the table. "This is more of a show. He needs a wife to vouch for his character."

Theodosia wiped her mouth of crumbs as she patted the tiny bulge in her abdomen. "The advertisement is cute, maybe even showy, but a man needs to be encouraged. Ester, I know you feel as if he betrayed you, but take it from me. You can't ask him to be less of the man he is. Go hear him out. See beyond your anger. Then let your heart decide."

When her parents had disowned her, he'd said to wait for a proper invitation. Was that what he wanted—for her to say she was wrong first? Ester picked up the paper again, returning to the horrid headline, BEX's SECRET. "How can I trust him again? He's still going to do dangerous things. And what if there is another lie he hasn't set right?"

Frederica grasped Ester's hand. "Faith, even a small bit, is needed for anything. Believe that Bex loves you. I hear love always finds a way."

Ester wanted to believe, but fear held her captive.

Theodosia rose from the chair as if her ankles weighed

hundreds of pounds. "Come on, Frederica. Ewan and your father should be done."

"What are Fitzwilliam-Cecil and the duke doing? That's an odd combination."

"It's for his father, the Earl of Crisdon. Since he's living in town, he's taken up with Simone. They are at his club. Crisdon forced both his sons, Ewan and Lord Hartwell, to attend."

"Is it still awkward, Theodosia?"

"It's getting better. Hopefully, it will get better by Yuletide when Philip gets his new sibling. Hopefully, he'll hear this baby's cries."

Ester hugged her. "Of course he will."

Frederica stacked the papers into a neat pile. "You think we can stop for bonbons? Can't you crave those, just once?"

Rolling her eyes, Theodosia hugged Ester again. "I don't know how she stays rail thin."

Frederica came to the left of Ester and joined in the hug sandwich. "I saw how Bex looked at you at the rally, and I so wish for a man, a decent one, to look at me like that. He's in love with you. Stubbornness or fear can make you miss your chance at happiness."

"I'll think upon it, but wear something fabulous for my party. You two will make it special. Maybe you can stand at my side to cut the cake."

Theodosia kissed her brow. "Would never miss it, and we'll be at your side, sharing your joy or pain, no matter your choice."

She gripped each of their hands and walked them to the door. "I've been blessed with the best friends a girl can have. Till the party."

Walking out of the parlor, her friends gathered their things from Clancy and stepped out to Theodosia's waiting carriage.

Ester watched the two-pair, and footmen aplenty, turn the corner. She was alone again. Wandering back to Mama's parlor, she passed Papa's door. No lights were on inside. He still hadn't the strength to be there.

Shoulders drooping, she went inside the parlor and flopped onto the couch. She picked up the stack of newspapers, her mother's personal collection of gossip pages. She flipped past the dreadful headlines and found Bex's advertisement. What must he think of her lack of response?

Mama came into the room with her arms folded across a gown of mourning gray, for the workers lost. Her silky locks were covered in a jet mobcap. "I told Mrs. Fitterwall to put these away."

"No. Please leave them, Mama. I'll do it."

Sitting beside her, Mama held up one of the papers. "There's no mention of the Croomes or your ill-fated marriage."

"Yes," Ester said. "I think we are safe from embarrassment."

"Oh, there's plenty of embarrassment." Her mother stacked the papers. "Arthur Bex is still your husband. That means he's family, and you've sent him away. But that is your business."

Ester sank into the couch. "But you were so quiet. I thought you were disappointed in me for marrying the nephew of a man who helped enslave your family."

Mama folded her arms. Her rings twinkled in the light as she twisted them. "Ester, Bex may be a lot of things, but he's not Captain Bexeley. I haven't disowned Bex, even if you have."

The words stung, but they were true. Ester brushed a loose curl from her braid. "He'll allow me to claim fraud to end this marriage. I don't have to accept his lies. You won't have to think of him as family anymore."

The frown on Mama's face was wider and deeper than she'd ever seen. "I'll send for Papa's solicitor, if that's what you want. That's your business, even if I think it wrong. I owe Bex my peace. I wish him well."

"Mama, what are you talking about? How has Bex given you peace?"

Mama unfolded the pages so that the worst headline, HERO UNMASKED, showed. "Did you read this article?"

"I don't want to read about how Captain Bexeley chose to drown fifty men for insurance money."

"Not even if one was your uncle?

"Papa's brother? No, he was murdered in the streets."

"No, my brother," her mother said. Her soft voice froze Ester's blood.

"How, Mama? What are you saying?"

"Bex is not his uncle. Next to your father, he is the bravest man I know." Mama rose from her chair and went to the closet and pulled out a small box. She sat back down with the wooden thing sitting on her knee. Her jeweled hand rested on the box, and Mama had that distant look in her eye, the one she had sometimes when she knitted.

"I don't want to upset you, Mama. But like you said, Bex is my business."

Ester stood and readied to go back to her room.

"You're stubborn like your father, Ester, but let's hope you don't get so rigid that you become like your grandfather. The man that was my father. He was very stubborn, cruelly stubborn.

Stubborn and wrong."

Blinking, Ester turned back. The woman had never spoken much of her father, just her mother and the enslaved in Jamaica. "Please tell me. Trust me with all of it. I'm strong enough to know."

The woman drummed the box upon her knee. "My mother was taken on the first raid of her village, and she came to Jamaica on the *Zhonda*, probably one of the ship's first voyages. She was sold to my father, who bought her because she wasn't as dark as the rest. He forced her to be his concubine, to give birth to children so he could give them to his wife, who couldn't have none. This man who was evil to the mother who bore me treated me like a full daughter, at first. His wife, Mama Rose, I believed she loved me, too."

A little too stunned to breathe, Ester listened with her whole heart.

"Birthdays were very important to my father. Maybe that's one thing that I hold over from him. He'd parade Mama Rose and me around the plantation. He put his big white hands about us in hugs so tight. So tight."

A hundred questions filled Ester's brainbox, but she saw her Mama's eyes drift, her face paler than ever, so she said nothing.

"He was good to me, but cruel to those darker than me. I tried to unsee his hands, unsee him whipping or nearly strangling his enslaved workers, but I couldn't unsee him slap a woman with my same eyes and my wide nose. That's when the whispers made sense. Maybe, why I pay attention to the gossip now."

"Your true mother?"

Mama rocked and nodded. Her jeweled hands lifted,

blocking some unseen memory from striking, and Ester swallowed tears.

"Father bloodied my mother's face—done with his big hands, his hands. Then I grew older and saw a lot more of what evil his hands, those awful hands, could to do to me. I was my mama, but just white as a ghost. He let me know that."

Ester dropped to kneel at Mama's feet and clasped the woman's fingers so tight, hoping Mama knew she was here, not Jamaica, and Ester had the strength to protect her. "Mama, I'm here. I could get your knitting to draw you back. Stay away from the memories. You've said enough."

"Sometimes, Ester, the fight is in your head. You have to win there to win anywhere."

A full sob broke, twisted free from her gut, deep and pained, and ushered from Ester's lips. She held on to Mama's knees. "I'm so sorry I judged you."

Mama patted Ester's head, smoothing curls. "Some things don't pass so easily." Mama's voice was low, but Ester heard her, and that was all that mattered.

"When your grandfather wasn't around, my true mama told me about her family in Africa who had escaped the *Zhonda* the first time it came. Her baby boy with a star birthmark above his left eye. He was learning to fish when she was taken by the *Zhonda*. Then she grew sick and died. Cholera, I think."

"The *Zhonda*." Ester lifted her head and caught Mama's eyes. "I'm so sick of that name. I wish I'd never—"

"Bex has memories that don't pass so easily. My story is Bex's, too. Mama tapped on the box in her lap. "You must see this. If I hadn't sheltered you and Ruth from these memories, maybe we'd all be stronger."

The box had to be a piece of the puzzle of Mama's story, and Ester held her hand, would hold her hand forever, so her mother would tell her story. "I'm here and I'm listening."

Fast blinking, as if she watched a play with actors in front of her, Mama stared ahead. She twisted a gold ring on her thumb. "My father took us to England. He needed to testify at a trial. A big insurance claim, about his lost shipment on the *Zhonda*. I saw the manifest papers in his things. One of the 'cargo' had a star mark above his eye. It could have been someone else, but in my heart, I knew the *Zhonda* had killed my brother, the last remaining part of my African family. The only part of my family left was an evil father who I thought loved me until he showed me he didn't."

Ester's throat thickened. "Is it Bex's story because of his uncle?"

Mama put a hand to Ester's cheek. "Mama Rose caught me crying. She knew what my father did in secret. She gave me a fist of money and told me to stay in London. She said I could be truly free here. I wouldn't have to fear *his hands* anymore. I took the money and I ran."

"Mama, you just stayed in London, alone? That's terrifying."

"It was, but I wanted freedom more than fear. Ester, it was hard for the first couple of weeks hiding, knowing if my father found me, he'd be so cruel, but I kept up with the trial in the papers to see when he left to go back to Jamaica." She opened the box and pulled out clippings. "I read in one article of a young man, barely twelve years old, who bravely testified against the *Zhonda's* captain, and all the evil the boy saw and tried to stop."

Ester was so shy she couldn't imagine standing up in front of strangers to testify. She drew her arms about her knees. "That's brave for one so young."

"It's worse, Ester. Bex had to testify that his uncle, the captain of the *Zhonda*, the man who'd raised him since he was six, was a killer, ordering the crew to toss my brother and the other men into the ocean to drown. Bex said many still had chains on them. Chains, in the middle of the ocean."

Ester couldn't swallow, couldn't breathe, couldn't imagine the terror of the heavy irons dragging a body down. But she also couldn't imagine the pressure a young, twelve-year-old boy was put under to do what was right.

Bex. Her poor Bex.

She took up the clippings and read the horrible truth, the young boy's terrifying testimony. Ester scooped up the paper that read HERO UNMASKED.

It said very much the same but added that he still struggles with being on that boat from age six, even though he had not known about his brothers' plight in the cargo below. Ester wiped her dripping nose. "Doesn't he know that a six-year-old couldn't have changed grown men?"

"Ester, I don't think anyone has ever told him. He was on that boat. He was almost tossed overboard, trying to reason with the first mate. Bex's account led to the captain's hanging. His uncle's hanging."

Ester picked up the box again and went through the clippings, landing on a caricature of the courtroom with a young boy drawn with slave's shackles labeled *"Zhonda"* about his neck.

Mama wiped at her blank eyes. "The captain was hanged

because of the large-scale fraud he tried to perpetrate on the insurance company, not for the killing of my brother or any of those men. Keep reading the papers. See the interviews of dock workers. They thought Bex a traitor to his own kind. At age twelve he was left all on his own, just for doing what was right."

Bex said that he wanted someone to believe in him. Ester didn't want him alone, but he still courted danger. "Then he's done enough. He should seek to be safe and build a safe, secure life."

Mama shook her head. "There's a guilt about surviving that haunts, just as there's a squeamishness about being powerless. I know it, for I was small when I watched my siblings being sold away. We Croomes live in this house and have freedom, but my plantation brothers may not have lived past fifteen."

It wasn't possible to hurt more, but Ester held her chest like it would explode. Everything churned inside—guilt, betrayal, and so much anger at herself. "Bex once said all he ever wanted was for someone to recommend him beyond his faults, to know he was good. I thought he meant his snoring, not this. I let my fears push him away. I betrayed him, Mama."

Her mother took a finger and swiped the tears from Ester's face. "He did what was right. Gave me peace for my lost brother, but it doesn't take the hurt from him."

"I didn't let him explain. My anger or stubbornness made me deaf to his pain. And to yours, Mama. I'll never forgive myself." Ester reached up and hugged Mama's neck. "There needs to be a better word to express how empty I feel inside. Mama, how could you be so strong and forgiving?"

Mama stroked her back in long circles that made her rings clink, then started to chuckle, but the laughter was bitter. "Strong? Forgiving? I ended up being the same as my father. I forsook Ruth. I couldn't stand her scandal and how it could ruin what your father and I have worked for—all those hours in Mayfair, *maiding,* all those late days in the warehouse, working and saving. I sent Ruth away—my own flesh and blood. Who's better, Ester? My father who sold off my kin, disappointed by the color of their skin, or a mother who sent away her daughter because she was disappointed by her daughter's choices?"

"Listen Mama, you're nothing like your father. It's not too late to take Ruth back in."

"Then it's not too late to do the same for Bex."

"But the risks? He won't stop taking risks."

Mama put her fingers light and easy on Ester's cheeks. "Life is risk. Find your strength, Ester. It's in you. It's in Bex, too. I saw *his hands* on you, and they were the hands of a man in love. I saw it from the moment he walked you back from the blacksmith's at Gretna Green."

He did seem more certain of their marriage than she did. And if she hadn't asked him to stop being brave, he'd be here at Nineteen Fournier.

Mama picked up the article scraps and put them back in her box, but she put the wooden container into Ester's palm. "Those hands of Bex's saved your father and four other workers. There's goodness in that man. Forgive him and then forgive your papa. He's flawed, too, but he loves you."

Clancy popped his head in. "Mr. Croome is looking for you, Mrs. Croome. He's dressed this morning."

Mama nodded. "Thank you, Clancy. I'll go to him when I'm done here."

The butler bowed and ducked out the door as if Mama had thrown a fireball at him. Maybe she had, in her own soft-spoken way.

"Just think on it, Ester. Oliver Arthur Bexeley isn't a perfect man, and neither is your father, but they need a strong woman to make them do better. I have faith in you. You're strong. You come from strong women who did what they had to do to survive. There's favor on your life because you're loved. Be that woman, Ester. Be brave and love."

She watched her mother leave, head high, rings glistening, then clutched the ring Mama had given her to wed Bex, spinning it on her favorite necklace. How could she go to Bex now, when she'd rejected him—twice? Sighing, she hugged her knees. No one was as brave as her mother. No one.

●●●

In his Cheapside flat, Arthur packed the last of his belongings. He wasn't sure of where he was going, but London had become unbearable. People didn't see the great actor, just a man to be pitied.

The only thing he could be thankful for was that Ester's name was kept from the papers. Phineas was true to his word about not disclosing their marriage.

Arthur looked around. Everything had been put away except his wife's bag. Ester. He missed her, craved the scent of her, but to see her face and know that there was no hope to love her was impossible.

His fault. He should've trusted her with his secret. Yet, how did he know he wouldn't have lost her sooner?

Opening her bag, he let his fingers sink into the fairy gown she'd worn when they'd eloped. It was soft like her nightgowns. Goodness, he missed her, her touch.

He pushed her gown back into the bag, trying not to wrinkle it, but that wasn't a talent a man like him had. Gowns were a wife's forte.

A knock at the door drew his attention. The hint of lilac that wafted from the dress made hope in his heart rise that Ester had spied the advertisement he'd penned in the papers and had come to talk, maybe forgive him.

But the next pound upon his door didn't sound feminine or shy. It wasn't Ester.

Exhaling useless air, he opened the door at the third knock.

Jonesy bounced up and down. "Wait a moment, Mr. Bex." The boy went to the steps and lifted a large box. The thing with the yellow sash bow seemed so big in his small hands. "Here it is, Mr. Bex. Straight from the Burlingame Arcade. The shopkeeper put the sketchbook inside."

Ester's sketchbook. She hadn't even thought to retrieve it. But who'd want to remember their crazed trip to Gretna Green?

Dancing for bandits, driving side by side, their first kiss, vows meant to be forever—yes, no one wanted to remember those things. Offering his helper a coin, he took the box. "Thanks, Jonesy."

"My pleasure, Mr. Bex. You're a good tipper. I have an errand, then I'll deliver it for you."

"Jonesy, I'm going to be away tomorrow. Will you be fine? How are you going to get along without my pennies?"

The boy frowned. "Don't really want you to go, Mr. Bex. Nobody tips Jonesy like you. I know that a lot of folks are saying mean things about you, but I don't believe 'em."

Arthur dug in his purse and handed him a guinea. "I'll miss you, my friend. Maybe you can get that footman position you want when you're not taking care of the things I need."

The smile on Jonesy's face evaporated. "No one trusts Jonesy like you. They don't see pos...possibilities."

"Any household would be privileged to hire you."

With a shrug, Jonesy put the coins in his pocket. "Don't care what they say about you, Mr. Bex. You're good. Will miss you something terrible."

Arthur watched the boy leave and it kicked what was left of his gut. London didn't have time for people like Jonesy. That feeling that he should stay and fight washed over him again, but it was best to go and gain some needed distance, where lilac and sketchbooks didn't make him feel so empty.

Before he could close the door, Phineas popped inside. "Bex, can I have a moment of your time. You haven't been keeping to your old haunts. I figured you and the wife needed your privacy."

"Phineas, I have plenty of privacy. My wife's still staying with her family."

The reporter took off his hat and fanned his sweating face. "The advertisement didn't work. Bex, I'm sorry."

Phineas pushed his hat atop his head with a swish. "Maybe we can write another article. And if you get your mother-in-law to participate, that would—"

"No." Arthur flailed his hands, out and in, out and in. "I don't want the Croomes bothered."

Phineas hung his head for a moment. "Well, I followed up with the doctor for you. Mr. Croome is still not himself. He's walking a little, but he's not out of the woods. The physicians think it's sheer force of will keeping him moving."

It was good to hear that Croome was mending, but that feeling of leaving Ester and Mrs. Croome unprotected should things become dire knifed his insides. Ester may have rejected him, but he hadn't rejected them. As stubborn as his wife was, she'd still need someone.

Getting tangled in his own logic, he picked up the box and pushed it to Phineas. "Take this to Nineteen Fournier. Today if you can. It's my wife's birthday."

"Yes, Bex," the reporter said, as he took the box and stuffed it under his arm and gripped the handle of Ester's bag. "Oh, I did some checking. The warehouse recently had gas lighting installed. Seems the housings were too thin, and the fittings leaked. With all the dust associated with the wool and cotton in the place, it was like gunpowder for a flintlock."

"The gas lighting was at fault?" Bex thought about the gas lighting business of the Jordan family. "Make sure you tell my wife about the lighting when you give her the present. That way she'll know her father wasn't at fault. You might get a story you can investigate out of it."

Phineas nodded. "If you change your mind about leaving town today, I know where you're needed. Wilberforce is going to attend a meeting at the White Horse Cellar to talk about abolition. The rally was a setback. He requested that you be there."

"Wilberforce requested that I come?" He held out his scandal-riddled hands. "Me? The talk of the town?"

"He truly thinks the fight for abolition is a young man's game. No one is more qualified to speak of the fight and its costs. The White Horse Cellar at nine. See you there. Another *Zhonda* could happen if slavery isn't abolished. Think about it, Bex."

Phineas tipped his hat and left with every trace of Arthur's wife but the scars on his heart.

He closed the door, dropping his head against it. He'd run all his life since his uncle's conviction. Maybe it was time to stop running. He'd lost Ester, but he hadn't lost the fight. The defenseless still needed defending. It didn't matter if he went to war with a broken spirit. He still could stop another tragedy and save another brother, so that no one ever knew the cruelty of the *Zhonda* again.

CHAPTER TWENTY-THREE

Performance of a Lifetime

Ester heard the musicians playing downstairs. The tunes they practiced sounded lively, perfect for a birthday celebration. It was her twenty-first, and the party would begin in an hour. Unlike all her other special days, she was miserable.

Breakfast had been done with a smile. Like always, the food tasted delicious, with the fluffiest biscuits she'd ever had and a splurge on beefsteaks, but she'd only taken a few bites. She found it hard to act happy when she'd never been more miserable. Yet, she'd become quite good at acting, even pretending to herself that she didn't miss Bex at all.

Liar.

When had she become a coward and a purveyor of falsehoods? Instead of answering Bex's advertisement or simply going to his residence, she'd stayed at Nineteen Fournier, hoping for her heartache to go away. Where was the bravery to love and be loved? Where was her faith?

"Miss Ester? You have a visitor downstairs in your father's study," Clancy said, his voice carrying to the third floor.

Her heart beat hard. Maybe Bex was trying one more time. She checked her hair, the position of her bonnet, the sash of her indigo-colored dress. She should put on something prettier, not last year's gown, for Bex.

Oh, what did it matter? Bex was here. In a flash, she was out of the room, down two flights of stairs, almost sliding in her new ivory slippers past the servants lighting the chandelier.

Trying to appear calm and aloof, not love-starved, she lifted her chin and knocked on Papa's door.

"Come...in." Father's words slurred, but his voice still had the masculine force that it always had.

Holding her breath, she entered, then released a disappointed huff. "Mr. Phineas, what are you doing here?"

"My business is twofold. I wanted to tell your father that I think the brass fittings on the newly installed gas lamps failed. With the dust of the wool and cotton in the air, a leak from a lamp could have caused the explosion."

"Jordan's lamps." Father took a moment and forced his lips to move without a slur. It was difficult with the burns to his face. "He put in cheap ones."

Ester headed to Papa's desk. "Mr. Phineas, are you sure? That's a mighty accusation. Your paper isn't known to get things right."

"Ma'am, I've been hunting the manufacturer, talking to the installers. I'm very sure. Jordan's gas lighting was at fault."

"Jordan." Papa fisted his hand.

Ester put her palm on her father's and squeezed. "Thank you, Mr. Phineas. My father prides himself on being good to his workers, not putting them in danger. This is good news, but what was the second thing?"

The reporter reached to the floor and lifted her bag, the one she'd left at Bex's, and a pretty parcel with a big yellow bow. "Bex wanted me to give these to you."

"Why didn't he come himself?"

"He's welcome," Papa said the words loud and clear. "The boy is."

Ester squeezed her father's hand again. Bex was welcome, welcome to everything, including her heart. She was tired of being afraid.

Phineas sighed. "He doesn't want to drag the Croomes into his fight. Some nasty reporter might follow him."

"He doesn't have to fight alone." The words slipped from her mouth before she could stop. Then she raised her head and let her protective nature reign. "Yes, he doesn't have to fight alone, at all."

"Maybe you should tell him before he leaves."

"What?" Ester covered her mouth for a moment. "Bex is going away?"

"Yes, but he might be at the White Horse Cellar tonight. There's another rally for abolition. Many people want him there, including Wilberforce. I hope he shows and defends himself."

Ester clutched the box to her chest. "Mr. Phineas, tell him he should fight. That he's a good man."

"My voice isn't the one he needs to hear. You've been to the Cellar. You know how loud it is in there. Those that want hate or are resistant to change—their voices are always loud."

"And voices trapped by fear will never be heard." Ester felt ashamed and scared and more in want of Bex's embrace than ever.

Phineas went to the door. "Happy Birthday, Mrs. Bex." The man tipped his hat and left.

"Ester."

"Yes, Papa."

Her father's upper lip went up and nothing came out for a few seconds. "Go to Bex. He made...mistakes. Still worthy of re-redempt—"

"Redemption?" Ester folded her arms about Papa. "I need to ask you something. You don't have to answer. I know it's not my business."

Papa nodded.

"Why a mistress? We'd just moved to Nineteen Fournier. I thought we were all so happy."

Her father looked down. "Forgot what made us work. Success can...can make you forget...struggle."

She swallowed hard and witnessed a vulnerability she'd never seen in her big, tall hero. "Why did you keep the letters? If you had destroyed them, I'd never have known. Mama wouldn't have read them."

"I knew." His shaky hand pointed to his forehead. "Up here. Needed reminder of the trust I broke. Mama, she...don't just trust any...anyone."

Ester swiped at the tears that came from his eyes. The fragility of love was so evident, so thick on his bruised lips. "Thank you for telling me, Papa. I'm so sorry for how I treated you."

He worked his mouth and said, "Sorry, for disapp...pointing." He held out his arms and she fell into them. She needed Papa's arms. She needed him.

The bear hug grew tighter. "Can't stand tall and proud for you anymore."

She knelt beside his chair. "Mistakes, they need to be forgiven, but Papa, you stand tall to me even when you are sitting."

He patted her shoulder. "Go to Bex. Tell him...sorry, too."

Putting a palm to her empty bosom, she shrugged. "Papa. He'll do dangerous things. I love him enough to let him go fight his fights, to be the man he is." Wiping her cheek, she rose and started for the hall before she felt even sadder about Bex.

"Wait. Ester. The gift."

She turned back. Fear ran through her. It would be something thoughtful that would break her heart all over again.

Sighing, almost praying that it was nothing personal, nothing that reminded her of how well he knew her, she took the box into her hands.

The ribbon bow came off easy in one pull. When she pried open the lid, her sketchbook lay open to pages with her dream name, *Mrs. Arthur Bex*, but underneath, the voluminous tissue paper wrapped something pale pink. She peeked at it, trying not to wrinkle any of the folds.

Papa grunted. "Well."

Joy swept over her as she lifted the collar rimmed high in lace. The rest of the dress, with lines of pearl buttons from bosom to hem, shimmered in the light.

"He bought you a dress." Papa fingered the falling sleeve. "Croome fabric. Good...taste."

It was more than good taste. It was the dress she'd designed on their elopement trip. Bex had it created for her but had it made with a high neck. Theodosia could calculate how many guineas it had cost, but Ester knew it was an extravagance for a humbled man of modest means.

"Ester. Can...go get him...now?"

The knock on the door was louder than her thoughts of agreeing with Papa.

"Come in," he said, clearer than before.

Clancy entered. "Mrs. Croome wants you both to come to dinner. The guests have arrived."

Papa struggled to his feet. Cane in one hand, he held his other out for her. "Go." He pulled her into a bear hug again. "Clancy...pull the carriage...my daughter must go."

Her stubborn heart beat fast, then went wild. She wanted her husband, loved him more than her fears. "A chaperone must come, Papa."

"You're married. Don't need one," he said.

"But I'm asking for one, Papa. I'm asking for you. Will you come with me and give me your blessing?"

His half smile returned. "Yes. Let me tell Mama."

They stepped out of his office to where Clancy stood. Smiling big, the butler held out his arm and helped Papa stroll the length of the hall.

The front door opened, and the groom announced the Jordans. Mrs. Jordan swept inside in a gown of gold. "Happy Birthday, Ester. Charles wanted me to tell you he couldn't make it."

Ester nodded, even as she sighed in relief. "Thank you, ma'am."

Mr. Jordan had a snide look about him. "I heard you've been doing some traveling. You should've stayed. The headlines these past couple of weeks have been illuminating."

He nudged his wife, and she giggled.

Surely, they knew about Bex, and Ester wished she had her ring on her finger and not on the coral necklace about her neck. "Yes, I only wish I could've shortened my trip to watch the installation of your gaslights. A reporter for *The Morning Post* thinks them faulty. It will make quite a headline once it's proved true. But you know some papers don't print truth."

The look, the audible swallow, was worth it, to enjoy each second of Jordan's sneer drop away.

"Does your father believe this lie?"

"Yes." Ester smiled big as she took the necklace off and removed her ring. Sliding it onto her finger, she nodded at the squirming couple. "He's waiting on proof, Mr. Jordan. It should be any day now. I wonder if Papa will sue to gain restitution for the workers that died."

"I'm not feeling too well," Jordan finally said. "Tell your parents sorry." He spun his wife around and was out the door before Ester could count to twenty-one.

She heard the cane tapping, getting louder behind her.

By himself, Papa came and stood by her side. "We...back before...time to cut the cake. Before midnight.

Yes, they had to have Bex with them before midnight, or at least by five past. Then their life together wouldn't just be a dream Ester had every night. It would be a wish come true.

• • •

Men packed the bottom level of the White Horse Cellar. Not a table up front was empty, but Arthur found a seat in the back. Covered by the low tallow light and his heavy greatcoat, he sat, wondering why he had come.

Yet, when Wilberforce offered his impassioned plea of the rights of every human, Arthur lifted his head and nodded in agreement. Just because he had failed didn't make the cause of abolition a failure.

Wilberforce raised a shaking hand to his face, cupping his

eyes. "You've heard my words, the ones of a man who is still in the fight, but now let's hear from a younger man. Arthur Bex, come forward."

The cheers stopped, and silence filled the cellar for exactly ten seconds. Then the boos started and lit a fire all the way around.

Arthur tried to rise, but his feet had turned to lead. He coughed and wiped at his face.

"Come on, Bex. Tell 'em." It was Jonesy. The boy must've snuck away from watching Bex's phaeton. So much for his one night in service as a groom.

The naysaying buzzed, thick like smoke in a warehouse, or like shouts against a boy testifying about murder. Arthur knew what was right, even if he was the only one. He had to do what was right. That meant he needed to stop hiding, to stand his ground and fight.

Now or never.

Arthur stood and moved through the crowd. He came to the chair that was being used as a stage. He leaped onto it and waved his arms and stared down the loudest accuser until all had quieted like an audience at Covent Gardens. "The stakes have never been higher. You must choose what's right, what's true."

"Sit down, son of a slaver."

The comment silenced the room. No doubt, everyone waited to see how Arthur would respond, but he hesitated.

"Bex was the slaver captain's nephew, and Bex tried to stop the atrocities. What have *you* done?" The voice was Phineas's, and it breathed new air into the Cellar's stench.

"Who in here is not related to a thief, a liar, or a slaver?"

Arthur's voice took command of the stage, making everyone go still. "If one in here can say yes, then you've deceived yourself. You've lied to yourself. No one is clean. We're all steeped in some secret sin."

His voice boomed. The echo of it rippled across the quieted faces.

He raised his hands, becoming Antony sending his men to battle and Macduff slaying Macbeth's evil minions. "Brothers, I've been ridiculed in all the papers, but I'm not the fight, just a speck of dust. Enslavement is a cobweb which sticks to every Englishman. The newspapers don't decry the chains cast on our brothers. They discuss the loss of coins from the *Zhonda*. If they could show you the chained men stacked like fish for the lure of guineas, then you would know. As the nephew of a slaver—the *worst* slaver—I've seen it. I saw proud men, proud brothers locked in heavy iron chains, thrown to their deaths. If you saw it, if you'd known the evil, you'd join me in the fight."

"You should know." The snicker lofted above the silent crowd.

"You turned on your uncle and let him be killed over cargo. The slaves were cargo. They endangered the crew. Crew comes first."

Arthur was losing them, but he'd not be stopped. "Brothers—"

"Crew come first. Crew come first. Lying actors last." It was a handful, not the whole room, but the angry voices were loud.

"Cargo doesn't scream. Cargo doesn't gasp for air as the weight of chains drags them to the bottom. Cargo isn't a man. Murder's not how you treat a brother."

"Traitor," one man said. "You got your flesh-and-blood uncle hanged."

"Doesn't murder require justice?" The woman's voice was low but grew louder. "Who'd not want justice for the killing of an uncle or brother?"

The shy voice silenced the crowd.

Ester? Ester's voice had done it.

She was in the back of the room, standing by her father. "Would any of you want your uncle to die, chains wrapped around him, tossed overboard to drown? The *Zhonda's* crew did that *fifty* times. Fifty murders witnessed by a young boy, a nephew who had the courage to try and stop evil. Who among you is that strong? None. But you sit in chairs or read papers and you mock him for doing what is right."

"Of course, you would side with the actor." A man stood and came toward her. "Look fellas, it's one of those runaway slaves. Let's get her and fetch a reward."

Before the blackguard or Iagos could get anywhere near her, Bex jumped between them and had a fist ready to do damage. "I can do more than act. Touch her, and you'll know how much of your life remains."

The man backed away and eased to his seat. "You're a big man, Bex, or whatever your name is. Get your maid and leave."

"Bex, we should leave," Ester said. "Why cast pearls before swine?"

"That one has a mouth on her." The drunk made his table of buffoons laugh.

But Arthur had to agree, because he'd kissed those lips and he wanted to again and again. "She does, a beautiful one." He took her arm and led her to a chair near Wilberforce. "Wait for me until I'm done."

Another man pounded on the table. "Hey, if she's up there, let her speak. Maybe she can tell us why we should listen to Bex?"

Before he could stop her, Ester bounced to her feet and faced the men. "Because I know Bex better than I know myself. If there's a hard path, one that will help others, he'll take the difficult road. He'll take on your burdens and make them his own. So, when he tells you abolition is the cause of his heart, it's true."

Her clear voice, unwavering in support, made a difference. A few started to clap.

The drunk stood once more. "Why should we believe this woman? She speaks good. Could be another actor."

She tugged off her glove and exposed her finger, the one showing her wedding ring.

Ester wore it again. His heart beat a little stronger, a little louder, but this could be Ester taking on a role to protect him. Acting would never do for Arthur. He needed her to love *him*, flaws and all. "You don't—"

Her smile, the light in her eyes, silenced him. "I'm Mrs. Bex. I'm his wife. We've been meant for each other going on two years—the niece of an enslaved man and the good nephew of his slaver. If I, who has more grievances than any, can stand here with my knees knocking and tell you of the good in this man, then you should know it's true."

The room went silent again.

Arthur took her hand and put it on his arm. "No one can undo the past, gentlemen, but we can do what is right, now. The slave trade beyond our borders, in our colonies, must end."

"What of America?" The voice was Phineas, and he seemed to be taking notes.

"The Americas aren't a colony anymore. That little revolution in seventy-six changed things."

The crowd snickered, and Arthur could feel they were with him again. "They'll choose their own path, but we can be a beacon of light. They can follow us, and the world can change. We are all brothers and sisters, trying to do what is right. That's our choice. Let's do what is right and push for abolition everywhere."

The applause started as he hoisted Ester in the air and tucked her safely at his side. He tipped his hat to Wilberforce and then to Phineas as he made his way to the back of the room.

"Mr. Croome, may I help you out of here?"

The man nodded. "Yes. Birthday cake, now."

The man's slurred command made sense. It was still Ester's birthday. He took hold of his father-in-law near his mourning armband and let Mr. Croome put his full weight against him as they made it up the stairwell.

On the main level, Mr. Croome grasped Arthur's lapel. "Son, can't fight everyone."

His heart warmed at the sentiment, son-ship. He hadn't belonged to anyone in a long time, but there was still someone who needed to claim him. Arthur looked over to Ester and drank in her smile. "I won't fight with your daughter anymore. She might take to the stage against me."

"Whoa," Croome said. "Don't look at her like that."

Arthur put her hand in his. "Sir, who else should I be looking at with all the love in my heart?"

"Fine. Come. Cake. Mrs. Croome." Ester's father was a big man, and if his shaking fist connected, it would have power. "We go now."

Jonesy popped up at his side. "Mr. Bex, you and Mrs. Bex ready to go?"

"I'm leaving town after I get this young man a position as a groom. He's loyal and dependable. He'd never lie or betray a trust."

"Jonesy is a good one, says Mr. Bex."

Mr. Croome rubbed his chin. "This fellow and I...have more in common...our good looks. Bex, come back for cake. Get us out trouble with Mrs. Croome...I'll hire him."

The young man jumped up and down. "Go for cake, Mr. Bex. Jonesy likes cake and a good job."

Ester took hold of Arthur's hand. His bare palm could feel her thin fingers sheathed in satin, melting into his. "Seems cake is a cause you can champion."

"Jonesy, help Mr. Croome into his carriage. Sir, I'll follow in my phaeton with your daughter, unless she wants to ride with you."

Her father, with Jonesy's help, climbed into his Berlin and slammed the door, but stuck his head out the window. "Cake before midnight."

The carriage started to move, and Croome's wonderful team of horses streaked forward in the night with Jonesy whooping for joy on the back.

Ester sighed. "Well, what do we do now?"

He put her palm in the crook of his arm and started walking around to the mews where he and Jonesy had left his phaeton. "I suppose we head for cake."

In silence, he hitched up his horse as she sat along the rail. When he had everything ready, he put his arms about her waist and lifted her onto the seat. When he took his place beside her, she had the reins in her hand and started his horses before he could stop her.

"You intend on driving me, Ester?"

She didn't say anything but kept the speed even.

He sat back and studied her beautiful form. "Have you been practicing? Your hand is steadier."

"No, but I've more peace about me. I'm not fretting or rushing to be anywhere. I'm merely riding with you. Bex, thank you for my present. It was very thoughtful."

He folded his arms. "Just because you stopped loving me, didn't mean I stopped loving you, or that I didn't think about you every moment."

"Arthur Bex, I've loved you for two years. You think that went away because I was mad? It didn't, just my hearing stopped. I didn't give you a chance to explain. I'm sorry, very sorry."

"Ester, what did you say that wasn't right? I take risks."

"A lot of things. I owed you a fair hearing. And yes, you face risks. In that cellar, many of them don't want change. You're in danger."

"Wilberforce has lived all these years. I'll be fine. After cake, I intend to do some traveling, anyway, and let tensions cool."

"I won't cool for you. My emotions have always been high-strung, irrational, really—all about you."

When they came closer to the Thames and the warehouse district, she slowed the gig, making the animals come to a complete stop. "I won't be fine without you. I was too stubborn to admit how much I need you. Too stubborn to see that you were trying to hide me from the ugliness. You and Papa are very much alike. Maybe that is why I love you both so much."

His heart began to beat a little faster, but the things that drew them apart where still there. "I'm a flawed man, Ester, not one of the heroes I play on the stage. I don't want to be the one to disappoint you. I can't stop fighting for the causes I believe in. Maybe the cost for us to be together is too high."

She crawled into his arms and grabbed his lapel. "You listen to me Bex-Bexeley. You love me, and you know it, and that's enough. I don't want you to stop being you. I believe in us, and I know you have to fight. You just need to be prepared for me to be at your side. If you fight, I fight with you."

He wrapped her in his embrace, drawing her to that space reserved for her against his chest. "I'll be as safe as I can be. I'll think through things. I'll prepare, even if it's merely a trip across town. You are my bride. I won't put lines on your forehead unnecessarily. I want to be with you forever, Ester. But I can't promise to run from danger. Sometimes the cause of justice is dangerous."

"I know, Bex. I know."

"But know, Ester, I will be as safe as I can. I want to come home to you. Your love is the home I need. Can we start again?"

"Yes. I'm saying yes to Arthur Bex-Bexeley. Yes, to us. I believe in us again. I found my faith to believe again."

He shifted and sank on one knee. "You proposed to me first, Ester, and now I propose to you. Love me. Love me like I love you. Every inch of my heart is yours. My voice, my body is yours. Be my wife for as long as we both shall live.

She clasped his hands and kissed his thumbs. "I love you, your strength, and how you know me. I love how you let me be me, and I promise to let you be you. We're better together." She laid her forehead against his. "I'll always want you, from this day forward for as long as we both shall live."

Who began the kiss, he wasn't sure, didn't truly care, but with her arms about his neck and access to her kissable throat, he was home. They'd found each other again, and this time he'd never let her go, never let anything but a blanket or a bathtub come between them.

A bell tolled in the distance. Twelve long gongs. "Midnight, and we are still here, Ester. This love must be true, not make-believe."

"Midnight." She bolted upright but stayed in the circle of his arms and took up the reins. "We have to get to Nineteen Fournier. I need to be home to cut the cake and you, you need to be at my side."

He sat, tilted back his hat, and let her take control of his phaeton. He'd take charge when it counted, when all the birthday guests were gone, when her parents had turned in and he and Mrs. Bex were quite alone.

EPILOGUE

Wearing her new salmon-pink birthday dress, Ester blinked a few times in a futile attempt to keep her eyes open while sitting on the couch on the parlor. She raised her arms and tried one more time to loop the thick wool yarn about her knitting needle. Tired from her long, long night, she yawned.

She and Arthur had made it to Nineteen Fournier well after midnight, but Mama had waited for them and made a great deal of pomp of the newlyweds standing side-by-side, cutting the three-tier cake with bliss icing.

Her mother had made it like a wedding cake, the one they'd missed by eloping. They had their first dance with real music, not merely to rhythms in her head or barge horns. Her husband was quite the dancer, something the papers had also reported wrong. But maybe he'd never had the right partner. For the twinkle in his eye had been perfect as he'd twirled her about the chalked floor. Then they'd disappeared to her room and made perfection.

Absence made the heart fonder, and his hand had known exactly how to wander. She chuckled. The pink room was too feminine, but Bex had made the best of it, whispering her name with that deep timbre in his voice.

What a wonder to have her own private concert with Bex, the hero of her dreams, and she willingly became his Juliet, his Katerine, and even Cleopatra—without all the betrayal and the dying. Ester felt blessed upon being blessed, to have the man she loved loving her, and she, all of him.

"Hold the needle more stiffly," Mrs. Fitterwall said as she refreshed the pot of tea. "Maybe if you get more sleep it would be easier for you."

The red-haired woman cast her a wicked smile before she scurried out the door.

Cheeks warming, Ester tried again to loop the yarn to cast a stitch, but it slipped. "Another fallen one, Mama. I'll never get this right. Mama?"

The woman stared ahead for half a minute before turning and looking in Ester's direction. "What?"

"The stitch, Mama. I'm failing."

Her mother picked up the twist of yellow yarn that was supposed to be a woolen baby's cap. "Good thing your friend's lying-in is at the Yuletide. You've a few months to practice, or that baby will be hatless."

The noise of the front door opening sent a tingle up Ester's spine. Bex had gone with Papa to look at the raising of the warehouse, and she was anxious when the two most important men in her life left Nineteen Fournier. "Hopefully, Bex and Papa have returned early with no incidents."

"Your father is getting stronger, but having your husband here, I think, is good for him. Papa loves his girls, but he always wanted a son. Hopefully, you and Bex will stay. We've plenty of room."

Having Bex about was good for everyone, but he hadn't said if he wanted to reside at Nineteen Fournier. "He lives in Cheapside. His flat is pretty nice."

"But can it compete with our bathtub? And you've no waiting for it here."

And the knowledge that everyone was safe within these protective walls. Yes, Ester wanted to live here. "Bex is considering it, as he decides what he'll do next."

The door to the parlor flung open and in came Frederica, carried by Lord Hartwell. His emerald green frock coat flapped from side to side as he came close to the couch.

Ester leaped up, dropping her foul needles. "Frederica, what happened?"

"I'm fine." Her friend's cheeks seemed flushed like she had a fever. "I am such a ninny to be spooked on my horse. I'm not a schoolgirl."

"She won't let me check her ankle," Hartwell said. "I think she needs a physician."

Tall Frederica looked so tiny in the man's big arms. Her deep ocean-blue riding habit had mud stains.

Lord Hartwell seemed very concerned, his face a riddle of fretful lines. "I escorted my father to the Duke of Simone's for an early meeting, when I saw this lady riding like a crazed rabbit. You looked very scared, Miss Burghley, barely able to hold on to your seat."

She pushed at her dark bonnet with its point like a pirate captain's hat. "Thank you, Lord Hartwell. You can put me down now."

The man startled, as if the concept was foreign to him, then eased her onto the couch. "You're lucky I am quick on my feet. I was able to borrow a horse and catch you, but not before your gelding tossed you into those bushes. Ladies, she demanded I bring her here and not to her father's."

"It was only a couple of miles." She blew at her falling curls.

"Maybe ten."

The man frowned and sighed at the same time. "Miss Burghley."

Frederica yanked leaves from the gold braid trimming her sleeves. "I don't want the duke to be concerned. He spent a great deal on my lessons. He'll be so upset to know I was thrown. I'm such a ninny." She tugged on her lapels as if that would right how disheveled she appeared. "You won't tell him, will you, my lord?"

"I'll keep your confidence, Miss Burghley, if you'll seek medical attention."

"I'm fine." Frederica rose, as if to prove him wrong, but wobbled like a lame pony.

The viscount folded his arms. "See how much worse it has become with the thirty-minute ride over here? I shouldn't have listened to you."

"It's my powers of persuasion, my lord." Frederica flopped into the side chair. "I'm good at persuasion. I just need to rest. Please don't tell the duke. I don't want him to be concerned. And don't tell your brother. Theodosia can't be upset."

Tucking his hands into his coat, he nodded. "As you wish. However, if you do not send me a note in a few days telling me you're dancing on the moon again, I'll consult your father." He nodded his head. "Mrs. Bex, Mrs. Croome. Send a note, Miss Burghley."

At the sound of the outer door closing, vibrating, Frederica sank fully into the chair, as if a pin had pricked and deflated her, letting all the hot air out.

"Dear, you look quite ill." Mama moved to her and put a hand on her forehead. "You feel warm. Let me send for a doctor."

"Please, Mrs. Croome—

Waggling her finger, Mama was already out of the parlor.

"Frederica, you're in Croome territory, so sit back and take it. My mother rules here. The strong woman knows best." Ester picked up the yarn again before putting the tangled strings on the table. "You're such a good rider. What happened?"

"I think," Frederica said, her voice sounding low. "Someone wants to kill me."

"What?"

Her friend lifted her swollen ankle up onto the table. "Well, he didn't exactly say those words, but something to the effect of if he couldn't have me, no one would."

"Did you hit your head, Frederica? That's not funny."

She rubbed at her brow. "Someone vicious is answering my newspaper advertisement. I received another threatening note saying he's watching me. The note described the dress I wore to yesterday's outing at the Burlingame Arcade. He had it perfectly, down to the gold pins in my hair."

"Someone is having fun. Since my marriage to Bex is more public, I think any of us Blackamoors that straddle the classes are gaining more attention. You saw Gilroy's awful cartoon of yesterday's meeting in the cellar." She held the picture up, resisting the urge to shred it. "I could laugh off Bex and I with a half-black, half-white baby, or even Wilberforce with a Blackamoor woman on his lap, but showing Papa on a table playing his cane as if it were a fiddle... That's outrageous."

"Horrible. How did Mr. Croome take it?"

"Papa hasn't seen it, but Mama has, and she's been very quiet. You being here will give her a distraction."

Frederica put her head back. "I'm glad my life crisis can be of use. Has your husband seen that dribble?"

"No, but he will. We have no secrets."

Leaning forward, her friend sat up, her mouth falling open. "None? Not even something for convenience?"

"None, Frederica."

She flopped again into the chair. "What am I going to do? This note wasn't in my box at Burlingame. It came to my father's house this morning. The duke will find out."

Ester stood and took hold of Frederica's palm. "Whatever this is, we'll face it. No one's going to hurt you."

Frederica shook her head, sending her tight ringlets jiggling. "The scandalmongers will ruin me. My father will disown me and make a new family with Miss Stevens."

Giving Frederica a big hug, Ester picked straw from her golden curls. "You're overreacting. This is some horrible joke. It'll pass. Stay here for the next few days. All will calm down."

Mrs. Fitterwall and Mama returned.

"Come on, Miss Burghley." They came on either side of her.

The housekeeper had Frederica lean more upon her. "Upstairs with you and soak that foot. The physician will be here soon."

Ester arose to help, but Mama's icy stare made her sit back down. "Miss Burghley will be down for dinner. You two can begin your scheming then. Jonesy says that the carriage has pulled up. You need to see if your husband will commit to living here. That's your one task. Ruth and her son will be coming at the end of the month. My family will be whole. That's my wish."

There was no out-talking Mama. "Yes, ma'am." Ester sat

back down and took up the horrible knitting needle again as the women helped her friend out of the parlor.

In a couple of minutes, the sounds of laughter came from the hall, loud, deep masculine voices.

Bex opened the door to the parlor. "Sir, you want to come inside here or to your study?"

"I'm going to let...you two have pri...be alone." He offered a big smile to her. "Daughter."

Ester smiled big, too. One of her heroes was walking a little better. The other gave her a smile that would melt icehouses.

Papa slid off his coat and handed it to Jonesy, then pushed his hat to the boy, too.

Jonesy stood proud, grinning in his new shiny blue livery as he loaded up his arms with their outer gear before dashing off.

Clancy shook his head. He didn't look happy, but he didn't look sad, either. Maybe he'd get used to all the additions to Nineteen Fournier.

"Clancy," Papa said, "help me to my study. Chess later, Bex. I...look forward."

"Yes, sir," her husband said. "It'll be my pleasure."

Ester laughed as Bex closed the door. "You know Papa will keep you busy until you tell him what he wants."

"What could that be?" He tugged at his cream and gold waistcoat as he sat beside her, yanking at his dark blue breeches, yawning loud and long.

She wasn't the only one who was sleepy, and that made her smile grow wider. "He wants you to agree to live here."

His face became serious with a hint of a frown as he picked up her awful needlework. "Well, you said you weren't a couch woman who could knit. You were truthful. What is it?"

"A cap for Theodosia's new baby-to-be."

He twirled the yellow thing about his pinky. "Yes, I can see that now. Will the baby have one tiny head or four?"

She gave him an elbow. "No. Don't even think that about a sweet baby."

Bex picked up the newspaper. "Well, you're already bored with me. *Tsk.* Checking the advertisement section for someone new?"

He flipped the paper open before she could stop him, and he landed on the fold with Gilroy's caricature of the abolitionist meeting last night. His expression became dour. "That woman looks nothing like you. Your curves are larger and more delightful. But you do look very well in your birthday...dress."

Face fevering, she shook her head.

He sighed. "Ester, I didn't want you and your father bandied about in the papers." He dumped the pages back to the table. "I'm more trouble than I am worth."

"Not possible." She reached for him, loving the scent of chamomile and honey on his breath. When she kissed his frown away, she leaned her head on his chest, that spot made for her. "Absolutely worth it. So much so that both my parents want to know if you will live here."

"You think you can butter me up, kissing me with the softest lips I've ever known?"

She smiled up at him, staring at him with confidence in their love. "Yes."

"Keep trying, then, Ester. It may help me come to a decision about something. The weather. Dinner? Something."

She elbowed him again.

"Will you quit? You're going to bruise a rib."

She shook her head. "Bex, I do want to be here. I feel like I'm getting to know my mother all over again. And it does my heart good to see Papa moving about with a sharp, clear mind, even if his speech isn't quite there.

Bex kissed her forehead. "Well, chess will involve vocal lessons. I'm going to see if practice can help."

"My sister, Ruth, and her son, they'll be coming soon. With you here, everything's complete, but I understand if you want to leave. As your wife, I'll go with you. I won't live without you."

"Not in a Cleopatra kind of way?" He eyed her suspiciously. "I know my love is powerful, but it shouldn't lead to a suicide."

She frowned at him. "Do you want another elbow to the ribs?"

"So violent, madam? Cheapside offers many things, but a family it doesn't. And you've hired my Jonesy. How can I get by without him?"

She elbowed him.

"Oh, and there are your parents. It is quite nice to have parents again."

She coughed and tapped her arm against his side.

"Woman, you might actually hurt something with those sharp lotion-needing elbows. Yes, Ester, we can stay. I'd be honored." He put his thumb to his chin.

"What? What is it, Bex?"

"The theater manager called. They want me to be Romeo in their next production. It seems they will be ending Antony and Cleopatra early. If I agree, I'll get six benefit nights for my troubles. He believes the scandal has made me a more famous man and wants to take advantage of my infamy."

It sounded like a good offer, but Bex didn't seem happy with it. Ester brushed his cheek. "But that's not what you want."

Taking her hand, he put it to his heart. "Wilberforce spent over eight thousand pounds to secure the votes for a seat in Parliament. One more run at the theater and I might have enough to try for this borough."

Her husband seemed very serious; his cobalt-blue eyes were bright and happy.

"What are you asking me, Bex?"

"You should really try calling me Arthur, especially if I run for Parliament under my given name. My now famous given name. Oliver Arthur Bexeley for Parliament. Living here, though not a requirement, would make sense if this is the place I represent."

"You would be wonderful, Oliver Arthur Bexeley, and I would love to build our family in this home." She kissed his finger. "But, I still like Bex. It's short and sweet. It's like a quick kiss."

He swept her into arms. "I'm a man given to strong passions. Will the intensity of our love frighten the residents of Nineteen Fournier?"

Cheeks burning, she pushed from his chest. "Not as much as your scaling of the walls to reach the third floor."

"Does that mean I'll always have an easy path to my bashful bride?"

"Always. We can do anything, survive anything, together. I have faith in you and me."

He picked her up in the air and held her as if she was flying. "I still love how you blush. I think we should go up to your room, our room, and shed it of its pinkness. Did I mention you are mighty pink, too?" His laugh was knowing and infectious. "Then I'll interview you, Mrs. Bexeley."

"Interview me?"

"Yes, I want you to practice saying my whole name. I'd like to test my skill at teaching you direct address, making you repeat, I love you, Arthur, I need you, Arthur. Yes, dearest Arthur."

Cheeks on fire, she shook her head. "Put me down...dearest Arthur."

With a kiss, he lowered her then led her to the door. "We have a pink mission, Mrs. Bexeley. Don't fret. We'll be most careful on this joint endeavor."

Tangling her fingers within his, Ester looked forward to all the things she and Mr. Bexeley would do together.

ACKNOWLEDGMENTS

Vanessa here.

I hope you enjoyed Ester's and Arthur's story. This one was special, because of the true history that I wove into this novel. I hope you were able to see the joy of reconciliation in this tale. But here is the history that I used to build their world.

Fournier Street is part of Spitalfields, London, developed by the French Huguenot immigrants dating from around 1720. The townhouses here were large but fell into disrepair and out of favor. I imagine by 1800s they could be assessable to lease or purchase by parts of the Blackamoor and mulatto communities of London, which had grown in wealth but could not purchase in areas like Cheapside or Mayfair.

The slave ship *Zhonda* is modeled after the *Zong*. The *Zong* carried slaves described as chattel from Africa in 1781. The trip, captained by Luke Collingwood, was overcrowded and under-provisioned. When the enslaved began to die of disease and malnutrition, Collingwood and his crew threw more than 132 men into the sea, jettisoning the cargo. An insurance claim filed on the lost 'cargo' was determined to pay more than the sale of the sick and malnourished men, but the claim failed. The judge, Lord Mansfield, ruled the *Zong* for negligence, so the captain and ship owner never recovered the money for this claim. Nonetheless, no one was held legally accountable for the deaths.

William Wilberforce (1759-1833) was a politician and abolitionist that played a pivotal role in the passage of the Slave

Trade Act of 1807. This formally ended England's role in the active slave trade involving the mainland, but not in English colonies such as the West Indies or South Africa. Wilberforce spent over £8,000 to ensure he received enough votes to become an elected member of Parliament, and used his position, his faith, and his money to promote the cause of abolition.

The cartoon described by Ester is called "The New Union Club," created by George Cruikshank in 1819. It depicts a wild scene of what everyone feared would happen if intermarriage increased and abolition won the day. The picture includes Billy Waters, Zachariah Macauley, William Wilberforce. See it at http://bit.ly/2ITp4nh.

Also see the picture of Josiah Wedgwood's Medallion, "Am I Not a Man and a Brother?" at my website.

In the game of seduction, the rules don't apply.

THE RAKEHELL OF ROTH

AMALIE HOWARD

As owner of the most scandalous club in London, the last thing the notorious Marquess of Roth wants is a wife. Keeping up his false reputation as a rake brings in the clients with the deepest pockets—money he needs to fund a noble cause. Even though everything inside tells him not to leave his beautiful, innocent wife behind at his country estate...he must.

But three years later, tired of her scoundrel of a husband headlining the gossip rags, Lady Isobel Vance decides enough is enough. She is no longer a fragile kitten, but as the anonymous author of a women's sexual advice column, she's now a roaring tigress...and she can use her claws.

Isobel decides to go to him in London, channeling her powers of seduction to make him beg to take her back. But she didn't expect her marauding marquess to be equally hard to resist. Now the game is on to see who will give in to the other first, with both sides determined like hell to win.

AMARA

an imprint of Entangled Publishing LLC